Black Mirrors of the Soul

Book 2 of

A THRONE OF SOULS

By Charles W. McDonald Jr.

Black Mirrors of the Soul © 2016 & 2017 Book 2 of
A Throne of Souls© 2016 & 2017
Library of Congress Registration TXu 2-032-142, TXu 2-045-297
(www.copyright.gov)
ISBN 978-0-9981177-6-8 available on Amazon Print Edition
3rd Edition featuring new maps, artwork, glossary content, additional proofreading and bug/error corrections.

Charles W. McDonald Jr.

Credits:

Very special thanks to the following for their feedback and contributions:

John Armond Howarth for the initial creation of Kellen, Goldenbow, Aaramus, Evanyil, Banthis, Rena Rectovich, and a few other characters important in the telling of this story. John helped awaken my creative thinking that further developed these—and other—characters, making the delivery of this work of fiction to you possible. With all my most sincere and best wishes, thank you, John.

The following Beta Readers:
Shawn Hudson
Brandy L. McDonald
for their very honest and constructive criticism in reviewing early editions of this novel.

Story by: Charles W. McDonald Jr.
Written by: Charles W. McDonald Jr.
Cover by: Larry Wilson
Edited by: Zora Alexandra Knauf
Proofread by: Jessamine Julian and Kathy Russel
Cartography by: Charles W. McDonald Jr., Wes Rand and Shady Curi
E-Book Conversion by: Charles W. McDonald Jr.
Publication Artifacts by: Charles W. McDonald Jr.
Other incrementally new artwork by:
Wes Rand,
Jonathan Elliott,
Michael Graham,
And Shady Curi

Charles W. McDonald Jr.

Dedicated to:

Brandy L. McDonald
& my twins: Raegen Gaites and Aiden Dylan McDonald

Charles W. McDonald Jr.

When all that is left of great miracles are the waning memories of distant accounts, now questioned by Men, shall I come to you in the one, undeniable breath of God that your tattered faith be renewed. For in the final moments, shall you need it.

Charles W. McDonald Jr.

Preface: A Reader's Guide to A Throne of Souls

Don't be horrified that there's a bit of an instruction manual at the beginning of this novel. I can assure you there's a good reason for it.

The complexity of weaving the intricate plot lines and asynchronous timelines of this story required the breaking of a *lot* of rules to bring this product to you. Some of those rules involve unconventional capitalization, emphasis strategies, more modern word forms (homeworld instead of home world), and intentional stylistic deviations from the Chicago Manual of Style. So, for example, there are many reserved words in this story (Humanity, Creation, Man, Mankind, Humanoid, God the Creator, etcetera). Those reserved words and phrases (such as titles of chapters or novels within this series) that will be consistently either capitalized and/or emphasized for this story and you might think *hey, that word shouldn't be capitalized or why is that phrase always in emphasis script*, but I assure you this is done with deliberate intent and should not be corrected to mainstream standards. This is not a mainstream story!

The bottom line is this: I'm not here to write like everyone else. I'm not here to placate the whims of the whore Gatekeepers of Deep State to win their phony, lauded praise from, at best, duplicitous and compromised people. I'm not here to rigidly adhere to boundaries established by others. I'm here to bring you something truly new and groundbreaking—but in *my* voice and *my* style. If that troubles you, perhaps you should find something more mainstream (or something with establishment's good housekeeping seal of approval) to read. But you're not going to find anything this thought-provoking written in the dark and intellectual void of the mainstream in the voice of the status quo. Groundbreaking content doesn't follow the status quo; else, it wouldn't be groundbreaking. George Lucas had to invent new special effects methods and new studio techniques to deliver the first Star Wars® trilogy because nothing like it had ever been attempted before. This is the space in which I find myself when writing the story of *A Throne of Souls* for you and for me.

I have written this entire series with the idea that eventually it would become a screenplay adaptation. As such, you'll see scene breaks that provide a 360-degree view of the unfolding events. This is especially true in battle vistas.

These unconventional scene breaks I've chosen to consistently handle in the follow manner:

$$* \quad * \quad * \quad *$$

Charles W. McDonald Jr.

The four-star mark (above) will be used denote a scene break of a brief period of time without switching locations or switching locations (roughly the same time) but staying on the same planetary body.

The preceding flourish bracket will be used to denote a scene break of a large time difference and/or a planetary body shift in location.

A simple carriage return of white space will be used to denote a change in perspective within the same scene. For example, in a large battle sequence, it's important to understand the perspectives of multiple key players as they are engaged in the fight—to see the same event from multiple camera angles, if you will.

I want to be as assertive as possible here: *please* pay careful attention to the ***time and location markers when and where they are provided***. It will greatly help you as the timelines begin to cross over one another asynchronously, and I promise it will contribute substantially to the whole story making perfect sense to you as the larger mosaic begins to paint itself. I'm not saying you *have* to take notes, nor have an eidetic memory. I'm just saying it will greatly help you deduce the clue drops and critical 'ah hah' moments I've woven into the story for those with ears to hear and eyes to see. And those who have gotten the most out of *A Throne of Souls* have had the trait in common of taking copious notes as they read the story. I've tried my best to standardize the following format for the time/location markers throughout:

(Specific Place, Planetary Body, Specific Time if Applicable)

If you look in the Glossary of Terms, I provide specifics on Time Stream examples and what they mean in this story. For example, I give a specific window of time for the terms 'Near Future,' or 'A Long Time Ago.' I'm going to give you a little more guidance specifically for this book since we're going so deep into the back-story of Damon. You'll see the time marker 'A Long Time Ago' frequently used for these back-story scenes, but as I'm stitching together the storyline I will show you some of Damon's back-story that is further in the timestream than another back-story scene also marked 'A Long Time Ago.' Let's say, for example, a scene from the year 560 precedes a scene from 530 by some 20 chapters. Rather

Charles W. McDonald Jr.

than give you specific years across multiple worlds and across multiple timelines crossing over one another, which would be even more confusing, I think the best way to anchor yourself in Damon's timestream is to pay attention to his abilities in that given scene. I'll make it obvious for you and you'll be able to figure out pretty quickly that this scene precedes another scene I described earlier in the book, because of his ability level and his maturity level. *A Throne of Souls* is a story significantly beyond just Damon, but Damon is the primary reason I'm providing this 'heads up' for you, because this book is going to go deep into Damon's history. I'll even be more specific in providing you a line of demarcation…. In the vast history that spans Damon's life, the line of demarcation for him—where it moves from 'A Very Long Time Ago' to 'A Long Time Ago' is when Damon met Dallia for the first time and had cause for the making of *A Throne of Souls*.

I cannot emphasize enough the importance of both the Glossary of Terms and the Glossary of Characters! I put them there for your benefit—not mine. There are so many unusual terms across so many different disciplines and subject domains, it's going to make your head spin if you don't use the Glossary of Terms, so please use it. For those who have read *The Wheel of Time by Robert Jordan*, this story has a comparable number of characters in it. Thus, please use the Glossary of Characters whenever you get confused about who's who.

You would have figured out some, or most, of the above as you read the story, but I thought it would be nice not to exhaust your effort figuring out the mechanics of telling the story. Now, we can get to *A Throne of Souls*—Book 2….

This is the Third Edition of *Black Mirrors of the Soul*. Why? With each new novel released in the series, I re-release the previous novels with updated maps, iconography, glossary content and so forth. I also use this opportunity for another glance at the content to ensure its integrity and delivery. This Third Edition includes all of the aforementioned updates and follows the release of *The Rise of Hope* (Book 4 of *A Throne of Souls*). It also includes another proofread pass from a seasoned editor with decades of experience. In essence, my goal was to get *Black Mirrors of the Soul* up to my fourth-novel standards, which it now meets. We're getting very close to the end now, and the conclusion of *A Throne of Souls* will be everything I have promised ***and much more***….

Charles W. McDonald Jr.

Contents

Charles W. McDonald Jr.

Charles W. McDonald Jr.

Charles W. McDonald Jr.

This Edition's Last Modified Date:
March 26, 2021

Maps:

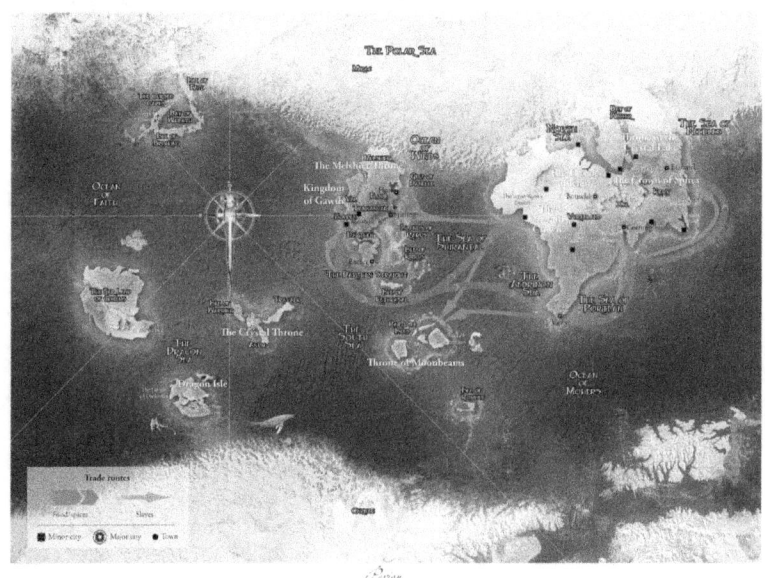

Charles W. McDonald Jr.

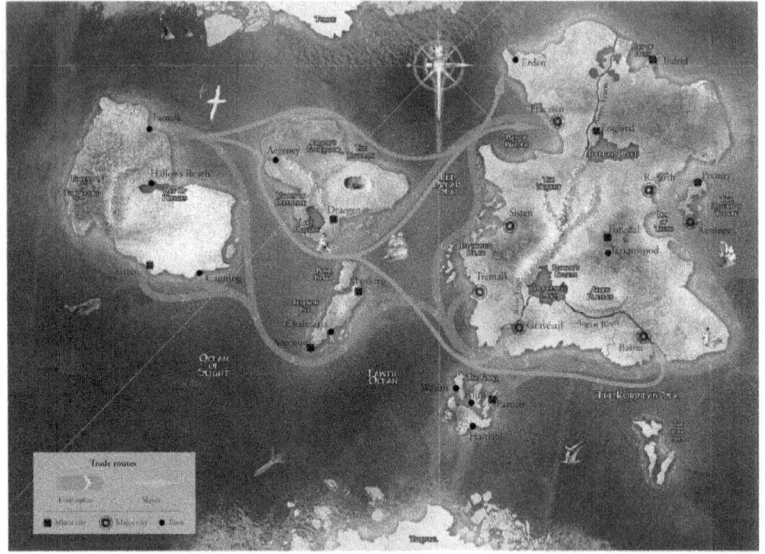

Kaleion

Charles W. McDonald Jr.

Charles W. McDonald Jr.

Eden

Charles W. McDonald Jr.

Pre-Flood Terran

Charles W. McDonald Jr.

Damon of Basrat - The Dark Knight of Magic

Damon the Banished - The Dark Knight of Magic

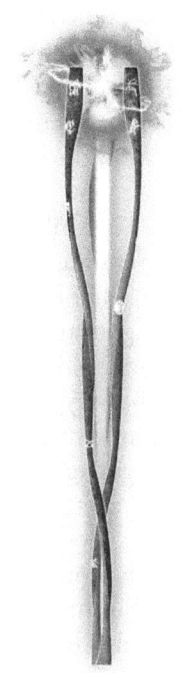

Prologue: The Cauldron of Hate

(South of the Aegen River, Kaleion, A Very Long Time Ago)

The chores were the chores, and it didn't matter how sweltering the work was in the blasted summer heat. Anything less than his best effort would see him punished, yet again. Severely! Brushing the hay straw off his brown wool pants, that no longer came down to his ankles, Kaylan checked the stack again, ensuring it was plumb and level against the barn wall, with all the excess hay picked up in a feedpail for the horses. His welts still throbbed from when the last pile of hay had fallen over. *That mustn't happen again.*

His starry-blue eyes shone like star-sapphire gems, taking in the dusky hues of the Kaleion sunset for only a moment as he ran his right hand through his wavy raven hair. Feeling the sweat on the back of his neck, running his matted handkerchief across it, then over his forehead to remove the sweat from his brow, Kaylan crossed off another of his many chores in his head, moving on to the next—collecting eggs from the roost.

His worn-to-the-knub boots kicking up dust along the dirt path between the barn, the chicken coop and the house, created earthen motes that filled his mouth and nostrils as he moved with all possible haste, this way and that. Enough to make him stop and cough the stirred up dust from his airway.

The sound of his father's footsteps coming up from behind, with his heels scuffing that very same dirt path between the barn and house, made Kaylan cringe inside—if not visibly so.

"WHERE ARE MY EGGS?!!" Keirill barked at his son, emphasizing his displeasure with his son with a slap of his huge hand on Kaylan's still-tender shoulder, knowing how much it would sting after his son's last punishment.

"Doing it now, Pa." Pivoting away from his father's iron grip, Kaylan moved with all the haste his thirteen-year-old frame would allow.

From just inside the barn doorway, Keirill examined Kaylan's haystacks, taking the measure of how his last punishment had drastically improved his son's work. He didn't take pleasure in castigating his son—at least he didn't think it so. Seren wouldn't approve, but then she wasn't here to express her disapproval....

Every day he intended to drive home his expectations for his son's development into a man. And his son *would* meet those very high expectations. No matter how many whippings it took, his son was going to understand what it took to survive in this world. His father hadn't been easy on him. He saw no reason to take it easy on Kaylan. No reason at all.

After his own experiences with *his* father, Keirill didn't even want a child, and he'd made that perfectly clear to his wife from the very beginning. Yet, still... there he was—scurrying about the barn, trying to prove himself worthy. Keirill's lips pressed together in a hard, thin line at the thought and how Kaylan had come into being. Now, his responsibility—alone—whether he wanted it or not.... Spitting into the worn path in the grass, Keirill silently cursed his dead wife.

Simmering as he retired back to his house, awaiting his eggs, Keirill contemplated his son's next sentence. He needed to be ready when his son failed him again, for he knew disappointment was coming.

Letting out a heavy sigh of relief at his father's departure, and the oppressive dark cloud of discontent that went with him, Kaylan moved with all possible speed gathering up the eggs. He knew his father wanted to keep the brown ones and sold the white ones. Going from hen to hen to hen, carefully collecting, but not dawdling, he'd managed to sort them into separate crude wire baskets that he knew he'd have to repair soon. Maybe moving a little *too* fast, as a gnarled wire from the white egg basket caught itself on the edge of the pen's enclosure, sending every one of them to the floor of the barn in a hasty, hot, and scrambled mess. Words couldn't escape Kaylan's mouth, not a single curse or expression of any kind. Just shaking from the tips of his bangs to the toes of his feet in terror, standing there looking at the profound justification for his next beating.

"WHAT'S TAKING SO *BLASTED* LONG?!" Keirill's bark hammered the barn loud enough to make the siding rattle against rusted framing nails already loose from weathering and wear. Noticing Kaylan using his body to shield something from his view, Keirill shoved his son's lithe body aside, looking at a week's worth of income on the dirt floor of his barn. Without a word, Keirill ripped his son's sweat-soaked, dirty-white tunic from his young frame, revealing a series of lash welts across his back, shoulders, neck and chest. Wounds already so much deeper than the flesh....

The fresh ones, still raised red with pus, threatened to burst and infect. Kaylan had stopped shaking as he walked over to the barn wall where his father liked to beat him—trying to comport himself for what he knew was to come. His body no longer shook in fear, but his hands couldn't calm themselves—shaking as he braced his young body against the barn wall. He knew his father detested the emotion of fear even more than he reviled the action of failure, so Kaylan tried his very best not to compound the forthcoming punishment.

Noticing his son taking responsibility for his actions triggered a faint and distant memory of a lesson from his own father—like unto a memory of a memory, shrouded in opaque justifications that no longer made sense. "Kaylan, did you do what you promised me you would do?"

"No, sir." His head faced the wall in obedience, awaiting the first strike. His knuckles pale-white as they tightly gripped the barn's frame studs to steady himself.

"And what have I told you about doing what you say?"

"If you don't do what you say, you're just a useless bag of flesh." A lesson he'd been taught many times, and severely so.

"That's right, and that's why we punish the flesh. If the flesh is holding us back, then it must be pierced and cut away." It hadn't gone unnoticed by Kaylan that his father had already picked up his whip from the opposite barn wall.

With his last words, the first strike came across his lower back, where he had the most severe wounds from the last several beatings. Kaylan's young body shook down to the tips of his toes, resonating with the stinging pain his father's whip had brought him. All of his senses suddenly lit on fire by the first strike of his father's whip, he could smell the worn leather and the sweat from his father's hands upon it. The bitter taste of dirt upon his lips and tongue suddenly more acute. The matted, dull-grey wood grain of the local pine used to build the barn more sharply in focus and defined, as if his tears were acting like a powerful magnifying lens. The hairs on the back of his neck, as well as his arms and legs all standing on end, intensely sensitive to his father's *hate* electrifying the air around him. In a terse and perverted way, he'd never felt more alive than when he was being beaten. The peril of death bringing life more into focus....

The next strike wrapped around his right shoulder to the right front of his chest, cutting him deeply and leaving ruts in his flesh as the blood began to seep out of the fresh wounds.

No longer contained to the inside, Kaylan's body began to visibly shake as the welled-up tears, he could no longer hold back, began to flow. As the first of his tears hit the tops of his dusty boots, quickly followed by a second and third, he couldn't help but look down. Watching his own tears streaking fluidic trails of vanquished *hope* in the worn and dusty leather just as the next strike came across the same right shoulder but over the top this time rather than around the outside. Those would leave deep scars as they merged with the previous ruts, driving the leather deeper into his young skin. Kaylan's tears flowed freely now, clearing the dust completely from the tops of his worn boots. His body was shaking so severely it was hard to concentrate on any thought at all except the one that always came to him as he was beaten. *When will I ever get it right, so I don't disappoint him? I'm sorry, Father. I'll do better. I promise.*

Somewhere inside, a part of Kaylan cursed those thoughts, and he began to hear whisperings; from where, he couldn't say, but as the next strike came, the whisperings became louder. Two words, overlapping one another again and again. *Fight* and *back*. The next strike of his father's whip landed on his outer left shoulder, wrapping around to his left pectoral, leaving a heavy stinging up and down his youthful frame. Whispers became shouts inside his thoughts. *FIGHT BACK! FIGHT BACK! FIGHT BACK! FIGHT BACK!*

The next strike came in exactly the same spot as the last, with Kaylan grabbing the black leather whip this time before it could recoil back to his father. Pulling it with all his might, his father's massive frame came roiling towards him in mid-air. It happened so fast, and then his fist was smashing Keirill's face in mid-air so hard it snapped Keirill's neck, sending his father flying back in the opposite direction, where his father crashed up against the wall in a slumping thud. *How did I...?* He didn't understand what was happening.

Kaylan just stood there for a moment, standing over the slumped body of his father, now coming to. *KILL HIM NOW!* Whispers no more; these were shouts, and they were *right*! Jumping on top of his father, Kaylan put his thumbs directly in his father's eye sockets, squeezing with all his might in a pinching motion between his thumbs and forefingers, watching his father's thick skull implode in his own hands and under the immense pressure of his own iron grip.

Spurts of blood, gore, and cranial fluid dotted and streaked down Kaylan's forehead and all over the barn wall siding. It was over so fast for the thirteen-year-old boy—now a murderer. Watching his father's brains running down the weathered wood planks of the barn wall and out of his crushed skull, Kaylan knew he couldn't stay here. *Was that a glint of hope and light amidst the violent bloodletting?*

Looking down at his hands, seeing them drenched in his father's bodily fluids, Kaylan stood silent for a few moments, contemplating his new freedom—his new future—as the gore of his boldness drained from his stained brow into his starry-blue eyes. Slowly, the blackness in deep charcoal-blue hues—a mixture of cranial fluid and blood—crept over the top of Kaylan's cornea, then his irises, turning them purple, then a smoky charcoal, then black. His only awareness was how upside-down his life had just been turned, and that staying *here* was not an option.

Moments later, after cleaning up in the house, grabbing a few necessities in a dirty wool sack he carried out to his side so as not to further inflame his freshly-beaten back and shoulders, Kaylan began heading east down the road to the biggest walled-city he knew—Basrat.

*   *   *   *

Walking all the way through the night, Kaylan was exhausted, and his wounds throbbed as his boots were almost totally worn through, but he had to put some distance between himself and his family's farm. The twenty-cubit-high outer heavy stone walls of Basrat before him, he tried to form a believable story—a mostly true story of his effort to forge a new life—just absent some of the more gory details. The city guard was coming up fast as Kaylan's position in line progressed.

"Aye, who goes there? State your business," the guard challenged the frail, old man hauling fruits and grains into the city in a wooden cart.

"Raken the Merchant," the man replied. "Bringing only the freshest fruits and wheat for the king's people."

"Unlikely." The guard briefly eyed his cart, kicking the wheels forward toward the gate. "Get," he ordered as the elderly man dragged his cart inside the city walls.

"Who goes there, boy?" The city guard paid little attention to what little threat a small boy could bring to his city, but something didn't feel right about the boy as the guard scratched the gnarled and matted mess of sweaty hair on the back of his over-sized skull.

With stirred-up dust in his now-black eyes from the merchant's cart in front of him, Kaylan tried not to cough at the guard. "Damon, looking for work." He displayed the guard his callused hands—a working boy's hands—turning them over for the guard.

A look at the boy's black eyes caused an alarming, taken-aback glare from the guard, "What the...."

Damon knew why the guard was staring at him. He'd seen the reason in the mirror when he was cleaning up, but he made no comment, only letting his desperation speak for him in his sullen and worn expression. He needed a break and he didn't have the words—nor the right—to ask for it.

Scratching the back of his head again, feeling the grit and grime of his already long morning rolling underneath his dirty fingertips, the guard wanted to reject the boy. Looking for any reason and finding plenty, he had all the justification he needed to send the boy away, but he really didn't look like the bad sort. He just looked...hopeless. Something worked on him from within. It was just a brief feeling, and then it was gone. "Aye, let him through."

Damon never looked back, only exhaling in relief as he crossed into the walled city of Basrat—his new home. His new origin.

(Austin, TX, Earth, Present Day)

His work on the next new fundamental for Dark Energy wasn't going as smoothly as had the one for Zero-Point, and Mira knew him frustrated by it. At least he had opened up to her about hearing the voices in his mind that came like 'prayers' he described. She didn't know what that was about, but with Damon, any number of things were possible.

"Are you hearing them even now," Mira asked, considering his beautiful black, smoke-rimmed gems.

Her eyes blinking more than normal as he considered what that meant, given what he knew of her, Damon longed to open up to her, but feared the abyss of where that could lead. Each were very different from the others—Dallia, Mira of old, Mira Castille of Earth, Evanyil, Victoria, Sijil.... All gave differing signals even though they were done with similar gestures. Each had a context and identity all their own. Each time, learning a new woman was like unto learning a new language—having the potential to be either thrilling or exasperating depending on the individual, but he didn't let the exasperating ones stick around very long.

This Mira was very special, and he knew it. He wanted very much to let her in, but he just needed to figure out the safest way to let that happen—if there was one.

"Earth to Damon, are you listening to me or just looking into my eyes, lost in thought again?" Lying in bed together, she longed for something more than mere pillow talk. She knew Damon's intellect was both broad and steep and it was so rare to find a man who could carry an intellectual conversation with her instead of her having to do all the work. This was one of the rare opportunities they had to actually get to know one another, and she wasn't about to let it pass her by.

"Sorry, I heard you…. Yes, I hear them even now. Even worlds away, I hear them asking me to heal this, or save them from that, or whether or not it's safe to fall in love again with someone new they just met. I hear my society, on the rim of Creation, asking for guidance…."

"And…?" Mira sat up, placing her right hand on his chest, "Are you going to give them the guidance they need?" Internally wondering if Damon were even qualified. His immeasurable power ran out in front of him like a great cantilever threatening to collapse, for its overhang was too long without support from the main body, that was the foundation of his identity, and his certainty.

He considered the question—in all its validity. *Who was he to provide guidance?* It was one thing for him to guide Radin in magic, but entirely something else to guide other Humans in life. *What example was his life for others to follow?* He needed the power of his new station to accomplish the Master Plan, but he wanted neither the responsibility nor the notoriety that came with it. Kellen was the one who sought infamy—not him. Yet, infamy found him far more often than it found even the mighty Kellen the Destroyer.

"I love your certainty of your own identity at such a young age. I miss that. It was so long ago; I barely remember it."

Now he was talking in riddles…. She loved his intellect…and his power, but often found herself in shaking terror at his ability to act with such mortal certitude and such quick decision-making. She knew and felt him a great doer of things, but she wondered if he foresaw all the outcomes of his actions before acting them out. "It's okay. You don't have to tell me if you don't feel like it. I can't say I understand, because there's no way I possibly could, but I understand feeling overwhelmed."

A big rakish smile from Damon involuntarily made her smile in kind.

Charles W. McDonald Jr.

"Thank you for that," as fond memories of Dallia stirred in his mind. He didn't want to share that part. Women didn't like being compared to one another. Men didn't either for that matter, but still the memory she raised was a good one.

"Thank you for what? Damon, what's going on in that head of yours?"

"I'm thinking there's a place I'd like to take you some day." Deflecting away from the topic of prayers and of his past was the best way out of this conversation.

"To your new planet?!" Mira's eyes were hopeful as her body leaned forward into Damon, now fully engaged in the promise of what could be.

"No!" His response was both terse and firm, causing her to recoil her head back into her pillow against the headboard.

She didn't understand what his deal was about not letting her go with him to the new world he'd made. It could really help her research, and she needed to find a way to make that happen. Turning her frown around, she shrugged off his rejection. Tracing ever-so-faint scars running across Damon's pectorals, shoulders, and neck, Mira freely thought aloud, "Why haven't you ever *Healed* these?"

His iron grip snatched her hand, immediately pulling her hand from his body. Rising from his king-size bed, Damon warned, "Some lessons are best left on the surface, where we can always remember them." His caution hung heavy in the air as he walked away from her out of the master bedroom without even looking back.

She knew Damon didn't fit the classical definition of bipolar, but the way he could swing from loving to completely shut-down terrified her. It was like walking in a minefield without a map of where the mines were buried.

Mira knew she needed to understand him better if this was ever going to work. She knew you didn't craft a Damon with teddy bears and flowers; Damon was forged in a *cauldron of hate*, and she feared, every day, exactly what that meant—for the both of them—her fears justified.

(One of Setinon's Moons, Present Day)

The fire crackled and hissed inside the maw of the cave as the night winds howled—more than powerful enough to sweep a man off his feet, carrying him away to oblivion. Inside a mountain or below ground was the only safe place when the great storms, that could last for weeks, bore down on the surface of the moon. These winds *would* carry the death of intense solar radiation and coronal-hole streams on them but for the transparent shield he'd placed over the maw of the cave.

The chaotic pattern of the fire's blue, orange, and yellow-green light danced off the third of his face not covered by the cowl of his hood. What could be seen were hard lines, dirty and rustic with weathering and age. A grey stubble formed a jagged goatee with a star-sapphire-like mole birthmark buried in the dimple of his chin. Tall, dark, and lean, he was still menacing if somewhat succumbed to the ravages of so very much time this mortal shell had already endured. Oh, he could have kept himself young and handsome with his magic, or even transferred his essence to another shell, but he had much bigger plans that required all his faculties focused on that outcome, rather than his vanity. Facing the mouth of the cave, he wasn't so far inside that he couldn't see crux of his anguish just above and beyond the far horizon. Setinon rose over his vista like a blue-green and white spherical jewel bedazzled with the glint of diamonds and gold—the millions of lights making up the endless city that adorned the planet, once his homeworld.

Hard, thin-pressed lips spoke of his pensiveness, while starry, bright-blue eyes backlit with smoke-rings of his ancient profession spoke of his imminent intent. Fiery embers—lighter than the frail air of the moon—made staggered stair-like trails, dancing before the intensity of his gaze upon the home of his *hate*.

Charles W. McDonald Jr.

Chapter 1: The Death of Men

(Southeast Corner of the Isle of Romney, Perion, Present Day)

lmost as far south into the Ocean of Mohers as one could go before reaching Carnac, the Isle of Romney had been both temperate and tropical—but that was before Radin had opened the First Seal, terrorizing the world with the Blood Night. Radin had left Royvan Miral specific instructions to find the Second Seal, no matter the outcome of the battle of Axum. Royvan didn't know who to follow: Talemar or Radin, but both wanted and needed the Second Seal, so it didn't matter. The only way through the decaying bleakness of the Blood Night was pressing through it—with whatever will remained.

It was as if they were lost deep in the bowels of a dark, dank cavern—the entrance sealed shut with debris. The only way forward was to move deeper into the mountain and hope for the best. They were committed now!

Looking up to the pale-red Blood Night sky Radin had brought to the world, Royvan Miral contemplated the words that kept coming to him in his dreams each night:

> And there shall be but seven trumpets, bearing seven messages,
> For all the worlds to hear, and all men therein.
> And each message shall be sealed up in itself.
> And woe unto the men of the worlds, for once the first is uttered,
> What will be will be swiftly, and nothing in Creation shall hinder.

Often, he contemplated that second line, 'For all the worlds to hear, and all the men therein,' wondering if Radin's words had been the catalyst of terror on other planets of Humanity. Shaking off the thought, bringing himself back to the world that mattered most to him right now—*theirs*—Royvan mustered the reserves of his resolve.

Looking to Kerrich, Levi, and Ham, each in turn, he knew their world was forever changed, and prayed for Radin's soul. If Radin still lived, and that was a big *if*, he was surely being tormented by that great and unholy *thing* that took him. That moment had changed them all—Royvan especially so. Royvan Miral was neither a man of faith nor religion. He was a believer in what he could see, touch, and feel in the here and now. But now, that he had firsthand knowledge of the extremes of what existed and interacted with them in their world; it had changed everything for him. This was it, and there was no denying it anymore, for any of them. He had all the motivation required to do what Radin had asked of him— even if Radin had never made the request at all. He didn't know if he was now a man of faith or not. *Am I now?* He contemplated the prayers of guidance and protection he'd offered for Radin. He wasn't sure what to believe in, except that his unique skills were needed now more than ever. He'd been entrusted with this most vital of all tasks…. People were counting on him and he trusted in those people, that at least one—if not many—had the proper intentions of getting Humanity on the other side of this…unmaking of Creation.

Tracing his fingertips over the stone sculptures of a ring of Nine Men, half buried and weathered by the relentlessness of time, Royvan Miral recalled his knowledge of ancient Ferian. It was a dead language dating back more than a thousand years and didn't always provide direct word-for-word translations. Some of what he was reading had no meaning in today's tongue:

'The Death of Men awaits you with the coming of the morning. East, as far East as the morning, you will find the doom of all men, for your age and the ages to come.'

It was a terribly inaccurate translation, he hoped, but the best he could afford from his memory of the dead, hieroglyphic language. 'Doom' could have meant 'darkness,' 'loss,' or 'void' in today's tongue, but none of those sounded good, and neither did the 'Death of Men.'

The ring of statues reminded him of the second ring on the holy grounds of Axum, but these were clearly not the same men as those depicted in Axum. The architectural style was vastly different as well. This ring was of a totally different time period.

"What does it say," Kerrich asked, dismounting to get a closer look for himself.

"Don't," Royvan Miral warned. "Get back on your horse. And tell Quin to get ready; we'll need a *Portal*...and a ship."

"Where are we going," Levi asked, looking between them—looking for a glimmer of *hope*.

"East." Royvan wasn't in the mood for details. It could only be one of a few places from the other pieces to this puzzle he'd been putting together over the last several years. Even before he found the First Seal, he had found clues to the location of the second, the fourth, and the fifth. And this wasn't the first time he'd seen similar warnings of the 'Death of Men' associated with the Second Seal. It terrified him, but they were already living in a world of darkness, and the only way through it was through it.

*   *   *   *

(Exeter, Perion, Present Day)

The four shades of grey stone that made up the Exeter manor gave a dead and muted contrast to the once green grass, now already turning brown as the pale-red rain of the Blood Night worked its acrid magic on the topsoil, killing every-thing. The cathedral vaulted ceilings of the East Wing of the manor only blended with the square architecture of the West Wing by the identical spired smokestacks with decorative stone rings around the top. The center square tower allowed light into the keep from five massive rectangular windows, each nearly two stories tall, but only red light poured through now, and any other time of day or night. *Cursed Blood Night*, Brigance thought as he tried to console Elise. This part of his job was the worst part. He had to shoulder an even bigger burden than just that of Elise weeping on his arm as he stroked her strawberry-blonde hair with his massive burly hand. For what little time he had spent with the young man, Radin had earned his respect, and Brigance would carry out Radin's last wishes. Plans had been drawn up, before the battle, for this very eventuality, and the fact that Radin could see beyond the now impressed upon him, even more, the need to carry out his will.

"I am with you, Elise. We all are. You can stay with us as long as you wish, and I'll see to it my finest men are watching you at all times."

"Tell me the truth," Elise demanded, punching his shoulder, knowing he'd barely feel it. "Is he gone? I have to know!"

"I don't know, but I can only relate to what I see and hear, not what I believe or hope for. Hope is not a strategy I subscribe to, and from what I saw, and heard, I'd say you should start preparing yourself for the worst." He hated delivering that kind of message to such a good woman as Elise, but she needed someone to tell her the truth, and from what Brigance had seen take hold of Radin and what he saw that *thing* disappear into…. There were just no words of comfort he could offer her that would have been fair to her…and her baby.

"GOD!" Elise howled, slamming both her fists into Brigance's chest, blunting his armor. Fresh blood dripped from underneath gold fingernails—like unto living gold-dust—dripping onto dried, crusted blood of the battle upon Brigance's armor. From Brigance's point of view, he could see all the hope and light in her once-bright eyes now shadow-cast and tear-laden as tears heavy with condemnation traced staggered trails of incomprehensible loss down his blood-stained armor.

"You have to take care of yourself now. You're carrying a child—his child and yours. You have to think beyond yourself now." He didn't have the words to provide guidance to an already brilliant and capable woman, but she needed help. These were not merely tears of loss. They were tears of crying out for help…and for answers.

He didn't know her full origin story, and she'd been very tight-lipped about her past, but he knew there was a lot going on behind those eyes that he wasn't privy to, and he wasn't sure he was ready to hear it should she have the courage to voice it. Still, he loved her like a sister, and he'd do anything to help Elise. Anything!

Brigance didn't know of her children, left behind on Earth to seek out Michael's reborn soul, so he couldn't comprehend her loss of *both* fathers of *all* her children.

She wanted to die, like so many of the men on the battlefield last night.

Charles W. McDonald Jr.

She deserved to die for leaving her children behind. Twice her God had punished her by taking the two loves of her life—the two that created children with her. Twice her God had broken her soul and her heart, and *she'd never forgive him for it. NEVER!* This was a cruel and unjust God, tampering with Humanity in such a way—this God the Creator of all things. In the shadow-laden vision of Elise's eyes, *he was the Creator of Nightmares.*

*　　*　　*　　*

His right hand draped across his waist, holding the star-sapphire-laden hilt of the great Starfire hung about his left hip. Talemar side-stepped wounded here, and triage carts there, as his eyes took in the losses everywhere he looked. He didn't even know where to begin as he counted the wounded while walking among what was left of his ranks, with Rowarc, who he'd made a General in hopes of bringing some unity to the army Radin had assembled. They needed unity in their leadership ranks now. Over four thousand dead, with twice as many wounded. Even with *Healing*, they'd be lucky to get back to thirteen or fourteen-thousand strong. It wouldn't be enough, and Radin hadn't even come close to solving the financial and logistical problems of keeping such an army, let alone mobilizing it for the battles to come. Radin had left a great deal unfinished, but he had also given the biggest sacrifice. Talemar needed loyalty, respect, unity, and organization above all things, right now.

"Where do we stand on Treasury," Talemar asked Rowarc, side-stepping another group of wounded. He still wore the Crystal Crown always. He had to send a message and ensure it was received in every corner of their forces—and beyond. As far as the message could carry.

"Terrible. Maybe two-and-a-half days at the most. Food for three days at the most. Now, I'm counting the six thousand men we took from King Aaron adding them back to replenish our own. I assumed you wouldn't want to release them from their fealty oaths they swore to you on the battlefield." Rowarc's eyes still watered over what he'd seen happen to his only son, firsthand. He could only hope Radin hadn't suffered long, but his heart knew otherwise. It was virtually impossible for him to get the image of that devil of filth and vile out of his mind. It haunted him every waking moment, and he knew it would torment him in his dreams—if he ever slept again.

"No and thank you for reminding me. That helps the count, dramatically replenishing our forces, but only if they can be trusted. Ensure the untrustworthy are executed publicly. I won't tolerate treachery or dissent in our ranks." Already hardening himself, the written and vocal legend of Talemar was one of mercy and goodness, but the reality had proven quite different. Having been through a great war before and knowing his failings, he wouldn't let his own historical reputation get in the way of doing what needed to be done.

"I'll take care of it." Rowarc tried to force the image of his son being snatched by that *thing* out of his head, but it consumed him, destroying his *hope*. *Could there be **hope** after what he'd seen?* He wasn't sure anymore.

(The Trident, Kaleion, Tens of Thousands of Years Ago)

He wasn't sure where they'd dropped off his brother, except that it must have been tens of thousands of lightyears away as he heard the gravity warp drive disengage some weeks after Alexelio had been abandoned on what he could only assume was another inhabitable world—at least he hoped it to be inhabitable.

As he materialized, handcuffed on the virgin landscape before him, Durial observed the beauty and majesty of the shape of the snow-capped mountains before him. His digital handcuffs disengaged, falling to the ground beneath him, allowing him to finally scratch the star-sapphire-like mole birthmark buried in the dimple of his chin. He felt the life energy of all that surrounded him flood his veins for the first time in as long as he could remember. A deep breath of the wondrous fresh mountain air and Durial felt renewed—reborn even. The ocher veil of his new homeworld's dawn made motes of dust glisten in embers of promise as he took in the unique shape of the mountain range's northern edge, ending in a great river feeding a massive downstream lake.

If his brother was this fortunate, perhaps they stood a chance at a brighter future. Wherever they'd left his brother, he would find Alexelio if it took him centuries. The Sentinels couldn't keep them separated for long; surely, they knew that. Banning magic wasn't necessary for technology to flourish. The two could co-exist. If only the Sentinels could see it their way....

Instead, he stood banished here on this new world. Looking around at the twin moons, both enormous in the sky above, this planet couldn't have been inhabitable all that long—a few thousand years at most, perhaps. Those moons would relax in their orbits over time. And time was what he needed to start building here anew, but only if....

Suddenly, a magnificent young brunette with high cheekbones and bright blue eyes, wearing only a one-piece black iridescent bodice with a plunging neckline cut high on her hips, materialized a few paces away from Durial. His wife and children had been killed in the raid that had captured him and his brothers. He couldn't help but feel both excited and ashamed at the intoxicating beauty of the young woman before him, but she was handcuffed the same as him. As he watched her handcuffs disengage, falling to the ground, their blue eyes locked with one another and he knew they had a chance here on this magnificent new world— together....

Charles W. McDonald Jr.

Part 1: Emrys Wledig

Charles W. McDonald Jr.

Through your promise and light,
I will do my best to pierce the night
That has consumed, by our own thoughts and deeds,
The Seeds of Humanity. Though, I fear the
Hatred and resolve of your judgment of Mankind,
For yours is the light of hope
And the despair of hate.

Charles W. McDonald Jr.

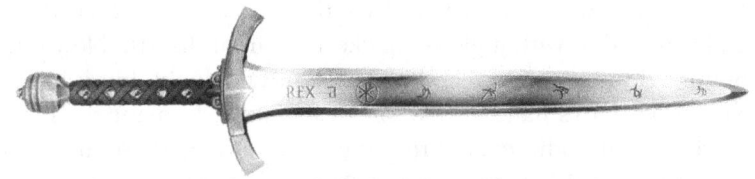

Chapter 2: The Lord Thy God

(The Vyran Wyrm's Desert, Perion, Present Day)

ven dozens of leagues from the North Sea, Elise could hear it raging against the northern shoreline of the continent and the Northwest region of the Throne of Knor. Here at the Northwestern tip of the mountain range, Elise retraced her steps from her first arrival here, following Damon's powerful wake to Perion. It was cold but warmer than it should have been this far north. The Blood Night was already taking its levy here too. She assumed there wasn't a place on the planet that wouldn't soon feel its blood-laden grip—choking out the lifeforce of the planet from the outside in. The pale-red hue of the sky provided little pure light, making it difficult for her to recognize the exact crevice where she'd hidden it, but she was beginning to recognize a familiar turn here or boulder there. Another familiar turn, followed by a recognizably unique boulder, and she was finally there—at the mouth of a cave, shaped like an upside-down V. She didn't want to leave it in the cave any longer; that would have been too dangerous, and she couldn't risk it falling into the wrong hands.

With welled eyes, Elise focused, using her magic to move the giant boulder on the shelf below and to the west of the mouth of the cave. As the stone rolled for her, obeying the request of the Arcane she gated through her left index finger, a section of the mountain, hewn by her magic revealed itself, along with a longer than normal Roman short sword with a wider than normal gold guard and an elegant hand-and-a-half grip. Not long enough to qualify for a longsword, it—like its custom, hand-made scabbard—had five runes of magic down the center of the blade's fuller. She hadn't bothered to bring the scabbard, for this blade didn't require it. Whatever its composition, it wasn't steel, and Michael's lab examination of it on Earth had proven that. The best labs on Earth couldn't determine its full composition.

Unseen hands brought the great weapon of Creation to her as it spun in the air until the Latin inscription on the other side of the blade could be seen. *'I am the Lord, thy God. Get thee behind me, Satan!'*

Charles W. McDonald Jr.

Her eyes could no longer hold back the tears as she recalled the last time her husband had held it, with it gleaming like a star in his hands. Now it was just a piece of burnished metal—a great and perfect sword no doubt, but it had only ever come to life in Michael's hands. It wasn't dead—only dormant she hoped. She had intended to see if Radin could bring it to life, but now those thoughts…. She couldn't even bring herself to contemplate them. A hard swallow as she choked that thought down, with tears cascading down her cheeks and onto the satin-sheen fabric of her soft, pale-peach shoes she wore to match her pregnant peach gown and cloak of pleated and pillowy cream. Her pregnancy had already taken from her the ability to wear the bodice-like, shimmering artwork clothing familiar to the female mages of her homeworld, now so very far away….

Even her beloved Michael didn't know her true origin story, and for that, she felt even more guilt. She'd always had a plan to tell him, of course. When the time was right…. Life marched on…. One pregnancy led to another and then their lives were full and happy and complicated by royal obligations of leadership and governance. And then there was the great war on Earth that robbed her first of even more time with her beloved husband, then robbed her Michael himself. The right time never came before *his* sands ran out of the hourglass of their moment to truly know one another.

Her time with Radin passed in the blink of an eye in comparison and she never got to tell him, either. *Was it really so hard? Truth right from the beginning?*

She needed to right this wrong. This series of wrongs…. She needed to put this mighty weapon of God the Creator's own making into the hands of someone who could do something with it, before all was lost.

No, she thought, *if Talemar is our last hope, then he needs all the help he can get.* There was no point in taking this home with her. There was no one there qualified to wield it. No one there who understood the stakes. Not yet…

(Kent, England, Earth, Present Day, Late Afternoon Hours)

His soft, purpose-built shoes hushed the sounds of his covert movements inside Leeds Castle, where he was well on the way of being kicked out of MI-6 for disobeying direct orders from Quincy Author Billings, Director of Clandestine Operations. His SRR Unit was still seven minutes out, but his Heckler & Koch MP5 felt comfortable in his hands as he progressed inside, where he knew his father to be held hostage by twelve or more active shooters. The six outside had already met

Charles W. McDonald Jr.

his eight-inch tactical combat knife, as he moved stealthily through the foyer to the sounds of the voices speaking in Farsi in the near distance.

He could hear what sounded like a young woman screaming, following the noise of a loud slap and smack of someone being struck hard. Her screams suddenly muffled as one of them asked why the checkpoint outside hadn't checked in on time—assuming his Farsi was still passable. Even with recent ops in the sandbox, he was more than a little rusty with the language, though his Russian was much better.

Making the turn into the Banquet Hall, he heard the voices getting louder, but not because he was getting closer to the hostages. The hail of bullets from the young, thick-bearded man with the angry brown eyes lodged in Michael's body armor, sending him flailing against the heavy door casings, but not before he returned fire with his silenced MP5. His rounds splattered the would-be terrorist blood all over the slim rectangular lower-level windows with arched tops. Even though his shots had been run through a silencer and killed without shattering the glass behind the jihadi, the terrorist's rounds had *not* been run through a silencer! The very distinctively loud AK-47's 7.62mm rounds were violently loud, especially inside chambered and cloistered structures with high-vaulted ceilings. Everyone in Leeds Castle knew where he was now, as he slumped down to the floor of the Banquet Hall, trying to gather his bearings—and his breath.

Running his hands over his chest, in-between the body armor, Michael verified nothing had pierced.

Quickly running over to the dead terrorists, Michael Anthony Day ripped the man's radio from his dying grip. At least he knew the source of the Farsi now, but that didn't help. He could hear hushed voices and footsteps rushing towards him at a fast clip, with the distinct smell of spent gunpowder perfuming the halls. Given what he knew of the meeting scheduled to take place, combined with the sounds of where the footsteps were coming from, he assumed they were in Thorpe Hall.

Throwing his back to the wall just inside the Banquet Hall—feeding his MP5 a fresh clip—Michael waited for the footsteps, listening for them to slow as they reached the other side of the entryway to the Banquet Hall. He knew they could already see their friend slumped against the wall bleeding out from their vantage, but…. *Shit!* Michael just barely caught the reflection in the glass, just in time.

Spinning, he fired just on the other side of the thick casing, hitting another young Middle Eastern man, this one with just a small amount of designer stubble for a beard. A double-tap to his heart, followed by a quick shot to his forehead, and he was out of the picture too, but Michael's own body armor caught another

Charles W. McDonald Jr.

round right in his left side, causing him to double over in the pain of the blunt-force trauma of his armor absorbing another close-range shot.

The pair had come down in standard two-by-two formation so the near shooter, opposite the man he had downed, had a good shot at him as he squeezed off another three-round burst at Michael.

Returning fire, Michael double-tapped the thirty's-aged terrorist in the forehead, dropping him opposite his younger jihadi brethren.

"Agh!" Michael let out a painful moan. He hadn't felt the round that grazed his neck, but he was vaguely aware of the blood leaking down his chest under his body armor. Funny how you often didn't feel the ones that struck for at least the first few moments, but it wasn't his first time being shot.

He hadn't been to Leeds for quite a while, but he still remembered the way to the Thorpe Room. Sprinting that way, he swapped in another fresh magazine. Approaching the Thorpe Room, he pulled out his tactical knife with his left hand, while his dominant right hand carried his MP5.

A glance off the once-mirror finish of his blade—now matted from blood he'd had to wipe—showed him the beautiful young strawberry-blonde woman he'd heard screaming before, gagged and bound to one of the antique and irreplaceable winged-back chairs, along with his father, the Secretary of State for Defence, the Leader of the House of Commons, and the Leader of the House of Lords. Standing behind them was a middle-aged jihadi with a robust and heavily graying beard, maybe 6'1," talking into a video camera while holding a scimitar to the neck of the Leader of the House of Lords. Two more jihadis by the tall rectangular, arched-topped windows—typical to Leeds Castle—plus the one talking into the camera, and the camera guy, meant there must have been a few more still searching for him or hidden somewhere else in the room.

Bouncing the image off the windows, then off his blade, he caught a glimpse of two more men behind the antique Victorian sofas, guns drawn toward the main entry. The high-gloss finish of the wood panel walls helped him see a little better around the room, but reverse images of reverse images made it hard to paint an accurate landscape. It was like live-fire practice in a funhouse, but with *much* more dire consequences.

Michael checked his watch. Still two minutes out, and this shitbag was about to stream the beheading of the Leader of the House of Lords on live feed! Right now!

Rolling a flash-bang across the wide hardwood floor planks of the Thorpe Hall Drawing Room, Michael chased the flash-bang into the room, standing in the doorway, shooting the men he most recently identified behind the sofas first, splattering their cranial fluid on the wood-panel walls. An immediate duck to avoid the scimitar thrown at him by the man behind the Leader of the House of Lords, Michael tossed his tactical knife weak-handedly at the cameraman—striking him in the neck, then ducked behind the cover of the sofas at the entrance of the room. He wanted to toss a grenade to wipe out the other two by the window, probably now hiding behind more priceless furniture, but he couldn't destroy Leeds Castle in the process of taking these guys out.

"You think yourself a Hero?"

Michael assumed the thick Middle Eastern accent had come from the man talking into the camera. He sounded, at the very least, unassimilated to the West—if not a refugee. *Syrian maybe...?*

Pulling out his .40-cal SIG Sauer ® P226, Michael checked to make sure there was a round in the chamber—having intimate knowledge of the 5.5lb precision trigger he'd had installed—he knew himself ready if he could just coax out a clean shot or two. Readying his last flash-bang, Michael leapt up from behind the sofas and tossed it to the last known location of the two by the windows. As the flash-bang flushed them out behind their cover with its concussive force, shattering glass all over them, Michael squeezed off two rounds, hitting each in the head while on the move. With only their leader left, Michael trained the red dot sighting on the middle-aged jihadi, taking a moment to talk to him in reply, knowing there would be no talking him out of his mission. But if there was a way to take him alive, he had to try. They needed one alive to give them answers, and he'd left a trail of dead bodies all the way to the Thorpe Room.

"I'm just here to make sure this thing doesn't go any more sideways than it already has." Michael knew reasoning with this asshole was an impossibility. Fanatics were, by definition, immune to reason. All this man cared about was his precious Allah, and Michael was about to send this shitbag to meet him. "Hey, tell me something...," Michael prompted, trying not to lose sight of the time, as he waited for the rest of his unit to arrive. But with it down to just the two of them, he was pretty confident he could take this guy out. The question was, could he do it without this asshole taking the life of one of the hostages first, or in tandem.

"What's that?" The middle-aged jihadi hissed at him in his thick and guttural accent.

Michael slow-walked backward nice and easy from behind the sofas back toward the entrance of the room, giving the man a wider berth—though never moving his red-dot-sighting of the terrorist's forehead. The jihadi had his AK-47 pointed directly at Michael with a Colt®-45 pointed at the head of the Leader of the House of Lords.

Charles W. McDonald Jr.

"Tell me what all this is about. Why are you here? What do you want," Michael asked, yanking his tactical knife out of the cameraman's neck as he backed his way toward the entrance of the Thorpe Room.

The middle-aged jihadi smiled knowingly as if to insinuate his knowledge of the rationale was beyond Michael's ability to comprehend.

It was all the opening Michael needed as he noticed the Colt®-45-barrel drift just enough at an angle away from its former target so as to give the hostage a fighting chance, but the instant had to be seized…. NOW!

A quick, smooth movement of his familiar P226, put the red-dot-sighting on the jihadi's left shoulder. Calculating the shot would point the jihadi's Colt®-45 even further away from the Leader of the House of Lords' head. Like taking a bank shot in pool, and hoping his geometry was sound, he took the shot in a smooth trigger pull, putting a giant hole in the jihadi's left shoulder as he returned fire in a death blossom of his AK-47 and two rounds fired from his Colt®-45, burying its rounds in the heavy door casing of the entrance to the Thorpe Room.

"Ugh!" Michael dropped to his knees as his vest took another two rounds from the AK-47 at far too close range. Seeing the terrorist swinging around the barrel of his Colt®-45 as he could no longer hold his AK-47 with his left arm nearly blown off from Michael's .40-cal tactical shot, Michael quickly raised the barrel of his P226 and fired.

"Ughhh," the terrorist groaned as his cranium was blown open from Michael's precision shot from his SIG® P226. Slumping to the floor behind the Leader of the House of Lords, Michael looked into the Leader's terror-filled and swollen eyes as his own eyes closed for the first time in minutes. God, he was tired, *and* sore, *and*…in trouble.

"Michael…." A familiar voice called out from the open doorway to the Thorpe Room, causing him to rise and pivot, acknowledging his superior from his SRR unit.

"Terry, sorry I couldn't wait." Blood all over his big stature, Michael didn't shrink away from his responsibility for all this. He'd take whatever punishment came his way…. His eyes made contact with Terry's and he could see the disappointment in Terry's face along with his grimacing disposition. It was a proper cock-up, and he knew it.

"Well…, a proper faff you've made," Colonel Terry Goodwin quipped, taking the measure of Michael's kill ratio, and the fact he'd left no one alive to piece this mess together.

Killing the camera feed, Michael walked over to the beautiful strawberry-blonde in the powder-blue and white lace summer dress, removing the duct tape and the hand towel they'd used to gag her. He slowly patted her pretty face, looking at the Leader of the House of Lords and the Leader of the House of Commons—the only two awake at the moment. Seeing she was now starting to come out of it, as she pulled her strawberry-blonde locks out of her face, Michael moved to the Leader of the House of Lords, David Wright, removing his tape and gag.

"Yes well, ace congratulations all round, but how about we cut everyone else loose. What's say?" David Wright retorted, causing Michael to resume cutting the thick rope ties with his bloody tactical knife, making the Leader of the House of Lords cringe at getting his hands bloody. "You can all have your brilliant chin wag later." David tried shrugging off the near-death experience with his quips, but he was shaking on the inside and immensely grateful looking around at Michael's work, walking over to the camera which he smashed to bits with a crushing stomp of his right foot.

"Right, well, we didn't really need that for evidence," team member Mason jibed, filing into the room behind the SRR Colonel.

"If no one else is going to offer it, I will," Janet Cook, Leader of the House of Commons, offered, "Thank you." Shaking Michael's hand as soon as he untied her.

Now, cutting his father loose, lightly slapping his cheeks to bring him around, he gave another look at the beautiful young girl in the powder-blue and white lace dress, now being doted over by David Wright. "Darling…." David petted her beautiful long hair. Michael wondered how a fifty-plus-year-old politician got off taking such a young wife.

"Ugh," his father starting to come around while his team members started the evidence collection process. "What happened," Michael's father asked, shaking his head as he came to.

"What were you doing here, Dad?" He didn't know all the comings and goings of his father—they didn't talk *that* often. Nor was it like him to be in some super-secret meeting with the top echelon of British Government Leadership and him to know nothing about it. His clearance was as high as his fathers'.

"Meeting with some of the political leadership. They say they found something near Shrewsbury." The words leaked and ached slowly out of his father, who was starting to show a bit of a shiner on his temple where they cold-cocked him.

"Not Shrewsbury. I told you it *must* be in *one* of only *two* places. Either the Berth in Shropshire, or in Wroxeter, at the seat of his ancient power," the beautiful strawberry-blonde clarified, though Michael hadn't the foggiest of what she was talking about.

Charles W. McDonald Jr.

"Whose ancient power, and who are you," Michael asked while trying to get the lay of the land, causing the Leader of the House of Lords to clear the room, evidence collection in progress or not—bleeding terrorists on Leeds priceless flooring or not.

"Michael, I'm going to read you in," David Wright announced with a tone of finality as he closed the distance with the man who'd just saved their lives.

"Read me into what, sir? What's going on, and what was this meeting about?"

"This meeting was to authorize a dig," Janet Cook added, still trying to comport herself after the near-death experience.

"THAT'S what all this was about?! A DIG?!" Michael scratched his head; more than just a bit of this mess wasn't adding up. "Wait a minute.... Digs are supposed to be authorized by the English Heritage. I see politicians and political appointees here. Well..., and her." Michael didn't do anything as gauche as to point at the beautiful strawberry-blonde, but his eyes might as well have been precision daggers.

"And her, yes...Michael Day, meet Elise Wright." The two exchanged glances across the room. "My daughter," David Wright concluded. "I can assure you the English Heritage will abide by our decision to proceed here."

"Wait, what are we..." Michael paused not wanting to get himself mixed up in this mess any further, "...I mean you, digging for?"

"Excalibur, of course," Elise proclaimed flatly with not a hint of jest in her voice, whatsoever.

"Phew," Michael offered with a none-too-sincere wipe of his brow, "I thought you were going to say King Arthur there for a second. You're just looking for his magical, mythical sword. THAT, I can believe."

No one in the room was laughing—not even a cough was offered to break the suffocating and uncomfortable silence.

Michael's father offering, "I don't know how the terrorists found out about our meeting, but perhaps that would be more up your alley to investigate, my son."

"NO," Elise barked, breaking in immediately, "I want *him* to help me. Make it happen."

David was already a breath away from Michael and in his personal space, looking to Janet, then to Michael's father, then to his daughter with a frown, "Very well, Mr. Day, your job from this moment forward is protection detail for my daughter. Anything," he started, looking directly into Michael's eyes as he continued, "and I mean ANYTHING, that happens to my daughter is on *you*." David's index finger now poked Michael's sternum to emphasize his point, he finished explicitly articulating Michael's new orders, "Do we have an understanding?"

Michael looked between his father and the political leadership, then to Elise, where his eyes couldn't move away, resigned to the fact he had been commandeered. "Understood, sir." He paused, knowing that wasn't quite ace enough for the man, adding, "Completely!" *What did I just get myself into?* Whatever it was, he didn't like the way the daughter of the Leader of the House of Lords was smiling at him like a giddy-eyed schoolgirl. *PERFECT! Just fucking perfect!*

About an hour later David Wright was in the back seat of his Rolls-Royce® forest-green Ghost Extended, being driven home by his personal driver, when a number not saved in his phone came across his government-issued, encrypted cell that registered as Regensburg, Germany.

He screened his calls religiously, but if someone had this number, it was an extremely remote possibility that this was some 400lb-hacker in his mother's basement as the American savages would say. "Yes...." Deliberately not offering any pleasantries nor name. If they knew the number they were calling, then they should know him.

"Good evening, Mr. Wright," with a click as if the call were being transferred or routed, the rich, elderly voice offered without presenting his name.

He thought he knew the voice, though. He'd heard it twice before—both times at very exclusive parties hosted at Waddesdon Manor. "Sir.... What can I do for you?"

"When they find it, you'll bring it directly to me." No explanation. No context. No possibility of conditions. And no tolerance offered for any deviance in the orders he'd just given to the Leader of the House of Lords as if he were little more than a foot soldier or pawn in a larger game of chess, where the major pieces were hidden out of sight—like unto an invisible enemy.

David's chin worked as he swallowed his pride and his great toil he'd spent most of his life attaining to his seemingly lofty position. He thought of a number of responses, calculating each of their outcomes five moves ahead, retracting each and every one of them as a quick route to being suicided by cloth tied to a doorknob. That was their way, after all.... No loose ends. Cooperate or die. Yesterday's news, if that. "Understood." No title offered in due respect for none had been reciprocally provided. A one-word response was all he deserved. Less was more in this case. That was the one response that would allow his life to continue, and his daughter's.

The call terminated with a click followed by another click, as if the transfer were disconnecting without another word.

David swallowed hard, considering the leaks and moles around him. *Had they sent the jihadis as a form of distraction, or warning? If they knew what his daughter was looking for, they clearly saw it as a threat to their continued way of life. Did that mean it might be an instrument to present cracks in their long-controlled matrix of control systems? Possibly. If they were so insistent that it be immediately turned over to them, did that mean someone that was part of the dig presented an imminent threat to their control matrix—especially with that weapon in their possession? Likely.*

He could only control what he could control, and no more. He needed to figure out a way to warn his daughter while keeping his other obligations. And keeping him and his daughter among the living.

And he needed to plant some disinformation individually amongst a tighter circle and see who leaked what information, and there he'd find his mole. Or moles.

Chapter 3: The Key to the Abyss

Wailing, moaning, and gnashing of teeth from those both living and not—both condemned and not—tormented Radin's every waking thought. Unfortunately, he was very much awake for every moment of this; sleep never to relieve. The cacophony of anguish never ceased. Crucified upside-down on a weathered and beaten, rough-hewn wooden cross, his feet bled at the ankles where they were pierced with a thick and rusty iron pike. His wrists never stopped throbbing, where they too were pinned to the old, thick wood that pricked at him everywhere about his naked body. He should have bled out by now, but death wasn't allowed here unless it served a purpose not his own. The molten coals just beneath his forehead kept him painfully aware of his surroundings, as did the trio of massive black scorpions keeping watch over him. Pincers erect and wide at the ready, Radin heard their clicking constantly in his thoughts, both conscious and not. His blood hadn't obfuscated both his eyes— not yet at least. He still had partial vision out of his left eye as he exchanged glances with the scorpion more than close enough to do him in, if it so chose. He wasn't just hanging from a cross. He was hanging on the balance between life and death—between the living of the physical shell and the immortal soul.

A glance away from his lethal tormentors fortuned a look of giant beastly feet with six toes each—each toe the size of his hand—walking right in front of him. A beastly and guttural laugh every time it passed him left him wondering how much he would continue to suffer. And for how long…. Time mattered not here. A thousand years, or a thousand moments, they were all the same, allowing his torment to last an eternity, regardless of how much linear time he actually spent

Charles W. McDonald Jr.

here.

Radin tried to take notice of everything he could—at least in between the very brief moments of clarity. Seeing the fiery, acrid demon's whip trailing across the hot coals that made up some of the ground here, he watched the Balak walk away behind him. He didn't know how long he'd have before the Balak returned to twist the spikes in his wrists and ankles again but looking off into the distance he noticed a great gate, more immense than anything he'd ever seen. It must have been more than a dozen times the height of the Balak, with twin doors—each mirroring the other—ten times the width of the massive Balak. The colossal charcoal gate displayed every known hue of grey misery against the backdrop of Hellish, lava-red leading up to it.

A mostly blank but cracked canvas of grey stone curtain wall—save the great blood spill-gates spaced evenly along the wall—sharply changed at the colossal door casings made of great overlapping chevron-shaped shields cascading down either side of the Gates of Hell. Each cascading shield column provided *false ladders of hope* for those senseless enough to think escape possible. Diamond patterns in positive and negative shades of grey checkered the field of each door to the Gates of Hell with a great living representation of what he assumed was the Dragon of Darkness writhing about the center of the seam—its tail moving before Radin's eyes as its eyes locked with his in a glowing repose of molten, amber *hatred*. Upon the checkered field of diamonds lay one circle high, another low, illustrating symbolism he didn't fully understand. Everywhere there were triangles and circles. It had to mean something…. The fierce, malevolent face of a great demon flanked by massive snakes formed the capstone of the gate he understood well enough as the blood spilled in rivers down and out the forked tongue of the demon atop the Gates of Hell. Great pikes marched along the top of the massive curtain wall displaying ever-decaying heads run through, so the top of the skulls fell just below the rim of the tips of the pikes. There were no images, tales, or nightmares that could have prepared him for the sight now before him. It was…terror incarnate. It was the inescapable and unrelenting agony of all who'd come before him and all who would come after. It was the Abyss of all things, living and not!

Even his flashes of the pure-white light amidst an endless crystal lake and booming voice had been silenced by this opaque termination of all things *hope*. The living energy of the Arcane inaccessible here; attempting to cast again was both futile and justification for more attention. More attention was the last thing he wanted!

The thud of beastly footsteps returning stirred coals around his head as the Balak slowly twisted his rusted iron spikes.

Charles W. McDonald Jr.

"AHHHHHHH," Radin cried out, causing the Balak to belly laugh; tufts of molten fire burst from its lips with each heavy guffaw. Radin's tears hissed as they fell to the coals below, offering more hot steam upon his ever-suffering brow.

Another great laugh from the Balak as he tossed dropped feces on Radin's feet, watching them trail sources of infection down Radin's bloodied legs and waist.

*　　*　　*　　*

(Evanyil's Domain, The Abyss, Time Neutral)

The long hallway of smooth, satin-finish, trapezoidal stone flooring was lighted smoothly and evenly by seemingly star-like portals in the apex of the ceiling, though each rib in the composition of the rounded, bone-like support beams held behind it a nasty surprise, hidden in shadow. It wasn't Kellen's first time here, but he hoped it would be his last. Every protection he had was up right now, and his most potent offensive weapons at the ready. He was channeling right on the edge of his capabilities, but he couldn't take any chances here. This place was dangerous—even for him.

The hall opened into an abdomen-shaped massive chamber with exactly nine other points of entry, not including the one he'd just come from—one of the antennae. The bulk of the other entry points representing legs. A pair of spiders twenty-spans-tall flanked Evanyil on either side of her throne of Human bones. Her ever-present poisoned dagger hung tight on her magnificent right hip. Seeing her here in the flesh, Kellen was immediately reminded of what Damon saw in her, though she was far beyond insane. She was genius to the extreme and radically dangerous. She acknowledged his entrance in much the way a child would acknowledge the existence of a pest.

"Evanyil, it's been a while," Kellen intoned, walking smoothly and confidently as he closed the distance between them only to see both spiders up and in an attacking position immediately as he got within ten paces.

"Sit," she ordered, immediately causing her familiars to heel. Her warning systems had told her of his presence, but she wanted to allow him all the way into her trap before she decided whether or not to kill him. She did *need* him after all—for now... He was an important part of her plans with Damon. But after that.... Then, she would re-evaluate Kellen's value to her and her future plans.

"I wanted to hear your plans, from your lips."

"Wow.... Your foreplay needs work, Kellen the Destroyer." She smiled, but she was furious inside, and her dagger ached to be freed upon his neck. *How*

Charles W. McDonald Jr.

dare he?!

"Yeah, well I'm betting my immortality and my legacy on your little plan, and I want to be certain we're all on the same page." His eyes looked left, right, up and down, almost constantly ever since he walked into the chamber. He might have been legendarily powerful, and immeasurably confident in his abilities, but he certainly wasn't comfortable with this 'visit.' Still, she'd never dare come see him on his turf, and arranging a neutral-site meeting had proven to take an eternity. She was stalling and he wanted answers. Now.

"Not like you to question your best and only pal." She was toying with him, of course, as her eyes danced with joyous foreplay of death and mayhem.

She knew he wasn't really questioning Damon. He was questioning her, and she knew it, but he was here, and she was bored, so *why not* toy with him...? Cocking her head ever so slightly, she rose from her throne in her shimmering and diaphanous black and silver bodice, letting her right hand fall to the grip of her familiar dagger as she began pacing around Kellen.

Kellen's eyes were now forced to follow her while keeping an eye on her familiars and all the entryways; it proved too much. He was spread too thin. He needed to force the issue. "Stop toying with me, Evanyil, or I'll pull out of this little venture of yours. You need me."

"*She* knows about our plans."

"She doesn't know the when, the where, or the how—only the who and the why."

"Exactly—the WHO and the why. Therefore, you can't pull out. You're already a named accomplice."

She was right. He was committed. Like it or not.

"I just want to hear the plan from your lips. That's all." Kellen's demands came across as a lack of trust of Damon. After all, this exact information had already been disseminated to Damon to give to Kellen.

"What do you want to know beyond the fact we're going to unseat her?"

"I got that part."

"What more is there to say?"

"How about who gets what afterwards? That would be a good start."

"Ah, now the legendary Kellen the Destroyer comes out to play." Evanyil rushed him head on, skidding to a stop inches from his face, where her beautiful, feminine fingernails tapped delicately on his cheek, just under his left eye.

He didn't like her being this close to him, and his eyes darted downward, carefully watching that infamous dagger of hers. *Still hanging on her hip—good.* He didn't want to let her see him freaked out, but he was way beyond unsettled inside.

Charles W. McDonald Jr.

He managed to force his eyes to make contact with hers. "You're insane."

Pouty lips acknowledged the truth of his words. It was a well-known truth—for centuries. "Crazy is as crazy does. What does that make you for being part of our little plan?"

"Suicidal." This was pointless. He wasn't getting anything beyond what Damon had already told him—less actually. "Good to see you, Evanyil." Turning to talk away from the crazed cave elf, Kellen was done.

Pouting again at the recognition of his futility, Evanyil sought more play time. She never had visitors anymore—at least none she hadn't killed.

"We were going to let you keep the key. Is that fair?"

The key to the Gates of Hell…. Now that would be a fitting trophy. And, an incalculable increase to his fame, and his legend. He paused in his tracks, turning to look back at her, obviously considering her proposal.

"Damon doesn't want it," Evanyil informed him grudgingly, adding, "… though it suits him more than it does you."

"I'll be in touch, Evanyil." With that he was gone, little shards of lightning bolts blistering her stone floor, chasing Kellen's exit.

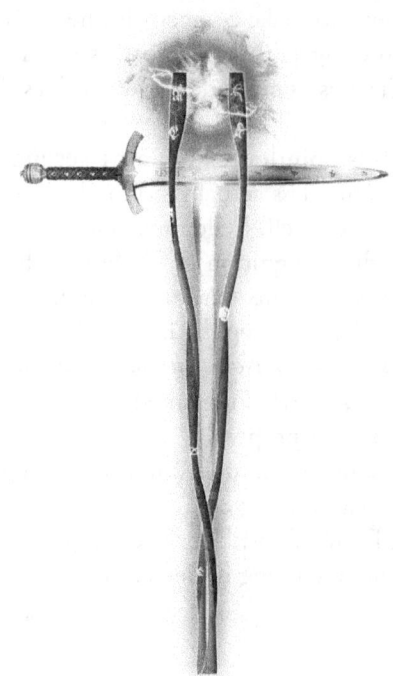

Chapter 4: A Bridge of Shadow

(Eden, Present Day)

Ron Stencowsky drove in another series of nails with his compressor-driven air-gun at the top of the roof truss that would become yet another new home on this alien landscape, calling out for the crane to bring in the next truss as he finished nailing the hurricane clips into the top of the truss. "Let's have it. Come on," Ron ordered. His crew of mostly Earth Humans had been very busy from the moment they arrived as the clear majority of construction equipment had been brought from Earth—though a significant amount of the building materials were not like any he'd seen before. Some of it was familiar territory, which made for easier work, but they had to experiment with some of the materials until they found the most efficient and eco-friendly ways to use them, as per Damon's governing laws.

Solar Powered DeWalt® digital media players blasted familiar tunes to work to. Country music seemed to get the best results with this crew, though he preferred classic rock. Ron wasn't sure how much of the planet was inhabitable, nor how far those *Portal* things had opened around the world, but occasionally he still saw one opening for more people to come through. Nothing like the first day, though, when hundreds of thousands had come through from Earth and several other worlds. It was going to be tough figuring out languages to work with everyone here, but Damon's laws also required every person to be able to speak at least two languages, so failure to learn another language wasn't really an option. For the most part, Damon's laws made sense, and he wasn't in the mood to start testing authority, especially reasonable authority that stayed out of their way to live their lives in peace. At least they were still alive, and that was something given his last images of Earth before he ran through the *Portal* to safety—to Eden.

Looking around again, never quite getting used to the alien landscape, Ron took in the little star and the huge moon in the skyline, along with the spiky spire-like construction of the alien life that ruled here before them. A giant spire, of a metal he didn't recognize, stuck out of the crust at a 22.5-degree angle. It must have been two hundred yards in length, and he didn't understand how it still stood like that without fracturing, especially with those diamond-shaped portals they must have used for windows weakening the overall structural integrity of the tower. A few of them had gone to investigate what alien structures still stood, in search of any living thing that might still present a threat. Damon had left weapons for them to use, M-4's, MP-5's, and the like. At least he had good taste in weapons and had left them a way to defend themselves.

Working beside Derek Willis, another ex-football player from the University of Georgia, the two of them worked together setting the next truss in place. Derek worked shirtless in the light of Damon's Star, its pale-yellow light glistening off the sweat on his young black, muscular frame. "How about a break, Boss?" Derek shot his boss a wink and a disarming smile. They'd been working for hours straight, but looking out across the new neighborhood under construction, there was still so much development left to do and so little time to do it. It was seemingly a never-ending job and they weren't going to get from here to there by killing themselves....

"Let's finish trussing this roof. Then we'll break." Ron used to be so much more carefree, but the Battle of New York had changed him, and caring after his men in their retreat to the American Resistance had taught him that life didn't allow for the mistakes of carelessness or carefree actions. It also taught him to think and work in deliverable sets. Now, he always tried to finish one job before starting the next and didn't like pausing in the middle of a job. It was just a different style and way of thinking, but it proved more efficient at getting things done, and there was so much to do here; that was really what they needed—to get things done....

Charles W. McDonald Jr.

"I want you and Charles to head out east again tonight, checking out those alien structures about ten clicks away. Don't spend more than an hour out there and get back before sunset." Ron oversaw all construction and security for New Georgia. It was the most responsibility of his entire life, but he was getting a handle on it.

"That's fine. Will do, Boss. But what are you expecting us to find out there?"

"Nothing," Ron replied flatly. "I expect you to find nothing, but that doesn't mean there's nothing to find."

That hadn't set well with Derek's stomach as it turned over, growling hungrily as they air-nailed the next truss into place.

*   *   *   *

Running the crane wasn't anything like back home, this one being solar powered and all, but Charles was getting the hang of it. It wasn't as peppy, but it was stable, and he had to keep an eye on reported energy levels on the dashboard of the heads-up display. It was a busy level of instrumentation keeping him on the edge of distraction, but the most important thing was watching the load and the tow-line. He had almost knocked Ron off a structure yesterday, but Ron could be a forgiving sort, when he wanted to be. He guessed it all depended on experience level. If he had claimed to be an expert on the crane, he'd bet Ron wouldn't have been so easy on him.

Picking up another truss and another tow-line, Charles began swinging the boom around, but as he boomed out at Derek's signal, his peripheral vision caught a flash of something. It was a light-blue flash, kind of like one of those *Portal* things, but this was definitely not that. This was much smaller, and there had been two of them close together, like a pair of eyes, bridged by shadow.

Charles W. McDonald Jr.

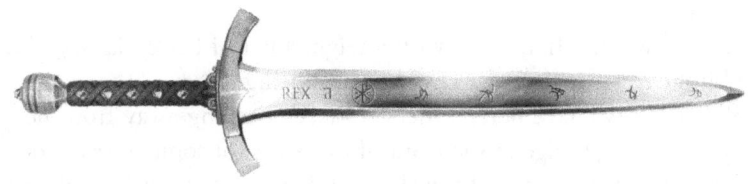

Chapter 5: A Legendary Sovereignty

(The lake at Baschurch in Shropshire, Earth, Present Day)

ow four weeks into their search, they were not worried about money, but the English Heritage was down their necks about the lack of progress reports and disturbing the surrounding countryside with digging. They had some twenty men, plus a detail from Michael's SRR unit. A military presence was part of the requirement from David Wright, someone to watch Michael, watching over his daughter. Six hours in the eighteen-footer, staring at the latest sonar technology available wasn't just monotonous, it was dull as fuck. Michael longed for a better assignment. *Even Syria was preferable!*

Standing beside this gorgeous young woman all day, inhaling her intoxicating perfume and not being able to do anything about it, was driving him over the edge. Far from the first time today, he considered throwing himself into the water, just to get away from her.

"All anyone is talking about is the impact of leaving the E.U. Everyone seems to have an opinion except you." Trying to break the deafening silence between them, Michael decided to strike up a meaningful conversation in an attempt to get to know her better.

"Oh, I have an opinion. You just never bothered to ask." Elise smiled, both coy and beautiful, standing entirely far too close to him for his comfort. She could tell it was making him uncomfortable, but she loved brushing up against him just to feel him squirm.

"Why is it always the man's fault," Michael challenged her, his right index finger right in her face nearly touching her nose. "Pot of rubbish you know… thinking I don't care enough about you to ask. We've been out here for weeks, and you've had plenty of opportunities to bring up your own opinion."

"You're working yourself into a dither." Brushing up against him again, pretending to pay attention to the sonar, Elise used her feminine charms, rather than her spells. She wanted to win him over without magic, but still longed for confirmation. All she had was a series of breadcrumbs—nothing solid.

Charles W. McDonald Jr.

"Stop doing that!"

"Doing what?" That came with a feigned bat of her eyelashes. Elise toyed with him 'til the sonar delivered a rare, but promising, beep.

"What do we have here," Michael asked, backing away from her, tussling the rapidly-hardening budge in the front of his pants for some measure of comfort.

Just a few yards from shore, Elise didn't understand how they could be getting a ping here, now. They'd been over this part of the lake dozens of times before.

"Great," Elise exclaimed, throwing her hands up in the air, just as the rain hit the sonar and started to come down in sheets, right as they were starting to make progress—par for the course. *This expedition sucks!* It wasn't supposed to go like this. For a brief moment, she considered casting to halt the rain, but that could create far more problems than it would solve. Besides, the source was so very weak here…. And unreliable.

Looking to the shore, Terry was waving them in. Michael threw his jacket over the both of them as the boat closed the distance between them to Terry's obvious displeasure, and Michael's. His pants were intolerably uncomfortable as Elise backed herself into him repeatedly—mercilessly. "Stop it," Michael barked at her, trying to make room between them without them getting soaked.

"Make me," she dared, turning to kiss him in front of God and everyone.

A brilliant flash of light in his mind's eye drew a vision of a great lake of blue crystal on a field of pure light, diamonds like grains of sand for beaches, with a booming voice from the far side of the lake somewhat masked in the shadow of two figures, shaking Michael loose from Elise. Now teetering on the very edge of the port side, Michael fell away from Elise into Baschurch lake with a splash of his hundred-kilo frame hitting the water, pelted by sheets of cold rain.

"*MICHAEL!*" Wanting to jump in after him, Elise considered it, but he disappeared from sight so quickly, and in water so shallow, she didn't understand how that could be.

"Do you see him?" Terry was at the shore's edge in a flash, taking off his boots, preparing to jump in right when a cluster of surfacing bubbles heralded Michael's trudging out of the water as the rain hailed down upon them.

Both could see Michael dragging something just under the water's surface. Terry's eyes growing wider as Michael approached, breaking the surface of the lake with the hand-and-a-half Roman short sword that was slightly longer than a traditional short sword. Pulling it from the water's surface, it shone like a molten star in Michael's hands as a booming voice—not from Michael—could be heard thundering from the sky, "I AM THE LORD THY GOD!"

Charles W. McDonald Jr.

Obeying the will of the Creator, the sheets of rain could not pierce the translucent and radiant shell of light surrounding Michael Anthony Day as he pulled himself from Baschurch Lake. Off in the near distance of the berth, a man could be heard, "God be praised, WE HAVE OUR KING!"

Looking at his friend and subordinate, unpierced by rain, and untouched by the water from whence he'd come, Terry was looking for the words that escaped him, as his mouth worked in vain. "I...." Terry wasn't the sort to be easily phased, but he was witnessing the impossible. "I think we better report this," Colonel Terry Goodwin suggested, trying not to appear too shaken in front of his men as he tossed Elise a tow-line, though he couldn't stop staring at the white-hot, molten star in Michael's hand.

The look on Elise's face was somewhere between knowing and *hope* as she helped Terry pull the boat to shore—her confirmation shining in Michael's right hand.

As Michael started to hand Terry what could only be Excalibur, he witnessed firsthand its fiery light go immediately dormant as soon as it left his own grip.

Like a crystallized moment of déjà vu for her, Elise had to stop herself from intervening. Though later than expected, this was right, and she felt the next piece click into place in her mind.

The sword still humming in Terry's hands, Terry wondered how it could be possible that it had been in the water all this time without a single spot of rust or decay on the surface of the metal. Looking as if it had just come out of the forge of Creation itself, it didn't sing for Terry, but it resonated electromagnetically pulling at the MP5 he had slung over his shoulder. Turning it over he tried to read the Latin inscription down the fuller, *Ego sum Dominus Deus tuus. Vade retro me Satana: 'I am the Lord thy God. Get thee behind me, Satan!'*

"Right.... Well...." Terry paused for a moment, searching for the words, "When we show this to the Prime Minister, I'll need you to be there to show them your little trick," Terry suggested, looking directly at Michael.

"You don't want to show Billings first," Michael asked, looking to Elise as the rain came to an abrupt halt, the skies clearing overhead as rays of the Sun pierced the clouds.

"Oh, I'm pretty certain we'll be showing both of them within the hour," Terry rebuffed while helping Elise out of the boat. Terry could be heard making the call to Billings over the secure comm-link as they headed for the Land Rover together—Excalibur in tow, now wrapped a plain, matte-white, linen cloth.

In the distance, maybe thirty kilometers away, they could see a rainbow

Charles W. McDonald Jr.

starting to form as the clouds parted around it.

Charles W. McDonald Jr.

Chapter 6: A Last Resort

(Exeter, Perion, Present Day)

 ooking at the scroll with Damon's broken signet seal, Michelle contemplated how this conversation might go, if it didn't kill her first, but they didn't have many options. *IF* Radin still lived, she couldn't save him, and she only knew one person—or *thing*—that could. She knew Damon a letch, so this unique visit called for a blacknet minidress she'd brought from Earth, never considering she might actually be able to wear it. Fluffing her long, wavy blonde hair and adding just a tad bit more rose lipstick, she velcro'd her Glock® G43 to the upper inside of her left thigh, just above the hemline of her dress. She had no idea if the seal would allow her weapon to go with her or not, but it was worth a shot. Literally…. Pursing her lips to get the lipstick just right, she broke the seal, falling to the floor immediately where she had stood.

(Damon's House, Austin, TX, Earth, Present Day)

"Damon, help me understand you better. I just don't get it."

She'd been on him, in her words, like a ten-pound tick on a two-pound dog, ever since he'd left the room over her tracing of his scars, and she wanted answers. *How could he possibly explain what he'd been through and how it affected him?* How it had changed the course of his destiny. *Had it really altered it that much?* It was the biggest mystery of his life. What kind of man *could he have been* if not abused as a child?

"What's the worst thing that ever happened to you," Damon probed her.

He didn't like where this conversation was going, nor where it could go with such a question of his own making, but if she truly wanted to understand him.... Darkness, despair, and hatred would have to lead the way. He didn't intentionally want to peel Mira's scabs—especially those not entirely healed, but she wanted to understand him—such was the way.

"I.... Damon, I don't feel comfortable sharing that."

"Then don't," tousling through the variety of T-shirts in his dresser drawer, he wasn't intentionally blowing her off, but sometimes space was required to allow a conversation to breathe. Standing there shirtless in his pale Levis® 501's, he gave the conversation of his unmaking the space it required.

She stood there behind him, alongside his side of the bed dressed in only a towel from her shower. He could feel her presence and the electricity between them interacting with his ever-present field of Arcane operating like a hemispherical shield around him.

Flip, flip, flip through his Android phone, looking for a specific song, Damon started playing *Staind – Tangled Up In You*, cranking up the song for the Bluetooth home audio system to pick up. Turning around to take Mira into his arms, he started slowly moving with her...with the music. "It's okay. You don't have to tell me. I was trying to find some relative equivalent between us, but I don't think there is one. I just want you to feel safe around me."

He felt the warmth of her pulse beating through her thumb pressed into the palm of his hand...the soft kiss of her fingertips gently caressing the back of his hand.

Her tears streaking his clavicle as she rested her head on his shoulders while they slowly moved to the beautiful music Damon had picked for them; she'd never in her life met anyone like Damon. Take away all his powers, he was still so unique that she struggled not to be eclipsed in the presence of his incredible soul. "I don't know what to say.... Can you just hold me a little longer?"

"You mean a lot to me, Mira. More than you know. More than I can put into words right now. I'll try to help you understand me, but it will take time. Time for both of us. Time for me to explain. Time for you to understand."

"We'll go at your pace, Damon. You lead. I'll follow you *anywhere*." Glistening bright sapphire gems miraged with tears of wanting and knowing just out of her reach, Mira kissed him as the song collapsed inward on itself and on them.

The *summoning seal* tugged so hard on his inner thoughts, the shuffle it caused in his feet nearly yanked him from Mira's arms. "I'm sorry, Mira. I have to go."

"Now?" She barely got the question out and he was gone. No *Portal*. Just gone. She was left standing there, wet hair, just blinking and staring at where he'd just disappeared into thin air, with their song severed mid-refrain, as his phone abruptly disconnected from his home's Bluetooth speakers.

(Damon's Manor, Kaleion, Present Day)

The bright LED daylight-spectrum bulbs in the three chandeliers of Damon's foyer were the first clue. The burned, dead grass visible outside was the second. The twin moons hung in the sky outside the windows of Damon's foyer were the third. This wasn't Earth, but Damon had clearly brought some Earth to wherever this place was. *Perhaps Damon's homeworld.*

Michelle noticed the middle-aged man attempting to sneak up on her from a hidden room to the right. "May I help you," Edgar Hastings asked, walking up beside her.

"Yeah, don't even think about sneaking up on me again," Michelle threatened, pulling out her Glock® and aiming it right at him. "I'm here to see Damon!"

"I see," it wasn't the first time someone had threatened his life before. Damon had all kinds of very dangerous visitors, but he recognized the lethality of her weapon straight away. "You don't need to shoot me. I'm his Chief of Staff. My name is Edgar, and I might be able to help you. Has Master Damon explained how his summons works?"

"Not to me." Still holding her gun on him, she painted his forehead with a red-dot laser originating from her weapon's sighting.

"I see." Unauthorized access was always a precarious position for Edgar. It wasn't the first time, and normally it resulted in the intruder's death, but something about her wasn't right. He had the means to take care of the problem, but her threats toward him didn't necessarily make her an enemy of Damon. And he assumed Damon's summing seal hadn't allowed for the physical transportation of a weapon. *A holographic representation*, he considered….

She hated this arrogant prick already, but she needed Damon, so killing him wasn't an option. *I could just knock him into the middle of next week. Damon would never know as long as I was careful not to leave any evidence….*

"That won't be necessary," Damon offered, descending the circular staircase from the second floor, still shirtless in his jeans in his haste to respond to the *summoning seal.* Damon waived off his Chief of Staff, causing him to retreat to the butler's kitchen.

She wasn't sure if Damon had read her thoughts. She wasn't sure how far his natural abilities extended, or even if he could cast without her foreknowledge.

"You know that seal wasn't meant for you. It could have killed you." Damon admired her from afar as he closed the distance between them—carefully so. She was certainly pleasant eye candy, except for the whiff of the undead she tried to hide with her sweet perfume. Normally, he couldn't stand the undead. Though, he found something in Michelle that made her presence acceptable around him. Perhaps it was a kindred likeness in the way they went about getting things done. She was a doer—like him and Kellen and Goldenbow, but there was something else about her that made him…respect her.

As he got close enough, she holstered the Glock® and, in a bold move, took Damon's hand, causing him to eye her sidelong, though he didn't retreat from her. "Radin was taken by a demon. I don't know his exact name, but he came out of the ground projecting a very clear thought into everyone's head, 'I've come for what was promised to me.'" She paused, trying to recall the events in detail. "Immediately before that, Eldrac had pointed his right index finger up at Radin, but a translucent web fell upon him, then Eldrac's remains left a symbol on the ground in a black ash." Taking a deep breath after getting all that out of her system, she looked Damon in the eyes, taking the measure of his handling of the news—wondering really if it even was news to Damon. He knew so much each time she'd been exposed to him, she wasn't sure how far his information network extended. She knew him not entirely omnipotent, but she also knew he liked to leave people with the impression that he was.

In her measure of him, she found…genuine concern in those smoke-rimmed black gems of his. Her keen senses picked up on his elevated heart rate and advanced rate of breathing. Damon was worried about Radin…. She could use that. She'd never seen him shirtless before, and his great many scars…. They were also very telling. She estimated them to be made by lashings—many, many lashings. And they were old—very old. And deeply rutted into his flesh.

"Describe the demon." She had his undivided attention, and this was always a possibility in dealing with stakes like this, but Radin being taken by a demon certainly qualified as unexpected, this early in the plan. He'd like to hear more about this translucent web that fell upon Eldrac—it sounded like a useful spell.

"Maybe fifty to sixty feet tall by twenty feet wide, with a whip of fire, huge wings, six toes on each foot—" Damon waved her off, interrupting her. He didn't need to hear anymore.

"A Balak. You're describing a Balak." Damon sighed, "Get me the spell of the translucent web that fell upon Eldrac just as he cast that spell that turned him to dust, and I'll handle the Radin problem."

"What was that spell Eldrac was trying to use on Radin?"

"Don't worry about it. I'll handle that." He thought Eldrac had stopped using *Damon's Damnation*, but he wasn't the only one that had gotten their hands on that spell over the centuries it had been in use. It was banned everywhere, but that just made it more infamous—more desired by Eldrac, and mages like him.

Damon would have to kill the immortal shell of the Balak, which meant he couldn't summon it—not without summoning his immortal shell here on this plane as well. The spell he could use to accomplish that was banned as well and every single time he used it, it had made him more infamous and always shone a brighter spotlight on him, and his activities. That clearly wasn't an option at this time, either. He had to go to the demon's home turf. Sighing as he weighed the options that he knew all sucked, Damon waved off Michelle, "Go get me that spell, and I'll take care of Radin. And Michelle...," he tsk'd with his index finger, eyeing her carefully, "...don't ever use my summoning seal again."

(Exeter, Perion, Present Day)

Michelle gasped for air on the floor of her room in the Exeter Manor, coughing as her unique lifeforce fled the copy of her body on Damon's homeworld, catching up to her mortal shell on Perion.

Charles W. McDonald Jr.

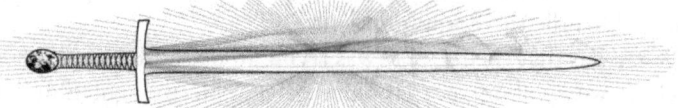

Chapter 7: Killing the Immortal

(Austin, TX, Earth, April 1ˢᵗ, Present Day)

Burning the golden arrowhead with a thought as his right index finger radiated heat from his *Pyrokinesis*, Damon summoned Goldenbow, not actually knowing if it would work from Earth. The molten metal filling the blue ceramic plate he'd set the arrowhead in on his desk, Damon looked into his liquified, golden reflection in the plate, knowing, from experience, it was time to ask for help.

"Babe, what are you doing," from behind him. He tried not to hide things from Mira ever since he had put permanent protections around her thoughts, as he had his own. They wouldn't protect her from every sort of mental probe possible, but it would make working with and around Mira more feasible...and safer for both. The encounter with the Dragon of Darkness on Eden was too close of a call. He had to take bigger precautions, but he also longed to be truly close to a great woman again, and Mira fit that description.

Recalling Michelle's description of the Balak, his mind worked the multitude of problems before him as the Master Plan threatened to unravel. One of Damon's many life-lessons-learned was 'don't be afraid to ask for help...and keep trustworthy people around you that *can* help.'

"I'd like you to meet a friend," turning to kiss a beautiful Mira dressed in hot-pink shorts, braless in a white T-shirt that read 'Sexy Nerd' with a graphic of a hot librarian, Damon looked around the room. *No Goldenbow. Hmmm, I might have to go back home.* Tap, tap, tap on his right shoulder from behind, causing him to turn back to the still-melting arrowhead. *Still, no Goldenbow.*

A snicker from Mira gave Goldenbow away. Spinning again, Damon saw Goldenbow standing beside Mira with his finger to his lips as if to shush her.

"Boy, you're fun to mess with, Day!" A million-watt smile from his incredibly lethal friend was a welcome site. "So, who's the babe," he asked, taking Mira's left hand to kiss it, noting her beautiful curves through the not-nearly-opaque-enough white T-shirt, long legs—her long brunette hair still wet from the shower. Damon could certainly pick 'em.

"Mira, this is Goldenbow, the most lethal assassin I've ever met." Damon presented, motioning to his friend dressed in only the most neutral of colors that seemed to pick up the neutral-tone hues of the room, making him barely visible even when directly looking at him. "You're in the presence of a living legend," he proclaimed, motioning to one of the books on his desk, *Kaleion Warfare After Goldenbow*.

"So, what's up, Day?" Another big smile from his equally larger-than-life friend and brother in arms.

"Why do you and Kellen call him Day," Mira asked, picking up on the commonality.

"Oh, that," Goldenbow paused, giving her that disarming smile again as he postulated with his right index finger in the air—remembering. "Kellen, Day, and I go waaayyy back! He doesn't let just anyone call him that. You have to earn that privilege, right Day?"

"More or less," Damon deflected, smiling as he ignored this part of the conversation as much as possible. But, he wanted to allow Mira her pleasantries and include her as much as possible.

Casting *Distorting Web*, Damon shelled the three of them for protection and encryption of the rest of their conversation.

"Uh oh," Goldenbow interrupted, "Damon wants to talk business now." Again, with the million-watt smile; again, directed at Mira. *What a flirt!* And it was working from what Damon saw of Mira's body language and the way she leaned her body toward him.

"I'm honoring my word to you. Phase I is complete. You're in the loop."

Both looking sidelong at Damon, knowing that *was not* really the case. The only one truly in the loop was Damon. Goldenbow testing, "So, what's involved in Phase II, then?"

Damon sighed, knowing that's where this would eventually go. "You know I can't tell you that."

"That's quite the loop, Day," Goldenbow quipped, making a pinching motion with his right hand meant to mimic jibber-jabber, obviously only meant to be shared with Mira, though plenty open enough for Damon to see.

"Just because we have to keep this compartmentalized doesn't mean you can't help me execute part of the Master Plan."

"Okay..., so, who needs to die," Goldenbow casually asked, winking at Mira, causing her to smile back at him, which then immediately made her internally question her Christian upbringing.

Two of the most powerful men in the Universe are casually having a conversation in front of me about assassinating someone, she thought. *Shut up and pay attention. This might get good.*

"Evanyil," Damon proclaimed flatly, carefully gauging Goldenbow's response to come.

Wow, this DID get good! Mira's blinking involuntarily halted, her eyes now staring at Goldenbow.

"Whoa!" Goldenbow got up, immediately beginning to pace—though making sure to stay within the encryption of the hemisphere of the *Distorting Web*—before answering, "But...."

"Can you do it, or not?" Damon's tone wasn't harsh, but it was abrupt.

"I mean, Day...." Goldenbow pausing, wiping the sweat already forming on his brow. Not a good sign. "I mean she's supposed to be part of all this...." Goldenbow motioning around the room with his hands. "Isn't she meant to be part of this MASTER PLAN of yours?"

"She is," Damon rebuffed. Totally emotionless. Expressionless.

"Am I part of your MASTER PLAN too," Goldenbow asked sarcastically as he stared down his long-time friend.

"Not in the same way," Damon smiled, being very careful how he navigated this discussion—and with good reason.

"Day, you've never asked me to assassinate a living goddess before."

"And I'd never consider asking anyone *but* you." Stroking Goldenbow's ego never hurt if you did it the right way and with total sincerity, of which Damon was an accomplished master.

"Sure, FUCK IT. I mean you only live once."

Standing before his long-time friend, Damon suddenly rested his right hand on Goldenbow's shoulder, "April Fools!"

After a bit of an awkward pause, Mira realized, "Shit! It *IS* April 1st isn't it?!" Mira looked at Damon like he was a total freak'n genius. "That's *so* fucking wrong!"

Goldenbow didn't get the April Fools part, but he knew Damon was fucking with him, as he eyed Damon back—wickedly so. "Ha-ha." It wasn't much of a retort, but not much of one was required given the look he was giving Damon. Damon would *pay* for that one.

Carefully measuring Goldenbow's reply and his entire handling of the initial request, Damon de-escalated, "No.... Seriously I do have a problem, and it does require your skill set."

No reply from Goldenbow, just a serious look, listening with a small shift of his weight from one leg to the other. Sometimes that signaled him pulling out a weapon, as Damon had seen Goldenbow do before without hardly anyone but the most careful and attentive, noticing.

Continuing, Damon offered, "Adena is a powerful witch on Perion, and becoming an even bigger nuisance for me. I know she's dispatched undead looking for me on Perion, and it's only a matter of time before they find their way to more sensitive areas." Damon could tell the conversation turning to the undead had already made Mira uncomfortable as she looked around the room, biting her lips, obviously trying not to intervene in the conversation.

"They're persistent bastards, and you know how I feel about dealing with undead," Damon concluded.

"Okay, why me? Couldn't you handle this problem?" It was certainly a valid question as Goldenbow still eyed Damon, more curious than ever. *Why does he really need my help?*

"Well, let me put it this way, which of the two problems would you rather deal with," Damon showing a viewing window to Radin in the Abyss surrounded by three massive scorpions, crucified upside down on a wooden cross amidst a Hellish landscape of immortals walking about everywhere, defiling all manner of the living and the dead.

"I think I'll take problem number one, thank you very much," Goldenbow jibed, trying to erase the all-too-fresh sight from his mind's eye. He'd seen a great deal in his very long life, extended by the likes of Kellen, Damon, and others, but Hell was where he drew the line. He'd never taken a job that involved The Abyss before, but if it meant helping Damon, he'd do it. It just wasn't his first choice. That was part of his reservation about neutralizing Evanyil. The Abyss was where he'd have to go if he was to accomplish that task and add in all of Evanyil's unique skills…you had yourself a real challenge on your hands.

"I thought so," Damon exhaled some of his building tension again, knowing what must be done. He was going to have to go visit Banthis—on her turf. He shuddered at the memory of the last time that had happened. At least, this time, his powers had grown exponentially, and he had a great deal more weaponry at his disposal. He'd be far more prepared this time around. "There's more to Phase II, where I'll need your help, but this is a start if you wouldn't mind taking care of it for me. We're reaching a point where we're going to have to start dealing with problems in parallel or the timing of the plan is going to be out of sync. EVERYTHING depends on the timing, so I'd appreciate you helping me deal with these problems simultaneously."

"Consider her piece removed from the board." The million-watt smile returned, allowing Damon to focus on the bigger problem at hand.

Charles W. McDonald Jr.

"You two are going to want to leave for this part," Damon warned, taking a seat at his desk, placing the *Staff of the Invoker* sidelong in his lap. Placing his signet ring—with his seal—on his right third finger so he still had a mechanism to link himself to this timeline if the worst happened and he lost the *Staff of the Invoker*, he concentrated. Damon's jeans and T-shirt disappearing before their eyes, replaced with long, elegant, charcoal-blue, diamond-patterned robes adorned with silver, living runes and embroidery of Kaleion and of his ancient profession. Closing his eyes as he focused, calling out to his wife—to Banthis.

(The Abyss, Time Neutral)

The giant open-air structure, sat atop a ground-work pedestal of skulls of all sizes, overlooked a large amount of the Abyss from its position closest to the Crown of the Dragon. The great misery that was the grey Gates of Hell with its massive curtain wall topped with pikes driven through decaying skulls of once great kings. Damon hadn't visited Banthis since her promotion to the right hand of the Dragon, nor had he desired it. Walking among the thirty-two scalloped Roman-style columns supporting the rectangular roof structure reminded him of a Roman Temple, with its colonnade along the front allowing for two tall rectangular open doorways. Intricate cornice work above and below runes he didn't fully recognize, but understood as angelic script, adorned an outer band of grey stone all the way around the structure. Beastly faces, raised on the uppermost cornice ribbon above each column, seemed to cry out from the stone in anguish. Walking inside the open doorway to the right, estimating it was probably at least a hundred feet to the top of the casing, Damon moved toward the immense dais atop a staircase of exactly sixty-six stone steps, a hundred yards wide at the starter step. He was roughly halfway up the steps before being greeted by a magnificently beautiful blonde having the appearance of an eighteen-year-old Human female, wearing a loose, color-shifting toga, revealing beautiful and seductive flesh hither and thither. Smiling at him, she said nothing but offered her delicate, girlish hand to guide him, which Damon cautiously accepted. Something felt familiar about her the moment her flesh touched his—maybe something in her crystal-blue eyes and the beautiful symmetry of her facial features. It was rare to see anything here with blue eyes, indicating she might be among the very few living creatures here, unless she was obfuscating her real eyes. Anybody could be anything here if they knew how, but the truly living had telltale signs, if you knew what to look for. You had to be at your utmost careful, at all times. Even still, you could almost never trust your eyes, and most certainly *never* trust your ears! Even now, he heard the seeds of doubt being sewn into the deepest recesses of his mind. All the voices sounding like variations of his own.

> *You'll never leave.*
> *You belong here.*
> *Remember what you've done.*
> *What you did to her....*
> *Yea, I know thee....*
> *Have you come to witness your great many sins?*
> *You're a monster....*

He couldn't shut the voices off, but he did his best to ignore them as he reached the top of the stairs, seeing the familiar faces of Banthis and their many immortal daughters. Spread out across the dais were a series of beds where all manner of debauchery, adultery, seduction, and casual sex—if one could call it sex—were in progress. It took a lot to get a raised eyebrow from Damon, especially when it came to sex, but Banthis earned one as she removed a stiff prosthetic appendage from around her waist she had been using to defile a young girl he immediately recognized as Leslie. *So, this is where Banthis had taken her....*

"Darling Love," Banthis smiled from ear to ear, not having seen her wayward husband *here* in a *very* long time. *Whatever brought him here must have been important*, she thought. "What brings you to our little slice of..." she paused almost having to correct herself, "...well, you know." Again, with another big smile for her husband.

Freeing his right hand from the beautiful blonde who escorted him up to the dais, Damon waved, showing a viewing window of Radin crucified upside down and the Balak that held him captive. "What's his name?"

A frown from Banthis, realizing he wasn't here to visit his family. "Voltor," a terse reply from his wife. She wasn't happy, and he knew it. A pissed off Banthis was a very dangerous Banthis. He needed to deflect. Fast!

"May I visit with my daughters?"

A smile immediately returned to Banthis' face. She could be whimsical to the point of insanity at times but had a dangerously clever, and quick, mind. Very dangerous. She showed, like Damon, plenty of elements of structure. She couldn't, and wouldn't have made it this far without it, but there was just something about Banthis that always left Damon...unsettled. He knew, beyond any shadow of a doubt, that *if* Banthis could experience love, she *did* love him. The question was: *what did love actually mean to Banthis?*

Charles W. McDonald Jr.

"Well, you *were* just holding hands with one of them." Banthis smiled at him knowingly. The beautiful blonde with the blue eyes smiled at him, admiring her father's good looks and the charcoal-blue aura of his radiant power against the dark misery of the night of Hell. Then it clicked for Damon—Leslie had been pregnant…from him. "They've just been calling me 'Daughter Number Seven' all this time. They wanted you to name me. Would you give me a name, Daddy?"

"Of course, My Love." *Nothing quite like being put on the spot by a child of yours you've never met.* Licking his lips in thought, knowing where he was, and who was in his presence, he considered taking a *big* chance. Looking at her, deep into her eyes, he took both her hands, pulling her to him lovingly where he gave her a full embrace, letting her nuzzle into his neck in a moment of comfort all but forbidden here. Pulling away, he looked deep into her blue eyes again. They were real. Those were hers—no doubt about it—a gift from his old self, from his childhood, and from Leslie. In her eyes, he recognized a piece of himself from so long ago, before the torment of the daily beatings had begun. Inside us all, there was something unmistakable, unique, and yet still recognizable. Inside his beautiful new daughter of fair skin and high cheekbones, he saw love, torment, disappointment, seething anger, and in this very moment…joy. "I'm going to give you a forbidden name, My Love. Are you sure that is okay with you?"

Banthis began shaking her head in disapproval, knowing the mind of her wayward husband far too well. She tried but couldn't read his thoughts. He had done something, and she could sense the shell around him even though she couldn't see it. He had incredibly powerful protections up.

"I just want a name that comes from you, Daddy…." She paused, blinking at him, savoring his chiseled good looks, seeing the attraction her mother saw in him. "Why is it a forbidden name, Daddy?"

Putting a finger to his lips, then waving her off, he proclaimed, "I name you 'Grace,' for your love may very well make me whole again." He knew it was a lie as soon as the words escaped his mouth. He was condemned, but if it lifted her spirits for a moment in Hell, he would give her that lie as a truth.

Seething from her dais, Banthis looked at her husband with far more than just disapproval. Her dank, ribbed wings stretched out, then cupped over her head, casting a great and gnarled shadow of her anger to slowly creep between herself and Damon.

"Thank you, Daddy, for such a beautiful name." She turned to her siblings proclaiming, "You can call me by my name now. I'm Grace." Damon's daughters stared between him and Banthis, looking for approval, not knowing where this was about to go. Bakris, his oldest, and most magnificently beautiful, golden-haired daughter, knew right away, rising from her bed where she had been tormenting an adulterous Human male in his middle forties. Blood dripping from her acrid and rapidly growing nails, her perfect nude flesh, and long, flowing blonde hair juxtaposed by her dank, black, leathery-ribbed wings. Regally, she moved towards Grace, spinning backward for the momentum she sought to decapitate Grace in one smooth motion of her extended fingernails—her severed head cascading down the steps past Damon. "Your name of *filth* has killed your daughter, Father," Bakris pontificated before them at the top of the dais, slowly licking and savoring Grace's blood from her fingernails with her long and pointed tongue.

It took a moment for Grace's body to slump where it had stood. Bakris' motion had been so quick and so lethal; it had left Grace's body temporarily suspended in her stance before it collapsed.

First horrified, then relieved, Damon knew this trip would leave yet another scar on his soul, and there it was. Hopefully, he could find his way out of here with Radin before the next scar left its mark. But for Grace, he was grateful. She had a chance now, albeit perhaps a slim one. "Perhaps I should do what I came for and leave," Damon offered, "...I could visit another time."

Her shadow retreating underneath her still-cupped wings, Banthis offered a slight and dismissive bow.

Walking down the steps, he'd never be able to remove the image of his daughter's severed head bleeding out on the steps below him. The seer of her fresh, warm blood as it struck the molten coals of the ground left little curls of puffy steam to further putrefy the scent of Hell. There it was: the second scar.

A distant flash inside his thoughts—one not experienced in centuries—and he nearly stumbled down the stairs. His protections, as powerful as they were, couldn't stop the prayers he felt being offered and flooding his cortex in a cascade of need, confusion, hope, and despair. He couldn't be sure if that had been the cause of the great flash of light in his mind, or something much more akin to a painful memory, but it was so hard to trust his instincts here. Here such things became more intense, but for now he had to ignore them to focus, or Grace would only be the first of many more deaths, and the unraveling of the Master Plan.

He felt as if something had come with these prayers, and he struggled to understand it. It was like a singing or a humming vibration just off in the distance of his thoughts. Whatever it was, it resonated inside him, and he needed to figure out how to either re-direct it or shut it off. He needed to be completely focused when he dealt with Voltor. Still not anywhere close to the edge of where the rivers Styx and Tsen crossed overhead then crossed again in deep chasms on the ground, he could see the great black scorpions guarding a naked body crucified upside-down in the far distance between himself and the great curtain wall of Hell.

*   *   *   *

A higher-level demon, the Balak was going to be enough of a challenge on its own. Gripping the *Staff of the Invoker* tight in his right hand by one of its three symmetrically coiled helix rods, he prepared himself as his black leather boots crushed the bloodied and decayed landscape of skulls leading away from Banthis' temple. Briefly looking back, he could see the far larger temple to the side of the one he just left, hoping she'd stay out of this. But with her—*it*—you simply never knew....

Bloodied and broken skulls—half-buried by their **own** sins, quarter-buried by their tormentors—paved Damon's way to meet Radin...and Voltor! Skyward, the River Styx, in acrid, emerald hues dusted with lit embers of justice for defiled acts, promised a literal cleansing to the bone to anyone unfortunate enough to come into contact. Crossing over Styx in mid-air, in helical skyward patterns, the River Tsen, in blood-amber hues of cursed hatred dusted with embers of justice for intent, promised just enough healing to maintain a life of suffering. Forever. Together, they fell in the far background before him, one against the curtain wall, the other against another long-ago-broken great temple of the one who shall not be named. Crossing over one another again in a great chasm in the foreground creating a barrier between the landscape of crushed, buried, and bloodied skulls and the burning embers of well-stoked coals, he didn't see Voltor, and that made him nervous.

He could already feel the intolerable heat and smell decaying flesh as he approached Voltor's domain, close to the Gates of Hell, marked by the likeness of the Dragon of Darkness protecting the great keyhole. Beyond the Gates of Hell, Mount Olympus stood guard between the fate of the damned, the selfish, and the righteous.

The crack of a skull breaking underneath his right leather boot made him look down, causing him to back away—quick! *That face*—or what remained of it, only about a third of the right side remained—he knew that face....

Focus, Damon! Focus or you're as good as dead here.

In the distance, he could see the heavy wooden cross buried upside-down in a mound of decaying feces, bearing Radin's body upon it, guarded by the trio of massive black scorpions who now gathered in a semi-circle before Radin, to greet Damon. Getting closer, he didn't see Voltor, but he could see the blood pouring out of a great wound in Radin's side and from his ankles—one crossed over the

Charles W. McDonald Jr.

other so the rusted iron spike could pierce both simultaneously. Denied clothes of any kind, Radin's nude body had been defiled everywhere with defecation and other means, intended to infect and persecute his wounds.

Another step brought Damon within thirty feet of the base of the cross, causing the center scorpion to inch forward toward him—its man-sized stinger fully readied. He needed a quick and easy method to prosecute these venomous servants while drawing minimal attention to his location. Another bolt of lightning coursed from the gathering storm overhead. For a brief moment, he could have sworn he had seen the likeness of the Dragon of Darkness in the fork of lightning that just struck the ground behind Radin. In the hackles raised on the back of his neck, he could feel the electricity in the foul-stenched air and sought to leverage it. Feeling the next massive bolt building in the expanding polarity differential of the gathering storm overhead, Damon waited for it, then directed the next strike as it bolted from cloud-to-cloud-to-ground, finding its landing point dead center the approaching scorpion—splitting it in half as its guts and venom poured out on the ground of ashen coals before them.

The remaining scorpions quickly retreated—he knew not where, but they practically vanished before him, offering him the chance he needed.

Risking his Master Plan, and everything else to stand here before Radin, Damon breathed a thought aloud, "Got yourself in a fine mess didn't you...."

Radin's tears couldn't clear the blood from his eyes, so he couldn't be sure what or who he was seeing, but a shadowy, tall, familiar shape, carrying a mighty rod in his hands, was trying to communicate with him in a language he didn't understand. All he could think of was to cry out, but the words didn't come—only a muffled gargle as his vocal cords struggled from all the blood in his mouth and throat. Suddenly, he felt the spikes removed and was freed from the cross, being uprighted somehow, but he was sure the tall figure wasn't even touching him. Released, but still suspended in air above the molten embers, Radin could feel the blood rushing from his head back into his extremities, though there was no way he could walk—let alone run.

"YOU?!" The only thing Damon heard was that foul guttural shout of familiarity, blasting fire right on the back of his neck, nearly piercing all his protections with the first blast.

Spinning to face Voltor, Damon wasn't in shock at the sight of him. It wasn't his first time facing down a demon, but it *was* his first time on *their* turf, and he had to keep his wits about him. Wasting not a second, he cast *Damon's Damnation*. Nothing. In his haste and unease, he'd forgotten one of the major tenants here. Almost no living things, thus virtually nothing sourced from Arcane would

Charles W. McDonald Jr.

work here. From here on out, he'd have to draw from Zero-Point, or his own raw power and artifacts.

A great belly laugh from Voltor, "Your feeble magic won't work here, War-lock!" His viperous words crackled in the air, though his mouth didn't move.

A crack of his great fire whip—some forty feet in length—and Damon was suddenly flying through the air ensnarled in its grip only to sling back toward Voltor's mouth agape to swallow him whole. He had half a second before he'd be a quick and easy meal. Reaching out to Zero-Point, he cast *Damon's Improved Shell 4*, creating a transparent sphere around him just as Voltor's teeth and jaws clamped down on him. Watching Voltor try to bite down on his shell in futility, Damon realized he'd only bought himself a few seconds at best.

Now standing in the mouth of the great Voltor, Damon shoved the *Staff of the Invoker* through his shell, piercing the roof of Voltor's mouth as he cast *Mind Blank* directly into its skull, simultaneously throwing a great lightning bolt down his throat to give him something to choke on.

Stumbling, Voltor released Damon from his iron vice of a jaw, causing Da-mon to spill down upon the crushed and bloodied skulls beneath—what remained of his protections still intact. He'd struck a mighty blow to the beast, but he had to kill its immortal body, or it would come back for Radin…and for him. Looking skyward to the great rivers Styx and Tsen crossing helically overhead, Damon rec-ognized the Dragon of Darkness in the distance—observing while in her Human female form from her temple. The magnificent brunette in revealing Roman robes seemed both simultaneously entertained and displeased.

Beside the Dragon of Darkness, Banthis and his daughters also watched; though no one interfered. Power struggles in Hell were nothing new, but an out-sider coming here to meddle—*that was entirely new*. And bold….

Pointing the *Staff of the Invoker*, channeling as much Zero-Point as he could source here, Damon cast *Sijil's Selective Elimination*, causing a column of acid fifty yards wide to engulf the immortal shell of Voltor. Nothing. *SHIT!*

Need a better plan, he thought. *Mind Blank* had stunned Voltor, leaving him unaware of why he was in a fight, but the *why* didn't matter now. *It* was in the throes of combat and that's all *it* needed to understand. Its fight or flight instincts were just as strong as a Human's, if not more so! Reaching into the inner folds of his black robes, he disappeared his *Staff of the Invoker*, pulling out a longsword that glowed like a star in depths of The Abyss—*A Crucible of Will*.

A sudden blast of fire from Voltor's whip and the last of his protections were gone in an instant. He was all but naked in Hell, his body spilling across the landscape of crushed skulls as his robes burned and charred about his body. With a thought, the fire was out. He still had *A Crucible of Will* in his right hand, and he meant to use it!

"VOLTOR!! Ego exscindo tuus vim vitae!" '*I destroy your lifeforce,*' Damon shouted, reaching out to the harmonic energy he'd been denying since the prayers had begun, casting *A Crucible of Will,* and all its embedded nobility, directly at Voltor.

Striking him dead in the chest, the great blow caused the chasm of Styx to widen with a cacophony of screams carried on mists of steam as Voltor's immortal shell collapsed down into the great crater of Styx—dead. Bursting out the back of Voltor's body as he fell into the chasm, a host of lifeforces escaped Voltor's *Throne of Souls*, heading directly for the Gates of Hell, save two.

Circling Radin's body one time, Damon faintly heard a female voice against the backdrop of the groans of Hell, "Forgive me," as the lifeforce trailed off out of sight past Olympus, now beyond the Gates of Hell. The other led a scorched path through the acerbic vapory air, heading straight for the great temple of the Dragon of Darkness.

Flamed eyes with reptilian, black slits acknowledged Voltor's death as the Dragon of Darkness transformed and took flight overhead, swallowing and consuming the wicked lifeforce that streaked to meet it mid-air.

Seeing Voltor's flesh being consumed by the acid of Styx, Damon used his *Telekinesis* to pull a *Crucible of Will* from Voltor's chest before Styx consumed the great weapon. Guiding it with his thoughts, he lifted *A Crucible of Will* out of the great chasm, hovering it over the crushed landscape toward him until it landed in the inner pocket of his robes where he pulled out the *Staff of the Invoker* to get him out of here!

Need to go, he urged himself, watching the shadow of the wings of the Dragon of Darkness creeping across the ground of skulls alongside his own shadow, Damon picked up Radin, tossing him over his shoulder. He tried to create a *Portal*. Nothing. Trying a *Gate* next. Nothing. *SHIT! Calm down,* he thought to himself, *very few living things here, therefore no Arcane.* Reaching out again to the harmonic energy provided by the prayers of his people, Damon walked through an immense *Portal* to Perion, dispelling it almost before finishing setting foot in Radin's War Room in Exeter.

Michelle, Brigance, Rowarc, and Talemar all came running at the sound of the horrific beastly screams echoing from the War Room where Radin's naked, beaten, stabbed, and bloody body lay on the floor next to Damon in his burned robes with blood and sweat dripping from his scorched brow and soot-laden face.

His vocal cords still caked with blood, Radin couldn't speak, though he moaned on the floor, bleeding profusely on the hardwood planks. Rushing back in a whirled blur, Michelle quickly had Radin's body wrapped in a grey field blanket. Prying his eyelids open to check his pupils, Michelle nearly jumped back. Radin's eyes looked…evil, their blackish-red irises terrifying everyone in the room.

"Oh, Creator," offered from Brigance Fireheart with a motion of his right hand Michelle didn't immediately recognize.

"It might take him a while to recover from this," Damon suggested, not really sure if he ever would.

"What did they do to him?" Michelle stroked Radin's auburn, blood-matted hair while checking his vitals and using his carotid artery to gather his pulse, which was coursing beyond any measure of control. If her count was right, it was nearly two hundred beats per minute.

"You don't want to know. Just get him cleaned up and give him some space." Damon proposed, "A lot of space."

"He'll never be the same again," a crowned Talemar intoned, shaking his head in disbelief.

"No…." Damon paused, "He won't." There was a potential, if used right, it could make Radin more powerful, but he had to survive what Damon knew would be ever-present memories of his torment first. And that was not a guarantee. Radin had seen the other side of the veil and lived to tell the tale. His knowledge of what he'd seen and lived through, if he could master it, could give him a potent advantage few others had.

Wraith walked into the room late, taking in the scene before him. "I owe you something." Reaching into his red, gold, and black robes, Wraith offered a piece of parchment to Damon.

Taking *Wraith's Return* in his grip and offering a simple nod in return, Damon made a *Portal* home and limped through. He needed to recover as well, and he needed to understand his new power and how to use it in concert with the rest of his mighty arsenal. His eyes couldn't help but glance back at a badly beaten and wounded Radin with his thoughts and emotions jumbled and raw. Rage, relief, *hate*, and *hope* among them, but as his eyes pulled away from Radin he didn't feel the courage of going to save him. He felt *fear*. Overwhelming, powerful, intense *fear*. It was all he could do to keep himself together enough for it not to show externally as his *Portal* whooshed to a close behind him, exiling him on Earth.

Charles W. M\(^c\)Donald Jr.

The Unholy Dragon of Darkness

Charles W. McDonald Jr.

Chapter 8: The Bleeding Crown

(Exeter, Perion, Present Day)

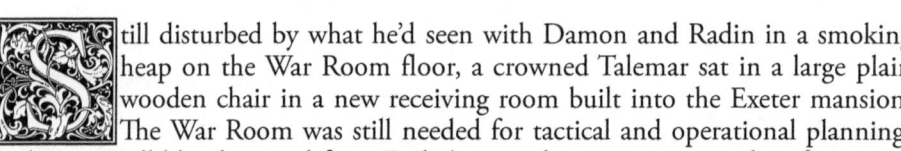

till disturbed by what he'd seen with Damon and Radin in a smoking heap on the War Room floor, a crowned Talemar sat in a large plain wooden chair in a new receiving room built into the Exeter mansion. The War Room was still needed for tactical and operational planning, and it was still blood-stained from Radin's wounds—not a proper place for receiving royalty. His messengers had gone forth across the world, spreading word of their capturing of the Crystal Crown and requiring fealty oaths of all kings, and stewards of all nations. Today, he was to receive Aegon, Steward of the Throne of Knor. As such, Sir Palomides' presence was also required. No one else in Talemar's reach knew Aegon better or had mentally jousted more frequently with Aegon than Sir Palomides.

Sipping his morning tea, Talemar sat down the cup to receive Brigance Fireheart and Sir Palomides. There was much business to discuss in preparation for their first head-of-state fealty oaths.

Brigance's leather armor felt vastly more comfortable without the chainmail, as he strode into the new receiving room, taking note of the newly-hung banners of Talemar's old house crest on each of the walls. Talemar's old crest of the Golden Dragon amidst a red background no longer fit. They needed a new crest more befitting the situation and times.

The larger and looming question was: *what are these times? These are certain-*

ly not the End Times prophesied, Brigance contemplated. At least, they didn't follow anything he'd learned in his youth and resembled nothing of any conversation he'd ever had on the topic—not that he was an overly religious sort. Prophecy had been stood on its side and flipped inside out by at least the duality between Radin and Talemar. The One didn't exist in its traditional framework afforded by prophecy. Things were no longer that simple. Neither was good or evil. Complex decisions from complicated motives and agendas of scarred people ruled the roost of this reality. Brigance longed for simpler times....

The reach and impact of Damon's interference was still yet to be discovered. It was as if the entire universe pivoted—or hinged—on Damon's Master Plan—a disturbing thought, fraught with peril.

Brigance offered a half bow to Talemar as he approached his seat before the grand fireplace and the massive, off-white granite mantle intended to be the focal point of this room. A new marble dais would be the new centerpiece, assuming they could get the funds to feed, clothe, and arm their men first. "Sir Palomides, as you requested, sir."

"First order of business, what is the status of Radin?" Talemar appeared business-like, in sharp, crisp, clean pastel off-whites with grey threads adorned with his old house crest, matching the banners hung throughout the receiving room. Soft charcoal leather boots propped upon a makeshift wooden—albeit elegant—footrest appeared more than out of place for his elevated station.

"Multiple *Healing* sessions still have yet to restore his ability to walk. His eyes...." Brigance trailed off, his eyes looking downward said all that was needed.

"Yes, well, we will say he's not feeling up to receiving visiting dignitaries at this time. If anyone asks, he lives, and he's doing well."

"Sir," vehement agreement from both Brigance and Sir Palomides as they simultaneously echoed their approval of the order.

They were both still Radin's men, and Talemar knew it. He might never be able to change that, but perhaps he could leverage it. "You wanted to offer suggestions for a new crest?" Talemar's eyes directed at Brigance with that as he motioned to the worktable he'd brought in, adorned with parchment and pen.

"Sir, the uniqueness of this is that we have two great leaders, one known to all, the other...." He didn't want to say it, but the men were behind Radin by a wide majority. Talemar offered an accepting nod, again motioning with his hand for Brigance to continue. "It's important in battles to know where your men are, how they're able to signal one another quickly on the field of battle, and to more easily single out the enemy."

"You're not telling me anything I don't already know, Brigance. Skip to

Charles W. McDonald Jr.

the part where you've made your point."

"We need, sir…," Sir Palomides adding, "…a unifying symbol of what we're fighting for. Of what we stand for. That is the life purpose of a standard."

"And what is your opinion of what that symbol should be, Sir Palomides?" Talemar had considered changing his crest long ago, but there had been no need for it. However, after capturing the Crystal Crown, the necessity of the matter had crept up in priority. Considering his question, he wondered if they were starting at the right point…. "What is it, Lord Fireheart, Lord Palomides, you believe we're fighting for?"

"We fight for the return of the morning, sir," Sir Palomides proposed flatly, seemingly obvious in tone.

"Are we," Talemar questioned legitimately. "We brought upon the world the Blood Night. With each Seal we break to bring about the coming of the Creator, we do untold and unspeakable things to another big piece of this world. And, quite possibly to other worlds as well." Another bright flash in his mind of the vast sea of crystal placid against a shore of white diamond sandy beaches and a booming voice of Creation off in the distance projecting upon him like a star even in the midst of all the surrounding white-out landscape. Each time, it was becoming increasingly harder to hide the effects. Shaking it off without visibly showing any outward signs of hindrance, Talemar considered their line of thinking. "Do you believe there will be a morning after we are done?"

Sir Palomides looked to his long-time friend, sidelong, wondering the very same. Talemar brought up fair points. It was hard to fight for a future state of glory when all they brought upon the world, or worlds, was despair. *Why were the Seals so hateful to Mankind?!* That was a broader, deeper question not being asked.

"Belief is a luxury," Brigance intoned with a certainty not held in the others, stepping over to the table to sketch a brief rendering for discussion. "It's what we project and defend that matters to the masses." Finishing his thought, Brigance put some quick finishing touches on his idea as it flowed from his thoughts to the parchment. Holding it up, Brigance explained, "WE are Justice for the Unjust. WE are the Trumpets of Amber Light. WE are the Bringers of the Morning." On his parchment, Brigance had brilliantly summed up their existence as an army and a new nation—a new kingdom. The center foreground was beset with the scales of justice flanked by rays of light originating from a sounded trumpet on the left and on the right a king's open-air court on the shores of the ocean—hearing two of his vassals on bended knee. Blistering beams of dawn's light on the horizon piercing a starry night sky formed the background. "Where darkness originates is irrelevant. It's what we do about it that matters," Brigance concluded. Sir Palomides smiled, standing alongside his friend, putting a hand on his shoulder in solidarity. Though, in looking at Talemar, Sir Palomides wondered if Talemar was the right man to receive this message. Talemar's face looked almost expressionless at the passion with which Brigance had delivered his brilliant proposal. *A hard man to read,* Sir Palomides considered.

"Your proposal is acceptable." Talemar didn't want to give Brigance too much credit, but it was brilliant. It was unifying, clear, and concise. It was a standard people would rally to with pride, but there was something missing. "I agree that things often come in three's, whether we want it so or not. That there is a symmetry to it." Rising from his seat to address Brigance eye to eye, Talemar continued, "I see three great Pillars of Hope on your standard. Who among us represents each pillar? Obviously, we have myself and Radin, and one could argue which person is which pillar, but who is the third?"

Brigance and Sir Palomides each looked to the other to answer.

"I leave you with that thought for both of you to chew on. I need to go see Radin for myself. It's long overdue." Walking out of the receiving room, Talemar left an awkward silence quickly falling upon them with only the hushed sounds of his leather boots on the hardwood floors to offer a reprieve.

*   *   *   *

Elise held Radin's head in her lap on their bed, gently stroking his hair in comfort; his eyes currently closed in thought or memory—one couldn't say. Standing in the open doorway of their bedroom, Talemar took in Radin's beaten body, with blood and puss-soaked bandages everywhere he looked. Except for the permanently maimed, he looked worse than almost any survivor of any battle he'd personally witnessed—even those of distant history from a life he barely remembered. The ripping out of the timeline by the Halls of Aaramus had done things to his mind—as if scrambling his timeline had also scrambled his memories and his psyche.

Crestfallen eyes a forerunner to Talemar's dark and weighty, yet soft approach, he needed to assess Radin's true condition, "May I enter?"

Elise said she had something to give Talemar when she first came back but hadn't brought it up again since seeing Radin in his condition. *Perhaps she never thought to see Radin alive again.*

"Of course," she offered, trying to sit up, while keeping Radin comfortable in her lap. She didn't know if Radin was even awake. His body had finally quieted enough to allow him some level of comfort, as his chest quietly rose and sunk with each labored breath Radin took. It took forever for his pulse to come down enough for his body to stop profusely bleeding on the sheets that had already been changed several times, as had his bandages. The efforts to infect his wounds had been *very* effective.

"If you'll indulge me a moment." Talemar sat beside her on the bed, offering to take Radin's head in his hands in lieu of her own. Elise offered little resistance, rising from the bed to walk around. Her legs had fallen asleep from comforting Radin for so long. Placing the Crystal Crown atop Radin's scarred head, Talemar cast into it and simultaneously into Radin, calling upon the power of their station as he began *Healing*. Radin's body began to violently spasm in his arms, causing Talemar to have to hold the Crystal Crown in place atop Radin's head. He felt the blood on his hands before he saw it, only now noticing Radin's bandages turning white as they dried out. Bleeding out his infection through the quartz-like pillars making up the Crystal Crown, Radin opened his Hellish red eyes, taking in Elise, in full, for the first time since he'd been rescued.

Gasping, Elise backed away from him almost involuntarily. She hadn't meant to offend him, or show fear of him, but it was just too much for her. Radin's child inside her and something yet still unknown inside Radin panicked Elise as she began heading for the door.

"Wait," Radin's plea causing her to pause, but it couldn't get her to turn back to look at him. The delicate fingers of her right hand already gripping the heavy door to his suite, he could see the reluctance and hesitation in her movement battling the need inside her not to see him this way as she closed the door behind her—leaving him with Talemar.

His eyes blinked a few more times, accepting Elise's reticence, before looking up to see Talemar's hands hovering over him and the Crystal Crown. His jaw moved and his mouth worked before his words came out labored, but with enough force as to show dramatic improvement. "Assemble everyone," he commanded, rising from the bed without stumbling. "I have something to say that I want everyone to hear."

Talemar rose alongside Radin, offering not a bow, but a nod of acknowledgment, never bothering to retrieve the Crystal Crown from Radin's head, where it still wicked out the spiritual and physical infections of Radin's wounds.

Chapter 9: The Three Pillars of Hope

(Exeter, Perion, Present Day)

eadership still gathering around him in the receiving room, Radin didn't feel nervous or apprehensive—only renewed in his determination for an end goal, frustratingly uncertain to him. Memories of Voltor still tormented him, and probably would be with him for as long as he lived. Even now he could feel the phantom torment of the spikes now removed from his hands and feet. Like the pain felt by the maimed, who'd lost an arm or a leg in combat, only to sense its continued existence in energetic form, even though no longer physically there. He doubted even death would free him of these memories, or his phantom agony.

"We're with you, Radin. Take your time," Lawna offered; still, the only one looking directly into those Hellish fiery eyes, she hoped not a true indicator of what lay inside. A slight nod of appreciation from Radin, and she was smiling, though a caustic tension laid over the room like a thick, infected blanket.

Looking to each of his leadership in turn 'til they locked eyes with him, Radin sought to make a point. They would have to get used to this. He had seen himself in a mirror, dressing in a full-length medium blue suede collared coat split down the middle exposing his light-grey pants. A series of heavy belt hooks ran up the center above where the coat broke in an upside-down V down both legs. The long sleeves terminated in thick cuffs angling back towards his forearms in silver cufflinks. It was far too hot, outside and in, for him to wear anything like that, and Michelle didn't understand how he wasn't sweating as she contemplated his thoughts—the last to lock eyes with him. Ykstherin couldn't, or wouldn't, look at him; instead busying himself fidgeting with a cane Radin knew he did not need.

"There are no words to describe…" Radin started, trying not to shiver, whether from the fever he thought was breaking or his adaptation to the somewhat average temperature of this plane of existence, "…what has happened to me, and what is to come. Save this…" He paused, looking around the room, settling on Brigance, "…we have a fight in front of us with a foe I don't believe is gone."

There were whispers and mutters around the room, mostly in the second ranks of leadership—field colonels and the like, though Wraith was looking directly at him.

"The demon, who you saw capture me, talked to me in moments of boredom, or vanity, telling me about how Eldrac was sending him the lifeforce of those innocent, and not. He told me that he had been growing in power and would soon be one of the most powerful in existence. In return, he would help Eldrac in this world, and others, to carry out his agenda. I witnessed Damon destroy this demon, and I remember seeing lifeforces escape out of the broken back of its body." More muttering as Radin concluded, "…And one of them—I'm certain—was Eldrac."

Mutterings turned to gasps as Wraith eyed Radin—with suspicion or skepticism, he couldn't say. Either way, there would be a private conversation with Wraith after this. Of that, he *was* certain.

"What bothers me more than Eldrac being released, whether back into this world or another, is the fact that **he** could rip a lifeforce out its destiny, permanently sending it to any place, person, or entity he sees fit. I was not aware such things were possible, but *this changes things for me*. I *will not accept* the very existence of such an ability. If we must destroy everyone, on every world, capable of such a thing, this is now a part of our charter. This is part of our mission, and we are going to do something about it, because I don't know if there is anyone else, besides us, who *can*." With that, Radin's eyes flamed, his head inclining to each of his leaders in turn; the Crystal Crown still bleeding his infections out of its tips for all to see.

"Where do we stand on financing our army," Radin asked, looking to Brigance and Talemar, taking note of his father's look of grave concern. They, too, would have to have a private conversation. He had half-conscious memories of Elise telling him of Rowarc's return as she stroked his hair, but his dad seeing him like this was not the reunion either deserved.

It had been memories of Rowarc's inner strength that had helped keep him sane in his moments of torment. That thought brought the closest thing to a smile he could manage as he returned his gaze upon Talemar.

"We were to receive Aegon moments ago but postponed that meeting to have this one. He was the first of our meetings with world leaders to discuss fealty oaths, finances, government requirements, and the like," Talemar offered flatly, not intending to insult; though hearing it again in his thoughts, it could have been worded more delicately.

"I heard some of the men discussing a new banner," Radin questioned, looking to Brigance.

"Aye sir...," he paused, trying not to let Radin's Hellish glare bother him, "...with your approval, we would like to use this." Brigance holding up a fresh-ly-stitched banner of hope. The center foreground was beset with the scales of justice flanked by rays of light originating from a sounded trumpet on the left and on the right a king's open-air court on the shores of the ocean—hearing two of his vassals on bended knee. Blistering beams of dawn's light on the horizon piercing a starry night sky formed the background. "Talemar suggested we name it the 'Three Pillars of Hope.'"

Looking to Talemar, Radin asked, "So who's the third pillar, if Talemar and myself are two?"

An acknowledging raised eyebrow from Talemar preceded, "That didn't take long." Talemar was once again seeing how sharp and quick the boy's mind was and how fast he caught on. "That was precisely my question from our previous meeting."

"I don't know if that's important or not at the moment. Perhaps it's the Creator himself. I can't say. What I can say," Brigance offered, motioning at the leadership around the room. "...If what you say is real, and a righteous person can be tormented, ripped out of the fate ordained by the Creator, and we don't do something about it, then there is no justice for the unjust."

Nods of approval around the room for Brigance with Ykstherin adding, "I don't think this should be discussed outside of this room. Certainly, not with the world's rulers—not yet." Around the room, more fervent nods of approval fol-lowed Ykstherin's suggestion.

"I think you're right about that, my friend," Radin replied, considering his wisdom. If they were to meet with Aegon, this *could not* be a topic of discussion. Eldrac would be enough motivation to extract funds, as would the rest of the Six the Dragon of Darkness had released upon the world if not upon all Creation.

"May I offer a suggestion," Sir Palomides proposed. "Sir, I am with you. I am your servant. However, for the purpose of this meeting with Aegon," he paused, trying to think of the right way to advise, "...I know this man. I think it

Charles W. McDonald Jr.

would be best if Talemar wore the Crown during our meeting with him."

Radin offered a slight nod to Sir Palomides, at least in reply to his out-wardly spoken fealty, but this first meeting with a world ruler outside their midst required a measure of caution mixed with an equal measure of boldness. "I will not start the meeting wearing the Crystal Crown," Radin declared, not knowing if it was done *Healing* him or not. Chances had to be taken, and Aegon had been kept waiting long enough.

Focusing as he reached out to the Arcane all around them, Radin changed all of Talemar's banners to the Three Pillars of Hope. A freshly stitched standard in Brigance's hands, suddenly suspended over Radin's head as he sat the Crystal Crown down on the worktable beside the single chair in the center of the Receiving Room. "I think Aegon has waited long enough. Please send for him," Radin commanded, taking a seat.

Talemar looked to Brigance and Sir Palomides briefly as they both looked to the Crystal Crown, sitting atop the worktable, no longer bleeding out Radin's infection. "Sir," Brigance Fireheart carried out the order, sending for Sir Aegon as he cleared the room of all but the most senior leadership.

*   *   *   *

Sir Aegon, dressed in light grey pants with a burnished burgundy jerkin, adjusted his black cloak, fanning his face as the young Captain Jac Haden came for him, sometime after he had been promised. This Talemar would answer for disrespecting his authority.

"Sir Aegon, we offer apologies and recompense for making you wait. We had a situation that required immediate attention and did not want that to interfere or interrupt your meeting with leadership," the fastidious captain offered.

Interesting word, leadership, he thought, noticing Talemar's name had been explicitly avoided. He wasn't a man for excuses, but he had seen many important meetings abruptly interrupted by matters of state; it happened. Better to have an uninterrupted session, especially on this topic, and if there was recompense.... *We'll see, but at least they are delivering a measure of respect*, he considered, following the young captain through a few turns into the meager receiving room. *Hardly fit for a world ruler*, he felt, with raised eyebrows taking in the mid-sized room with the high ceilings and the single chair beside a small working table holding the most powerful artifact on the planet. Immediately questioning why Talemar wasn't wearing it, Sir Aegon took in the young man in the chair before him, with the eyes of a demon. Shuddering inside as he locked eyes with Radin, Sir Aegon questioned the wisdom of answering this summons.

"Sir Aegon, you've been made to wait intolerably long, and we want to make that right," Radin began with Talemar, standing off to Radin's side and not knowing where he was going with this, but already he didn't like it.

Nodding, with an ever-so-light, almost non-existent, bow, Sir Aegon offered platitudes, "Respectfully, sir, I was curious about the condition of my men you took into battle and wanted the opportunity to meet the man in person, as well as the Great Talemar, of course." A deeper and more pronounced bow to Talemar as Sir Aegon gathered bearings on this new political landscape. This wasn't what he had expected, but Sir Aegon thought fast on his feet, and trusted his instincts.

"As recompense, we offer you the Crystal Crown," Radin declared flatly to a series of coughs from around the room—Talemar searing Radin with his eyes. "Assuming you can place it on your head, you may walk out of here with it...," Radin paused, putting his right index finger in the air, "...but if you cannot, and I can, you will commit every man you have to serve me. You will immediately collect a new five-percent tax, which you will pay to me every week without fail. You will immediately surrender a third of your entire treasury to me. And you will take the oath of fealty, right here—right now, to serve me as one of my most senior generals equal in rank to Sir Palomides, answering to Lord Brigance Fireheart." Radin smiled at him, eyes blazing like unto roiling lava, "Risk-reward, Sir Aegon. Do you accept my recompense challenge?"

A brief and measured shake of the head from Talemar expressed his displeasure and disapproval, but a cut-off smile from Brigance said he had been listening when Sir Palomides had educated him on the tendencies of Sir Aegon's ambitions.

Walking in very measured steps, Sir Aegon approached Radin and the table, picking up the Crystal Crown. The dried blood at the tips didn't match the descriptions he had seen in historical manuscripts, but he believed it genuine as he began placing it atop his head. Feeling it pushing back against the top of his skull, the more force Aegon used, the harder the Crystal Crown pushed back. Grunting, Sir Aegon took a long moment further examining the Crystal Crown before relenting to place it back down on the table with his left hand.

A sigh of relief from Talemar preceded a knowing smile from Radin, as unseen hands snatched up the Crown, placing it atop Radin's shoulder-length auburn hair. "I believe you owe me something, Sir Aegon," Radin tersely reminded, again taking his seat in the sole chair in the Receiving Room.

"Whether or not I approve of your tactics, I do recognize your authority and do hereby swear fealty to serve in the capacity you described before these witnesses."

"And…." Radin encouraging Sir Aegon to follow-through on his word.

"You will have my troops, the five percent additional tax, and a third of my current treasury…," he paused, "…I assume you'll want to send someone back with me to collect from the treasury."

"I will, and if he isn't returned to me completely untouched with a verified third, yours will be the shortest tenure of a senior general in history."

Offering a full bow this time, with a kneel all the way to the floor, Sir Aegon briefly glanced to Talemar on his way back up, just in time to catch Talemar snatching the Crystal Crown out of the air where Radin had tossed it to him.

"Behold," Radin proclaimed, providing a suggestive nod to Talemar. Taking his cue from Radin, Talemar quietly, smoothly placed the Crystal Crown atop his auburn hair. "Our prophecies were wrong. Our history misguided. We are forging a new path, and these are our tenets." A wave of his right hand caused fire to blaze around the Three Pillars of Hope banner he'd suspended in mid-air above his head. "Bear witness to the Three Pillars of Hope that we will bring upon this world. WE are Justice for the Unjust. WE are the Trumpets of Amber Light. WE are the Bringers of the Morning." The words boomed out of Radin, aided by the Arcane flowing through him with enough volume to shake the floor General Aegon stood upon. "Go forth, General Aegon. Go forth and tell everyone what you have seen! You are dismissed!"

Pivoting immediately right where he stood, General Aegon nearly ran out of the meager receiving room.

A raised eyebrow from Talemar as he tossed the Crystal Crown back to Radin. "You should continue to wear that until we're certain your wounds are fully healed," Talemar proposed, slowly striding towards Radin.

"Thank you." A rare moment between them. That and the *Healing* had changed his view of Talemar, but he didn't know if their working relationship would hold or not. They had dipped their toes in the lake of friendship but had not yet swam in it. Twice already their relationship had been severely strained. He wasn't sure if it was his growing confidence in himself that Talemar feared, or that he genuinely might have had more capabilities than even the Great Talemar, and perhaps they both—in some way—knew it. Either way, they were more powerful together than apart. Of that, there was little doubt. If they were going to hunt down everyone capable of condemning lifeforces to unending torment, they would need a truly powerful and cohesive force. He felt Talemar helped towards that end.

"Well played, sir," General Palomides complimented Radin with a broad smile. "I rather think word will get around. I'll be your representative to go back with him and verify the third of the treasury if you like. I would know his coffers best."

"Thank you, General Palomides. You have my leave." Radin gave his general a dismissing nod of approval as General Palomides headed for the exit, chasing after General Aegon.

Trying to hold himself together, Radin was utterly shivering inside within his three layers of clothing. Cold sweat formed on his brow, and he felt clammy throughout his entire body. No one seemed to notice yet, but he wanted to retire before anyone did. "Talemar, would you please continue setting up meetings with the rest of the world leaders?"

Talemar tried not to stare at the cold, blue fiery wisps of flames left in the wake of Radin's footprints as he trekked towards his room, as he exchanged worried glances with Lord Fireheart.

No longer suspended by Radin's *Telekinesis*, the standard of the Three Pillars of Hope fell to the floor, directly on one of Radin's still-flaming footprints. The flames licked at the cloth of the banner, but the Three Pillars of Hope refused to burn.

Chapter 10: The Circle of Losses

(Exeter, Perion, Present Day)

adin's room was quiet, and, for a change, he was finally alone with his thoughts. *Forgive me*, the only thought on his mind. He remembered much of the battle that resulted in him being captured by Voltor, but the thing that haunted him was the memory of being in the womb of someone other than who he had known as his mother—someone other than Arella. That combined with the knowledge of Vosh being killed, and the pieces were starting to fall into place. He had asked for his father to be brought to him only moments ago, but the knock on the doorway's casing to his suite made him question his readiness.

"Come in." Radin rose from the bed, trying not to move as he stood bedside. He didn't need his father worrying about him leaving fiery footprints everywhere he walked.

"How are you feeling?" Rowarc offered an apprehensive smile, attempting to allay his own concerns.

Charles W. McDonald Jr.

"Like I just became everyone's worst nightmare." His body had just been broken by a great and powerful demon. There was no other way to put it, and he didn't know if anyone would ever trust him again. He saw the way everyone looked at him—the way his father was looking at him right now—like he was no longer Human. "Some of who I was still exists deep inside, and right now I'm trying to understand that part of me. Can you help me?" Wanting to add 'Father' to the request, but he knew better.

"Sounds serious when you put it that way, but of course, anything. Name it."

"Tell me about my birth."

"Your mother told you that story a dozen times, or more—I'm sure of it."

"I want you to tell it. Please."

An apprehensive sigh from Rowarc, as he eased to the foot of the bed to take a seat, gathering his thoughts on where to begin. "I wasn't there," he began in resignation and acknowledgment of his negligence as a father. He felt ashamed. Who wouldn't…? Failing to be there for the birth of his only son! Radin deserved better than that. He deserved the whole truth.

Shaking his head in acknowledgment, Radin was grateful for the honesty. Maybe he would get some answers after all—and with them, peace. "Go on, please."

"The first time I saw you, you were a few weeks old. I returned from an expedition. Your mother was just starting to show when I had left, and you were early—very early. I had always assumed you were just healthy stock to have survived an early birth and growing so well, weeks after being born, almost caught up to where you should have been. I mean I never questioned—'til recently—whether you were mine or not. You had my eyes and a healthy resemblance in the face. I guess I don't know what to say." He didn't know. Inside he was shaking—trembling at the thought that this wonderful boy he'd known and raised might not be his. "Look, I don't know if that's the information you were seeking or the reason you summoned me, but I never had a single doubt or reason to believe you were anything other than my son, until recently. Even if it were so, you're still my boy."

"Just the truth is all I ask. You're still my father, no matter what." Rowarc was the only father he'd ever known—and a good one at that. Rowarc had taught him a great many life skills, and he longed for Rowarc's inner strength right now. Though, he wondered if it were true that there was never a single doubt in Rowarc's mind all this time. *Could that have explained why he was so distant after mom's death? After Arella's death,* he corrected himself internally.

"What made you ask? Something happened with all this…." Rowarc mo-

Charles W. McDonald Jr.

tioned up and down his son's body, ending at his eyes.

"I think Vosh is…was…my mother. The question is, why did she give me to Arella?" He had to stop himself from calling her 'Mother,' then, frowning, he felt guilt over not doing so.

"Why Vosh?" Putting together the pieces in his head, they were beginning to fit around that answer, but *this* was *his* son regardless. Radin was still his responsibility, and Radin needed reliable counsel, now more than ever.

"Vosh spoke to me, and I felt something—a memory I can't explain it any other way. The memory felt so real and yet so faint—so distant. Like a memory of a memory of a birth—my birth."

"A memory of your birth?" That was hard to imagine, but so many things were possible with magic. It was hard for someone like him to understand what, if any, limits magic had.

"Difficult to explain, but more like a feeling combined with a memory. I was unconscious from Voltor's torment when Damon came for me, and yet I still heard and saw so many things I still can't explain."

"Well, I don't know…," Rowarc was searching for the words, but he wanted the honest and open communication to continue, "I'm worried about you. I want to help however I can. I'm here to listen and counsel." Rowarc thought about it for a brief instant, knowing if he had just been through something so traumatizing, he wouldn't want to talk about it so soon.

Rowarc could see the deliberation in Radin's expressions as the tall stock of an unknown genitors carefully calculated what he had both the stomach and heart to reveal.

Rowarc paused, seeing the molten-flamed eyes of this fine young man—no longer his son—wondering what his feeble attempts could do for Radin. "What would you like me to call you? I think you could still use good counsel, and I want to be that for you—someone you can count on."

"I'm still your son no matter what. You raised me. You cared for me. And yes, I'd like your counsel as long as you would like to provide it." Sitting down on the bed with Rowarc, Radin let out a sigh like the one of his father moments before, smiling at the recognition of the resemblance. "I think I'd like to be alone with my thoughts a little while if that's okay." Just as soon as the words escaped his mouth, Radin regretted them. This was an impactful moment for both, and silence wasn't the answer. *There will be much more regret to come,* he realized while looking into Rowarc's watering eyes.

Rising from the bed, Rowarc offered another tense smile without comment.

Charles W. McDonald Jr.

A moment of Radin thinking beyond himself made himself ashamed for not thinking of this sooner, "I'm sorry for your loss. I mean if I'm not yours, then that means your child is—was—lost." A thought, and possibility, Rowarc had already entertained, quickly shoving it deep down inside himself. There wasn't time for that right now, but perhaps there would be a chance to mourn his circle of losses later—the loss of two children in one conversation. It was impossible to find the hope for their future together in that.

"I love you, my son," the words he couldn't say when they last parted in Stirling. His mouth worked at the emotions the words had immediately brought to the surface as his jawline tightened with his attempts to pull himself together.

"What if I called you, 'Dad?' Whether I'm your blood or not, you're the only man I could ever see as my dad."

A heavy nod of acceptance as Rowarc proudly took on his new title, though he didn't have the words to reply.

"Do you remember taking me quail hunting shortly before Mom's death?" It was a mistake calling Arella 'Mom,' but he was still lost in an emotional tide that stormed the shores of his consciousness.

"Yeah." A managed smile from Rowarc as the old memories stirred—if painfully so. "You were so miserable out in the elements. We didn't catch a damn thing."

"You're wrong, Dad."

Rowarc's smile vanished, not knowing where this was going.

"That was one of the best moments of my life. One of my fondest memories. That my dad, the legendary Rowarc d'Aguillon, wanted to spend all his time with me—just me. You couldn't have done anything more important—in my eyes—than doing what you did with me that weekend. As children, all we want is your time. Gifts are one thing, but your time is so much more. You can't fake care when it's spoken through the passage of *your time* invested in *your child*."

Wow! How has my son grown up so fast, so intelligently, and so strong? This is an impressive young man. Son, or no. "You have my time. Whenever you need it. I'll be there for you. I swear it!" He couldn't stay anymore. His eyes were already watering, and he wasn't going to let Radin see him cry. Pivoting away from his brilliant son in kind one last time, Rowarc walked out, wondering if the war they'd started would allow the keeping of his promise.

Charles W. McDonald Jr.

Illirian Starfire

Charles W. McDonald Jr.

Chapter 11: A Favor Earned, A Debt Paid

(Damon's Manor, Kaleion, A Long Time Ago)

eviewing his second surprise for Chara, Damon worked feverishly at the desk in his hidden study, ensuring all of his best weapons were at his disposal. The Dragon of Darkness had provided Chara's location, and she wouldn't remain there forever. He had to strike soon, to right this most recent wrong she had visited upon him and eliminate this painful thorn in his side, once and for all. *Damon's Surprise*, as this custom spell was titled, only worked on the undead, and specifically only one type of undead, but it was beyond lethal, and if *Damnation* failed, this would not.   Only a slight variation on *Damnation*, it was meant to snuff their lifeforce out of existence—just as useful as decapitation, but without the need to get too close where Chara was more physically lethal.

Gating the symbols through his right index finger, he made yet another improvement to the spell, just for Chara. The more limited its scope, the more potent he could make it.

"Always working so hard." He recognized the soft, sensual, feminine voice immediately as Illirian, and didn't bother wondering how she managed to get into a study only he should know how to even find, let alone enter. He knew better. Illirian was one of few in existence more powerful than he or Kellen, and he never underestimated her. He often wondered the limits of her power that only seemed to find their thresholds politically.

Turning to acknowledge her, he began putting on a shirt to cover his scars. Illirian, stepping forward, stopped him from covering himself. "Don't. You don't have to do that with me." She was close now—too close. Her sweet perfume filled his nostrils, with her lush body so close as to touch his.

"Did you need something," he asked, looking her right in her golden eyes, allowing his black eyes to follow and trace her curves.

"You MUST stop using *Damnation*," she implored, tracing physically the scars across his clavicle that were more scars on his soul. "Are you sure you don't want me to *Heal* these?"

"They can't be *Healed*," Damon flatly proclaimed, recalling all the times he had tried. Perhaps if they were physical scars, they could be. He knew them to be physical manifestations of an internal wound he could not even access or discuss, let alone *Heal*.

Wanting to weep for him, she understood him better than anyone since Dallia, but he wouldn't accept her pity. That would enrage him. He accepted her presence, and sometimes her closeness, but *love* between them was as forbidden as one becoming the other, as love often required—at least so in part. Even the greatest changes in Damon's behavior wouldn't allow it. He was condemned, but she always thought there was a way inside Damon that would allow her to minimize the casualties of his destructiveness. *If love were the only way in, surely wouldn't that be allowed, or at least justified?*

"I will use whatever I must to destroy Chara. She must be dealt with. Permanently!"

Delicately caressing his chest, beginning to run her golden fingertips along his shoulders, Illirian argued, "I'm only saying, it would be in your best interest to use whatever means you have, other than *Damnation*, to bring her down. Have you thought about putting her in *Stasis*…?" She paused, her fingertip now on one of the heels of his scars where the whip had crossed in slashing directions on his body, "… I could even go with you. She wouldn't stand a chance of getting away from both of us."

It was a more than fair offer, and Damon was considering it, whilst wishing Illirian would stop tracing his scars. He hated being touched there, by *anyone*. "Thank you for your offer, but if I don't personally take care of this problem, I'll regret it for the rest of my life. And yes, I have considered using *Stasis*, but that isn't punishment enough for the wrongs she's brought upon me—the wrongs she's brought upon Dallia. You know what Dallia meant to me! You know I'd been trying to make peace with Chara! Why did she have to destroy Dallia that way? You weren't there. You didn't see what she did to Dallia. I hope you never have to experience anything like that."

She hadn't been there. She hadn't seen the bile of Chara's work. She'd failed Damon in that way. Even now her mouth worked, trying to find the words to get him to let her in. She desperately wanted to help Damon. It was best for everyone if she could find a way in, but she'd seen Damon's obstinance before. His ownership of a problem was absolute, and this was by far the biggest problem—the heaviest of all burdens. "Does personally *have* to mean, without the help of others?"

"In this case, yes!" The look they shared—locked in a loving, caring glare—transcended mortal coils of good and evil, creating new shores of bonds, everlasting between them. "But, thank you, Illirian. Thank you. I mean it. Your offer means more to me than you'll ever know. It means a lot to Dallia too. She thanks you…from her grave." This time his mouth worked to struggle through the memories of Dallia. "I'll only use *Damnation* if I must."

"Every single time you use *Damnation*, you bind your soul with a shadow even I cannot undo. I know you are committed to Banthis now, and I know you think that life with her could give you what you want, but I also know you are not fully the darkness personified you try so hard to be. You were not made to be this Damon, but with each casting of *Damnation,* you revoke another thread holding you to this plane of existence. I don't know if you're doing this because you feel justified from what happened to you as a child, or what happened to Dallia, but there is only so much forgiveness left in all Creation for you. He will not allow you to continue ripping his children out of their designated fates."

Removing her hand from his shoulders, Damon threw his shirt on, turning to face her, "Thank you." He paused, looking her in the eyes again, "Thank you for trying to protect me, but please do not ever risk yourself, your future, or your forgiveness for me. I'm not worth it. Your life—your future—is more important than mine. You've done more than enough for me already." Placing his right hand on her chest, in between her breasts, the extent of his palm barely touching her pale peach summer dress, Damon sent Illirian to the most remote—though still safe— place on Kaleion he could think of.

*   *   *   *

Charles W. McDonald Jr.

Within the Bay of Witches, on the far side of the world, Illirian was unceremoniously dumped on the white sand beaches. It must have been three hours past dawn here, and the ocean crashing against her ankles matched the tears streaking down her face—tears for Damon's fate.

*   *   *   *

(Chara's Manor, The Haedron Mountain Range, Kaleion, A Long Time Ago)

Directly below the battlements of the left-flank eight-sided tower, Chara's sitting room offered a beautiful view, even through the narrow, crossed archer windows on each of the walls. It wasn't a pure octagon design, rather a rectangular construction abbreviated with four beveled edges on each wall, creating an elegant but militarily brute construction.

Chara's favorite color, blood red, adorned her sitting room with eight banners—two per main wall, making the off-white stone pop with color. Each banner bore her crest of a prostrate man before an obvious female figure all in shadows. Hours past dusk, she felt more alive now than any other time of day; she was at her peak. The tinging of the little bronze bell at the end of her fingertips summoned her male servants; they were all male, of course. Setting the bell down at the large map table to her left, Chara contemplated her plans to take over the neighboring kingdom. A meeting with King Amos, scheduled a few hours from now, would prove pivotal.

Looking at the map's iconography, Chara wondered where her manservant was. Men were sublimely stupid submissives, while women were cunning thought-leaders, brought about to change the world. They couldn't be more different in Chara's eyes, save one, of course—Damon. The *only* thing she admired about Damon was that he didn't fit into her mold of what other men had proven themselves to be: useless fools.

Damon's possible locations both entertained and bothered her. She knew him well enough to know he'd be coming for her. When last she saw him, his body was broken about the headstones in the church's graveyard. She hadn't had the time to go look for him, but she had made the time to develop a bit of a surprise for him—if he still lived.

About to ring the service bell once more, indicating the death of another of her manservants, Chara frowned at the nude male eunuch walking into her

Charles W. McDonald Jr.

sitting room. She didn't bother naming them, renaming them, or calling them by whatever names they may have gone by before. They were all 'Useless' to her so that's what she called them—all of them—'Useless.' "Useless, another moment and I'd have to kill you. You know this."

"My apologies, Your Majesty." She wasn't royalty—far from it. Yet they would die horrifically if they ever addressed her without her assumed title. "How may I serve you?"

"Go get dressed. You need to show me you can dress appropriately for serving our guests this afternoon." Chara tsk'd with her left index finger, warning, "And, you're responsible for dressing everyone else too. Don't fail me."

"Of course, Your Majesty. Useless will do a good job."

"We'll see...," she chided from her dais.

Her stomach didn't growl—ever—but she knew she was hungry. A blur, and she was outside, feasting on a doe she smelled only an instant earlier. It wasn't as rich as Human blood, but it sustained her until she could feast on the king and his men later tonight. Scheduling the meeting in the middle of the night had been a coup on her part, but she knew Amos would bring a healthy contingent to protect him; whatever it was, it wouldn't be enough.

A blur and she was back up in her tower, taking a seat before the dry husk of the doe collapsed to the ground outside. Blotting her face with a white towel that lay on her map table, Chara picked the fresh venison from her teeth.

* * * *

There wasn't much space between the back wall of the sitting room and Chara's throne, or the back of her dais, for Damon to sneak in, but he knew as soon as he set foot through the *Portal*, she would sense it, and the element of surprise would be forever lost. He had one shot at this.

Creating a *Light Orb* that would follow him, floating beside his right cheek so Chara could clearly see it was him, Damon adjusted the stoles of his charcoal-blue robes and picked up the menacing *Staff of the Invoker*, that crackled with the bliss of the power he gated through it with his right hand. Tossing the *Staff of the Invoker* to his left hand, the flowing, over-sized cuffs of his sleeves jostled in the anticipation of combat.

He had to be slightly closer for the ranged spells of *Damnation* or *Damon's Surprise* to work, so it was now or never.... Casting *Damon's Improved Shield*, he walked through, *Staff of the Invoker* in his left hand, leaving his right hand free to cast *Damon's Surprise* simultaneously.

Charles W. McDonald Jr.

*　　*　　*　　*

About to ring the bell again with her right hand, Chara suddenly dropped the tiny bell to the floor, feeling ill enough to sick up her blood meal right there on the dais. Blood spewing from her mouth agape, Chara looked behind her black leather, winged-back chair, seeing her arch nemesis, dressed in his finest mage regalia, lording over her—smiling ear to ear.

"Hello, Chara." *Damon's Surprise* had failed obviously, but a mere thought and his *Telekinesis* snatched *Damon's Contained Blast*—in scroll form—from his inner-robe pocket into his right hand. Even before Chara could react, the white-hot explosion violently blew her out of the room, up against the corridor wall—some forty paces away—with a crushing thud producing a battered, debris impression of her body in the stone wall. Another thought, and his *Telekinesis* snatched a *Mind Blank* scroll into his right hand just as he'd discarded *Damon's Contained Blast* onto the floor. Casting the *Mind Blank* scroll in his right hand, leaving Chara stunned, blinking and stammering, trying to regain her bearings, Damon mocked, "Are you okay, Chara? You don't look well."

Extending his right hand out in feigned help to his arch nemesis, Damon was surprised to see her so confused as to begin reaching out to him as if he'd actually render aid to this vile creature. Channeling both *Damon's Surprise* and *Damon's Damnation* simultaneously caused a light amber stream of fire to erupt from Damon's right index finger as tiny lightning bolts rode the stream of fire all the way to the floating target before them. Hitting, engulfing, then wrapping around Chara as *Damon's Surprise* did its work, dismembering her carotid arteries and spinal cord right at the cerebellum—effectively decapitating her without removing her head.

Her once-beautiful body collapsed into a dead, grey husk before him, bursting into a black ash symbol on the stone floor—the Seal of Banthis. A whisper on an unnatural wind confirmed receipt of his gift, just as that same wind cleared her remains from the floor. Chara now obliterated, with her lifeforce claimed by Banthis, brought the first smile to Damon since his last day with Dallia.

That broad, savored smile of killing a mortal enemy slowly crept across his face—Damon savoring his vengeance—just as Useless came to check on the crushing noise Chara's body had made slamming against the stone wall. Turning to the eunuch, Damon commanded, "Tell me everything, or I'll keep you alive a thousand years just so I can make you suffer that long."

Nodding in violent agreement, Useless took all the time necessary to tell Damon of Chara's plans to meet with King Amos and of all her treasure and their secret locations. Useless was suddenly useless no more.

Charles W. McDonald Jr.

(Perion, Present Day)

It didn't matter how long he was gone; it had felt like another eternity in suffering for Eldrac, and that young lamean would pay for *all* of Eldrac's torment. He had found a new home for his hatred—Wraith Silverstring.

Climbing the hilltop where he'd been set free once before, seeing the blackened path of his fire that had raced toward the children he'd killed playing in the field, he gathered his bearings.

The Blood Night consuming the planet didn't help. He barely recognized where he was, but he knew enough, and most importantly he knew where to find Wraith.

Looking down at the black and red signet ring, given to him in his torment, he felt its power—her power—coursing through his veins. And, power he would use.

Chapter 12: The Wrong Choices

(Damon's Manor, Kaleion, Present Day)

ooking out the six-over-nine windows, Mira wondered how extensive the blight damage to Damon's homeworld was and how long it would take before photosynthesis made right everything Damon's Star had made wrong. The daylight spectrum LEDs of the foyer's chandeliers seemed far more than just an anachronism, knowing the technologically-backward world that lay beyond the horizon.

Damon had given her free reign to go wherever she pleased within his estate and grounds, and the great Gold Dragon down in the cavern foundation had rent her entire reality to shreds in one terrifying moment. She didn't know what to make of her new reality, nor of Damon, but she knew nothing would ever be the same.

Taking the railing with her right hand, she ascended the circular staircase heading back up to his secret study on the fourth floor.

A moment later, about to pass through the secret passage of the barren, tiny square room, she could hear a feminine voice talking to Damon on the other side. Not wanting to interrupt, Mira listened covertly at the hidden door's edge.

*   *   *   *

"It isn't the first time I've asked you to stop using *Damnation*, but I don't know how else to explain it other than there are forces about to intervene, and I don't think I'll be able to hold them off much longer," Illirian Starfire pleaded with Damon with outstretched arms that desperately needed to cling to him.

"You've done far more than you ever should have to protect me. I thank you for that, and I'll never forget it."

Rounding Damon's desk to sit atop it, Illirian parted her white and gold full-length dress, allowing her to sit directly in front of Damon, ensuring she interrupted his work.

"Really," Damon protested, with a disapproving look. "This is important work, Illirian."

"So is this," Illirian motioned between them, emphasizing their own conversation.

Pushing aside the parchment of the new fundamental, Damon made more room for Illirian. "You have my undivided attention."

"Good, I report on you. You know that right?"

"To whom?"

"That doesn't matter. There are others interested in your work that I answer to. That's all you need to know."

"I was aware, but obviously, I don't know the details."

"The details are that your all-out assault on the status-quo will not be found acceptable to a great many of those above me."

"So, let them come for me then. You think I fear the outcome of my transgressions? I've been planning for the manifestation of those consequences half my life."

Shaking her head in frustration, Illirian took Damon's face in her hands, smoothing his cheeks. "Yes, but *I* care about what happens to you, you insufferable dolt."

"Why? You know we cannot be. You've said it a thousand times before."

Performing the forbidden, Illirian kissed Damon, caressing his tongue with hers while her fingertips soothed against his face and neck. Breaking off the kiss, Illirian pontificated, "Damon, sometimes we make the wrong choices to get to the right place."

Charles W. McDonald Jr.

"Tell them, if I'm successful, a new balance is precisely what they'll have. It should settle into an acceptable equilibrium—an acceptable outcome for everyone."

"Really?" Illirian dubious at the last, offered a suggestive smile. "You've promoted yourself to a deity, and you think that an acceptable new balance?"

"Tell them if they take me off the board now, a permanent imbalance is exactly what they'll have. Tell them to examine my motives, and actions, and then ask if they are not consistent with one another. You know my motives better than anyone. Explain it to them. I need you to buy me some time."

"I used to know your motives, Darling, but honestly, I don't know anymore. This whole deity move caught me completely by surprise. I just couldn't see you ever wanting that kind of responsibility."

"Yes, well, about that…," Damon paused, smirking, "…let's just say it was a means to an end, rather than my first choice." He allowed himself to get close to her, taking in the unique sweet scent that was Illirian. Wanting to kiss her back, he deliberated, pulling back away from her. "I don't want to use you. I told you before, don't risk yourself for me. I'm not worth it, and I meant it. I still mean it."

"I'll always do what I can for you. You don't even have to ask." Shaking her head, trying to reconcile her feelings for this man, Illirian gave voice to her internal struggle over Damon, "There are parts of you I detest, but there are equally beautiful parts of you I adore. More than anything, I respect you…I think more than anyone I've ever known." Getting up from the desk to leave, Illirian offered, "You *are* worth it to me, Damon."

*   *   *   *

Tears streaking down Mira's face, she contemplated how she could compete with someone he'd known for centuries. How could she build a bond to overcome one forged over hundreds of years? How could she contend with a near goddess in beauty and intellect? Then, a moment of realization came upon her in but an instant. If Illirian could save his life, she believed the whole better off with Damon than without. Damon was far from perfect. He was terrible, cruel, ruthless, and terrific all at the same time, but he was a difference-maker, and, with the right influence, he could….

You can't change someone like Damon, you moron! Mira berated herself internally at the thought. She couldn't compete with Illirian. That was a simple fact, and she knew it. Maybe she needed to start distancing her heart from Damon, so he didn't shatter her to pieces. Maybe she needed to go all in with her love for

Charles W. McDonald Jr.

him and make sure he knew it, unquestionably. Steeling herself, wiping her tears from her face, she'd made her decision, confident it was the right choice. Walking back into Damon's secret study through the hidden doorway of the barren and tiny antechamber, Mira smiled at Damon, noticing Illirian's absence, though her scent lingered.

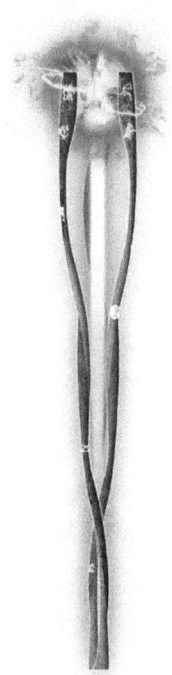

Chapter 13: The Author of Damnation

(Exeter, Helios Manor, Perion, Some Hours Later)

The knock on his door would have woken him if he could have slept.

"Come," Radin blurted, running his right hand through his hair, still laying on his bed.

Ykstherin, dressed in his usual matte gold color, but not of wool this time—just a long sleeve shirt with pants somewhere between a burnished gold and charcoal. "I wanted to check on you."

"Seems like that's all everyone wants to do—check on me." Exhaling in frustration, Radin wondered if he'd ever have the trust he once enjoyed. His Hellish eyes certainly didn't help. He had already tried to change them back, to no avail. They were a gift he couldn't return, even if a gift he never wanted. "Everyone wants to see the Hellish Freak."

Not really understanding the 'freak' label, Ykstherin assumed Radin had been in the company of his Terran friends again.

Charles W. McDonald Jr.

"Yes, well, that's not how I see you."

"I guess I should say 'thank you' then." He hadn't intended for that to come out so sardonic, but he was still very young, and his words still came out without the forethought he knew they required.

"This new charter you brought us...I thought we might talk about that." Ykstherin licked his lips, briefly looking at the ceiling. He wasn't thirsty—just uncomfortable. This would be uncomfortable—for the both of them.

"I'm listening." The words still came out tinged with suspect and acrimony, even though this was the man that had come to save him—both in the real world and his waking dreams. His time in Hell had changed him. There was no getting around it, and it wasn't going to be easy to change himself back—if he even could.

"Do you remember me telling you I knew of Damon—of his work?"

"Yes, I still have some of my memories." He hadn't meant to let that slip out—that he was missing some of his memories, while others had been accentuated. Too late now.

Ykstherin noticed, his eyes drifting right then left as they registered the comment for later use. "I don't know quite how to put this to you."

"Just say it...."

"To my knowledge, and I could be wrong, Damon is the author of the spell that was used on you by Eldrac."

Radin's face went immediately blank—emotionless, registering that the *author of all his suffering was Damon.* A painful silence fell upon the room like a disease of shadow.

An awkward moment later, Radin, rising from his bed, headed to the front of his room.

"Radin, where are you—"

"We're done here," Radin replied flatly, heading for the dresser where he kept Damon's scroll. Without thought, he brought the edges of the seal together, only to break it again; his body collapsing on the floor before Ykstherin.

(Damon's Manor, Kaleion, Present Day)

Finding himself in the familiar surroundings of Damon's foyer, Radin took a hard right, descending the stairs of the butler's kitchen three steps at a time, skidding to a stop right in front of Edgar Hastings, Damon's Chief of Staff. "Tell Da-

Charles W. McDonald Jr.

mon I'm going to his balcony on the fourth floor. I'll be waiting for him. Make sure he gets the message immediately when he arrives."

"Sir, we haven't fully finished the remodel up there yet. Wouldn't you prefer—" Edgar didn't get to complete his suggestion, interrupted by Radin's index finger now pointing inches from the end of his nose.

"Tell him, Edgar!" Radin shot up the stairs of the butler's kitchen, then through the foyer's main staircase, again three steps at a time, finding himself on Damon's unfinished balcony, waiting for Damon. His fingers fidgeted, wishing he'd taken the time to bring Dallia's staff with him through a *Portal* instead of using Damon's *summoning seal*. Haste would get him killed, if Damon didn't kill him during this confrontation.

If Radin was going to confront Damon, he needed to be beyond full strength, and he still hadn't fully recovered from Voltor's torment. At least he had the Crystal Crown, yet it felt different here. Feeling the crown atop his head, he verified it was there, though he couldn't source much more energy than without it. *Great, it's limited to Perion*, he thought.

After a few moments, having a clear view straight through the open Ritual Room, he noticed Damon strolling across his seal in the floor of the Ritual Room in full mage regalia. He'd never seen Damon like this—carrying a mighty metal triple helix staff that could have intimidated all on its own. Damon looked...God-like.

Reconsidering his approach, Radin's mouth worked, but the words came out a bit jagged and uncertain, "I n-n-need to know something"

"You're welcome," Damon's tone was agitated, allowing the spherical tip of the *Staff of the Invoker* to point directly at Radin; a hazy charcoal-blue aura around Damon's signet ring appeared as it gripped one of the helix metal rods of the *Staff of the Invoker* tightly. The *Staff of the Invoker* cast its own charcoal-blue hemispherical aura large enough to encompass both him and Damon combined.

Undeterred, Radin barked out his indictment, "Are you the author of *Damnation?*"

"Yes," Damon replied straightforwardly, wanting to say more, but what more was there to say...? His spell had caused Radin more torment than his mind, or body, could ever calculate. It was heinous—his spell. So was he.

Spinning to face the gardens, or to face away from Damon, Radin had no reply. He was crushed under the weight of this betrayal, looking for a way out. Damon could not be allowed to become the enemy—that would be the end of all of them. Damon could kill them all with a thought. His purpose seemed crystal clear hours ago, and now....

Charles W. McDonald Jr.

"I warned you of what I was." Another moment of truth offered by Damon, still not helpful as Radin was still seeking a way out of this without having to go through Damon—without the impossible.

"You mean what you *are*." *Not helpful*, Radin's inner thoughts screamed at him.

"Right...," Damon paused, reflecting on the long and bitter shadow that was his past, "...what I *am*." The words came out resigned and weighty with condemnation—for himself. *The Staff of the Invoker* no longer pointed at Radin, instead leaning against Damon on his right side, though its terrifying aura still engulfed them both.

More awkward silence—the second time in only minutes—this time from Damon.

"I told everyone that we would hunt down and destroy everyone we found using this spell because it's so wrong on so many levels. How could you?"

Damon started to respond, but Radin interrupted, "I mean this thing redirects a lifeforce from its intended fate."

"It can, yes. I made it specifically for Chara, so in her case, she was fated for the Underworld, one way or the other. I was just directing her soul to a specific...*entity*—ensuring she stayed where I put her." That was the best adjective for describing his *wife*, in *this* conversation. "I merely accelerated and directed her more expedient arrival there."

"But, you used it on innocent victims as well?"

"I did." Damon's candid reply took Radin off guard. He never got used to Damon's blunt nature. Radin exhaled heavily, again running his right hand through his hair, trying to think of a way out of this future of death about to swallow him whole.

"When was the last," Radin asked, thinking aloud, "...Tell me everything. Please. I need to know."

"I use it when I have to. It's one of the most lethal weapons I've ever built." Damon paused, thinking of how he might be able to turn this around. "You still are not powerful enough to protect your thoughts, so I can't show you everything, but will you come with me?" Offering a *Portal* between where they were standing and Damon's Seal of the Ritual Room, Radin saw a beautiful, lush world on the other side of the *Portal*. "Please," Damon offered, seeing Radin pick up his feet walking in his direction.

Charles W. McDonald Jr.

(New Georgia, Eden, Present Day)

The other side of the *Portal* confronted Radin with an utterly alien land-scape—somewhere between a modern society of Earth and something…beyond that. Ancient yet advanced architecture jutted out of the ground at 22.5-degree angles in the background, while fresh and continuous modern construction flooded the foreground. Everything was new—the city streets, businesses, houses, schools, even what looked to be buildings dedicated for the treatment of those with medical needs—albeit most in operations while still under varying stages of construction. Built in operational stages or wings. He'd never seen anything quite like it before, nor had he seen any reactions like those offered before them now.

They had *Portal'd* in between a new commercial district under construction and a residential neighborhood on the opposing side of the street. Crews of men on both sides of the street scurried about both houses and businesses alike making all manner of construction noises that ceased the moment Damon and Radin had walked through Damon's *Portal*.

Human men, women, children, along with elves, and other species of life he didn't recognize, all prostrated on the ground before them—before Damon. He didn't recognize many of their languages, muttered in awe, but he could tell they were in mesmerized by the way they looked at Damon—and him.

Touching Radin's head, Damon cast *Linguistics* allowing Radin to compre-hend the mutterings: "It's Damon." "He's come." "He came to help us."

A great gathering of all species began to congregate around them as an old-er man approached from the commercial side of the street where he'd been talking to another worker under the awning of the medical facility. His walk was slow and labored with a limp from an apparently injured right leg that still bothered him greatly.

"Master Damon, thank you for coming," Ron Stencowsky offered with a full and respectful bow. "Will he be staying with us? Would you like us to make accommodations for him?" Ron looked to Radin, running his handkerchief over his balding, sweaty head.

"No, this is…Radin. He won't be staying at this time, but if he comes, you are to treat him as my representative and surrogate. Radin, this is Ron, my Construction and Security Director. He's also got a good mind for military tac-tics." That detail Damon offered with a half-smile and a nod towards Ron.

Ron immediately offered a full bow to Radin, "Of course, sir. Anything you ever need. Just ask." Ron looking nervously between both Damon and Radin, as he considered Radin's *real* relationship with Damon. Call it healthy skepticism.

Charles W. McDonald Jr.

Call it battlefield senses, Ron trusted his instincts, which told him never to trust anything at face value—from anyone, especially Damon. His relationship with Damon was a complicated one. Damon had performed feats of miracles that both impressed and awed, but his aura was…terrifying…and magnificent. Jumbled and juxtaposed thoughts as Ron tried to comport himself before his living god.

"Ron, would you tell Radin the story of how I brought you here?" An odd question coming from Damon, but if your god asks you directly to do something, you do it. He still had trouble associating that title and that relationship with Damon, but Damon had saved him. He'd saved them all.

"Of course, sir." Ron looked between them, wondering, "Does he understand what a thermonuclear explosion is?"

Damon shaking his head, performed an illustration, casting *Damon's Far Reaching* immediately followed by *Shockwave* far off in the distance over the water. With only Arcane as the source, a quarter-strength, five-hundred-kiloton explosion just beyond the edge of the horizon lit up the ocean, yielding a massive mushroom cloud and a concussive blast that eventually rushed over them, disheveling clothes, causing everyone to look at Damon in fear. "Sorry," Damon offered after the concussive blast washed over them. "Sometimes a demonstration works best…."

A moment later, still licking his lips and not wanting to see another of Damon's *demonstrations*, Ron told Radin, "Our world was at war—everywhere—tearing itself apart. It was our apocalypse—our End Times. Suddenly, these *Portals* opened everywhere all over the world—our world—their world…. Just in time to save us from explosions like what you just witnessed, as well as other manner of cataclysms." Ron motioned to all the species, men, women, children, and elves gathered around them. A glance from Ron at the statue of Damon behind them, caused Radin to spin around, looking.

"Upon our arrival, we found those, along with all this construction equipment and material that we've been using ever since we got here. We've been building pretty much non-stop, day and night, since our arrival. Damon gave us an efficient government, rule of law, allowed us to elect our own leaders. He provided enough technology to get us off the ground. Free-energy-driven electricity and renewable electricity devices all over the planet. The tools and equipment to build the world as we see fit. Weapons for us to protect ourselves. Damon saved us. He…." Ron didn't finish the thought, but he really didn't have to. Looking to Damon, that level of honesty was all Damon was looking for as Ron received an approving nod from his god.

There it was. Radin had wondered why Damon's appearance had changed; how he looked even more intimidating than the day they first met. Damon had

made himself a deity…. He'd taken upon his shoulders the futures of all the people, and races of beings, he saw before him and far beyond the horizon, in every
direction. "Why?" Radin asked, wondering what could ever make Damon take on
such an incredible burden, given everything else he knew to be on Damon's plate.
How many people were here, and from how many different worlds?

Damon motioned for Radin to walk with him. "I'll be back," Damon
proclaimed to the gathered crowd. "I will address some of your concerns before I
go—I promise." Ron offered the both of them another full bow as they started to
walk toward the shoreline, a few miles off in the distance; *Shockwave's* mushroom
cloud still dissipating out over the water.

"Whatever I was, I might very well still be—especially when the need
shows itself," Damon explained, thinking of how best to explain why he, himself,
was struggling with this internally. "I'm a condemned man, Radin. I know that.
However, I've always had standards. Always had an ethical compass. Say what you
mean—do what you say kind-of thing." Damon paused again, reaching into his
own psyche for an explanation. "Whatever I was, isn't it possible for me to become
more?"

"More what?" It was a legitimate question for such a weighty conversation.

"I can't risk showing you much more, Radin, but do you believe, after seeing all this, that I have a bigger plan for all of us?"

"I don't know what to think about you. You're a complete enigma to me."

"To me too," Damon chuckled, putting a hand on Radin's shoulder as
they walked closer to the beach, illuminated by his thermonuclear explosion on the
horizon. "There is no way for me to set right everything I have done wrong. That's
not possible—even for me. Let's just say I look at the world, and the Universe, differently than I did in my youth. I have changed and I continue to evolve. As we
all do…."

"Look at which world differently," Radin asked, motioning to the alien
landscape all around them.

A brief snort of acknowledgment from Damon as he thought aloud, "I've
been traveling among worlds quite a while so that's a fair question. Let's just say
which world might not be as relevant as you think." He needed to address Radin's
biggest concern before sending him back. He knew it had been tearing Radin
apart at the seams, and he wanted to give him an answer that was both plausible
and believable. "*Damon's Damnation* was immediately banned on my homeworld by
the Council of Mages. That, unfortunately, had the effect of making it infamous,
which led to other mages learning of it, then taking it with them to other worlds
where it was banned there as well. If I could have foreseen these consequences, I

would never have created it. However, I cannot unring that bell. We are where we are. I can, however," Damon paused again, now standing in front of Radin, "... offer you my assistance in leveling the playing field."

"You're going to have to talk in terms I can understand, Damon. I don't have the same level of exposure to other cultures."

"Right," Damon considered, reconsidering his approach. "I'll give you a list to start with, of magi, or lameans as you call them, that have been known to cast my *Damnation* spell, and I'll give you the resources you need to put an end to them—permanently." He felt a little more explanation was required, continuing, "I don't think killing these magi is going to work. I believe we're going to have to put them in a kind of *Stasis*—for now at least. As you can see, by looking around you, I've got quite a lot on my hands now so I won't be able to help you as much as I would like, but if you still wish to continue our lessons, I will leave that up to you."

It was still a lot to offer, and it got him away from the precipice of dueling with Damon to his own certain death. Damon was offering Radin a way out. Considering the consequences of the alternatives, Radin saw little else, but he needed time alone to think and consider. "I'm not sure about the lessons just yet but thank you. Thank you for saving for me—for not leaving me there." Radin choked up before him, wanting to offer more of a gracious response, but given how he got where he had been, he felt it might have been enough. Their relationship was complicated before this; now it was a riddle, wrapped in an enigma, and shrouded in paradox.

There it was. Not recognition. Not gratitude. Damon was happy to see the acceptance in Radin that Damon had been the one to come for him—to save him. That Damon had been the one to risk everything to come get him when no one else could or would. It might go a long way towards helping the Master Plan, but Damon still wasn't sure if their agendas were aligned or not. Only time would tell.

A smile from Damon accompanied by a touch of his hand on Radin's chest and Radin was gone—sent away.

Walking back to the gathering that had patiently waited for him at the roundabout, in front of the freshly constructed city streets, Damon offered his best smile, but he couldn't seem to soften his intimidating aura. The Humans and elves were easy to read; he had been around them all his life, but the 22B Humanoids were a bit tougher to read. Their homeworld, Kepler 22B, was thought to have been a savior homeworld for Earth when their End Times came, but it turned out their End Times was in-progress as well. Much shorter than Earth Humans at an average of just over five feet in height, 22B's had wider almond-shaped eyes with

Charles W. McDonald Jr.

tepid grey skin, large heads, and very slender bodies. Similar to the Zeta Reticuli greys in shape and size, but not nearly as hostile or manipulative. They brought with them a lot of tech, including FTL, but Damon had forbidden the use of FTL, for the time being. He wanted them to focus their talents on getting Eden off the ground and in order, ensuring the planet's well-being was being watched after by a semi-advanced race. Especially from an energy perspective. He didn't like how they could communicate with him telepathically either, but he felt like he had warned them sufficiently about staying out of his head. Still, he kept up his strongest mind protections at all times ever since his last encounter with the Dragon of Darkness.

Standing before the gathering, Damon extended his left hand—his right still holding the *Staff of the Invoker*. "I've heard many prayers of concern about the possibility of indigenous life threatening your families. I've come to answer those prayers of concern. Tell me more about the problem. Show me."

A few clicks from one of the androgynous Greys, and *Linguistics* translated for the gathered audience. "We've seen them mostly around the hours of dusk. They have pincers for hands with long, poisonous tails, and hard exoskeletons. They're quite tough to kill, even with the weapons you left us. We never go out in raiding parties of less than four anymore."

Looking to Ron Stencowsky for verification, Damon inquired for more details, "Have you captured one of them that I can examine?"

"We have, sir," Ron struggled, not knowing how to properly address his new god. He was still having trouble processing it all.

"Show me."

Walking off together, the androgynous 22B-Grey, Ron Stencowsky, and Damon all headed inside the still-under-construction hospital bristling with the latest medical technology the 22B-Greys had to offer. Listening to the Grey speak through the translator as they moved through more complete wings of the hospital, it described advanced robots in every operating room he passed, along with the latest portable blood chemistry diagnostic equipment—the size of a small tablet— each capable of performing genetic profiling for tailored medicine and pharmacogenomics. Passing a bio encryption lock, using facial recognition and a retina scan, they entered the secured wing of the bristling new hospital, made from heavily fortified concrete and titanium. In some rooms, they were prototyping 3D printers capable of printing both metal and organs alike. In others, they were prototyping robotic doctors for remote checkup and general medical capabilities. Passing another layer of security, this one using facial recognition with a finger scan that *wasn't* reading fingerprint swirls, they proceeded deeper into the research and development wing of the hospital, where the Grey explained they were working on cures for diabetes, cancer, and Alzheimer's Disease among many others. A fifteen-foot by eighteen-foot sterile operating room, with another one of those advanced robots, housed the captured indigenous species in question.

"Mhmm," Damon commented as he looked over the creature's exoskeleton being surgically peeled back by the robot's pincers after the laser had done its job. "Is this one smaller, larger, or average in size, compared to the others you've seen?"

"The ones my men encountered were bigger, sir." That from Ron, but Ron had heard of accounts where they were much smaller too. The one on the operating table was about five feet in height, Damon estimated. It had big, glossy-black eyes like unto a shark's eyes, that flashed light blue at times.

"You haven't seen the most interesting part yet," Ron warned. "Show him," Ron instructed the Grey, reaching for the light switch. As Ron hit the lights, it took a second for Damon's eyes to adjust. Nothing unusual. Then he noticed the indigenous creature missing from the OR.

"Well, that certainly explains a lot," Damon thought aloud as he observed the creature disappear right in front of them. It all made sense now. Never once had Damon seen or felt a presence anywhere on the planet, and *he had explicitly looked* for them. *How deep underground must they have gone to hide from his scans, and how had they survived being slung out of their star's orbit? And, for how long?* His best estimate was that it was slung from orbit within the last ten years or so. Surely, they couldn't have survived that long. But, in all the times he had been here, there was virtually no light, except the light he brought with him, until he created the Yellow Dwarf that they now orbited. If they had been anywhere on the surface, he wouldn't have seen them, given their ability to be invisible in the absence of light, but still, he should have sensed them. "Hmmm, that makes me think of something. Here, let me try something. Leave the lights off a moment longer." Damon held up the *Staff of the Invoker*, reaching out to the Zero-Point all around him, casting *Damon's Improved Foresight* to probe the being. Nothing. He was going to have to work on that. If he was this close to it, and he still couldn't sense it with his magic, then that was going to be a problem. "That's one hell of a stealth capability that thing has."

"Yeah," Ron commented. "My men said they didn't see them 'til they were right on top of them, and if you hadn't left us those weapons, we'd all be dead by now."

"If I had known these were out there, I would have taken care of them before I brought you here. Or, I would have just found another planet. Tell everyone I'll help fix this. Tell them to look for their nest—recon only. When you find them, break this seal." Damon handed Ron a black wax seal with his symbol. "I'll come immediately and take care of the problem. Meanwhile, tell me what other weapons I could bring you that would help."

Hitting the light switch, Ron walked back toward them as he watched the creature reappear on the surgical table. "Lasers are useful on them, as are depleted uranium rounds."

Damon nodded in acceptance. "I'll see what I can do." Using *Telekinesis*, Damon instantly produced two sample vials, handing them to the Grey, who clicked in acceptance. "I need you to harvest these DNA samples and grow it for me at an accelerated rate—say fifteen years per orbit. Can you do that for me?"

Linguistics translating the clicks in real-time, "Of course, Savior. I will do as you wish." The Grey felt the frozen samples in its slender, four-fingered hands, placing it in its white lab coat.

"That's my only sample. Getting another is not an option. So, don't disappoint me."

The Grey shook its large bulbous head in complete understanding, its black almond-shaped eyes, blinking in terror at even the thought of letting Damon down. The responsibility of dealing with him directly terrified it, but that was the price of running in circles so close to the sun—sometimes you got burned.

"Let's head back out," Damon suggested, then paused abruptly, his *Telekinesis* instantly producing another transparent cylinder in his right hand. "The instant you have the completed genetic analysis of that creature in there..." Damon pointed back to the OR, continuing, "...put the report in this cylinder and close the lid. The cylinder will find its way to me. It will help me deal with these things for you. Understood?" Another vehement shaking of the bulbous head in agreement, and they were all heading back out the secure corridor the way they had come in.

Walking back out toward the main lobby of the hospital, Damon noticed a beautiful, young, and all-too-familiar figure tapping her heels just on the other side of the secure zone.

The double doors hadn't even stopped swinging to and fro behind them when Damon was verbally assaulted.

"Where the FUCK have you been the last couple of years," Mira exclaimed, her eyes caustically accusing Damon from a few feet away, as her right foot was in full fidget mode, tapping her heels on the glazed, hygienic, Terracolor® flooring.

Ron looked to Damon as if to disavow this woman, shaking his head at her in violent disapproval. Even the Grey wore an expression of horror, and Ron thought that impossible.

"Mira, it's a little difficult to explain right now. So—" Damon was gone—swallowed up by the ground underneath him, not even leaving a seam to indicate where he had been.

"YOU GODDAMNED MOTHER FUCKER!!!" Mira smashed both her heels, jumping up then down on the sterile flooring of the hospital lobby. "FUCK!!!" Storming out of the hospital, broken heels in her hands, Mira fumed while Ron and the Grey wore semi-permanent mortified looks about them.

The demigod that was the maker and destroyer of worlds, who had stared down the Dragon of Darkness one on one, would rather run from Mira than face her wrath....

(Austin, TX, Earth, Present Day)

A thud, and Damon was deposited unceremoniously to an ungraceful landing in his master bedroom in Austin. A look through the window treatments, and he could see it was daylight outside. Sighing heavily, he heard a familiar female voice call out from the kitchen. He could hear Mira's footsteps approaching.

"I haven't quite finished unpacking yet...," Mira began, still a few feet from their master bedroom, wondering where Damon had gone to after arranging to send her home from his manor on Kaleion.

"There you are," she squealed in excitement. Another heavy exhale from Damon caused her to take a step back. "What's wrong," she asked, looking into those *black mirrors of the soul.*

"Can you make me a promise and keep it?" Damon didn't know quite how to approach this subject, but it was an inevitable backfire of his Master Plan.

"I don't like where this is going." Her heels started tapping.

SHIT, he thought, as he watched her habitual fidgeting begin.

"I've told you before, I can't tell you every single part of my plan, because you can't protect your thoughts from being scanned. Do you trust me enough to believe me when I tell you that your safety and well-being matter to me? That you matter to me?"

"Now I really don't like where this is going!"

"Just answer me," he challenged, staring into the brilliant, fiery soul behind those starry, bright-blue eyes of hers.

"Yes, I believe you care about me," she admitted, finally after a long mo-

Charles W. McDonald Jr.

ment, though wondering the extent to which he cared about her. She was in uncharted territory with Damon and it utterly terrified her.

"There will come a time when you doubt that, but I want you to remember this conversation and realize the truth is here in this conversation we are having right now. Mira, I love you. With everything that I am, or ever will be, I *do* love you."

Mira practically leapt into Damon's arms, hugging him. "You fucking better not be lying to me, Mister, because I love you too." Abyssal tears fraught with the terror of falling all the way inward on Damon—of giving herself completely to him—traced Damon's cheeks as her face mirrored his in a moment of glorious confinement.

Chapter 14: Becoming Immortal

(Somewhere Hidden in the Carpathian Mountains, Earth, Present Day)

The expansive reach of Rena Rectovich knew fewer boundaries than the absurd proportions of her hidden estate within the Carpathian Mountains. Rena had sent one of her many Cessna Citation Hemispheres for them—all blacked out of course, as was Rena's style. The pilots were under direct orders not to disclose any location information, except Lawna knew them to be flying into Brașov, Romania. Now eight months pregnant, after the successful IVF implants, her three baby girls threatened an early entrance into the world, and Rena wasn't going to have any of that—at least not without her direct supervision, and control. Michelle needed to be under the care of her best physicians, and only the best medical facilities would do. A hundred percent success ratio on the IVF implant wasn't supposed to happen, and Michelle wasn't excited to be delivering triplets, but such was life.

Dating back to even before the IVF harvesting, there was talk of a super-secret project that had Rena's direct involvement. The rumors had only gotten more intense since that time, and both wondered if, and how, they were being played.

Even now Lawna could see Michelle's eyes intently focused out into the distance beyond the runway coming up to meet the wheels of their Hemisphere.

"Cessna Hemisphere for your thoughts," Lawna jibed, while probing.

"Ha! You don't own this absurdity."

"No but I betcha I could take it from them. Care to make that bet?"

"No. And, no you're not going to shoot anyone either." Michelle glared at her wife accusingly though with a managed smile—knowing her all too well.

The wheels screeching as the Hemisphere touched down at 115 knots, Michelle's pregnant body ebbed with her plush seat's vibration of touchdown in Rena's

Charles W. McDonald Jr.

domain. "Just the same concerns I've had since Rena propositioned us…. I mean you don't throw this kind of money around if you're not expecting something in return, right?"

A nodding Lawna obviously agreed with Michelle's assessment, recognizing the need to abruptly mute the conversation as handlers began approaching. "We'll continue this in a little bit."

Their intense recruitment into Rena's organization had been no secret. Rena had been quite upfront about her wishes to have both for their weapons and tactical experience to be operational leaders in Rena's immortal army. Michelle wasn't ready to take that step yet, and neither was Lawna. But Rena had done for them what no one else could do: give them children from both their DNA. *They owed Rena more than they could ever repay.* A thought that weighed heavy on them both as Rena's handlers showed up in black pantsuits with white blouses to 'escort' them to a waiting blacked-out, bespoke, sweptail Rolls-Royce® Phantom Extended limousine on the tarmac. As the handlers bent over to help Michelle, Lawna noticed their holstered Glock® hardware tucked away underneath their black business jackets.

It was a tense yet scenic ride for a while as they continued gathering their thoughts on Rena's expectations of them, and for them. What would be Rena's price for all this generosity and spoiling of them?

Now under the canopy of hand-hewn Italian marble, Lawna helped Michelle into the golf cart that had been waiting for them. Michelle felt as big as a whale, struggling to get her awkward pregnant body out of the limo into the open back seat of the golf cart. Lawna always giving her that tense *'are you sure you're okay'* smile. She wished Lawna would stop doing that; it made her more nervous than she was already. As if she were about to burst right there under the canopy.

"Mrs. Blade," the tall, dark-haired man in the white lab coat began, addressing her formally, "I'll be your primary OBGYN while you're here. I'll be heading up your delivery. My name is Dr. Foust. I'm going to give you a cell phone." Dr. Foust handed her a jet-black, gleaming new Android phone. "This has my entire staff programmed into it. You'll see their titles next to their names. If you need anything, just send them a text. They are here for you, and you are their top priority. You're not to do anything yourself, not even go to the bathroom. Do I make myself clear?"

Smiling, Michelle liked the idea of total pampering, but she hated being told what to do, and she hated, even more, the undue and excessive attention Rena was thrusting upon them. Surely there would be a cost for all this, and she wasn't sure she was ready to pay that bill just yet.

It was only their second time here, so Rena's hidden estate still carried a lot of mystique as the golf cart carried them down cavernous hallways cleaved out of the side of a mountain—with the interior finished in Italian marble and bullet-proof Lexan® everywhere they looked. Now passing an armory wing dedicated to the development of new weaponry, Lawna noticed the latest M-4 variant spraying rounds at a two-inch armor plate—the rounds fully penetrating. There was a con-siderable amount of noise emanating from those test range rooms, but still more than reasonable sound-deadening for being so close. An estimated hundred yards into the mountain and a sharp left turn found them approaching the medical wing that was, for the most part, void of anyone requiring medical attention. It looked to be mostly just R&D, save the one pristine Operating Room (OR) they passed with several technicians setting up the latest in delivery equipment. One of the technicians tested a robot's visual interface with another technician broadcasting "test, test, test" from a booth somewhere else in the facility.

Another right, two lefts, and another right turn and they found themselves in the medical suite wing passing one sterile room after another, adorned with multiple 70" UHDTVs. A staff of two nurses—one blonde, the other brunette—prepared a large double suite. One of the suites having a regular king-size, four-post bed—the other the latest in hospital stretchers with big urethane wheels and a magnificent plethora of gadget-like buttons. The blonde approached the cart, helping Michelle to her stretcher, saying, "Mrs. Blade, this is your call button," showing her the sterile plastic cylinder object with the red-button tip—attached to the stretcher to make it mobile. "If you're within arm's reach of this button, you're to use this to call for help if you need anything, even going to the bathroom. If you're not within arm's reach of this button, please use the cell phone you were provided to text anyone on that list of medical personnel. If someone isn't assisting you in 30 seconds, something has gone terribly wrong." The blonde smiled at her with a wink to defuse the tension. "My name is Amber, and this is Cindy," Amber intoned, motioning to the 5'3" busty brunette at her side who was now helping Michelle out of her full-length grey coat and white maternity dress into a hospital gown. The 5'7" slender dirty blonde continued, "When our shift relief arrives, we'll come in and do another round of introductions, but don't worry about re-membering who to text or call. Just send anyone on that list a text, and there's also a distribution list you can text as well. We're all on 24-7 call while you're here with us."

"There you are…," the heavy Romanian accent called from the doorway, causing Michelle to pivot to the seemingly late-twenties, raven-haired beauty. "There's my precious babies. Oh, I can't wait…," Rena Rectovich doted as she

Charles W. McDonald Jr.

smoothed her black cocktail dress against the outside of her thighs.

"Hi, Rena," Michelle sighed, trying not to let the moment get carried away. At just an inch shorter than Michelle and with the same gorgeous sparkling blue eyes, they could have been sisters, except for the raven-haired beauty having lived many centuries before she was ever born.

"I came as soon as I heard of your arrival. I'm so happy for you, Darling."

"Mother, please." It was an offer of respect, calling her Mother, even though she hadn't been turned yet. Rena had done more for her and Lawna than she would ever be able to repay, but Michelle still worried about the price tag—constantly.

"Thank you for everything, Mother," Lawna offered, approaching from the other side of the suite after dropping off her duffel bag of guns and fully-loaded ammo clips on the king size bed.

Turning her cheek to receive kisses from her latest recruits, Rena hugged Michelle. Contemplating what was to come, Rena gave the doctor a sharp eye as if to prod while hugging Michelle.

"You are so very welcome, my darling," Rena extended, "Anything you need, just ask. We're here to make this a pleasant experience. Your babies will be here soon! Are you excited yet?" Turning to her medical staff, Rena urged, "Doesn't she look radiant?" The entire medical staff offered sharp and immediate nods of approval, trying to look busy in front of Rena.

"Mother, why are we here? This all seems…*excessive*." Michelle wanted to be grateful, but the more doting that went on, the more concerned she got.

"NOTHING is too good or too much for MY girls," Rena pontificated with a scolding index finger, causing the staff to fidget even more. "Have you given more thought to my offer?" Rena tried not to bring it up too often, but persistence was in her nature, and more than nine hundred years hadn't changed that aspect of her much.

"It's practically all we have thought about," Lawna replied for the both of them. It was the truth. It had been nearly all they talked about the last eight months, leaving little time for planning or talking about the future of their lives together with a new family. *What future would they be allowed to have by becoming the tip of the spear in Rena's immortal army anyway?*

"Well," Rena turned to Lawna, "I don't want my offer displacing thoughts of my precious new babies. That should be your top priority, so I'll leave you two alone. Take good care of them, Dr. Foust." The last wasn't a request, causing the doctor to nod sharply in violent agreement.

"What Mrs. Blade needs now is stress-free rest, and I don't think we're doing a good job on the first part of that so let's get out of their way." Dr. Foust began shooing staff out of their large medical suite.

A moment later, with their suite now cleared, Michelle exhaled, "Jesus that WAS stressful. It felt like I was carrying a fourth baby there for a minute."

"I hear ya, Shelle." Lawna started pulling little circular pads out of her duffel bag, each about the size of a pin head, pulling a sticky pad buffer off the back as she began sticking them to various places in the room and doorway.

"I don't think Rena would like you installing spy gear and operating tradecraft in her facility," Michelle quipped, smiling at her wife.

"I don't give a *flying fuck* what Rena wants. I'm here to protect you, and that requires me knowing what the fuck is going on."

*   *   *   *

Standing by the OR still being set up for Michelle, Rena's index finger was right in Dr. Foust's face, "You're not the expert in this field, doctor. I am. It would do well for you to remember that…. You will do as I say, or they'll be finding pieces of you all over these mountains a hundred years from now."

Dr. Foust, offering a full bow, "Of course, Ma'am, I'll make the necessary preparations."

Rena spun and was gone in a blur, leaving a gale of unnatural wind in her wake.

Dr. Foust exhaled for the first time in seemingly forever, regretting being recruited into Rena's agenda regardless of how well it paid. Then, of course, he was given the offer you cannot refuse.

*   *   *   *

(About an hour later)

"Now Mrs. Blade, I'll be setting you up with an IV catheter to get some fluids in you," Catherina offered at the start of her night shift, tapping the veins on the back of Michelle's left hand to begin the stick. Michelle didn't trust redheads—they were all more than just a little crazy from her experience, so she wasn't hot about the idea of a redhead sticking her with a big needle.

"What's in the IV," Lawna questioned, tapping the bag to examine its contents.

"Just a saline solution to keep up her fluid levels."

Charles W. M°Donald Jr.

Lawna turned the bag, reading the contents label *NaCl 0.9% / 1000ml*. Lawna didn't trust anyone, but she didn't know what to think about being in Mother's lair. *Still, best not to trust anyone*, she thought, eyeing the redhead nurse threateningly.

"Any contractions, Mrs. Blade?" Catherina manually checked her pulse, holding her hand opposite her IV.

"Barely anything noticeable. Just some light ones." Michelle examined the examiner.

"Mhmm, and how far apart?"

"Maybe 30 minutes," Lawna replied for her wife, reading the digital layout of the monitoring equipment, paying close attention to the baby heartbeat monitor and the blips and beeps that followed.

"Mhmm, okay, well we need to be watching the timing more specifically, and once we get to twenty minutes, or less, apart, you're pretty much in labor at that point."

*   *   *   *

(Two hours later)

"OWE! OOOOH SHIT! GODDAMN," Michelle screamed, waking Lawna out of the chair she'd pulled up beside her wife.

In an instant, Lawna's hand was on the call button pressing the shit out of it 'til the medical plastic cylinder broke in her hands.

"Goddamn, that one was painful." Michelle still squirmed, trying to find a position on her side that gave her some level of comfort. Less than thirty seconds later, Dr. Foust was standing in her doorway with Catherina—and Rena.

"Okay, Mrs. Blade, we're going to start wheeling you into the OR now. Just relax, and everything's going to be fine. Deep breaths." Catherina now at her side, manually taking her vitals while Lawna lovingly stroked Michelle's hair.

Unlocking the brakes on the urethane wheels of her stretcher, Catherina began pushing Michelle towards the OR with a male orderly—Dr. Foust with the IV, with Rena and Lawna in tow.

"OOOOOH SHIT," Michelle felt the contractions coming fast and hard now as she began her delivery breathing.

*   *   *   *

Charles W. McDonald Jr.

Rena and Lawna watched pensively from the sterile confines of the hallway via the OR's viewing Lexan® as Catherina began switching out Michelle's IV at Dr. Foust's orders. Lawna's grip on the windowsill tightened to the point of leaving nail marks while Rena observed Lawna's reactions.

Only moments after switching out the IV's, Michelle's body began contorting on the surgical table as they began rushing to put her under general anesthesia, two OR nurses holding Michelle's body to the operating table.

"What's happening?" Lawna ran to the doorway to the OR, threatening to burst in without scrubbing. *Why hadn't they let her into the OR to begin with?* It was always customary to have the spouse in the room during delivery. Something was going on.

"It's okay, Darling. We have the best care available here, and we're prepared for anything." Rena's assurances fell on deaf ears. Lawna was fuming; her right hand resting on the Glock® in the holster, nested in the small of her back.

"I think a cesarean is what they're going for now," again Rena trying to comfort.

"A CESAREAN!" Lawna howled, "We didn't talk about that being necessary. Why are they doing *that*?"

"Darling, I could interrupt the doctor to get you an answer, but I think it's best if we let him focus on Michelle. Don't you agree?"

Pensive lips pressed together on Lawna's face expressed only a fraction of her dissatisfaction at the increasingly tense situation as her grip tightened on her Glock® in the small of her back.

The incision ran across Michelle's lower abdomen as Dr. Foust smoothly and expertly moved the scalpel, piercing Michelle's epidermal layers.

Now back at the viewing window, Lawna was barely aware of the blood on her neck as her grip on the windowsill loosened with her body slumping to the floor in a dirty blonde heap.

Now standing over Lawna's body, who had already begun thrashing on the floor, Rena gave the go ahead nod to Dr. Foust through the bulletproof pane of Lexan® as he started the next IV bag of Rena's own blood. Licking her fangs as they began retracting back into the roof of her mouth, Lawna's blood still oozed from their razor-sharp tips.

*   *   *   *

(14 hours later)

Charles W. McDonald Jr.

"You have all the genetic material you need then?" It wasn't really a question from Rena, and the doctor knew it. He knew her expectations intimately as she had been so very less than elegant in the way she had voiced them days before Michelle's arrival. This had been in the planning for years. The ability of her immortal army to operate in daylight was at hand—finally. Nothing was going to stop Rena from this moment. Nothing and no one!

"We have everything we need, ma'am. We've already begun taking stem cells from all three of the newborns, as you instructed."

"And what symptoms are the babies displaying so far?"

"None, ma'am. Just as you thought."

"Good. See to it I'm notified as soon as either of the proud new parents begin to wake. Ensure they are given at least 2000ml of fresh blood while their transformations complete. They're going to be my super-soldiers."

"I'll see to it personally, ma'am."

Rena was gone in a blur, and another unnatural gust, that perfumed the sterile hospital air with a scent somewhere between jasmine and formaldehyde. Dr. Foust hadn't taken a single breath during their entire conversation. Only now did he finally exhale, allowing himself to breathe. *What have I done,* he wondered, walking down the medical suite corridor to check on the now immortal Michelle Alexandra Blade.

Charles W. McDonald Jr.

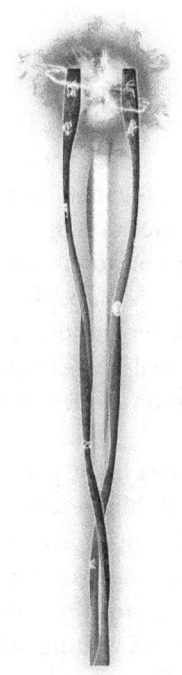

Chapter 15: The Birthday Boy

(Austin, TX, Earth, Present Day)

It hadn't been easy, asking such a huge favor from one of her many ex-boyfriends, but this was a special occasion, and the sky was the limit, as was the massive new charge on her AMEX®. Now whisking eggs for an omelet in Damon's kitchen, Mira plotted. *What do you give to the man who, quite literally, has everything and anything he wants?* Quietly, she busied herself as Damon walked shirtless into the kitchen from the master bedroom.

"Tell me how you like your eggs, Day," Mira boldly asked with a dastardly smile as she whisked eggs to a fluffy and frothy perfection, trying not to give anything away while toying with him by using the nickname Kellen and Goldenbow used with him.

A sidelong glare, but not skipping a beat, he replied, "I'm sure however you make them will be delicious." He was starving, and specific in his tastes—rarely ever without granular opinions—but he wanted to see what she could do with little-to-no guidance. He wasn't testing her, but if she was going to mess with him,

Charles W. McDonald Jr.

he could mess with her.

Enjoying the view of one of his cobalt blue UNTUCKit® shirts unbuttoned all the way down the front of Mira as the only thing she'd bothered to put on, Damon licked his lips at what he might be having after breakfast.

Angling the cuffs of Damon's shirt back so she didn't get it too messy, Mira turned on the fancy, commercial gas-range burner, beginning to heat the skillet for the omelet while she prepared green onions, tomatoes, mushrooms, and grated cheddar cheese in separate ramekins off to the side.

"So, I've been thinking…," Mira began with a wicked smile, as the clarified butter began melting in the skillet and the scent of sautéing onions and mushrooms perfumed Damon's commercial-grade kitchen.

"This can't be good," Damon chided, yet offering a playful smile back at her.

"You told me you really don't know your birthday, right?" It was a one-off, pillow-talk discussion she'd had with him recently as her delicate fingertips expertly tossed diced Roma tomatoes into Damon's All-Clad® D-5 skillet.

"Yessss." He held on to that one, wondering where she was going with this. The scent of her expert cooking was making him hungry, as her sexy, practically nude movements against his range was wetting other appetites.

"Well, how about today?" She paused, spinning back away from him as she tossed the onions, mushrooms, and tomatoes in the skillet to the hiss of well-heated ghee. "More specifically, how about tonight?"

"I'm almost afraid to ask." He glowered at her, moving to her side to turn on the light on the hood and then its fan, which she always seemed to forget.

Intentionally looking away from him—nonchalantly as she played at breakfast being the sole focus of her attentions—she let her offer linger in the cooking-scented air as if it were…merely an afterthought. "How would you like to go see *Metallica* tonight, in Dallas?"

"Are you FUCKING with me?!" Damon beamed, his *black mirrors* sparkling to life.

"Well, yes, but not the way you mentioned. Front row. Center." Now she was looking right at him. Her starry-blue eyes and silky, shimmering brunette hair cascading off her shoulders the sole focus of Damon's sexy and powerful gaze.

Damon pulled Mira to him so hard he almost crushed her, whispering in her ear, "Thank you."

"Well don't thank me yet. We're both probably going to be deaf after tonight." She spun back to the ramekins, getting the rest of the ingredients for his birthday breakfast, "Can you *Heal* deafness?"

Charles W. McDonald Jr.

"I'll risk it with you!" Mira was always full of surprises, but this…. This was a special woman!

(Kaleion, Present Day)

Damon still had a few hours before the concert and much in the works still left to execute. A visit to Kellen was required, so he might as well get it over with. Kellen's castle reminded him of Warwick on Earth, but far more sinister—the stones were all varying shades of a matte-charcoal finish. He was going to go through the front guard tower this time—no sneaking up on Kellen that might cause unpredictable outcomes. Kellen didn't like that, though he did it to everyone else—including Damon—all the time. A few flag signals and hand gestures from the tower to the keep and back, and he was being let in through the massive oaken gate doors that vertically raised up into the gatehouse by heavy iron chains.

Kellen the Destroyer, himself, stood in the main entry of his keep, dressed in a light tan leather jerkin over a dark-grey long sleeve shirt with midnight-blue pants. *That can't be good*, Damon thought, considering the very personal greeting.

"Ra," Kellen called out from the double-door entryway of his keep, smiling at Damon with mischievous gesturing. "To what do I owe the pleasure…?"

"Business this time," Damon replied flatly, smoothing his mage robes. He had to get comfortable wearing them again after so much time in Earth garb. The people of Eden wouldn't respect their deity dressing in T-shirts and jeans. It was time to clean up his act and get back on plan.

"So, what's up?" Fidgeting with his hands and forearms, he was obviously hiding something from Damon and the surprise visit had caught him off-guard. *Kellen was always hiding something*, come to think about it.

"I wanted to ask you to prepare to use *Damnation*," Damon proposed flatly, not wanting to give away any more detail than he had to. The fewer people who knew any real operational details of the Master Plan, the better.

"I'm always prepared with that, but I haven't used it in forever." Kellen's gaze was multi-level in its probing of all things Damon. From his stance and body language to gestures, eyes and expression, Kellen weighed it all in very specific measure, reading the legend in between the lines of Damon's subterfuge.

"I need you to be prepared to cast it seven times, simultaneously, with a 50 percent contingency ratio." That was a lot more specific and was bound to raise questions.

"Okay, tell me what the fuck is going on, Day." Kellen's gaze became more prosecutorial as his body language tightened.

"I need you to prepare—at your level—meaning no delegating the work this time, however many scrolls you need to accomplish the goal I just set."

"That's it. That's all I get. No explanation." Now his body language was as tight as a coiled viper—ready to strike. Kellen, however committed to the Master Plan he was, clearly didn't like being used in this way.

"I need to be the recipient of the souls. Please." Now, Damon was asking a lot. This might not go as easy as he had wanted. He could see how wound up Kellen was and knew he needed to defuse the situation.

Kellen scratched the stubble of his chin—thinking. "Who's the target?"

"You know I can't tell you that yet," Damon began, watching Kellen the Destroyer's gaze squint at that. "The less you know the better it is for both of us—and Goldenbow. It's going to take you a good long while to prep those scrolls, and that is why I'm giving you this information so far in advance."

"Okay, Ra. Sure." Kellen wasn't satisfied with that lack of an explanation, and his tone expressed as much, but, as his visit to Evanyil had already proven, he was committed to the cause, as it were, so he had to make the best of this. But, he was filing this one away…for future use…for now. Damon had never led them astray. He'd led them into plenty of problems, but never anything they couldn't handle, and usually the reward far outweighed the risk. Damon was always careful about that. He could tolerate the subterfuge…for now. But this was going to require further looking into. Damon's secrecy was creating unacceptably large blind spots and Kellen's future and that was a problem that could not be allowed to go unaddressed.

Kellen is giving up too easily. Not good, Damon thought. He didn't like keeping this stuff compartmentalized any more than Kellen, but this information was… dangerous.

"When we're done, I'll make all this up to you. I promise," Damon offered with a genuine smile for his old friend.

"Oh, I know," Kellen countered with a twisted smile, further unnerving Damon to the core.

Maybe Damon could defuse this a bit.

"If there is anything you need, please ask me. Other than details about the plan, of course." Damon offered another genuine smile for his friend, hoping this would help.

"I'll do that," Kellen replied flatly, his lips in a thin, pressed line. If Kellen were playing Poker, he wasn't offering a tell of any kind. Just standing there with his hands open and off to his sides. His hard face expressionless.

"Well, you know where to find me," Damon offered in a parting smile, turning to walk back through an obfuscated *Portal* he opened with but a thought—its far side opaque to Kellen's view.

"Toodles," Kellen quipped with a chaotic grin as Damon walked through.

Frowning, Kellen closed the main double-doors, scratching his chin in contemplation. Seven *Damnation* spells simultaneously…. *Hmmm*, he thought, heading upstairs to begin working on the scrolls he'd need for this task. *Why seven?*

*   *   *   *

(Damon's Manor, Kaleion, Present Day)

His private study was as it was when he last left it. The mighty *Staff of the Invoker* in the corner of his study, leaning against the bookshelf that was the curved wall opposite his ritual room.

Walking over to it, his left-hand fingertips traced its helical rods to the iolite sphere that floated untethered at the top—twisting this way and that with a charged hum of immense power.

Facing the desk he spent so many thousands of hours at righting wrongs done upon him all his life, memories of Dallia came back to him as they always did in the presence of his most powerful artifact. Memories were a powerful thing, invoking emotions and scents nearly a thousand years old in an instant. Even the hairs on his arms tingled—partly from the power of the *Staff of the Invoker* and partly from powerful emotions roiling to the surface that was the wave of Damon's destiny crashing upon the shores of the *throne of souls* that threatened Creation. And its unmaking.

Memories of Dallia were always and inevitably followed by those of Banthis, who came to fill the gaping void of his broken soul. Jumbled feelings of love and lust juxtaposed sympathies of a twisted and warped view of reality he knew to be at the core of Banthis. As well as suspicions of complex and contorted motives he didn't yet know the full of their impact. Upon him, or the Master Plan.

Blink. Blink. Blink. His consciousness registered his study desk in front of him, but his sense of time was…off. His fingertips still rested upon the violet iolite sphere atop his *Staff of the Invoker*, but his memories were…jumbled and entangled, like a plate of a spaghetti. No longer clearly focus as they were only a moment before.

A *Portal* to Austin and Damon was walking through. To Earth. And to

Charles W. McDonald Jr.

Mira. *Staff of the Invoker* again at his side.

A whoosh of air as the *Portal* sealed up on itself, Damon walked past the angled granite countertop island of his Austin kitchen, heading toward the master bedroom, as his senses felt…off.

Hearing Damon's entrance, Mira walked out of the bedroom to greet Damon.

"Wow!" Damon admired, thoroughly checking out the tight black mini-dress and soft black leather CFM (Come Fuck Me) boots that terminated mid-thigh on Mira. The back of his thoughts were trying to figure out what wasn't right, while his Mira-facing consciousness acted as if everything was as right as rain.

Turning around for him by the island countertops, she motioned to the backless cutout of the dress.

"Nice." Damon pulled Mira to him, kissing her as she responded in kind.

"You like?" She knew the answer, but she wanted to hear him say it.

"I love it!"

"It kinda says 'let's fuck at a metal concert,' doesn't it?"

Chuckling heartily, Damon admired her spunk. "Yeah, it does! We'll have to do something about that! I like the boots with it. Very Texas of you!"

"Thank you."

"When do we need to be there?"

"*Metallica* comes on at nine. Concert starts at eight."

Damon looked at the Thermador® wall oven-microwave combo for the time, noting it was just after seven. He'd lost a couple of hours somewhere…. "No time for a car ride up there. You said it was the American Airlines® Center?"

"Uh huh," Mira nodded joyfully.

"I've been there before, so a *Portal* shouldn't be a problem, but we need to be prepared to drive back just in case. It would be helpful if your world believed in magic." Damon was thinking, the wheels in his head almost visibly turning.

"What's going on in that head of yours, Damon? I don't like it when you get that look."

"I have an idea," Damon smiled broadly, unnerving Mira while trying to be in the moment with her, letting go of his concern over the loss of a couple of hours.

"What are you going to do," she asked, watching him enter her personal space with his nose an inch from hers. Her eyes looked into his gazing at hers as she felt his fingertips in the small of her back, pulling her to him as their lips touched and electricity followed along pathways of their shared excitement.

An instant later and she was thrust to sit upon the island countertop with Damon's kisses trailing down the inside of her left thigh as her head threw back, with the tips of her brunette hair spilling upon the colorful granite of Damon's kitchen island. Her thighs involuntarily clasping around Damon's face the moment his kisses touched her most sensitive places. The soft caress of his tongue upon her sensitive flesh sending little electric shockwaves throughout her body each time it made contact. Her fingertips running through his raven hair between her legs, clutching at clumps of hair in response to a lick here and a rake of his teeth there.

*   *   *   *

Damon made the short walk to the master bedroom nude, returning a brief moment later in his *Metallica* T-Shirt, sporting an illustration of *Ride the Lightning*, and a pair of his stonewashed Levi's® 501's.

A moment later, coming out of the master bedroom, leaving the *Staff of the Invoker* behind, but keeping on his smoky black and red signet ring, Damon was ready for *Metallica*. *But, was Metallica ready for Damon?*

*   *   *   *

(Downtown Dallas, TX, Earth, Present Day)

He brought them in around the back of the parking garage on the northeast side of the AA® Center, dispelling the *Portal* quickly as they walked onto N. Akard, but there were already so many people around someone was bound to have seen more than they should. *Oh well, that could serve a purpose too*, he considered. 8:45, he looked at his Android, locking the screen to slip it back into his pocket. They were cutting it close, and he was sure he'd have to move an asshole or two out of their very desired seats.

Cutting through the traffic of Humanity of *Metal Militia*, Damon held Mira in tow as he split the crowd with his menacing looks. He could look exceptionally evil when the occasion demanded. People were actively getting out of his way as he wore his fiercest scowl, letting his nails go to their normal liquid gold state as his eyes burned like smoky black coals.

Five minutes later found them at their seats—occupied, of course.

Charles W. McDonald Jr.

"Let me handle this please. No one needs to die tonight," Mira pleaded with hand gestures, a pouting expression, and an almost knelt body as she faced an angry Damon, who was clearly in the mood to kill. Pivoting around to the two early-thirties and very large squatters in their seats she pulled out their tickets with an expectant expression. One of the squatters looked to be an MMX fighter, and the other a biker type, both sporting their fiercest leather over *Metallica* T's and a fuck-off scowl.

Approaching confidently but non-threatening, Mira smiled, "Hi, guys. Would you mind if we checked our tickets against yours?"

"We're not moving. You should have gotten here earlier," MMX threatened, making his biceps and pecs pop on demand before them.

Standing behind Mira, Damon's eyes lit aflame in varying black and amber hues of death as he lifted his right index finger just above and behind Mira's neck and clavicle.

"And, don't think your cocksucker of a boyfriend's going to intimidate—" MMX's trachea already beginning to collapse, he couldn't finish his insult. Suddenly pulling his friend with him, MMX cleared out of their seats, walking away as fast as he could, without appearing to run.

Giving a final look back, seeing Damon's chaotic, fuck-you grin, MMX frowned in search of another place to squat for a better view of the concert.

Spinning to see what Damon was doing behind her, Mira scowled. "You didn't have to do that."

"Do what?" Damon's sudden schizophrenic switch from heinous back to sweet, frightened Mira, but she wasn't going to let it spoil the evening. This concert had cost her a small fortune, and she was going to enjoy it!

Before they had time to settle in, the familiar opening riffs of *Unforgiven III* pierced the darkness of the AA° Center as *Metallica* had slipped into position behind a black-curtained stage. Furious pyrotechnics went off right in front of them, perfuming the air with spent powder and excitement, as the heavy rhythmic chords of the song took hold of the throngs of metal worshipers in their unholy temple. Damon was in *his* Church, banging his head to the furious beat. *"Why can't I forgive me,"* James Hetfield howled into his microphone as Kirk Hammett's guitar solo burst to life, shattering eardrums throughout the arena with astounding energy. Damon, held his left index finger in the air, causing fireballs to explode above stage, matching the notes of the guitar solo. Hetfield and Ulrich looked to one another in confusion, as if that wasn't part of their usual pyrotechnics display. Spinning his drumstick and motioning for Hetfield to keep going, Lars threw his right hand in the air in a devil horns symbol as he kept on performing.

Charles W. McDonald Jr.

Gradually, Damon amped up his display for the crowd. Progressing from unplanned fireballs to cloudless lightning bolts—during *Ride the Lightning*—striking down from the top of the AA® Center just feet away from Hetfield, Ulrich, and Hammett on stage, causing Hammett to check again with the band and see if they wanted to continue. Undeterred, Ulrich kept urging them to keep going. After an hour of ever escalating displays that challenged the crowd's acceptance of what was even possible with pyrotechnics, the chords and riffs of *Fight Fire with Fire* sent shockwaves of metalgasms through the crowd of *Metallica* worshipers. As the fury of Kirk Hammett's speed metal guitar riffs accompanied Hetfield's chorus of "*Fight fire with fire, ending is near. Fight fire with fire, bursting with fear. …We all shall die,*" Damon recalled his most vivid memory of the Dragon of Darkness and summoned her awesome winged likeness above of the first few rows, breathing black, ethereal flames down upon *Metallica*. The whole summoned apparition filled the AA® Center to the top of the roof—its jagged black scales and razor-sharp teeth each nearly five feet in length, its wingspan nearly a hundred feet. Pointy and serrated spikes, twice the size of grown men, running up its spine, its body roughly thirty-five percent of its overall mass, the likeness was uncanny, though no one in the audience had such familiarity with the Dragon of Darkness itself—save Damon.

Looking amongst themselves in obvious terror, not knowing what to make of a concert that was like nothing they'd ever experienced before, *Metallica* concluded *Fight Fire with Fire* to continued roars of the crowd—some in obvious panic over the display they couldn't even begin to rationalize. Chaos breaking out in certain sections of the AA® Center with some people climbing over others to get out as fast as they could while others looked at their roach clips, still burning in their hands, as if something had gone horribly wrong. The scent of potent, spent weed pervasive enough that Damon considered the very real possibility they'd both get a pretty severe contact high, Damon looked around at the pandemonium he'd caused and said nothing as Mira just scowled back at him.

Having seen more than enough, *Metallica* wasted no time with an encore, rushing for the side exits of the stage, and not looking back.

Damon smiled at Mira as the lights came on, dispelling, with a mere thought, the Dragon of Darkness illusion overhead.

"WAS THAT REALLY NECESSARY," Mira barked at a volume twice as loud as necessary, obviously angry at Damon and barely able to hear herself screaming.

Damon nodded with a dastardly grin, taking her by the elbow as they exited the AA® Center, heading for home. His sermon sufficiently delivered. The question was: *would it make a dent in the disbelief of a world so completely enthralled with*

Charles W. McDonald Jr.

technology?

Charles W. McDonald Jr.

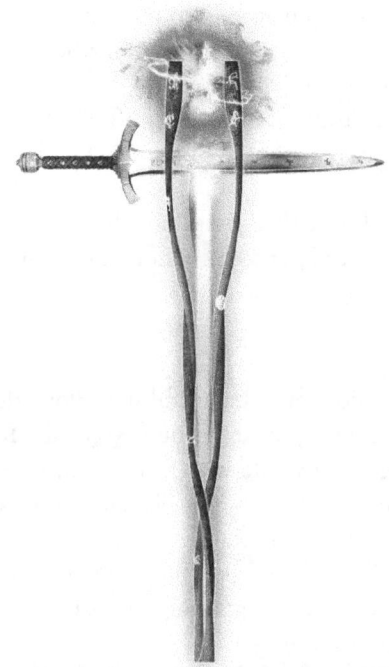

Chapter 16: The Creator of Injustices

(Exeter, Perion, Present Day)

adin's lifeforce crashed back down into his mortal coil, where it had dropped to the floor after cracking Damon's Seal. No matter how many times he had visited Damon by way of his *Summoning Seal*, Radin never got used to the return, and he wondered the damage it might be doing to his body and soul—not to mention the complexity of their already tumultuous relationship. Gasping for air as Ykstherin helped him up, Radin's eyes lit like stoked amber coals.

"Easy. You were gone quite a while." Ykstherin slapped Radin's back a couple of times, prompting Radin to breathe.

"I think I'd like to go for a walk," Radin declared, struggling to stand for a brief moment. He wasn't sure if it was the lack of sleep making his return to his body more destabilizing this time, or the changes his body was forced to go through from his time in torment.

"Of course, but you shouldn't go alone." He looked to the doorway just as

Charles W. McDonald Jr.

Lynn Marshall skidded to a stop before Radin's room.

"Is he okay," Lynn asked, slinging her shortbow over her right shoulder as she helped Radin walk to the door.

"I'm fine," Radin protested, brushing off Ykstherin, "Would you set up a meeting with the leadership in a couple of hours? I'd like to update them. Things have changed."

Ykstherin frowned, but that was often the case. *When had a visit to Damon not changed things*, Ykstherin thought as he handed off Radin's care to Lynn.

*   *   *   *

The courtyard outside, once beautiful with flora and vine, was now barren and desolate against the backdrop of the Blood Night sky Radin had brought upon his homeworld. Walking side by side with Lynn, Radin held no comfort in being responsible for the death of her husband—Ethan—and wondered the degree to which she held him personally accountable.

"How are the children," he asked, trying not to look her in the eye. He tried not to look anyone in the eyes anymore unless the intent was to intimidate or kill—such were their impression now.

"Terrible. They miss their father. I can hardly get them to talk anymore. They keep everything inside, and I fear for the quality of what little future they might still have."

"I destroyed their future," Radin admitted knowingly. He was right. He had done incalculable damage to everything and everyone on Perion. It was all on him, and he knew it. The question was: *how far did the destruction of his leadership reach? Where were the shores of this ocean he suddenly found himself upon?*

"You did what you had to do." Giving him a managed smile, she took his arm as she continued walking beside him. "Do what you must to bring us on the other side of this Darkness, Radin. I still believe in you."

If Radin's tear ducts still worked, he might have cried, but those stopped working just as his ability to find sleep. "Thank you for saying that."

"Do you believe that this is the end of all things," Lynn asked, not knowing if she could stomach the answer.

"I don't know what lays on the other side of these events that are to come. Change is the only certainty. A new balance perhaps. I can't say for sure. I know our prophecies were wrong and cannot be trusted to guide our future actions. We'll have to adapt to the new landscape we find ourselves in, and just trust our judgment in each decision branch that we face."

Charles W. McDonald Jr.

"That's why I believe in you…," she admitted flatly, "…it's your judgment I trust better than the rest of the leadership—save maybe Brigance." The last she offered with a knowing smile—hoping he'd take it the right way. Brigance had been a friend of the family a very long time, and she knew him well, but she also knew Radin listened to Brigance, and that made Radin's judgment even more trustworthy. "You should spend one-on-one time with Gareth and some of the others as well. I think it would really help you as much as it would help them."

"Are they beginning to doubt?" Radin wouldn't blame them at all if doubt was starting to creep into the ranks of the leadership. It was hard to show them a working plan for a future that hinged so dynamically upon his every move—and Damon's—but maybe the new information from Damon would help him develop that working plan with a bit more fine-grain detail. He needed to show confidence and belief in what they were doing. He needed to demonstrate conviction in their actions, or the ranks would disintegrate into a fractured abandonment of *hope*.

"I think they really need to hear from you—personally." Lynn looked him in his eyes of wickedness—still evidence of his torment—offering a genuine smile of belief as they continued walking through the bare gardens of the Exeter Estate.

Moments later, Radin caught sight of Wraith standing in the foyer, waiting for him. "I'll catch up with you later, Lynn. Thank you for the walk." Smiling at Radin, offering a familiar nod of acceptance to Wraith, Lynn excused herself from their private conversation.

"You look like a man who's got something on his mind." Radin cut through the tension in one sentence, noticing the brooding intensity written all over Wraith's face.

"If this Blood Night is but the first of many curses to fall upon us, I'm not sure I'm on the right side of things."

"You question the intentions of a Creator who would put us through such a thing," Radin proffered, wondering the same thing himself.

"Forgive me, but I do."

"Admittedly…. I've wondered that myself."

"You have to understand, and I've been trying to think of how best to explain this to you before seeking you out, but I don't really have a dog in this fight, Radin. I'm not trying to change the world. It worked fine for me the way it was."

"The world was changing underneath your feet, you just didn't know it yet. Ignorance of the change doesn't prevent it from coming down upon you like rubble inside a cavern. Either way, the exits are still blocked."

"If we're going to use that analogy, I never would have been inside the cave if it weren't for you."

Charles W. McDonald Jr.

A fair prosecution of Radin's actions, and he knew it as soon as it left Wraith's lips. He was the bringer of doom upon them all—Wraith and Silura included. He was directly responsible.

"What is it you want?" It was time to cut through the crap. Radin's cup of self-judgment was already full. He didn't need the judgment of others to cause it to overflow. There was still much worse to come, and he couldn't burden himself with more self-pity.

"I want to see a vision that gives me a level of confidence that my help is aiding the right team, and I want one hundred gold coin per month for my, and my wife's, services. We bring more to the fight than five thousand of your best men, and we expect to be compensated accordingly."

"I see." Radin was used to the mercenary mentality. He'd been around it growing up, meeting some of Father's friends. *Some of Dad's friends*, he corrected himself internally. "You'll have your coin, up front every month. I trust you to make good on it." Radin gave Wraith an intense look of expectance, prompting a response.

"I will. Both Silura and I will make good on it." Wraith shifted his body in response to the uncomfortable nature of their discussion.

"As for the justification of your support, I'll do only what I can and not a scrap more." Radin shifted too, into an air of confidence, though he had little to offer, given the topic. "There is no map illustrating the beginning, middle, and end of this journey—only questions, doubt, change, and death. I know it is not right that there are those out there that can alter the fate of one's destiny for their own profit or gain, and I mean to correct that scale no matter the cost. I mean to get to the other side of the End Times to whatever new balance might exist at the end of all things. Damon has offered to help us find and capture those who have a history of casting *Damnation*, and I intend to accept his help in doing so. If that isn't good enough for you, then you know where to find the door…." Radin didn't enjoy delivering this message in that way, but it seemed necessary from his point of view. He just hoped it would be enough, for now, to hold them together.

"It is…for now." Wraith didn't enjoy bringing up this unpleasant topic, but his motives were his own, and he wasn't here to make right all the injustices of a cruel and intolerant world. Let the Creator himself deal with that. After all, it was the Creator who created these injustices in the first place.

Charles W. McDonald Jr.

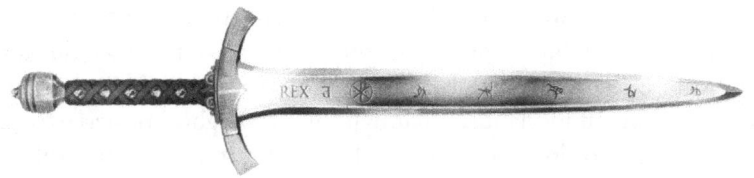

Chapter 17: The Archbishop of Canterbury

(10 Downing Street, London, England, Earth, Present Day)

rying not to be intimidated by the millions of Pounds' worth of paintings and furnishings in the Green Drawing Room of #10 Downing Street—a place he never hoped to find himself for fear of it being the end of his career—Michael Day busied himself, looking up at the magnificently ornate ceiling medallion centered around a priceless Tiffany and Co.® chandelier. Standing on the room's royal-blue rug with cream and silver accents, beside one of the two royal-blue opposing sofas, Michael tried not to stand too close to Elise, though she had a habit of getting uncomfortably close to him.

Quincy Arthur Billings and Terry Goodwin stood side by side in front of the sofa opposite Michael and Elise as the door from the inner hall opened. The Prime Minister walked in, followed by David Wright…and the King of England.

SHIT, Michael thought. *My career is over!* He wished his father was here. Maybe his political ties might have saved him, but it was too late for that.

"All right then, let's get on with it, shall we…," the Prime Minister chided, looking to Billings.

"Right, sir. Terry if you would, please." Billings motioned to Colonel Terry Goodwin, who held the sword they just pulled from Baschurch Lake, as he began unwrapping the plain, matte-white cloth to reveal the remarkable hand-and-a-half sword that was not a sword.

"My God," The Prime Minister gasped, taking another step towards the ancient relic. "Has there been any analysis of it yet? Any authentication? Carbon dating?"

"Sir…," Billings interjected, "…they pulled this from Baschurch Lake just over three hours ago. There hasn't been time for any of that yet, but I can assure you it's already been ordered and is being set up as we speak."

"That won't be necessary," King Harold proclaimed, never taking his eyes off the sword as he privately read its inscription from a far position, close to the doorway, "…it's Excalibur."

Charles W. McDonald Jr.

"Your Majesty, we can't make hasty proclamations like that. We need to run tests," the Prime Minister protested, now reaching out to take the sword that was not a sword into his own hands. Taking the sword from Terry, the Prime Minister felt it humming in his hands; it felt light, not too light, just perfectly balanced. A swing via the flick of his wrist, and it whooshed through the air, still humming in his hands. "Whatever it's made of, it's magnificent. And you found this *in* the water?"

"Yes, sir. Well.... I didn't...," Terry clarified, correcting himself, "...Michael did." Terry motioned to Michael innocently enough, but every eye in the room was on him now.

Boy, this was rapidly getting uncomfortable! Thanks Terry, Michael thought.

"And, sir, I believe you should allow Michael to offer a demonstration."

Fuck you, Terry! It had only been a thought, but the way everyone looked at him he wondered if he had actually just said 'fuck' in front of the most senior leadership of England. His career *was* over! Terry smiled innocently as he recovered the sword from the Prime Minister, offering it to Michael for a 'demonstration.'

Reaching with his right hand to claim the sword that was not a sword, it immediately burst into a molten white hot star in Michael's grasp inside the Green Room of 10 Downing Street as jaws dropped and prayers were suddenly, silently mouthed.

"My God." The Prime Minister's mouth agape, looking at Michael Anthony Day basked in the light of the star that was the one, true Excalibur. There could be little doubt, yet his analytical mind was having trouble accepting what he was seeing.

Almost staggering again, trying to hold onto his balance, Michael heard the calling—the pure-white light, the placid crystal lake and the booming voice of Creation itself off in the distance from the far side of the lake—a tall figure standing beside a voice shadow-cast in the light of a Humanoid Sun. Too much for him to maintain his balance, Michael let go, handing Excalibur to Elise as it immediately cooled, allowing the room to dim in a moment of awkward and powerful silence.

The impossibly-hard-to-quash romantic stare, however brief, between Elise and Michael, caused David Wright's attention—in the form of a scowl—to be more focused on Michael than the incredible display of the magic of the Sword of Creation right before their very eyes.

The king stood silent, pensive, and yet knowing—as if somehow expecting...or remembering. Licking his lips in deliberation, his words came out weighty but without hesitation, "Well, I think we've seen quite enough. I'll abdicate," King

Harold offered, starting to walk for the door.

"But, Your Majesty…," the Prime Minister protested with waving hands as he chased after the king, "…you can't…."

"Better call The Archbishop of Canterbury and have him ready Westminster Abbey for the Coronation of Michael." The former king was nearly out the doorway now.

"He's not even nobility," David Wright angrily chided, approaching Michael to separate him from his precious daughter.

"He is now. So says the Sword of the First Kings." With that the former King of England walked out of the Green Room, the Prime Minister hot in tow, leaving a fine faff for Billings to sort out.

(Exeter, Perion, Present Day)

"So, what's this meeting supposed to be about," Lawna questioned Wraith standing in their suite's doorway, lustfully eyeing Michelle's curves on fully display in a tight-fitting archery outfit of forest-greens and browns with ties up the center of her bosom holding it together.

"Radin needs to talk to leadership about his plans, after his meeting with Damon." Smiling at Michelle, who did not reciprocate in kind—rather busying herself cleaning *Bad Intentions* in her lap. Wraith regretted not sending Silura in his place to deliver the message.

"We'll be there," Michelle countered, running the clean white cloth swab through the muzzle using a long, metal stem.

The feeling of the tether between Michelle and Amanda—the first of the triplets—slammed home like a great hammer on an anvil, causing Michelle to gasp as she looked to her wife. She could feel her daughters again, and she would have smiled if that hadn't carried with it an ominous meaning. *Why could she suddenly feel her daughters now?* It was as if….

They needed to speak to Radin and Talemar…immediately.

*   *   *   *

"I don't know what it means exactly," Michelle tried to explain, but there were just so many variables that could not be drilled down to root cause from their current assignment and location. She was struggling to understand the possibilities herself. She wasn't a scientist. A linguist, an Operator, and a tactical expert maybe, but Michelle was out of her depths with the possibilities that faced her now.

Looking between Michelle, Radin, and Talemar, Lawna took a stab at summarizing what they knew, "Look.... I don't know how it works any better than Michelle, but when we were 'transformed,' we developed an innate ability to 'feel' each other's presence—including that of our children. The tether to our children was especially powerful. I can feel them as well, but not like Michelle. I should say I *could* feel them, but not while they were on different continents—or different worlds in this case—like Michelle. If Michelle can feel her tether to them now and couldn't all this time we've been here, then either the tether has been tampered with, or someone was shielding them and no longer is." There were other possibilities Lawna entertained privately and would discuss with her wife when not in the company of others, but those possibilities had far-reaching implications she didn't even want to consider.

"Or, they're now on Perion," Talemar proposed to the surprise of everyone in the War Room, scratching the fresh goatee he was working on growing.

"Or, they're now on Perion," Michelle breathed Talemar's comments aloud—whether to hear them again for herself or to reinforce his idea—none could say. It was a dangerous thought. All of them were, but the last most especially so. *If they were here, who had brought them, and why?* The Blood Night was incredibly lethal and dangerous—even to their kind, and neither of them knew how robust their girls would be in comparison to the full conversion both Michelle and Lawna had experienced.

"Or, you're not operating in the time—" Radin didn't get to finish his thought for his captain's urgency.

"You need to come quickly," Captain Jac blurted, interrupting the obviously tense conversation, pleading Michelle and Radin with his distressed eyes.

Charles W. McDonald Jr.

Part 2: Legacy and Legend

Charles W. McDonald Jr.

Chapter 18: A Promise Kept

(Damon's Manor, Kaleion, Present Day)

Working in the familiar confines and secrecy of his hidden fourth-floor study allowed Damon to make quick progress on the new custom spell; this one was somewhat familiar to others he'd made in the recent past, so he was able to make quick work of it. Gating the last few symbols, he let out a long sigh of relief, knowing Radin wouldn't be strong enough yet to cast either this new one or the existing spell he would bring to settle his debt between them. He would have to do something about that.

"I can't read any of that," Mira admitted from behind, putting her hands on him for the first time in hours as she began working out the massively tense knots in his scapulae.

"You're not meant to. You're not a mage. Arcane is a language as old as Creation itself, as far as we know." Far older than script found in the Egyptian Book of the Dead, the Thoth Tablets, the Seven Tablets of Creation or even Atlantian scripts of Earth. Far older than even the oldest texts from Durial himself on his homeworld, or Xaldran's Tome of Perion. Possibly even older than Angelic Script, no one really knew the origins of it, though it was found throughout most of the worlds of Creation in the oldest texts on those worlds.

"I've seen you do things where I didn't really know if you were actually casting or not. Do those things require Arcane?"

"I've had natural abilities in *Telekinesis*, *Cryokinesis*, and *Pyrokinesis* since childhood."

Charles W. McDonald Jr.

"You must have been a delightful childhood friend." Mira smiled, trying to cut the obvious tension he bore between his shoulders any time he discussed his youth. It wasn't the first time she probed about it, but she had always been rebuffed by his changing of the subject or simply leaving the room to avoid the topic. *Progress*, she thought, *came in small doses with Damon.* He was going to be a long-term project. "So, do your natural abilities help your ability to cast?"

"It doesn't work like that. They're completely separate threads of use and alteration of energy and matter." Turning to face Mira as he pulled her to sit in his lap, Damon explained, "However, I'll grant you, everyone I've seen with a natural ability like mine learns the art of magic at an enhanced rate and at a scale not ever achieved by those who cannot. They make the most powerful mages of all." He wanted to help her understand, but it wasn't easy explaining something like this to someone who couldn't cast at all. "Think of it this way. With my natural abilities, I'm projecting a power from within, using my mind. With magic, I'm just a conduit, channeling and shaping energy that exists all around us to borrow its force and then quickly release it back into the field from which it came."

"And how does all this work with, or complement, the prayers you're getting all the time?"

"It doesn't. The prayers are complicating things more than I anticipated. The best analogy I could give you is playing guitar."

A frown and more blinking from Mira. *What could Damon possibly know about playing guitar, and upon what shores did Damon's knowledge finally find their limits?* "Honey, I don't play guitar, but I know people that do. Explain the correlation."

"Think of it like this...magic might be like playing guitar with a normal tuning: E, A, D, G, B, E. However, if you're like Jimmy Page, and you want to make your music really unique, you alter the tuning of some, or all, of those strings. What happens when you do that?"

"It changes the default sound...?" She wasn't confident in that being the right answer, but it was still a correct answer.

"Yes, but what it really does is change the rules of playing guitar. In other words, an E-chord is no longer made the same way it was under normal tuning. The same for a G-chord, etc. In other words, when Jimmy Page did that, he had to re-learn how to play guitar all over again. And with each time he made a different instantiation of an alternate tuning, he had to re-learn it again and again. Not easy, I can assure you! The same goes for these different uses of energy. My natural abilities fall under one set of governing rules for playing the 'energy,' where 'energy' is analogous to the 'guitar.' Then Arcane, or magic, would fall under a different set of governing rules, and prayers yet another set of governing rules. So, with each I

Charles W. McDonald Jr.

must relearn the rules and adapt them accordingly. So, switching between them, especially with any kind of pace, is really tricky. Using them in concert with one another even trickier."

It was a great explanation, but it made her only that much more uncomfortable around his power and brilliance. She was no intellectual slouch, but dating and just being around Damon was a lot to take in. "Well, I'm still having a hard time rationalizing my dating a deity. I grew up believing there was one and only one God—God the Father."

"This is a very philosophical discussion we're treading into here. I'm not sure this is a great idea." Damon had vastly superior information on this topic he already knew to be fact. He wasn't sure Mira would be so ready to accept such facts. That it might do untold damage to her psyche and obliterate her belief systems entirely, leaving her rudderless upon an ocean of the archetype of Creation already fraught with storms of the uncertainty of the unmaking of all things.

"I can handle it. Communication is the key to any relationship—even one as crazy as this one."

"Deities have loved mortals for as long as there have been both. It's not as uncommon as you might think. There are hundreds of gods, though most will concede to the fact that there is likely only one true Creator of all that we see and experience around us. Even a great many of your scientists believe that the simple mathematical odds preclude the absence of a Creator. That Creator God goes by many names—God the Father being one of them. The Father of the Beginnings being another. Personally, I don't know what to believe. When I was young, I didn't believe in an afterlife of any kind—good or bad—Heaven, nor Hell."

"And what do you believe now?" Her massaging of his shoulders had stopped as she stood right behind him and to his right; her soft breath upon his earlobe.

"I believe I'm getting hungry. Can you ask the staff to bring us up some food while I finish up," he asked, putting his new spell—*Copy/Paste*—on his desk.

Leaving the hidden study through the secret passage into the small, naked antechamber, Mira headed downstairs just as she heard what she knew to be a *Portal* being used from behind her. Looking back at the naked antechamber and the seamless secret doorway that only allowed a select few entrants into his private study, Mira knew Damon had left her again—she knew not where. His obfuscation of his own belief system had left her troubled. She knew he had been to Hell, so obviously, he had to believe in that. *If Hell clearly existed, surely some manner of Heaven does too.* Mira tried to convince herself of such while making her way down the circular staircase to the lower levels of Damon's manor.

Charles W. McDonald Jr.

*   *   *   *

(Fort Bragg Armory, TX, Earth, Present Day)

The *Portal* hadn't been too far off the mark, even without previously being here before, but Damon had leveraged the *Portal's* viewing capabilities to scan the desired target before walking through to the other side. Texas was just as hot as his homeworld. Luckily, he had taken to wearing jeans and a T-shirt the vast majority of the time—his full mage regalia no longer practical except in certain circumstances. He could hear soldiers a few aisles over, but he was basically where he needed to be—standing in front of hundreds of wooden crates of NATO 5.56mm—tracer, FMJ, 25mm APEX, and armor piercing. At ten thousand rounds per crate, he only needed one of each kind. Using his natural *Telekinesis* abilities, he stacked the crates one atop the other, suspending them above the ground so they wouldn't make a sound as he shoved them through the *Portal* to Exeter, Perion.

*   *   *   *

(Exeter, Perion, Present Day)

Captain Jac's jaw dropped, seeing the four huge crates coming through a *Portal* bigger than any he had seen since the battle at Axum a few months back—not to mention the tall, broad man with black eyes and strange garb. "Uh, get Lord Fireheart. NOW," He ordered the light-of-foot corporal, in leather armor and green jerkin, who took off running into the manor.

A moment later, Brigance Fireheart walked out to greet the man he knew as Damon. Though he didn't relish seeing the man, he did recognize what Damon had brought with him. Looking him up and down, not really knowing what to make of the obvious other-worldly attire, Brigance didn't extend his hand toward Damon. Instead, standing a few paces away with arms much folded. "I believe you are Damon. Correct?"

His *Linguistics* spell taking over for him, Damon's speech translated as he spoke, "I need to speak to Radin and Michelle. Quickly, please."

Brigance turned to Captain Jac, ordering, "Captain would you fetch them please, for our guest?" With that, the young captain burst into a full run.

"Thank you for saving Radin." Whatever Damon was, or wasn't, to Brigance, his actions had helped a friend—many of his friends. He just wished he understood Damon's motives better. Perhaps a private meeting between them could

Charles W. McDonald Jr.

be arranged, but that was for another time. There had to be something else going on with Damon that he didn't like, but he just couldn't place it. Until he could, Brigance would never trust Damon the way that Radin apparently did.

A moment later and Radin was walking out with Michelle and Captain Jac—Radin looking at Damon incredulously as his eyes roamed over the massive crates of ammunition. Cold blue flames continued to burn in the wake of Radin's footprints, though there was little grass left to burn, thanks to the Blood Night. Everywhere one looked, the ground was the color of a pale-red dirt or clay, rather than its normal lush landscape of life.

Damon admired Michelle walking toward him in her best tight-fitting green and brown ranger outfit with a recurve bow slung over her right shoulder. Figuring he would get her gift out of the way first, Damon announced, "Yes, well, ladies first I suppose," he offered, motioning to the many ten-thousand-round crates of ammunition he'd brought for them.

"What's the occasion," Michelle asked, wondering what her cost would be for the badly needed resources. After the Battle of Axum, they were practically down to nothing on the ammunition front.

"I heard you were going hunting," Damon smiled, intentionally not elaborating. "Radin, if you would come here please; I brought you these," Damon offered the two scrolls including two custom spells, one old: *Stasis*. And one new: *Copy/Paste*. Damon whispered in Radin's ear, "Both of these are beyond your capabilities right now, but if you would work with Talemar, I'm pretty sure he could teach you the *Stasis* spell we discussed the need for last time we spoke."

"And the other?" He wasn't comfortable whispering in Damon's ear, but he intentionally kept his voice down so as not to carry beyond their immediate vicinity.

"Allow me a demonstration," Damon declared with an excessive flourish, cracking open the tracer round case with his *Telekinesis*, causing one of the rounds to pull from its band and float in the air towards him where he snatched it out from the air with his right hand. "This spell is called, *Copy/Paste*, and it has three modes of operation, each successively more difficult than the last. I'll demonstrate them in progression." Focusing on the metal and chemical compounds contained in the single NATO 5.56 round he now held in his right hand, Damon cast *Copy/Paste*, producing tens of thousands of new identical rounds on the ground before them in hundreds of neat piles, each stacked about three feet in height by six feet in width by four feet in depth all over the ground around them. "That's mode one. Here's mode two," he followed, causing hundreds of rounds at a time, each coming from the new piles that he had just produced, to burst into the air, with their caps

Charles W. McDonald Jr.

igniting from an unseen hammer as they shot off into the tree line in the distance with a deafening sound equivalent to several of Michelle's firearms going off simultaneously.

Despite the seriousness of their conversation only moments ago, Michelle's smile was practically ear to ear as she nearly experienced a whole-body orgasm right there in front of everyone, now admiring Damon in an entirely new way. He was courting her Operator-half with every glorious round he exploded—perfuming the outside air with the scent of freshly spent gunpowder.

A crowd of hundreds quickly gathered from outside their surrounding tents and encampments as the demonstration escalated, now gathering everyone's attention with the last burst off into the tree line, now fully ablaze from Damon's tracer rounds.

"I see you liked that...," Damon offered, looking at Michelle's tight but quivering body, "...but this is my favorite part. This is mode three." Having gone through nearly all of the rounds of ammunition Damon had just created, Radin wondered how Damon would be able to continue the demonstration. As if to answer, Damon lazily tossed the single round he held into the air, waiting 'til its nose pointed toward the tree line, then cast mode three of *Copy/Paste*, causing modes one and two to act simultaneously, as one round became hundreds and then tens of thousands as he mowed down the tree line in a thunderous hail of tracer gun fire. As silence eclipsed his thunderous demonstration, with the exception of a few large trees collapsing off in the distance, Damon simply smiled, offering a slight bow to the crowd, now with their mouths agape—Michelle looking quite literally weak in the knees as she smiled from ear to ear. The trees that were not on fire crackled and split, crumbling to the ground from being mowed in half by the tracer rounds.

"I FUCKING LOVE IT!" Michelle exclaimed, almost giddy with excitement, continuing, "Radin, you HAVE to learn how to do that! You have to!!!"

"Don't get too carried away. It might take you years before you'll be able to do it, and I doubt if Talemar will ever be able to. But, he might be able to help you break down the spell enough to learn modes one, or two, or both over time." Damon thought for a minute about their relationship and the complexity of it, now with the author of *Damnation* information out there, "...or we can work on it together. Over time. If you want to resume your lessons. I leave it up to you. Either way, it's yours," Damon offered, motioning to the scrolls now in Radin's hands. "And it doesn't just work on ammunition," Damon continued to explain, "it works on any organic, or inorganic matter, but the more familiar you are with the compounds of whatever you're trying to copy, the easier it is to paste." He considered Radin's lack of familiarity with those terms, adding, "...the easier it might be to replicate."

Radin nodded, "To what do we owe this incredible generosity, Damon?" Radin's tone wasn't kind, but it wasn't disrespectful either—just matter-of-fact. And duly suspicious, given everything he knew of Damon's sordid history. His eyeing of Damon wasn't cold or spiteful, but it was far from trusting. Whatever Damon was, historically, he appeared to be trying to make up for it. But then, he knew Damon fully capable of killing immediately, even now, without even a morsel of remorse.

"I told you I was going to help you with a list of names and a means with which to resolve the problem. I'm fulfilling my promise," Damon proclaimed flatly, offering another piece of paper, pulled from the back-left pocket of his jeans; there were a few names burned into the paper as if Damon carved their names with his thoughts rather than writing them. For what purpose, Radin couldn't say.

Noting Eldrac's name at the top of the list, confirming what he already believed—that Eldrac still lived—Radin offered a half bow to Damon, looking to Brigance and Michelle, but not showing it to the others yet. He wanted to talk to leadership about it and formulate a plan, though he felt his place in the leadership slipping. Even now, before Damon, he saw the questioning glances shared between Brigance and Michelle with their eyes on him and Damon—watching their interactions. It didn't give him confidence in barking out orders or assembling leadership to hear him speak or give orders. He needed to find a better way—a more collaborative way. He wanted them to feel invested in the joint decisions that needed to be made to go after these…disgusting lameans.

"Thank you for keeping your word, Damon. It is appreciated." He wasn't whispering in Damon's ear, but his tone was soft and recompense for having doubted Damon earlier. Each time he'd doubted Damon, he'd been proven more wrong than right. *Was that more a reflection on his lack of judgment or on Damon's enigma of a personality?* He couldn't say, but he was going to have to start giving Damon more credit where credit was due, and he wondered if doing so meant he was now, more than ever, within the sphere of Damon's Master Plan than he'd considered before….

The sound of more trees collapsing to the ground in a burning heap off in the distance brought Radin back to the here and now.

Radin offered a knowing and expectant glance to Damon, his eyes wandering off into the far tree line that blazed to a point he knew would burn tens of thousands of hectares, if not immediately dealt with.

"Yes, well, I suppose I should deal with that." Damon considered summoning a *Storm*, but then thought about the lightning and their proximity to the ocean, thinking of an alternate and better solution. Casting *Damon's Far Reaching* to augment the reach of his abilities, Damon held both hands overhead, using a *Hydrokinesis* spell as he pointed out toward the ocean and the Darthen Straight, pulling a funnel of water directly from the Darthen Straight in a column two hundred feet wide as he formed a great hand of water over the burning trees. Damon's right hand now pointed at the tree line; bringing it downward in a sweeping motion, he caused the giant water hand to crash down onto the burning tree line, completely extinguishing the fire in mere moments.

"Thank you...," Radin genuinely offered, looking at the paradox that was Damon before him.

Looking into the heinous flames Radin now took for his own eyes, Damon knew Radin's suffering had changed him forever, but at least some of the original Radin still lived inside the young man before him.

Whatever their relationship would, or might, become depended on careful grooming and complete transparency. Outside of his relationship with Goldenbow, this relationship with Radin was proving to be one of imminent importance as he was starting to find a place for Radin in his Master Plan. If he could learn to trust his own instincts about what he'd seen of the many possible future timelines and their perilous outcomes.

(Kaleion, Present Day)

For this meeting, and this message, Damon had briefly returned to his manor to create a more formal aura. And that aura required the *Staff of the Invoker* he had brought back from Austin. He was starting to carry more and more frequently as the stakes grew.

Never before had Damon come to visit Kellen's keep back-to-back times. Something was up as the signal tower flashed flags back and forth between the keep and the gatehouse, causing the massive gate to rise again for the tall, dark, ominous Damon in full mage regalia, carrying his now ever-present *Staff of the Invoker*. He was running in circles too dangerous—even for him—to be without it too frequently. It wasn't the first time these guards had seen Damon, but the charcoal-blue aura from the *Staff of the Invoker* bathed him in wicked intent, as the ground gave way underneath Damon's black leather boots splitting under the pressure of all the energy Damon was now carrying with him. Reaching out hundreds of miles, Damon sourced all the Zero-Point field he could find, aggregating it with

Charles W. McDonald Jr.

the energy of his worshipers and all the Arcane he could find for hundreds of miles. The *Staff of the Invoker* hummed under the weight of all this energy—its aura seven times greater than normal as its hemisphere of terror cast its darkness upon Kellen's keep centered on Damon as he approached from the main gate. He wasn't taking any chances with Kellen, and Damon needed to send a very specific message.

With this amount of energy, Damon could wipe Kellen, and his entire estate, off the map, and Kellen knew it as he personally opened the door to the keep—deciding not to escalate the situation by drawing all the energy he could draw—which was considerable without aid of artifact.

"What's up, Ra?" Kellen needed to defuse the situation, though he wasn't sure what he'd done to cause Damon to come looking for a battle, other than answer the door in his full charcoal-grey mage regalia. In fairness, he had been planning to leave right before Damon showed up.

Handing Kellen the most dangerous thing he'd ever received, Damon fulfilled his promise. Even Kellen the Destroyer didn't know exactly what he was looking at—not at first. The elegant and complex scroll work, in what he knew to be illuminated styling, worked like a doorway in the back of his mind.

A terrorizing sneer slowly crept across Kellen's face as his ancient and Archmage mind began probing the possibilities of what this door might access. "Useful...," Kellen breathed aloud—his wicked smile now ominous.

"You're welcome," Damon offered with a half bow, knowing he wouldn't get the 'thank you' he so richly deserved for honoring this most dangerous of promises. "I won't bother teaching you how to use it. It works just like the fundamental for source, except it allows you to source the Zero-Point Field—instead of Arcane. If you want to learn how to use it, study the Zero-Point Field, but this will make your practice and use of it more stable than without it."

"Thank you," there it was. Words almost never uttered by this none-too-closest of friends, yet one of the oldest among them.

Another half bow from Damon in acknowledgment as he began to turn and walk away only to pivot back in hesitation. "Now you really are Kellen the Destroyer, The Midnight Morning." He didn't normally reference Kellen by either of those titles. He had so many, after all. Even Damon didn't know the full of Kellen's many great atrocities. A thought he'd ponder as he started to walk away, knowing he'd just given one of the most dangerous weapons possible to one of the most ruthless men in existence. Perhaps, even eclipsing himself....

"Hey, Ra," Kellen blurted, trying to get Damon's attention before he left.

Turning back to Kellen, as if to answer his friend with his eye-to-eye glow-er, Damon paused.

"We're okay, right?" It was a legitimate question. Damon's manner had been...odd, to say the least. Leaving a lot to the imagination about what might be going on in that highly complex and layered psyche of his.

Walking back to his old friend, Damon transferred the *Staff of the Invoker* from his right hand to his left, only gripping one of the triple helixes as he always did, though never letting go of all the energy he was holding. Extending his right hand to shake Kellen's, Damon replied, "Always." Less was frequently more in Damon's book—especially when it came to Kellen—his intended and unspoken message had been received loud and clear. With that, Damon casually broke the handshake, turning to walk away as he tossed the *Staff of the Invoker* back to his right-hand grip, walking away from Kellen, splitting Kaleion's crust underneath him in his powerful wake.

Charles W. McDonald Jr.

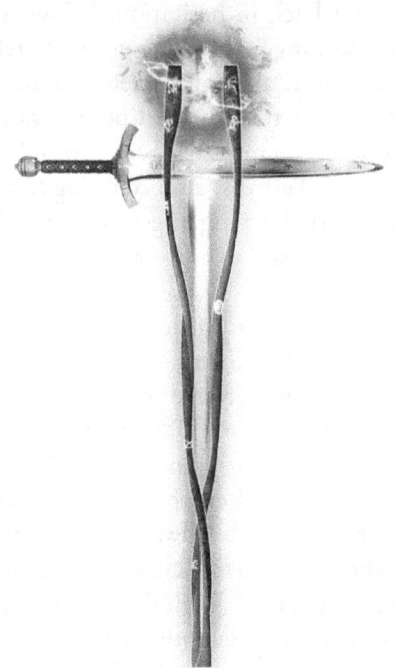

Chapter 19: Six – Part II

(Dragon Isle, Perion, Present Day)

Being freed carried with it so many forms of both euphoria and confusion. Confusion over what to do in his new body and all the great many sensations that came with it, and euphoria in the ability to cast once again—to feel the glorious power channeling through his veins, even if the veins weren't *really* his. He had been given a plan and had also been given a major role in it; he meant to execute that plan, to the letter....

Middle-aged, tall, lean, and muscular, with silver-grey hair and fire eyes, Castlin of old dated back to before the great war with Talemar, and hearing of Talemar's return had made his blood boil. Though, things were vastly different now. Then, they were pitched enemies, knowing where the other stood. This time, he wasn't so sure. As with the changes in his body, times and circumstances had also changed. Now it was about agendas, and he'd heard a great many things about this new Talemar and the young boy he ran with, leveling their all-out assault on the status-quo. That didn't sound like the conservative Talemar he once knew. Perhaps

Charles W. McDonald Jr.

there was a bargain to be struck, but he'd have to see. His orders had been clear and didn't leave much room for rogue interpretations. Still, an ally was an ally, and one less person to fight on the greatest of all battlefields to come was a net win, in anyone's books....

Creating scroll, after scroll, after scroll, Castlin prepared to execute the plan in earnest. Castlin's appetite had failed to return with him since his release. His body still had not yet eaten—only worked. Everything he had was going into this plan—every coin, every part of his being, every resource, and every effort. He would use magic to sustain himself if necessary, in order to maintain focus on executing the plan he'd been assigned. The ancient monastery carved into the side of one of the northernmost eighteen mountains of Dragon Isle, so old it pre-dated how the island received its name, with its crumbling colonnade of blue-grey marble, offered a magnificent view of The Hands of Darkness—two great footprints in the island made by a great and ancient dragon of almost immeasurable size.

There were so many ancient scores to settle but preserving his role and status in the plan took top priority, above all other goals. Perhaps one goal could service the other—in time. Sitting at a small desk, carved out of the same stone as the colonnade and columns, Castlin made no effort providing himself luxuries of any comfort. Listening to the ocean beating at the Hands of Darkness shoreline a short distance away was more than enough to calm and clear his thoughts, enabling him to focus on the task at hand.

Another rune burned into the parchment of *Damon's Damnation* as he rolled it up, placing it into a slender silver cylinder next to the three others already at his side. He could produce one scroll every few days, and it wasn't nearly enough yet to accomplish the kill list he'd been given, nor to complete the plan, but it was a start. He needed to keep going. Fortunately, his torment taught him the lack of necessity for sleep.

An unnatural gale of wind much colder than capable given the tropical climate, made the hackles on the back of his neck stand on end.

Pivoting where he sat to face down the intruder, he immediately prostrated himself on the broken stone colonnade of the ancient structure in ruins.

"Great Princess, how may I serve?" He didn't dare look at her, for he knew Lilith's appearance all too well. Beyond the mere beauty of a goddess, her perfect nude flesh walked barefoot on the dead grass of the Blood Night, causing it to curdle beyond death into a pale and disgusting footprint of bile enough to make Castlin involuntarily sick up in his prostrate position, vomiting onto his hands.

Her greenish-black serpent tail hissed upon Castlin's convulsions, baring its deadly, venomous fangs at him as its eyes burned molten amber with reptilian

Charles W. McDonald Jr.

narrow vertical slits to match those of the great Lilith, whose blonde locks down to the small of her back blew toward Castlin in icy fingers of death, carried on the unnaturally cold gale she brought in her wake. "Eldrac has failed...." Her lips didn't move as she transmitted her thoughts telepathically to Castlin—speaking only through the hateful aura of her eyes.

Wiping vomit from his face with his sleeve, Castlin offered, "I am here for you. What would you have me do?"

"Plan. Plot. Prick. Deceive..." He could tell by looking at her gaze she wasn't done, as her hate-fueled eyes grew wider with her last command, "...and RECRUIT!"

Suddenly producing a cape of fair flesh—whether hers or stolen from someone else, he couldn't say—Lilith swirled counter-clockwise into a great chasm that swallowed her whole to the sound of a thunderclap above, as great waves crashed upon the Hands of Darkness behind Castlin. The chasm that swallowed her as gone as any thoughts he may have once had of leveraging his freedom for settling old scores. This new brewing war would require different tactics to produce old outcomes.... Assuming old outcomes were still desired. He still couldn't see all the pieces moving on this great board before him. He knew her primary goal. She'd been quite specific about that. Remove Damon and his allies from the battlefield at any and all costs. But her more obfuscated desires and motives she'd kept just below the surface. *That* is where he sought to be of greater value, and if he couldn't at least guess at what those were, his desired status would still remain forever out of reach. He needed to get back to work. He needed to follow his orders. But most of all, he needed to get inside her mind and start thinking like her.

Assuming it wouldn't drive him mad.

Charles W. McDonald Jr.

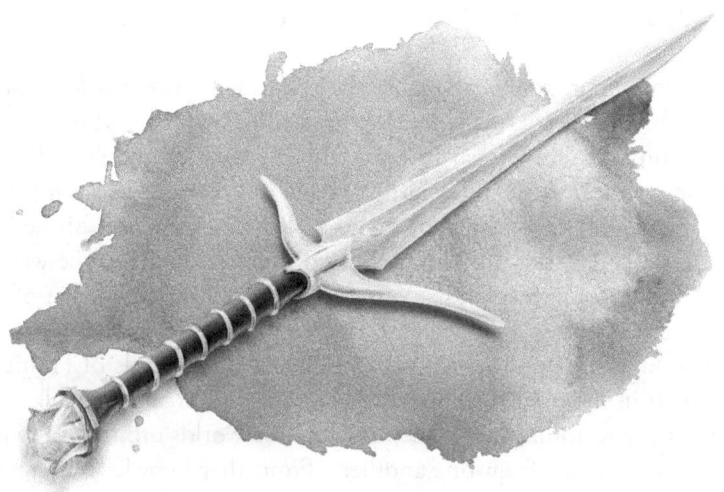

Chapter 20: The Seeds of Humanity

(Exeter, Perion, Present Day)

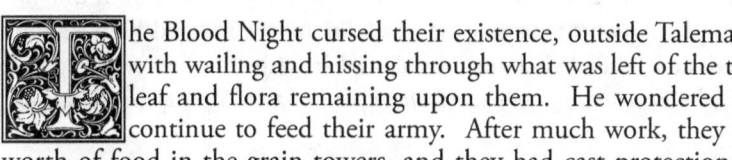

he Blood Night cursed their existence, outside Talemar's two windows, with wailing and hissing through what was left of the trees that still had leaf and flora remaining upon them. He wondered how they would continue to feed their army. After much work, they now had a year's worth of food in the grain towers, and they had cast protections on the seeds to keep them from being eaten or decayed by worm or disease. Still, the Blood Night would kill them all long before they saw their way to the other side of this long punishment ahead of them. If the Creator had intended the breaking of all Mankind before his arrival, he'd made proper work of that, with only the First Seal—The Scroll of Carnac.

The fury of gunfire moments ago brought Talemar out of his concentrated reading of Xaldran's Tome, but he had since settled back in for the long read of what would be Xaldran's greatest legacy. He needed to absorb this Tome of Power. He needed to understand why it was such a threat to Adena, and her kind. *Or, had Adena just been amassing great relics, for power's sake?* Both were possible, given what he knew of the great witch.

Yes, there were many unique spells—some of unknown origin—that would help him and Radin deliver upon their goals, and he supposed that Adena

Charles W. McDonald Jr.

could view those as a threat to her existence. Yet it wasn't groundbreaking in any way he could see.

He came upon knowledge of entryways into *The World Below and Between*, but that was hardly new knowledge. After all, he had sent Mora to that place during their raid on Eldrac's keep a thousand years ago. He didn't understand how it worked, or even if it was truly a part of this world or not. Or even this plane of existence. He merely knew the path there, and if he ever found himself there, he wasn't sure if he could find his way back; that's how little this place was generally understood. Even this tome didn't provide much more knowledge of the place than what he already knew.

Then he came upon it—the chapter labeled The Seeds of Humanity. He wasn't an expert in the topic, but between Damon, Radin, and Michelle, he'd come to understand the relationship between inhabitable worlds orbiting stars in the sky and their stellar distance from one another. From that knowledge, he assessed he was essentially looking at a star map, indicating five homeworlds, labeled as the Seeds of Humanity. One was Perion, another what he knew to be Terran (Earth), another Graelon, another Kaleion, and the last, labeled Setinon. He wasn't sure about these distances he was seeing and how they translated into a distance he could comprehend, but they seemed relatively clustered around two of the spiral arms of what was referred to as a Galaxy—each world's star systems toward the outer bands. Contemplating why that was the case, Talemar wondered how Xaldran would have gained such knowledge and not shared it with him so very long ago. More importantly, he considered, *who would have planted these Seeds of Humanity, and why scatter them so?*

He noticed some markings beside each world, though he wasn't sure what to make of them. It wasn't numbers or script, more like a series of dots with an occasional symbol. He didn't know what to make of it. He would need to show this to Ykstherin and get his opinion, but he could feel its importance. This might have been what Adena was after—now the only question remaining was: *why?*

*   *   *   *

Carrying Xaldran's Tome with him to the leadership meeting, Talemar contemplated sharing this knowledge and what it would mean. This was…dangerous knowledge, and he knew if he shared it with Radin that it would get shared with Damon. However, it was highly unlikely Damon was unaware of such knowledge. He might very well have been the source for Xaldran to write it down in the first place. He knew Xaldran to have run in very dangerous circles in his very extensive past, so it wasn't beyond the realm of the possible. Still, that didn't make the knowledge any less dangerous. If one had the capability to travel to all these worlds and knew of their significance in the grand scheme of things, one could wipe out all of Humanity for all time, with no hope of recovery. The very thought made him shiver as he entered the makeshift receiving room now in full décor, proudly displaying the bold and colorful standards of the Three Pillars of Hope.

A crowned Radin sat in the lone chair, beside the table of maps and iconography. Michelle and Lawna stood side by side, appearing closer than typical for them—whispering to one another. Ykstherin and Brigance stood next to and slightly in front of Michelle and Lawna on the west side of the room, Brigance fidgeting with new Three Pillars of Hope tabards adorning his gold-clad breastplate. Rowarc stood beside Radin, on his right side, opposite the map table, while Gareth stood to his right, slightly behind him. Wraith and Silura stood side by side near the entryway, fidgeting, as if they were planning on a quick exit.

By Radin's natural *Telekinesis*, The Crystal Crown floated as it lifted from Radin, now moving towards Talemar where Radin allowed it to fall upon Talemar's head gracefully. "Thank you for letting me use it to *Heal*," Radin stated with a nod to Talemar, who returned the gesture with a confirming nod of acceptance. Radin stopped short, failing to mention that no amount of *Healing* was going to make him whole again. He wanted to be strong for Elise, as she made her way into the room. She hadn't intended to be late, but there was so much on her mind, as her eyes darted around the room, taking in who was where, as much as they were now taking in the fact that she was starting to show.

"I want you to know, fully, my condition, as it surely will make itself known to you by rumor, if not by other means," Radin continued, though pausing as his eyes continued to follow Elise. "I have not been able to sleep since my return. So far, I haven't noticed a significant side-effect of this, but I am having to use magic to maintain a certain level of focus. I would appreciate regular *Healing* from some of you in that regard as time goes on. I hope we will eventually be able to resolve the issue, but if not, I think the bulk of the leadership decisions should fall to Talemar, for the foreseeable future." That was received with a level of murmuring around the room, though Ykstherin, Wraith and Silura offered nods of support as Radin continued, "I know many of you wonder about the condition of my mind and my thoughts, so I'll address that. I am consciously aware of memories of Voltor and his torment upon me. I am learning to deal with it—to focus it into something…useful." That was met with more intense murmurings around the room, as many contemplated its meaning. "Now, with all that set to the side for the moment…" It wasn't—not by a long shot, but Radin was determined to plow through regardless. "I met with Damon as soon as I became aware that he might be the original author of *Damnation*—the spell Eldrac tried to use on me twice, in the Battle of Axum, causing his own demise." Murmurings turned to outright accusations and outbursts around the room, causing Radin to raise his right hand, hushing people around the room. "Let me just start by saying, Damon is not what you think he is. He's not what I think he is. I doubt he's what he thinks he is. He is…unique and he is…changing." Stone dead silence fell upon the room; everyone's eyes locked on Radin's Hellish pools, even though it sickened them to do so. "Changing in a way perhaps he, himself, doesn't understand. This is a man who has earned his infamy ruthlessly dealing out death, destruction, and mayhem. This same man has now created a world—a sanctuary—for us and others like us to go and live out our lives in peace, safe from the vials of judgment of the Creator." He paused, thinking of his own role in delivering death and destruction as he continued, "…the same vials of judgment we brought upon this world." That came out soft, and somewhat accusatory of his own actions. "That I brought upon this world."

Talemar's steel, blue-grey eyes shifted in processing thought. He interrupted, "What does all this mean exactly? Where are you going with this?"

"I don't claim to know," Radin admitted, only recounting his experience, trying to relay his own interpretation to this important audience and gathering. "Damon immediately, and without reservation, admitted to being the sole author of *Damnation*. He didn't shy away from that fact at all. He explained that it was created to deal with a specific enemy who killed his first wife: Dallia. You've seen me carry her staff, which Damon freely provided to me to use as long as I wish." Nods around the room preceded more murmurings. "He admitted the infamy and banned status of *Damnation* made it more desirable for others of ilk to use. He further admitted that had he known the reach and sordid outcomes of his work, he would have found another way to deal with the problem and never created *Damnation* in the first place. And I, for one, believe him." More nods as the murmurings grew louder, into near outbursts. Searching his memory for Damon's exact words, hoping it would help with his intended goal, Radin continued, "In Damon's own words, 'she (Chara) was fated for the Underworld one way or the other. I was just directing her soul to a specific…entity.'" The murmurings calmed, though everyone's eyes stayed on Radin, listening attentively. "It gets better," Radin offered, continuing, "'Whatever I was, isn't it possible for me to become more?'"

"Now…," Radin paused, clearing his throat. He was starting to choke himself up to the astonishment of those around him. *Creator, my relationship with Damon is ever complicated!* "…To his credit, Damon has offered, and already delivered upon his promise, to give us a list of those capable of casting *Damnation* and known to have done so on more than one occasion. Eldrac we already know about, but this...," Radin pulled the list Damon had provided, continuing, "...is now a substantial part of our tenets." *Collaborative thinking*, he chastised himself for stating something so unitarily. However powerful he might become if he believed Damon, he was still being a pushy, annoying brat who hadn't yet earned his stripes. He needed to find a better way with this team. "If you'll indulge me, I BELIEVE, this list is a good part of the reason we've been assembled. I BELIEVE that such a power as this..." Holding the list up in the air for the rest of leadership to see, he continued, "...should not go unchallenged. If I'm wrong, tell me I'm wrong. Speak up. I want to hear everyone's thoughts, who cares enough to speak."

Michelle looked around the room, seeing the thinking in progress, but already having formed an opinion of her own. "There's a lot of power assembled in this room, and on these grounds. This kind of force needs to be applied intelligently, thoughtfully, and be made adaptable to the situational fronts it will face, regardless of what world it may be on. We haven't yet adapted to some of the foes we know we will face, but for now it makes sense to eliminate pieces off the battlefield that we know are capable of doing unnatural things to a lifeforce. However, there will soon come a time, in my opinion, where we'll have a larger understanding of the battlefield, the players on it, and may need to shift resources to attack problems that might have a bigger impact on the war as a whole. I mean, we still don't know exactly what we're fighting for. I see the new banners, and they're great. I know what the banners stand for, but are we really doing that or are we an extension of Damon's army, doing as he wills? I don't see them as one-hundred percent compatible, but I don't see them as mutually exclusive, either. Damon is the catalyst here, and all I'm saying, is that while the banners are nice and the thoughts behind them just, Damon's larger goals might peel us off to do things that might very well put us at odds even with our own proposed tenets."

That was a lot to chew on, but Michelle, as usual, was on point. Scratching his stubbled and weary face, Radin considered all she'd brought up, adding, "You're not wrong, and if I knew more about his plans, I'd share it. If you'll indulge me to hazard a guess, I'll do that, but keep in mind, it's just a gut feeling."

Everyone looking at him expectantly told him to continue. Clearly, he had their attention.

"When I used to hunt with my father...," Radin looked to Rowarc who smiled back at him, "...he always told me the most dangerous game was wounded game. I see Damon as a man wounded by the loss of Dallia. I've seen her grave on his estate, and the flowers kept perfectly manicured around it. I've seen her perfectly kept room as if a monument or museum describing his love and longing for her. I've seen the look in his eyes when her name is mentioned, and the pain behind them. This is a dangerous man who's not done delivering his wrath. I think some of this new equilibrium he keeps talking about has to do with paying a debt still owed to his beloved Dallia."

Nods from around the room indicated they accepted his supposition as fact. Even those who didn't know Dallia, or Damon, could comprehend the thinking, given the information laid out before them.

"I never knew Dallia. I only know Damon. And even then, just barely so. However, I can understand both his thinking and his motives. He has admirable traits, even if his methods are…ruthless, brutal, and at times…cruel. If his wrath is intended to settle this ancient score, and he's still accumulating power and resources for what he hints at will be the battle of all battles, one would have to assume that his foe is both powerful beyond imagination and an enemy to us all. An enemy of Humanity…."

More sound thinking added fuel to the leadership conversation, and thoughts as the room digested the new information—slowly, like a snake.

Beaming with pride over the rapid growth of the man he'd raised as his son, Rowarc asked, "What does your gut tell you about Damon? Is he a good man?"

"No." Radin's eyes followed around the room as the consequences of that one word chased its acceptance in each person present.

Whispers and mutterings around the room escalated with Radin's forthright admission.

"Then why are we engaged with him? Shouldn't we pull back and chart our own course?" Elise delivered her line of questioning with passion, motioning to the others around the room, as if trying to sway them. Her own thoughts and knowledge of Damon ever present in the back of her mind.

"It hadn't been my intent to cause a crisis of conviction in this meeting, but I can see that is where we have gone, so I'll leave it up to the room to make this decision. As much as I understand Damon, and want to help him, and moreover to stay out of his way of delivering his justice upon whomever is the target, I will do as the room—as this team—wishes."

Clearing his throat, Ykstherin had remained conspicuously quiet during all of this, but he felt somewhat responsible for bringing Radin's attention to the fact of Damon being the author of *Damnation*. "I, too, have done unspeakable things in the name of love."

It was a shocking admission as open mouths around the room attested, many looking at him sidelong and anew.

"We have not walked the path of Damon's circumstances and are unqualified to judge him. He will, as we all will, be judged at a time appropriate to the Creator."

Wraith and Silura looked down at the floor simultaneously as soon as the word 'judged' was uttered, apparently in an affront to their beliefs.

"You said, with confidence, you believed he was not a good man. Correct?" Ykstherin looked to Radin for confirmation as if to drive home his point.

A singular nod from Radin told Ykstherin to continue.

"You yourself said he was 'changing.' Do you believe he could ever be, in Rowarc's assessment given to you, 'a good man?'"

Radin thought about the question for a moment. "I believe he has developed, over a very long lifetime of wrongs done upon him, a sense of what he believes is right versus wrong and that he tries to do what falls under his interpretation of right. It isn't as simple as my father teaching me right from wrong and then following that path. His sense of wrong comes from wrongs done upon him by those both 'good' and 'evil.' His sense of right comes from uplifting experiences shared with forces of both shadow and light. He's a conundrum shaped out of intersections of circumstances, spanning generations.

Let me put it this way, and this is really the best way to think about Damon.... If not for his circumstances, I believe he could have developed differently into a man both myself and my dad could admire...and call a friend."

Mouths were now closed around the room, many pressed in hard, thin lines in contemplation.

Radin looked to Talemar, noting his silence during the entire conversation, offering him an attempt to speak up with his eyes. Though Talemar's eyes diverting down at the floor at Radin's gaze suggested he had nothing further to add.

"We haven't done this before, but I think it makes sense to do it now. If we are to be the Justice for the Unjust, then we now have a place to start," Radin proffered, holding the list of names up for the room to again see. Thinking, Radin's eyes darted around the room, settling on Talemar. "I think Damon risked far more than just his life to save me. I think he risked his Master Plan. I think he risked everything to save me." He had to stop as his mouth worked, recalling Voltor's torment of him and the vague memory of Damon casting a great, gleaming sword into Voltor's chest, obliterating his tormentor's immortal shell. "I'd like to call for a vote by a show of hands. Those who think we should continue to follow Damon until we have good reason not to, please raise your hand." Choosing not to raise his own hand so as not to influence the vote, Radin started to tally the raised hands, but noticed Michelle stepping forward to get everyone's attention.

"May I offer another piece of information to consider," Michelle's voice projected throughout the room—cutting through the pending votes—causing everyone to heed. "I just think we also need to consider the state of what's outside. I mean that big pale-red sky outside and all of the living things suddenly dying. We need a status on the Seals. We need to understand how much longer we might need to survive what we've already started. That may impact whether we move at Damon's pace or at a pace more requisite to our survival."

Nods from around the room conveyed everyone's agreement with Michelle's clarity and logic.

"Talemar, what news have we of Royvan Miral's progress," Radin asked.

"He's following clues from several years of research. There's no one more qualified for the task. Last I heard, his clues led him into the southern hemisphere."

"That's not much to go on. It could be weeks, months, or even years, but I doubt we'll survive years, so let's assume it will be weeks or months. Anything beyond that is moot," Radin pontificated, though not from a place of arrogance—merely a place of necessity. He knew they wouldn't survive years. He hoped they would be able to hang on months, and even more, he hoped they wouldn't need to. *Hurry, Royvan Miral. Hurry! Please.*

"So that's the best we have to go on right now. What is the vote count to follow Damon until we have good reason not to do so," Radin reiterated. Again holding back his own vote, Radin tallied the raised hands.

Gareth, Ykstherin, Rowarc, Michelle and Lawna—albeit much slower to raise her hand than Michelle—Brigance, and Talemar raised their hands, in that order. Radin finally raised his, making the count eight to three, with only Elise, Wraith, and Silura voting against—if tepidly so.

A look of fondness shared between Radin and Elise wasn't stopped by her counter-vote. They shared a child together. They cared for each other, and he knew he needed to make time for her—whether or not they still had a future together. That was a conversation he'd been putting off—intentionally so—but needed to show the temerity and the backbone to get on with it. Elise deserved that much.

Moving his eyes from Elise to the rest of the room, Radin concluded, "Very well then. We have work to do. Talemar and I will find out what we can about the lameans on this list as we continue preparations for the army and opening the remaining seals, which we can only hope will bring us to the other side of this nightmare that I started." Solemn looks at his last two words, as he only said

Charles W. McDonald Jr.

what others were thinking, or had thought. But as soon as he said it he wished he hadn't, knowing it hadn't been helpful.

Burly hands grasped Radin's shoulders from behind as he rose from his seat; he knew hands that big could only belong to Brigance.

"You did good. You're learning. Don't be so hard on yourself. Men your age weren't meant to shoulder this kind of burden. Lean on those around you and let them help. Delegate everything you can," Lord Fireheart suggested through the voice of his own experience.

A nod from Radin expressed his appreciation at the wisdom that came with Lord Fireheart's experience.

Talemar grabbed Radin's left arm with his right hand, whispering into his ear, "I have something you need to see. You and Ykstherin both…." Motioning with his eyes to Xaldran's Legacy close at his side, Talemar beckoned Radin with a burning weight he obviously didn't feel comfortable sharing with the rest of leadership. Turning back to the room, locking eyes with Ykstherin, Radin motioned with his index finger for him to follow as they walked the roughly fifty paces to Radin's suite.

The last inside Radin's suite, Talemar closed the door, then closed the distance between them, opening the Tome to the chapter "The Seeds of Humanity." "This is something that Adena made several attempts to get her hands on back during the Great War when Xaldran still lived. I can't say for sure where Xaldran got this information from, or even if it was his writing, but it *does* look like his writing."

Running his eyes rapidly over the text and turning to the star map on the very next page, Radin immediately recognized what he was seeing, making the correlation between this and the star map Damon showed him months ago. "This is a star map, and I recognize these locations, well, three of them at least. Graelon and Setinon, I don't. What are these markings next to the planet names?"

"Yeah, I wanted to ask you both about that. I have no idea." Talemar looked between them, hoping for answers.

Shaking his head, Ykstherin replied, "I've never seen markings like that before, but that isn't the first reference I've seen to Graelon. That *is* the first reference I've seen to Setinon, and Setinon appears the furthest out of all of them."

"Or the genesis of the others, making the rest colonies." That was an interesting perspective from Radin, showing his rapid maturity on the topic. The others nodded—seemingly impressed. "Do you think we should ask Damon about this?"

"That was my thought," Talemar offered. "I don't think we're running much of a risk exposing him to something he didn't already know. I don't think we're running a great risk of destroying all Humanity by showing him this. I mean from everything you've said about him…." That offered with a knowing glance to Radin.

"What does the text say about this map? Does it provide much perspective?" Ykstherin liked Radin's idea of Setinon possibly being a mother to its colonies and wanted to see if that text had any merit.

"I'll admit not having had time to read it all. I just ran across the star map right before the meeting, and some of it's in ancient tongue. I'd need Royvan Miral to translate it. It does talk about the Seeds of Humanity being spread across worlds intentionally for the survival of the species. Then there are other references to great punishments of exile handed down from the *Eye of Time*. Then still others of a temporal war with a great threat, beyond all others…" Talemar paused, sharing a look of wonderment between himself and Radin.

Radin could tell everyone was internally chewing on the 'temporal war' comment. His own knowledge, or lack thereof, said it was better not to say anything on it until he talked with Damon.

"It gets better…. It also talks about future knowledge of this great threat that could destroy them all—thus scattering them to increase the odds of survival." Talemar paused, taking another breath before completing his thought, "Who 'them' refers to is a little mysterious to me, but I *think* 'them' refers to the greatest of their lameans."

Then it hit him, like a flash in the foreground of his mind, one of those symbols next to Setinon. Talemar had seen that symbol…from the Halls of Aaramus! The alarming memory immediately caused his right brow to furrow as he tried to recall where he'd seen it.

"You're thinking something." Radin saw it written all over the crowned Talemar's face.

"I don't know. I need to check something." Pulling a blank piece of parchment from his back pocket, Talemar began scratching the symbol next to Setinon on the parchment, making note of it for future reference.

†¤‡-ˌÆ‡:˘Œ

"It doesn't look like any Arcane I've ever seen," Ykstherin proffered, immediately getting affirming nods from both Radin and Talemar.

"I don't want to rule anything out, but if Adena knew about the existence of this, that alone makes her a threat. She's far too crazy to be an ally with this kind of knowledge."

"Agreed," from Talemar.

"Agreed," from Ykstherin.

"I don't want to do anything without talking to Damon about this first, but it wouldn't be a bad idea to start drawing up a plan to take Adena out of the picture. Have Brigance work on that with Wraith but tell them not to act on it until they've spoken with me." Affirming nods from Ykstherin and Talemar as they recognized Radin's tactical mind in action, even if Talemar and Ykstherin had infinitely more experience between them. Still, he chastised himself internally for being so quick to take charge again. "Or, at the very least, we could hold another vote on taking action on Adena."

More affirming nods from Talemar and Ykstherin. Looking between them again, they could see Radin was still trying to piece this great puzzle together.

"Thank you for this information, Talemar," Radin offered as he pensively continued to digest the information. "I feel like it could be helpful, but I'm still struggling to understand how, exactly. That's where I think Damon can help us. What do you think we can do with this new information? How would *you* leverage it?"

"I've been giving that some thought as we've been talking. We need to understand more about this *Eye of Time*. We also need to understand if the term 'them' was in reference to the greatest of their lameans as I had proposed, and if so, does that threat still exist today? Where does that threat originate and is it a bigger threat to us than the lameans on Damon's list? This story—if Xaldran is the one recording it—is far more ancient than anything I've ever considered before. That means if the threat still exists, its origins must be…nearly eternal." The last came out slow, measured, and barely breathed aloud as Talemar's contemplation of the timeline in play stretched even his understanding and imagination.

"That is a lot to consider," Ykstherin proposed, looking between them, impressed by both. "I can look into the *Eye of Time*, if Damon doesn't have answers for us there."

"Agreed," Radin nodded, adding, "I'll discuss this carefully with Damon, gauging his reaction and information sharing to each section before moving on to the next so as not to reveal all we know all at once before knowing where Damon will fall. I don't believe Damon to be a threat in this regard—and hold him more of an asset than a liability—but I still think caution is warranted, especially with the weight of this information. Talemar, could you please continue to find out what you can from Xaldran's writing and piece it together with what you understand of Adena, her agenda, and her knowledge?"

Charles W. McDonald Jr.

"I can."

Talemar could see Radin's mind still churning....

"Something else?"

"I'm just thinking, I don't know how far, or for how long, we can trust critical objectives to Wraith. Let's keep this information between us for now. I'm not saying we don't tell Wraith and Brigance before they engage Adena. I think we should, but I also think we might want to just create the plan to take Adena out, rather than make the plan and execute it. Let's come back to that when we know more about this new information." Internally Radin already had begun berating himself a prodigy of Damon. This was how Damon would have handled this situation, and it unnerved him to be thinking in such a manner.

"Agreed," from Ykstherin.

"Agreed," from Talemar.

From the look Talemar was giving him, he knew there would need to be more explanation about his sudden lack of trust in Wraith.

Circling back to the previous topic from the larger meeting, "I noticed Eldrac's name on the list given to you by Damon. What are we going to do about him?" A more than fair question from Talemar, and one Radin had been considering a great deal as he seethed at the mention of Eldrac's name—almost as much as the name of his most vile tormentor, Voltor. Radin noted Talemar hadn't bothered asking how it was possible for Eldrac to even be a problem, given their last sight of him. Apparently, Talemar knew a great deal more than he was letting on.

"We're not going to do anything about him. I'm going to ask Damon to settle that score for us all, and he's going to do it." There wasn't a hint of doubt in Radin's voice as he drove home that command; if not directed at the others, it might have simply been directed at himself.

Ykstherin dubiously coughed into his hand as Talemar just looked at Radin, questioning his sanity and lack of sleep, and how one might be feeding the other.

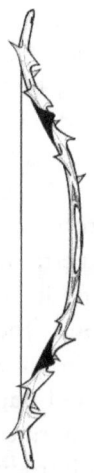

Chapter 21: Scouting the Mark

(The Crown of Spires, Perion, Present Day)

Dusk at the Crown of Spires was magnificent, even if the divination tile causeways were still under repairs from Radin's previous assault some weeks past. Goldenbow moved gracefully in the underbrush that had, for the most part, escaped the full wrath of the Blood Night. His color-shifting ranger gear made him nearly invisible as he barely disturbed the green blades of grass and long fescue beneath the causeway. He hadn't found the source of their fresh water yet, and he had already completely scouted the southern side of the Crown of Spires, well past Adena's quarters, but that wasn't surprising; looking at the lake to the northwest, he expected to find their source of fresh water on that side of the compound, anyway. Really, he wanted as good of a count as he could get on Adena's camp to see how many threats he was dealing with, and whatever that number was, he needed to bring it down significantly before acting on Adena herself. He needed to best mitigate the risk of reprisal, or aid, and leaving half or more of them living was just too dangerous. What he needed was a high body count—plus the mark herself. That was the ideal scenario, but things didn't always go that way, even with all his experience working for him.

A little further west and he came upon a series of well-disguised aqueducts dumping fresh water from the Crystal Lake into a series of aquifers. The Blood Night had taken its toll on all the leaf and flora intended to fully disguise both, starting to kill off some of the vegetation at the root system, and revealing some

Charles W. McDonald Jr.

of the man-made structure descending the terrain down toward the Crown of Spires. It wouldn't be easy to take apart the aquifer enough to see where the end point of the water was, but he needed to be sure his toxin would do its job. This is where having someone with him would actually be helpful for overwatch while he worked, but he preferred working alone. It had kept him alive all this time, so why change now?

Muscling his short sword in between a series of interlocking rocks that formed the top of the aquifer, he expertly levered the rock to move without disturbing too much of the gravel around it. It wasn't enough noise to disturb anything and only confirmed his suspicions. The water was being purified by the gravel, and likely at the source, by magic, to prevent poisoning from the Blood Night, then collecting into a great bowl carved out of stone with a series of cheesecloth and pebbles over the top for further purification. He couldn't see the extraction point, but this was the right spot to introduce his lethal holotoxin, concentrated from the seeds of castor oil plants on Earth—commonly known on Earth as ricin.

It had been a favorite of Goldenbow's ever since he discovered it, following Damon on one of his many trips there. Big secret or not, he wasn't going to allow Damon to drag him and Kellen blindly into the Abyss—as it were—without effectively spying on him enough to get an idea of this Master Plan of his. From what he'd seen of it so far, Damon had lost what was left of his mind, but that was for a discussion at a later time with both him and Kellen present. For now, he'd promised a kill, and a kill he was going to deliver. One milligram of ricin was more than enough to kill a Human, if ingested. He had to account for the dilution of the water, and the very distinct possibility that some, if not many, of these witches regularly ingested various poisons to build tolerances to them. *Why not?* He had. It was smart, and it was an even smarter way to kill, if a tad bit indiscriminate.

Propping up the large stone with his short sword, he opened the 2000mg vial of holotoxin, dumping all of it into the water supply. He'd seen enough. He knew his desired point of entry to remove Adena from the board—permanently— and needed to allow time for the ricin to do its job. Maybe a few days to let the panic seep in. He knew Adena would have a separate water source just for her and her closest companions, and she'd have tasters as well, so the likelihood of this reaching her was slim to none. He'd have to come back to finish her off, but for now he gently lowered the stone back into place, erasing any signs of it ever being disturbed as he broke the seal that transported him back home without a flash or sound of any kind.

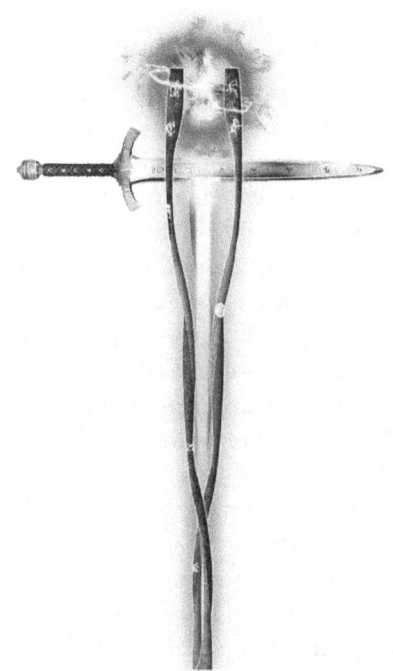

Chapter 22: Off the Map

(The Far East Ocean of Mohers, Perion, Present Day)

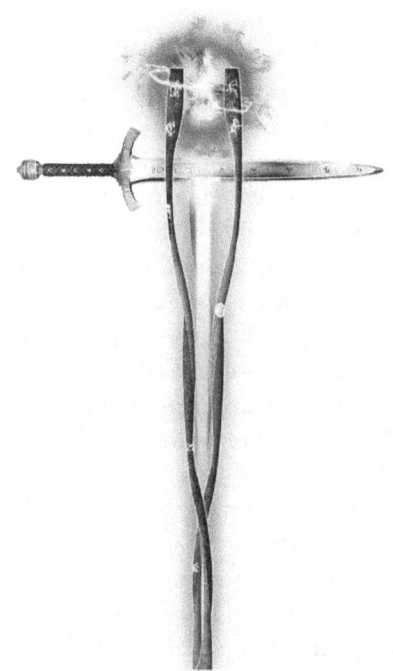either Royvan Miral, nor any of his team, had ever been this far east in the Ocean of Mohers. It seemed almost the edge of the world, for they hadn't seen land in weeks. Fortunately, their frigate was large, holding months of provisions, and Royvan Miral had seen to it they had a proper crew for this adventure, but none of them had sailed this far south and east, either. There wasn't a fear of the world being flat, or any such nonsense, but fears of terrifying sea monsters, fears of never seeing land again, fears of the Blood Night bringing on another fierce storm—those were all justifiable. The last storm had ripped the main topsail to the point where it wasn't salvageable. They were now using the only spare they had and counted themselves fortunate the storm hadn't destroyed the mast.

Now in the captain's quarters, checking his map of Perion against the captain's sea charts that held *far* more detail, Royvan knew roughly where they were, but without sight of a known landmass any time recently, he couldn't be certain.

Charles W. McDonald Jr.

Royvan estimated they were two thousand leagues south of the southern tip of The Needles, and if they were to have a shipwreck of any kind, no one would ever find them. He'd seen what he knew was the same school of sharks following them for hundreds of leagues. Maybe they knew something he didn't. Maybe they were just being opportunistic—or hopeful—or both. Either way, he didn't like it.

Checking his best guess at their current location against the clues and evidence he'd collected over half his life, he felt they should have found it by now. Osalin was a mythical island of legend and only mentioned in two books out of the hundreds he had read throughout his lifetime. He had nothing to compare it to, if it even existed at all. Supposedly, great magical artifacts had originated from there, making their way to the far corners of the world. Supposedly, it was an ancient home to the most reclusive of lameans—and the most dangerous. He hoped to find nothing but the Second Seal of course, but he also hoped for a great many things he knew not possible. *Why would this be any different?*

Captain Therigish Flinn slammed the door to his cabin, cursing about his crew—a topic of frequent swearing. He was always swearing about something. His dark green linen pants matched his eyes, and his dirty-white, long sleeve shirt matched his matted, harshly-weathered skin. His short cropped, black hair sported just a touch of salt and pepper graying that couldn't hide the jagged scar over his right cauliflower ear. Whatever had happened to him, it surely wasn't pretty at the time it happened. He reeked of sea and fish; they all did. It perfumed every corner of the ship, and Royvan Miral was sick of it. If he never ate fish again, he'd consider it a miracle from the Creator.

"I'm having to spend *all* my time just keeping the men and their stupid superstitions in line." Captain Flinn dropped his ever-present long dagger on the map table of his cabin; the dagger's burnished and pitted bronze scabbard looked as if it had sailed around the world at least a dozen times with him, or more. "We should have hit land by now. Another day of this and I'm going to turn us northeast back into the main shipping lanes."

"I paid you—" Royvan didn't get to finish his thought before he was cut off; the captain scowling at him and pacing around the map table to look him right in the eye.

"Gold don't help you when you're dead!" The captain's mouth twisted as he blurted out his harsh truth.

"You sound as superstitious as your crew, Captain." Royvan Miral delivered his title contemptuously, glowering back at the captain. He had paid the captain and his crew a hefty fee to find Osalin—not to turn back when it got uncomfortable. Royvan had a point, delivering it at the captain with his usual soothing tactfulness.

"How do you know this place even exists," the captain challenged, contemplating the possibilities. *Osalin*, he thought ruefully. *Not likely!*

"If you doubted its existence any more than I, you wouldn't have taken this job. You know these seas as well, if not better, then anyone. You're telling me you've never wondered about Osalin's existence?"

"Oh, I've wondered about it, but there's never been a shred of evidence—not even gulls. No ships sailing from this far southeast—not ever."

"So....We ARE further southeast than you've ever been then?!!" Royvan had been lied to by the captain. Now he *was* worried. He desperately wished for Quin's presence—or any lamean that could *Portal*. Thinking briefly, then dismissing the idea of abandoning this path. The Blood Night would kill everything and everyone on the planet. The only way through this Hell was forward. They needed the Second Seal! This was the right place! Looking the captain directly in the eye, Royvan warned, "We're staying this course, Captain, until I say otherwise. I've killed harder men than you!"

Sneering, Captain Flinn considered the numbers he had with his crew over Royvan's men; he *did* have the numbers. Flinn could take them, kill them and drop them into the sea where they'd never be seen or heard from again, but he needed time to execute *that* plan. Buying himself time, the captain replied, "Very well, Royvan Miral. We'll stay the course. For now...."

"GULLS! GULLS! LAND HO! LAND HO!" The shouts coming from the First Mate, outside the cabin, on the whipstaff.

Another sneer from the captain as he dismissed his immediate need to kill Royvan Miral. *Another time perhaps,* the captain thought, as Royvan Miral bolted for the cabin doorway, heading out to the main deck for a view.

Chasing Royvan outside, Captain Flinn noticed the gulls overhead—some circling his frigate and crew in search of food—some heading back to the southeast. "Maintain heading. Follow them home," the captain ordered the first mate, who echoed his captain's command to a giddy crew, quickly forestalling the chaotic thoughts of their own demise.

"Very well, Mr. Miral. We've honored our part of the bargain. There's your Osalin," the captain offered ruefully, motioning to the white sand beaches of the crescent-moon-shaped land coming into view.

Royvan Miral replied with his eyes and the hard look of determination at the prospect of getting through to the other side of the Blood Night. Even here, in what should have been broad daylight at the edge of the world, the reddish-pink hues of the horizon, seemingly in perpetuity, threatened the existence of every liv-

Charles W. McDonald Jr.

ing thing. Soon, nothing would grow—anywhere.

     Probably closer to Dragon Isle than to The Needles, they might as well have been off the map, for they were close to nothing, except maybe saving what was left of Humanity.

Charles W. McDonald Jr.

Chapter 23: A Throne of Souls

(Damon's Manor, Kaleion, Present Day)

Getting up to head to his secluded study, Damon left Mira's nude body undisturbed in his bed. The master bedroom only existed outside of normal space—space created by Damon's magic at the time the manor was built. Its direct entryway to the secret study was the only way in, or out, of the master bedroom for it didn't exist in the square footage of the footprint of the manor. If it had existed in normal space, it would have to co-exist in the same space occupied by the entry to the Ritual Room and the Ritual Room itself. It had taken Mira a while to figure that out, but with Damon, the possibilities were endless.

He had to overcome a profound limitation in *Damnation* which prevented the caster from condemning the soul to the caster's property. There were already three instantiations of *Damnation*, but fortunately only one ever got published. The others were more heinous—more powerful. Still, he needed to get past that limitation. He needed a fourth instantiation of *Damnation* to build his own *Throne of*

Charles W. McDonald Jr.

Souls.

Thus far, the limitation had proven to be like breaking the FTL barrier—damn near impossible. It was his fourth day working on unraveling the limitation into components he could deal with one at a time, but he was getting nowhere with it, and that was frustrating beyond belief. If he couldn't do this, Phase II wouldn't be possible—not without help. And help would require the release of compartmentalized information. *Unacceptable*, he thought, sitting back down at the larger of the two desks in his study. It was really a solid red oak worktable—not a desk per se.

Looking at the *Staff of the Invoker* radiating charged flames of its evil charcoal-blue aura in the corner of the study by the hard bed that he used in his youth, Damon's memory drifted to thoughts of Dallia and the magnificent gift of love she'd made from nothing. The gift of her love alone had been enough as his first wife—the very first person to see him as anything more than evil; the very first person to accept him as he was. Though he still bore the scars about his chest, back, and shoulders, because they were more scars on his soul than his body, Dallia had been the first, in a series, to help him get past that *cauldron of hate* that forged Damon into existence. He was Damon, fully and completely now, whether born Damon or not. The nameless one had become less than inert to him. He was dead.

Yet Dallia had coaxed out the being before Damon—though he couldn't recall his name. She had coaxed the Damon—post Dallia—into being more than the *cauldron of hate* would tolerate. Her love worked on him to this very day; with each use of the *Staff of the Invoker*, she was there with him. It terrorized everyone with its aura and its presence, but it terrorized Damon with its inextricably associated memories of his loving Dallia. It was the living and inerasable reminder of Dallia…and her death. He loved the *Staff of the Invoker*, and he detested it with every fiber of his being.

"That is a brooding and very thoughtful look." Illirian's presence did not startle him this time, even though he had been deeply lost in his thoughts.

Wiping his face, ensuring he got his eyes, though not sure whether or not he'd actually shed a tear, Damon wasn't in the most welcoming of moods—even for Illirian. "You came for a reason?" That hadn't come out right, and Illirian instantly recoiled at the viperous statement, rising from the seat opposite Damon's worktable where she'd suddenly just appeared—her red-gold dress a reflection of her magnificent hair.

"I can go…," she replied, looking back at him as her beautiful eyes threatened to leave.

A heavy sigh from Damon announced he was thinking about it, but a

Charles W. McDonald Jr.

longing look from Damon beckoned her, without words, to stay.

"Talk to me, Damon."

"Who am I?" That was the most unique question she'd ever heard from Damon, clearly in a crisis of identity.

Without hesitation, she proclaimed, "You are Damon of Basrat, The Dark Knight of Magic, Wielder of the *Staff of the Invoker*, God of Eden, Maker and Destroyer of Worlds, Author of *Damnation*." The last title she could have left off, but it *was* who he was—just as inextricably linked to *Damnation* as the *Staff of the Invoker* was to memories of Dallia.

A single nod from Damon his only reply.

"Having second thoughts?" Illirian's question more a counter than anything else. Not mocking, though it might have pricked his ears that way.

Of course, he was. It was a stupid question coming from an infinitely brilliant woman, yet it was intentional. Her motives were hers alone, but if she could leverage a weakness to supplant his plan with her own, he was sure she'd see that as a win-win.

"This isn't just about me and what I want. You know that," Damon chided with glimmering *black mirrors of the soul*.

"So, you *are* beholden then." Her tone rose to become as erect as her body in her tight dress; her form she knew perfectly distracting to Damon's eyes.

"Not the word I would have chosen, but the end state is bigger than what I wanted."

"What was the deity move all about anyway? Did you expect to get absorbed into her pantheon?"

"Ha!" A disgusted snort from Damon, though he could see how Illirian's thought processes had brought her to that conclusion. "Like I said, I never wanted that responsibility. It was a necessity."

"Well want it or not, you won't be allowed to operate much longer as an independent." Her arms folded over one another as her glower made itself felt. There were simply too many blind spots Damon had no insight into, whatsoever. He couldn't possibly believe himself immune to the consequences of his actions.

"We'll see…," determination replied on Damon's behalf as he began to run the calculus of his actions, past, present, and future through his mind. "Besides, I won't need to operate much longer as an independent."

"Yes, yes, and then what?" Illirian held up her head, not putting on airs; more an effort in wicking the truth out of Damon's camouflaged machinations.

"Divination isn't my specialty. You know that."

"This isn't about what future you *see*, Damon. This is about what future

Charles W. McDonald Jr.

you're *planning*."

"Compartmentalized. You know that as well."

"Well, with all this compartmentalized information, I really don't see how I can help you: in seeing who you really are, in executing your Master Plan, nor in reconciling your immortal soul with your actions."

"If you could see, for a moment, past the bitterness and disappointment of being left out of the loop, perhaps you could leverage what you know of me, my past, and my actions and help me reconcile with my feelings."

It was a more than fair request from Damon. She could indeed do that, and she could use her powers to probe his feelings, but she wanted to hear him say it out loud, or at the very least make some acknowledgment trending in that direction.

She would try for the whole of it first. "Very well then, Damon. What are your feelings?"

A heavy sigh concurrent with a tilting nod of the head instantly told her that was a futile request.

"Okay then, what is the confluence between your feelings and your history of who you've been?"

Damon could answer that, but he didn't want to. "I know I was a monster. That's a given, but is that what I am?" *Sometimes you had to do things you despised to get to the place you longed to be or to right wrongs done upon you in far greater scale.*

"Those I report to believe unequivocally that yes, that is who you were, are, and ever shall be." She hadn't intended for that to come out as a perpetual rebuke of him, but it had....

"They're right." Of course they thought that; he could leverage that fact and would. The clock was already ticking with that in mind.

"I don't believe so. For all their divination and peering into you from afar, they don't know the half of you." Her chin tilted down at the last as if to smote their haughty beliefs of things they knew nothing about.

"Your optimism won't save me from what I must do." He was cursed but knew what had to be done. He'd seen it....

"You act as if you have no control over your own actions. We both know that isn't so. Whatever outcome you truly desire, regardless of what outcome you may have planned for yourself, point your rudder in that direction and row." The daughter of a mariner, she frequently used maritime analogies regardless of whether or not the analogy fit.

More brooding from Damon as she took the seat beside him, smiling at him. "Would you like to know the real reason I came to visit you?"

Charles W. McDonald Jr.

"Please." A breath of fresh air in the conversation—a breath of honesty—could be uplifting, Damon thought, turning in his chair to face the always plotting, but beautiful, Illirian. Her red-gold hair shimmered against her cheeks, drawing his eyes to her immaculate features as she often did.

"Two members of the Council of Mages are gone—two that would have voted in your favor. I fear that before the Council replaces them, they'll hold a vote on you."

"Oh." As if Damon didn't have enough problems to deal with—now this! The chair of the council of mages had wanted him off this planet long ago. They had the numbers now. *Great*, he thought. "Vosh is one I'm sure of—who's the other?"

"Mora," she replied flatly, receiving a knowing nod from Damon. "I might be able to persuade them to leave you alone."

"DON'T!" Damon protested, rising from his seat before her. "I've said it before, and I'll say it again. I'll need you for much more important things than matters of avoiding conflict between myself and the Council of Mages. Don't waste effort on matters of the Council of Mages. I could wipe them off the face of the planet if necessary."

"Please don't do that," she pleaded, knowing better.

"Don't worry but thank you for the warning. It was only a matter of time after the experiment."

"Yes, well, I wouldn't use *that* in your defense, for sure." Getting up, checking the bed to see Mira still asleep in Damon's bed, she turned back to Damon, giving him a kiss before disappearing without a trace.

Another heavy sigh from Damon as he resumed his seat, his thoughts, and his work on his newest instantiation of *Damnation*, but with a different viewpoint. Something Illirian had said in her maritime analogy made sense. Rather than trying to break *Damnation* into re-usable components, then fixing one of those components in a re-assembly effort, he could try re-writing the entire thing from scratch.

With renewed focus and effort, Damon pulled the blank parchment to begin working again on an entirely new spell, *A Throne of Souls*. But, for that, he'd need a very old source book—*The Book of Souls*.

Charles W. McDonald Jr.

Chapter 24: The Dark Knight of Magic

(Damon's Manor, Present Day)

Throne of Souls now complete only a few hours after starting, Damon looked over to his bedroom for the first time in hours to see Mira gone. She couldn't have gone far. A knock on the other side of the small false anti-chamber sounded like Edgar fidgeting outside.

"Come," Damon didn't like interruptions, often intentionally giving the appearance of being very unapproachable to his staff. Those who worked for him needed to fear him. Fear was useful, but so was trust, and Damon was sparing with that precious commodity.

"Master, Radin is in the spell test room requesting an audience." Edgar Hastings announced, trying to keep himself as small and unremarkable as possible while just inside Damon's secret study. He didn't want to set foot in this place. He disliked being anywhere close to that damnable staff.

Damon hadn't been internally summoned, meaning Radin must have traveled here on his own. *Interesting*, Damon thought, rising from the table to follow his Chief of Staff down to the third floor.

Charles W. McDonald Jr.

Opening the closed doors to his spell test room, Damon found Radin practicing *Damon's Bigger Boom* causing two overlapping hemispheres—one of fire, the other of lightning—to explode violently near the far northwest corner of the room. Damon was impressed with Radin's development, watching the ferocious energy from the twin ten-foot hemispheres get absorbed by the test room wall, ceiling, and floor materials.

Damon didn't flinch when Radin turned to face him with those eyes of Hellish torment flaming inside his worn eye sockets. He'd seen far worse. He'd personally known worse. Still, it was a more than odd juxtaposition to the gold and silver jerkin he wore, matching his finely embroidered grey linen pants. The jerkin displayed some new crest he hadn't seen before, obviously meant to deliver a message in threes.

"You didn't use the seal this time," Damon postured.

"No, I didn't. I hope that's okay." Radin didn't want to step on any unseen, or implied, rules of Damon. That could be dangerous, and he needed Damon. *They* needed Damon.

"Sure. What did you want to see me about?"

"Well," Radin cleared his throat, delivering the hammer, "First, I wanted to know if the reason you've been helping me is because I'm your son?"

Wow!

Damon hadn't been expecting that. Damon knew of course, but he assumed he had some time to deliver that message when the timing was right. If Radin knew, then others would soon know too, and that could complicate matters. It could even be deadly…for Radin.

"Yes." Damon paused after that frank and simplistic reply, contemplating how far he needed to go with this delicate information. "Vosh had good reason to shield you from your lineage. We rarely saw eye to eye, except on that. Our relationship was volatile to put it mildly, but sometimes relationships that are torrential can be fulfilling in an odd way—if only for a short time. They flame out fast—those kinds of relationships." He paused again, letting Radin soak in the facts. "You deserved the love of a real family that would raise you properly. You deserved better parenting than a tumultuous relationship could offer. We simply were not stable enough a couple to do right by you. And, people close to me have a way of getting killed with regularity. The fewer people who know your lineage, the better."

"Mother is dead." It was Radin's first time using that familial title in association with Vosh, but Damon deserved to know if he didn't already.

"Yes, I saw her when I slayed Voltor. Her soul is free now. She's free of torment." Damon considered the ease with which he'd delivered the news of Radin's mother—his former lover. For himself, Damon had lost so many around him, the number of great losses had dulled even the most intimate of senses that should still be sharp and sensitive. Not that Damon lacked sensitivity. He still had it on some levels, but on others it was vacant or at best…sparse.

Nodding acceptingly, Radin took a few steps, closing the distance between himself and Damon 'til they were within arm's reach of each other, looking each other in the eyes. "I need to understand who I am, and that means I need to know who you are—precisely—without secrets. Please." Radin's sincerity blew Damon away. If his excellence at Magic and similarly hard-chiseled features weren't good enough measure that Radin was his stock, his forthright nature alone would have made him question whether or not Radin was truly his.

"Funny you should ask that question. May I quote a close friend of mine in replying to that?" Internally questioning himself about the status he'd so freely assigned to Illirian Starfire. *Is she your friend?*

A single nod from Radin told Damon to continue, "I am Damon of Basrat, The Dark Knight of Magic, Wielder of the *Staff of the Invoker*, God of Eden, Maker and Destroyer of Worlds…" He wanted to stop there, for Radin's sake, but the reply wasn't authentic without it. Illirian was right to include it in his accolades, "…and Author of *Damnation*." The latter had come out softer than the former which had been far more assertive.

"What made you become these things? What, or who, drove you into this?" Radin motioned up and down Damon's body as if to encompass all Damon was, is, and would ever be.

"When you allow yourself to love, you open a doorway to the Abyss. When you trust, you open the door for betrayal. When you need someone there by your side more than anything or anyone, and they're ripped away from you because of the incredibly dangerous circles you run in, you feel like you might as well have killed them by your own hand. The burden of this grief is a crushing knowledge—suffocating and toxic to one's soul. Its abrasions never heal. They are wounds that only fester in the infection of your own guilt." Damon's mouth worked wanting to continue, but he'd said enough. Whether wisdom or warning, he'd delivered his own indictment of how The Dark Knight of Magic came into being.

Looking down, then into his son's eyes, he wasn't finished. "I'm often called a monster. I'll let you decide whether or not that is truth, but I will say that the real monsters among us are the *ones who never loved* and *those incapable of love*. Love is worth staring into the Abyss, Radin. Friendship is worth the risk of

Charles W. McDonald Jr.

betrayal." The loss of Dallia wounded him deeply—blackening a large chunk of his heart in perpetuity. Still, he never once wished he'd been absent her love. Not once. Not for a moment. She'd exposed the very best facets of his being, hewn by the magic of her own soul. Had Morden, Castlin, Adena, Chara, or Xarn ever experienced such a thing? He doubted it. There were so many that fell into that category, and he was grateful, each day, he'd escaped that categorical depravity of monster.

"I don't know what to think about our relationship. Are we family? Are we friends? Are we mortal enemies?"

"Radin, this knowledge is dangerous, and you have to be careful with it. It can get you killed. It can get you far worse than just death. That's the first thing I would recommend. With regard to us, I see nothing has changed really. I mean to exact my revenge upon very powerful forces—far more powerful than you can possibly imagine. I mean to cause a new equilibrium to take root for all times. I mean to—" He had to stop himself. *Compartmentalized information*, he thought. "It's in your best interest and mine to work together for as long as our goals are compatible and complementary."

"Does being your son make me immune to your…revenge?"

"No. You wouldn't be the first of my offspring I've killed." *Was that really true?* He definitely felt responsible for Grace's death, but it was Bakris' hand that had done the deed, and she was better off for it—at least her soul was. Still, if it delivered the truth of the monster he was and is, he'd allow Radin to have that lie as a truth.

"I see." How else was Radin supposed to reply to that chilling fact? How would he reconcile who he was and would be against the backdrop of horror that was Damon's existence? Before coming, he wanted to resume his lessons with Damon, but now…. Would he get dragged into the vortex of Damon's guilt, anguish, and hatred, or could he pull Damon back from the Abyss? They *did* need each other.

"Father, would you tell me what you know about these markings?" Picking up Xaldran's Tome off the test floor, opening to the page with the star map, Radin showed Damon the markings unique to each of the five worlds of Humanity. Specifically pointing to the markings beside the star system marked Setinon, Radin continued, "I've never seen markings like this. They don't look like Arcane to me."

$$†¤‡- {}_{\text{,}}Æ‡:\,\breve{}\ Œ$$

Charles W. McDonald Jr.

"They're location markers for traveling between worlds." It had only taken Damon a mere instant to recognize the familiar markings. Though he briefly considered holding back information that could easily get his son killed, he thought better of it. Radin had specifically asked for no secrets. And, therefore, Damon would try to be as forthcoming as possible—at least where it didn't put the Master Plan at risk.

"But how would I translate that into anything I could use to *Portal*?" Radin wasn't asking the right question, because he didn't understand.

"Not by any means of travel you'd understand. These are location markers for *The World Below and Between*. It's another plane of existence. No one knows who built it or why. It predates me. It predates anyone I know, but if you know where you're going, you can use it to travel between worlds in a very short time without aid of a *Portal*. Useful if you're using it to move armies without the aid of magic, or if you have mages that aren't powerful enough to *Portal* between worlds. However, you can also get lost and spend the rest of your life down there trying to find your way out. Going back the way you came doesn't work there. Kind of like the Halls of Aaramus in that way. The other thing they share in common is suspension of time, because time is a directly-correlated component of spacetime manifold, and space itself is dimensionally altered there, and in the Halls of Aaramus."

"Is it possible Aaramus would have created this other plane?"

"Oh no, I seriously doubt it. That lich is far too self-centered for any of that. *The World Below and Between* I think was created from altruistic intent, but just poorly executed. That's why I don't trust it. You'd do well not to trust it either. Stay out of there. Even *I* might not be able to find you if you ever get lost down there."

Taking another look at the star map and the context provided in the text, Damon asked, "Would you leave this here with me to study? I can share my findings in a few days."

He had something Damon wanted. He needed to seize the moment. "I want Eldrac gone. Permanently. I want you to take care of it for me. For us."

Furrowed brow from Damon at the demands being put upon him—son or not. Still, the Tome was worth studying. "Fine. Consider it done," he confirmed, taking the Tome from Radin.

"There's one more thing," Radin added, eyeing his father as he gauged his response.

"I'm listening."

"Have you ever heard the term, *Eye of Time*?" Watching Damon's reaction

Charles W. McDonald Jr.

carefully, Radin made note of the thin, pressed lips and the calculating look in Damon's eyes.

"Was that term mentioned in here?" Damon raised the Tome again.

"It was."

Immediately, he retracted the Tome, sending it somewhere unspoken with his magic as it was suddenly gone in a flash of silvery-blue light to raised eyebrows from his son. "I'll get back to you on that," Damon offered, keeping his cards closer to the vest than ever.

There were several ways Radin could respond to that. He considered each of them briefly. He could challenge Damon, probing for information he clearly didn't want to—or didn't feel he could—offer. He could guilt or maneuver him into offering a piece of information, but he felt as if Damon had been used a great deal throughout his life and didn't want his father looking at him in that way. Or, he could try to build something with this very unique man. He could try to give him space and try to understand him. That was how he would want to be treated in this scenario, so that would form the framework of his next maneuver with this brilliant man.

Radin wanted to offer Damon a very personal response. "The more I use Dallia's staff, the closer I feel to her. She was…an amazing woman." With that, he opened a *Portal* home, walking through it to leave Damon to his thoughts and to Xaldran's Tome.

Damon's mouth worked, wanting to reply, but the words wouldn't come for him before Radin was through his *Portal*. All this internal anguish and strife…. He needed to kill someone. He needed to take out his frustrations on someone worthy of their weight. Now was as good of a time as any.

Heading back up to the fourth floor, he found Mira sitting in his study, reading a book she shouldn't be able to read. Glowering at her, he went right by her to the bedroom-facing part of the study, where he began putting on his full mage regalia. Picking up the *Staff of the Invoker* with his right hand, holding one of the triple helix rods, Damon proclaimed, "I'll be back. There's a problem that requires my immediate attention." With that, a *Gate* opened in the floor of his study, quickly swallowing Damon. He was gone.

"I don't even get a kiss goodbye," Mira chided to the walls, sitting at the worktable with her book, *The Chronicles and Tales of Damon year 530-650* by *Toren Merch*. Their language wasn't too far removed from Latin—a language she'd spent most of her high school and college years mastering. A look into early Damon was proving to be…enlightening. Dating all the way back to his graduation, yet failing to explain who he was before, it was somewhat frustrating. It failed to explain how

Damon became Damon in the first place. She knew he wasn't born that way. At least she hoped not.

Turning the page to start the next chapter, "*The Conflagration at Castle Burgentine*," she continued her search for more insight into her Love—her Damon—disappointed to read the first paragraph starting with Kellen the Destroyer, The Midnight Morning. She detested that man!

*   *   *   *

(Isle of Romney, Perion, Present Day)

The rubble mostly buried and weathered by the relentless cruelty of time against the landscape of rolling beachside hills, Damon couldn't be certain this was the place, but if Eldrac was still the Eldrac he remembered, he'd be rebuilding his manor on familiar ground. Looking across the small section of the South Sea that separated the main part of the island from a small barrier reef, he could see a great mansion being built atop the rocky basin of the barrier reef island. Everywhere Damon looked he found the result of the Blood Night unleashed by the Scroll of Carnac in the dead forestation, the sea washing up dead sea-life upon the beach, and dead fowl falling from the pale-red sky above. *My son did this.*

No, the Creator did this, he corrected his internal thoughts immediately. The Creator of all things, and the Creator of Injustices had levied this toll of hypocrisy and his spiteful meddling on Humanity. But he wasn't here to make right the Creator's great prophetic atrocities. He was here for Eldrac.

Using a divining window to zoom across the South Sea, he peered into the crew building Eldrac's new manor, searching.

"Looking for me, Damon?" Eldrac had met Damon many times before, but given the knowledge imparted him from she who set him free, he knew why Damon was here and he had the advantage this time….

That came from behind him. In his haste, Damon hadn't put up any of his usual protections. *Too late now.*

Spinning to face Eldrac for the first time in forever, his facial features were the essentially same each time he'd been reborn, or repurposed. No longer the short-cropped, scruffy platinum hair, goatee and mustache, he was more blonde with silver highlights with a very full beard this time. Still lithe and weathered with harsh gold eyes wrapped in fiery hues and deep, grayed eye sockets. No longer in the forest-green robes he used to wear in the past, but instead in black and charcoal silk pants with red seams and a forest-green, long sleeve jerkin, he was still very much recognizable as the Eldrac he once knew. Especially with the hostile sneer of condemnation as he glowered back at Damon.

Casting offense only, Damon simultaneously charged the *Staff of the Invoker* with Zero-Point reaching out thirty miles into the atmosphere while using *Telekinesis* to yank a scroll from inside his silver-runed robes of a Kaleion Archmage.

Before the scroll could land in his hands, a great thunderclap of sound emanated from a conical vortex a short distance out in front of Eldrac between the two, obliterating Damon's hearing and causing his ears to bleed violently at the concussive force.

Nearly letting go of the *Staff of the Invoker*, then gripping it tight to prop himself up, he pulled the scroll off the ground where it had fallen, casting *Mind Blank*. Nothing. Eldrac appeared unaffected—his protections now up and escalating as this was quickly becoming a pitched battle to the death.

Another concussive sonic blast from Eldrac shattered both of Damon's ear drums, causing him to lose his balance, but not before unleashing *Damon's Sonic Blight*. *If Eldrac wanted to use sonic weapons—so be it*. *Sonic Blight* amplified by Zero-Point energy and the *Staff of the Invoker*, unleashed a terrifying sonic boom at ground level, ripping through all of Eldrac's protections in an instant, blasting his body to the other side of the island. Its terrific sonic blast shook the construction of his new manor, as construction workers fell from their high-perched positions on great scaffolds.

The terrain didn't allow for him to see where Eldrac's body landed, and he was deaf now so he couldn't hear where it had landed, but he assumed it was on the rocky, pebble beach on the other side of the island.

Simultaneously pulling another scroll from his robes with his *Telekinesis*, Damon opened a *Portal* to the far side of the island, walking through and casting *Damon's Improved Shield v4* on the other side of the *Portal*, causing a semi-transparent shimmering hemisphere to follow him everywhere just outside the charcoal-blue aura of the *Staff of the Invoker*. Looking around, he didn't see Eldrac, but he was right, he could see blood all over one of the giant rocks forming the rocky beachline on this side of the island.

Suddenly, a massive column of white-hot fiery acid struck down from the sky, hitting his shield, hissing against it; the acid denied penetration, though it stuck to the shield like napalm as it moved with Damon. That had come from up the hillside. Eldrac had already moved back inland. Damon's balance was destroyed; he couldn't run, or really walk all that well either. Opening another *Portal* to where he assumed Eldrac would be, Damon walked through—*Mind Blank* scroll and *Staff of the Invoker* in hand.

Charles W. McDonald Jr.

The other side of his most recent *Portal* brought Damon to a spot about 300 yards inland between a set of rolling hills where he didn't immediately see anything of note. Calling out with his thoughts and hoping there were still living things in the air that could help, a flight of crows overhead began spiraling over the area in the pale-red sky of the Blood Night, searching on Damon's behalf. Seconds later, he witnessed them diving headlong, showing Damon the way. Eldrac was nearly back to the barrier reef side of the island, likely running back to his manor under construction to get something he needed to aid him in combat. Casting *Shockwave*, Damon obliterated what remained of Eldrac's new manor with a massive thermonuclear explosion approximately twenty-five miles from Damon's current location. The concussive force, this close, would have been enough to blow his ears apart. Instead, he leaned into the pending shockwave, watching Eldrac's body being blown backwards, several hundred yards—nearly all the way back to Damon. Between the damage of *Sonic Blight* and *Shockwave*, Eldrac's body bled from wounds over every inch of his body—his silk pants frayed, burned, and singed. Looking as if his chest had imploded, Eldrac barely drew breath on the ground, now only a few feet from Damon.

Finishing him off, Damon cast *Mind Blank*, immediately followed by modality number 4 of *A Throne of Souls*. Damon couldn't hear the thunderclap, but he could see the warping of reality around him as the air shimmered, then heaved, then tore in the space occupied by Eldrac's body, leaving only ash in the shape of Damon's Seal—a center-filled pentangle inside a pentagram inside a pentagon inside a circle. The winds from *Shockwave* blew Eldrac's ash to the four corners of Perion as Damon *Portal'd* home, but not before feeling the very first instantiation of the *Throne of Souls* he'd built for himself, to receive the benefit of his own work. Eldrac's soul now lived inside Damon—circling and passing through Damon's chest again and again and again, like an angry and violent source of power. Never to be reborn again....

Stepping into his secret study, he collapsed before Mira, bleeding all over the floor. He could see Mira attending to his wounds in obvious concern but couldn't hear anything she was saying. He just looked to the ceiling as a smile slowly crossed his lips. He wasn't sure how many he'd killed with *Shockwave*. It was a highly indiscriminate weapon of mass destruction, but had it served its purpose. Eldrac was gone—forever. And..., having wrought all this violent destruction and chaos, Damon was starting to feel like his old self again. Though in the background of his thoughts, his personal *Throne of Souls* was making him feel like an entirely new man.

Charles W. McDonald Jr.

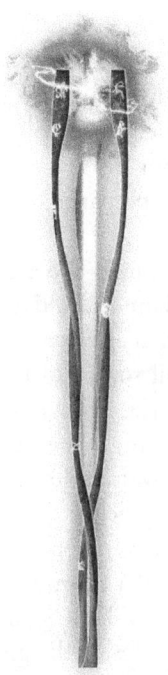

Chapter 25: A Present – Part II

(Damon's Manor, Kaleion, A Long Time Ago)

auldron threatened from a sprawling position on the massive cavern floor in the first of the subterranean levels beneath the bedrock foundation of Damon's manor. It threatened from any position, really, and constantly plotted what it would do to Dallia when, not if, it escaped. Its decayed black scales—each the size of a full-grown man—shone with a matte, gritty finish in the light of the stoked amber coals of Kasrael's forge.

The Titan, Kasrael, continued to work the trio of highly enchanted adamantine-steel ingots into rods as it had for weeks. Working them one at a time, this, the last of the three, was being pushed through a triangular die at the far end of the giant anvil via a large screw that Kasrael turned consistently so as to force the rod through at an even pace. Now with the screw press fully extended, pushing the last rod nearly all the way through the triangular die, Kasrael grabbed the now triangular rod on the other side of the die, pulling it the rest of the way through. He didn't want to quench until he was done shaping it. Right now, it was nearly a ten-cubit-long triangular rod, matching the other two, though without their twisting revolutions, nor their permanent charcoal-blue glow the other two already possessed. This staff was about three's—three triangular rods, twisted in exactly three revolutions each, in a triple helix assembly. Beads of sweat rolled off Kasrael's half-naked mass of a body as he put the last of the three rods into the forge to re-heat it to a perfect hot amber glow, preparing to form the three twisting revolutions it required to mate to the other two.

The soft clap of feminine leather shoes on the bedrock staircase descending into the subterranean cavern proclaimed Dallia's arrival as she tossed back the hood of her sky-blue robes, revealing her half-elven heritage in the form of her beautiful-ly soft pointed ears—the perpetual source of her own insecurities. Her pale-pink lips and song-like voice enthralled Kasrael, while revolting Cauldron.

"How is Kasrael this evening," she cooed, approaching the well-stoked forge, recoiling slightly at the heat wafting from it. She was right on time, and very necessary for the next stages of the process.

Kasrael grunted gutturally in reply, motioning to the third rod now re-heating in the forge, causing Dallia to smile broadly enough to add the light of her beautiful elven features to the dim lighting of the cavern workspace.

Pacing to the work surface beside the great anvil, she picked up the second of the glowing rods, nearly collapsing to the floor with rod in hand due to its hefty and cumbersome nature. "I keep forgetting how heavy each of these are."

Kasrael smiled at her, taking pride in his craftsmanship.

"The enchantment will take away at least seventy percent of the overall weight, so this is good. The heavier it is, the more enchantment it will hold." It was still going to be the most challenging artifact she ever made and would require all of her skills to be in top form when she performed the actual enchantment.

Still, it would take a heft of a man to be able to wield it even with all the weight the enchantment would remove. Damon was going to get a workout with each use of it. *He's going to love it*, she thought, smiling as she set the triangular twisted rod back down on the metal work surface, beside the great anvil. *There's **never** been a staff like this. None that I've seen*, she thought.

Pulling the hot amber triangular rod from the forge, Kasrael set the bot-tom end into a jig form on the floor he would use to hold it in place. Grabbing the top of the rod with a heavy-duty, purpose-built wrench—it was now becoming all too obvious why a Titan was needed for this job—Kasrael began to twist the tempered rod in a counter-clockwise manner.

Casting to further stabilize the rod as soon as Kasrael began twisting, Dal-lia's magic ensured Kasrael's revolutions were perfectly symmetrical, and the triangular rod stayed true during the final shaping process. This was a complex job, and there were lots of things that could go wrong. They'd already had to start over on the first of the rods twice before they got it to twist correctly, so that it would form the proper triple helix configuration.

A satisfied grunt from the Titan, and he pulled the twisted rod out of the jig form footpad. Carrying the mammoth twisted rod over to the oil, he ensured it was pointed due magnetic north as he smoothly lowered it into the quenching oil with a pair of heavy blacksmith tongs. It hissed and popped in the oil, causing the oil to bubble for a moment as he left it submerged, then quickly pulled it after it had soaked the precise amount of time. Checking it with his metal file, another satisfied grunt meant it now had the look of properly hardened, folded, and shaped metal.

It was still quite hot as Dallia took the last of the hardened twisted metal rods into her delicate hands, but, for the first time ever, she could now hold them all together side-by-side-by-side, demonstrating the triple helix configuration for Kasrael as a satisfied smile crossed his weathered face—proud of his finest work yet. "Would you hold this in place for me, Kasrael?"

A grunt and the Titan's massive left hand held the three rods equally spaced wider apart at the top than at the bottom where they all three nearly touched—only two of the three rods glowing with that ominous charcoal-blue hazy aura resulting from Cauldron's breath. A view from above would have made it appear like a great metal cylinder was cleaved into three equal pie shapes at the bottom where all three triangular-shaped rods came together. Pulling a nearly priceless and perfectly spherical fifty-carat iolite gemstone from her pocket, Dallia placed the iolite sphere at the top where the rods were furthest apart, providing just enough space for the magnificent gemstone to rest equidistant from each rod, though never touching. The gemstone, between violet and purplish-blue, was the perfect mate to the charcoal-blue aura of the triple helix rods, and it would serve the purpose of housing the bulk of the enchantments required to hold the staff together since there were no brackets or manner of fastening to physically hold the individual components together.

"That's perfect, Kasrael," Dallia praised, obviously satisfied with the test fit and then pulling out the third rod for Cauldron to do its job. Not trusting the beast to work nicely with Kasrael, she used her magic to suspend the raw, helical rod mid-air before Cauldron, giving the ancient black dragon a look of expectation, causing it to rise ungracefully and ungratefully from the cavern floor.

The first burst from the Dragon's mouth still took Dallia by surprise even though she was expecting it. It surely would have burned Kasrael again, and her for that matter, *if* she hadn't been using magic to suspend the rod before Cauldron at a safe distance. Cauldron was blatantly careless as he provided a wide dispersion of black and fiery hot, tacky acid. It burnished and etched the hardened metal immediately, causing it to hiss violently while suspended mid-air by Dallia's magic. A blast of air from Dallia's magic air-quenched the rod, removing its acidic component while allowing other elements of Cauldron's magical breath to seep and soak their way deep into the hardened metal. Dragons were creatures of magic, so their breath was one of the most coveted things in Creation—especially when it came to creating powerful relics.

A *Light Orb* from Dallia allowed her to examine the acid-etched pitting in the newly twisted helical rod before proceeding. It nearly had that perfect gritty, burnished look she was trying to achieve. Damon was a man of hard, faceted, and gritty edges. She wanted his staff to look and feel like him—to have the depth and beautiful dark luster of his eyes. She wanted it to have the classic manly V-shape of his body—leaner at the bottom, wider at the top. The pitting in the metal represented the wrongs done upon him—incapable of penetrating the impenetrable metal of his soul all the way through. The three helical revolutions of the three triangular rods served not only the purpose of providing more metal for enchantment but also represented the three Damons she knew. The Damon of *hate*. The Damon of *hope*. And the Damon of unconditional adoration. The *Staff of the Invoker* was a complex piece, but no more or less complex than the great man for whom it had been made.

Two more hot breaths from Cauldron, spaced apart for examination purposes, and the newly-twisted rod now held the same permanent charcoal-blue ethereal hue of the first two as it became virtually indestructible. The more heat and other elements applied to it from now on would only make it that much stronger, in perpetuity.

*   *   *   *

Dallia assumed Damon was likely off to meet with Evanyil, but he often left without telling his wife where he was going—with whom, or for how long. It was as if he wasn't married, but she loved Damon the way he was, and she would never change him. Still, it was the perfect time to get this done while he was out and about.

Sitting on the floor in his secluded fourth-floor study, Dallia lifted the three six-and-a-half-cubits tall, twisted helical rods with her magic, floating them towards one another, forming the desired tapered triple helix configuration while simultaneously floating the violet-blue iolite spherical gemstone to the top of what would become the mighty *Staff of the Invoker*. As the rods came close to one another, nearly interlocking with one another at the bottom, their individual charcoal-blue hues became one giant hemisphere of ethereal terror, pulsating with a dark life all its own, as far out in perimeter as it was tall. It was enough to cause Dallia to push herself back on the floor so as not to be within the reach of its intimidating hemispherical aura.

Its black-dragon energy already hissed and popped with a power most promising. Howls of timelines and planes unseen but still nonetheless there cheered and jeered at the moment they already knew most pivotal. 'Twas like a tangential intersection of future's past bifurcating the already wicked hemisphere of terror of what would become Damon's mightiest weapon of *hope*. And chaos.

Blinking and wide-eyed, unsure if she should even attempt making this *thing* more powerful than it already was, Dallia began to clear the mental space in the room for the long series of her enchantments that would make this terrifying thing into a great weapon of her undying love for Damon. It would be the perfect anniversary present for the man who had everything, and he would love it. *He'd better love it!*

Charles W. McDonald Jr.

Part 3: The Fatal Momentum

Charles W. McDonald Jr.

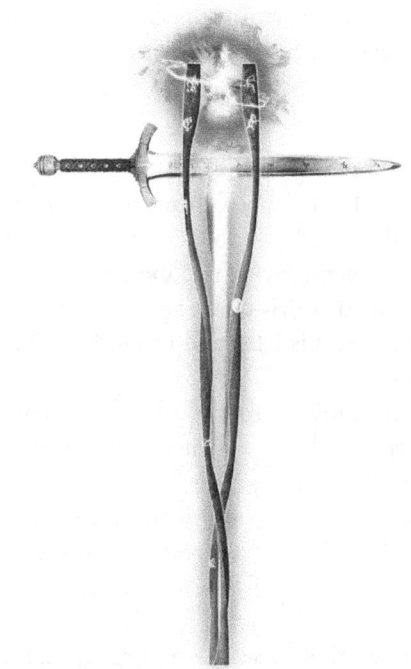

Chapter 26: A Rogue Threat

(Inside the Negi Caverns, Eden, Present Day)

ven though daylight outside, Derik Willis watched Ron's six through the FLIR sight atop his NATO 5.56 M-4 while Ron examined the archives of the indigenous, yet alien, race that lived here before the planet was pulled from its natural orbit. *Pulled by what* was the question that needed the most urgent answering.

Running his hard-labor-hewn fingers over slender, silver disks most closely resembling a thick nickel, Ron Stencowsky estimated hundreds of them lined one side of the angled wall that buried itself deep into the crust of the planet, connecting to dozens of subterranean levels and chambers in the caverns below they didn't want to explore—yet. Whatever this place was, it was relatively close to the point of entry and exit—near the maw of the great cavern—which made it 'safer' for them to explore. Perhaps it was a library, or an archive of some kind, but the highly organized catalog of slender silver disks might hold some badly needed information. Gathering them into a series of plastic containers Ron had brought with

Charles W. McDonald Jr.

them, he Sharpie'd® their location within the catalog system on the outside of the plastic container before placing it securely in a leather satchel at his side, slung over his left shoulder.

The 6'1" broad-shouldered, muscular Eric Striker stood just outside the maw of the cavern which blended itself into one of those great 22.5-degree angled spires with diamond-shaped windows. The yellow-dwarf rays of Damon's Star glistened off the sweat of their trek making ember-like pools on Eric's matte-black skin. Swinging his tactical M-4 around, looking through the sighting with his sharp brown eyes, Eric used his left hand to motion Charles to put some hustle into Ron and Derrick inside.

He didn't like the movement both he and Charles were seeing in the still-budding northeastern tree line of spruce and dogwood. The scent of magic-enhanced pollination everywhere.

These hard-exoskeleton indigenous beings were practically invisible except for the movement of brush and those flashy damn eyes of theirs. In the darkened space between the foliage, he'd already seen their unmistakable eyes. Watching. Observing.

"Tell them to move their asses," Eric urged, maintaining the mental focus it took not to shoot, even though his sense of fear beseeched him otherwise. These things were damned hard to kill, and he didn't want to start something he feared they might not be able to finish. Going out in heavily armed parties of four had helped bring down their casualties, but these things were not friendly, and he hoped Ron was finding a better way to kill them.

"You guys done fucking around in here?" Charles' blatant disrespectful tone never came without warrant. His eyes darted around the room as he swung his illuminated M-4 around, allowing its rail-mounted tactical light to fall directly on Ron.

"Did you see something," Ron asked, motioning for Charles to point his barrel downward, rather than right at him. Charles was a former football player from the University of Oklahoma, not tactically combat trained by the military. He could be a hell-of-a-shot with a long riffle, so Ron tolerated his lack of tactical skills and decorum.

"Yeah, I saw something. I wouldn't bother you if I hadn't seen something. Another pair of those flashy fucking eyes. They're watching us. We need to get the fuck out of here. Like now."

Charles W. McDonald Jr.

"I need a couple more minutes." Ron accelerated his pace, but was just as meticulous as before, cataloging where he found each set of disks. More importantly, he grabbed what he thought was the player. A shimmering metallic object with a glossy sheen shifting from charcoal to midnight-blue to forest-green—just like the metal structure of the building itself—looked to have an opening the exact size of the disks. Mounted inside a console with dozens of other black-box-like components, Ron scooted down underneath the console, taking his pocketknife to the mounting brackets, breaking what he hoped was the player module free. He didn't see a viewing screen anywhere, so that could be problematic when trying to play these archives back, but he didn't have time to sit here and diagnose every fiber-optic cable running to and from the player and the console desk unit.

Turning back to face the exterior, Charles looked for the creepy eyes that had been observing their movements. He heard the module pop out of the console into Ron's hands, causing him to look back, motioning again for them to move their asses.

Player module and a few hundred archives in tow, Ron walked out of the 22.5-degree angled spire building connecting to the Negi Caverns with what looked like transparent color-shifting metal.

Derek walked butt-to-butt backwards out of the building, following Ron out with Charles on point. Whatever Ron had collected, Derek hoped it was worth the risk.

*   *   *   *

It had taken about thirty hours to figure out how to rig the solar power supply to the alien media player, and fortunately it provided its own holographic display, so there was no need to route a monitor to one of the many fiber-optic cables. They were only using two of the twenty cable ends as it was. God only knew what the others were for.

Making out their language had been an exercise in total frustration. Even the short 22B-Grey aliens were having a hard time with it, but their chief scientist sat with Ron and the newly elected president, Abel Tetrien. Abel's common language, most closely resembling Latin, had been relatively easy for Ron to learn—to a degree. He'd had a couple of semesters of Latin in college, but that was a hell-of-a long time ago. The 22B-Greys—forget it. There was no learning that cryptic shit! He let them communicate with him telepathically, while understanding the apprehension of others to do so.

Now watching the fourth archive, of hundreds, the chief scientist's eyes

Charles W. McDonald Jr.

blinked. Ron had never seen its eyes blink, except in terror of being in Damon's presence.

"What do you see?"

Pointing its slender arthritic-looking right index finger into the hologram, the indigenous aliens had marked the object, though he couldn't make out what the markings meant. A black spherical object with a shimmering set of rings all around it like unto a pebble thrown into a pond of still water stared back at them; its rings reflected the position of the stars behind and around it.

BLACK HOLE—the thought shouted into Ron's mind by the chief scientist as it put its hand back at its side. Ron Stencowsky was no damn scientist. He wasn't even a high-IQ guy with a bunch of fancy degrees. He was just a regular dude with a lot of responsibility for keeping people alive on this strange world. And, as the frames of the archive moved forward, it illustrated frame-by-frame the location of the black hole as it moved through the star system. *FUCK ME*, Ron thought, looking to the president.

"Show me where we are in relation to that thing," Ron demanded, looking to the chief scientist, causing it to extend its index finger again. He could barely distinguish any difference between the location of the black hole and where it was pointing right now.

TOO CLOSE—the thought shouted into Ron's mind and Abel's simultaneously. Probably what pulled the planet out of its orbit to begin with. A rogue threat that could kill them all. Damon had put them all downrange with a black hole loaded for bear and aiming right at them.

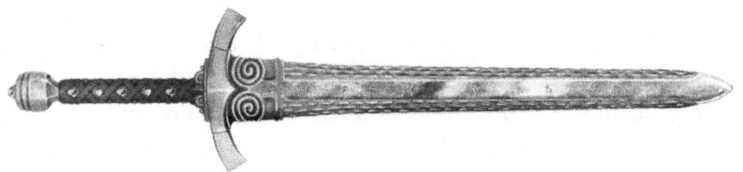

Chapter 27: A Right Proper Faff

(Dover Castle, Earth, Near Future, 6 p.m. Local)

Working outside the castle walls in one of the auxiliary buildings he'd converted to a multi-car garage, King Michael Day rolled on his padded creeper out from underneath his '69 Pontiac TransAm 400CID (Cubic-Inch Displacement) HO (High Output) RAM-AIR induction muscle car, cursing at the main seal he'd been having trouble with since he got the car a month back. He was going to have to pull the engine again and rebuild it—again. More than a bit nasty cold outside, Michael had the garage doors cracked open a bit for fresh air but had the space heaters cranked up inside.

The news played on the 70" SUHDTV mounted in the garage as Michael rolled across the newly treated urethane garage floor, getting up and heading to the large stainless steel worktable beside his Cornwell tool chest. The cobalt blue of the 18-drawer 84" tool chest exactly matched the twin blue racing stripes running the entire top length of the impeccable cream-colored TransAm. A series of valves, floats, jets, dials, gaskets, and screws laid out before him on a urethane mat organized in a fastidious manner as he prepared to rebuild and re-jet the 4BBL 750 CFM, ELECTRIC CHOKE Edelbrock PERFORMER SERIES® carburetor. Looking over all the intricate parts laid out on the clean mat, Michael let out a heavy sigh. *A bit of a faff*, he thought to himself, starting to piece the carburetor together, thinking about the next steps.

Thinking ahead to pulling the stock intake manifold and replacing it with the beautiful new Edelbrock Performer® intake manifold he had sitting on his tool chest, he heard the breaking news over the telly. Picking up the satellite TV remote, he turned up the volume, listening to an agitated reporter bark out the latest atrocities of the new American president in a proper British accent.

Every bathroom break was reported with breathless outrage as the cheap prostitutes of the Deep State tried to convince everyone who'd listen just how dangerous this new president was. It was 100 percent negative news. All the time, and it was wearing thin. Even on him.

Charles W. McDonald Jr.

"Looks like 'the Beast' is preparing to take the new President down the street to the 'White House'," the dark-haired British Ken-doll reported, over-enunciating every single word. "We'll follow the motorcade the entire way, and we're covering every detail of this major event as the new US President returns from his most recent, historic trip to the halls of Congress. We're following reports he's already issued some significant new orders to his military commanders who also attended this meeting with Congressional leaders, and we'll have that report to you as soon as we verify our sources. Stand by for more on that."

Shit, Michael thought, setting the carburetor body back down on the mat. *What have you cocked up now?*

"Your Majesty," Billings addressed Michael from the side entry into the garage, standing in silhouette in the open doorway casing—the sunset behind him casting an amber glow around his slightly portly elder frame.

"I've got a bad feeling," Michael breathed aloud to himself, walking towards Billings. "What did he do?" It wasn't really a question of who or when—only what, where, and impact. The why was irrelevant; he couldn't condone half of the man's rationale—if there was any—though he knew the man's intentions to be right and just. Unfortunately, the road to Hell was paved with good intentions as the saying went. *So true*, he thought ruefully waiting for what he knew would be *bad* news.

"The White House is informing us, out of courtesy, of their intentions."

"Intentions to do what exactly?" *Here it comes*, he thought, bracing himself internally.

"They intend to deploy 'Iron Dome' throughout locations in South Korea and permanently station the USS Abraham Lincoln and USS Gerald R. Ford Carrier Battle Groups off the Korean peninsula."

"Oh," Michael accepted, wiping his brow, "…is that all?" Michael let out a sigh of relief, turning to walk away. That wasn't so bad. The North Koreans would consider that an act of war, but they considered our breathing an act of war too, so *fuck 'em.*

Billings hadn't left, and Michael could still feel his friend's presence lingering in the shop with him as he cleaned and sorted parts.

"He's ordered the USS Ronald Reagan to essentially park itself just off the Chinese man-made island in the South China Sea."

Shit. There it was. He'd been waiting for the other shoe to drop. He started to ask 'why,' but realized the futility of the question upon consideration. "So, I'm guessing he *wants* to provoke a war…?"

Billings just shook his head in resignation. Billings felt the same way too, but what could they do? The American public had spoken and so had their new president.

Michael sighed in frustration, leaning with his hands on his worktable in front of his many carburetor in pieces. Knowing there was something more to this chess game the American president was playing. He'd met the man in person. Felt like he'd come to know the man. Understood his motivations and the rudder of his long-held principles. There was something else going on here and he was certain of it. Either, he was maneuvering pieces for sleight of hand, or to flush something out, or to *act* like he was following the traitorous advice of the Human trafficking, drug running, organized crime syndicate, Deep State CIA whilst really driving a more important operation somewhere else.

Whether brilliant or insane or both, he needed to hear it directly from the horse's mouth and not one of his many traitorous, infiltrated handlers.

The carburetor might have been a *bit* of faff, but this....This was a *right proper faff*, and he needed to get on the phone with the American president to understand what was really going on. These surface maneuvers were something other than what they seemed.

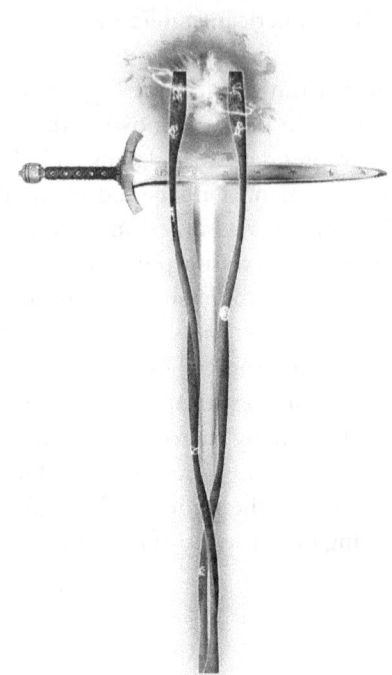

Chapter 28: The Knowledge of Suffering

(Exeter, Perion, Present Day)

Abeautifully showing Elise, radiant in her maternity, graced the doorway to the room she used to share with Radin, knocking on the door casing, holding what looked like a sword or rod in her hands, wrapped in plain, matte-white, linen cloth. The white linen popped against the bright red of her maternity dress. Almost no one dared to wear red anymore with the Blood Night threatening to kill everything on the planet, but with her strawberry-blonde hair, it suited her, and she made anything look beautiful. He missed her.

"Come." Radin patted his bed beside him where he sat up, motioning for her to come sit beside him. "Please."

Setting the item down on its razon sharp tip in the corner of the room beside the doorway, she leaned it against the wall, still cloaked in linen, and walked over to sit beside him. "Talk to me. You've kept almost entirely to yourself since you returned."

Charles W. McDonald Jr.

"I mean—," she began, before Radin cut her off.

"You mean since I was *returned*." He hadn't meant to cut her off, but his thoughts were a jumbled mess—especially around her. After all, there was a significant difference between the two, especially given the circumstances. He could see her recoil as he looked her in the eyes, knowing how evil his own eyes must have appeared to her.

Trying to recover her thoughts from his startling gaze, she began again, "I mean, you've been hurt immensely and maybe there's a way for me to help. Can you tell me about it?" It was the first time she'd ever asked for him to recount any of his suffering. She wanted to allow him time, *but how much time was enough time to recount his torture? Was it even therapeutic to discuss such things?*

"I've stopped trying to lie down to sleep. I only lie down to allow my body to rest, but sleep is impossible. I know that now. I've come to accept it. I use it to my advantage, thinking, planning, using my mind while letting my body rest." While true, it was still very unnatural not to sleep. Deep sleep brought with it healing for the mind—for his consciousness. It allowed brief moments for the consciousness to free itself of the body in natural ways that opened doorways to know and understand things the flesh could not. Especially as a lamean, or mage as Damon's profession would relate, it was vitally important to exercise the mind and to let it rest. *How would this new condition of his affect the future of his development?*

"Okay, tell me about your thoughts then. What have you been thinking in all this time you haven't been able to sleep?"

"I've thought a lot about you. How I've missed you. How you've come here looking for a man that I cannot be. I've thought about how torn you must feel, and how you may feel as if you've betrayed the man you really love."

"I really love you, Radin." Tears welled in her eyes, but his only burned a Hellish flame. That's all they ever did now. It was impossible to read his emotions with those perpetual eyes of Hellfire, but she still loved him. She would never stop loving her Michael either—no matter what. They were different and distinct— Michael and Radin—just as her love for each of them was different and distinct. *Wasn't it possible for one person to love more than one other? And for the love of each of them to be real and true?*

Radin took her hand into his, caressing the back of her hand with his fingertips the way he used to, in order to calm her. She looked beautiful in her motherly glow. *Damon was going to be a Grandfather*, he thought ruefully. *Not funny* was his next thought.

He couldn't say the words back to her. His mouth worked like he was about to say something, but he stopped himself, trying to rationalize what could

Charles W. McDonald Jr.

not be rationalized. Oh, he certainly felt the same way—he just couldn't say it. Seeing what love had done to Damon had changed him deeply. He didn't know if he could ever love after seeing what love had done to Damon. He needed companionship as much as, if not more, than any other man, but she needed her Michael—not him. Baby, or no, just saying you love someone didn't make it a working relationship—even if it were true. That's what his mind had been trying to wrap itself around while unable to sleep. It took a lot more than just love to make a relationship work. Mostly it took heavy doses of investment in time in each other and endless communication. At least that's what his better senses were telling him. He didn't really have the life experience to know that to be true. And he wasn't good at reciprocating either time or communication, yet. *She deserved better.*

"I've been thinking you should go home." There it was, the blunt of it— the blunt of his feelings pushing her as far away from him and as far away from trouble as he could.

Tears began running down her cheeks as Elise acknowledged the truth for the first time since she'd come here, but before she could do as he asked, she needed to be certain.

Walking to Excalibur—the Sword of the First Kings—Elise removed its scabbard of white linen, unveiling it before Radin for the first time.

Radin's eyes widened in recognition. *Had he seen it in one of his many dreams?* Like the moment of déjà vu when your memories of old collide with a memory of tomorrow, seemingly planted by the hand of Creation so that when the thread of that moment happened, one could realize its importance—its awe-inspiring *divine* providence. To recognize the beautiful fluidity of time in its nonlinearity.

It spun around, held suspended in air by Elise's magic as the other-worldly inscription came to bear before him. Suddenly, and for the first time since his return, the pure white landscape before the great still lake of crystal with the booming voice of Creation, flooded his every thought, pushing out everything else. Deafening and all-consuming in its iron grip of Radin's consciousness.

Dazed, Radin nearly fell as his body slipped off the bed. Catching himself before he hit the floor, he was suddenly back in the room with Elise and the magnificent sword that was neither long, nor short—nor heavy, nor light. It was perfection as Elise floated it toward him.

"Would you do me a favor and hold it in your hands? Please..." Elise eked out her request, choked up by her thoughts of Michael and trying to suppress the emotions that threatened to overwhelm her.

There were no words for his reply, but slowly Radin's right hand closed around the hand-and-a-half magnificently burnished grip, feeling its power hum in his hand. It resonated with pure energy as he expertly wielded it—the blade slicing the air with its perfect balance.

Though, Excalibur never gleamed in Radin's grip. It had rejected this master, just the same as it would reject all others.

The tears came like a burst dam, overwhelming Elise as she collapsed to the floor in a heap with the knowledge of her suffering. Michael Anthony Day was forever gone. Her king was gone. His kingdom had been destroyed. Forgotten. Baby or not, Elise wanted to die.

Through the torrent of her own tears, she couldn't see Excalibur had completely healed Radin's eyes, finally bringing his suffering to an abrupt end. Hers was just beginning.

Charles W. McDonald Jr.

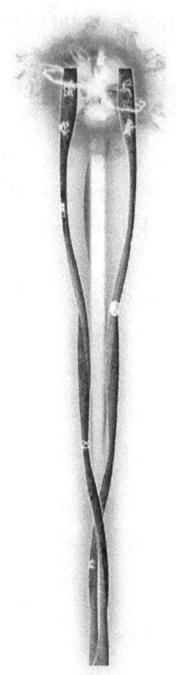

Chapter 29: Banished

(Damon's Manor, Kaleion, Present Day)

After Mira broke the seal summoning Kellen's aid, his *Healing* of Damon had helped, but Damon had not been the same in his recovery. He had been very…fatalistic. Nihilistic. That was the best word to describe it. Kellen mentioned something about being summoned to the 'Council of Mages'—whatever that was, and then Damon's mood just altered immediately, like a light switch. First, he was fine, even happy, then dogshit. She wasn't sure if it was his hearing still bothering him, making him so agitated, or this 'Council of Mages' thing, causing him to be such an…asshole. All Mira knew was, she wanted her old Damon back.

"I don't understand what's going on, Damon…," Mira implored with outstretched hands towards her love. "Tell me what's happening."

Damon answered by getting back into his elegant, full-mage regalia, grabbing the *Staff of the Invoker* angrily, with a look on his face she could only describe as 'pissed.' A *Portal* suddenly appeared inches from Mira's face, displaying a recog-

Charles W. McDonald Jr.

nizable Austin skyline that appeared to be mid-morning, whatever day it was on Earth. Frowning, now *she* was pissed. "You're getting rid of me?" Mira, hands on hips, accosted the Dark Knight of Magic.

"If you'd like to take a book or two with you while you wait for me, that would be acceptable."

'Acceptable?!' Did he really just fucking say that? Mira smoldered in Damon's private study, radiating an aura equally menacing to that of the *Staff of the Invoker*. Well…almost as menacing.

"I'm not asking. I'm telling you. You need to go. I'll come back for you."

Damon was being a terse little turd with her, and he knew it. It had to be intentional. Damon was very deliberate about all his moves. Especially how he treated those around him. Everything was purposeful. He didn't take a shit without a plan. *But why is he being such an ass?* It bothered Mira to no end, *how he could flip on a dime like that…?* She knew he wasn't bipolar.

"Fine…." She put down the book she'd been reading on his chronicles of terror as if *not* reading about him would send him a message. He was stone-faced as she walked through his *Portal*; her Android phone began buzzing with messages as it synced with the local cell tower on the Earth side of the *Portal*.

"I—" Mira was cut off before her intended loving statement instead became, "*Fuck you*," as the *Portal* whooshed to a close, exiling her on planet Earth.

Damon's hearing still wasn't right. He thought he heard Mira say, "Fuck you," but the constant low humming at the base of his eardrums was like a background itch he just couldn't scratch. *Must be*, he thought to himself. It was driving him nuts. He'd have to have that checked, but often *Healing* recreated rather than mended—like new stem cells—organic compounds. It was quite possible the *Healing* made his hearing better than new. Or built new pathways that didn't previously exist. It was also possible *A Throne of* Souls was altering his chemical makeup. Too many new variables in the equation to isolate the root cause. He needed to get it looked at, but he had bigger fish to fry right now, and deep fry them he would. *Council of Mages*, he thought to himself. *Those self-important, self-righteous, pompous, arrogant….*

The Council of Mages was older than Damon and comprised of mages both on and off world, though its rulings only held scope on his homeworld. It had been established for the purpose of education, knowledge sharing, control, mitigation of threats, publication, and, in his case, especially, more than one occasion of banishing his custom spells as well as a level of supposedly hidden archives. It wouldn't be his first time before the Council of Mages, and likely wouldn't be his last either. He knew that as he fully charged the *Staff of the Invoker* to the point it hissed and crackled with energy as he walked through the *Portal* to Sisten.

The great citadel of Sisten sat atop a beautiful green hillside of farmland both in and outside the city walls. A bustling metropolis of trade, education, and political power, it was the perfect place to establish what constituted as law and order for mages. Everything one needed, one could find here. Taking in the green health of the land, he wondered how the damage from Damon's Star hadn't reached this far with its damaging rays, or if the Council of Mages only cared about protecting this little corner of Kaleion.

White and grey stone construction of the citadel's forty-cubit-high wall matched the white and grey stone construction of the Hall of the Council of Mages. Shaped like a great dome with a perimeter colonnade around the outside, with a massive arched entrance preceding the great dome, it reminded Damon of the architecture of the Jefferson Memorial in Washington, D.C. It was, at least, twenty cubits taller than the citadel walls, and perched on the highest part of the hill within the city walls. Meant to be the heart of the city, the Hall of the Council of Mages seemed impervious to the bustling activity going on everywhere else throughout the city. It was quiet and waiting for Damon. That was bad, and he knew it as he approached, beginning to ascend the white and grey marble stairs leading to the massive ash double-door entryway.

Inside, the resonating hiss of the *Staff of the Invoker* quickly became the only sound—as if in a vacuum—as he navigated the few turns toward the rotund auditorium. Guardsman, garbed in the twelve colors of magic, opened the great red-mahogany-stained ash inner doors leading to the great round hall bearing exactly thirteen chairs along a twenty-cubit-tall, rounded perimeter, such that the audience chamber on the floor was dwarfed by the Council of Mages sitting high above, along the perimeter wall leading out to the colonnade. Though not entirely familiar with all of them, he recognized them all. *They* certainly recognized *him* as their eyes immediately went to the still-hissing and crackling *Staff of the Invoker* that should have been respectfully silent here. Damon had come loaded for bear.

Scanning from left to right all the way around the room, he made note of each of the attendees as if cataloging them for future identification. Rary, in red robes, well past middle age, never cared for Damon; he fidgeted and feigned at taking notes while never taking his eyes off Damon. Kellen, of course, sat next to Illirian; both feigned pleasantries with one another while disdaining each other's company. Kesla, a descendant of Evanyil's family tree with her very dark tan and sweaty yet beautiful elven flesh, had known Damon the longest of those not named Kellen or Illirian, but their relationship had been platonic, so he wasn't sure how she would vote. *Perhaps platonic was best in that regard*, he thought to himself.

Charles W. McDonald Jr.

Morgern, in charcoal black and silver robes and of the same school as Damon, had helped Damon on more than one occasion, so that was another vote he hoped he could count on as they exchanged familiar nods and glances with one another. Sijil, the half-elf whom he hadn't seen in years and hadn't expected to see here today, exchanged very familiar glares with Damon, though not as intimate as he had hoped for, given her former-lover status. Vosh's chair was empty, as was Mora's next to hers. He knew what had happened to Vosh personally, but he'd only heard what had happened to Mora. He acknowledged their name placards, but internally wondered how voting in absentia would be counted. The great elf Nigel, in pale yellow robes, was no friend to Damon, frequently trying to conspire against him, so he knew how that vote was going to go down. Acknowledging one another with the briefest of declarative stares, Damon held back a sneer when making eye contact with Nigel. It was enough to make Nigel's pointed ears twitch in anticipation of the vote to come. Raaseth, just as tall as Damon, wearing green robes, appeared much older than the last time Damon had seen him—perhaps middle-aged now. They had worked together in the past, exchanging spells and crafts, but he had no idea which way Raaseth would vote. *A swing vote*, Damon thought to himself. Leaning the *Staff of the Invoker* back away from Raaseth, Damon offered a measured bow, though Raaseth didn't deserve it. Raaseth acknowledged Damon with a half nod of his own. That was ten so far, and the tally was five for, two against, and one swing. *Not good*, he thought to himself, as he carefully examined the final three.

Mirak, the chairman, wearing slightly translucent robes of air, bore the oldest appearance with his graying black hair and hard, weathered looks. Amrys, in color-shifting robes of time, flanked Mirak, and while not quite as old, still appeared twice the age of Damon if not more so. Damon barely bothered acknowledging either of them, knowing their votes already, though he held the *Staff of the Invoker* leaning back away from them to keep his threat level down. Finally, the beautiful Dilys, in her gold robes, similar in stature to Illirian with similar red-gold hair and magnificent blue eyes offered Damon a coy, knowing smile as he offered her a nearly full bow in return. He smiled at her as he met her beautiful and engaging gaze.

"Damon." Mirak addressed him first, of course. "You have been summoned before the Council of Mages yet again for your crimes against Humanity. How do you plea?"

"Perhaps I should hear the charges first. Wouldn't you agree that more just?" Damon cavalierly dangled his future before the Council of Mages, offering a slight bow before their totality.

"You are charged with reckless endangerment of the world, Kaleion, by the creation of Damon's Star. How do you plea?"

"Oh that...." Damon tried not to laugh. This was serious business after all. "Guilty...?" It wasn't really a question, but his tone made it come out that way.

"Court reporter, annotate the defendant acknowledges his guilt for the record, please." With that, an unaccompanied quill began scribbling on parchment in mid-air, obeying Mirak's orders.

Damon didn't like how this was proceeding, leaning the *Staff of the Invoker* forward as it hissed, coming back to life in Damon's hands—its hemispherical aura expanding with the pulse of Damon's hatred. He didn't want to invoke them into action, but Damon frequently used the *Staff of the Invoker* for non-verbal communication. Given the reaction of most of the room backing their chairs away from the three-quarter-circular bench, Damon assumed his message had been both received and understood.

"The defendant is permitted testimonial explanation of his guilt," Mirak stated in formality, peering down his aged and slightly wrinkled nose at Damon.

Damon sighed heavily, thinking on the fly of how he'd relate this to the Council. "It was not my intent to harm anyone with my prototype. What you saw was the result of a *Light Orb* spell scaled up slightly." Coughs from around the room at that statement caused Damon to pause briefly in thought before he continued. "I did take several precautions, including shielding the construction materials of my test room, which had never failed me before that incident, shielding myself, and shielding the entire manor as well. Unfortunately, it was more energy than I had anticipated, and it scaled up far greater than I had estimated. However, it was my first attempt."

"First attempt at what? Where did all this massive energy come from to scale a *Light Orb* so?" Raaseth was dubious and being coy in his phraseology of that question—not so coy as Damon's reply.

"A new energy source that works where living matter, or belief in magic, is *not* required."

A sudden burst of murmuring from around the room save Illirian, Kellen, and Sijil confirmed Damon's suspicions that none present had experimented in this field before. They all knew Damon too well, though they, and Kesla too, eyed Damon suspiciously and expectantly.

"And have you stabilized this new energy source," Raaseth asked knowingly with an expectant expression.

"I have," Damon replied flatly, intentionally offering no details.

"I motion the defendant's sentence be commuted upon his delivery of said new energy source to the Council for further study," Raaseth proposed, looking around the chamber for support.

"I second," Rary dared, looking down upon Damon from on high.

"A motion has been offered and seconded. We will have a vote," Mirak matter-of-factly stated.

"Don't bother. I shan't provide it," Damon coolly rebuked to approving nods from both Illirian and Kellen.

"Very well," Mirak stated, attempting to gather order in *his* Hall. "Damon has offered his plea and his subsequent testimony. Are there testimonies either for or against to offer to the Council?"

Illirian stood immediately, waiting for the chairman to recognize her.

"The Chair recognizes Illirian Starfire, Watcher of the Runes of Fate."

"Thank you, Chairman." Illirian paused in deference to the chairman's position, offering, "Damon is not a threat to Humanity. You fear him because he's grown beyond your power to control him. I know Damon, and he's only a threat to those who would intentionally come against him. Damon has taken in- nocent lives in his past. This is true. Damon's Star killed thousands of innocent lives. That is also true. However, Damon didn't intend to kill with Damon's Star. It was an accident. It was never meant as a weapon, set upon Kaleion. He loves this world. He took precautions to prevent many more deaths, and in any form of experimentation there are risks. Many have killed innocent lives while experiment- ing with magic. Where are they? Why were they not summoned here along with Damon? You summoned him only out of the scale of his experiment and your fear of him. I know Damon has intentionally moved his experimentation off world. Is that not the actions of someone behaving in a more responsible manner? If Da- mon wanted to destroy this world, he could have done it already."

Kellen visibly cringed at Illirian's last statement, looking around the room, taking in the varying reactions—from Raaseth's look of shock to Mirak's look of disgust to Nigel's look of anger. Illirian kicked Kellen while taking her seat, prod- ding him to speak. A heavy sigh escaped Kellen the Destroyer as he rose to offer testimony and character witness for Damon. Public speaking wasn't his thing, but he *owed* Damon, and Kellen paid his debts just the same as Damon.

"The Chair recognizes Kellen the Destroyer."

"Thank you, Chairman." Pausing only briefly, Kellen spoke boldly, "I know Damon to be a man of his word. If he says he will do something, it's as good as done. When the incident happened that made Damon's Star, I came to him, in- stantly that night, to find his manor in ruins. Damon loves that manor. He loves the ground around it, and he loves this world. He never would have caused all that destruction to the things he loved, intentionally so. He gave me his word he would cease experimentation with unknown power sources while operating on our home-world. He agreed it was best to do so, and I absolutely believe he will continue to operate within those self-imposed limitations. He also agreed he would resolve the problem of Damon's Star, and he did. Who else do you think *Dispelled* Damon's Star if not the man standing accused before you now? He's no longer a threat to Humanity. He never really was." He wanted to add something else for the Council—something they needed to hear. "I agree with Illirian though, that Damon is really only a threat to those who come against him. If you vote to punish him, I won't save you from his wrath. Consider yourself duly warned."

Nigel didn't like that, neither did Rary, Raaseth, or Mirak. *Was it possible that Kellen's last statement had turned the tide against him?* That hadn't been Kellen's intent; however, the frowns and furrowed brows across the Hall were getting more intense by the moment as the situation appeared to be escalating beyond Damon's control.

"Anyone else," Mirak asked, again looking down upon Damon from his ivory perch to see his black eyes stoking like amber coals as the *Staff of the Invoker* leaned threateningly toward him, fully charged to the point of crackling and warping the air around Damon all the way to the three-quarter-round circular bench. He didn't know how much energy Damon held at the ready, but he fathomed it might just be more than even he could summon.

Sijil cleared her throat, though did not stand.

"The Chair recognizes Sijil of Charms and Thunder."

Leaning forward in her chair, Sijil testified, "While not familiar with the events that created Damon's Star, or those leading up to it, I am *very* familiar with Damon. Damon has changed over time. He's grown. Some of the best men grow with time. They consider their failings of the past as valuable lessons, never to forget or repeat. They move forward with the knowledge that they can do better. *That* is who Damon is now." A nod of Sijil's head to Damon below as she continued, "However, Damon is not without old flaws and old habits. One of which is to 'slay thine enemy.'" She paused letting that last line sink in, "The Damon I know would revert to old habits if the Council made itself *his* enemy. I will not save you, either, should you vote against Damon. I will not be a part of making Damon *my* enemy, for he is my friend. Even though we are no longer together, I will not come against him. I see no point in that." She felt like more needed to be said, looking around the room, knowing the Council almost as well as she knew Damon. "Damon is not a good man. I don't think he knows how to be. Damon is ruthless, cunning, and immeasurably powerful. Damon is definitely a threat, but not to Humanity. He's a threat to those who place themselves, of their own choosing, in his way. I urge the Council to reconsider their decision to enact *any* form of punishment."

"Thank you, Sijil, but one's power or vengeful capabilities does not make one immune to the law." Mirak nearly cut her off, looking down upon Damon to see his sneer growing more hateful by the moment. "Anyone else, before I call for the vote of Damon's sentences?"

Sentences, plural. That's not good, Damon thought, looking around the room, especially at Raaseth.

"Very well then...." Mirak offered one last look around the room holding his gavel high before dropping it on his bench three times to the thrice wood-on-wood clap that echoed throughout the chamber of Damon's fate. "The question for the roll call vote is, 'Does Damon represent an imminent danger to Humanity on this world?' Yeas or nays only, please."

Looking around the room from Damon's left to his right, Mirak called for the roll, one at a time:

"Rary?"

"Yeah."

"Kellen?"

"Nay."

"Illirian?"

"Nay."

"Kesla?"

"Nay."

"Morgern?"

"Nay."

"Sijil?"

"Nay."

"Nigel?"

"Yeah."

"Raaseth?"

A long pause as Raaseth looked down upon Damon, making direct eye contact with him....

"Raaseth," Mirak prompted again, angrily calling for his vote. "Yeah or nay, Raaseth." Mirak directed his response urgently to the hush quiet of the room. The guardsmen glared between one another, then to Damon, then to the *Staff of the Invoker*, still hissing like a terrifying coiled and angry viper.

A last shared look into Raaseth's cool brown eyes then the fatal word escaped his thin, hard-pressed lips, "Yeah."

Stunned looks shared between Sijil, Kellen, and Illirian as an icy blanket of death crept over the room like a crypt. The rest were just a formality.

"Chairman votes yeah. Amrys?"

"Yeah."

"Dilys?"

"Yeah."

"Very well. The affirmatives have it, by a roll call vote of six to five with two in absentia." Mirak hastily read Damon's sentences. "Damon of Basrat. You are hereby **convicted** of being a threat to Humanity on this world and are hereby BANISHED from this world, henceforth, **never** to return via any mechanism whatsoever for the rest of your natural, or unnatural, life."

Damon's sneer turned to a full-fledged, hate-brimmed glare at Mirak as he turned his icy gaze upon everyone who voted against him, searing the memory of this seminal moment and their face into his mind's eye...*forever*! The Hall was dead quiet. The only thing that could be heard was the resonating hiss and electrical pops of the charged energy held inside the *Staff of the Invoker* and the low guttural growl coming deep from within the bowels of Damon's throat through his hateful gaze.

Mirak slammed his gavel down on the bench, getting Damon's attention away from his locked glare upon Raaseth. "Damon of Basrat!"

Damon replied only with the hateful glower he'd been saving for Raaseth, now directed at the chairman.

Mirak took a moment, thinking how best to enforce the Council's punishment of banishment. Illirian, Kellen, and Sijil were some of the most powerful members of the Council, and yet they feared Damon. A stroke of brilliance made Mirak's face light up with a soft glow as he addressed Damon directly, "Damon, I want you to give me your word that you will never again set foot on Kaleion for the rest of your natural, or unnatural, life. Do I have your **word** on it?"

Damon's sneer turned into a frown as he thought about how he could carefully phrase his reply, "Mirak, Chairman of the Council, I do hereby make you a personal promise that I will never set foot on Kaleion, after gathering my possessions and leaving in accordance with the Council's decision—as long as we *both* shall live."

That garnered thoughtful looks from around the room. One could almost see Mirak reflecting internally on Damon's words and their exactness. It wasn't exactly what Mirak asked for, but it would have to suffice for now. This was precarious at best and he needed to exercise caution in the execution of Damon's sentencing.

"Damon of Basrat, you are hereby stripped of your rank and privilege of a

Charles W. McDonald Jr.

Mage of Kaleion and ordered to surrender your robes and signet rings to the Council, hereby ***immediately***. Henceforth you will be known as *Damon the Banished*—never again *Damon of Basrat* or *Damon of Kaleion* or *an Archmage of Kaleion*. Let the record show it." The mid-air quill writing Damon's sentences into the record obeyed the chairman's will and his gavel stroked the bench again at the last of his verdicts.

Punishments. Plural. Damon thought in a deeply reflective moment. There it was. The last straw. Nearly everything he'd fought for his entire life was here on Kaleion. Dallia was here on Kaleion. Her spirit still roamed here, and he didn't know if she would follow where he would be forced to go. He felt those words in his head from when he was a boy, being unrelentingly whipped by his father, overwhelming him. Unlike so many others who fell victim to their own adrenaline, Damon grew cold and dismembered from his own consciousness in moments of *hate* and rage. His heart rate slowed as the calculus of his revenge consumed his thoughts. His face twisted in an unspeakable anger as this moment of finality drew itself out—as if time itself had slowed to the rate of his own slowed respiration.

"You want my robes?" Damon slammed the *Staff of the Invoker* down on the stone floor of the Hall, cleaving it in two as he delivered *his* sentence upon the Council, "*Come and take them!*"

Recognizing that look in Damon's eyes, Sijil, Kellen, and Illirian were all instantly gone in less than a second, quickly followed by Kesla and Morgern.

Again, he charged the *Staff of the Invoker* with all the Zero-Point he could reach, causing it to hiss and crackle again. Just as he leaned it forward, he witnessed a semi-transparent hemispherical shell slam down upon him, squashing his staff's aura, obeying the downward stroke of Mirak's right index finger as it fell upon Damon—one in sync with the other. Damon panicked, trying to reach the Zero-Point he'd held only an instant before. He sensed the charge still held in the *Staff of the Invoker*, but he knew he couldn't recharge it without any power source. He couldn't feel the energy source from the prayers, Arcane, Zero-Point, nor any of his followers either. Whatever this shield was, he'd never encountered anything like it before. He tried reaching down through the floor, but the shield must have continued underground, completely cutting him off. He had to find a way to pierce the shell. It was his only way. The cunning Mirak had successfully caged him.

He could see the others discussing between themselves but couldn't hear their conversations. They were motioning between themselves and Damon, apparently discussing what to do with him.

The words from a life so very long ago screamed in his thoughts. *FIGHT BACK! FIGHT BACK! NOW!* Reaching down into himself, he felt Eldrac's power within his reach. He still had a chance. Using Eldrac's soul and his fully charged

Staff of the Invoker to amplify his own natural abilities, he formed a transparent spear with his *Telekinesis* atop the *Staff of the Invoker,* shoving the tip of the staff against the semi-transparent, spherical shield around him, feeling the shield crack just a little with that first stroke. Again he hit it…. Hard! Now hearing some of the conversation from outside the shell as those who had noticed Damon's progress gasped, drawing their gaze upon Damon once again. Again he hit it, causing the shield to shatter into jagged-edged pieces of energy that dissolved on the Hall floor.

Nigel immediately began forming what he could only assume was an offensive spell he'd learned from Morden, only to feel his skeletal structure being squeezed to the point of popping as Damon made a pincer motion between his right thumb and index finger causing Nigel to burst into a bloody mist. Instantly drawing everything he could, Damon held each of them tight against their chairs with his amplified *Telekinesis* while simultaneously floating himself up to be at eye-level with them. His *Shield* wasn't as thorough as the one Mirak had just used on him, but he slammed it down on them nonetheless, engulfing them in their seats while he considered what to do with Mirak.

Only a moment later, "I know what I'm going to do with you," Damon hissed at Mirak like a snake—his *black mirrors of the soul* blazing at the chairman. He heard footsteps behind him, causing him to spin around, catching the guardsmen attempting to leave. Suddenly they too found themselves motionless on the broken hall floor, suspended by Damon's unseen hands. "You're going to witness and record everything I do here, and you're going to go tell everyone: every mage, every bard, every steward, every historian, every teacher, and every soothsayer. Or, what you witness me do to him…," Damon tsked and motioned to Mirak, "…will happen to you." The guardsmen wanted to nod in violent agreement but could only acknowledge with the sheer terror in their eyes, wondering what judgment was about to befall Mirak.

As Mirak's body carefully floated down from on high to the broken hall floor below, Damon cast *The Rack*, forming a black ethereal torture rack with a foot housing on one end and a neck housing on the other—in between the two an ethereal table. Everyone watched in horror as Mirak's body was ominously positioned by Damon's *Telekinesis* between the two ends. Both halves of *The Rack* clamped around Mirak's head and feet, closing shut with a smooth click on either end. Using his natural abilities in *Pyrokinesis*, Damon set fire to Mirak, allowing his robes to burn into his skin until the hall was perfumed in the acrid stench of burned flesh and charred wool.

Inside Damon's *Shield*, as *The Rack* began to stretch Mirak's burned body to the crack of joints, cartilage, and bones. Mirak's tormented howls could be heard well outside the colonnade and outside the stained ash double doors, though no one was coming to save him. Damon was just getting started as he kept a close eye on Mirak's condition. He would not allow Mirak to die—not easily so. He'd *Heal* Mirak if necessary, but Mirak's suffering was only beginning.

Slowly, *The Rack* stretched Mirak's fourth-degree charred body as Damon's *Shield* held him cut off from Arcane. One-by-one Damon used his *Telekinesis* to tear off a toe here, a finger there, 'til none remained—blood splattering almost every square millimeter of the transparent shield Damon held around Mirak. He was taking his time as the Council of Mages—or what remained of them—watched in abject horror from on high. Mirak's breathing had slowed dramatically. All his screams, howls, and groans had taken almost everything out of him. Damon knew Mirak wouldn't be able to continue to the next phase of his sentencing. Dispelling his *Shield* around Mirak, Damon briefly approached what remained of Mirak, casting *Healing* as his right hand touched Mirak's chest, causing it to upheave violently while restrained and stretched inside *The Rack*.

"Let's see if we can get to that fancy *Shield* of yours...." Damon trailed off, probing Mirak's tortured mind for the *Shield* used to cage him moments before. "Ah, there we go...." Using some components from *Healing* and others from *Forget*, Damon robbed Mirak's mental images and memories of a spell he knew all too useful.

A sneer from Damon as he looked up at Raaseth, glaring at him as he continued, slamming his *Shield* back down upon Mirak. The new *Shield* was clean and transparent, allowing a full view as Damon's *Telekinesis* tore Mirak's genitalia off, uncleanly so, leaving his still-blackened scrotum attached to his perineum as it dangled beneath his broken body. Slowly, Mirak's entrails were pulled, by unseen hands, from within his body as they began piling in a nasty and putrid coiled heap of filth on the once-hallowed stone hall floor.

"On Earth, they called this the Purification. It was a sentence handed down by English priests to the unrighteous, making them pure to enter Paradise." Damon smiled broadly, proudly continuing his sentencing as he puffed himself full of prideful air. "You're welcome...," Damon proclaimed to a groaning, panting Mirak whose eyes were frozen wide in torment so absolute.

Damon cocked his head, tilted in the curiosity of never having actually seen a Purification ceremony before. The mass of Mirak's entrails, both large and small intestine alike, lay still steaming on the Hall's floor. Mirak wouldn't survive but seconds longer, he estimated. Dispelling his *Shield* over Mirak once again, Damon used Mode 4 of *A Throne of Souls*, causing what remained of Mirak to turn to black ash in the shape of Damon's symbol on the Hall floor as he felt his Throne of Souls accept Mirak's lifeforce—locked away forever. Purified or no, Damon en-

Charles W. McDonald Jr.

sured Mirak would never enter, or see, Heaven—if it even existed at all.

Joined in tandem with Eldrac, Damon would use Mirak's lifeforce to do his own bidding and further his own Master Plan.

Raising himself to the council members' level in order to carry out their sentences, one-by-one Damon used Mode 4 of *A Throne of Souls*, ripping their lifeforces out of their intended fates as they forever became his property—his battery—his energy, to do with as he saw fit. Saving him for last, stopping when he got to Raaseth, who struggled at Damon's *Shield*, trying to break free, Damon asked, "Was your vote worth it?" Damon now looked down at the pile of ash that had been Mirak, awaiting Raaseth's reply.

"You're a monster, Damon. A monster and a menace to Humanity. *Some-one* had to do *something*," Raaseth indicted, realizing it was probably the last thing he'd ever say—that Damon's face would be the last thing he'd ever see.

Leaning in threateningly over Raaseth, Damon pointed his right index finger inches away from Raaseth's curled nose, saying, "No, Raaseth, I'm *your* mon-ster. I'm *your* judgment. You, and people like you, spent my entire life going out of their way to *wrong* me. To *prick* me. To *bleed* me. You could have stopped at banishment and lived, but you had to *insult* me. You had to *defile* me. You had to try your best to *break* me. You had to *make a point of me*." Damon prosecuted Raaseth in a *staccato of hate*, escalating in bitterness with each count in his begrudged indictment.

An instant later, with a stroke of his hand, Raaseth was nothing but ash in his great leather council chair, now in the form of Damon's symbol as Damon quickly accepted Raaseth's immortal soul as his own property in perpetuity.

Damon floated back down to the broken stone floor of the Hall, walking toward the guardsmen as he released them both, again charging the *Staff of the In-voker*, "GET OUT…," he growled at the guardsmen, "…and tell EVERYONE. EVERYONE, YOU HEAR ME?!" They never looked back to acknowledge Damon for fear of a fate far worse than death.

Running out of the stained ash double-doors as fast as their feet would car-ry them, Damon chased their exit out of the Hall of the Council of Mages, casting and causing an ethereal charcoal-blue version of his right hand to scale thousands of times larger than actual size as it formed over the dome of the Hall. Switching the *Staff of the Invoker* from his right hand to his left, Damon raised his right hand, forming a fist as he watched the ethereal hand above the Hall mirror the motion of his right hand. Again and again and again he pulverized the Hall of the Council of Mages into dust, rubble, and ruin with his fist of judgment 'til there was nothing left but the groaning and weeping of those who did not get the chance to escape.

Charles W. McDonald Jr.

"Come and take them...," Damon growled hatefully, walking back the way he entered the citadel as his deep scars pulsated and seethed with the fever of his loathing. The evil charcoal-blue aura from the *Staff of the Invoker* reached out some fifty cubits in front of, and behind, Damon—only a small measure of his malice as the tectonic crust of Kaleion gave way, and split, in his path. Now, far behind Damon, another massive colonnade support column collapsed, shattering in his wake. In the streets, men, women, and children ran from Damon in terror, clearing a path for his **hate**.

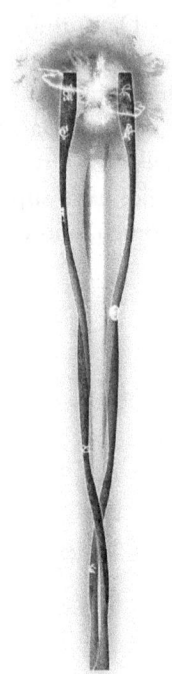

Chapter 30: Damon's Farewell

(New Georgia Hospital, Eden, Present Day)

The prismatic-shaped amber rays of sunset from Damon's yellow dwarf star were just as beautiful here as on Kaleion, though that middle-aged star was more than twice the size. Still, melancholy filled Damon as he checked in with his chief scientist at the still-under-construction research wing of the New Georgia hospital. Clicks from the alien Grey immediately translated in real-time by Damon's *Linguistics* spell.

"The Rogue Black Hole will need to be dealt with soon, and I have the results from the tests we ran on the exoskeleton of the indigenous race we found." Damon took the paper-thin tablet from the alien Grey, looking over the recognized compounds within the exoskeleton and nodding as he scrolled down through them.

"I think I can improve our ammunition to penetrate that," Damon offered flatly to the senior leadership team of Abel, Ron, and the alien Grey they'd come to know as 22. "A 25mm APEX round made of both tungsten and depleted uranium should be able to penetrate this exoskeleton," Damon added.

"Fuck yeah." Ron's military critique may have been explicit, but he liked the way Damon thought sometimes. He was an expeditor—a doer. Ron liked that about Damon while detesting many other of his characteristics.

As much as he wanted to continue the military banter with Ron, it was time for Damon to drop the bomb on them, "I'll be coming to live with you here on Eden." Only a few words, but they instantly caused a sense of panic among leadership, as their breath could be heard and felt in their anxiety of the moment and what it meant to have their god living among them.

"This...," Damon produced a hologram of his manor and surrounding grounds on Kaleion, continuing, "...is *sacred* ground to me. No one will be permitted to build anything within fifty miles of its location. I'll be taking prime ocean-front real estate along the peninsula cliffs to the southwest. No one will be permitted to visit without prior authentication and permission. Ensure all inhabitants understand these rules as I've relayed them to you."

"*No* exceptions," Abel asked, looking at Damon, knowing the man better than Damon thought.

Damon did consider Mira, but he was too furious right now to think straight. He needed time to calm himself. He needed time to reflect. "None. I'll post an exceptions list at some point in time, accessible to the public, but not now."

Ron Stencowsky considered the possibilities of their deity living among them, thinking back to his TV-based knowledge of Egyptian history. That hadn't worked out so well for the Egyptians when Akhenaten took them from a polytheistic society to a monotheistic society, claiming to be their living god among them. Damon was immeasurably powerful and could do great things for them while living among them, but he feared Damon's sphere of influence could doom the newly revived planet that was now their new home. Shining a beacon of notoriety and infamy on their new homeworld didn't bode well for its other inhabitants. Kaleion being the most recent example of that. Responsibility for tens of thousands had changed Ron, causing him to speak up, "You know I am gracious for your saving us. I do wonder about how safe it would be for us living so close to your power and sphere of influence."

Abel, shaking his head in rebuke at the question, calmed himself as Damon put a hand on Ron's shoulder, saying, "That's a fair question, Ron. I'm not in the mood to go into details now, but I promise I will do so soon enough. Suffice it to say, I didn't come here to destroy. I came to defend. And," Damon paused, looking into Ron's eyes, making him entirely uncomfortable. "*You want* my defenses, don't you?"

Charles W. McDonald Jr.

"Yes," Ron lied, looking down and away from Damon's terrifying gaze.

"The people will be overjoyed you're coming to live with us," Abel deflected. "When can we make the announcement," he asked, looking questioningly at Ron.

"Tomorrow morning," Damon pronounced, exiting the secured area of the research facility alone, leaving his senior leadership behind as they looked to one another in shared disbelief. And shared concern.

*   *   *   *

On the southwestern peninsula of the same continent, Damon had a bit more daylight to work with as he took in the pristine ocean panoramic views with the snowcapped mountains marching their way north on the other side of what would become known as Dallia's Bay. Weather had taken root, and the rainfall had been plentiful, as the ground here was as fertile as any he'd seen anywhere. There wasn't an indigenous structure anywhere within sight, so he hoped this would be a suitable place. Given the Blood Night and everything Radin had started there, Perion certainly wasn't an option. He knew Graelon wasn't an option, having been there before. He liked Earth, but it was too limiting to his abilities and would likely dull his strength, and his lifespan. Eden made the most sense to him without going back to his research and finding another suitable world, and that could take time—time he didn't have. Time the Master Plan couldn't afford. Eden was where he'd make his stand, even though this banishment from his homeworld hadn't been part of his Master Plan. He had to adapt, as did the rest of Eden.

Magic was available in plentiful quantities here, and he could foster that. *Yes*, he thought to himself, *banishment might have been a blessing in disguise.* Quickly realizing his betrayal to Dallia's spirit, Damon looked down at his clinched fists, seeing his fingernails cutting into his own flesh as the blood began to run out of the palms of his hands. That word, '*banishment*,' still invoked the blackest of all hates from within. He needed to find a way to calm himself. He needed to right himself. He couldn't make progress on the Master Plan if he was constantly thinking about more wrongs already visited upon him and beyond his control.

Thinking of placement, some five hundred yards from the cliff that dropped down to the ocean below, Damon used *Improved Foresight* to probe the bedrock below, wondering how deep he'd need to go to accommodate Dallia's work below his manor—*four hundred feet perhaps?* Charging the *Staff of the Invoker* with only the energy held within his *Throne of Souls*, Damon amplified his *Telekinesis*, scooping out of the crust of Eden, a massive lump of fertile green grass, dirt, rock, and sediment, moving it in a single object out over the ocean where he lowered it into place, creating a small man-made island just offshore. A gaping crater remained before Damon, ready to receive a home he simply couldn't live without. He had only estimated the dimensions of his manor, but it looked approximate in size— close enough to refine and work with when he would bring his entire estate in tow.

A *Portal* opened to Kaleion as he quickly walked through to his foyer on the other side. "Edgar," Damon summoned, looking around seeing an empty and desolate manor before him.

A moment later, his chief of staff ascended the stairs out of the butler's kitchen. "Sir, my apologies for the delay." His weary eyes looking this way and that, trying not to directly connect to Damon's black pools of hate, and his damning gaze.

"Where is everyone," Damon growled.

"Quit, sir." Again looking down at his own shoes to keep Damon's gaze tangential and peripheral to his own vision.

"Excuse me?!" Too many problems. Too much hate roiling inside him. He was about to blow a gasket and he knew it. *Think Damon! Count to twenty and think.*

"Word of what happened in Sisten spread here, and they all quit... Fled, rather." Edgar's eyes darted this way and that—anything to prevent himself from connecting with Damon's gaze.

Damon looked down at his hands, seeing the blood flowing from his clinched fists, again cutting into the palms of his hands.

Edgar Hastings's eyes ran to Damon's clinched fists, saying, "I didn't think you'd want me to execute them all. Was I wrong in that assumption?"

"No," Damon admitted, thinking aloud. "I was going to ask you to empty the manor of personnel, but it appears that might not be necessary."

"I'm the only one left, sir. Would you mind my asking why you want to evacuate the building?"

"I'm going to move the entire estate, grounds and all. As one unit...."

Edgar's eyes briefly popped at that, but then he considered the reasonable nature of it and the known power of the man standing before him, "Of course, sir. Would you like me to leave the building then?" Edgar thought a moment, about the Human moment before him, offering, "Where are *we* going, sir?"

Opening a *Portal* to the crater awaiting them on Eden, Damon showed Edgar the landscape and vistas of their new home.

"Why, it's magnificent, sir. Far more beautiful than here. I should be delighted to continue my service for you there. If you'll have me?"

Charles W. McDonald Jr.

Damon's hand rested on Edgar's shoulder, "I wouldn't want anyone else running *our* estate, but you. I'll introduce you to President Abel, and he'll help you build a new staff. He's from Kaleion, actually, so you two should be able to work well together and he speaks our common tongue." Damon thought for a moment, looking around one last time outside the windows of his estate. Some of the ground would look familiar, because he'd take it with him, but the sky would not. This was the last time he'd ever lay eyes on Kaleion. "Go ahead Edgar and wait for me on the other side. I'll be along, estate in tow."

Edgar obeyed without question, never looking back, and rather excited about the new and magnificent alien world that lay before him as he heard the *Portal* whoosh closed behind him, exiling him on Eden.

Remembering Hadron, the Gold he'd left in the first subterranean sublevel of his manor, Damon walked outside, using his *Telekinesis* to excavate an exit for Hadron to escape. A moment later the great Gold creature of Durial's magic burst into the sky, free, as it looked back at Damon only briefly before disappearing into the western sky and blending into the dusky shades of the Kaleion star.

His manor now completely evacuated, Damon focused, drawing everything he could. This would be a multi-step process requiring more energy than he'd ever held before. Moving people across worlds was one thing, but this....This was something entirely different.

"Don't go yet, Damon." The soft and familiar feminine voice of Illirian called to him through puffy white, low-hung clouds, though he couldn't see her.

Looking around for her in every direction, Damon wanted the familiarity of their relationship for a brief moment.

"Don't go yet. Sit down in the grass. Listen to the wind whisper through the trees."

It was an odd request from Illirian carried on the winds of Kaleion, but meddling or not, she knew him best, so he did as she asked, sitting down a few hundred yards in front of his estate, onto the crisp grass not yet fully recovered from Damon's Star. The gentle winds of Kaleion flowed through Damon's shoulder-length raven hair as rays of his home star pierced the clouds, falling upon his face in ocher veils of pollen.

"Don't let go of this moment, Damon," Illirian whispered to him on the winds that caressed his weary face. "Let it sink in and remember. This is home."

Lifetimes upon lifetimes cascaded inward upon Damon in his thoughts as the memories of all his past adventures, past loves, past friends all called to him over the great chasm of time. Choosing to remember the good, *that* was what he wanted to take with him. That was Illirian's intent.

Charles W. McDonald Jr.

One after the other, the memories came to him. Memories of his first kiss with Dallia upon a picnic blanket on the hill a few hundred yards behind him and receiving the *Staff of the Invoker* on that same blanket, on that same hill, a little over a year later as husband and wife on their anniversary, tugged at Damon to stay. The memory of his first spell to the eastern horizon toward Basrat and of his first meeting both Dallia and Mira at the college, where he had taught not far away, called for him to make peace. The memory of meeting Kellen, Goldenbow, and Illirian for the first time, on these very grounds, beckoned the realization of Damon's farewell.

The lump forming in Damon's throat, a recognition of the anguish of the reality and finality of this moment, was quickly quashed by Damon's determination not to be beaten or defined by this moment. He'd already been defined by a crushing moment of hate so very long ago at the hands of his father. His hatred and subsequent revenge of Chara had further shaped him, solidifying the path upon which he now found himself. Damon was done letting powerful events shape him and his path—however emotive they might be. *He* would do the shaping now—in his own image if necessary.

Each of the memories seared into his mind; recording them for posterity, Damon rose to complete the task at hand.

"Thank you, Illirian…," he offered to the wind, "…for making me take pause."

Appearing only in ethereal form, she kissed him remotely, using only the air around Damon to briefly form her corporeal body. "Do what you must…," Illirian's form intoned, warning, "…and hold no regrets from this moment of necessity. You are more than Kaleion. You are more than the sum of beautiful memories compiled here. Take them with you and let them make you stronger."

A long pause from Damon, filling his lungs with the familiar air of his homeworld. His *black mirrors of the soul* glistened in the light of *his* sun with the weight of *his* heart. "I will," Damon breathed aloud to the winds, to the sunset, to the moons, and to the magnificent horizon of Kaleion for the last time. No anger, nor hatred, crossed Damon's face, only a look of finality and commitment, quickly followed by a look of inner peace. The constant humming in his regenerated hearing from the *Throne of Souls* within grew silent as the new path before Damon smoothly clicked into place in his Master Plan.

He wondered if he could still be the same Damon without Kaleion. Damon of Basrat was his first, real identity. His identity was so intertwined with being one of the most powerful Archmages from Kaleion. Now he was Damon the Banished. Perhaps he could be an even better instantiation of himself now—without Kaleion. If he could learn to leave with a proper farewell. If he could learn to leave without allowing the weight of this moment to crush him.

You're entirely too sentimental, he cursed himself internally, looking to where Dallia's grave marked a permanent memorial on his estate. If he was going to say goodbye to Kaleion, he needed to learn how to say goodbye to Dallia. Dallia belonged here. He didn't have the heart or the strength to disturb her. He had to learn to say goodbye to her....

A final look back to the west, to the physical cave entrance of *The World Below and Between* where he'd first met Evanyil so many centuries ago, made him wonder if he had the constitution to carry the weight of all these memories with him—whether for posterity, for sentiment, or for the cherished fondness he felt for all these companions. Some of them had found a way to move beyond Kaleion and build new lives elsewhere. *Why was his own farewell so personally gut-wrenching?* He didn't believe in reincarnation, but everywhere he walked on these grounds he felt Dallia. He didn't know what to believe. There was evidence of so many possibilities in the *architype of Creation*. He wondered if the reason this was so torturous for him was because it was more than just his farewell to Kaleion. It was Kaleion's farewell to him. It was *Dallia's farewell* to him.

Charles W. McDonald Jr.

Chapter 31: The World Below and Between

(The World Below and Between, Time Neutral)

Mora felt the power of the life source of Arcane flowing through her veins as powerfully here as any other world she'd ever visited. It was definitely there, at the edge of her mind's eye, ready to be tapped. She'd heard both Damon and Eldrac speak of this place, but never thought to find herself here, nor did she have reason to come here on her own. It felt like a month, maybe more, since Talemar had sent her here, and she hoped to find a way out soon, but her magic, however powerful, had failed in getting her out thus far. In fact, it had been so long since she'd studied or properly rested, she felt her once-great skills waning and spiraling toward oblivion—powerful and available sources of energy or not.

Even now, as she walked among the massive stalactites dripping from the roof of an immeasurable cavern, avoiding the stalagmites built up upon the cavern floor as she found her footing to the next road ahead. *Another fork in the road*, she thought. This newest fork brought her a three-way choice. There was no map. No insight. No possible way of knowing her way around. Only yesterday had she left a small village of underworldlings, trying to buy her way out of here with all that she had left—her body. Nothing. There was no hope for her, except her own wit and skill. She'd have to find her own way out.

Wearing only a small patch of cloth across her breasts and waist that she formed from a dried mushroom head, she longed for a good pair of shoes, as her feet were ripe with rot. So much of this place was dank, dark, and inhospitable.

Charles W. McDonald Jr.

Worse, she knew she was being followed. For how long, she couldn't say, but Mora trusted her senses, and they screamed at her every waking moment, like eyes in the back of her head—warning.

    Left, she thought. *I'll take the left fork this time.* The last two forks she'd taken right, and she didn't want to find herself walking in circles down here. She began to question her instincts and her choice in the fork, thinking the right looked more hospitably lit.   Just as her feet made her decision for her, jutting left at the last moment, she heard a hiss from behind. Pivoting immediately, she saw nothing. *I'll take that as a good sign*, she thought ruefully. *If you wanted me to stay and didn't like my choice, then I must be onto something.*

*   *   *   *

    Some hours later, though she had no real sense of time here without the sun or moons to guide her way, Mora came upon another small hamlet, though this one appeared distinct from the outset. She didn't recognize the language on what she had been told, by one of the underworldlings kind enough to speak to her, were directional markers—if he hadn't been lying to her. She'd seen markers like these before but hadn't been able to establish their meanings. The markers were not helpful if you didn't have the map to go with them, and she barely had cloth on her body, let alone traveling gear, or a map. *That would have been entirely too useful*, she caustically considered.

    All manner of ilk greeted Mora as she made her way through the filthy huts of displaced Humanoids. Mostly trolls and cave elves here, wherever *here* was, eyed Mora wantonly as the small patch of cloth she bore as clothing clung to her beautiful, sweaty figure. Not having eaten well since being sent here, had made her body far more lithe and lean than she was used to, but she still had some of her curves and tried very hard not to flaunt them as she walked among the under-worldlings, speaking in languages she'd never heard before. Passing a table of trolls devouring some manner of cooked rabbit, Mora's stomach growled aloud. She was starving, but she'd rather not make a deal with trolls, especially if she couldn't com-municate accurately with them. As bad as the cave elves were, trolls were worse.

    Walking past the signpost, with the arrow pointing out toward the far end of the village, Mora made note of the strange symbols she'd seen in a different or-der at previous villages:

✝¤‡-ˌÆ‡:˘Œ

Charles W. McDonald Jr.

Walking through the open doorway of the straw and mossy hut, Mora was shocked to find the first Human she'd seen since being banished here: a young man, not so tall as Damon yet taller than Eldrac, with long auburn hair and steel-blue eyes. He couldn't have been much older than his early twenties, dressed in a regal cream and grey jerkin made of fine linen she thought might have been Elian, bearing a great crest. The center foreground was beset with the scales of justice flanked by amber rays of light originating from a sounded trumpet on the left and on the right a king's open-air court on the shores of the ocean—hearing two of his vassals on bended knee. Blistering beams of dawn's light on the horizon piercing a starry night sky formed the background. Not a crest she was familiar with, but he obviously had both wealth and power, making her wonder what he was doing down here.

His charcoal-grey pants provided perfect contrast to his perfectly tan skin, and the cream and grey jerkin in combination with his beautiful eyes provided just the pop of color she found attractive in a man. *Was he her ticket out of here?*

Approaching his table, he was apparently in the middle of a conversation with a magnificently beautiful dark cave-elf dressed in a matte-sheen black body-suit with ties up the front and the most amazing and surreal violet eyes she'd ever seen. With platinum-blonde hair spilling down her back in braided waves, she was beautiful—for a cave elf.

What could they be doing down here? Mora didn't want to interrupt, but they had food and they had means. She didn't have much of a choice. *How should I approach this?*

In her best Perion common tongue, Mora proposed, "Can you understand me?"

"Of course," the handsome, young man replied instantly. His cave-elf companion—if that's what she was to him—appeared irritated, looking down at Mora's feet. "What can we do for you? You look...hungry," he surmised with his eyes following the cave-elf's, to her sore and rotted feet.

"Oh, fine sir. You have no idea. Would it bother you if I ate with you?"

"Sit." The young man offered Mora a seat beside him, opposite the dark cave-elf becoming more irritated by her presence by the moment. "Evanyil," the man confidently snapped his fingers at her, drawing her intense violet gaze upon him, and away from her. Mora was grateful...for both the food and the inclusion as she devoured the smoked rabbit, or whatever it was, before her.

"I'm just saying that Damon didn't mention that being part of the plan, and if he had, I would have said, 'no,'" Evanyil picked up their conversation where they'd left off at Mora's interruption, eyeing Mora's animalistic appetite with an indignant smirk.

"If I had to answer for every action Damon hadn't openly declared, I wouldn't have time for anything else," the handsome, young man retorted, this time the name tickling Mora's recognition as she safe-swallowed a large chunk of rabbit in starvation.

"Damon, what about him?" Mora's second interruption hadn't been received any better from Evanyil than her first, as Evanyil eyed Mora threateningly. *What is it with her? I'm just trying to get some food in my stomach!*

"I'm sorry…." The beautiful, young man turned to Mora. "How do you know Damon of Basrat?" Maybe beautiful wasn't the right word for him, but Mora loved his chiseled features and *those eyes!*

Wiping her hands clean with the white linen napkin beside her, Mora offered her hand to the young man, "I'm Mora. I've met Damon before once with Eldrac." The last met with a raised eyebrow from the young man.

He needed to approach this carefully, even though he far surpassed Eldrac's abilities now, and Eldrac was no more.

"I'm Radin. What was your relationship to Eldrac?"

"Wasn't really a relationship. I was more his property and confidante than anything else," Mora explained, tearing off a piece of bread.

A mocking cough from Evanyil at the last from Mora, provoking a nasty stare of her own right back at Evanyil. *Seriously, what is her problem?*

"Well, then, I hope it won't hurt your feelings to know that Eldrac is gone," Radin informed, gauging her response carefully. He barely remembered his life before Damon, but vaguely recalled being a more trusting sort when his life revolved around Rowarc—a man he never had reason to doubt was his father. *Was he always so suspicious or was that the result of working so closely with Damon for the last couple of years? Or, was it the mission for which he'd been training—his very reason for being here?*

"Gone where," Mora asked with both curiosity and delight in her eyes.

"Gone—never to return—gone," Evanyil answered, this time with a smirk on her face as she exchanged knowing looks with Radin.

"How? Who?" Mora wanted details and these people had them. *How long have I been down here?*

"Damon….," Radin replied flatly, raising an eyebrow at Evanyil as if testing Mora's response at that.

"Wait! Damon *killed* Eldrac? Why?"

"Well, not *killed* exactly…but *permanently destroyed* for certain." Evanyil almost giggled in her reply, tickling her fingertips together left against the right in a prayer-like motion above the table.

Charles W. McDonald Jr.

Mora sat silently, chewing on her bread, contemplating. Damon *destroyed* Eldrac! *WOW! I must have been down here a long time!*

Radin had a good sense of people, and Mora had prompted his inner threat senses to sound off, but he wasn't sure of the right thing to do with her. Still, Evanyil *detested* her, and that meant she couldn't be all that bad. "What say we get you out of here," Radin suggested to Mora, smiling.

Practically leaping into his lap and arms, Mora kissed Radin's cheek, daring Evanyil's scowl as she glared back at the beautiful cave-elf from her position under Radin's chin.

Suddenly, the largest black spider Mora had ever seen crawled up onto the table, eyeing Mora threateningly, quickly flanked by another of equal size on the opposite side of the table.

"HEY," Radin warned, confidently snapping his fingers at Evanyil demandingly, as if ordering her. "Enough of that!"

Evanyil's scowl traversed from Mora to Radin as her familiars disappeared below the table. Mora wasn't sure whether or not to be grateful now that they operated outside of her line of sight. She preferred those monster spiders being where she could see them.

Casting *Healing* on Mora's festering feet, Radin offered his hand in helping her up. "That should feel better. I think you should be able to walk easier now, but we better get you to a place where we can get you some new clothes." He smiled, trying not to let his nose turn up at her smell. He wasn't sure how much time had passed since she'd bathed, and surely, she'd grown nose-blind to her own foul stench, but he could see the beautiful woman she once was and could be again.

"You're just like your father...," Evanyil mocked Radin with a cheeky and knowing smile, eyeing his saving of Mora suspiciously, pondering his ulterior motives, for Damon surely would have had one—if not many.

"What did she mean by that," Mora asked, walking away from the table with Radin, arm in arm whilst still chewing on some bread she'd taken with her.

"Don't worry about it. Nothing really." Radin smirked knowingly, admiring Mora's shapely figure, thinking how nicely she'd clean up. "She's crazy. Don't pay attention to her." Radin made a twirling motion with his right index finger pointed toward his ear cavity.

Leaning against Radin's shoulder as they walked, Mora felt safe for the first time in forever, since long before Eldrac—since before Damon, though the fact they knew Damon bothered her. Mora never knew what to think of Damon. He always did what he said, and that was what worried her about him! However, there were certainly worse people to be around...like Eldrac—or Anna—or Cas-tlin! Thinking about those three and the circles they ran in, she looked at Evany-il anew.... There was something tremendously off about Evanyil as she glared knowingly back at Mora, Evanyil's eyes piercing straight into her and through her. Evanyil had the look of knowing something she wasn't about to share. A look of pending chaos. And doom.

*   *   *   *

Walking past the few huts that remained of the small village, Mora and Radin encountered a couple more post markers: one pointed further out to another cavern tunnel, the other pointing back whence they came. Seeing those same sym-bols, though in different orders, she wondered what they meant as they entered the tunnel of what she hoped was the way out.

Avoiding the tunnel's stalagmites as they still walked side by side, Mora noticed the tunnel make a large downward dip in elevation, then a large sloping rise. Coming over the rise, what she saw caused her to halt immediately in her tracks, tugging at Radin's arms.

(Setinon, Near Future)

As far as Mora could see were buildings like nothing she'd ever seen before, jutting out of the ground in magnificent and highly artistic, fluidic metal designs. Brilliant lights of every color imaginable lit up the skyline in magic-like imagery that went all the way to the horizon and beyond. Radin had to practically drag her out of the cavern tunnel as she shrugged almost instinctively, trying to avoid the floating carriages whizzing past her head, flying through the air in perfect order and harmony, as if bound on unseen pathways.

"Welcome to Setinon," Radin proclaimed, motioning to the city of metal, glass, and technology eons beyond that of Perion, Kaleion, Earth, or even Eden. Phase IV of the Master Plan was about to begin.

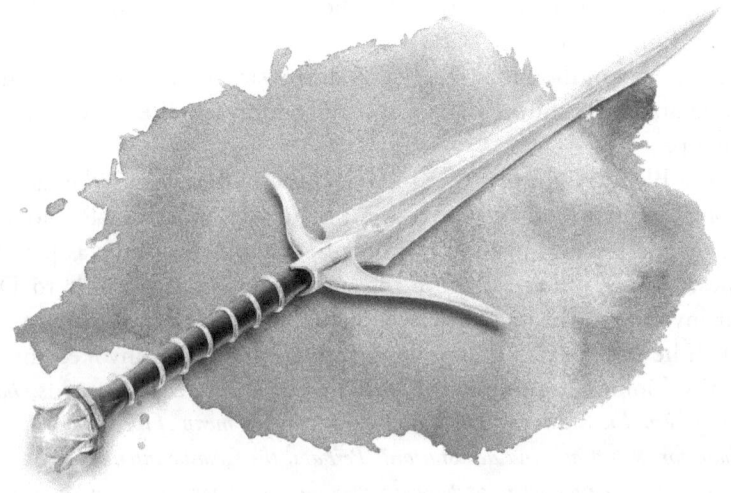

Chapter 32: Filling the Void

(Exeter, Perion, Present Day)

owarc and Ykstherin had come to carry Elise away from Radin's suite. She was a total wreck, and Radin understood her suffering, almost better than anyone else could. Elise wanted to die and Radin knew that feeling all too well.

"Sir," the welcome distraction of Lord and General Brigance Fireheart's throaty voice of the hulk in the doorway of his suite brought Radin out of his trance. Brigance smiled while making eye contact with Radin. "I see you're feeling much better."

"I am," Radin realized. He *did* feel like a new man, charged with an energy he couldn't begin to describe. Whatever it was, it resonated through him like a fluidic current—not entirely unlike the root of Arcane itself.

"Am I interrupting anything?" Brigance could see the fire of Radin's soul returned to his eyes rather than those flames of hate he once recently bore.

"Hard to explain. I need to walk and clear my head. And, I need to find Talemar." Radin started for the doorway, putting on a crimson red cloak that fastened to his embossed shoulder plates that bore their new crest. Brigance cleared the door casing for him to walk past, quickly following in pursuit.

"Troop count is up another three thousand. Treasury is keeping pace.

Charles W. McDonald Jr.

Barely," Brigance offered, showing Radin the latest numbers from his leather folio he took with him everywhere.

"And what of the Blood Night?" A downward look from Radin, along with his fidgeting about his chin, spoke of how uncomfortable the topic was for him to even bring up.

"The Blood Night is taking its toll. Even with magic, we're having a hard time keeping enough food in production just to feed ourselves, let alone the surrounding general public." It was a hard truth—people would die as part of this... End Times. Radin didn't attribute the viciousness of the scrolls to Damon— only their invoking. The viciousness he had a hard time attributing to anyone— even though he felt the Creator speaking through him as he invoked the Creator's words. Still, looking around at the outcome of the Creator's words, *had all this suffering truly been The Creator's intent? If so, what did that mean of the Creator? What reason could he have for such death and devastation? Perhaps, the Creator intended to punish the vile and guilty, cleansing the planet to prepare the way for a brighter tomorrow—though it seemed such an indescriminent manner of cleansing, punishing the guilt-ridden and innocent alike. Perhaps, it was the Creator's intent to make The End Times so awful that no one would ever invoke the End Times out of the arrogance of thinking they were 'The One.' But hadn't he done so himself? Out of his own guile?* Or perhaps, he was 'The One' and he was just doing what he was fated to do. Or, he was just one of a great many playing his part in a whole only the Creator could see. There were so many unanswered questions and possibilities.

He wasn't the Creator and could only fathom at the wisdom on display in the pale-red sky of hate that had darkened their once-beautiful world. He'd come to accept it. There was little choice. People would die either way, but with Damon's plan, *perhaps* there would be a brighter tomorrow—if there was a tomorrow. Seeing Eden had totally changed his impression of Damon. If Eden was their future, he could accept that, though he wondered how many would survive between now and then, and *why was Damon waiting to save them as he'd saved the others? Was he operating, in some way, out of time?*

He mulled on those possibilities that bothered him almost every waking moment. There were so many questions relating to philosophy, biology, cosmology, religion, physics, and metaphysics he didn't understand. He needed an in-depth conversation with Talemar, Ykstherin, and Damon—altogether—to address the larger forces at play and to light a pathway for them. Their prophecies were wrong. There was no roadmap. And, they badly needed one.

"Sir." Again, Brigance brought Radin out of his own deep, internal contemplation. Radin's thoughts barely felt his own anymore as he walked the halls with his most senior general, wondering when the time for bloodshed would come again. He knew it wouldn't be long. They were preparing for the inevitable, *but when would the inevitable show itself?* That was the other big question that haunted him.

"Sorry," Radin apologized, smiling to offset Brigance's concern. It wasn't working. "Where's Talemar? I haven't seen or heard from him in a while."

"I believe he's in the courtyard, last I checked. He's been working with the archers... Training them."

"What about Royvan Miral? What's the last word we have of him?"

Brigance just shook his head, "I haven't heard from him in months, sir. Last I heard they were getting on a ship heading east."

"East? That's it?"

"That's it, sir. East was all he said."

"Hmmm...," that didn't set well with Radin. Without knowing where Royvan Miral was, it would be hard to know the status of the scrolls without resorting to witchcraft. His face contorted at the thought. Without knowing the status of the search for the Second Seal, he couldn't project any confidence of getting through this mess, or a time for doing so to those following him and Talemar. That was critical to holding his army together. They knew they could get the food and clothing they needed by being part of his army. That had certainly helped in recruitment, but they had to have *something* to believe in, not just someone. And, Royvan Miral had the 'something' they required. *Or would have*—he hoped.

"If you'll permit me to freelance in thought a little, sir."

"Go ahead. You know I trust you, General."

"Well, sir.... I believe Talemar knows more than he's letting on. And, it's not like Talemar to allow such loose ends as what we've seen with Royvan Miral. Yes, I believe Talemar holds trust in Royvan Miral, but I also believe Talemar is not telling us everything he knows." Brigance didn't enjoy leveling that accusation without evidence. That wasn't his style, but neither was holding back a critical gut-feeling either, and usually his gut was right.

"Thank you." Radin smiled at his general. "Is there anything else you require of me?"

"No, sir. Should I tell everyone you're busy and not to disturb?"

"No, that won't be necessary. I'm just going to look for Talemar."

"Very good, sir. I'll leave you to it." Brigance offered, trailing off behind Radin, taking a left and another right, heading toward the War Room.

Heading toward the courtyard, Radin made it roughly twenty steps before being caught in the corridor by the familiar voice of his father—by *Rowarc*. He corrected himself mentally at the thought.

"Radin," Rowarc called after the young man he still took for his son.

"How's Elise," Radin asked, pivoting back to him.

"Sleeping. We gave her something to knock her out."

"I'm on my way to see Talemar. You want to walk with me?"

Rowarc tried settling in beside his son, walking confidently beside him, but not entirely confident in his relationship with the bright and powerful young man that used to be his son. His aura had become bold and assertive—a measure of the budding power inside him.

"Did you want to talk to me about something else before I asked you about Elise?"

"I had something brought from the Inn, a rocking chair I used to rock you to sleep in. I was thinking about having them put it in your suite—if that's okay." Rowarc offered, looking into the steel-blue eyes of his son, so very grateful to see them finally healed from his tortuous experience not long removed. Whether or not Radin was physically healed, he worried about Radin's psyche. Some wounds never healed. No matter the arduous and relentless passing of time.

"Yes, I'd love that. Very much," Radin realized, stopping to place his right hand on Rowarc's shoulder. "Thank you."

"I'm here if you need to talk, Son." There it was. Claiming Radin as his son, whether he was or wasn't. It was the truth—at least in Rowarc's eyes.

"I appreciate that, Dad." Radin could accept, internally at least, calling Rowarc 'Dad,' but not 'Father.' 'Dad' was a familial term of endearment, while 'father' was a term of biology. Damon was Father, so Rowarc could be Dad. Or so Radin's logic rationalized in his own thoughts. It may have seemed a crazy rationalization, but to Radin it helped him make sense of his history and distinguished the necessary boundaries for his life to move forward. "I don't think this is something I can talk about with you." That came out more insulting and exclusive than intended, but it was the truth.

"Then talk about it with Damon, but you need to talk about it." Whether intending it to come out as advice or not, it had that ring to it, as he played back his own words in his head.

"You're right," Radin admitted, knowing he did need to discuss this with Damon sooner than later. Elise's sword had healed him, finally making him feel almost whole again, yet memories of Voltor *still* haunted his every waking moment.

"Do you think you'll be able to sleep now at least?"

"Don't know. I'm not even remotely tired. In fact, I feel like a new man," Radin replied, continuing toward the courtyard.

Charles W. McDonald Jr.

Raised eyebrows from Rowarc at the last, wondering how in the name of the Creator someone could go weeks and months without sleeping, then be *Healed* and not crash right where they stood. It was unknown territory for them, but he'd seen magic do both miraculous and unspeakable things. Somehow, he wasn't sure this quite fell under the realm of magic.

"Maybe you could do something for me?" Radin thought aloud, pausing mid-stride, nearly at the courtyard.

"Anything." Rowarc stood ready, eagerly anticipating his son's request.

"Morale is a delicate thing, especially among thousands of men, many of whom are here only because we have food where others do not." Radin stated the facts knowingly. "I need to know when morale is trending in a dangerous direction and at a dangerous pace. In time to do something about it, and it might not be a bad idea for you to develop a plan to mitigate morale from getting to that point in the first place."

"Consider it done." Rowarc smiled, internally frowning at the thought. Morale wasn't good, and he knew it. The Blood Night wasn't making this an easy task, but he had his role to play, and he was going to help his son in any way possible.

There was more Rowarc wanted to say—perhaps in search of a moment of inspiration in a world teetering in the balance, he could see it in Rowarc's eyes. Radin was still trying to figure out who *he, himself,* was, and he wasn't sure he was the right person to inspire at the moment.

"Thank you, Dad. I'll catch up with you later," Radin assured, turning to walk into the courtyard.

Inside the courtyard, Radin could see a host of new archers, most of whom he didn't recognize, acing the bullseye from over a hundred paces away. Another set of targets, some two or three hundred paces beyond, were set up for some of the more advanced students as Talemar, Michelle, and Iain Longbow managed their development. Seeing Lynn Marshall acing shots at the furthest targets surprised him, to the point of raising an eyebrow. *Wow, what a shot*, he thought as she held her perfect bowman form 'til the arrow pierced the target more than three hundred paces out.

"How long have you been out here working with them," Radin asked, walking up behind a crowned Talemar.

"Weeks," he reported, turning back to watch Lynn.

"She looks like your star pupil," Radin complimented, looking at her downrange damage.

"She is," Talemar replied flatly with a smile, though something looked a

Charles W. McDonald Jr.

little off about that smile of his. It wasn't one of a proud mentor.

"Anything I need to know," Radin asked. It was his first time being able to catch up with Talemar in quite a while, and he still wasn't sure about their relationship. He'd gone out of his way to reduce the tension between them and cooperate for the good of the cause, but Talemar wasn't his first choice of men to take into battle with him, and he felt like Talemar probably knew that.

"The new units are shaping up nicely, and the original units are stronger than when we took them into battle at Axum. I'm working with Brigance on a series of maneuvers to coordinate archers with infantry, and Michelle is working on teaching the best of the men hand-to-hand combat and close-quarter combat. She's building an elite unit for what she calls 'Special Ops.' She's incredibly efficient at killing," Talemar offered flatly, though in a tone unbefitting the serious nature of the compliment.

"I'm not sure who's more efficient at killing—her or Lawna," Radin mockingly coughed into his hand, wondering how he became so cold so quickly—suddenly having to dismiss yet another thought of Voltor permeating the front of his thoughts. "Out of the list Damon provided, I wanted to discuss with you my thoughts on the next target. We don't have the Second Seal, and we'd be better served eliminating the threats on Damon's list while we wait. I also wanted to ask your thoughts on sending Royvan Miral help in his search." Radin wasn't trying to infer anything, but the sheer facts dictated that Royvan Miral was both the linchpin and the bottleneck. If there was anything that could be done to further assure his success, he'd hope Royvan Miral didn't take it as an afront that they'd meddled in sending him help.

"I think sending Royvan Miral help is a great idea. With the Blood Night doing so much damage, the sooner we get through the Seals, the better. I hope…" Talemar paused at the last, scratching his head in contemplating what devastation the remaining Seal's would bring upon them all. "If you want, I'll take care of that for you," Talemar offered, intentionally failing to mention that he'd secretly placed a tether on Royvan Miral to locate him wherever he'd find himself. None of them knew the precise location of the Second Seal, and that would make sending Royvan Miral help very problematic if he hadn't thought ahead. Still, he didn't know if Radin lived or not when he'd made it, and still today didn't know how their relationship might develop. Radin was entirely too close to Damon, and that was plenty enough reason to keep his tether to Royvan Miral a secret. Making Radin come through him for the Seals was safest for everyone, given what they'd already seen. Maybe some private analysis of the Seals by Royvan and himself would be prudent before anyone spoke the words within. Either way, Talemar was carefully building some hedges in protective layers he hoped Radin would understand *if* he discovered them.

"Tell me who's on the list that you're thinking about, and I'll give you my thoughts," Talemar deflected, while Radin had been chewing on his offer to help Royvan Miral.

"Morden, Morvan, and Kirkus were the three I was thinking about. From my research, Castlin is very powerful, but a loner—not the kind to go about amassing threats or building an army. The others…. I don't know any of their agendas, or if their agendas are their own or someone else's and they're just following marching orders. My point being, I think we can come back for Castlin at any time and have nearly the same enemy to deal with. Morden, Morvan, and Kirkus I think are the kind that would be building up their defenses."

"Kirkus for sure…," Talemar agreed, having had personal knowledge of Castlin going back well over a thousand years, though it felt like yesterday to him. "…I've heard of him at least, and he will definitely become a threat to us sooner than later. Morvan, I'm not so sure, but I can find out. I assumed he was dead. Morden, I only know by reputation, and from his reputation you'd be wrong about him. He's very much a solo operator like Castlin, but that's because Morden doesn't need help."

"What are you two talking about," Lynn interrupted, taking Talemar by the arm, romantically cozying up beside him.

"You were great out there," Talemar praised, beaming with pride for her, bending down for her to kiss him on the cheek.

Radin cleared his throat, not to interrupt their affection, but just to reaffirm his presence in front of them. Smiling at them both, Radin offered, "How long have you two…?"

"About a week," Lynn replied for the both of them, smiling between them. It was the first time he'd ever seen Lynn smile, though he hadn't really got to know her while her husband—Ethan—still lived.

Good for him. Radin thought about how long it must have been since Talemar had someone to care about—someone to care for him. *Good for both of them.* They needed each other and there was no substitute for being needed by another. Though it made him miss Elise that much more. *You're being selfish,* Radin admonished himself internally. "Well, I didn't mean to interrupt." Radin looked between them, then focused on Talemar. "Get back to me soon about your decision, and we'll figure out a plan from there. Why don't you bring Brigance, Michelle, and General Palomides with you when you're ready to talk about it?"

"Done," Talemar promised, walking arm in arm with Lynn, escorting her back to the residence quarters of the keep.

"They're a cute couple." Michelle snuck up on Radin, proving once again how lethally silent she could be without even trying.

"What about you? Surely you have someone you care about," Radin probed, never really digging into Michelle's private life 'til now. Though, he often wondered about her and Lawna.

"I like your eyes better like this," Michelle complimented, slinging *Bad Intentions* over her left shoulder as she left him without answering his question.

Radin frowned, left to wonder if Michelle was flirting with him or not. She was such a mystery to him and ordinarily he thought of her as a beloved sister.

Still, he missed Elise!

*   *   *   *

He wasn't sure if Elise had been given enough time to recover, but he didn't want to leave it with her the way circumstances had provided. Giving her door casing a solid knock, he could hear her stirring in the bed. He thought about just opening her door, but he didn't think it was right given the uncertainty of who they were as a couple. Then he heard her faintly from the other side of the door, "Come."

Opening the door and walking inside, he wasn't sure what to expect. Elise was radiant though her eye sockets were still swollen and purple from crying…and stress.

Wearing a delicate off-white robe, she crossed her legs and sat on the edge of her bed facing her dresser on the opposite wall. "What's up," she asked, not really knowing what to expect from the tall, young man who still made her weak with his mere presence. My, how she loved his hair, the way it cascaded around his face…and those chiseled features of his. He was like a much better version of Damon. A good version of Damon, without Damon's harsh characteristics.

"I didn't like how we left things between us," he began, in uncharted territory with her.

"I don't know who or what we are anymore," she confessed, staring down at her bare feet.

"Hey, you can look me in the eyes now you know," he offered, delicately trying to lift her head to look at him with his right hand as he sat beside her.

"Sorry…." This was awkward for her, as she knew it must have been equally awkward for him. Even as she felt their child kicking her from within, she felt completely lost in whatever relationship this now was. "I guess I'm just a little lost."

"You and me both," he breathed aloud, smiling at her as he tried to cut through the tension. "Why don't you tell me about your husband?"

"You sure you want me to talk about this?" Her weary eyes blinked, considering whether she could handle this discussion, let alone him.

"We're not going to get anywhere if we keep hiding things between us."

Radin clearly inheriting some forthright qualities—whether from Rowarc or somewhere else, Elise couldn't say.

"Michael Anthony Day was my whole world," she started even now wondering how much she could safely say. She wasn't sure what Damon did and didn't know, and how information might flow between Radin and Damon. She knew it was possible Damon had interfered with events that led to her husband's death. Without knowing the whole of the puzzle, she had to be careful, given Radin's proximity to Damon and his Master Plan. "I left my children behind to see if it was possible he still lived, even if it was only his lifeforce."

"I see," clarity and comfort being two entirely different things as he was the one now looking down at his feet. "How did that searching for Michael lead to me?"

"A clue here and there, following the path of least resistance. Like water. But there was one *big* clue. I imagine Michelle and Lawna might tell you they found something similar, if not exactly the same thing."

"What's that?"

"A pair of handcuffs."

"Pardon me?"

"It wasn't the handcuffs themselves, but a mention of them. It was something I had seen before when searching for Excalibur."

"You're losing me. What's Excalibur?"

"The sword that *Healed* you. It's thought to have been forged by the Creator himself."

"Oh. Never heard of it."

"It's an Earth legend. A mythos."

"So, I'm still lost, how did Excalibur lead you to the handcuffs and then to me?"

"When I was researching Excalibur, I twice came upon a mentioning of handcuffs being the only thing immune to its power. When I arrived here, I started following some smaller clues that again led me to mentioning of handcuffs immune to the power of Arcane and their indestructibility. And there was something else in those books?"

Charles W. McDonald Jr.

"I'm listening."

"There was an illustration of you."

"WHAT!"

"No name. No location. I had to go town to town, city to city, tracking you down. I used magic and even witchcraft to narrow the possibilities, but eventually I came to Stirling expecting to find you, and instead, you found me first."

"What made you think I was Michael?"

"Do you...see things?"

"I see lots of things.... Help me out here?"

"A great lake of crystal with brilliant shores of diamonds the size of grains of sand with a booming voice from beyond the lake on the far shores..."

The vision came to him like a bolt, causing his body to collapse into Elise. The reality of it, causing his mind to flash back and forth between the room and somewhere else he knew to be just as real.

"Radin? Can you hear me?" Elise snapped her fingers, holding Radin upright.

"How.... How did you know?" The question eked out past his now-labored breathing.

"Michael told me about them one night when I confronted him about it. He'd be walking along just fine, side by side with me, then suddenly lose his balance. I thought it might be a disease or a medical problem. Then I saw similar signs in you. It just made me think.... I guess I was stupid to have hoped for something so crazy."

"You're far from crazy. You might be my best anchor to sanity out of this whole gaggle we have working with us."

"Even if I drive you crazy?"

"Dad said that's what women do."

Punching him in the shoulder, she added, "I don't pretend to know what it means, but it's more than either of us had to go on a few moments ago. So, maybe it's helpful for us both."

"So, if Michael and I are both plagued with these visions, what does that mean?" He thought about it for a second before correcting himself, "If Michael *was*. Sorry."

"It's okay. I still have a hard time believing he's gone, but I've come to terms with it. You mentioned that I should go home. I'm honestly at a loss. I can't bring my children here to this mess with the Blood Night, and I don't want to raise another child without a father. I'm torn. I don't know what to do, except whatever I do, I must do it with *all* of my children. Together."

Charles W. McDonald Jr.

The question remained open and something he wondered if it would find a better, more knowledgeable audience with Damon. Too many questions and not enough answers, but he still tried to balance his Q & A sessions with Damon with a fair balance of value so as not to be the ever-inquisitive pest—even if the pest was Damon's son. Still, there was a much bigger question on his mind that needed an answer from Damon, and it was of paramount importance to his understanding of himself.

Charles W. McDonald Jr.

Chapter 33: Damon's Rift

(Damon's Estate Grounds, Kaleion, Present Day)

A massive and cavernous crater greeted Radin upon his next visit via *Portal* to Damon's manor, or what used to be Damon's manor. "What the...?" Radin muttered to the winds of Kaleion. "Not good," he thought aloud. Radin didn't know exactly how to get to Eden. *How would he get in touch with Damon? More importantly, where did Damon go? And why did he take his entire estate with him?*

Looking around the former estate grounds, his eyes fell upon the headstone of Dallia's grave—undisturbed. *Had Damon left Dallia behind? Why would he do that?*

Searching the crater for signs, he wondered if he could trace where the manor had gone, but before his focus led him to the answer, he found a scroll with a familiar symbol left behind, half-hidden under a rock—its seal unbroken—Damon's symbol in blood-red wax. Taking a deep breath, Radin broke this new seal for the first time. Blackness!

Charles W. McDonald Jr.

(Damon's Manor, Eden, Present Day)

Damon's foyer looked the same, but the view outside certainly didn't. A much more impressive ocean-side view, but without all the trees and vegetation he'd grown accustomed to seeing on Damon's homeworld where the vegetation had thousands of years of growth. Here, it looked both old and simultaneously new, like an ancient world with newfound life and growth. There were trees outside, but some were only budding while others appeared as if they'd been there a dozen or even a hundred years.

"Like the view," Damon asked, walking up from behind. It was apparent that Damon had been doing some work outside, from the soil on his hands and his attire—jeans and plain white T-shirt. *Was Damon gardening?* The idea was both laughable and simultaneously horrifying!

"I'm impressed, Father. I love it."

"You don't have to call me that."

"Would you prefer the Dark Knight of Magic?" Radin quipped, smiling. He knew Damon would prefer that title, but he also knew Damon well enough to occasionally needle him.

"That *is* one of my favorites," Damon strutted toward the massive dining hall, causing the double doors to swing wide open for him with his *Telekinesis*.

"May I ask what precipitated the need for the moving of your entire estate?"

"Your father has earned a *NEW* title!" Damon smiled, motioning around to the greatness of his new dining table, the top made of solid blue-grey granite with fissures of white and opals of red; the massively thick granite top was supported by acid-etched adamantine-steel similar to the *Staff of the Invoker* triple helix rods.

"And what would that be? And what happened to the old formal dining table?"

"Moving sale—everything must go." Damon smiled, taking a seat as some beautiful girl younger than Radin began serving them in an outfit he could barely call a 'uniform.' "I'm now known as 'Damon the Banished,'" Damon proclaimed, flourishing his arms at the new title, though no longer smiling.

Radin only nodded, not knowing what to say; he could sense this was bothering Damon a *lot* more than he was letting on. "Why were you banished from your homeworld, Father?"

"A mishap." Damon wasn't looking Radin in the eye anymore, instead

Charles W. McDonald Jr.

busying himself with his refreshments brought by his very young, and very inappropriately dressed, maid. When Damon was terse in his responses, you were getting close to the threshold of pissing him off, so Radin dropped it.

"You found the Seal at least," Damon offered, motioning for Radin to at least partake in some of the food and fine wine being served. "What made you come looking for me?"

"I wanted to know more about my..." Radin paused, not wanting to use the word mom with relation to Vosh. He didn't know Vosh. He felt for her and realized her a hopefully good person, but she was not his mom. "...Mother. And...I thought we could resume our lessons."

A furrowed brow from Damon at the first, followed by a broad smile at the last, caused him to settle in between the two, "Your Mother, Vosh.... She was a far better woman than I deserved. I don't know why I attract good women for relationships and corrupt women for sex. Perhaps it's because the worst women don't know how to have a relationship, or don't care to. I assume good women are attracted to me for the 'bad boy' syndrome. Who knows?" Damon's sexist and womanizing arrogance on full display, Radin chuckled into his warm bread, allowing Damon to continue. "We fought all the time, but that just made the making up that much more intense. It was a crazy relationship, but she cared about you a great deal. She sent me notes about you every time she would check on you growing up, telling me how big you had gotten, how healthy and happy you looked. She watched over you most of your life, but I bet you never saw her."

"So, tell me about the amulet. What does it do?"

This time Damon nearly choked on his food, clearing his throat. "That. You don't need that thing. Don't worry about it."

"I know you took it from Elise and never brought it back."

"I said I would return it, and I will. You know my word is good," Damon challenged, threateningly. Very much not liking his integrity being brought into question.

"I want to know why it's so important to you, and why Mother took it from you." Radin was putting together the pieces nicely, causing Damon to recalculate his next move in real time.

"Your mother was around when I first started building the plan I'm executing today. She knew I needed the amulet to execute the plan, and she hoped you would be a better steward of it. That's my best guess."

"That doesn't tell me what it does, Father."

"No, it doesn't." Damon wasn't offering any more details, son or not.

"I wish you trusted me more. You're asking for a great deal of trust from me, Father."

Sighing into his coffee cup, Damon wanted to do more for his son, but sometimes if you couldn't offer the chicken they really wanted, you offered fish instead. "How about I teach you one of my favorites? *Damon's Rift...*," Damon proposed, ominously, with a wink and a smile.

"That doesn't sound like a nice spell, Father," Radin jibed, eying Damon sidelong.

"*Oh, it's not*," Damon played along, legitimately anxious to show his son the nastiness that was *Damon's Rift*. It hadn't been banned, but banishment of it had been vigorously discussed by the Council of Mages. *Hell Gate* was similar and *did* get banned, among many others. That didn't stop their usage, at least not by Damon.

*   *   *   *

"You'll need to use your staff for this one," Damon informed, watching Radin snatch Dallia's staff from the far corner of the spell test room as it shot into Radin's right hand via his *Telekinesis*. A smile from Damon in recognition of the talents his son had inherited, as well as the right-hand dominance they held in common. Radin's grip on Dallia's staff was even similar to the way Damon held the *Staff of the Invoker*.

"Good," Damon coached, adding, "Crouch down, without letting your knees touch the ground, making a singular striking motion downward from the crouched position all the way to the ground, letting the tip of your index finger touch the ground first. Like this." Damon demonstrated, continuing, "After you source, you'll want to imagine splitting through the planes, creating a direct line between here and there. This is called imagineering and we've discussed this in other instances before. This will work the same way. Since you've been there before, you should be able to execute this spell rather easily. Can you focus on that location without it causing you problems?"

It was a fair question, and Radin felt like the answer to that question was a very solid 'no.' Still, he wanted to try. He hadn't been able to stop thinking about Voltor since his return, so at least if he could channel those thoughts into a useful spell, he'd have something positive out of it—sort of. "I think so," he deflected.

"Good." Damon didn't like being lied to, and he didn't want to have to teach his only living son the same lessons his father had taught him—especially not in the same ways he'd been taught. Not that he ever would use those same techniques that had proven so scarring—both physically and emotionally—upon

Charles W. McDonald Jr.

himself, but Radin *did* need to understand the importance of being reliably honest. And how it affected your relationships with those around you. Brutal honesty was useful, especially when making others fear you. "So, let's say you've got the source, and you've imagined splitting the planes to the destination, your target isn't the floor, the person you're trying to send into the rift, nor is it the plane of Hell either."

"Then where do I send the target?"

"This is what makes the more powerful spells difficult, Radin. You have to start thinking in a more dimensional, higher-functional way."

"Okay, but that didn't answer the question."

"If we operate in three normal dimensions, plus time as the fourth where space and time are one fabric—or manifold—which one of those do you think would be the location of this particular target?"

"None of them."

"Very good!" Damon beamed, legitimately proud of his son. "Now, what makes you say that?"

"Because the laws of physics, as you've explained them to me, don't apply in Hell."

"Good. This is where your actually having been there is an advantage to you, and I want you to use that advantage against those who come against you."

Radin nodded, acknowledging his father's coaching. "There obviously have to be other dimensions outside of the four we normally operate inside of," Radin estimated, looking at his father for his concurrence.

"There are many theories about that very topic, and I can tell you for certain there are at least eleven dimensions for sure. Some theories say as many as twenty-six."

"I'm not going to ask how you know with such certainty about the eleven, but how do I know which dimension to assign the target value to?"

"This is where art meets science and intellect meets creativity. This is why the truly great mages are so rare, because it stretches and exercises every possible corner of your mind. I want you to picture this...." Focusing on the interdimensional illustration he wanted to make for his son to grow his powers, Damon traced the image in the air in front of Radin with his right index finger, etching a four-dimensional model in mid-air.

As he continued to sketch for Radin in mid-air, he coached, "I'm not going to bother going into the minutia of bosonic versus fermion and supersymmetry, because it's far too deep into the weeds for what you need to know right now. Suffice it to say that as we double each number of points in a set, we add another dimension just like I'm doing right now. Thusly, if we assume Hell must operate within the dimensions we know exist, what we're looking for is an anchor point in our set of points that is representative of that dimension in which it was built."

"And how do we know that dimensional point?" Radin thought about his question, correcting himself immediately, "...or rather set of points?"

"Because we know Hell encompasses a time-neutral zone of inhabitance. We also know that it must accommodate for all possible start and end points. Another way of looking at this is that, if I draw an illustration with five or six or seven dimensions in 3D space, that doesn't mean that said fifth, sixth, or seventh dimension is THE fifth, sixth, or seventh dimension, but that they are representations of other dimensional space. Does that make sense?"

"It does." Radin followed Damon's illustration, but it wasn't easy for him.

"So, as an example, I've drawn a four-dimensional model for you, and you can say that one of these dimensions represents time, though I didn't technically draw time itself. Make sense?"

Radin nodded, accepting Damon's explanation, still trying to imagine where he could possibly be going with this.

"Now, let's talk about membranes." Damon let his four-dimensional model stay where it was in mid-air, while sketching a 3D illustration of a sheet of energy that ebbed and flowed like a living thing. Drawing another 3D sheet of energy right atop the other, he began contorting the new sheet into an elliptical paraboloid.

Damon then began drawing one elliptical paraboloid after the other, at-taching them at their base to the living sheet of energy floating in the air so that the open ends of the elliptical paraboloids were all facing upward away from the living energy sheet. "Each one of these elliptical paraboloids represents a universe. We, and everything we know and love, exist inside one of these elliptical paraboloids. The main-body, membrane sheet of energy spawns the Creation of each universe in what is called the multi-verse. Let's assume the top membrane sheet of energy is the eleventh dimension, and the other ten are either a part of what's inside the elliptical paraboloid or other space that is interacting with the elliptical paraboloids in one way or another."

"Okay." Radin nodded, accepting, still wondering where this was going.

"Where do you think Hell exists in this illustration?"

Radin pointed to the underside of the main-body energy sheet membrane, opposite to the side attached to the bases of the elliptical paraboloids.

"Very good. You see things in negative space—things that are not there.

Charles W. McDonald Jr.

That is a sign of genius by the way." He wasn't intentionally complimenting his own offspring for the sake of proving his own genius, but it certainly could have been construed that way. "Just because we can't immediately see it, doesn't mean it isn't there. Remember that."

Radin nodded again, now looking forward to the rest of Damon's illustrative explanation.

"So, if we look at the underside of the energy sheet, opposite the base of the paraboloids, creating another sheet like this...." Damon illustrated another semi-liquid sheet shimmering in the air below the other one that was meant to represent the eleventh dimension. He then connected the eleventh-dimension sheet to the one representing Hell via four points—one on each end of each sheet—then filled in the space between the two sheets graphically. "This is the plane of existence for Hell, the Halls of Aaramus, *The World Below and Between*, etcetera."

"Wow." The realization of the moment and the lesson and the memories of his time in Hell all collided inside Radin's mind as he reached out to touch the graphical representation of the plane of Hell. "Does that mean that Hell and these other places exist in a twelfth-dimensional space?"

"It could, but that's not important to the casting of this spell. What's important is that you understand where *we* are in relation to where *it* is. Picture that in your mind, compounding it with your own memories of being there, then use the sourced energy to rip the fabric of spacetime to go from here to there. Are you ready to try?"

"I think I understand. Like this...." Radin tried putting the pieces together in his mind, reaching out, sourcing as much energy as he could to split the fabric of spacetime in Damon's spell test room. On Radin's first attempt, he formed a ten-foot-long by three-foot-wide crack in the air just above the spell test room floor, since he knew he couldn't actually split the floor itself or the floor would have dispelled *Damon's Rift*, out of which came acrid sulfur smells and lava-like molten-red light. Dispelling it immediately, Radin didn't get to see or feel the pressure that was already beginning to rush into the void he had created.

"Very good, but you have to leave it open longer for it to do its job. If left open a little longer, it would have sucked whatever was within one-hundred paces down into the rift. I've used it many times, and it's great when you're in combat with someone very powerful or there's a great number of enemies. The odds of them being able to avoid getting sucked into the rift are very small, and once they're sucked in, they're toast," Damon paused at the thought, "...quite literally." He finished with a smile at the last thought.

For braggadocious reasons or for further illustration, Damon, without

Zero-Point or aid of his staff, opened *Damon's Rift* wide enough and long enough to fill the entire room. This time he held it open, standing as close to Radin as comfort would allow so that Radin could see the protective shell *Damon's Rift* invoked around him, protecting him from being sucked into the rift. "Keep practicing, and that's what you'll be able to do soon. It's a useful spell, no?" Dispelling *Damon's Rift*, he tried recalling anyone who'd ever successfully cast it before on the first attempt besides Radin and himself. He couldn't think of anyone—not even Kellen.

Putting a little distance between himself and Damon, Radin didn't know whether to be excited or horrified at what he'd just learned from his father. Yes, it was a useful spell, but he needed to use it judiciously given his own personal experiences. "Thank you for teaching me, Father."

"You're welcome."

"May I ask you something about your banishment that's been bothering me?"

"Of course." Damon really wished he wouldn't, but he knew these kinds of questions would come up, regardless.

"They couldn't possibly enforce their banishment upon you, so why leave?"

"Because I said I would." Now was the moment to deliver that lesson from his father, but in *his* way, *not* his father's. "If you say you're going to do something, you must do it. If your word cannot be counted upon or if you're not reliable, you might as well not exist. Reputations can be a useful tool, but if you're known as a liar, that is not useful. If, however, you're known for ALWAYS doing precisely what you said you'd do…. That is VERY useful, indeed."

Damon let that sink in, noticing Radin's accepting nod before continuing, "Besides, it felt like a chapter of my life had come to a natural conclusion, and sometimes you need to know when to just let things go. I could have pushed it by staying. I could have fought back against those who tried to enforce the banishment. However, I've got bigger plans, and my attention needs to stay focused on them. So, if leaving lets me stay focused, then leave I shall, and I did." Damon's black eyes betrayed him as Radin caught Damon deep in thought.

When Damon was in the mood to provide answers, he provided excellent ones that made sense. No matter what anyone else said, Damon was a rational actor, and the more time he spent around his father, he knew that for a certainty. Letting go of that subject, Radin came back to the lesson topic. "How did you learn all this…laws of the Universe…or multi-verse stuff anyway?"

"Research… Lots and lots and lots of reading." A pregnant pause while he admired his son, noticing his fully healed eyes. "And then more reading." He smiled again at Radin, adding, "Glad to see you're fully *Healed* now."

Charles W. McDonald Jr.

"Yeah, it was this sword that Elise had. I just held it one time, and that's all it took."

Suddenly Damon went from happy-go-lucky to dead serious in another of his instant mood swings. "Where is this sword right now?"

"I don't know, Father. Elise has i—" Radin didn't get to finish his sentence before Damon was swallowed into a *Gate* right in front of him.

Charles W. McDonald Jr.

Chapter 34: The Chairman

(Paradise, Time Neutral)

Everywhere light poured into his spacious chambers. From under the great and elaborate oak double doors inlaid with honey-stained walnut and gold, and from the oculus atop the vaulted ceiling held up by buttressed Roman-style columns adorned with cherubim, and from the cathedral stained-glass windows, the light of being this close to the Creator would not be denied.

"But sir, he destroyed the entire Council. All of them! Well, all who voted for his banishment, at least. He destroyed the Council!! It literally doesn't exist anymore, and other candidates for their replacement refuse to re-form it in fear of what Damon might do to them if they did." The red-haired, gold-eyed beauty in diaphanous gold robes adjusted the iridescent mantle atop the Chairman's chest and shoulders, helping him prepare for the next Council of the Architect gathering. Appearing lost somewhere between the ages of eighteen and forty, her advice spoke of experience centuries beyond her appearance, but her impatience still got the better of her at times. She wasn't as elegant, nor as capable as Illirian, but she was far closer to the Chairman, and that mattered far more to her.

"*That* Council is no longer our concern. This one *is*." His aura radiated like the sun, but she was used to it as she brought him his high-mountain ash walking cane, a fitting accoutrement to his very long grey beard ending in a somewhat scraggly tip at his sternum. "Has anyone asked the far more important question that requires answering? That being, how did Damon destroy six of the most powerful mages in existence all at the same time?"

"I have been considering that, and it appears some of the Council's record survived, along with two witnesses. Apparently, Damon has discovered a new energy source, or, more accurately, has figured out how to tap that energy source in lieu of Arcane," she added, bringing him a very weathered, and extremely old shofar dating back thousands of years, which the Chairman slung about his left shoulder, letting it rest on his left flank and hip.

"We saw this coming—some of it at least. Damon is pivotal in bringing about the prophecies of the worlds of Humanity, but he is not fated to survive beyond that. We have seen it, and I am confident in that viewing. He will serve out his justice for all time, and we need to ensure we don't lose Illirian to his fate. Otherwise, I see no reason to intervene in the Damon matter beyond that." The Chairman gave a final adjustment to his very familiar shofar, allowing it to rest more comfortably on his aged and ancient frame, not really needing to look in the mirror, though there was only one in his chambers. He knew what he looked like. After seeing one's own image for thousands of years, it was etched into every corner of his memories. It wasn't really arrogance in the Chairman's voice that bothered Arella; she assumed it was just him exuding his confidence. Looking into Arella's eyes with his own eyes like unto a perfectly heated ingot of metal ready to be worked on a blacksmith's anvil, the Chairman ordered, "...but I want an answer to this new energy source of his. I want to understand what he's doing with it, and his plans. Ensure we get that information—whether by Illirian or not."

"I understand perfectly. I will take care of it personally, if necessary."

"No, you will not. You will stay away from Damon. You will allow the forces of nature we have put in place to repel you away from him. We need a more suitable source of intelligence in this matter—one more tailored to fit into Damon's circle of influence. I have someone in mind we can use."

"Of course, I didn't mean to overstep my authority, sir."

"Your enthusiasm is appreciated, child...," The Chairman coolly chided while offering his most affable and unflappable expression. "...But it won't save

Charles W. McDonald Jr.

your lifeforce from Damon's path of destruction." He didn't want to scare her, but Damon was truly dangerous. Especially to her.

"And what of Illirian? Won't she object to this other influence on Damon?"

"Not if she doesn't know." The Chairman adjusted a small leather pouch about his waist, hung from very weathered and dark tan leather belt, holding his grey and white linen robes together.

"I understand," Arella replied, bowing before The Chairman.

"Assemble the Council. I want an update from Illirian. She's been far too coy with us for far too long, and I want more direct answers to my questions *this* time."

"Of course, sir. I'll take care of it." Another full bow for the right hand of The Father of the Beginnings....

(Gravêstil, Kaleion, A Very Long Time Ago)

The shipping and merchant town of Gravêstil always had some two hundred ships or more in its harbor as well as a military presence of some fifty thousand or more, belonging to King Aelon's family. Merchants trading in molasses, fine cloth, slaves, spice, and alcohol flooded the city from all over the world, but Damon's focus today was inside the great-walled Naval District. He didn't like working for Illirian. He didn't trust her. Her motives were always tightly held secrets, and he didn't have time for her mind games. Nor her meddling ways....

People cleared the way for him as he walked with intimidating purpose in full mage regalia. Even without a staff, which he wanted badly but hadn't found just the right one yet, he would bring enough firepower with him to bring this merchant lord to his knees. *Oh well, everyone had some dirty work they needed doing.* He scowled internally, pondering Illirian's motives for using him to do her dirty work.

"Aye, mages are not allowed inside city walls without written permission. State your purpose," the middle-aged city guardsman challenged Damon while simultaneously motioning for backup.

Damon didn't immediately reply, instead examining the height of the guard tower, number of archers, and his actionable options to get inside the walled district without a *Portal*. He could use magic to get inside the walls if necessary, but there were protections over the walled district, and he'd rather not deal with that unless he had to. His calculus told him the conservative move was the better play here. Producing a decree with a red wax seal, he handed it to the city guard, awaiting his reply.

Examining the seal on the wax, seeing it was of the high merchant of Gravêstil, the guard scowled in immediate distrust of Damon, but didn't have the gravitas to open the sealed decree he'd been handed. "You'll have to wait here while we have a runner check with the merchant lord."

He didn't want to blast his way in, but the situation was circling perilously close to that outcome. He wasn't close enough to cast *Suggestion*, and they had some twenty archers with crossbows pointed at him right now, with more reinforcements on the way—of that he was certain. "I come on business from Illirian Starfire, Ruler of the Rod of the Nine, Watcher of the Runes of Fate."

That name they definitely knew, causing the guardsman to motion his archers aim off of Damon.

She had said he could mention her name if necessary. Like pretty much all things, people would find out sooner or later it had been him even if he killed every living person here, and eventually they might even link his visit to Illirian. So, it was best just to not play coy about *him* being *her* emissary.

"I am to be her emissary in negotiations with the merchant lord, High Seat Robert Tomerian."

"Beg your pardon, sir. We were not informed of your visit." Motioning again to the gatehouse guardsmen, he added, "We would still like to send the runner ahead of you. Who may I say is coming to visit the merchant lord in these negotiations?"

"Damon of Basrat."

A hard gulp in three of their throats said they'd heard of him. The others might not have, but he was sure they would be generous in their embellishments of his notorious acts. A swift kick of dust followed the hasty footsteps of the slender young archer, now turned runner, tasked with the message of Damon of Basrat on the merchant lord's doorstep.

Damon walked slowly behind the runner, allowing plenty of time for the word to reach Tomerian. How he would be greeted would tell Damon a great deal that Illirian intentionally had not. He readied himself with one protection spell after another, anticipating the worst. Passing a set of rotund twin towers, their battlements littered with archers, down Seaside Road, the runner fled before him, making a hard left, away from the retainer wall and the ocean, toward Nightingale Way and the merchant lord's estate. Along the way, Damon passed all manner of housing for the more esteemed merchants, fishermen, and noblemen of industry— some seventy buildings in all within the walled district. It was temperate this close to the sea, and Damon was sweating, but there was enough stench in the air from the fishermen's wharf to more than overpower any other odors.

A few more buildings down Seaside Road, and he made the left turn to follow the path of the runner, now in full sight of the merchant lord housing—a great three-storey estate with a colonnade supported by some twenty marble columns. Damon estimated it to be maybe more than a hundred paces left to right and fifty or more paces deep. *His place is nicer than mine*, Damon realized in detest.

Built upon a foundation higher than all the other buildings around it—perhaps to allow for sublevels—Damon ascended the twenty wide steps up toward the colonnade. As he topped the last few stairs, he could make out the man Illirian had described—fat, wealthy, wearing far too much gold, bald, with a smile you knew you couldn't trust as soon as you saw it.

"Damon, may we get you some refreshments on this hot afternoon," Robert Tomerian offered, showing Damon the way through a side door from the colonnade into a private office where Tomerian apparently conducted business meetings. The walls were littered with shelves of maps, sea charts, iconography, sailing manuscripts, and all manner of conversion charts from languages to money.

It was intolerably hot after the walk, and he admonished himself for not using the *Portal* to begin with. He didn't need to play games with this guy, whether Illirian did or not. Still, he couldn't trust this man, and it would be just like Tomerian to *poison* him. "No, I prefer if we just get to the matter at hand."

"Well that's just it my dear Damon, I haven't any idea why you're here. Illirian made no mention of this, and the decree you gave to the guards was empty when I opened it."

Not surprising, Damon thought. He assumed it was a fake when Illirian gave it to him. He only needed it to get inside.

"I'm here, Merchant Lord, because you're a thief and a swindler, and taking from Illirian Starfire will not be tolerated a moment further."

The fake smile on Tomerian's face vanished instantly at being called out by this...outlaw!

"You lack manners, sir. You cannot come into my house and insult me!"

Standing now to emphasize his physical statue over the short and fat Tomerian, Damon towered over him; he was fully capable of killing him with his bare hands in his instant assessment. Illirian hadn't explicitly authorized his assassination, but she hadn't forbid it either. He didn't like this man—not one bit. Damon could respect a thief, but he couldn't respect a swindler, liar, nor a hypocrite. Allowing the pause of silence to make Tomerian uncomfortable, Damon delivered the message from Illirian, "Illirian knows you've been stealing from her, an extra twenty percent above your agreed contract, for nearly a year now. She knows you've been building an army to remove the king." That was only the half of it, or she never would have sent Damon, but the second half he'd held back intentionally, waiting to see Tomerian's response.

"So, you're meant to be Illirian's enforcer then?!" It wasn't really a question from Tomerian; he knew better, and he knew himself caught. It was only a matter of time, and he was surprised he'd been allowed to carry on this long, anyway. At least he'd prepared for this inevitability. "Words of your misdeeds have reached my ears, I assure you, but I am not afraid of you."

"Oh?" *The balls of this fat lummox*, Damon calculated, examining the merchant lord again.

"Have you met my mage counsel, Morden," Tomerian offered with a broadening smile turned sneer.

Morden. Damon had heard that name before. Illirian had failed to mention that little tidbit of information.

In walked a man, looking some ten years older than Damon. He was a full hand shorter and had a hard and weathered face, carved of hate—the kind of face one gets when consumed by the toxicity of a violent obsession. Sunken sullen hazel eyes in deep furrowed eye sockets proclaimed Morden's disdain for Humanity, but his presence and stature proclaimed his love of wealth and power.

"We finally meet." Morden, apparently not impressed with Damon's physical stature, came perilously close to Damon, though not so close either couldn't cast. Damon held his ground, staring him down, paying no attention to Tomerian. Morden, in his pale green robes with gold seams and embroidery, carried with him a tall staff, taller than Damon actually, of high mountain ash, twisted and gnarled like Morden's own face. "I heard about you working with Kellen, but Kellen is not here. *Is* he?"

"Morden…," an intentional pause from Damon as his black eyes became backlit with a charcoal-blue fire of his father's execution, "…I'm going to *enjoy* killing you!!" *Damon's Contained Blast* blew Morden clear out of the room, shattering the twin glass and wood panel doors leading out to the colonnade. Unseen hands snatched a scroll from inside Damon's robes; the scroll landing in Damon's right hand as he followed Morden's body outside into the colonnade. Damon cast *Mind Blank* at Morden before he could escape, causing Morden to stagger as he tried to right himself to combat Damon. Discarding the spent *Mind Blank* scroll, another scroll leapt into Damon's hands from within his robes just as Morden tried to cast *Portal*. In that moment, Damon could see the threads of energy fail before them both, confirming Damon's suspicions about the protections over the walled city.

Charles W. McDonald Jr.

Morden would have to fight Damon or physically run. That thought brought a twisted and savored smile to Damon's face as he closed the distance between them, casting *Summon Lightning*, which caused a burst of lightning to erupt out of a cloudless sky, shattering Morden's shimmering protective shell.

Morden needed to gather his wits, or he was as good as dead. He knew Damon's reputation well; so far, he'd proven to live up to it. *I've got something for you, Damon.*

Physically reaching into his robes, quickly snatching a scroll from within, Morden cast *Guillotine*, causing ten huge handle-less scimitar blades to rush Damon from mid-air, some of them slicing through his protections, gashing his face, robes, shoulders, neck and mid-section.

Blood poured from Damon's wounds, causing his twisted smile to turn into a snarl as he rushed Morden straight on, physically tackling him, throwing Morden to the ground, landing one punch after another—some with his *Telekinesis*—some with his bare fists now bloodied at his knuckles with chunks of Morden's flesh.

In all his long life, Morden had never seen *anyone* fight like Damon. Damon's fists landed about his face, neck and chest with a voracity he'd never before experienced. Damon was a ruthless and furious *killer*—driven by a *hate* beyond anything even *he'd* experienced—and Morden thought that impossible. Damon didn't just fight like a mage. He fought like a man possessed! And he was surely going to die by Damon's hands if he didn't escape. He needed distance and he needed it NOW! Casting *Gate*, Morden was swallowed, snatched from Damon's grasp of *hate* before his next punch could land, leaving Damon only staring at the fissures in the dirt where Morden had just been.

Haven't seen that spell before, Damon realized, immediately searching for Morden. Damon had a feeling he'd know—all too well—Morden's location soon enough, for he didn't feel like Morden's pride would let him run from a fight—especially a fight with him! Bringing his protections back up to snuff, Damon cast *Damon's Improved Shell,* immediately followed by *Damon's Improved Foresight,* as he searched for Morden. A huge column of fire ripped through Damon's shield as he simultaneously found Morden in one of the twin rotund towers, peering out one of the archer openings, not quite at the top of the tower. His robes scorched, his stole and mantle still burning, Damon cast *Damon's Cube*, encasing and trapping Morden inside a transparent cube, as Damon made a smooth upward motion of his open right hand.

Shit, Morden thought, slamming his fists against the transparent walls of the cube that imprisoned him just as writhing squid-like, venomous tentacles erupted from the floor beneath him, gripping and sinking their stingers into his flesh as his blood splattered against the transparent walls of *Damon's Cube*.

A chaotic grin crossed Damon's bloodied, beaten, and burned face as he waved at what was left of Morden after being ripped apart within his cube.

Walking back to the colonnade and into Tomerian's office, seeing the sheer terror in Tomerian's eyes, Damon gripped Tomerian with his *Telekinesis*, throwing his body up against the bookcase-wall as he began collapsing Tomerian's trachea with an upward motion of his right index finger.

"I don't think Morden will be interrupting our meeting any further," Damon sneered, knowing it was time to get what he'd really come for.

Gargled gasps for air escaped Tomerian's mouth in a word he thought was '*anything*.' Relaxing his *Telekinesis* grip on Tomerian's neck, Damon emphasized his point, "You WILL give me *anything* I want, or you'll *wish* for death." An emphatic nod of agreement from Tomerian told him that he was now in a more cooperative mood. "Good...," Damon breathed in Tomerian's face, getting to his point, "... you possess a chest found by an expedition nearly a year back. That was something that was explicitly supposed to go to Illirian should you ever find it. This chest doesn't look like any normal chest. Do you know what I speak of?"

"Yes," Tomerian struggled to eke out with incredibly powerful unseen hands crushing his voice box. "I can show it to you...," Tomerian paused, thinking of how he might survive this. "IF you'll let me go, I'll show it to you."

Relaxing his *Telekinesis* further, but not completely—only enough to allow him movement as Tomerian fat body slumped to the floor, Damon followed Tomerian to his desk. Pulling a key from his right pocket, Tomerian opened the lower right drawer of his desk, producing another large key on a thin leather loop—probably meant to be worn about the neck. Pulling out that key, Tomerian moved back around to the front of the desk looking like he was about to move it. "It's in a floorboard beneath the desk," Tomerian informed, causing Damon to blow the desk to shards with his *Telekinesis*.

Charles W. McDonald Jr.

Tomerian frowned, remembering who he was dealing with. If he wanted to live, he needed to just give Damon what he wanted and get out of his way. Kicking one of the wooden floorboard panels with his right foot, Tomerian revealed another keyed wooden panel beneath it as the first wooden panel uprighted itself at a ninety-degree angle upon its hidden interior hinge. Damon's *Telekinesis* snatched the large key from Tomerian's tight grip, as Damon remotely slid the key into its lock, physically taking a few steps back, expecting a trap. A smooth click of the key unlocking the panel allowed it to flip upright in the opposing direction of the first panel, revealing something unlike anything Damon had ever seen before. Most treasure chests, if that's what this thing even was, were made of wood and iron. This thing…he had no idea of what materials were used to create it, but it flashed numbers, symbols, and characters about its perimeter. The whole thing couldn't have been much larger than one cubit, by a three-quarters cubit, by a half-cubit in thickness. It was mostly black, though color-shifting, with no obvious lock or opening of any kind. Damon frowned, examining it as he pulled it out of the hidden panel with his *Telekinesis*. "Have you ever opened it," Damon asked, staring down Tomerian, expecting an honest answer from the man, for once.

"NEVER, I don't know what's inside it. I don't even know where it came from. Well originally, anyway."

"Where did the expedition find it, and did they find anything else like it?" He had to give this back to Illirian, because he promised he would, but he didn't say anything about returning anything else, and this had piqued his curiosity.

He could see Tomerian thinking of how he'd lie to Damon, causing Damon to start crushing Tomerian's trachea again, this time followed with a hard gut-punch from Damon's right fist. "Don't lie to me, Tomerian. You won't like how that ends for you. I know you to be a thief and a liar. You've got this one chance to change your ways. Don't waste it!"

"A very small island…. I don't even know if it's on any of the sea charts. Deep in the Ameryth Ocean, south of the equator by some four hundred leagues."

"And my other question: did they find anything else like this?"

"A pair of handcuffs, but I don't have them. The captain of the expedition kept them. Said he'd barter them to buy a new ship."

Damon ripped Tomerian's body apart with his *Telekinesis*, causing body parts and blood to mist outward in all directions as he left Tomerian's office with what he'd come for. Taking very brief notice of the tower where he'd left Morden, he couldn't see Morden's body. Perhaps his tentacles had ripped his body apart; the cube was certainly bloody enough to indicate that might have been the case.

Walking out of the walled district the way he'd come in, he didn't say anything to the guards, and they didn't say anything to him—only making note of his bleeding, battered, and burned body limping out of the city, where he cast *Portal* as soon as he was on the other side of district barrier wall, disappearing into the superheated shimmering air.

Pulling the seal of the pale-pink rose with white leaves on a tan circular clay-cast circle, Damon shattered the seal in mid-air, crushing it with his *Telekinesis*, waiting in his fourth-floor secret study as he took a seat at his worktable. His wounds were noticeable now as the adrenaline of combat fled his body and the pain intensified.

A few moments later, a knock came on the far side of the secret study, on the other side of the decoy room wall.

"Come, Illirian," Damon announced, wincing at the pain of just talking.

Illirian stepped through the decoy wall, her silky legs, ivory dress and body seemingly appearing out of nothing on the far side of his study. "My goodness, I missed a good fight, it seems. I'm guessing the other one looks worse off."

Damon only smiled, producing the little peculiar chest from his still-smoking robes.

"I *knew* he had it," Illirian snapped with a scowl on her face, quickly turning to a smile as she took the box from Damon. "Let me at least *Heal* you for doing this for me," Illirian offered, setting the box down on Damon's worktable to lay hands on Damon's mantle as her fingertips made direct contact with Damon's scarred neck. He felt entirely uncomfortable letting *her* get this close to him, but she did have a smooth touch as he felt her *Healing* surging through his body, sealing up wounds and both taking energy from him as well as shooting *her* energy into him. Slumping in his chair after she finished, Damon knew it would take a day or more of hard sleep to recover, though he was thankful as he watched her pick up her package, walking around him to now stand in front of him.

Examining the man who'd done what she could not, Illirian wondered what future uses she'd have for this man—this Damon. She couldn't trust Kellen, and she felt an immeasurable disdain for him anyway, but Damon.... She would have much further use of Damon.

Extending her right hand to shake his, Illirian proposed, "I like you, Damon. You're unique, and you know how to get things done."

Extending his own hand to shake hers, he found another of her clay seals in her palm.

"Take it...," she offered with a slight pause, continuing, "...always keep one on you. You never know when you might need me." With that she turned, walking out of his study. Damon found himself involuntarily checking out her

Charles W. McDonald Jr.

legs and taut ass as she exited his study. *Stop it*, Damon admonished himself. *You can't possibly have anything to do with that woman!*

Now he needed to figure out how to find that island and see what else was left behind.

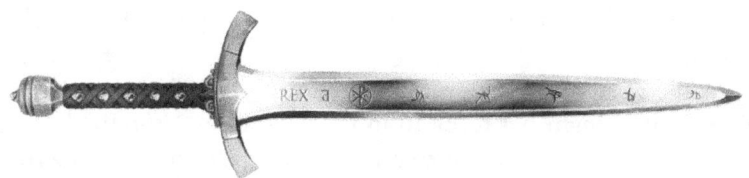

Chapter 35: The Halls of Aaramus – Part II

(Exeter, Perion, Present Day)

Her eyes opened slowly in her room, now separated from Radin, though not at her request. Her mirrored dresser facing the foot of her bed reflected her sunken eyes—now fully cried out. Sitting up in her bed, swinging her feet over the edge to let them dangle, Elise looked over to the corner of her room at Excalibur, thinking only of Michael. She could not think of her husband without crying, and she could already feel the tears coming again as she felt another presence suddenly enter the room—and not through a *Portal*. Looking up and expecting the worst, she wasn't disappointed seeing the 6'4" dark and ominous frame of Damon leering over her.

"What do you want, Damon? I'm not in the mood for you."

Raised eyebrows from Damon at the gumption of her less-than-kind greeting.

"Very well. I came for Excalibur."

"You can't have it." Elise rose to her feet, flooding herself to brimming full of Arcane to Damon's protest as he waved her off.

"Stop. Don't embarrass yourself. There's no reason for all that."

Embarrass herself! The arrogance of this man knew no bounds, she thought, putting herself between Damon and Excalibur. "You still haven't brought back the amulet yet. Why should I let you have Excalibur?"

"True, and I still need the amulet, but you also know my word is unbreakable, so you will get it back. I guarantee it! For the good of what is to come, you need to trust that I am trying to save Excalibur for the future." He thought about how much he could reveal of his Master Plan—not much. "Would it help if I told you I was going to take it to the Halls of Aaramus?"

"Why would you take Excalibur to that…that lich?!!!"

"Because that's where I found it," Damon answered simply, not offering further explanation.

"But you didn't find it. We did—on Baschurch Lake."

Charles W. McDonald Jr.

"And how do you think Excalibur found its way into Baschurch Lake for you to find in the first place?"

The pieces started falling into place in Elise's mind as she examined some of the pieces that brought her to Earth in the first place. "YOU?!" It wasn't really a question or expletive, more of an epiphany moment for Elise, as the truth of her role in his plan struck home.

"Exactly…me. Now, I need Excalibur if you would be so kind, please."

"You got Michael killed," she added.

"No, Michael got Michael killed. He had no business being on that battlefield."

Sitting back on her bed, she didn't really give Damon permission, but he moved forward, taking Excalibur. It didn't sing, glow, or resonate in his hands—only dead metal of unknown origin in his grip.

"Would you like to know the sex of your baby," Damon asked, looking at a confused and befuddled Elise. Her eyes answered where her lips could not. Casting only the probe part of *Healing*, Damon never laid hands on Elise, only pulling the information from her body with his right hand, saying, "It's a boy and he's very healthy." Damon smiled at the idea of knowing he'd have his first grandson, though he couldn't share that information with Elise. That would be too much for her in her current condition, as he examined her trying to put together the pieces in her head.

Before Elise could protest, Damon and Excalibur were gone, leaving Elise to ponder the breadcrumbs that led her to Earth in the first place and the son currently kicking her and tumbling inside the warmth of her womb. *How far back had Damon gone to execute his Master Plan, and how much more of a role did she have to play in it?*

(The Halls of Aaramus, Time Neutral)

Damon knew the way in—the precise location of the halls themselves—a forbidden place to materialize unless you knew Aaramus, personally. Damon had contributed far more to the Halls of Aaramus collection than any other, and Aaramus knew it as he arrived only seconds after Damon. Two of the most feared mages in all Creation now stood head to head and toe to toe inside the Halls of Aaramus next to the sword collection as Damon extended Excalibur to the lich for examination.

Decrepit bones with faltering and fettered flesh took Excalibur as Aaramus instantly authenticated the immortal weapon of Creation. "Mhmm," his only response with a long unnecessary breath for the undead. "What do you require in return, Damon the Banished?"

"Your absolute secrecy in any knowledge you have of my plans. You will not share that knowledge with anyone or anything, living or not, immortal or mortal."

A staggered and raspy laugh struggled out of the lich's dead excuse for a mouth, noting the precision of Damon's request. "You have it," the lich offered, adding, "Are you certain there isn't anything else you require?" Aaramus toyed with Damon the Banished as his dead eyes looked over to the staves across the hallway.

It took Damon a moment to realize what was going on in the crazy lich's psychotic mind until he followed those dead eyes to the *Staff of the Invoker* leaning proudly in a place of honor among hundreds of other staves as it cast its terrifying aura engulfing all relics around it. Aaramus laughed out loud, placing Excalibur in a similar position of honor among his most impressive collection of swords.

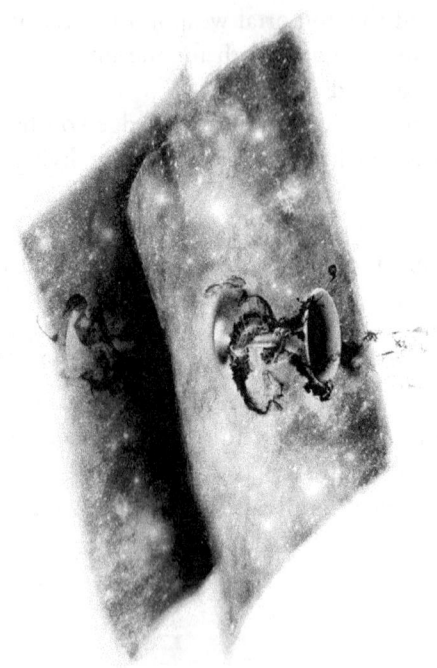

Chapter 36: The White Hole

(Damon's Manor, Eden, Present Day)

Damon contemplated the rogue threat he'd been shown some days ago by Abel and his chief scientist as he worked the soil for his roses in the front of his manor. More than mere busy work, he needed something to calm his thoughts and keep his mind focused on his Master Plan without allowing himself to get enraged over his banishment. Besides, his new ocean view was worth the move, and the trees were growing at an incredible pace now that he'd personally addressed their growth rate. Looking out to the north-eastern sky, to the far right and above his yellow dwarf Protostar, of his own making, Damon could sense the threat that was coming. Whether Eden's orbit to the Black Hole or the Black Hole came to Eden, the threat was coming, and he had personal stakes in saving this world now.

"In all my life, I NEVER thought I'd see this." Illirian's soft and sweet voice came from behind him.

Damon immediately pivoted to Illirian, brushing his dirty hands on his

Levi's® 501's, careful not to get his plain white T-shirt too dirty. "What can I do for you, Illirian? I'm a little busy, as you can see."

"Why are you gardening, Damon? Don't you have staff for that?"

"Why are you here," Damon asked in less than a nice tone, causing Illirian to frown in response.

"Very well, I'll get right to it. Damon, you need to come home."

"Excuse me... Wasn't it *your* Council that banished me from Kaleion?"

"Not *my* Council. Besides, it doesn't exist anymore, anyway. You made certain of that. And, the person you made the commitment to no longer lives. You even made your commitment based upon both of you living. Well, he's dead. You made sure of that too."

"I know what I did, and I know what I said."

"YOU CAN COME HOME, DAMON!"

"I like it here." Damon turned away from Illirian, returning to tending to his flowerbed, looking at his view of the beautiful blue-green ocean beyond.

Kneeling beside Damon, only inches away from his face, Illirian drove home her point. "Damon, you left an immense power vacuum in your wake, and there are mages warring one another over who's going to be top dog in your absence." Illirian paused, thinking of the disastrous unintended consequences of the Council of Mages. They had thought Damon's banishment would *protect* Kaleion, but the real result for Kaleion was total chaos. Damon's presence had kept volatile forces in check. With Damon gone, all bets were off. "Damon, Morden will probably win this war and remake the world in his image. Even as we speak, half the planet burns as a result of this war."

"Sounds like the world I knew is gone anyway. Why go back?" It was a fair question from Damon, but it was impossible not to think of Dallia and the love he left behind to be scorched by Morden's hatred and insatiable ambition. He wasn't intentionally trying to be a thorn in Illirian's side or a stumbling block to her wishes, but he had bigger fish to fry right now, and Morden wasn't his problem.

"Did you not just hear a word I said?" *What would it take for her to get Damon engaged? He was so far removed from the world he once adored.* It was as if he no longer cared, and she knew that wasn't the case!

"You're more than powerful enough to take on Morden by yourself," Damon surmised while intentionally avoiding her desperate gaze, adding, "Why don't you do it?"

"I'm not allowed to intervene. You know that. It's part of my station."

"Oh well." Damon pretended not to care, moving to the other side of the garden, only looking at Illirian to deliver this warning, "...and don't mention *that*

Charles W. McDonald Jr.

name to me ever again!"

"Morden," she asked, not really asking. "Morden. Morden. Morden. MORDEN!!!"

"Now you're being petulant—very unbecoming of you *AND* your station." Damon delivered his harshest ever judgment of his friend and comforter. He was right, but that didn't make it okay.

A long moment of awkward silence between them as he tended to the white roses on the left side of his manor.

"So…," Illirian thought as she was putting together the pieces, "…is this part of your Master Plan too? Morden tearing apart your homeworld?"

He thought about it. She wasn't entirely wrong, but she wasn't entirely right, either. He knew there would be a power struggle in his absence, but he was too busy trying to find the right state of mind to say goodbye to his homeworld—to Dallia, and to everything else he'd left behind. "If you want me to save people from Kaleion, and bring them here, I'll do that."

Another long pause as Illirian came to terms with the fact that this *was* Damon's best offer, and he meant it. Her homeworld was lost—another casualty of Damon's Master Plan.

"What about Kellen? He could take care of Morden," Damon offered, knowing better.

"He's too busy with your Master Plan to deal with Morden. You know that." He did. "The only other mages that could have dealt with Morden, you killed at the Council—horribly so, from what I heard."

"Come and take them," Damon whispered quietly to his blooming white roses under his breath, vividly recalling his dismemberment and purification of Mirak.

"What was that?" She heard him well enough but wanted an explanation. Actually, she wanted him to vent. Venting from Damon could be very cathartic, and from his gardening, it looked like he needed some psychiatric help.

"Nothing," Damon deflected, adding, "I'll save those I can from Kaleion who will prove useful in building this society I'm developing here." Not like it was any sweat off Damon's back; he'd already done it or was about to do it—pending one's perspective in the fluidity of time. President Abel was one such he'd saved from Kaleion with the use of the time manipulation amulet he'd 'borrowed' from Elise.

"I'd appreciate you saving as many souls as you can, Damon. Thank you."

Interesting, he thought, *the use of her word 'souls.'* More for him to ponder, but his roses kept calling out to him for attention.

Charles W. McDonald Jr.

"Is that it then?" He hoped that was it. He was done being examined under Illirian's scrutiny.

"I don't want to take up any more of your precious gardening time."

With that, Illirian was gone. As he looked back to confirm, Damon finally exhaled, sighing deep in thought. His homeworld was lost to Morden, but he wouldn't lose Eden. *No matter what*, he thought looking up at where the rogue black hole should be—on a collision course with his world. One thing in all that conversation had really bothered him. He didn't know the state of Dallia's grave. Had Morden's chaos disturbed it? He couldn't live with himself if he had allowed that….

"Can I bother you for a moment, Father," Radin asked from the front doorway of the manor, arms folded over one another as he leaned against the open-door casing.

Geez, why can't people just leave me be for five minutes, Damon thought, forcing a smile for his son. "Sure. What's up?"

Stepping down the stairs of the entrance to Damon's manor, Radin informed, "So we're thinking about going after Morden. What can you tell me about him?"

Ugh, that name, Damon thought. Twice in the last ten minutes when he hadn't heard that name in decades before. Forcing another smile, Damon jibed, "I bet he remembers me," fondly recalling the beating he'd delivered to Morden on more than one occasion. "Be sure and tell him I sent you with all my best wishes."

"Seriously, Father, I need details."

"Okay, he's way beyond your skill level. He's filled with more hate than you can possibly imagine. More driven by power, wealth, and sheer accumulation of shit than you can imagine. And, he knows ways of killing you that will make you beg for a quick death."

"Gee thanks. I'll get right on that," Radin quipped, but inside he was thinking, *What is wrong with Damon? Why is he gardening when there are so many bigger 'fish to fry' in Damon's words? And why would Damon give me a list of names I couldn't possibly hope to deal with?*

"Okay, how about this?" Damon wanted to help his son, but there was so much going on in his world at the moment, and he needed to clear his mind to prepare for what needed to be done. "Don't negotiate with him. Don't even talk to him. Just attack. Hit him with *Mind Blank* repeatedly until it works, then drop your most lethal spells on him as fast as you can, but DO NOT HESITATE with this man." Damon thought about it for a moment. *What did Morden fear about him the most?* "And, Radin, when you attack I want you to totally commit yourself to killing him, no matter the cost. If you must physically beat him to death, do it. If you must crush his skull with your bare hands, do it. Use your natural abilities in conjunction with your spells. Bring significant help with you. Have protections up that protect you specifically against metal and fire; those are his favorite weapons of choice." Damon continued, recalling his last interactions with Morden. "And don't let him run. He'll want to attack you from a distance but stay on him. Be the ten-pound tick on the two-pound dog."

Radin furrowed a brow at the obvious other-world slang coming from Damon, not really knowing what to make of it, but feeling he knew what Damon meant. "Thank you, Father. That was very helpful tactical advice."

An awkward moment of silence between them as Damon pulled another weed from the flower bed, rolling the stone border back into place.

"Father, if you need to clear your mind, would teaching me how to more effectively use *Mind Blank* help?"

Damon thought about it a moment. *What am I doing out here? Killing time? Escaping the inevitable? Trying to understand why my staff is in the Halls of Aaramus?* "Sure, let's go upstairs," he suggested, getting up from kneeling in the soil of his garden as he brushed off his hands and pants.

Moments later in the spell test room, Damon coached Radin on the use of *Mind Blank*. "This isn't a terribly complicated spell, so your only misuse of it is really in where you're placing the emphasis. It's part *Shield*, part *Suggestion*, and the rest are unique to *Mind Blank*. What you need to do is place emphasis on the power you put behind the *Suggestion* components." Before Radin could protest, Damon illustrated his point on Radin, casting *Mind Blank* with enough voracity to leave Radin stammering and faltering for his footing. "Sorry, but there was really no other way to make my point. Not like we can just create a lightning bolt in the test room and watch it dissipate against the test room walls. You okay?"

Radin used his hands against the spell test room walls to gather himself upright. "No. No. I get it, Father."

"Just remember, it only buys you maybe a short moment, and that's all the window of time you have to strike. But if you strike while *Mind Blank* is active, then their protections will be useless in most cases. So, have your most powerful weapon queued up right behind the *Mind Blank*, ready to go."

He didn't want to bring this up, but Radin wasn't like Damon, and it needed to be said. "Can you be ruthless?"

"What?"

"You heard me."

"No, I heard you, Father. I'm just trying to understand."

Charles W. McDonald Jr.

"There's nothing to understand, except with this man—Morden—you'll have to be ruthless, or you'll be dead. Can you be ruthless, like me, just for a little while?"

"I suppose so, Father."

"I was hoping you'd say 'no,'" Damon admitted under his breath, looking down as he thought about what he was asking of his son. Damon waved off his son in protest, cutting off his response, adding, "Just while you're in combat with Morden, you can't hold anything back. Don't assume anything. Verify. If you see a body, blow it to Hell. Obliterate him entirely. He's very cunning, but if you're always the attacker, you can get him off balance, and that's where you want him."

"I understand." *Do I?* Radin hoped he understood. Facing Morden sounded like he was biting off more than he could chew, but people that could and did cast *Damnation* had to be eliminated one-by-one if necessary, and at great personal risk if necessary.

"Take Michelle, Lawna, and Wraith with you. Only the strongest killers among you with killer instincts will do. Leave that sniveling boy scout Talemar behind. He'll only get someone, not named Morden, killed."

"He's actually very talented, Father." He didn't understand the boy scout comment, but he gathered from Damon's prior comments about Talemar that Damon didn't think too highly of him.

"I never said he wasn't talented. There's a difference between talented and someone that has a killer instinct. Talemar does not have a killer instinct. Michelle does. Wraith does. Lawna does. Take them with you."

Do I have a killer instinct, Radin wondered of his own capabilities. Obviously, Damon felt like he did, or at least had the potential for it, or he would have said something about it. *Were being ruthless and having a killer instinct one and the same,* he wondered. He was still so young, and all this was coming to him so fast. Radin looked at his father—really looked at him—even in simple clothes he was... *ominous.*

"Like the shirt, Father." He didn't really. It looked like something wholly inappropriate for the great and ominous Damon to wear, regardless of what he was outside doing. "It's the first time I've ever seen you wear white."

That was it!!! The answer to his rogue threat. He'd only been gardening because he didn't know how to fix the black hole problem. He had hoped clearing his mind would provide the answer, but it was his son that had provided the answer, after all.

"Shiiittt." Damon's epiphany slammed home. He needed to talk to Mira—like now. Without preamble, Damon vanished before Radin.

Charles W. McDonald Jr.

"Uh…. What did I say," Radin asked the barren, shimmering black walls of Damon's spell test room.

*   *   *   *

(Austin, TX, Earth, Present Day)

Damon's materialization in his Austin, TX kitchen caught Mira off guard, causing a near miss of her fingers with the hefty but well-balanced Santuku kitchen knife she held in her hands as she cut veggies for her solo dinner. "Shit, Damon!"

"Sorry." Damon unconsciously wiped his hands on his jeans again.

"I need to get you a goddamn bell or something."

"Ha-ha." Damon looked around, noticing *her* redecorating of *his* place. Soft touches like impressionistic art paintings and prints hung about the house with some new furniture he assumed he'd paid for in one manner or another, along with some fine china and wine glasses. "Like what you did with the place." He wondered if this meant she thought they were married or not. Nevertheless, he got a beaming smile out of her, so it was worth it. "We need to talk white holes. Got a minute?"

"Ugh, random topic, but okay…."

"So, theoretically, every black hole in this universe is a white hole on the other side of the universe's membrane. Correct?"

"Well…. kind of. It's often thought to be a white hole in another universe, but that's only true if the membrane of another universe is touching our universe's membrane at that location where the black/white hole appears in each universe respectively. If a black hole was created by the gravitational collapse of a star, then no, it's likely not a white hole on the other side. And, technically we've never observed a white hole before. They're strictly theoretical and violate the net entropy laws of thermodynamics."

"Yes, exactly. See, that's why I needed to talk to you."

"What exactly? Where are you going with your question, Damon?"

"I have a black hole problem in *this* universe."

"Okay?"

"I'm struggling with how to fight a gravitational force that strong."

"Okay?"

"But, if it's really just an energy problem on the other side of the membrane, then that's an easy fix."

"So, you're going to go to the OTHER side of our universe's membrane?!!!"

Charles W. McDonald Jr.

"Yes," Damon matter-of-factly replied, observing Mira's dubious look in response.

"Damon, our laws of physics only apply WITHIN our membrane. How are you going to even continue to exist? Without the laws of gravity, strong and weak forces, etc., your atoms will fly apart outside of this membrane. You will cease to exist."

"True, but I have an idea."

"Do tell." Mira walked around the gleaming island, leaning into Damon to hug him.

"I have never created another plane of existence before, but I know people," Damon paused, cringing at that word associated with Aaramus, "I know of some who have. And, I would think they would have already solved this problem before."

"Okay, let's say for a minute, you could exist outside the membrane of our universe, and you're staring at this big white hole on the other side. Then what?"

"That's a good question, but...," *Damn that was a good question.* Damon considered his options. He wasn't sure if Zero-Point would work, or not—likely not—but Dark Energy.... Nor was he certain if the energy provided by his worshipers would exist there or not either. But, his *Throne of Souls*—that would still be usable, if *his* atoms held together. He could create a transportable shell to work within while outside the membrane but getting back might be the biggest problem of all, assuming he could even fix the white hole from the other side.

Raised eyebrows from Mira, expecting a better response from her brilliant demigod boyfriend.

"Okay, so maybe it's not such an easy fix after all."

"No shit." Mira walked back to the island and cutting board, watching Damon stew over his options while she continued her food prep. "You never explained your little black hole problem. I'm assuming this has something to do with Planet X, the same planet I've not been allowed to visit." Holding the knife pointed at Damon, she recalled their last conversation. "And what was so damned important you had to kick me out of your manor anyway?"

"Oh that...." Damon still struggled with being banished, and he didn't want to bring up that topic again. "I'll make it up to you."

"Mhmm. Bullshit." Mira's foot began fidget tapping as she continued cutting vegetables.

Shit, he thought, knowing what that meant. *Women are complicated!*

"Seriously Damon, going back to your little black hole issue, you can't just throw massive amounts of energy or matter at it, or you'll make the problem even

Charles W. McDonald Jr.

worse. The black hole will be able to convert any energy you send at it into matter, making it a meaner problem to deal with."

Chopping her carrots, Mira continued pondering Damon's black hole problem. One that many physicists before her had pondered with no solid answer in sight. "There's a theory out there, that I read from Ted Jacobson and Thomas Sotiriou, suggesting that if you feed a black hole enough angular momentum and charge, you can destroy its event horizon, but that doesn't mean you'll destroy the black hole, and no one has any level of certainty that feeding it so much angular momentum wouldn't make the problem worse when, and if, it settled back into its steady state."

"You're just full of good news," Damon quipped, taking one of the island bar stool chairs as he watched her prepare *his* dinner. He just realized he was hungry.

"With Hawking radiation, we know that all black holes, even the super-massive ones, will die on their own over time, but I get the feeling you don't have a few billion years to wait."

"Um, no."

"Have you considered healing the membrane to strangle the black hole, or white hole, right out of existence? Assuming your little black hole friend didn't come from an exploded star...."

The wheels immediately started turning in Damon's mind. *Now there's an idea, but how would I do it?* "I haven't, but that sounds promising."

"Well, technically the black hole isn't really a tear in the manifold of our spacetime, but I don't know if I really believe the mathematics or not."

"I'm listening. Go on."

"We only use the term singularity out of our own ignorance of what's really happening at scale. Newtonian physics is useless, and so is Einstein's General Relativity. We just keep getting these divide-by-zero bullshit answers that we know simply cannot be. We know space really is finite. We know that minimum and maximum energy is finite, and so is minimum and maximum mass. We can define the mass of pretty much any black hole, so we can't accept something finite giving us infinite answers to simple questions like, 'How long would it take for an object to cross the event horizon and be sucked into the singularity itself?' That's simply unacceptable and contradictory to what we know has to actually happen."

"You're not getting any disagreement from me. It's total bullshit."

"Well, my point in saying that is, I think our ignorance of what's really going on is getting in the way of providing some really useful solutions to this problem."

Charles W. McDonald Jr.

"So, you're suggesting an experiment with the black hole before we decide how to deal with it. Study it for as long as it's safe, then act only when we have to."

"Exactly." Mira was a sharp cookie, and Damon knew it. She smiled at how they finished each other's thoughts. "Don't hold me to it, Darling, but I think what our study will find is that the way to tackle this problem is by dealing with the manifold of spacetime on which the black hole has manifested itself. Heal the manifold, and you solve at least the black hole problem, and the white hole problem too, if there is one on the other side of the membrane. If you heal the membrane, theoretically, you should be able to cut off the black hole at its source like a noose around its neck."

"I like it." Damon winked at her, once again admiring the fantastic mind that came with that hot body of hers. He missed her.

"I do think, if it's possible without it being too risky for you, that as part of our study of this black hole, you should try viewing it from the other side of the membrane to verify if we're dealing with a white hole on the other side or not. Can you use one of your viewing portals to do that without actually physically leaving the membrane to go to the other side?"

"Another great idea, Mira." Damon smiled at her, truly impressed. "Maybe. I've never tried that exact use-case for a viewing portal before, but it's worth a try."

"Do you know for certain this black hole is a problem? I'm assuming this involves your little Planet X."

He couldn't hide that from her anymore. Besides, if they were going to work together on studying the black hole, she'd figure that out sooner than later. "Yes, it's possible that it might still be close enough to the star system of Eden, that it could affect its orbit and then I'd have to start all over again. Which I really don't want to do."

"Could we study it from Eden?"

"NO!"

"I don't understand, Damon. Why can't I go to your new planet? What's going on there you don't want me to see? You know I don't like secrets between us."

"NO!"

Mira frowned, thinking of how she'd get Damon to change his mind, but the Damon she knew was a stubborn one—not inclined to change his mind any time soon. "If you say so, but you do want my help to study the black hole, right?"

"Absolutely. If you'll help me. I'd greatly appreciate that." *And I know hundreds of millions of other people that would appreciate it too*, Damon thought, smiling at his very bright girlfriend.

Charles W. McDonald Jr.

"As a backup plan, would you be able to move Eden, creating another star?"

Another good idea from Mira, but not a practical one with all the life already on it. He didn't really have a place for them to go that wouldn't severely fuck up the timeline. It would be easier to just find another inhabitable world. "I will start working on a backup plan right away, but I do believe we have some time before we *must* solve the black hole problem."

The wheels were clearly turning in Damon's mind as he watched the Santuku knife crisply and neatly cut through the veggies Mira prepped for dinner. Something about the way the pendent LED lights reflected off the mirror finish of the knife rolled over in his thoughts, almost like a stir-stick mixing a drink of possibilities within his consciousness. *How had the indigenous race survived years on Planet X after being slung out of orbit? All that time without liquid water, atmosphere, warmth or light? There must be an immense set of tunnels underneath those spired structures*, he surmised. *Maybe killing them isn't the best option if I want a really viable, and easily executable, backup plan. Maybe I need to talk to them and negotiate a truce.*

"Staying or going, Damon? Hello? Earth to Damon?" His eyes focused again on the mirror finish of the knife as Mira's voice brought him out of thought.

"Sorry, um…Staying," he offered, causing her to beam for him.

"Good, I bought something special to wear for you," she teased.

"Goodie." Damon visibly licked his lips at the thought of taking Mira right here, but his stomach got the better of him. *Wait 'til she finishes cooking your dinner*, he calculated.

Part 4: The Fatal Spiral

Charles W. McDonald Jr.

Chapter 37: Ring Out

(Just outside Coronado, California, Earth, ~2300 Pacific, Present Day)

"Stop. Get off me," Raegen protested, pushing back against the rough and weathered looking young man now holding Raegen by her butt as he pushed her back up against the brick exterior of the nightclub.

"You should have worn a longer dress, baby." Anthony had had a few drinks, sure, but he knew what women really wanted. Besides, he was a great looking virile young man. He forced a kiss through his excessively thick designer stubble beard, moving his hands to pin her hands to the brick wall to get her to stop struggling so much.

"FUCKING QUIT IT," she screamed at him after biting his lips hard enough to draw blood, swiftly kneeing him in the balls. She knew it was a bad idea to follow this shithead into the alley, but he was cute and garnered a measure of trust from her over the last couple of hours talking to him in the club.

Moving his hands away from her to protect himself, Anthony never felt the wound, but could feel the blood pouring out the side of his neck and trundling down his V-neck, black T-shirt, even pouring down his back as consciousness quickly evaporated for him. Everything swirled and then he was on the ground.

"Shhhhh…," Michelle Alexandra Blade warned Raegen with a finger to her blood-stained lips as she resumed feeding on what remained of Anthony. In mere seconds he became a shriveled dry husk of bone and flesh, rapidly discarded by Michelle to be deposited at her feet. "You didn't see anything," Michelle continued her warning. "Don't make me regret saving you."

A vehement nod of agreement from Raegen told Michelle she understood. "Thank you," Raegen replied, quickly running out of the alley trying not to think too much about what she'd just witnessed. After all, she'd had more than just a few drinks.

Wiping her lips with an embroidered handkerchief she'd taken to carrying on her at all times now, given her new disposition, Michelle put the bloodied handkerchief in a Ziploc® baggie, shoving it into the back-left pocket of her tight-fitting jeans. Throwing Anthony's body into the dumpster, where it belonged, Michelle needed to get back to the BUD/S (Basic Underwater Demolition/SEAL) barracks before someone noticed her missing. Rules or not, she had to feed, and the meal she needed wasn't on the menu at the base.

*   *   *   *

(BUD/S Training, Coronado, California, Earth, 0430 Pacific, Present Day)

Having passed Physical Screening Test (PST), and SEAL Officer Assessment and Selection (SOAS) with Lawna in stellar fashion, Michelle was fulfilling the destiny laid out before her by Rena—becoming super soldier leaders in Rena's immortal army. Having a Letter of Recommendation from POTUS didn't hurt either—excluding the exceptionally high bar being placed on them at BUD/S, which was already ridiculous because of their gender.

The brass ship's bell, atop a singular white pole, angrily greeted Michelle as it had every day since arriving at BUD/S, silently taunting her to do what so many had already done—to ring out and end this nightmare. Three rings of the simple brass bell were all it would take to end her misery and suffering, but she never considered it—not even for one second. Recalling what she'd told Rena before leaving for California, "I'm not ringing that goddamned bell," and remembering Rena's response of, "And that's why I picked you, Darling," gave her a measure of confidence as she stared the bell down, heading out toward the beach, knowing the water temperature to be deathly chilling this time of the morning. She didn't care. Her metabolism had radically changed in her transformation and she knew there was nothing the SEALs could throw at her that could break her physically, but mentally, that was another story. Even by her standards, this was going to be demanding and require all her faculties—vampire physiology or not. This was only Phase 1 of BUD/S—the highest washout rate—where less than 35 percent advanced to the next stage.

"Oh, here comes hot shit Blade," SEAL Instructor Alvarez commented as Michelle fell in beside Lawna, Rikers, and Castillo at the front of the formation, boots in the water as everyone fell in for the morning run along the beach, accumulating almost 200 miles in just over five days. Michelle didn't reply. She said as little as possible, letting her actions do the talking. She'd hoped she'd earned some level of respect from the men, but she also needed the respect of the instructors.

A moment later, and they were running to the fast and steady cadence coming from Instructor Alvarez, maintaining boots in the water the whole way, ensuring they got maximum resistance from the sand, the lapping foams of the ocean, and the fatigue setting in from Hell Week. Never being allowed more than four hours of sleep a night with twenty hours a day of intense physical training wasn't really a problem for her or Lawna, but it was making it excessively hard to work as a team with the others who were having a much harder time of it. Teamwork and mental fatigue were their weakest scores, and EVERYTHING was scored here. Every conversation. Every outburst. Every reaction. Everything was a test here, and failure was a regular occurrence, or at least it appeared that way from the instructor's responses and instant, relentless judgments. But the most common denominator of success was those who wanted it the most, and Michelle wanted this—more than anything she'd done before in her life. Not for Rena. Not for Lawna. Not for her daughters, but for her and her country. She was a part of Rena's immortal army now, but she was an American first; Rena knew it when she recruited Michelle, so she'd just have to deal with that fact whether Rena liked that about her or not.

She'd already witnessed three candidates ring out just yesterday. Now, after their run, they sat six abreast in the water with a huge twenty-foot, thousand-pound log in their laps, forced to work together to do sit-ups in the water with the log across their arms as resistance. For some reason this exercise appeared easier for Lawna and Michelle's group with them strategically sitting on each end— they didn't need the help of the four in the middle, and that just made getting through the exercise easier. It made Michelle wonder if they were helping candidates make it through the program that should have rung out. That could be a problem later if they really were depending on them as a Team's member.

SEAL Instructors Alvarez and Camden could both be heard over their bullhorns encouraging candidates to DOR (Drop on Request) or 'ring out' as it was known, encouraging the inner voice of each candidate to quit. *Who could blame the instructors for doing this?* They would likely have to serve on missions with some of the very people they were right training now, so they wanted only the very best to progress and to stop wasting their time on everyone else. They wanted the highest possible washout rate and relished each ring out with acrimonious joy.

Almost on command, Candidate Vickors dropped his helmet liner at the foot of the brass bell, ringing it three times in succession. Now Vickors' team had to work harder without his help on the log.

"ANOTHER FUCKING QUITTER," Instructor Alvarez chided over his bullhorn. "THANK GOD. I was tired of wasting my time on that pussy!" His last word shouted directly in Michelle's right ear, in emphasis.

"HOW ABOUT YOU BLADE? YOU'RE A FUCKING PUSSY, AREN'T YOU?!" Again, emphasizing the derogatory sexist remark directly in her hyper-sensitive ear drum with the bullhorn.

The ringing of his bullhorn-augmented voice in her ear would be ever present for the next several hours until her healing took care of it. Still…. No reply, only angrier sit-ups. She wouldn't even acknowledge him with her eyes.

"ARE YOU EVEN HALF AS BAD OF A BITCH AS YOU THINK YOU ARE, BLADE?!"

No reply, not even a glance. Just angrier sit-ups.

Instructor Alvarez furrowed his brow at not getting the reply he'd wanted. He'd made no bones about it. Women had no place as an Operator, but they'd got the grant, followed all the rules to get here, and were now the prototypes. If Michelle failed, especially with all her significant advantages, then no woman had a chance at doing this. There was more at stake here than just being a super soldier for Rena.

Instructor Alvarez moved to harass someone else, but he'd be back. Soon! Michelle knew it. Lawna knew it. Her team doing sit-ups with her knew it.

Sure enough, moments later he was back in her ear with the bullhorn, after fifty log-resistance sit-ups. "I don't think Blade's group is tired. They don't look tired to me. Keep going. Give me another fifty."

That was it. "YES," she barked, not even bothering to look at him.

"WHAT'S THAT BLADE? YOU GOT SOMETHING FOR ME?!"

"You asked if I was half as bad of a bitch as I thought I was, right…? The answer is YES. I AM."

All four team members in the middle of the log almost simultaneously shook their heads, discouraging this exchange.

"STOP," Instructor Alvarez ordered, causing Michelle's team to immediately halt their sit-ups. "OKAY, BLADE. LET'S FIND OUT." He barked back at her, circling her ominously. "GET UP!"

Tossing the entire log off their laps at once, causing it to safely land away from their legs, Michelle was instantly in Instructor Alvarez's face, eye to eye, staring him down. Tossing his bullhorn into the sand, Alvarez struck with amazing speed, even for Michelle, punches to the gut and ribs, as she was being tossed to the sand with a leveraged maneuver executed almost as fast as she could move.

Instantly she was back on her feet and right in his face. Trying to make a similar move, this time she blocked his fist and hand maneuvers in a blur, ensuring she blocked them with enough force to give him bone bruises, if not hairline fractures.

What the hell? Instructor Alvarez wondered exactly *what* he was facing, taking a step back to regroup, as he shook his fists and arms in an attempt to try to ignore the pain of his blows striking what felt like iron with everything he had.

Candidates and instructors alike had gathered, some cheering for Michelle. Others cheered for the instructor. Some even placed bets, but in a surprising move, Michelle stood down, coming out of her combat stance, offering Instructor Alvarez her hand as if to shake it. "You're really good," she genuinely complimented. "I know I need to be mentally tougher to fight alongside you. Will you help me with that?"

"Oh damn…," one of the candidates could be overheard saying, breaking the awkward silence between Instructor Alvarez and Michelle.

"Sure, Blade," the instructor brushed himself off, picking up his bullhorn, completely reassessing the woman before him, compared to his previous perception of her. He was pretty sure she'd broken his wrist, but he wasn't about to show any weakness in front of her, or his candidates. He could get that fixed later. "We're going for another run. Form up." Candidates hustled into formation along the beach, preparing for another long run in the water.

Maybe just a tad bit more respect was all she'd accomplished, but this was about the long game, not just Hell Week.

*   *   *   *

(Damon's House, Austin, Earth, Present Day)

"So, you wanted to know more about the plan, right?" It wasn't a question really, as he rolled his body toward Mira, pulling her to him in his bed.

"Of course. You know that." Mira blinked, observing his every breath, those unique eyes of his, and the scars he wore like a badge of honor, or an acceptance of his own fate.

"Do you remember the viewing window I showed Goldenbow of the crucifixion in Hell?"

"I wasn't aware it was in Hell, but it certainly looked Hellish, and I was afraid to ask about it."

"It was Hell, and that was my son. His name is Radin. He lives on another world."

Charles W. McDonald Jr.

"Oh my God, Damon, why didn't you tell me? I'm sorry. Is he…?" She trailed off with that one. It didn't seem appropriate to ask if someone just crucified upside down was 'okay' or not. The obvious answer was 'no.' The next question in her mind was, *how many children does Damon have by how many different women?* Maybe she'd hold off on that question for now, for fear of the truth….

"He's alive. I brought him home."

Mira pondered that. Damon literally going to the lengths of entering Hell to save his own son. *Was Damon 'good' or 'bad' or 'none of the above…?'* Whatever Damon was, the circles of his past had ensnared him into a life not of his own choosing. At least that was how it seemed to her, but she needed to know more.

"My point in bringing up the viewing window into Hell was, I went to see someone there. Someone not my son."

"Oh? Who?"

"My wife."

"*Pardon me?*" WIFE! WTF, Damon?! She tried not to let her thoughts scream at him through her eyes, but she was failing, miserably.

"Banthis. Her name is Banthis, and before she introduces herself to you, I'd rather you hear the story from me."

"Oh, I better hear the whole goddamn story, right fucking now!" Mira pulled the bedding around herself, sitting up in the bed, never taking an eye off Damon while hurling visual daggers in his direction.

"Many centuries ago, I lost my first wife, Dallia, to an enemy named Chara. I was lost for a time after that. Dallia meant everything to me. She was…." He didn't really know how to put his love for Dallia into words. He didn't have to. By the way Mira was looking at him now, she knew.

"Yeah, well, anyway…. I was in a very dark place, and I'm not Mr. Nice to begin with, so you can draw your own conclusions. Banthis came to me. She gave me what I needed at the time. We connected in a way I can't connect with other women. I know that's not the kind of thing you want to hear, but just as I can't connect with you in the way I connect with her, I can't connect with her in the way I connect with you." He suddenly wished he had *Distorting Web* up for that part of the conversation. Too late. He was certain Banthis had heard that part.

A massive web, the size of the entire room, suddenly appeared over Mira and Damon, engulfing their master bedroom, shifting and pulsing with life and an energy all its own. Mira blinked, still not used to the power Damon could wield with a mere thought—at least she hoped that was Damon's magic.

"Sorry, for the rest of this conversation. I'd prefer it stay encrypted and between us."

Charles W. McDonald Jr.

"I'm listening, Damon. Tell me everything you can, please. I want to know." Blink. Blink. Blink. Her eyes darted from the *Distorting Web* to Damon's iron glare, shrouded in mystery and weighted in more emotions than Mira could count.

"I have six daughters with Banthis. They're all wonderful, brilliant, beautiful, and talented in their own way. No, that's not all of my children. Honestly, I couldn't tell you how many children I have, but let's say a number greater than ten wouldn't shock me."

A hard gulp from Mira as she tried to take it all in stride, but her blinking rate definitely increased after that.

"This is the part I'm least proud of, so hold on. Don't leave me. I need you. I love you. I know I'm not everything you wanted, but I can be much more if you let me try."

"I'm not going anywhere Damon. I promise."

"Don't make promises you may not wish to keep, Mira. Let me finish."

"Okay…." Another hard swallow from Mira told him to continue, but her withdrawing further into the bedding said she was terrified of what was to come.

"In my obsession to kill Chara, in all of my hatred and revenge for her taking Dallia from me, I made a spell. A spell unlike anything anyone had ever made before. A spell so horrific it was banished on multiple worlds. I was nearly banished from Kaleion twice for this one spell. This spell that would allow me to take one's soul and send it to whomever I wish. Souls are power, and power is useful; it became a balance-of-power issue with its very first use."

"You used it on more than Chara, didn't you?" She was following along and keeping up, but her mind wandered into very dark places very quickly with this conversation and the little gold cross dangling between her breasts felt…awkward.

"Yes, but it had to be tested first." Damon's expression was flat—matter of fact, while Mira's was…terrified.

She didn't want to hear about the test. She was afraid of that knowledge and she wanted to just skip right over it, if possible. "And after it was tested…? After you killed Chara, did you still use it?"

"Yes."

"Do you still use it today?" Mira's glare expectant as she observed his every move and gesture. Every part of his body language was tight. Close to the vest.

A long pause from Damon….

"DO YOU STILL USE IT TODAY, DAMON?"

"Yes."

Charles W. McDonald Jr.

Immediately she jumped up from the bed, starting to put on her clothes as the *Distorting Web* moved slightly in size and position to ensure they were both completely covered for what remained of the conversation.

"Back then I used it to elevate Banthis. Now, I'm using it to gain strength for what must come next."

"And what's that?"

"I'm going to destroy the Dragon of Darkness."

"You're going to what?"

"You heard me. She knows it too."

"The Dragon of Darkness is a woman?"

"He, she, *it*, is whatever it decides to be. Whatever form suits its purpose."

"May I ask why you feel you need to do this?"

"That's really complicated."

"I'm here. I'm listening. Tell me." She paused, adding emphasis, "Tell me, or I'm gone."

"I told you not to make promises you may not wish to keep."

A know-it-all glance from Mira rebuked his 'told ya so' remark.

"If I die now, the way things are, Banthis and I will be crushed by her. By it. By...you know."

"Is the Dragon of Darkness another name for what we might call Satan?" Her fingers held her little gold cross, trying to make a connection to that which was both far and near. A connection to something more of her parents than of herself.

"*IT* goes by many names—probably over a hundred names just on your world."

"You can't destroy Satan, Damon. He's literally a necessary evil in order for people to behave."

"We'll see...."

"What are you not telling me, Damon?"

"Does your Bible not talk about your body being made new—a life in Paradise—after the End Times have concluded and God the Creator defeats the Dragon of Darkness and all his, its, her surrogates?"

Mira blinked, somewhat shocked at Damon's knowledge of her own religion—a religion she'd left far behind most of her adult life since embracing science. Maybe knowing one meant knowing them all, *if* Damon was right. "Okay, continue...."

"My point is, what if all those prophecies were wrong? What if the End Times are not the end of *all* things? What if there is a life beyond for your mortal coil—not just your lifeforce? What if there was never intended to be a true defeat of Hell and its operatives? What if God the Creator needed the Dragon of Darkness for more than just to keep us all in line?"

This philosophical debate was intriguing but unsatisfying, given what was really on her mind, "What is your end game?"

A brilliant question from his very bright girlfriend made him briefly take pause—proud of her. "I'd like to have a life beyond the End Times that is not underneath the thumb of the Dragon of Darkness. I don't want to have a life beyond the End Times where I'm always looking over my shoulder. I want some level of freedom for myself and everyone I love. I want a new equilibrium where the gods of old *have been replaced by those more fit to lead*."

There it was. Damon's Master Plan, or at least an executive summary of it, laid out before Mira. Only Evanyil knew more, and she'd helped build the plan from the very beginning, so many years before. He'd left out a lot of the details of the how, the when, the where, and so forth, but her demigod boyfriend had much bigger plans than she'd ever considered. And now, suddenly she wished she didn't have this knowledge.

"What is our future, and why won't you let me go to Eden?"

A frown from Damon as he considered, *when will Mira ever be happy?* He'd just laid out a tremendous amount of incredibly sensitive information before Mira, and yet it wasn't even close to enough. *How could he convince her to drop the Eden situation?* Damon shivered internally at the thought of Mira going to Eden with him. That could be bad....

Charles W. McDonald Jr.

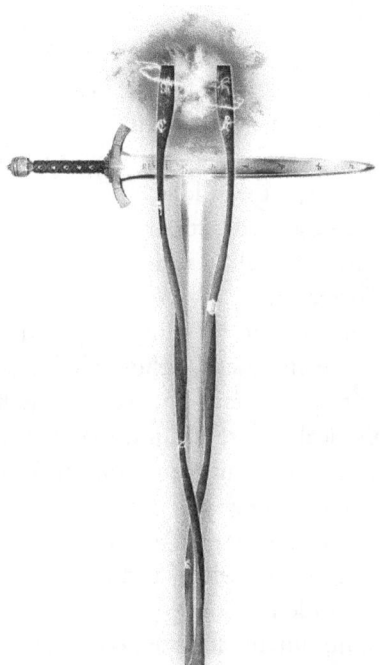

Chapter 38: Morden

(Exeter, Perion, Present Day)

"I don't care what Damon suggests. Silura's going with me. She always goes with me, and there's a very good reason for that," Wraith protested to the group, but especially to Radin. He didn't understand Radin's relationship with Damon, but it was too close and too cozy for his liking. Damon could NOT be trusted, regardless of his forthright nature.

"I don't want to argue with you, Wraith. I'm only saying that Damon's rationale was that when we go face this Morden, we need to take people with 'killer' instincts, and Silura doesn't strike me as that type. Does she have a *'killer'* instinct?"

It was a fair question, if posed in a less-than complimentary way, causing Wraith to postulate and reflect for a moment, frowning. He'd known his sister wife his entire life and they were mirrors of one another. He definitely had little-to-no hesitation to kill, and since his sister was often his mirror, *did that mean she didn't?*

Charles W. McDonald Jr.

"I don't think Damon was trying to exclude anyone as much as he was trying to ensure we have the best chance of success with the least number of casualties. Damon definitely wants Morden dead! Of that, I can be absolutely certain," Radin added, looking at Michelle, Lawna, and Wraith, each in turn.

"Did he offer any tactical advice on how to kill him," Michelle asked, slinging *Bad Intentions* over her right shoulder.

"He did. Very specific advice, actually."

"Well, let's have it," Michelle encouraged, motioning with her arms to come forward with the information.

"He emphasized the need to be completely ruthless, to always be the aggressor, to be prepared for fire and metal—those are his favorite weapons—and to be prepared for him to try to put distance between himself and his targets so if we can press him by being physically close to him, that could be advantageous for us. I was thinking about closing in on him from multiple directions—boxing him in. And, I was wondering if Wraith had a spell that could contain him or prevent him from using a *Portal* or *Gate* to escape or gain a distance advantage?"

"I do. I haven't used it in a while, and it's probably not powerful enough to work on someone like Morden, but if you give me some time, I can update it and see if I can make it more suitable for the task." His eyes blinked, still contemplating his sister's capabilities and mental toughness for this task before them.

"We don't have to do this right this moment, but the sooner the better." Radin was anxious to notch his belt with Morden and the others on Damon's list. He was going to deliver the suffering for a change, and Morden seemed a fitting target for his building acrimony.

"Can you give me a few hours? I'm not really sure how long this will take. I haven't even looked at this thing in forever." Wraith was talented and fast, but not *that* fast. They seemed ready to hang Morden by his balls right this very instant.

"A few hours," Radin agreed with a singular nod, thinking of what he needed to do to get his affairs in order before facing down Morden.

(Gravêstil, Kaleion, Present Day)

The crimson haloed glow over what used to be the magnificent and ancient walled, port city of Gravêstil couldn't hide the bald Morgern from Morden's next volley of fireballs laced with steel shards, exploding outward from their epicenter, upon the legendary Morgern. Metal shrapnel immediately shattered the last of

Charles W. McDonald Jr.

Morgern's shields, ripping through black and silver robes, sending him into hiding as Morden witnessed the great flash of silvery-blue light where Morgern once stood as the dust and violence of his spell dissipated.

"THIS IS ME LAUGHING AT YOU, MORGERN. CAN YOU HEAR ME LAUGHING?" A boisterous belly laugh of gloat pierced Morden's ever-present, hate-filled sneer as he swung his pale green robes with gold embroidery around, pivoting some hundred-and-eighty degrees to see a brilliant flash of golden light off in the distance—on the eastern side of Gravêstil, outside the inner-city walls.

Is he repositioning himself, Morden wondered. Surely Morgern had seen enough. He was no match for the great Morden; he had to know that by now!

The oceanic breeze out of the southwest carried so much of the debris of his hatred across the landscape, it was hard to see details of the once great city, now in ruin. Still on the Aegen River side of the once-great port city, Morden dusted himself off; at least he was upwind from the upheaval he'd wrought. Even *he* didn't like seeing Kaleion this way, but they needed to learn to submit—whatever the cost! He couldn't tolerate any further insurrection….

A smooth downward stroke of his ash staff began super-heating the air in front of him, but as soon as the first silvery-blue flash of light appeared, it was snuffed out of existence as the air in front of him unbent, returning to normal right before his hate-filled, sunken eyes. Something was very wrong. Scrutinous eyes left, then right, under the cowl of his hood as he contemplated what had just happened. *Shields*, as he considered the possibilities, slowly turning around.

"Hi there," the beautiful feminine voice of the busty blonde offered in a common tongue not entirely accurate for Kaleion, caused Morden pause as he took in her strange, outer-worldly, black pants and a low-cut, black top.

She appeared to be on the safer end of some sort of strange weapon now tracing a red beam of light directly to his forehead.

ACK! ACK! ACK! A three-round burst of metallic projectiles bounced right off the shield, directly in between his eyebrows as Morden quickly realized this wasn't a social call. A slow frown turned into a sneering smile as he folded his arms, waving his index finger admonishingly at the beautiful blonde. *Linguistics*. "I do not know you. But that will not save you." A wave of his staff shot forth expanding scimitar blades aiming straight for the beautiful blonde's pretty little head.

It took nerves of steel not to flinch, but she trusted Wraith as she watched the blades bounce off his shield one after the other 'til the fifth one stuck inside the

Charles W. McDonald Jr.

shield—piercing it, stopping only inches from Michelle's nose. That earned Wraith a dirty look from his hidden position behind Morden as she returned fire, this time with her grenade launcher, smiling at the classic sound of the pump-action release of *Bad Intentions*.

He barely had time to see the large metallic object—this one much larger than the other projectiles that nearly split his skull—launched from the under-mount black cylinder coming to rest on the heavily worn cobblestone path just a few spans away. ***BOOM!***

Lawna chuckled from her elevated sniper position—a rooftop some three hundred spans away—watching Morden's body being flung high into the air by the high explosive grenade launched from *Bad Intentions*. Waiting for his body to reach the apex of its arc in mid-air, she exhaled, squeezing the trigger of her Barrett® .50 cal. ***BOOM!*** Easing into the massive recoil, she saw the sizable arc of the blood spurt from her direct hit of the moving target but couldn't see where Morden had landed, behind a set of buildings where Wraith had positioned himself.

From his vantage point, just southwest of Michelle but northeast of the main port, Radin watched as Morden's body flung high into the air, causing him to lose his grip on his staff as Lawna's weapon struck him mid-air, sending him nearly in an opposite direction toward Wraith's position. He didn't like those odds. Wraith was powerful, but he was no match—one on one—for even a wounded Morden. Still, he couldn't *Portal* or *Gate* without Wraith releasing his grip on the city. It would take time, but he immediately took off running to close the gap.

Pushing himself off the ground, Morden felt the gaping wound in his left leg—barely still attached. Without his staff to aid him, this was appearing less and less like a fair fight. He wondered who among his many enemies had brought these off-worlders here to deal with him. *Not Morgern. Not Kellen. Not Illirian. Then who?* Weighing the possibilities, Morden righted himself on his left side in the alley, noticing a shimmering hole about fifty paces in front of him on a slightly elevated position. *Hmmm.*

Wraith couldn't be sure if Morden had noticed him or not, but he *could* see Morden's lips moving. BLACKNESS!

Charles W. McDonald Jr.

What looked like a small, tactical nuclear device to Michelle went off behind where Wraith had been positioned, and in between Wraith and Lawna. The incredible outward explosive force blew Michelle backward at least a hundred yards before the massive sucking sound of the explosion's search for more oxygen drew Michelle's body back toward the epicenter where fire began raining down from the haloed crimson sky.

In full stride, and nearly to Michelle, Radin was suddenly blown backward as he felt all the air ripped from his lungs, just before passing out.

The building suddenly collapsed underneath her elevated position, swallowing Lawna whole as she fell four stories with rubble following her on the way down.

Morden's advanced shields held—purpose-built to be used in conjunction with *Damon's Shockwave*. He could deal with them now but leaving and gathering more research on them seemed the smarter play—for now. A wave of his hand produced the expected result this time as silvery-blue flashes of light superheated the air in front of Morden as he escaped—severed leg in tow, minus one ash staff relic of incredible value to him—not to mention the treasure he'd plundered from Morgern a few moments earlier. *They'll pay for that!*

Part 5: The Distorted Continuum – Part II

Charles W. McDonald Jr.

Mira Castille

Charles W. McDonald Jr.

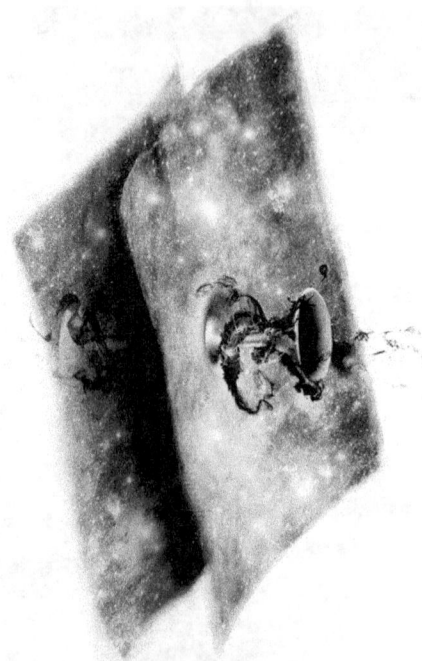

Chapter 39: Mirror

(Damon's House, Austin, TX, Earth, Present Day)

"Fuck you, asshole," Mira shouted, slamming down her fist on the granite island countertops so hard she wondered if she'd cracked the surface. Actually, her fist hurt now too. *A hairline fracture?*

"Necessary," Damon asked, standing within arm's reach of Mira's anger, though questioning the wisdom of such, as the conversation had quickly escalated to insults.

"GO fuck yourself!" Her right foot in full-blown fidget mode now, threatening to tear a hole in the tile flooring.

"You kiss your mother with that mouth?" Damon's glower from his nearly full-foot height advantage over Mira didn't intimidate her one bit. She stared him down with all the tenacity of Morden, and twice the gumption. Mira was no ordinary woman, and she wasn't about to settle for anything less than what she wanted.

"I sure as fuck won't be kissing you." Love or not, she was pissed. And wanted some fucking reasonable answers! An explanation at the very least.

Awkward silence between them momentarily became the impetus for Damon to yield a little ground to Mira. "What will it take for me to make this right between us?"

"You know what I want, dammit!" Her beautiful blue eyes flared at him in the daylight-spectrum lighting of his kitchen, with her lips pressed together, expectantly.

"I'm not taking you to Eden!" He could feel the electrical tug-of-war going on between them, charging the air in both acrimony, and need. This war of will would soon rip them apart, or weld them together.

"Why the fuck not, Damon? What are you hiding from me?" Mira wasn't the jealous type, but the thought of him having one or more lovers on his little experimental world jumped to the front of her consciousness. They had talked at length about Banthis, but from what he had described about that situation, she didn't get the feeling this was about Banthis. This was something different, or someone different.... "Is it Illirian? Are you fucking her too?"

"No! And jealousy doesn't suit you. You know I'm not the monogamous type, but I have kept my sexual distance from other women since we started dating. Just for the record and all!" That came out more spiteful than intended, causing the radiating aura of her glower to superimpose over his.

"Then I don't get it. Why can't I go to Eden with you?" Again her eyes observing every little move of her lover's body and his body language. From the toes of his black leather boots to those raven bangs hung low over those beautiful black eyes of his, her eyes walked over every inch of him, expecting a new level of that famed honesty of his.

"I'm done with this conversation." He started to walk away, causing Mira to resort to a different tactic.

"I want to understand everything there is to know about this man that I love with everything I have. Can't you see that?" Tears welled in Mira's eyes as the words invoked the feelings deep within her, "I ache for you, Damon. I'm in physical pain when I'm not with you. This is far more than love for me, Damon. Don't you get it...?"

Stopping dead in his tracks between the kitchen and master bedroom, Mira's confession shattered his will to protect her. Pivoting back to her hard beauty, Damon caved before her adoration. "I'll do it. I'll take you there, but you must stay on my hip at all times. You're not to go anywhere where I cannot see you in my direct line of sight. Got it?"

She didn't understand the reason for the explicit nature of his condition,

Charles W. McDonald Jr.

but it was progress. "Got it!"

"I need to spend some time there. I'm not sure how long we'll be gone, but why don't you bring an overnight bag for us both?" He felt the emotional whiplash from her demonstrative pivot on a thin dime, but at least they weren't hurling insults at one another. And her foot had ceased its fidgeting. Progress....

"I'm on it." Tearing off towards the master bedroom to gather their things, she kissed Damon, caressing his arm, already plotting how she'd stay longer on Eden.

(Presidential Palace, New Georgia, Eden, Present Day)

"Sir, she just won't go away. I've tried to get rid of her," President Abel's assistant, Casey Williams, informed. Her beautiful brown eyes and straight brown hair in a well-pressed business-like skirt with cream-ruffled top marked her the pretty, but consummate, professional. Her tone sounded exasperated.

"Did you tell her I'm in the middle of a meeting?"

"Twice!"

"She's not going away, is she?"

"No, sir. I'm afraid not." Casey's arms folded over one another said she was tired of this being her problem and ready for it to become his. Let him deal with this crazy bitch for once.

A heavy sigh from the president. Ever since Damon had saved him from Kaleion's chaos, he'd often wondered if he would have been better served being left behind to deal with Morden rather than Mira and everything else on his plate. "Send her in...." Abel's tone was...resigned, as his eyes looked down at the massive paperwork requiring his attention.

"This oughta be good," Ron Stencowsky offered. "I'm staying out of it, just so you know."

"Sure, Ron. Show that legendary backbone of yours," Abel chided, causing Ron to frown.

Strolling in, looking her finest in a tight, black, sheer minidress with flowers in all the right places, Mira immediately reminded the president of what Damon saw in her. "Mr. President...," Mira offered with a brief pause and barely a nod of acknowledgment for Ron. Ron, and his men, had been playing interference, trying everything they could to keep her out of the president's office, and quiet too. Well, so much for his efforts. She was here now, and she was going to have her say. "You know what I'm here for."

"I do, and the answer is still 'no,' per Damon," the president informed her flatly, adding, "Damon said he would post an approved list of visitors soon, and I'm certain you'll be at the very top of that list, but I'm also certain he has his reasons for needing privacy at the moment. I've known Damon far longer than you, and I can tell you for a fact that man doesn't do anything without a good reason."

"I don't give a flying juniper fuck what his reasons are!" Mira flared before them, adding, "I'm his goddamn girlfriend—practically his wife! And I want to see him right fucking now! If I must, I'll walk all the way there in heels. I don't care if it takes me forever. I don't care if I have to...." She didn't need to finish. She'd made her point as obvious at the sign of the president waving her off in protest. Though, she knew she'd stretched the truth with their relationship status. Even she didn't know what their relationship status was, and that was the whole point of this meeting with Damon. To find out. Damon had just disappeared years ago. No note. No goodbye. No explanation. And she wanted—she *deserved*—that explanation.

"I really don't understand what all the lack of patience is about, but I'll contact him and make arrangements. Will that suffice?"

She wasn't sure if she was being lied to or not. He was a politician, after all. Looking between Ron and President Abel, she didn't know quite what to make of it, but she was going to finish making her point. "Today! I want an answer today, or I start walking towards his manor, if necessary. And Damon will do far worse than kill you if you let me get hurt on my way out to his manor. Are we clear?"

"Perfectly. Crystal clear, Mira. Will that be all?"

Her pivot toward the door to the presidential offices expressed her dismissal of him, and this conversation.

A moment later, in a Mira-cleared office, "Wow, she's got spunk," Ron quipped.

"Is that what you call that," President Abel asked, adding, "On my world we had a different word to describe that."

"Sir." Casey cautiously poked her head back into President Abel's office, not wanting to follow that disaster that she'd overheard moments before.

"What is it now?"

"I'm so sorry, sir. I think this is urgent and merits your attention."

"It isn't Mira, is it?"

"Ummm. No sir. Definitely not Mira."

"Send them in...." It couldn't be worse than Mira. Whatever, or whoever, it was.

Melissa walked in, her youngest son in tow with him looking around the office of the president, making note of all the splendid artworks and fine craftsmanship, though not overwhelmed. "Mr. President." Melissa offered a curtsy—sort of, obviously not familiar with Kaleion customs or formalities.

"Melissa, isn't it?"

"Yes, Mr. President." She beamed for him, surprised he remembered her.

"We've met a few times here and there. What can I do for you?"

"Mr. President, this is my youngest son, Lance. Say hello to the President, Love."

"Hello, President Love," the adorable Lance offered with his best imitation of his mother's horrid attempt at a curtsy. Maybe three years old, Lance still wore the clothes he'd worn the day they'd arrived on Eden, though obviously still well-maintained out of necessity. Lance had been unable to process the new alien world without the familiarity of his old clothes, leaving Melissa little choice but to do what mothers do—help their children adapt.

"Uh," Melissa started to correct her son, only to see President Abel waving her off.

Moving out from behind his intimidating, ornately hewn birch desk, President Abel squatted down on the floor with Lance to get himself down to the child's level. "Hi Lance. How are you? You can call me Abel."

"Okay, Abel Love." Lance still had his mother's hand in his left hand, while he nervously fidgeted his right index finger in his mouth in a self-soothing manner.

The president smiled broadly at the cuteness on display before him, offering his hand to Lance to hold with his right hand, encouraged when Lance immediately accepted it. "Did something happen you want to tell me about?"

Lance nodded slowly, though sheepishly looking at Abel in the eyes.

"It's safe here. You can tell me anything. No one will hurt you."

"I went down into the tunnels with the Negi."

The boy's English was not fully enunciated, but Abel could make out the gist of it.

"With the what," the president prompted for clarification in his best Earth English, which wasn't that great, though 'going down into the tunnels' got both his attention, and Ron's.

"The Negi; that's what they call themselves. They've been here a very long time. They want to know how long we plan on staying on their world."

Ron got out of his chair, now sitting down on the floor with the president, facing the innocent boy before them. "Hi there, Lance. I'm Ron."

"Hi, Ron. I know you. Everyone talks about you. You're like Bob the Builder®."

Not really getting the child-like reference to the cartoon, Ron still smiled back at Lance. "What else can you tell us about your trip down into the tunnels? What all did you see down there? Were the Negi nice to you?"

"Yeah, I guess so. They kinda showed me around and stuff. I saw lots of what they called, 'pods.'"

"Can you describe these 'pods?'" Ron was curious. They all were.

"They had to go into these machines that kept them alive down in the tunnels when the bad thing happened."

"Did they talk about what that bad thing was? Did they explain it to you," President Abel asked, questioningly looking to Melissa.

Lance shook his head no, adding, "They can talk to you without moving their lips. They told me a little about how their machines worked, but...," he paused unsure of himself and what to say. "...They want to talk to you."

Ron looked questioningly amongst them, wanting a clarification. "They want to talk to us," he asked, pointing between himself and the president.

Lance shook his head no again, adding, "They want to talk to Abel Love."

President Abel smiled broadly at the boy, but inside he was all frowns and furrowed brows, considering what the boy had just told him. The fact that they had killed so many of them already but had allowed the little boy to live to deliver their message was troubling, though he was grateful. Perhaps a truce was possible between them. Communication was always the first step in negotiations, and he was a master negotiator, but he wondered how great his negotiation skills would have to be to get the Negi to allow them to stay. Permanently.

*   *   *   *

(Damon's Manor, Eden, Present Day)

A silvery-blue flash of light bent and rent the superheated air just inside the foyer of Damon's manor, enabling Damon and Mira to walk through from Damon's house in Austin. The sound of Damon's early warning systems went off immediately, alerting his staff to the presence of someone appearing inside the alert perimeter via magic. An instant later, Damon's chief of staff appeared by way of the butler's kitchen.

"Good afternoon, sir. How are you? Will you and Ms. Mira be staying

Charles W. McDonald Jr.

long this time," Edgar Hastings asked while all smiles for heels and business-skirt Mira.

"I'm not sure Edgar. We've got some business here, and as soon as we're done, we'll be off again. How's the staff situation shaping up?"

"Quite good, sir. We're almost back at full complement. There's been a flood of people requesting to work for you. I'm just finishing a few more interviews, and I think I'll have the full staff, plus a couple of spare candidates just in case." It was always best to have spares where Damon was concerned, since people had a nasty habit of quitting or dying around him—or worse.

"Anything Mira needs, make sure she has it, but I need you to help me keep an eye on her while she's here. She's not to be alone for even a moment. Do I make myself clear?" That appeared to be directed at Edgar, but Mira felt Damon's eyes on her with that statement as well.

"Perfectly, sir," Edgar replied dutifully, not really understanding why, but perfectly understanding the outcome, if Damon's orders were not followed.

"Can you have dinner brought up to my bedroom?"

"Certainly, sir. Would an hour from now work for you?"

"That's fine, Edgar. I'm going to take her for a walk around the grounds, then we'll be upstairs."

"Of course, sir." Edgar offered with a dutifully measured bow.

"Bye, Edgar," Mira offered, yielding her overnight bag for him to take upstairs.

A moment later, they were walking on the grounds outside, Mira admiring Damon's handiwork in the garden. "It's so beautiful here. How did you get the photosynthesis to take hold so quickly?"

"I have a spell that allows me to extend my capabilities, or the capabilities of a given spell a tremendous distance. I used that in combination with a spell called, *Life*. Effective, huh?" Damon offered, motioning out before him to the trees, flora, and lush green grass everywhere on his oceanfront property. "It will still take months and years for the trees to look like they've been growing centuries, but they're doing nicely."

"It's beautiful, Damon. You should be very proud of what you've done here, but you still haven't told me the big secret of why you wouldn't allow me to come here with you, and why am I not allowed to be alone...."

"Look, it's complicated, okay. I've told you that I can't tell you every detail of my plan, and you know why."

"Banthis."

"No, not Banthis. Not entirely."

Charles W. McDonald Jr.

"You might trust Banthis, but I sure as hell don't." Mira still had trouble digesting the origin of Banthis and the idea of Damon sending her *souls*. She knew a lot of Damon's past was horrific by his own admission, and Damon wasn't 'turning a new leaf for her,' but he wasn't descending further into Banthis' grip, either. At least, she hoped he wasn't.

Walking around the perimeter of the manor to the unobstructed view of the ocean out over the cliffs before them, Damon took Mira's hand, taking a deep breath of the salty ocean air.

"It really is beautiful here, Damon. You really outdid yourself."

"Thank you." He appreciated the genuine nature of her compliment, but he was avoiding the inevitable. *Maybe just a little longer and she'll drop it*, he thought. "I've always been great at destroying—comes with the territory of my specialty. But creating is so much more difficult, and challenging. This represents the best and most complex magic I've ever done."

A crunch of brush behind them announced Edgar's hasty arrival. "Sir, an urgent call for you." Edgar handed Damon a cellular device looking very similar to, but more advanced than, an Earth Android smartphone. Only 3mm thick and made entirely of transparent aluminum—looking only like a small sheet of glass with a holographic image—Mira wondered how Damon had managed to build a network infrastructure superior to Earth so quickly on Eden.

"Abel, what's going on?"

Damon's rich and throaty voice sounded both concerned and agitated. She didn't know who Abel was, but it sounded important.

"Uh huh...." Pause from Damon. "Uh huh...." Another pause. "Nuh-uh!!"

Mira frowned, observing the urban slang from Damon. He'd been spending too much time on Earth. *And what was he so vehemently opposing with this Abel anyway?*

"You didn't hear me, Abel. I said fucking '*no*,' and I meant it! Not right now!" Damon, clicked the red end call icon, hanging up on the president.

"So, who's Abel?"

"The elected President."

"Oh." Mira blinked rapidly, involuntarily fidget tapping her heel on the ground beneath her, not really liking that her boyfriend was powerful enough to curse out the president of a newly elected government. It was all so unnerving, being around Damon and running in his circles. It was...treacherous footing to put it mildly, and she struggled with her identity being this close to him.

"Let's go eat. I need you," Damon offered, pulling her to him as he kissed

Charles W. McDonald Jr.

her before the ocean view. At least now she wasn't asking about why she couldn't be left alone here on Eden anymore.

*　　*　　*　　*

Food and sex always helped Damon focus, and already thoughts of dealing with the rogue threat of the black hole, not far enough from his senses for comfort, were rolling through his mind. *What if I…?*

"What are you thinking about?" Mira stroked his legs with hers under the covers, snuggling into Damon.

"A different solution than healing the manifold of spacetime on the other side of the membrane."

"Do tell."

"Well, like we said you can't throw more energy at the problem or you could make it worse."

"Yeah…."

"What if we threw velocity and direction at it?"

"I'm not following." Mira wasn't following, but then the light came on just as Damon was about to open his mouth. "No, you fucking can't be thinking…."

"I'm thinking we fix a black hole with another black hole, only this one already has escape velocity sending it, and the other black hole with it, out of harm's reach." He paused for a moment, admiring his destructive genius and that's really where this came from—his destructive intellect versus his newfound creation intellect. "If I can't destroy it, I can sure as hell move it out of our way and send it somewhere else to become someone else's problem—albeit a much bigger and nastier problem than it ever was before, since the two would inevitably merge with one another."

"Damon, you can't. Let's find a more elegant solution to the problem than a hammer. I believe the manifold idea is capable of solving this problem, and think of what it would mean if we could actually do it?"

"I'll tell you what, I'll give you three hundred days to give me explicit details on how to heal the manifold, or otherwise solve this problem. That's about as long as I can hold off before we act on this problem, but if I don't have specifics by then, I'm going with my plan, regardless of how risky it might be to neighboring star systems. Deal?"

"Deal….," Mira replied sheepishly, not wanting to think about the consequences of her failure and how many people, or lifeforms, she might be responsible for killing if this much bigger problem found its way to an inhabited star system.

Charles W. McDonald Jr.

She needed to get up and walk around. She thought better on her feet, anyway. "Can I go for a walk if I stay inside the manor?"

Damon visibly cringed at the idea of letting her out of his sight, but he could also see she was troubled by their conversation. Perhaps a little relaxing of his leash might help settle her nerves. "Stay inside, Mira. Don't make me come looking for you."

"I promise." Slipping out of bed, she walked to the dresser he'd given her to use, pulling out a cream-colored robe with lace and flowers, tying it at her waist as she tried maintaining calm 'til she got on the other side of the door where she let out a deep sigh of relief. She never got used to Damon's control, or his power. How he casually talked about things that could destroy entire civilizations made her rethink their relationship and her role in being this close to him. She needed to think, and while pacing wasn't her style, she needed the space away from Damon to make her decision—to weigh the pros and cons of being around him, or this close to him.

Thinking aloud was dangerous, but she couldn't help herself, "If I stay with him, at least I can influence him by being his better conscience." She paused before she rounded the circular main staircase, descending in her bare feet on the magnificently-stained ornate hardwood steps comprising the staircase. "If I go, he won't have my knowledge to tap into anymore, and that lack of knowledge could enable very bad and destructive decisions to be made. Something horrific could happen, and it would essentially be my fault." A few more paces and she reconsidered, "He'd just find someone else to replace my knowledge—someone with less of a moral compass even. God, what should I do...?"

"Pardon, Miss Mira?" Edgar had stunned her out of her pros and cons contemplation, as he was ascending with a tray of food for Damon with a scroll teetering on the edge of the silver serving platter.

"Oh nothing, Edgar. Just talking gibberish."

A suspicious look from the chief of staff said he knew better, but he also knew better than to make an issue out of it. "Damon said I could go for a walk if I stayed inside the manor. I was thinking about walking around on the first floor if that's okay."

"Certainly. If Master Damon said it's okay, then it's perfectly fine. Do you need anything?"

"No, Edgar. I'm fine. Thank you for asking." A disarming smile from her and she hoped it was enough to make him forget whatever he might have heard.

"Of course. If you need anything, just go down the staircase in the butler's kitchen on the right side of the foyer and you'll find the servant's quarters down there. They'll get you whatever you require."

"Thank you, Edgar." Mira smiled, continuing her descent. Somehow her interaction with Damon's chief of staff served as catalyst for her decision—to leave Damon. Now she just had to figure out the mechanics of doing so. Extracting herself from Damon wouldn't be easy. Running through the horrific scenarios of 'goodbye' in her head, she rounded the staircase, setting foot on the magnificent, massive tiles that made up the foyer of Damon's manor. The tears welling in her eyes couldn't explain the vision before her…and why she was seeing double.

"What the FUCK!" Future Mira called out to present Mira from Damon's front door, practically kicked open by future Mira in stiletto CFM boots and a tight-wrapped black bodysuit—with a holstered and silenced Glock®-29 on her right side.

The scenarios of why Damon didn't want her to come to Eden suddenly slammed home in an instant for present Mira as she stood horrified and shocked at the future Mira standing before her. *WTF!* Carefully she closed the distance between her and herself, momentarily pausing in disbelief at what and who she was seeing. "What has Damon done," she asked herself aloud.

"What do you mean? You don't know?" Future Mira was closing the distance as well, running through *Timecop* scenarios in her mind, wondering if all that bullshit about the same matter not being able to occupy the same space at the same time was true, or not….

"Know what?" Present Mira's beautiful blue eyes blinked, trying to piece Damon's time-manipulation mosaic together in her mind's eye.

"Tell me, what's the last thing you remember?!" Future Mira insisted, obviously the more aggressive instantiation of the two, but given what she'd been through over the last few years, it was totally understandable. The apocalypse hadn't been kind to her on Earth, and Damon's abandonment of her hadn't helped, either.

"Last thing I remember about what?" Now standing just a few feet apart, present Mira felt woefully out of the loop.

"Earth," Future Mira hissed at herself.

"Earth is fine. What's the big deal?"

"Fuck me!" Future Mira was piecing it together. She hadn't even considered this possibility…. "What is your classification at UT right now?"

"A junior. Why?"

"Fuck me! Damon, what have you done?"

"What are you talking about?" Now future Mira and Mira were within arm's reach of one another, just outside the gaming room off the left-side of the foyer.

"Let's go in here." Future Mira motioned to the gaming room where she started to walk, hoping Mira would follow. "I don't want Damon to hear this conversation. He's here, isn't he?!"

"Yes."

"Mira, please come here. We need to talk," future Mira pleaded, using the calmest tone she could manage.

Following future Mira into the gaming room, future Mira slammed the door shut, closing them both inside.

*   *   *   *

The door to the gameroom opened just enough to let Mira out, ensuring she locked the door from the gameroom side before firmly closing the door behind. Adjusting her cream robe, Mira headed upstairs…to *her* Damon.

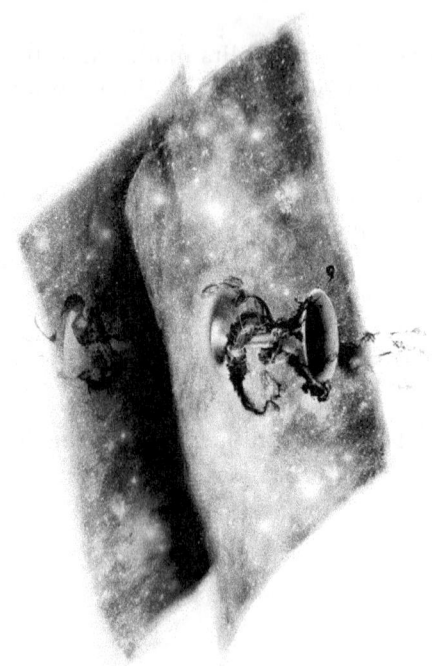

Chapter 40: Black Mirrors of the Soul

(The World Below and Between, Near the Kaleion Marker, Time Neutral)

amon never trusted anyone, or anything, down here. Trust could be fatal. Besides, *what had trust ever done for him?* He followed the arrangements, sitting at the steps of the temple, waiting for Evanyil and her even more crazy sister, Lorianus. Elves were dangerous and slippery with the truth. Cave elves, on the other hand, didn't even make an attempt at being coy. They merely killed you if they didn't like you. Still, if Evanyil was all she was alleged to be, she could be useful. Though, the idea of a partner did require a level of trust he wasn't yet comfortable with. This would be a trial run. *Let's see how she does, and we'll go from there*, Damon cautioned himself as he waited.

The strange light given off by the vegetation of this dangerous expanse made him take pause. The interior of the city seemed darker, more dangerous, than the outer that butted up against the native plant life of the massive caverns. He was warned never to travel here until he'd become far more experienced and powerful. This was no place for a beginner. Even seasoned mages died here, and

Charles W. McDonald Jr.

many were lost forever, but supposedly Evanyil could help him find the way out. He tried staying as close to the markers as possible, but even that didn't guarantee his safe exit. Hopefully Evanyil could do what had been claimed of her by his contact.

Sitting on the steps of the temple, he watched others go by, elves and trollocs alike, even the occasional Human, though that was much less common down here. Turning his attention temporarily back to the temple's entrance, he could see a figure moving in the shadows—definitely female—and unquestionably beautifully shaped. Just as quickly as she appeared, she was gone—perhaps inside. He couldn't tell.

Sighing, he turned back to face the street, regretting his decision to wait here for Evanyil. *What am I doing? I don't need her, or her even more unstable sister. I'd be better off on my own.*

"I think so too."

The sultry voice of Evanyil was more than enough to make him jump out of his skin right there on the spot. Spinning around and rising to his feet before he knew it, Damon found himself confronted by the most beautiful woman he'd ever seen. Her satin yet shimmering black skin was perfection as was her ageless youth. Her perfect symmetry, unique and glowing violet eyes, shimmering platinum braided hair to the small of her back, and her stunning curves would turn every head—man, woman, elf—everyone. She appeared not even twenty summers of age. They say first impressions are everything. Damon's first impression of Evanyil in the flesh was…. WOW!

"Ummm. I'm Damon." Not wanting to threaten her with his size, he sat back down on the steps.

"Yes, you are." Evanyil paced around him, or *for* him; he couldn't quite tell. Suddenly, unexpectedly, she kneeled eye to eye with him. "Those are pretty black eyes. Wherever did you get them?"

"You could say I killed someone for them." Not a lie, but not the whole truth, either. He wasn't sure about her yet.

"I heard you killed your father for them." Her beautiful violet eyes flashed with the delivery of her well-sourced intelligence on the matter.

She had good sources—as did he. "Where's Lorianus?"

A directional nod of Evanyil's head pointing behind Damon caused him to pivot and look behind, seeing Evanyil's much bigger and fiercer-looking sister all decked out in the finest elven ranger gear money could buy. Evanyil was soft, sultry, chaotic, and amazingly stunning. Lorianus was muscular, broad, toned, and deadly quiet in appearance. She'd managed to sneak up on them, on him anyway,

Charles W. McDonald Jr.

with little-to-no effort.

"*This* is the mage?! He doesn't look like much to me," Lorianus chided, looking down at Damon from her higher-ground position on the temple stairs, causing Damon to stand where he towered over her, even with her elevation advantage.

"Try me," Damon warned, never blinking as he stared Lorianus down.

"Okay, maybe he's got some balls. I'll give him that." Lorianus backed down, giving Damon some space.

Pivoting back to Evanyil, only to see she was gone, Damon started to wonder what was going through her mind. *Was she toy*— Before he could finish the thought, he felt Evanyil's tongue in his left ear. Before he could protest, she had him weak everywhere but that which he couldn't yet control. There he was pulsing as Evanyil's licking turned to sensual kissing of his earlobe while caressing his neck.

"Hmmm." Evanyil suddenly pulling back left Damon frustrated and confused. "Well, he's going to be fun to play with at least." Evanyil moved around him again—this time down the steps as she started walking away from him, swaying her perfect hips in a tight, shimmering black bodysuit that also showed off the long, poisoned dagger she was known to wear at all times. "Coming, Damon? You do want to get out of here, right? I mean, we've got work to do—don't we?"

A heavy sigh from Damon didn't reveal everything currently going on in his head about Evanyil—that was far too complicated for one physical gesture to fully express. *What was he getting himself into with this cave elf?* She was going to be his undoing, but she *was* magnificent to listen to, and to look at.

(Damon's House, Austin, Earth, Present Day)

The house was just as she remembered it. Though Mira was experiencing a serious case of déjà vu, she was still able to maintain her cool thus far. Damon hadn't noticed yet, and that was a good thing.

"What's wrong?" Damon's sudden appearance behind her startled her almost to the point of back-kicking him and driving her heel into the roof of his foot—an involuntary response she had to fight with everything she had, as he wrapped his arms around her waist.

"I love you, Damon." Spinning around, she kissed him in what felt like the first time in forever, remembering what they once had, as it all came flooding back to her in an instant. Nuzzling into his neck, she missed the comfort of knowing no one could hurt her ever again in his presence. Her missing of Damon couldn't be expressed in words, but her body practically tried to crawl inside him as she pulled him as close to her as she could.

"I love you too. Are you okay? You've been looking out the window like...."

"I'm fine." She had to cut him off quickly and get her shit in gear or he was going to figure it out. His intellect was as sharp as hers, and he was infinitely more experienced. "So, what more can I do to help?" *Yes, that's the right approach. Distracting him with helpful thinking, words, and action....*

"Well, now that we got the whole Eden visit thing off your chest, if you can get me the manifold healing details in the timeline we discussed, that would be helpful."

Uh-oh, she remembered the white hole discussion they had, but not the timeline for a deliverable for healing the manifold. *When had that happened, and why can't I recall that conversation?* A faint tickling in the back of her mind like a memory of a memory told her she'd already provided Damon an answer to that question, but she couldn't for the life of her, remember the details of that answer. Wave-particle duality perhaps, that was the answer to so many problems, but it wasn't detailed enough to resolve something like this.

Another absence in her memories bothered her beyond comprehension as she tried to recall how and why they broke up in the first place. *How and why did I become separated from Damon and suddenly finding myself in the plains of West Texas as the first bombs started to fall?* Somehow, she felt her leaving Damon wasn't entirely of her own making.

As if stirred by her continuum-distorted memories, a twinge poked at more than just her thoughts, as the new—or rather old—wound at her side began to throb. The bullet had gone clean through. She had made sure when she shot herself not to hit anything vital, but it had left a nasty scar in her left flank. *Pull your shit together woman. NOW!* "Anything else? You don't have to play your cards so close to the vest anymore. You know that. We've shared a great deal. I can keep a secret. You know that."

"Perhaps." He considered it. He had shared a great deal with her, but he couldn't be around all the time to protect her from being scanned. "I'll tell you what, with the protections I've already given you, I can protect you from being scanned for about a month, but I'll have to renew the magic from time to time to keep everything intact, so your thoughts won't be readable by anyone or anything. If you allow me to do that, then I can share more. Sound fair?"

"I understand the precautions you're taking, and I'll keep my mouth shut.

You can count on me."

Focusing as he reached out to the Zero-Point source field, Damon cast *Mind Shield*, leaving a charcoal-blue aura of his magic encircling Mira's skull that only he and other very experienced mages could, or would, notice. It wouldn't protect her from being scanned by the Dragon of Darkness, but if the Dragon of Darkness were in front of Mira, that would present a far bigger problem than just having her mind scanned. Still, it would encrypt her thoughts and their conversations, but it also meant he couldn't probe her thoughts anymore, either.

Staring into his beautiful black shimmering eyes—his *black mirrors of the soul*—Mira sought comfort from the memories of the life he'd saved her from, not long ago. She tried to hold back the flood of horrible memories that always came rushing back whenever she thought of the apocalypse on Earth, and she didn't know if Damon's spell would prevent him from reading her memories or not, but they were just beyond the horizon of her preeminent thoughts. If he could read her thoughts, he would know, but his beautiful black eyes looked back at her with nothing but unconditional love and adoration, and all she could do was nuzzle into his chest again—safe once more in the comfort of her Damon, as she felt the reverberation and bravado of his sexy voice begin to tell her more of his closest-held secrets about the Master Plan.

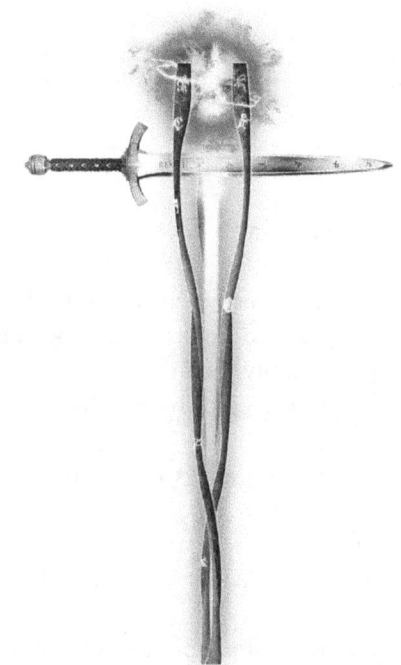

Chapter 41: Phantom Lust

(Place of Defiling, Perion, Present Day)

It wasn't sure what exactly *it* was seeing. Oh, it was Anna, alright—sort of.... *But why was she devouring a deer?* She'd snapped its neck and begun drinking its blood. He, *it*, didn't understand.

Her rebirth hadn't been kind to her, and the Dragon had made it clear there wouldn't be another. This was her last and final chance to serve, or the punishments would be far worse than she could imagine, and she could imagine the unfathomable.

Letting the dry husk of the deer she'd fed on drop to the bloodied grass below, Anna tried to understand.... She had all the thirst of before, and nearly none of the strength and powers that had come with this other-worldly affliction. It wasn't right, but then right and fair were not in the Dragon's vocabulary. There was only servitude and hope for a lesser suffering. Still, there were rewards—of a sort. They were doled out sparingly and only to the most deserving. *Eldrac would never see them! Castlin neither! Xarn—phaw! She wasn't even as useful as the deer she'd just*

Charles W. McDonald Jr.

killed. If anyone was going to succeed, it needed to be her. And, there *would* be successes. She'd learned from the last time.... She knew the greatest of the threats among them, and she was going to deal with the dirty-blonde first, and foremost.

(San Diego, CA, Earth, Present Day)

"Rena, I don't get it. We're not even out of BUD/S training yet. What's the fucking rush?" Lawna struggled to understand Rena's plans, *but what was so different about that?* Rena always gave only the information needed to execute her plan, but revealing her plans wasn't in the cards—ever. That part of working for Rena sucked!

"Darling, you've always been able to focus on more than one thing at a time. I'm sure this will be no different." Rena Rectovich casually sat on Michelle's bunk beside Rena's obvious favorite, staring down Lawna expectantly.

"How are my babies?" Michelle's first and only concern was always her girls. Rena could relate.

"I brought more pictures." Rena pulled out her Android phone, showing Michelle and Lawna more adorable pictures of their baby girls. All three of them.

"Why haven't you sent us these?" It came across accusatory and leverage-like from Lawna, but Michelle waved Lawna off with her eyes.

"Darling, I took these just before getting on the plane to come see you. I can make sure you get pictures every day, if you want. I won't ever hold anything back from you."

Yeah, like you didn't hold back on the little becoming immortal piece of information, Lawna accused internally, then wondering if Rena had unspoken ESP talents. *Likely.*

Their barracks wasn't the best place for this conversation, and Michelle doubted Rena even had permission to be in here with them, but she was grateful for the very recent pictures of their girls, if not for the simultaneous tug on her loyalties. She had duties to the United States of America and the U.S. Navy SEALs. They were less than two weeks from graduation and deployment. There was simply no way they could even get out of BUD/S long enough to do what Rena was asking. She didn't understand why Rena had sent them to BUD/S training to begin with if they were going to become U.S. Government Property. *What was Rena thinking?*

"Look, Rena...," Michelle began with the use of her name, rather than the required familial title of 'Mother,' to Rena's flash of disappointment in her eyes. "…Thank you for coming to see us. We appreciate the pictures, but we're trapped here. We simply cannot leave." Given the intensity of the special forces' installation all around them and the current alert level status—DEFCON 3— Michelle's logic was unassailable. A fast-rapping knock at the door to Michelle and Lawna's quarters caused them both to look terrified at Rena, who remained calm and collected. And immovable from her current position on Michelle's bed.

"Come," Rena offered, not thinking twice about the fact that she wasn't supposed to be there.

"Here, Blade." SEAL Instructor Alvarez held out a sheet of paper with an official JSOC seal at the top center part of the header. His eyes ran across their quarters, making direct eye contact with Rena, but not saying a single word about it. "We've got orders to take the top of the class with us. That includes you two."

"The South China Sea," Michelle breathed aloud in disbelief. *How had Rena?* Michelle looked at Rena, truly astonished at her reach and influence inside the walls of the US Government. *Who did she know? Better yet, what did she have on them?*

Even the scent in this room was…off.… Every single time he'd been alone around either Michelle or Lawna, his nose picked up hints of both something sweet and something…stale. Here too, with her, he smelled it again. Not quite the same as the other two, but definitely in the same category of weird. *Ignore it,* he prioritized his thoughts internally. "Get your gear. We're feet wet in six hours." SEAL Instructor Alvarez tried, unsuccessfully, not to slam their door in frustration upon exiting their quarters.

"There. See. Problem solved." Rena brushed her hands together as if she'd been toiling all day in the soil of her garden in the Carpathian Mountains.

Michelle and Lawna looked to each other, then to Rena. Rena gets what Rena wants. Always!

Dallia, Enchantress of Winds

Charles W. McDonald Jr.

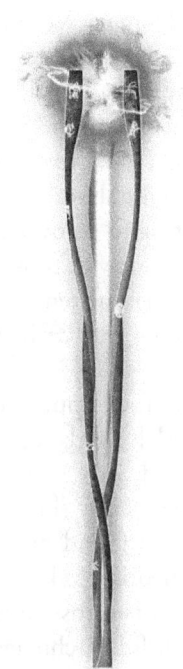

Chapter 42: The First Sentence Commuted

(School of Invocation, Kaleion, A Long Time Ago)

he first day of school was awkward for everyone—faculty and students alike. Yet it had come like lightning through the crisp morning air—raising the hackles and nerves of even the most seasoned among them. This was a dangerous place, after all. Young kids, some of immense talent, wielding incredibly powerful tools like a babe with a meat cleaver. Last semester had ended with the death of four students and two faculty members. Already there were rumors of their replacements. One of the rumors was not to be believed! *It simply could not be!*

Dallia busied herself, examining her fingernails—like unto living gold dust—pondering both what might be and when this faculty meeting would be over, so she could be about her business. She had over a dozen students in her homeroom class this year—over a dozen! *What were they thinking with that kind of class density! Did they want to get more faculty AND students killed?!*

A cleared throat from Dean Thackerly surreptitiously called the room—

Charles W. McDonald Jr.

and the meeting—to order. "Welcome. Welcome. I'm so glad to see so many familiar faces this year." Another nervous clearing of his throat proclaimed his own apprehension—perhaps in the confirmation or dismissal of the rumors swirling about the campus. Tense eyes darted around the room in anticipation of Dean Thackerly's announcements. "As many of you know, the unfortunate incidents at the close of last semester have brought about some necessary changes in both faculty and protocol, so we'll be wanting to go over everything with a fine measure of care this year, and I wanted to cover a few of those items with you this morning."

A not-so-random cough broke the tense silence that followed Dean Thackerly's qualifying remarks—*from Miriam Transum* he thought, but he couldn't be sure. She'd covered it up pretty fast.

"Yes, well…. I suppose it's time to put to bed all the rumors."

More tense exchanges of sidelong glances between faculty members as they hung on Dean Thackerly's every word.

"You all know we have two faculty slots to fill—in both Components and Field Application. Well, we actually found one exceptional talent easily capable of filling both those roles, simultaneously. He'll have quite a full load and a wide exposure to a great deal of our students across all levels, so I expect you to give him your full support as he joins us with full Archmage status, and we're very fortunate to have a man of his…" He paused, searching for the right word, clearly in a state of conflict about the announcement that had come down directly by order of the Council of Mages and there would be no pushing back on this…recommendation, "…Experience."

*The rumors **were** true….* Dallia tried to process it as she smoothed the pleats of her sky-blue robes. *Am I sweating?* She felt like she was. This man, if true, was dangerous! He had no business in a school—teaching others! *My God, what were they thinking!*

"Ladies and gentlemen, please give a warm welcome to our newest faculty member…. Damon of Basrat." The dean, quickly yielded space at the front of the room, appearing positively mortified and beside himself and he tried to balance his sense of responsibility to the safety of his faculty and students with his hierarchical pecking order in relation to the Council of Mages.

There was no applause—only gasps and mutterings as the centuries-old room of grace and elegance burst into huddles of several private conversations. Some faculty members, Damon overheard as he confidently strode into the room, appeared to be in not-so-silent prayer.

Faculty eyes darted towards him, daring only the briefest glimpse of the menacing sight of Damon in perfect and magnificent full-mage regalia, pacing confidently towards the front of the room, where he leaned against his silver-runed-cuffed hands on the leading edge of the ornate and heavy table. His charcoal-blue robes in three primary shades—darkest at the three-stage mantle, mid-shade and more metallic-marbled purple upon his shoulders, and a lighter diamond embroidered pattern down his chest with charcoal stoles of frightening silver runes that cascaded off of him in radiating waves of dread. He knew what the runes meant, and so did they. They were runes of ruin. Of destruction. Of unmaking. Of the dire and the dour.

His ominous reputation had preceded him like a great cantilever hanging over their heads, precariously balanced on Damon's mood. And his ruthlessness....

Scanning over the room, Damon took note of the one they called Hastil; his brown eyes locked with Damon's *black mirrors of the soul,* as Hastil tried not to look down, but failed. Hastil's eyes quickly darted downward, smoothing the pleats of his red robes, adjusting a gold sash that didn't need adjusting. Damon knew his presence wouldn't be easily accepted—if it was ever accepted at all. Yet the Council of Mages had ordered it. The bargain had been struck to commute his sentence of Banishment, and so here he was. Ready, willing, and able to teach the next young crop of mages all he could to the shock and horror of everyone. Standing at the edge of the table alongside Dean Thackerly, Damon scanned the room, locking eyes one at a time with each of them in turn. The black-robed Durial—named so after *THE* Durial—was his biggest competition and his biggest threat as they locked eyes blue to black. To his credit, Durial didn't look down or look away. At least someone among them had a pair of balls. The rest *did* look away and look away quickly—Miriam, Lucilla, and Servilia; none dared more than the briefest of glances. Damon saw them as lovely in their own right, and they shouldn't have had such reason to fear him, but reputations were a dangerous weapon, and Damon's was both honed and sharpened by many years in the field with Evanyil, Kellen, Goldenbow and the like. Their reputations further stoked his own.

Damon carried his reputation with him like most mages carried a staff—at the ready. He would use whatever advantage he had in combat and do so both callously, and without hesitation. While this wasn't combat, he couldn't believe *this* was the faculty responsible for raising the next generation of mages until his eyes fell upon the beautiful half-elf at the end of the table, tracing imaginary rings in the pleats of her deep V-neck, sky-blue robes. He slowly drank in every facet of her beautiful features. From the platinum-blonde waves cascading down to the small of her graceful back, to her large breasts strained tight against the front ties of her robes, to her slender frame, Damon had never seen anyone like her before. He held his demanding and expectant gaze upon her…waiting.

Charles W. McDonald Jr.

Dallia felt Damon's eyes upon her and could sense his presence from across the room. His scent filled her half-elven nostrils and their acute sense of awareness. The electrical charge of his aura was profound…and permeated the entire room, as if to claim his ownership of everything and everyone inside it, tugging at her soul from within. Her elven ears could hear his breath upon her neck as if he was standing behind her—hot and palpable. Her mind warned her to keep her head down. Not to look at him. But her body was already craning her neck upward. Her heart…. She didn't want to know as her beautiful green-gold eyes slowly locked with Damon's black pools. She'd never met anyone with black eyes before—especially not anything comparable to his. They were like dark gems of magic—not something given to him by birth or biology—more like something given by the Arcane he'd wielded as a young child. *Were all the rumors true? Had he killed his own father with magic at thirteen?* She didn't want to know. She wanted to pull her eyes from him, but she couldn't. She just kept staring into his soul from across the room, searching her instincts for how to deal with this incredible…man.

"Yes well…." Dean Thackerly broke the long-held silence again, adding, "Damon and I have spoken at length about his skills and experience and what he brings to us here at the college. Damon has a singular passion for those with innate capabilities in *Telekinesis, Cryokinesis,* and *Pyrokinesis*. And, as the only one of the faculty with any of those innate capabilities, he has offered to work with any student demonstrating skills in these areas. I think that was a fine act of volunteering from our newest faculty member, and I encourage your support in bringing to him any student that might qualify. Damon, the floor is yours."

His black pools still locked on Dallia, Damon offered, "I may not have been your first choice. I'm sure you've all heard a great deal about me. But, what you haven't heard may change your perception, and I encourage you to seek me out directly to allay any concerns you may have. I think you'll quickly find there's much more to me than hearsay and innuendo. And, I look forward to learning all I can about each of you, in turn." A nod from Damon directed at the magnificent, platinum-blonde half-elf caused her to smile against her will, though she quickly erased that smile before her peers. "You'll find me a reasonable man, and my word is iron. I hope to make everyone around me better, and I hope to learn at least as much as I teach. I look forward to the exchange of knowledge between us."

"Well said, Damon. Thank you." Dean Thackerly didn't wait for any opposing argument to surface before terminating this line of discussion, besides he had to get to the new protocols, and classes were starting in a few moments. With

Charles W. McDonald Jr.

a nod, he encouraged Damon to take a seat so he could finish. As Damon walked down the length of the burnished and polished oak table, he took the only open chair, opposite the beautiful half-elf who again locked eyes with him, watching his every move. When the orders had come down, he was furious with the Council of Mages. *How dare they force him to teach and remove him from the field that had brought him so much wealth and power?!* Yet, staring into the eyes of this beautiful woman, for once he was grateful to the Council and their commuting of his sentence. A wink at the beautiful half-elf caused another involuntary smile from her. This time it wasn't erased as easily, nor as quickly as before. *Progress perhaps…?*

She had no idea how to categorize Damon other than lethal and incredibly dangerous. Ominous. Commanding. A general among Archmages. Yet there he was, taking his seat opposite her, while her entire body tingled inside as if she was alive for the very first time. That raven hair and long bangs over those smoky eyes. That smile. That throaty, larger-than-life voice. Those chiseled features. *My goodness, was he ever a physical specimen?! Control yourself, Dallia!* She wanted to, but a great part of her wanted to know more about this notoriously dangerous man. *Why was he so dangerous? What led him to kill his father? What happened to his mother, and was there anyone else left in his family?* So many questions about him piled up almost instantaneously in her mind. She couldn't help but be curious about him—fascinated by him. *Am I obsessed already? Did he just wink at me? Why am I smiling like a giddy school girl? Stop it! Control yourself, woman!!!*

He couldn't be certain—intentions were so hard to predict and analyze on the fly, but she might just be the only 'good' thing in his life—assuming she said, 'yes.' *Don't be a fool, of course she'll say 'yes.'* His ego never one to disappoint. He shot another wink her way—this one far more flirtatious than the last—this time invoking an ear-to-ear smile from the lovely platinum-blonde half-elf. He wanted to know her and everything about her. There were these inexplicable moments in Damon's life when he could just sense his life was about to change in a very big way, and all his senses were screaming right now. Still, he couldn't help it. Fate or no, he was going to ask this woman out—and soon. Suddenly, his vision was cast into doubt as this light-blue aura appeared all around the beautiful half-elf before him.

Something was different. She didn't know what it was, but all her senses were suddenly on fire, and her body felt warm all over. Glowing. Dallia struggled to understand what was going on with herself as much as she struggled to under-

Charles W. McDonald Jr.

stand this Damon of Basrat before her. *Why was she still smiling at him so? Geez!* It was as if she'd lost all control of her own emotions—and bodily responses—around him. *What was he doing to her?*

Charles W. McDonald Jr.

Chapter 43: The Hand of Fate

(Graelon Colonial Outpost, A Long Time Ago)

While never before being exposed to such technologies, Damon knew, or at least had supposed, such things were possible. He didn't know exactly what he was looking at, neither outside the chamber, nor inside, but he knew it was a meld of both technology and magic—powerful beyond imagination. He could only wonder at who might have built such a thing, and for what purpose.

Mira was a different story. While his equal in every measure of talent, she'd not traveled as extensively as Damon had with Kellen, Goldenbow, Evanyil, and Illirian. He was simply more experienced and had been exposed to more possibilities. Mira could see the supposition in Damon's expressions as he was already putting together the pieces she could not. Her long, elegant black and gold robes, between dress and long coat in design, flowed about her firm, taut frame as she tossed her long brunette hair this way and that in the faltering twilight. Considerably shorter than Damon, the top of her head barely came up to his chest but looks could be deceiving. Mira had all the appearance of a delicate, magnificent woman, but appearances were very deceptive when it came to Archmages, and Mira was one of the most lethal Damon had ever encountered. Together, they were virtually unstoppable—or so they hoped.

They *had* already come through the hard way, as it was—through the traps—via the only known, or visible, entrance to them, from the valley below. Now inside the great chamber with the two man-sized niches broken and unleashed—their titan bodies broken and blown to pieces across the interior of the

Charles W. McDonald Jr.

chamber from Damon and Mira's combined powers—they could see the incredibly detailed model of the School of Invocation before them, and the cavern entrance concealed by powerful magic beyond. His *Staff of the Invoker* wielded in his right hand, as always, Damon quickly paced to the edge of the cavern entrance. Holding up the *Staff of the Invoker*, leveraging its hemispherical aura to project light against the cavern wall in search of more traps, Damon carefully proceeded to the edge of the entrance eyeing the great and ancient city in ruins below, as if blown to bits rather than crumbled from the relentless weathering of time. Pacing back to the model of the college, and the center console beside it, Damon's mind was rapidly at work filling in the blanks—of which there were many—with the best assumptions he could surmise. Best he could discern, from the number of blind turns they had made getting up here, they must have come from the other side of the valley through the traps. If he had known of another entrance he certainly would have preferred to take it. Still, *why was this place built, and precisely by whom?* Those questions were just as paramount in his mind as was the construction of the center console before him.

"I can see the wheels turning behind those pretty black gems of yours," Mira prodded, hoping he'd volunteer his thoughts. She had no terms of endearment for him, though she'd never loved anyone the way she loved Damon. He was simply Damon to her. There were really no suitable words to describe him other than... Damon. The silver flashes behind those blue eyes of hers flashed from Damon to the center console, hewn from the cavern's stone, which bore inlaid handprints—one male, one female.

Making it through the traps had already proven a near-death experience for them both, and she wondered how much more Damon had left in him and how much more it would take before they could leave.

"This wasn't built with magic alone." Damon traced the male handprint without letting his skin touch the honed-stone surface of the console. "This is something more." Examining the tiny holes at the end of each fingertip and the small lens-like protrusions coming out of the console at each of the fingertips as if to read or identify, Damon drew further conclusions based upon things he'd seen while working for Illirian. And things he'd seen before on Earth. Wherever, whatever, this place was, they had managed to bridge magic and technology—to a degree at least—and he was beginning to wonder if it had been their undoing. "I've seen something like this before. It's ancient."

"But this looks very advanced." Mira was sharp and beginning to put together the pieces, but clearly Damon knew something he wasn't sharing just yet, and it was not helping the situation. They needed to get out of here—fast. That

Charles W. McDonald Jr.

meant they needed to share and combine all their knowledge, on the fly.

"Oh, it is. That doesn't mean it hasn't been here for thousands of years."

"You're not making any sense."

"Can you put your hand in that," Damon asked, motioning to the female print. "Let's do it together. Simultaneously. On the count of three."

"Damon, we don't even know what this does. This is crazy."

"Trust me."

Damon wasn't crazy, but he was a fast actor. A doer among doers. Occasionally, his execute attributes outweighed his better judgment of standing pat. Still, the clock was ticking, and they needed to get out of this place. This place that had already come perilously close to killing them both multiple times in the last couple of hours. In the absence of better ideas, she nodded in agreement, hovering her right hand over the console indentation of the female handprint while Damon hovered his left hand over the male indentation.

"One." Damon started the count.

"Two," Mira relayed.

"Three." Damon slowly lowered his hand into position in sync with Mira lowering hers. As soon as their fingerprints touched the fingertips of the indentation, Damon felt a slight tingle and could see lights flashing underneath and through his skin, casting prismatic images of light in the shape of the bones constructing his, and Mira's, fingertips on the ceiling of the cavern chamber. Lights danced under their fingertips and on the ceiling, projecting internal images of their finger structures in amber and white hues against the dank-gray of the chamber's honed-rock ceiling. A smooth mechanical click, and the projections immediately ceased as the cavern suddenly plunged into a dead calm.

Scanning the immediately observable area for the source of the click, Damon noticed something different about the clock tower in the model of the college. The clock face was slightly ajar—pushed outward. Reaching into his charcoal-blue, diamond-patterned robes, Damon pulled out a silver telescoping rod he used to open the agape door of the tower's clock-face, revealing a small amulet—one-half the size of Damon's palm. Scores of princess-cut diamonds filled a rounded background of a unique type of gold, looking as if it had been melted with other metals, giving it the appearance of fluidity and weathering, though it was perfectly smooth, clean, and neat. Navigational arrows of the same gold, though seemingly incorrect in number and direction, lay atop the field of diamonds pointing outward toward the perimeter of the amulet. An emerald-cut ruby, with some sort of scarab inlay, lay atop the navigational arrows. Another set of navigational arrows—exactly five and made of a different material than the gold—pointed inward toward the ruby.

Charles W. McDonald Jr.

Each of those five navigational arrows bore a rune marker unlike anything Damon or Mira had ever seen before. It looked as if the bottom navigational arrow had a hook where it had once been hung at the end of a chain, as if intended to be worn around the neck. By whom, why, and for what purpose, were all important questions that needed answering, though clearly not something likely to be answered now.

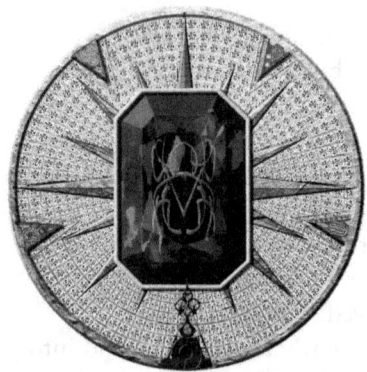

Handing the unknown amulet to Mira, Damon leveraged the *Staff of the Invoker*, throwing up the last of his protections. His internal alarms were sounding off at their loudest since they'd arrived and given the horrific voracity of the traps they'd already been through, that made him extremely cautious as he proceeded looking through the model for other things that might have changed with the click they'd initiated from the console.

Looking down at the mastercrafted amulet, Mira's beautiful silvery-blue eyes flashed, capturing the charcoal-blue aura of the *Staff of the Invoker* sparkling off the facets of the large ruby centered upon the ancient artifact. "What do you suppose it's for?"

"I don't know, but I've got a bad feeling about what happened here," Damon postulated, briefly looking back to the cave entrance he had just visited.

"You're not telling me everything again. What are you thinking?" Her eyes looked heavy and worried, nearly afraid.

"I'm thinking somehow the merger of technology and magic led to this place ripping itself apart."

Looking throughout the model of the college for more signs of disturbances from the hand-scan, Damon was still trying to understand both what happened here and the purpose of this place. It bore all the hallmarks of a time-capsule—

Charles W. McDonald Jr.

as if trying to explain, but only to the right person, what happened here. Circling around the model of the college to the opposite side, Damon noticed another anomaly: the other side of the clock tower barely ajar—but not the face of the clock—the entire side of it from top to bottom. Using his silver telescoping rod again to pry the side ever-so-gently open, he could see a slight reflection of light from the *Staff of the Invoker* off a shiny piece of metal within the clock tower. "Hmmm," Damon considered aloud, trying not to move any piece of the model more than absolutely necessary. "What have we here…?" A small metallic orb made of five curved silver bars revealed itself from within the model of the clock tower, not quite one-third Damon's palm in size. He'd never seen anything quite like it before, noticing it housed—or rather caged—a star sapphire gem within the silver bars running up and down the longitudinal lines of the orb. Unable to resist the urge any longer, he reached inside, carefully grabbing it between his thumb and forefinger, hearing another smooth click as soon as he did so.

"I don't like that sound." Mira looked everywhere observantly, trying to identify what changed with that last click, and finding nothing—obviously unsettling to her from the concerned expression on her otherwise beautiful face.

Damon didn't like it either; he scanned the model, the pedestal, and surrounding chamber for anything that looked different than it had only a moment before. "I don't see anything different," he admitted, putting the small orb into the interior pocket of his charcoal-blue robes.

"I don't either. We've been lucky so far. Let's not push our luck any further."

"Agreed." With a thought, Damon's *Telekinesis* smashed the model to dust before them setting off a whoosh of hushed darts from all around the chamber aimed at them. Bouncing off of Damon's protective shells, none penetrated, but Mira immediately collapsed to the chamber floor, unresponsive with a dart sticking out of her throat—its point of entry already red and swelling with each passing moment. *Poison*, Damon knew, as he lifted her body with his *Telekinesis*, floating her toward the cavern entrance so he could keep his hands free if they encountered any more traps.

(Graelon Colonial Outpost, Present Day)

Standing in the place he swore he'd never set foot again, all the memories of his beloved Mira came back, wave after wave of regret and anguish causing a

Charles W. McDonald Jr.

hard, thin-pressed line to form on his already stony, multi-cultured face. The dust he'd collected last time had proved useful and powerful, just as he'd suspected. In the rush of being forced out of here the first time, he hadn't had time to confirm any of his suspicions about the construction of the model. Analysis of the dust indicated 20 percent Polytetrafluoroethylene, 30 percent transparent aluminum, and 50 percent unknown compounds. Whatever those compounds were, it was a catalyst as it was both explosive and burned hot like magnesium under certain test conditions—nearly always sticking like a Molotov cocktail, but with much more devastating effects.

Once more, standing before the model he crushed to dust with his *Telekinesis* so very long ago, Damon cast every protection he had with the *Staff of the Invoker* held tightly in his right hand, as he slowly began to move the layers of dust, looking for what he knew he'd missed the last two times he'd been here. There were answers here. He knew it. And, he needed those answers...for Eden...for Mira... for Humanity. Slowly, carefully, his *Telekinesis* removed layer by layer of the model's dust, funneling it into a small gold box he had placed on the chamber floor. His eyes sparkled as the glint of metal reflecting the aura of the *Staff of the Invoker* could be seen, slowly being revealed millimeter by millimeter. He'd seen such an artifact before when working for Illirian and had such an artifact in his secret fourth-floor study but seeing this here only confirmed a few things he already knew, also raising more questions than it answered. The unremarkable silver rod, not quite half the length of Damon's forearm, sparkled in the light of the *Staff of the Invoker* calling out to Damon from several feet away as his *Telekinesis* slowly picked it out of the dust, spinning and rotating it as it floated toward him, suspended in mid-air. "What are you doing here," Damon asked, only half expecting a reply. Carefully, he reached out to grab it with his left hand, expecting to feel its warmth and resonant energy, but instead finding something totally different as the holographic message started to play some six feet out in front of him.

A weathered, middle-aged man of obvious power and status sat behind a glass—or what appeared to be glass—desk with huge frameless, infinity-like monitors seemingly suspended in mid-air displaying a bleak status of dead, dying, and destroyed. His uniform, if it could be called such, had the appearance of what he could only describe as something akin to what he'd seen on *Battlestar Galactica* and *Space: Above and Beyond*. "I.... We are the descendants of the four brothers Durial, Alexelio, Pierio, and Adamian. My name is Fondro. I am the Colonial Outpost President. If you're seeing this message, I, and likely the rest of us on this outpost, are the casualties of our own ingenuity."

"What happened here," Damon breathed aloud, listening intently to the message-in-a-bottle housed inside the brushed metal rod.

"It is important that you understand each brother was instructed to keep magic alive, but in their own way—eventually destined to bring a justice to their captures equal in measure to *their* sins. I don't know what happened to the other brothers, but Pierio, the brother banished to Graelon, kept magic alive with the intentions of merging it with the most powerful technology. He instructed several outposts be built where the most extreme talent and possibilities could be tested. This was one such outpost."

"There *are* more…." Damon considered the possibilities, wanting to know more—hoping they were not all like this.

"Our experiment started to go wrong shortly after the college was built and the knowledge disseminated. The knowledge of building and replicating technology—at scale—through the use of magic. It built unforeseen pathways into the technology, creating an artificial intelligence unlike anything we'd ever seen before—unlike anything the brothers had seen before. On Setinon, there were accounts of AI carrying the brothers to the stars, but this new AI was infused and emboldened with the ability to control Arcane."

"Wow!" Damon's jaw dropped as the possibilities of such capabilities slammed home in his thoughts. *That's what happened to this place! Just imagine the possibilities of AI being able to cast…. It would be like a toddler wielding a chainsaw!!! So, it wasn't the Forkettes after all….* His mind ran with that idea as he continued listening intently.

"Magic was banned on Setinon tens of thousands of years ago. Apparently, they had some knowledge of the possibilities we encountered on this outpost, or perhaps had already encountered them in their distant past. We lost contact with one of the other outposts, a few months ahead of us in experiments, and have warned the others of our situation, including the Graelon homeworld. We can only hope they will heed our warnings. We can only hope what started here doesn't spread and become the unmaking of Humanity itself."

Damon visibly gulped, wondering about the *Amulet of the Five Gates* and whether he should immediately destroy it. He couldn't. He needed it. It was crucial to his Master Plan. He needed to understand more.

"If you're playing this message, that means *you are a direct descendant of one of the four brothers.* It is *your* responsibility to deliver *a* justice they no longer can. It is *your* responsibility to ensure that what happened here does not spread. It is your responsibility to save us all—or those of us who remain. Our mages did what they could. They honored the brother's family name, revolting against Humans that the AI controlled and the AI itself. It was a noble fight to the death, but the AI was

Charles W. McDonald Jr.

too strong, too numerous, and too lacking in mercy or Humanity. It proved too cunning in its use of Humans to do its own bidding and too ruthless to know or understand its limits."

Damon looked around nervously. *Had the magic-wielding AI survived? Was it watching him?* He needed to get out of here while he still could. Damon wanted to hear and see more, but right now he needed to ensure his knowledge and this message survived this outpost. Throwing the plain silver rod into his inner robe pocket, he immediately headed for the cavern entrance—*Staff of the Invoker* in his right hand.

Standing at the edge of the cavern entrance, he looked around, more observant than ever before. Seeing the same ancient city in ruins in a totally new light, he looked around for signs of movement, seeing and hearing nothing as he allowed his *Telekinesis* to lower him slowly to the valley below where he could *Portal* out. Silvery-blue flashes of light superheated the air right in front of him as he wasted not another second, stepping through to his Austin home and to Mira.

The quarter-millimeter wide-angle lens didn't have to move much from the cavern entrance to capture Damon's exit in vivid detail. It had only taken less than a nanosecond for the facial recognition software to mark him as a direct descendant of Durial—and as the same man that had been here now twice before. The aperture snapped shut, then reopened like a Human reactionary blink—a fused behavior centuries in the making as the intelligence behind the lens worked the calculus of understanding the descendant of brothers of the *Father*. *It* didn't yet fully understand, but it *was* learning.

Chapter 44: A Future Warning

(Lancaster Castle, Lancaster, England, Earth, Present Day, 7:40 a.m.)

The castle didn't open for another two-plus hours, but Rena had just made a very recent and very generous donation to the curator, so negotiating a visit outside of normal business hours hadn't been a problem. Their assigned guide, a twenty-six-year-old brunette named Elizabeth, who could have stood to lose a couple of kilos, still had the most amazing million-watt smile Rena had ever seen. Elizabeth nervously showed them the exclusive tour, though eyeing Rena and her magnificent lithe blonde companion in both suspicion, and curiosity.

Amber trumpets of the glory of the coming morning cast prismatic rays upon dust-motes suspended in the vestibules between chambers of the fourth floor of the keep at Lancaster Castle. Rena's right hand trailed behind her; fingertips spread wide and feeling the warmth of dawn on her skin still felt...renewing to her. There were physical and metaphysical things the Sun did to a Human physiology, though she wasn't really Human, anymore.

Her greatest contribution, centuries in the making, made all her soldiers capable of operating in full daylight, and she savored the fruits of her work, as the dust particles flowed around her seemingly delicate fingers.

"What was it that brought you to Lancaster Castle so early," Elizabeth asked, trying to make polite conversation between providing the executive guide content she'd committed to memory not more than a few months back. Still, it was a great job, and she was happy to have it.

"Oh, we don't sleep all that much," Alisa commented, giving Mother a knowing and barely observable wink in between the moments of Elizabeth's at-

Charles W. McDonald Jr.

tention. She wasn't sure why Mother was so intent on coming here—just that she needed a distraction, and they needed to get in and out 'without issue.' Alisa knew exactly what that meant, having worked closely with Mother before, but Mother didn't provide details that often. It was her prerogative, of course, and proving her loyalty over and over should get Mother to open up to trusting her a little more over time. She could be patient, after all; she literally had all the time in the world....

Rena trailed behind Alisa and Elizabeth as they began their descent down one of the circular stair turnpikes. Running the numbers in her head, she figured a six-minute descent, plus a two-minute window of opportunity for Alisa to stall before she'd have to return to the group. Eight minutes wasn't very long, even with her abilities, but she had a very good idea of where to look. Alisa felt Mother's disappearance and distance increasing as she continued blocking Elizabeth's view. They continued their descent while Elizabeth chided, trying to maintain balance on her heels amidst the awkwardness of the steeply-spiraled stairs. "Everyone wants to see the drop room. Some morbid fascination with all the hangings I guess, but we'll hit that on the way down."

"Oh no, not necessary. We can just go to the bottom and continue from there," Alisa deflected. *Good luck, Mother...*

Now in the basement of Hadrian's Tower—built circa 1210—Rena had reason to believe it would be buried in the thick walls...*but where...? Less than eight minutes and ticking.* Rena's heightened senses worked through her fingertips as she ran her fingers along the now ancient mortar and stone wall, looking for anything that might give away its location. Her pupils focused in on every abnormality in the centuries-old mortar, knowing—or rather believing—it had been centuries since it had seen the light of day. Then she saw it: an ever-so-slight variation in the color of the mortar—a good indication it had been repaired, and the repair looked...old. *Have to risk it*, she thought, bursting through the wall with one sure blow from her right hand, crushing the stone to dust with a loud and echoing bang. She hoped she was far enough away from Elizabeth that she hadn't been heard. She liked Elizabeth and didn't want to have to kill her. *No time for worrying about that*, she chastised herself internally, brushing the disintegrated stone to the floor, looking for perhaps a box.... She wasn't sure they would have left it unprotected. More likely it had been placed in a box of some kind when it was buried.

She would have to clean herself up as the dust and mortar was getting all over her smooth black dress and heels. Then she felt it...the push-back of some-

Charles W. McDonald Jr.

thing firm wedged in-between stones. She didn't want to burst another stone. The first had already made such a racket. Intensely, she dug at it with her nails—now protruding lethal weapons as they extended three times their normal length, aiding her digging. Rapidly digging around the wooden box, she could see it now with her enhanced vision and could smell it too. The air was stale and ancient as she stirred it thoroughly, whisking dirt, dust, and debris into an ever-growing pile on the floor of Hadrian's Tower. "There you are." Finally freed, the box was too big to hide on her person, but a flick of her wrist and the ancient lock was shattered. She wasted no time opening it. If there was a trap, she hoped her abilities would help her avoid it. An instant later, she was looking at a plain silver rod, slightly longer than half the length of her forearm, wedged in between two wooden clasps meant to hold it in place in the box. Beneath the silver rod was a pair of handcuffs that appeared both ancient and futuristic. The metal looked burnished and old, even scarred, whether by acid, chemicals, time, or natural weathering she couldn't immediately tell. The digital readout looked...like nothing she'd seen before. She quickly removed both items and dug at the box's edges, both interior and exterior; she wanted to be sure it contained nothing else before she would be forced to discard it.

Suddenly she could hear her name being called from halfway across the castle. *Time's up*, she thought. In a whirl, Rena was gone, leaving the greatly-disturbed pile of dust and debris to float and settle all over Hadrian's Tower.

She stopped a few paces away from Alisa and Elizabeth, hoping the rapid movement had cleaned most of her appearance so she wouldn't have to eliminate Elizabeth. Turning the last corner between herself and them, she comported herself with absolute calm, but just enough curiosity to explain her disappearance. "My apologies, Dear...," Rena explained, "...it's such a beautiful place, I couldn't help myself from taking a peek. To get a better feel for my...investment." *That should put the issue to rest.*

"Of course, Ms. Rectovich. Is there anything you'd like me to personally show you?" She wasn't about to bring up how unescorted visitors were not permitted in the castle for any reason regardless of their...generosity. After all, she needed this job, and good feedback from a wealthy patron couldn't hurt. Though a look up and down Rena, and she looked a little...disheveled, but still amazing. Maybe it was a few of her jet-black hairs slightly out of place, but she was probably looking for a bathroom. Not uncommon.

"Darling, I hate to be going, but as much as I love this place and would

Charles W. McDonald Jr.

love to see every millimeter of it with you, I have an 8:00 a.m. call I have to be on. Would you mind if we come back another time to finish?" It was two minutes 'til, and good thinking on her part if she wanted to avoid killing Elizabeth.

"Of course. I know you're quite busy. I'd be delighted. Here's my card. Just call that number at the bottom left or send me a text message and I'd be happy to give you another personal tour, even during hours if you like." Elizabeth handed the card to Rena, who instinctively turned it over, examining both sides—so much time spent in Japan she'd picked up some habits of respect from their culture.

"Wonderful," Rena offered with a full and sexy smile and a bit of a wink as she looped her arm in Alisa's, nudging her toward the main exit as she popped her Bluetooth® in her right ear to fake a quick call.

Outside, Alisa opened the right-rear door to Rena's Rolls-Royce® Phantom in her one-off color of majestic Rena Blood-Red. Rena climbed inside the comfort of her beautiful Bespoke® cream interior with starlight headliner as she pulled the plain silver rod from her little black purse barely big enough to hide it.

Climbing into the driver's seat, Alisa looked back, wanting a glimpse of what this trip had been about, only to see the most peculiar—if unremarkable— little silver rod barely the diameter of an average male index finger. "What is it, Mother? I don't understand...."

"A future warning, Dearheart.... A future warning." Twisting the plain silver rod in her hand, confident Elizabeth couldn't see them through the dark-tinted windows, Rena contemplated its age, construction, and purpose—especially the handcuffs.

As Alisa drove Rena off Lancaster Castle premises, she considered how her chief scientist would be busy cracking the code of how these things worked and what they were for, but she already had an idea. You only made handcuffs for one reason...well two maybe; a sex-laden smile crossed her beautiful face while her thighs simultaneously rubbed one against the other in an emerging sense of arousal. Now, she needed sex. That made her think of Michelle.

Charles W. McDonald Jr.

Chapter 45: Descendants of Destiny

(Setinon, Near Future)

adin understood the absolute urgency of his mission and the fact that the Master Plan hinged on it. Failure could mean the end of all things—worst case scenario—or a very severe bump in the road—best case. Damon trusted him with this mission, and he wasn't about to fail, but not failing started with blending in. So, the plan included a good story along with some fake identification and currency—only problem was he hadn't counted on picking up Mora along the way.

Not everyone here was marked of course, but *nearly* everyone was, and that alone was going to make it hard enough to blend in if they didn't get some proper clothes—*fast!* He could make them of course, but he couldn't risk setting off any warning systems likely in place to detect the use of Arcane. His instincts for casting or using his natural abilities in *Telekinesis* had to be intentionally suppressed. There was Zero-Point, of course, but he didn't know if their warning systems would pick up that as well.

He had to remain sharp, relying more on his wit and charm than ever before. Usually having a beautiful woman around helped, but in this case, he feared it would just draw more attention.

This group of merchants looked as reasonable as any of the others, and he didn't want to travel much further into the perimeter of the city dressed like he was or her *undressed* like she was. He wasn't sure what all of the merchants were selling. One of them looked like an advanced communications booth—another like a place for wearable tech that had some 'clothing' as well, but not like the booth next to it. Perhaps they were synergetic, being located side by side, like they were. *Who*

Charles W. McDonald Jr.

knew?!

     It was difficult for him to get used to the way all the *pods*—that was the best word Radin could think of—moved in cohesion with one another like a hive-driven intelligence, carrying their cargo to their coordinated destinations. Directly underneath one of the unseen pod pathways, Radin approached what he hoped was a clothing merchant—if those things suspended in mid-air before him could be called clothes—while automaton pods whirled past them overhead at terrific speeds. The transparent identicard presented a head-to-toe hologram of Radin, as required by law, activated by his fingerprint as he handed it over for inspection, but the lack of a government-certified lithographic-code on the back of his hand marked Radin a neophobe. He wasn't the only one; there were thousands of them that lived beyond the city, but none dressed like him. His charcoal-grey pants and cream embroidered jerkin made him stand out like nothing the merchant ever seen before.

     "What wanting," the slender woman in skin-tight, color-shifting, nanite clothing initiated, though Radin knew he wasn't hearing or understanding her correctly. *That was going to be a problem.* He couldn't leverage his magic to translate. He'd just have to adapt.

     Looking directly into her obviously enhanced eyes, Radin noted her glowing teal irises orbited by lithographic pathways comprising her corneas. Her perfect pale skin and iridescent platinum hair made him question whether she was Human, or just 'enhanced.' Trying a minimal exchange in his common tongue, he replied, "Black dress," with his best attempt at a disarming wink while tugging on Mora as he brought her forward by her forearm as if presenting her to the merchant.

     The woman eyed Mora up and down; she'd seen far more scantily-clad women in public before, but this one looked…road-worn beyond belief, making her eye the handsome auburn-haired young man even more suspiciously than before. He had nice eyes and seemed nice, but he was less than gentle in the way he handled women. *That could be a good thing*, she thought placing the nanite dress against Mora's body. It wasn't black at first, but it changed from silver to gold to black as Mora considered different color options internally—without ever voicing them.

     "Wow." Mora couldn't help it. Radin warned her to keep quiet, but it was like magic—this technology. Stripping completely nude right in front of Radin, Mora slipped the nanite dress over her skin, thinking it might feel metallic or anything but smooth, but surprised to feel its Elian-like qualities. That was the closest she could relate the sensation to—Elian. It felt…so sensual against her flesh and

Charles W. McDonald Jr.

made her tingle everywhere it touched, as if directly interacting with every node of her skin.

Seemingly satisfied with Mora's new color-shifting nanite dress, Radin eyed the female merchant, using his fingertips to draw out the 5'7" Mora's long brunette hair—scraggly and unattractive as it was, hoping the merchant might have a solution.

The merchant's teal eyes flashed and shuttered almost like what Radin knew to be a camera lens. That concerned him. *Was she taking photos of them?* He was warned there would be surveillance everywhere, so it really didn't matter. The risk was the same, either way—extreme!

Running her fingers through the brunette's lovely but worn, shimmering, black hair, her eyes connected with the neophobe's crystal-blue ones, wondering if they were real. They could have been enhanced, but they would have been far more expensive than her own if they were. She was beautiful, and she wanted to help her be even more so, but she was growing more skeptical of the two by the moment. Reaching into an unseen pocket in her skin-tight color-shifting outfit, the merchant pulled out a tiny glass container filled with what looked like millions of carbon-colored grains of sand. Twisting the black lid, she poured its contents on Mora's head, causing a shimmering coat to fall over Mora in wave after wave of dried cleansing.

Mora felt the tingle of whatever the substance was prickling at her hair and skin and only what could be described as both a euphoric and invigorating sensation tickling her nerve endings from head to toe.

Taking in the stunning and shimmering beauty that now stood before him, Mora looked…new in every way a Human could. Her skin looked like perfection. Her hair shimmered as if freshly washed. Even her eyes looked more vibrant and alive. Radin could only quantify the difference in what he knew to be standard definition versus ultra-high definition television from what he'd seen in the presence of Damon at his manor on Eden. "Wow!" He looked between Mora and the merchant, surprised at his own comment after warning Mora to keep quiet, but Mora was stunning now, and it was hard to ignore! He'd hoped to blend in after this, but now she stood out even more than she had before. They'd just have to adapt. Maybe picking up Mora along the way wasn't a good idea after all. The best way to blend in was to look like her husband, and right now he looked like anything but that.

Eyeing what he assumed were the male bodysuits, Radin trailed his fingers over them, thinking of the color he wanted, and one by one they adapted to his projected desires. He wasn't sure how this technology worked, but Damon didn't

Charles W. McDonald Jr.

warn him of technology that could read thoughts. That was news to him—and dangerous news at that. If clothing could read projected thoughts, he was certain there was more aggressive technology that could probe and read thoughts deeper than surface-level.

Looking around, he noticed a changing booth and took one of the nanite body suits with him. A moment later, Radin came out to catch the merchant eyeing Mora with a newfound lust. He didn't have time for that. Mora didn't say anything…verbally, but her eyes did as she ogled Radin from head to toe in his skin-tight bodysuit that suddenly shifted from grey to red to charcoal-grey with red trim as he tried to get the hang of dictating his desired appearance to the nanites. Walking up alongside Mora, he put his arm around her, resting his left hand on the small of her back as he offered his identicard one more time for payment.

A couple of taps of his identicard to the merchant's, and the transaction was complete—seemingly to her satisfaction, but he still didn't like the way she observed them walking away—like she was taking mental notes of them, or something. A final look back and a last attempt at another charming smile for the merchant, and they were quickly out of sight, around the corner and down the next block. He felt like this task might have been more difficult than he first considered, given the handicapping of not being able to use any of his abilities. Still, it was vital, and it had to be done. Moreover, Damon had convinced him it had to be him that did it. As much as he'd been let in on the Master Plan, he still wondered what Damon *wasn't* telling him, and whether or not it was going to get him killed on this mission.

Block after block of metal and glass—if it was glass at all—elegant architecture stretched so far into the sky he wondered if there were what was known as space elevators carrying workers into the heavens—literally. The city went on seemingly forever, as if it covered the entire planet. He knew that not to be the case, but it was close. *How could the planet sustain such a population? Where did they ever find the space to grow the food they needed? They might have used synthetic food to solve that problem.*

Damon had provided the location of the building in question—the Central Records Repository in the heart of the Governing District. Some of the signs and marker posts he could make out. Some reminded him of the markings he saw in *The World Below and Between*, but some were far more complex and confusing to him—like unto a lithography written from both left and right perspective toward the center. Perhaps even steganography. It wasn't easy, but his preparation had been helpful. About thirty to forty percent of it he could make out—at least he thought he could.

Charles W. McDonald Jr.

This building, with its pastel satin-white-finish stone edged in a cobalt-blue matte-finish metal trim, looked like some sort of a courthouse. *We're getting close*, he thought, looking up to see the pale-white stone turn transparent, then opaque again, making him frown in wary awe of their technology.

A couple more buildings down, and the marquee—if you could call it that—read *Central Records Repository and Historical Records Division*. He wasn't sure about the Historical Records Division, but given what he was looking for, this had to be the place. A look up offered him a similar architectural appearance to the courthouse he passed a moment earlier—perhaps built at a similar time by a similar architect, but this building was much taller, narrowing to a golden spire at the top. The same transparent-to-opaque, pale-white stone was used with similar metallic edging, but the trim on this building was more like worn, glossy black finish than the matte cobalt-blue finish of the courthouse. The courthouse was more broad and sprawling. This building made much better use of vertical space, having one of those lines that stretched into the heavens. Damon said they were made of carbon nanotube construction, or something like it. That allowed them to be incredibly strong, light, and durable over incredible distances.

Knowing this was the place and getting access inside were two different things, entirely. A tug from Mora brought his eyes back down to ground level, where they were being observed by pairs of guards on every corner visible—six pairs in all. Each of them wore similar nanite bodysuits, mostly black with blue, white, and silver trim marking them as governing authority. *Shit!*

Radin barely got out that thought, and they were already being approached. A brief look down, and his bodysuit had gone transparent on him. *Shiiittt!!!* It took concentration to keep the nanite cohesion in place. He just wasn't used to it, and now it showed. *Think, Radin! How are you going to get out of this?!*

Fuck it! Reaching out to Arcane with everything he could find, surprising himself with how much he could flood his body even here, Radin channeled—not for combat, but to make a point. Summoning four—no more, no less—bolts of lightning that simultaneously struck from a cloudless sky upturning streets, drainage, and a highspeed rail subway infrastructure system below, shooting up out of the ground into street-view, Radin had delivered his message.

"WHAT ARE YOU DOING," Mora screamed at him, backing away as if to distance herself from him, but it was too late.

Smaller, faster, and armed automaton pods—with government markings ripped around all sides of the building, surrounding them instantly. A burst of dust-like material from one of the security pods, and suddenly Radin and Mora found themselves caught in a net of shimmering nanite construction—neither of

Charles W. McDonald Jr.

them able to feel the source of Arcane anymore. Radin could only hope his other spell had gone off as well as the lightning, because their work here was done before it ever got started. Damon had warned him of the risks, and he still took the job. *Fuck*, he thought. *Well, let's hope this works.*

Minutes later, they were in custody and being processed for incarceration. They were back in the courthouse building they had passed only moments before. Somehow, he didn't think they were going to get off lightly in their sentencing. At least they hadn't been separated yet, and he wasn't sure why that was, only that there had been a brief discussion about it. He'd only understood a few words, but it was something about the results of the blood tests from when they were taken into custody. Then he heard it—a word—a name really, and one he'd been expecting to hear. Durial. And the word 'descendant,' but the way that word was used made it sound like they were both descendants of Durial and someone by the name Alexelio. Names he had heard before and he was finally starting to put some of the pieces of this vast mosaic together. *Damon had been right all along, but he certainly hoped he had been wrong about what needed to come next.* Still, it wasn't going to do anyone any good if he couldn't find a way out of here, to do what he came for.

He started to wonder if this had been a one-way trip—a suicide mission. Thinking about possible escape routes off world led him to other thoughts.... He wondered, *does the government know about the entrance to The World Below and Between, and if they do, why do they allow it to remain...?*

Charles W. McDonald Jr.

The Living Goddess Evanyil
The Architect of Chaos

Charles W. McDonald Jr.

Chapter 46: The Old Us

(North of the Trident, Kaleion, A Very Long Time Ago)

nly pretending to sleep under the comfort of the largest elm he could find, Damon kept one eye open at all times—as per the norm. He trusted Evanyil and Lorianus completely, of course, but they were entirely too close to the mark this time, and the Steward of Engêstal had his men everywhere—all the way to the Trident, looking for them. Damon wasn't sure how he'd found out about the mark on his head, but there would be no element of surprise *this* time. Fortunately, he'd learned a long time ago to live without much sleep.

As the dawn crept over the far Ragarth horizon, soon-morning rays of promise danced upon the subtle and soft waves of Daedrid Lake beneath them. Majestic amber, purple, and gold hues of the coming dawn chased the twin moons across the Kaleion sky over the opposing horizon. Damon swore he'd never seen one of the moons as massive in the sky as what he saw last night in full repose. He didn't quite understand the mechanics of how the moon could grow in size from one full moon to the next, and he'd heard many such suppositions about it, but most of them leaned on the supernatural. He was a proponent of a more prosaic, scientific explanation. The wobble of the moon about its axis in relation to the wobble of Kaleion about its axis, and so forth. Science and math were *always* more reliable than beliefs and witchcraft, and really the only true methodology for predictable findings.

It was *old* beliefs and *old* ways of thinking that had led them to *this* place

Charles W. McDonald Jr.

and to *this* specific mission. He didn't care for witchcraft, but if the steward had in his possession what he was rumored to have, then that would prove a very big payday indeed. Beyond that, the steward held title to many lands as far south as the Aegen Plateau—where Damon intended to build the greatest estate Kaleion had ever seen. Killing two birds—or one steward—with one spell never hurt, especially when the rewards and stakes were this high.

For now, they'd staked out a position just north of the lake on the tallest hill for leagues around, so they could see the steward's forces coming, but large thickets of forestation along the way made that a more thorny task, causing both Lorianus and Evanyil to make brief scouting expeditions north and westward while Damon studied and prepared. He was advancing at an amazing pace—even ahead of his own torrid schedule. Already he could *Portal* them—at will—practically anywhere on the planet. It was a useful tool for certain.

"Whatcha look'n at?"

Damon practically leapt out of his skin as he stood on the lakeshore. He had to focus not to fall into the lake from Evanyil startling him so. "Would you stop that, please?" He pivoted in frustration to see those magnificent violet eyes staring at him lustfully through those beautiful platinum bangs. *WOW*. He never tired of looking at Evanyil. His eyes had grown so familiar to her stark, dark beauty, his eyes had trouble noticing most other women. If he ever found another woman as magnificent as Evanyil without her...idiosyncrasies, he'd *have* to marry her.

"Stop what, Sweetie," Evanyil asked, taking his hand in hers, gently petting the back of it as if he were her pet.

Was he?

He wasn't going to tell her to stop *that*, but it made it hard for him to concentrate on the mission—very hard! "What did you find?" He managed to eke out the question through her superimposed distractions. This time he actually managed to both see and hear Lorianus coming out of the tree line a few hundred paces to the left. She must not have seen or heard any of the steward's men, to be moving with such a cavalier nature.

"I found two groups of the steward's men moving toward the lake, but not in a direction where I think they'll run across us. They're over that way." Evanyil pointed toward Ragarth in the distance.

Hmmm. That made Damon question the steward's intellect. The steward's men should have been searching the high grounds currently held by Damon and his party. *What was the steward thinking? What games was he playing with them?* "What about the steward's keep?"

Charles W. McDonald Jr.

"Oh, he's got at least one hundred men guarding that place, a drawbridge as the only point of entry with a three-storey curtain wall. I counted two dozen archers with a hard-covered battlement, four dozen infantry, and four dozen cavalry. And…" She held onto the last, wanting to be sure Lorianus was in range to hear what she had to say next. "…Horigarth. I saw him training some sellswords in the inner bailey. Well, wounding them was more like it, but clearly they needed some encouragement."

"Horigarth, huh? I've been looking for him." Lorianus joined them at the lakeshore, her back to the lake so she could watch the tree line from a distance while they continued their conversation. Evanyil wasn't much one for 'keeping an eye out.' She preferred using her elven hearing to hear any impending threats, and she was more than fast enough to get out of the way before anything bad happened—most of the time. Damon had always been there for when that hadn't worked. They made a good team for that, and many other reasons.

"I thought you might like that. What did you find?" Evanyil moved from petting Damon's hand to pressing her body into his from behind, delicately tracing her fingertips just underneath his mage robes just above his waistline. Tracing the outline of his frenulum down to his glans, she felt him pulsating against her caress, making her smile wickedly.

Feeling Evanyil's very aroused breasts pressing—pointing really—against his lower back, Damon was struggling to focus. *Is she messing with me again?*

Raised eyebrows, tossing her bow over her left shoulder, Lorianus struggled to understand the relationship between her crazy sister and this…man. "What did I find? Well, the biggest tracks I've ever seen for starters and leading right up mural towers on the northern curtain wall. The western curtain wall and mural towers back right up against the natural protection of cliffs leading down to the River Tsaen. They knew what they were doing when they built that place. Only one way in and one way out, but it bothers me that those big tracks just disappeared more than a thousand paces from that point of entry."

"They used a *Portal*." It wasn't a guess from Damon. They had a dragon. And a mage. *This just got more interesting*, Damon considered, as the delicate tracing of Evanyil's fingertips found the hardened tip of his arousal as she toyed with him just above his beltline. This had to stop, or he had to take out his frustrations on Evanyil. Their relationship had been…complicated, but it hadn't escalated to sex, yet, and he was trying to avoid that with her, but she was…determined to fuck with him. He just couldn't figure out if it was literally or figuratively, and right now they didn't have time for this. Pushing her hands away from him so he could pivot out of her grip, Damon freed himself from Evanyil's distractions. Good

Charles W. McDonald Jr.

thing too; the arrow just missed him as it whistled past his right ear between him and Evanyil, immediately causing Evanyil to disappear so fast into the northern tree line he thought her a blur as Lorianus crouched where she was, nocking and loosing an arrow so fast Damon could barely see its trail screaming off into the tree line at her target.

A thud from the near tree line accompanied a man falling from a thick tree limb only to watch a hail of arrows launched simultaneously upon command of someone just beyond his line of sight.

Damon's Improved Shield up just in time caused more than fifty arrows—which would have turned him into a pincushion—to bounce off his protective shell, redirecting them into the lakeshore around him. He needed cover, but not as bad as Lorianus did. She was hit already in her bow tension arm. That was going to make return fire complicated at best. As Damon extended his *Improved Shield* over Lorianus so she could more easily lay down return fire, he concentrated on the brittle underbrush all over the ground of the eastern tree line. Using his natural abilities in *Pyrokinesis*, Damon dastardly grinned as dozens of paces of the eastern tree line suddenly burst into flames.

Damon could see and hear the steward's men scurrying out of the tree line—some in retreat further back into it. Eight were dumb enough to try and rush Lorianus. Five of which she managed to mow down before they made it thirty paces from the tree line. A brief moment of focus and Damon's *Telekinesis* snatched a scroll from his inner robe pocket into his right hand as he called a giant bolt of lightning from a cloudless morning sky to obliterate into mist the remaining three Lorianus couldn't get to in her wounded condition. "THEY AREN'T DONE WITH US YET," Damon called out to Lorianus a few paces away, searching for Evanyil in the tree line and not finding a single trace of her, but knowing she *was* out there.

"MOVING TO COVER," Lorianus barked, also looking for her sister. She couldn't see her either, but she could *feel* her. It was too quiet, and that was when Evanyil was most lethal.

Then he saw Evanyil emerging from the eastern tree line, side-stepping the brushfire that was only just beginning to consume some of the trees. She held what looked like a severed head in her right hand, her poisoned dagger dripping trails of blood from her left hand as she closed the distance between them. Covered in splatters of blood from magnificent head to toe and all over her black bodysuit, Evanyil sauntered toward them, though occasionally looking off to the northern tree line as if expecting another assault.

"A trophy," Damon asked, as she got within earshot.

Charles W. McDonald Jr.

"A message," Evanyil replied flatly. "One I'll deliver soon enough."

Damon nodded in approval of the idea. That was the *old* way of doing things, and he approved. It had a certain *panache*—succeeding in getting attention. And Evanyil was *all* about attention!

"I think we should take that as an invitation, don't you…." It wasn't really a question from Lorianus. She knew better, but she needed help with her arm. She couldn't break off the arrow and pull it out of her arm by herself. But she didn't have to ask. Most of their communication was non-verbal, especially between Damon and Evanyil. Damon was already tying off a tourniquet around her arm, just above the wound. He knew it was going to bleed a lot when he pulled out the arrow's shaft. He thought about giving her something to bite down on before he broke the tip of the arrow of so he could pull the shaft through, but he knew her well enough. She'd been injured far worse than this before, but this was still going to hurt…a lot!

Snap! The bloodied arrowhead now in Damon's palm separated from its shaft. Tossing it into the lake, Damon leaned down and filled a cup with fresh lake water, which he quickly boiled with his *Pyrokinesis*. "This is going to hurt." Damon tossed the hot water on Lorianus' wound, pulling the shaft from her bloodied arm in one smooth, quick motion.

A grimace and tears from Lorianus, but not a sound, as she knew Damon would try his best to save her arm. *Healing* wasn't his forte, but Damon was learning fast and already far more powerful than he should be. Unseen hands snatched another scroll from within Damon's robes, as he cast *Healing*, gating it through his left hand, which covered her wound. She had to sit immediately, right where she stood as the *Healing* started closing her wound, and she felt the energy Damon described as Arcane flooding through her body, rushing to the wound.

"You'll want to remove that tourniquet now, so the blood will rush back into the healed area and carry the Arcane through your bloodstream."

"Thank you," Evanyil offered sincerely, sitting down beside her sister while looking up at Damon with those magnificent violet eyes of hers.

"Thank you," Lorianus agreed. "They're going to pay for that," she proclaimed while wiping the tears from her eyes. It might not have been her worst wound, but it still hurt like hell. And fresh in her mind.

"What do you think," Damon asked, his black eyes locked with Evanyil. "You think he's going to send more men to flush us out or sit back in his keep waiting for us. He's been a little unpredictable. I can appreciate his line of thinking. He's not stupid, after all."

"How long before she can be fully functional again," Evanyil inquired of her sister's wounds while devouring Damon with her magnificent violet eyes.

"A day…maybe two," he suggested, knowing they didn't have that long to wait. They had to move on the keep in hours—not days.

"I'm not going to be the one that holds us up. Let's go kill this fucker!" Lorianus was pissed!

A smile from Evanyil as she kissed the side of her sister's face. "Let's go kill this fucker," she agreed. "Slowly." Sheathing her bloodied poisoned dagger and picking up the severed head of the regiment lieutenant the steward had sent to kill them, Evanyil knew exactly how she was going to deliver her message to the steward.

Something about that sexy saunter and swaying of those magnificent legs and hips in that satin black, bloodstained bodysuit of hers—all the while gleefully swinging the former lieutenant's severed head in her right hand as she descended into the tree line—gave Damon pause of who he was actually working with. Though, the steward had something he wanted—something he needed. And there was no doubt of him wanting a fight to the death to keep it.

*　　*　　*　　*

(Ten Hours Later)

The grey, white, blue, and sand-colored stone—quarried on site out of the eastern plateau of the River Tsaen—looked both old and intimidating in the four-storied form of Fort Tsaen. The grounds were mostly an oblique square perched atop the cliffs overlooking the River Tsaen below, with two of its rotund mural towers traversing the length of the riverside, while the other two formed the ends of the eastern curtain wall. An outer, shorter curtain wall, made of the same blending of the varied colored stone in near-perfect rectangular bricks, marched around the inner curtain wall, making the obliqueness slightly more pronounced and able to provide enough space for an outer bailey for fortified protection and training of the steward's men. The center of the inner bailey was formed—on its southern boundary—by the less-oblique square keep's northern mural towers and keep wall extending both east and west by the inner curtain wall joining the keep's wall center-length, going outward several hundred paces to the corner mural towers that formed the perimeter of the inner curtain wall, where it made its southern turns on both the eastern and western legs. The front of the keep—only accessible by the drawbridge on the outer curtain wall—had two massive oak doors set inside a three-tiered, cathedral-shaped archway using only the blue stones to form a stark and majestic contrast to the grey, white, and sand-colored stones forming the bulk of the keep and curtain walls. At each corner, a blue-stone brick hash was formed by setting one blue stone brick going in one direction atop another going in the opposite direction, filling in the negative space with the grey, white, and sand-stone colored bricks. The same contrasting pattern was repeated in a decorative, checkered inlay above the archways and inside a decorative alcove between the archway and the decorative checker plate, where a statue of the Steward of Engêstal watched—with outstretched sword—surveying all lands to the south.

He owned lands east and north as well, but it was *unusual* for the center of power for such a large swath of land to be at its northern perimeter, as was the case here. Normally, the center of power was more centrally located, but his reputation for ruthlessness had made up for his lack of strategic, relative positioning. The tactical advantage of building here was obvious, even if the steward's land grab exceeded his would-be reach. Still, it had taken decades to build this place, and it was formidable, if a little dated and conservative.

From the southwestern tree line, Damon could see the significant challenge before them for the first time. Evanyil and Lorianus had already scouted it out, but now seeing what they had gave him pause, but also gave him some ideas. "They were smart to clear the tree line as far back as they did. There must be at least a thousand paces of open ground between the tree line and the outer curtain wall. Fertile ground for picking off an invading force."

"It's just as nasty on the northern face. Trust me." Still holding the severed head in her right hand, Evanyil stood on Damon's right side. He was tired of that head bleeding on his robes.

"Is this as close as you got last time or did you get closer," Damon asked—his black gems sparkling in the moonlit night, as he flexed forward in a kneeling position beside Evanyil.

"Oh, I can get as close as you want, Sweetie. Just say the word."

"That didn't answer my question. I was wondering what else you could tell me about what's inside the inner curtain wall?"

"I didn't get *that* close."

"My guess is the dragon was brought in by *Portal* to the dungeon or one of the lower levels of the keep—probably somewhere below the inner bailey."

"The *what*?" Lorianus fidgeted with her bow, kneeling beside Damon opposite Evanyil.

"Dragon. What did you think those large footprints were?" He offered Lorianus a managed smile, but his mind was on the fortress in front of them. And the daunting task of taking it without a siege force.

Charles W. McDonald Jr.

"I don't know, but you didn't tell me you thought it was a dragon!" Lorianus smiled back at him, though she was certain he could see into her concerned thoughts.

"Having second thoughts?" Evanyil posited to both of them.

"If you're not concerned, I'm not," Lorianus offered with another managed smile.

"Oh, I'm concerned alright. This will be my first time in combat with one, but I'm wondering how long it will take for them to get that thing from where its being held to where we enter the keep. There are lots of tight places in there that we can use to kill off a large number of his forces where that dragon will be useless. That's where I think we need to enter."

"You're thinking like one of those mural tower circular stairways or something like that," Evanyil suggested, as her violet eyes flashed in anticipation of the task in front of them.

"Exactly!" Damon's eyes were as intently focused on the fortress as were Evanyil's, as he began the process of imagineering—in his mind's eye—how he'd *Portal* into a place he's never been. Imagining the first moments of their invasion, step by granular step.

Watching Damon's mind quietly work the problem in front of them, Evanyil asked aloud the question she knew he was asking himself. "How do you *Portal* into a place you've never been?"

"That's the tricky part and why I was asking how close you got. If you could describe it for me, I could extrapolate the difference based on what I'm seeing in front of us and safely get us really close to where we want to be."

"Hold on to that thought, Sweetie. I'll be right back." A lick of his earlobe, and she was out of sight. He had no idea how she could move so stealthily fast without aid of cover from the tree line, but it was nightfall, and being a cunning, lithe cave elf in a black bodysuit *did* help. The night was *her* element. He had seen her leave and tried to follow her trail as far as he could but lost her about halfway across the open field between the tree line and outer bailey curtain wall.

Next thing he noticed, the count of guards along the battlements dropped by two, then four, then eight—all without a sound or warning shot being fired. It was still too risky for him to attempt closing the distance in the open field. He could *Portal* to the most inner part of the keep he could see, which was just the other side of the drawbridge, but then Evanyil wouldn't know where to look for him. The matter was settled soon enough—not by Damon's decision, but by the nocked crossbolt arrow pointing at the back of his skull an instant after the crunch of a tree branch behind him.

Charles W. McDonald Jr.

Instinctively, his hands wanted to go for the pocket inside his robes, but he fought that instinct, slowly raising them behind his head, turning slowly to face the two guardsmen that had gotten the drop on him just forward of one of the steward's regiments sent looking for them.

He said nothing about Lorianus, but he assumed she'd taken off right after Evanyil and had been so quiet about it, he hadn't even noticed her absence—until now. A moment later, Damon's hands were bound behind his back, as he was being shoved into the open field and being marched toward the steward's keep.

Lorianus had seen Evanyil working along the covered battlements, taking out guard after guard, and hadn't even noticed Damon's capture until seeing him being marched toward the keep. Clearly the steward's men were still working behind them. That meant Lorianus needed to move in and move now. They'd be expecting her to assault the front and save Damon, but she knew there had to be another way in. The steward was a clever man, and he wouldn't have built this place without a safe exit away from the obvious point of entry. She just needed to find it. She'd try east, then back south, flanking the steward's men, then back north along the river, but she needed to move fast. The steward wouldn't keep Damon alive long—if he was as clever a man as she gave him credit.

Inside, the grey and cream ensigns edged in sand-colored rope trim with an embossed gold dragon laid atop a field of crushed red roses marked the first-floor great hall as belonging to Emry Luca—the Steward of Engêstal.

The great mountain of a man, Horigarth, swept Damon's legs out from underneath him with one smooth motion, causing Damon to hit the stone floor, landing on his kneecaps. *Ow. You're gonna pay for that.* Damon didn't have to say much more than what his *black mirrors of the soul* shouted.

With Horigarth's broadsword pressed horizontally against Damon's throat, the steward pressed Damon for answers. "Where are your two companions? The two dark elves...?" Emry paused, mocking, "I think this mage prefers the company of *elven* women and *dark elves* at that."

That met with manly, hearty chuckles around the hall from the regiment who'd just captured Damon.

Damon's icy stares of hate silenced each one of them in turn. At least his reputation was working for him. *Where is Evanyil?* Looking around the hall, not just for Evanyil and Lorianus, Damon was trying to understand where the dragon could be. They were clearly on the western, riverside of the keep, from the views

Charles W. McDonald Jr.

he was seeing on the left side of the hall. The right side of the great hall had a stone partition open at both ends of the room, with descending and rising stairs on the northern end. His view out the southern opening of the room was obstructed by Horigarth, and the fact he couldn't move his head without drawing blood against Horigarth's broadsword. A balcony ran across the full length of the western wall, likely to the mural tower staircases on both the northern and southern ends of the keep. *Lots of points of entry,* Damon considered, running the calculus in his thoughts as he chose to answer the steward's questions with a stone silence.

"Well…," Emry paused in the briefest of consideration, adding, "…if he's not going to talk, then I guess he doesn't need his tongue."

Damon could feel Horigarth's smile beside him, accompanied by his foul breath. Hearing Horigarth unsheathe his dagger was the last incentive Damon needed as his *Telekinesis* shoved Horigarth's broadsword away from his neck, while rolling an unseen pressure wave outward from his body in all directions, tossing everyone from their positions, including Emry, who was tossed up against the far northern wall of his great hall.

Now confidently striding toward Emry, his hands still bound behind him, Damon closed the distance as if his hands *were* free. *I don't need my hands to kill you, Emry.* He wasn't *trying* to project his thoughts, but the steward suddenly looked as if he'd heard them spoken aloud.

Stomp. Stop. Stop. He could feel Horigarth rushing up from behind him, his massive feet thundering on the stone floor, then suddenly, nothing. He didn't stop closing the distance between himself and Emry and never had to look back to know who had stopped Horigarth dead in his tracks. He had help, and he was sure they were already doing their job. For a man mostly without trust, he *trusted* Evanyil and Lorianus. They wouldn't leave him alone to die.

"So, you wanted to remove my tongue, did you?!" Damon towered over Emry, glowering at him. Though not as tall or mountainous a man as Horigarth, Damon was physically and psychologically imposing as he leaned over Emry, snapping the rope that bound his hands behind him with his *Telekinesis*, his right index finger now in Emry's face. "Where is that dragon of yours?"

"Don't kill me," Emry pleaded, "I can make it worth your while, Damon."

"Oh…? *NOW* you're willing to negotiate?!"

A guttural roar came from the eastern side of the hall, where Damon had noted the ascending and descending stairs a moment before, accompanied several thunderous footsteps that shook the keep to its foundation. Those footsteps picked up pace as a smile quickly crept over the steward's face. The glint of golden scales reflecting off of the glass of the western wall windows confirmed Damon's worst fears. Suddenly, the severed head of one of the steward's men landed in between Damon and Emry, immediately wiping the steward's grin from his face as it rolled around on the floor, dancing in the reflection of the gold dragon now coming for Damon.

Soft-footed with her bare elven feet on the stone floor, they never heard her coming as four arrows quickly took out four members of the regiment in the great hall with head and neck shots, as Lorianus smoothly unsheathed her long-sword, rushing Horigarth from behind and to his left.

Killing this arrogant mage was going to make his week, and he was definitely keeping the head for a trophy. Those black eyes and long, girlish black hair would look nice with his head on a pike. Gathering his balance, Horigarth, in his brown pants and forest-green leather jerkin over a tan tabard, started rushing for Damon until he was knocked off his feet, suddenly flying sideways toward the western wall in a thud as his massive body crunched up against the inner stone wall of the keep.

Unseen hands rapidly snatched the exact right scroll from Damon's inner robe pocket into the grasp of his right hand as he immediately cast *Damon's Improved Shield*, discarding the scroll just as another flew into his hands enabling him to immediately cast *Amplify*. Using his *Cryokinesis*, Damon formed a conical beam of ice directed at the Gold stomping its way into the great hall from the northeastern entrance, meeting a burst of fire erupting from the fury of the Gold's mouth in a deafening roar that blew Damon backward just with its concussive force. The *Amplified* cone of ice pierced the fire, driving the Gold backward, seemingly angering it, more than affecting it. A hard gut-punch to the neck from Damon's *Telekinesis* further got its attention, if Damon didn't have it already. NOW it was *really* pissed off!

Thinking he'd escape before the dragon tore his great hall apart, Emry tried to get up, finding Evanyil's poisoned dagger a breath away from his throat as she smoothly, silently came up from behind him. "Where ya goin'," Evanyil mocked, snapping his left ankle in half with one quick, hard kick to the side of his stance, forcing him to sit back down, crying out in pain. Evanyil's poisoned dagger now pressed against his scrotum through his slacks; Emry wasn't going *anywhere*.

Charles W. McDonald Jr.

Gotta think fast, Day. How do you kill a Gold dragon? Fire's not going to help you. Summon Lightning is going to be diminished going through all this stone. Think fast. He had to right himself from being blown backward by the concussive force of the dragon's roar, but an idea quickly came to him that just might work. Forming a great spear with his *Telekinesis*, followed by another *Amplify* scroll, Damon thrust the ethereal spear into the soft underbelly of the Gold, causing it to cry out as he could now see it bleeding liquid living gold dust onto the stone floor of the hall. The very substance of magic, itself.

Backing up, recognizing both the power and ingenuity of this mage, he knew he was bleeding now, but he still had his primary weapon, and he was going to use it. A deep breath forced more blood through the gaping wound in his chest, but the fire he laid down ignited the mage as he took another deep breath, preparing another assault.

Damon's robes now burning, he cast them off with his *Telekinesis*, simultaneously snatching the last of his scrolls as his robes flew toward the western wall, now completely ablaze. His charcoal-grey slacks and deep-blue cavalier shirt now revealed, Damon did not retreat. Instead, closing the distance between him and the great Gold. His last big weapon in his right hand, Damon cast *Ball Lightning*, sending a sphere of lightning the size of Damon's head to rush toward the Gold at incredible speed; it was nearly three times the size of the Gold's head when it struck the Gold right where he'd wounded it before. Kneeling almost to the floor, Damon held his right hand out palm up, trying a spell he'd never before used in combat, as he lifted his right hand, summoning a series of squid-like venomous tentacles to rip and tear at the Gold's hands, scales, and feet.

He'd seen this spell before and knew his primary weapon useless against it. Normally, he'd just take flight to avoid them or use his teeth to rip them apart, but his strength was fading from the gaping wound in his chest. Looking to the mage eye to eye, then to Emry, he tried to communicate non-verbally with the mage who'd bested him. If they'd been outside, on open ground, the outcome might have been different, but he couldn't change that now. Again, he looked between the mage and Emry.

Damon wasn't sure what to make of it, but before doing anything else, he

Charles W. McDonald Jr.

Dispelled the tentacles before they ripped the dragon apart. Taking the non-verbal cues from the great Gold, Damon looked to Emry, really looking at him this time. *How had he known what Damon was thinking when he started approaching Emry moments before?*

The massive pommel of Horigarth's broadsword struck Lorianus square in her suprasternal notch, shattering her sternum with a single blow that cracked loud enough for the whole hall to hear it. Backing away from Horigarth enough to give her space to swing and maneuver was difficult with him charging her for the kill shot he desperately sought. Still, a shift to her left, then another hard and fast shift to her right got him off-balance and charging her in the wrong direction as she took advantage of it, bringing her longsword over the top and down upon Horigarth, slicing him open at the base of the neck. The shock on Horigarth's face said it all—bested by a woman—by an elf! As badly as she wanted to bring the longsword back across his throat, she didn't have the strength, and her chest was already throbbing in agony; she could feel her lungs filling with fluid from her internal wounds. But Evanyil's dagger suddenly slamming into Horigarth's left temple ended the fight—and Horigarth.

She hadn't wanted to interrupt Lorianus, but this wasn't the time for egos. Survival had to come before egos, whether her sister would forgive her, or not. Tossing Emry to the side and down the steps, she stood enough to gain a throwing balance and stance, releasing her dagger where she stood.

"Where do you think you're going," Damon pressed Emry, who was already attempting to scurry away on one leg, propping himself up against the wall with his right hand. That's when he noticed the signet ring. That wasn't like a ruler's ring, at all. It wasn't a crest or a seal of any kind. Tearing Emry's ring finger off with his *Telekinesis*, Damon brought the ring to within a pace in front of him where he reached out and grabbed the finger to pull the black and gold signet ring from Emry's finger, which he tossed aside and behind him, now closing the distance between him and the great Gold, as he slipped the signet ring upon his own right ring finger. At first it didn't fit, then it swelled in size to accommodate the size of Damon's ring finger. Then he heard it, *I'm Hadron*. The recognition in the slit pupils and fiery cornea of the Gold before him immediately confirmed for him the source of that message.

"I'm Damon," he replied aloud to the great Gold before him, continuing

Charles W. McDonald Jr.

to close the distance and now only a few paces away.

"You need to kill that thing, not keep it as a pet, Damon." Evanyil's voice carried behind him—not commanding—but not leaving anything to suggestion either. "Don't get too close to it!"

Communicating only non-verbally with his companion, he gave Evanyil a full open palm pointed backward at her to tell her to stay back. "I'm not going to kill you if you promise to end this fight and help me find what we came for."

A snort of fire from Hadron's nostrils preceded an *agreed* projected back at Damon.

He didn't know if he could *Heal* both the dragon and Lorianus, but the dragon was the key to cooperation, and he could use a dragon like this for generations to come, if not longer. He wasn't sure how old this one was, but he knew they could live practically forever. Laying his hands on the wound he'd caused, Damon cast *Healing* directly into Hadron's wounds, feeling the gaping hole closing almost instantly.

A horrified Emry watched on, cursing, "You can't help him! I forbid it!"

His foot suddenly slamming Damon to the left and out of his way, Hadron set Emry ablaze with one breath, collapsing back to the floor from Damon's *Healing*.

"Um, we kinda needed him." Damon looked perturbed at Hadron, righting himself after being tossed aside like a doll.

I know where he keeps his most prized possessions. That book is what you came for, is it not?

"It is."

You'll find it one level down, just below ground level. There are four chambers. One chamber contains the treasury of taxes. One contains a library of scrolls—mostly history, deeds, titles and such, but the one you're interested in is the first chamber along the eastern wall as you head back south down the hallway below.

"What's in the fourth chamber?"

I was asked to protect those three chambers at all cost. He never told me what was in the fourth, and I never asked.

Pivoting back to Evanyil, Damon asked, "Is she going to be okay, or do I need to take care of her right now?"

"Go." Lorianus didn't sound convincing, coughing up blood when she said it, but she also wasn't going to be argued with either.

"More of the steward's men will be along any moment. Can you guard the staircase and Lorianus?" That was directed at Hadron. He glanced back to Evanyil, communicating with her non-verbally again with his eyes that suggested they check

Charles W. McDonald Jr.

out the chambers one level down—immediately.

No one will get past me.

Waving Evanyil past him, Damon gave the go-ahead nod.

"Let's go." Evanyil was already halfway down the staircase, not waiting on Damon.

Downstairs, Damon got a better feel for Hadron's description: two sets of double-doors on the left, along the eastern wall, two on the right, along the western wall. He was making an assumption about which one was which as Hadron hadn't been all that specific. Three of the oak double-doors, inset in a cathedral-shaped archway, had similar locks, including the first on the eastern wall—the one Hadron specifically extolled as containing what he, and Evanyil, had come for. Each of those locks looked as if activated by a simple large key, something Evanyil could pick with relative ease, but the second double-door along the western wall—the riverside wall—looked almost seamless and had no discernible locking mechanism.

"What do you make of that? That has to be the fourth chamber Hadron spoke of?"

"Well, I didn't get to hear any of that conversation. To me it just sounded like you'd lost your mind and started talking to yourself, so you're going to have to fill me in a little bit. Good to know you're on a first-name basis with the dragon, though!" Evanyil smiled at the last jibe, knowing Damon would take it in stride.

"Did he—sorry, your pal Hadron—bother telling you which one has the book?"

"That one." Damon pointed back to the first set of double-doors along the eastern wall.

"Then why aren't we opening that one, first?"

"Because I've got a feeling. That's why."

"Oh, pardon me. I thought I was the one that always went off *feeling*."

"Shut up and open the door." Damon looked perturbed, but she knew better. He just didn't like being argued with. Either get in line or get out of his way. That was Damon's thinking, and she knew that, but that didn't prevent her from challenging it from time to time, just to see how much she could get away with.

"Hmmm." Examining the seamless double-doorway beneath the cathedral-shaped archway, Evanyil didn't know quite what to make of the lock, because she couldn't find one. The traps were relatively easy to find, and they were nasty. Something about the traps didn't look right, though. They were all set to the left side of the doorway. Most of the time, at least on a double-door, if there were traps, they'd be set in the middle at the point of entry. Another, "Hmmm," from Evanyil made Damon stare this time.

"Hmmm what?!"

"Hmmm, I don't think this door opens the way it appears."

Damon knew of spells that could reveal, remove, and even set traps, but he hadn't learned those yet. His sole focus had been *Healing, Portals,* and combat. He wasn't going to be much help, and that meant relying on Evanyil. "I trust your judgment," Damon offered, stepping back and giving her space to work.

The unexpected compliment brought a smile to Evanyil's face as she ran her soft, delicate fingertips along the left edge of the doorway, never letting her fingers touch as she tried to assess the location of the trap's trigger-points. "Looks like two trigger-points. Hang on."

A moment later, and she was convinced. "Do you think you can shield us both?"

"Why?"

"Because I don't think I can safely trip these."

Wow, a trap Evanyil can't safely disarm! That was shocking! …And disturbing. *What's behind this door, anyway?*

Casting *Damon's Improved Shield* to encompass them both, Damon had to get a little closer to Evanyil—close enough to where his hands were on her hips— only emboldening her to grind herself back against him. *She's incorrigible!* "Better now," he asked, whispering in her ear.

"You tell me." She leaned herself back into him as she activated the triggers, causing spikes to shoot out of the walls, bouncing off his shell. The door didn't budge, but she'd considered that possibility, going back to the idea that this door may not open the way it appeared.

Now with that trap disarmed, she took a closer, longer look, seeing if that had been the last of the traps, before she took a very close look at the opposite right side of the doorway. "Hmmm." Another thoughtful look as she pushed her delicate fingers into the tiny gap between the door itself, and the doorjamb. One more time on the left side of the doorway, and Evanyil slid her long pick into the left doorjamb, flipping the well-hidden latch, causing the entire double door to slide right as a single unit.

"Hmmm indeed," Damon added, hoping they found whatever traps might remain in the next few brief moments before the shield dissipated, but the steward had gone to *a lot* of trouble to protect the contents of this room. Suddenly wishing Hadron hadn't torched Emry, he was left to figure out the 'why,' himself.

Charles W. McDonald Jr.

Beyond, lay nothing special about the chamber itself. Its construction was the same as everything else here—grey, sand-colored, and blue stone uniform bricks with some decorative hashing, laid in an overlapping manner. However, the sheer volume of the scrolls and books before him—five rows of casings, four shelves per casing—along with the meticulous inventory system put in place, made Damon question the value of what might be in the other chambers. Examining the illumine-like indexing system for a moment, it appeared to go primarily by topic, then by era, then by region, then by ruler. The topics were…fascinating! Ranging from magic, to witchcraft, treasure, trade and commerce, folktale, legend, lineage, and to a topic most notably labeled 'leverage.' He'd have to come back to that one, but under lineage was a sub-topic labeled, 'the tree of life.' "Wow, what have we found, here?"

"A bunch of boring stuff. I'm going to break into the other chambers while you fiddle around with all this…," she hesitated only a brief moment—probably a reflection of her disappointment—before continuing, "…ancient gossip."

Ancient gossip, he thought, *humph. Who puts traps and hidden locks on ancient gossip?* No, there was something significant in here, and he was pretty sure where to start looking: 'leverage.' Still, it was 'the tree of life' topic he first ran across as he traced his masculine fingertips across the weathered leather spines of the books before him, then he felt it at his feet.

Looking down to see what his boot had struck, Damon noticed the unremarkable book laying on the floor with one corner of the book on the bottom rung of the bookshelf as if it had been dropped—recently so. "Hmmm," he thought aloud, looking at the title, *The Book of Souls* by Daedrin.

*   *   *   *

Nearly an hour later, Damon emerged from chamber of 'ancient gossip' as Evanyil had proclaimed it, but not before securing several artifacts in a remote location via *Portal*. He'd have to come back to those later, but Evanyil had been entirely too quiet. As he made the turn back north up the hallway, he noticed the chamber opposite on the eastern wall looking very similar in design with the same row and count of casings and shelves. A brief look inside, and he could see a similar fastidious manner of bookkeeping and inventory. This steward was a meticulous sort. Now he understood how he'd gained so much power, so quickly. That and the 'leverage' topic of materials he found in the other room had answered a great deal of questions for him. The contents here were more benign, current, and of an accounting type. Still, there was something very important he wanted here.

Charles W. McDonald Jr.

A flip through a few documents told him he was in the right place as he found the various deeds of title to lands the steward held all over the continent. "Ah, there you are...." Damon smiled, recognizing the deed for the lands just east of Gravêstil Lake. "You're coming with me." He smiled again, sliding the deed into his front right pocket, moving back north up the hallway to the treasury, where he found Evanyil laying in a pile of gold coins halfway to the twenty-span ceiling, rolling around in it as she tossed coins in the air, letting them rain down over her lush curves in her blood-streaked, black bodysuit. Laying on her back, half-buried in the pile of gold and silver coins, Evanyil kicked her left leg up into the air, tossing a handful of coins for them to roll down her leg and thigh, striking her pelvis in waves of monetary ecstasy.

"Am I interrupting a coingasm?" He'd seen stranger behavior from Evanyil, of course, but her mischievous savoring of the moment made him question his allegiance—if only for a brief moment. Besides, she was gorgeous when she was like this. And, she wasn't the only mischievous and dastardly member of their little band of terrorists.

A flash from those violet eyes of hers, turning her body toward him atop the pile of gold coins, "*You* could be giving me something *much* better than a coingasm...."

"Aren't you the least bit worried about your sister? You know, *the other* cave elf upstairs?"

"Damon, if there was ever a time for us to have sex, it's now, Sweetie. Come here...." Those beautiful curves. Those thighs slowly rubbing one against the other. Those sultry violet eyes, and mussed platinum hair were all calling to Damon—as was her right index finger lingered on the ties that strained to hold her bodysuit together, tugging at them as taut curves of her naked breast came into his lingering and lustful view. Evanyil's magnificent violet eyes watched him watching her as another tie became undone, fully exposing both her breasts and her very victory-aroused, fully-erect nipples. Pulling her body suit off her taut body, only down to, and around, her midriff, she wanted Damon to do the rest. The scent of her aroused sex filling the chamber from floor to ceiling.

A slow and uncontrollable boil built up inside Damon as he cautiously closed the distance between himself and the most beautiful incarnation of a woman he'd ever seen. It wasn't as if he'd never considered making their relationship a sexual one, but they worked well together. Completed each other in so many ways. He didn't dare assume the same woman could complete him in that way too. Life didn't work that way. His father had taught him that; even if his father had failed in every other way, he'd been right about that...so far. Now within her grasp, feeling her hot breath on his neck, just under his ear where she licked him as she brought her thigh up and around to close around him, tossing her own body up into his lap as he simultaneously sat down, they quickly found themselves in a coupling release of intense sexual tension, months in the making and something entirely beyond their ability to control.

*   *   *   *

Evanyil wasn't the cuddle-after-sex type, and neither was he, really. Besides, she was too busy giving herself more coingasms, rolling around nude in the pile of gold coins. Putting his slacks back on, Damon left the treasury shirtless, curious about something he'd seen back in the first chamber they'd opened; he wanted to revisit that. He knew he'd missed something the last time he was in there.

Now back in the vaulted library, Damon searched the topic 'lineage,' looking back as far as the records went—about twenty thousand years. Assuming the records could even be accurate going back that far, he started comparing what he was looking at to the 'tree of life.' Noticing the birth and entrance into the tree of vital beings such as dragons, elves, duragar, and trollocs alike, it all originated with a man by the name *The Life Bringer*. There looked to be an almost direct correlation to *The Life Bringer* and the arrival of dragons—among other creations. It also appeared as if there was an early near-extinction-level event where *The Life Bringer* had three children—two boys and a girl—with only one of the boys surviving, leaving a noticeable void in the tree as it moved around the death of one of the boys and the girl, as if in mourning.

"Where did *you* come from?" It wasn't like Damon to talk to himself, but his question was a burning one. He didn't believe in the idea of *Ex Nihilo*—creation from nothing. *So, where did The Life Bringer come from? More importantly, where did magic come from?* He understood magic—at least he thought he did—but it had to come from somewhere, from someone. There were just bigger questions here than he had answers for, but he knew there were answers in here—somewhere—if he only knew how to look for them.

*   *   *   *

(Atop the Aegen Plateau and East of Gravêstil Lake, Kaleion, A Few Hours Later)

Charles W. McDonald Jr.

Surveying the land to the east in good measure, Damon knew this was the place. Dawn was already in the process of evaporating the heavy dew drops on the long green grass and fescue, where Damon now stood. The verdant, fertile ground, landscaped with tens of thousands of ancient but well-distributed trees atop the highest grounds east of the Trident stood out like a field of opportunities stretched out before him. A brief look back to the west, and the twin moons were being chased over the opposite horizon. With natural fresh water sources both north and west and thousands of acres of fertile hunting ground, it would be a hard place to siege or cut off. There were natural hills large enough to present a series of berms to the north. With the Trident and Gravêstil Lake to the west, the only real approach was ascending the Aegen Plateau from the south and east. It would make a defensive position—not the best he'd ever seen—but given the magnificent view, it was a beautiful piece of property for *his* future needs. He'd soon be powerful enough that no one would dare attempt a conventional assault, anyway. Drawing in a deep breath of fresh mountain air, Damon considered, *it's perfect!*

"Observing your spoils, Damon?"

The soft, feminine voice—as delicate and disarming as it was—made him immediately pivot as one of the spoils of his latest conquest leapt out of his singed and mangled robes into his right hand as he readied himself for combat.

The voice, as beautiful as it was, didn't do her justice. He still wasn't expecting the red-gold angel in cream and gold robes before him. He didn't believe in angels or demons, but he *somewhat* believed in good and evil. He'd seen both— well, evil at least. *Was she an angel?*

Just above her large breasts on the right side, he saw a crest on her robes of a pale-pink rose with white leaves on a tan circular background. Maybe two hands shorter than he, she was the most beautiful woman he'd ever seen, next to Evanyil. Still, she looked and felt like the enemy, and the flow of Arcane filled his entire body as he began to cast.

"*I surrender*," she exclaimed, dropping to her knees before him, her hands outstretched toward him in forfeit.

Not knowing what to think, Damon was taken aback. His right hand held the *Summon Lightning* scroll tight-gripped in his hand as the Arcane seared into his palm. He'd already cast the spell. The energy had to go somewhere. Arcane demanded it.

Suddenly Damon's right hand was struck by the lightning he'd summoned, as the raw power of his split-second decision to save the woman slammed into his right fist, knocking him to the ground in a blistering agony.

Charles W. McDonald Jr.

His eyes opened slowly, one at a time, to see her red-gold hair spilling over his face, upside down as he awoke with his head in her lap.

"I shouldn't have surprised you like that. I'm sorry. I won't do it again," she lied while caressing his beautiful, long, black bangs. Peering into those ominous and beautiful black eyes of his.

"How did you know who I was, or even where to find me?" Damon struggled to get up, but she didn't try to stop him. Instead, choosing to merely observe the difficulty of his recovery from striking himself with his own lightning. His hand was numb and stuck open. He couldn't feel it at all, let alone close it or make a fist, and he could see symbols from the scroll embossed into the palm of his hand.

"You are Damon of Basrat. You killed your father, and with good reason. You were once known as Kaylan. I know a great deal about you, Damon, and wish to know more." She paused, looking at him carefully—looking into those *black mirrors of the soul* his father had given him—or rather Damon had claimed. "You fought your own instincts to protect me. I am grateful, Damon. Thank you." Those beautiful gold eyes of hers, matched each of her ten gold fingernails—like unto living liquid gold dust.

"Argh…. You're welcome…. I think." He struggled as his eyes still seemingly spun, having trouble focusing on her.

"I'm Illirian Starfire. It's a distinct honor to meet you, Damon of Basrat."

"Illirian Starfire! You *are* the fucking enemy! What are you doing here?" He questioned—if ever so briefly—the wisdom in saving her.

"Don't let the soft features fool you, Damon. I could have easily killed you, and I had the element of surprise. I didn't. What does that tell you?"

"That you think you can use me."

"Wow!" *His mind is even quicker than I thought.* His reputation, though…. She'd have to drill into that a bit more.

"Wow, I'm right, or wow, that was blunt?!"

"Uh. Both." His reputation for being brutally honest was certainly proving to be accurate. She'd never met anyone quite like him. *Was there still room to shape such a man? And his future?*

"Just because you're beautiful, don't think you can use me, Illirian." Now standing for the first time since the lightning strike, the feeling was starting to come back to his right hand, but the scar of that symbol was going to require magic to remove, as he looked down briefly at it, then to the magnificent red-gold angel before him. He wasn't sure what to believe about angels and demons and the like. He wasn't even sure about an afterlife. He just knew enough that peo-

Charles W. McDonald Jr.

ple made choices, and often those choices led to disappointment—frequently his. Still, something about her.... In that raw moment to strike himself, instead of her, he still felt like it was the right choice. His gut told him it was the right decision. *We'll see*, Damon considered, eyeing her suspiciously.

"What if our interests overlapped? Would it then be, as you said, *'using'* you if we both benefit out of a *partnership?*" She hesitated, using that last word as it formed in her thoughts, but when she delivered it verbally, she delivered it with staccato emphasis to drive home the idea—if indelicately so. Damon wasn't the delicate type. He might very well appreciate the boldness of the delivery itself.

"I'm listening."

A broad but genuine smile from Illirian nearly prompted a smile from Damon before he caught himself enough to scowl instead. One needed to be fierce in negotiations—never showing satisfaction until the deal was inked—and the ink dry!

"There's a ship I've been tracking for quite some time. All the way from the Ocean of Slight." Her eyes briefly looked off—far off—to the west, with that mentioning.

"Wait, you want me to go halfway around the world?" Damon instinctively pointed off to the west, where Illirian had just looked.

"No, Damon, I want you to learn how to listen before you act." That was a bit too harsh—even if totally on point. "I'm sorry...," she offered before she continued, "...you're an amazing talent, Damon. And, someone that knows how to get things done. I think your actions will more closely match your interests if you listen a little more and talk a little less."

"Fair enough...." He didn't like the lecture, but he was smart enough to know she wasn't wrong. "Continue please." He knew his biggest weakness was his lack of experience, and from her gold fingernails, he could tell that was something she *could* help him with. He was truly interested, and if this was really Illirian Starfire, he could learn...a lot. And fast.

"The Steward of Engêstal knew a great deal more than he let on. I know this because he was working for me until I found out he was pilfering valuable intelligence and artifacts from me, thinking he could hide it and grow his own wealth and power all the while using my access and my contacts to do so. You just did me a huge favor, Damon. Whether intentional or not. Now, the first thing you'll need to do is go...." Illirian Starfire leaned in close as she continued, her beautifully toxic perfume lingering in Damon's nostrils, permanently imbuing that scent, and that sensuous sensation between them, with her beauty—forever recognizable as unmistakably Illirian Starfire.

Charles W. McDonald Jr.

(Austin, TX, Earth, Present Day)

He'd managed to bring a good deal of his most important documents with him from Eden, so he didn't have to keep going back and forth so much. This way he could keep Mira close to him without keeping her close to Eden and all that could go wrong there. Still, he hadn't looked at this manuscript in centuries. There'd been no reason—'til now. But after his most recent visit to the Graelon Colonial Outpost, Damon thought he was in a better position now to look at the old manuscript with fresh eyes and derive fresh answers. Looking at the lineage tree once more, he traced the lineage branches with his fingertip, branch by branch from *The Life Bringer*—who he now knew as Durial. The numbers weren't adding up in his head. He knew the population of Kaleion well, along with the approximate timeline and average birth and death rates. Just doing the math in his head, he could tell something was off, and that void in the tree of life diagram was… troubling.

He'd seen invisible ink before, and this wasn't that. Usually invisible ink left telltale signs of indentations where the illumine had applied pressure to draw or write. There were no such telltale signs in the void that fell directly below who he knew to be Durial. There was, however, a magical equivalent of invisible ink. A wave of his left hand revealed answers he hadn't expected, causing his eyes to grow wide in attention and focus as it immediately became clear why it was no wonder he'd missed these signs all those centuries ago. He should have revisited this document long before now. It might have changed things. When he'd first discovered this document, he had neither the knowledge, nor skill, to know what to do with it.

Still, the direct lineage from the supposedly perished children of Durial led almost immediately, straight to a name he knew all too well: Seren—his mother. His mother was a direct descendant of Durial—one of the four brothers banished from Setinon because their magic could no longer be safely contained or controlled. But Damon's name was not listed in the tree of life. It stopped at Seren, or rather traversed around her. There were other names he recognized after having been revealed—who would be distant cousins—Illirian Starfire among them. *But why had these names been hidden? Were not the other descendants of Durial just as important as he, or Illirian? Kellen's name had not been hidden, and Kellen was as much a descendant of Durial as he.* There was another hidden name he recognized—by legend and works only; he'd never met the man and didn't know if he still lived or not. Daedrin.

Charles W. McDonald Jr.

The author of the source material for what would become the making of *A Throne of Souls.*

Listening to Mira's hot shower running in the background, Damon's calculus brought more questions than answers as he continued looking over the tree of life of Kaleion. *Why had they really been banished? Why not simply kill them? Why bother separating them if it was known they could travel between worlds? Had they assumed they wouldn't be able to find one another? Surely, any race powerful enough to be able to do so many of the things they had done would be smart enough to know better than that. Why would my mother, as powerful as she was, have anything to do with my father? If Durial had created dragons, and Pierio had created a race of AI capable of casting, what were the other brothers capable of, and what had they done? What else was a part of their legacy that I don't know? And how can I leverage that to execute the Master Plan?*

He did have one potential answer to his last internal question, though that answer only raised several more questions. Daedrin. *Is he still alive? Where is he? Who is he? How does he fit into this equation? And will he help, or stand in my way?*

He needed to do more research, and he needed to talk to Illirian.

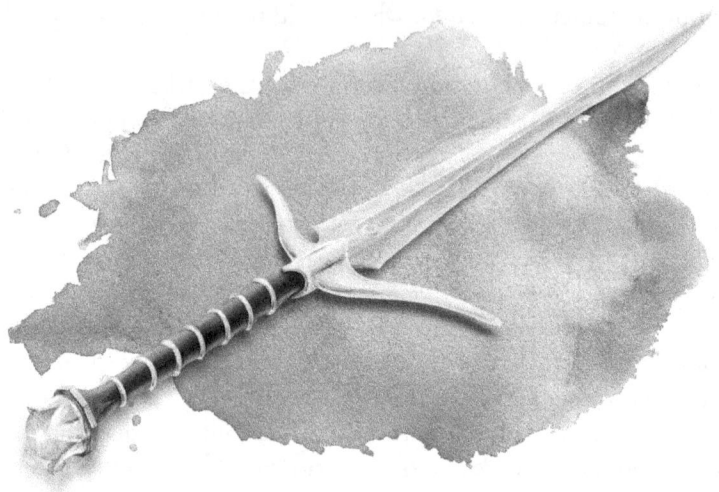

Chapter 47: Keys and Hatred

(Osalin, Perion, Present Day)

acing down the natives, angered by his arrival, Royvan Miral had to rely on his instincts. The fluent usage here of the ancient dead language of Ferian had him out of his element. His soft leather boots crunched on the dead grass beneath him, and he knew what he needed to do. The only thing he could do. There were hundreds of them, and their hatred lay on the edge of the knife in whether to kill him, eat him, or listen to him.

Prostrating himself on the dead grass before the natives, he immediately held out the rough-hewn gold scroll case of the Scroll of Carnac—opened—the First Seal missing from its ancient sarcophagus.

Barely off the ship still moored in the crescent-shaped port of Osalin, Royvan Miral hadn't dared offload the rest of his men or gear. Instead choosing to face down the angry natives alone while Captain Therigish Flinn stood atop the whipstaff. Watching.

With bones pierced through what could only be described as their very stretched nipples, Royvan considered the pain each must have endured to have such features, and the ones appearing to give the orders looked to be the most severely disfigured as if it were a badge of distinction and honor to have endured such torment. All were shirtless, both men and women, proudly displaying the varying levels of torture they had endured—all bearing spears on long pikes for weaponry. The men wore what looked like grass skirts, open in the back, while the women wore a rough-textured hemp sarong covering them down to their toes. Some of the men were painted in dark and painful tattoos. Others looked too young or didn't have enough stature to carry that apparent honor. For most, their skin appeared leathery and sun-worn, though it was apparent the Blood Night was working against that as even the most weathered were beginning to show signs of going pale, and weak. Clearly starvation was beginning to set in here too. He could leverage that.

He understood fragments of the whispers around him, now prostrate on the ground before them as one of the elders approached.

"Blasphemers," one of the elders reflected aloud in a broken Ferian.

The angry mob hissed at him almost in unison to the elder's accusation.

Think fast or you're dead, and Humanity with you. Extending the rough-hewn gold scroll casing to the elder before him, Royvan Miral offered in his best attempt at Ferian, "The One has sent me. He opened the Scroll of Carnac and brought the Blood Night. I am his emissary."

The angered mob backed up at the last word. At least his Ferian was working.

"Why open," the elder asked, as he approached a few steps further toward The One's 'emissary.'

It was a fair question, and one he'd considered from the moment Radin had done so. He knew it had to do with Damon and some great plan of his, but he wasn't about to translate all of that madness.

"The One saw the end of all things. He's trying to save as many as he can before the end comes for us all." Royvan Miral wasn't sure if he'd translated that correctly or not, but he could see the thought behind the elder's weathered eyes and face. "I give this to you." He again offered the scroll casing to the elder, who finally reached out to touch it but refused to take, or hold, it. Instead, he backed away from it, almost hissing as if it were a vile thing. Perhaps it was.

"The One sent me to you for the Second Seal because he knows the only way to end the Blood Night is to open all the Seals and summon the Creator."

Shaking his head angrily in response, the elder began backing away and the mob began closing in.

"It is the only way!" Royvan Miral suddenly found himself standing, nearly towering over the elder in a threatening manner, but the spear through his side was a much bigger problem now as he was bleeding out of his right flank all over the dead grass beneath him. As the elder stowed his bloodied spear back at his right side, Royvan Miral collapsed to his knees before the elder, and this time he wasn't getting up.

A glowering stare between the man atop the whipstaff of the unwelcome ship in their harbor and the elder said it all. Already the captain was climbing down from the whipstaff, heading into his cabin as the elder looked down at the now collapsed Royvan Miral laying on his side at his feet.

Damned Royvan Miral wouldn't listen, and now he'd gone and gotten himself killed by angry savages. He needed to get his men, and his ship, out of here, but he needed supplies. He'd counted on resupplying if he'd found Osalin. Well, here they were. *Now what...?* The options staring him in the face were all bad ones. He didn't have the men, even with Royvan's men, to fight off an all-out assault from the lot of these savages. They'd just killed the only man capable of speaking their language. *Too light to sail. Too dangerous to stay.* He needed to find a way to negotiate with them. *But how?* He needed the night to think on it.

"What are you doing in here?" Kerrich slammed the door to the captain's quarters behind him, nearly shattering the doorframe...and the door. "We have to go save him!"

"Save who? Royvan Miral is dead. You saw the spear go through him, same as me."

"We have to do something. We must try to talk to them. Maybe they'll let us bring him back to the ship. Maybe we can treat his wounds...."

Lots of maybes. I don't deal in maybes. Maybes don't keep you alive, and maybes have a propensity to get you killed, just like the maybe existence of this damnable island. Maybe Osalin does exist. Oh, it exists, alright, he considered ruefully. *Now what?!*

*　　*　　*　　*

He felt clammy all over, like his skin was crawling with icy sweat. He was vaguely aware of voices, but the language.... It was hard for him to even focus on the conversation enough to tell what it was. It was more like mumbling as he became aware of a moist towel laid atop his forehead as his flank throbbed underneath bloodied bandages.

His eyes still closed as he tried opening one of them, not recognizing any of his surroundings. It was an actual building—not a tent or anything he'd attribute to the angry natives that had wounded him. He shuffled his hands at his sides, trying to get some leverage to lift his head to look around.

Charles W. McDonald Jr.

"Don't move," the male voice from a blurred darkened figure warned in perfect common tongue, approaching Royvan Miral from his right side, pushing him back down onto the surface of the table. "You'll pull your stitches."

Now looming over him, the blurry figure crystallized somewhat into an elderly man—probably in his sixties—wearing dark-grey robes with long white hair and bright blue eyes. As he laid back down and the old man's hand retreated back to his side, Royvan Miral noticed the gold fingernails and assumed he'd been *Healed*. More importantly, he assumed he'd found his way to the people that might know the location of the Second Seal. *Was this one of the ancient lameans he'd heard so much about?* "I'm Royvan Miral. Who are you?"

"Yes, Mr. Miral. I know who you are...." A brief pause followed, as the old man peeked under the bloodied bandages. "And why you are here. We need to change your bandages again. I need you to roll over on your left side, please."

A guttural moan left Royvan Miral as he worked his body to twist onto his left side with the aid of the old lamean who had a hand on his back, away from his wound. "Why did you save me if you knew who I was, and why I was here?"

Pain shot through Royvan Miral from his flank all the way to the tips of his toes as the bandage was ripped away from his wound and the laceration suddenly doused with alcohol. The gash at his side throbbed a bright-red, as he looked upon it for the first time, realizing it was probably infected. Maybe he hadn't been *Healed* after all.

"No, Mr. Miral, I haven't *Healed* you yet." The old man confirmed Royvan's thoughts and his own ability to read them. "You wouldn't have survived *Healing* in the state you were in."

"You mean I was in *worse* shape?"

"You were dead, Mr. Miral. You had no pulse. The poison from the spear had done what it was designed to do."

"How did you bring me back without *Healing* me then?"

"I need you to bite down on this." The old lamean shoved a small wooden chuck into Royvan's mouth, shutting his jaw around it as he simultaneously flooded Royvan Miral with Arcane from the tips of his toes to the fine ends of his hair, causing him to convulse uncontrollably in the old man's grasp.

"How is he?" The familiar, virile young voice burst into the room through the door closest to Royvan, as Royvan Miral spit the wooden chuck from his mouth at the site of a crowned Talemar walking into the room.

"How did you find me?"

"You're welcome." Talemar gestured to Royvan Miral's now *Healing* wound even though he hadn't been the one to *Heal* it. Well, not this time.

Charles W. McDonald Jr.

"I feel like I'm at a loss here." Royvan Miral tried to put the pieces together, staring between the two powerful lameans.

"Not at all. You did your job. You found *them*. I found *you*." It was simple logic from Talemar, but Royvan couldn't help but feel used as his side sealed up before his eyes, though it still throbbed, whether in phantom pain or not.

"Mind catching me up, then?" He didn't know how long he'd been out, but clearly there had been conversations between the old lamean and Talemar, and he wanted to know where things stood.

"They've agreed to hear us out, but I wanted you to be a part of that conversation, so we were hoping you'd recover, and it seems you're tougher to kill than you look." It might have been feigned flattery from Talemar, but it worked. "Now, get some clothes on and meet us outside." Tossing Royvan's pants at him unceremoniously, Talemar pivoted and walked straight back out of the room, leaving Royvan alone again with the old lamean.

"You gonna tell me your name?" Royvan Miral eyed the old lamean from his half-elevated position as he worked to upright himself enough to put on his pants.

"My name is Daedrin, Mr. Miral." It was a bare-bones response to a much deeper question, but he was clearly done talking as he followed Talemar out of the room, letting Royvan Miral get dressed to join them.

*   *   *   *

Outside, Talemar sat on a crate of fresh fruit looking to have been brought from Exeter, under a lean-to built against the plain but hardened structure where he'd been taken to *Heal*. It wasn't much more than four thick walls made of mud-bricks, reinforced with wood and metal, but it was the only thing he could call an actual structure in sight. They were clearly on the edge of the world, and not his first time doing so, but Royvan Miral was clearly at a disadvantage here and was grateful for Talemar's unplanned arrival. Unplanned from his perspective, at least.

"The food we brought for you is yours whether you help us, or not. However, if you don't help us, this will be the last fresh fruit you'll ever see. You'll starve to death. We all will." Talemar fired off his opening salvo, but his expectations were anyone's guess as his face was stony and hard to read—even for Royvan Miral.

"I appreciate the gesture," Daedrin offered, but quickly countered with those cool blue eyes. "I could simply go to another world and take those I care about with me." Looking between them, knowing they knew the same thing he knew…the existence of other inhabitable worlds.

Charles W. M℃Donald Jr.

"You're not going to escape this problem by going to another world. It will find you there, too," Talemar countered knowingly, though his eyes didn't give away much more than what he'd already offered.

"Oh, how so?" Daedrin, whether merely skeptical or testing, wanted the argument of logic—not presumption. Facts—not educated guesses.

"Some of the prophecies say this is the end of all things on all worlds—the great unmaking of Creation," Royvan Miral offered, knowing the prophecies had proven to be inaccurate, or incomplete, on many levels, and therefore untrustworthy.

"Prophecies or not," Talemar abruptly added, knowing Daedrin would respect evidence more than vague ramblings of a prophecy that may or may not be accurate. "If you know of other worlds, then you likely know of the Seeds of Humanity."

That had Daedrin's attention as his bright-blue eyes focused on Talemar, listening to his every word.

Talemar clearly had Daedrin's attention where he wanted it now as he continued, "You will not escape this, and neither will we. You know of the one called Damon?"

Daedrin's eyes now swelled with his attention level answering non-verbally.

"Good then. He means to bring about the End Times on all worlds of the Seeds of Humanity, so there will be no escape for you, or any of us."

That wasn't true. It wasn't like Talemar to lie. *Was he lying?* Royvan Miral considered the game Talemar was playing with Daedrin. While it may not have been true, it was irrelevant the moment the First Seal had been opened—if you believed the Seals were meant to affect all of Creation, as had been prophesied. He must have been playing a dangerous game with Daedrin, hedging on his unconscious belief system.

"I know of the End Times already being in play on three of the known worlds. Where did you plan to go hide where Damon's reach and that of the Creator won't follow?" Talemar paused briefly, calculating the wisdom in delivering this next piece of information—or rather his own supposition. "Damon means to go to war with the Creator and bring about something he calls a new equilibrium. Personally, I think he's mad. Regardless, whether you are for Damon, or against him, that's your choice, but staving off the End Times isn't a viable option now that the Scroll of Carnac has been uttered. I haven't yet decided for myself on which side I will stand, but I'm not on the side of leaving things the way they are now. The First Seal has been used, and it cannot be unused. We *must* open the rest and let Damon and the Creator settle this matter between themselves, if need be."

Charles W. McDonald Jr.

Talemar was treading on some very dangerous ground here, and Royvan didn't understand where he'd gotten all this knowledge of Damon's supposedly true intent, all of a sudden. From what he knew of Damon, Royvan felt like Talemar might be having a casual relationship with the facts.

A long awkward pause of silence settled under the lean-to as Daedrin considered the possibilities. He knew a great deal of Damon of Basrat—The Dark Knight of Magic—and wondered what ever led him to believe that opening the Seals of the Creator was a *good* idea. "The Seals were imbued with their powers by the Creator, not by Damon. It *is* possible their reach goes beyond Perion." Daedrin didn't know that for a fact, but he had always considered that a possibility. No one really could know until the words were spoken. They weren't there when the scrolls were made. No one even knew if all the Seals were on Perion, or if they were disbursed among the Seeds of Humanity. He'd considered the very real likelihood that some might be on his own homeworld. "I haven't left Perion since the Blood Night fell. Has it spread beyond Perion?" Daedrin's eyes instinctively looked skyward to the roof of the lien-to, but really beyond.

"I have not seen it with my own eyes—the effects of the Scroll of Carnac on other worlds. I only know that other worlds are experiencing their End Times concurrently with ours." Talemar knew more—at least he thought he knew—but he wasn't going to offer that information, since revealing it wouldn't advance his position.

Talemar's thoughts were even more transparent than the legendary adventurer to Daedrin's left. He could use that, but Talemar's logic was accurate. Still, Daedrin felt like he was being used by Talemar—and by proxy—Damon. *Why would Talemar be helping Damon?* It still posed more questions than answers. And the more he thought about it, the more he trusted Damon more than Talemar. "Maybe we should have this discussion with Damon...," Daedrin proffered.

"If I may," Royvan Miral offered, looking between them. They didn't have time for involving Damon. They needed to move faster, or they were all as good as dead. Everyone and everything was counting on them. "This message has been bothering me for some time now. Years. I can't explain it. I simply come to, and it's there...usually etched into the ground where I'd slept.

I don't know if this means anything to either of you, but I'm telling you I personally believe there isn't a place you'll be able to go and hide from this," Royvan Miral explained while writing the thought etched in his mind into the dirt below the lean-to.

And there shall be but seven trumpets, bearing seven messages,

Charles W. McDonald Jr.

For all the worlds to hear, and all men therein.

And each message shall be sealed up in itself.

And woe unto the men of the worlds, for once the first is uttered,

What will be will be swiftly, and nothing in Creation shall hinder.

Looking at the familiar message in the dirt, Daedrin's decision had just been made. "I will take you to the Seals that are the keys to the unmaking, but I do not see in you the *hatred* to open them."

Seals—plural. What is he talking about? Royvan Miral's mind suddenly flooded with possibilities.

Daedrin's *Portal* seared and rent the superheated air with silvery-blue flashes of light revealing an overgrown landscape of what must have once recently been a verdant green paradise now virtually destroyed by the pale-red Blood Night sky above. Still, the roar of a waterfall filtered through the other side of the *Portal*, calling to them as Daedrin walked through to the other side. Moving was still challenging for Royvan Miral, but this was what he had come for, so he managed a slow walk to and through Daedrin's *Portal* with Talemar quick on his heels.

Now on the other side, the *Portal* vanished with a whoosh behind them without a single motion from Daedrin. The grass, flowers, and vegetation must have been above knee height only a short time ago, before the coming of the Blood Night, but now crunched underneath Royvan Miral's feet, as dead as he was said to have been a short time ago. He saw a few trees hither and thither still fruit-bearing and assumed they must have been kept alive by Daedrin's magic—and powerful magic it must have been, to swim upstream against the will of the First Seal.

Slowly he walked, trying to keep pace with Daedrin and Talemar, who passed him, trying to keep up with Daedrin, maintaining both men in sight— one forward, and one back. They moved along the perimeter of a crescent-moon-shaped pool of fresh water that fell from a twenty-storey drop waterfall above onto blue stones below. The water appeared still untainted by the Blood Night, and Royvan Miral could see clearly all the way to the bottom, still containing some level of life, as he saw the occasional fresh-water fish moving in the water. It was the first fresh-water fish he'd seen since the coming of the Blood Night. Clearly there was a level of magic alive here pushing back against the Blood Night.

Forward Royvan Miral pressed 'til his side throbbed near enough to make him falter, but still he kept pressing forward until they approached the right side of the waterfall where there appeared to be about a gap the span of a man length-wise between the water itself and the stone face of the cliff. "Stay close to me," Daedrin instructed, walking right into the waterfall between the water and the cliff-face. Keeping close on Daedrin's heels, Royvan Miral and Talemar followed into the roar of the rushing water cascading down all around them. Unable to resist the temptation, Royvan Miral outstretched his left hand, letting the fresh-water cascade in betwixt his fingertips to suddenly feel a tingle rushing throughout his entire body, starting at his fingertips and circulating through his bloodstream, giving him new life. His side no longer throbbed, and he could more easily walk and keep pace with Talemar and Daedrin in front of him. *What is this place?*

A quick, ducked turn to the right, into the cliff, and Daedrin quickly disappeared from sight. Talemar looked back at Royvan Miral, touching the cliff-face where Daedrin just vanished, and he felt cliff and rock pushing back at him until his hand traversed further down, where he felt nothing but air, though his eyes lied of the rock they saw before him. Ducking just as Daedrin had done an instant before, Talemar trusted and hoped and thrust his body into the cliff-face, disappearing just as Daedrin before him. Royvan Miral had seen and experienced a lot in his lifetime, so this wasn't quite as shocking for him, but he wondered how much magic it would take to push back on what Damon and Radin had begun as he felt around for the camouflaged edges of the cliff-face then ducked into the cliff as Talemar and Daedrin had done before him.

Now in a narrow cavern entrance, he clearly saw Talemar and Daedrin as they resumed walking deeper into the bowels of the cliff. A few dozen more paces, and the hall opened up into a great chamber, hundreds—if not thousands—of spans across, and high. He had heard of space created out of nothing by magic, and he wasn't sure if that was what he was seeing now in front of him, but the front of the ancient city cut into the face of the rock looked...undisturbed—and unmistakable in style. This looked similar in style to the ring of figures on The Isle of Romney that had led him here.

"Welcome to Osalin," Daedrin offered with a flourish, moving his hands ethereally across the great thirty-storey pillars that flanked either side of the ancient stone architecture forming the entrance of the ancient city. *Osalin isn't an island,* Royvan Miral considered. *It's a city.* Nine smaller ten-storey columns formed a colonnade front with what looked like a fifteen-degree sloped roofline cascading right and left of a center apex toward the great, flanking thirty-storey pillars.

Now inside the main structure, past the colonnade, they moved down a series of ancient halls, left, then right, then down, then right, then right again, then down again. So many turns, Royvan was lost already, until they found themselves in a room decorated with great, five-storey inlaid columns of polished maple with round rungs attached at the columns in three spots. Gold shafts traversed the length of the room, looping through each of the rungs. Between each polished maple column were purple banners embossed with red and gold symbols—symbols he'd seen before. *Are these the root of Ferian?* They looked like what had been described to him as the fundamental runes of magic, but different somehow. A table was center offset of the rectangular ceremonial room; at least he assumed it was ceremonial. It certainly had that feel to it.

Great and regal purple curtains adorned each of the short ends of the rectangular room. As Daedrin approached the offset table, he moved something Royvan didn't entirely see; it looked, perhaps, like a small stone. Suddenly the great curtain at one end of the room began pulling back, revealing another segmented room of the same design, but this one square rather than rectangular. It was more like the entire room was one great ceremonial room, but the great curtain appeared to have some ritualistic purpose in hiding the square room beyond. Like a veil to be lifted during the ceremony. Within the square room sat a chest exactly centered in the smaller segmented room. Both Talemar and Royvan Miral stood gaping at the chest as Royvan worked his mouth, struggling to come up with the words to describe what he was seeing. The chest itself looked to have a burnished, metallic sheen, but it wasn't here, and then it was, and then it wasn't, and then it was. Winking in and out of existence of their reality, the chest was decorated in beautiful metalwork illustrating flowers and vine similar to what must have lived outside the waterfall before the Blood Night. The sides of the chest were decorated in architecture similar to what Royvan had seen entering the ancient city, with the colonnade carved into the rock of the cavern.

Royvan Miral considered asking why it winked in and out of existence, but internally he also considered this ceremonial room might forbid speaking. Immediately he put his fingers to his lips so Talemar could see his indication for silence, causing a smile on Daedrin's face as he reached his hand toward the chest just as it winked out of existence, only to see it immediately snap back, out of sequence at his request. Daedrin never touched the chest, though the flower-adorned lid opened as his fingers came within a breath of its metallic surface. A soft glow came from the interior of the chest, and Royvan never saw what came next as he suddenly found himself out of time back in hallways ascending and turning, exiting the bowels of Osalin with the Second and Fifth Seals in his hands. Halting right where he stood, mid-steps, Royvan Miral tried to recall the last few moments that had given him the Seals, but they were gone. Wiped from his memory—or never really experienced—which one, he couldn't say, but he had what he'd come for—and more. Looking at each of their designs, Royvan noticed neither held the same construction, nor design, as the Scroll of Carnac. His left hand held what looked, and felt like, a solid stone cylinder etched with two languages—one ancient Ferian, the other he'd never before seen. But the Ferian clearly spoke of the Death of Men, making that one clearly the Second Seal. In his right hand, he held a similar shape and size solid cylinder of wood. It should have been dust by now, and yet it looked old and worn, but like it could last another thousand years. It had inscriptions in five different languages—one of them ancient Ferian. He wasn't sure exactly what it was describing because his eyes couldn't look upon it for more than an instant. Twice he tried to focus his eyes upon the inscription, and both times the inscription moved with life so much as to make reading it impossible, but what he was seeing fit the only description he'd ever found of the Fifth Seal. Perhaps it was something else, but right now he had to keep pace with Talemar in front of him or he'd never find his way out of this ancient and holy maze.

Moments later, emerging from the bowels of Osalin, Royvan Miral spoke for the first time in recent memory, "You said earlier, you didn't see in us the hatred to open these keys. What did you mean by that?" That obviously directed at Daedrin, who halted, pivoting where he stood at the second step down from the colonnade, now looking back up at Talemar and Royvan Miral.

"I meant that now you hold the despair of all Mankind in your hands. I meant, I hope you are prepared for the judgment of Mankind, and of the Creator, for speaking the words that will kill us all." He thought about it for a moment, knowing that wasn't a fully complete response. "…Or save us all depending on how you look at it."

Feeling the weight immeasurably beyond the stone and wood cylinders in his hands, Royvan Miral looked to Talemar, asking, "Are we doing the right thing?"

"I can't say, but we're doing what *must* be done." Talemar hastily split the air in front of them, forming a *Portal* back to the crescent-moon harbor where they could gather their men and do what precisely must be done.

Charles W. McDonald Jr.

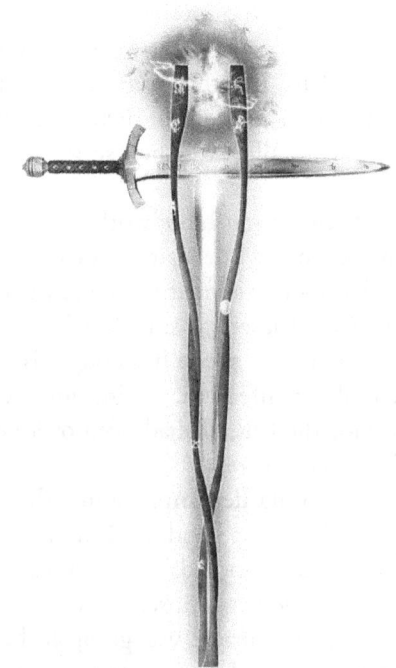

Chapter 48: Consequence of Disappointment

(New Georgia Hospital, Eden, Present day)

The beautiful, but highly functional, sterile aesthetics of the emergency room erupted into organized chaos as soon as she was urgently wheeled into a four-bay triage pod. She had no identification on her, but they immediately knew *who* they were working to save.

It was all hands on deck, and the hospital's ER crew frantically worked over the beautiful, young brunette laying before them with a gaping gunshot wound to her left flank. The bullet looked to have gone clean through but had expanded—mushrooming—on the exit wound and would leave a nasty scar if she lived. The duty nurse visibly cringed at the thought. *She has to live!!!* The implied, *or we all die* was a given. They all knew who this was. This was their living god's girlfriend—his love.

How or why Damon would have left her to die in his own manor wasn't being questioned right now. Maybe he didn't know. The president said he'd made many attempts to reach Damon but hadn't been able to get through to him yet to

Charles W. McDonald Jr.

notify him of Mira's condition. As the president paced just outside the ER, they all knew he was waiting for the news to share with Damon that Mira would live, and now out of critical condition. But they were far from that moment as the IV of blood started flowing into Mira, and four of them worked in counting unison to pivot her body onto the gurney to allow the duty surgeon access to see the exit side of her gunshot wound.

A designated runner nurse ran bloodwork samples for testing so fast she nearly ran into the automated door while waiting for it to open. A statistics nurse scanned the wound with what looked similar to one of the transparent flexible cell-phones, causing a phased array of lasers to scan Mira's wound, producing a three-foot-by-three-foot holographic image above her body. The duty surgeon frowned at the exit wound's potential for infection, calling for the team to carefully roll her back flat, prepping her for the OR. It had been over an hour since she'd been shot—best guess—and she was in distress.

"We're gonna do a cannula decompression," the support surgeon called out to the team, holding out his right hand awaiting a fourteen-inch needle that the duty nurse to his right produced immediately into his waiting hand.

Monitoring her vitals as he began inserting the decompression needle into Mira's chest, the support surgeon knew it was going to be a delicate balance be-tween getting her stable enough to cut her open and operating immediately enough to find out where all this blood loss was coming from. It was possible it had gone clean through missing all vital organs, but they wouldn't know for sure until they cut her open and verified that. Still, she'd lost a ton of blood, and they hoped that was only due to the time from gunshot to treatment.

The androgynous grey five-foot presence of Eden's chief scientist loomed much larger in the triage pod, causing involuntary glances from the triage staff. 22B, as it had become known, stood far enough out of the way to observe, though close enough to provide telepathic guidance to the surgical staff. Projecting a copy of the holographic scan of Mira's wound close enough where it could study it in detail, 22B used its long, delicate fingers to work its transparent tablet to zoom into various spots within the hologram, looking for evidence of grazed, or punctured, vital organs. It was, of course, extremely familiar with Human physiology by now, after having examined them for so many decades up close and living among them for nearly a year already.

22B's facial expressions, such as they were, usually didn't give away much. They were pretty hard beings to read, but as Mira's body was being wheeled past it, 22B looked worried and fearful as the gurney's large urethane wheels left tracks in Mira's blood covering the floor of the triage pod. Still, it fell in line behind the duty surgeon and the gurney heading into the OR to save Mira's life…and theirs.

*   *   *   *

(Isolation Chamber, Chief Scientist's Section of the New Georgia Hospital, Eden, Present Day)

More than thirty advanced computers, including quantum computers, monitored the subject's condition. Growth pattern analysis displayed across three 3mm-slim, interconnected displays, forming a large cohesive dashboard of vital information which tracked the subject's every moment of development. Damon had been very specific, and the consequence of his disappointment made quite clear. His chief scientist wasn't about to test its God's capacity for forgiveness. 22B wasn't even sure if Damon had that capacity at all, and that wasn't for it to question. It had a job to do.

It had been touch-and-go in the OR with Mira for well over two hours, but she looked to be coming out of critical condition sometime in the next few hours if they'd done their job right. Jumping from one near-death experience to another, 22B worked its transparent tablet causing the three, interconnected dashboard displays to change, isolating a specific set of growth parameters, and activating a large wall display along the twenty-six-foot length of the interior leg of the room. Circling the eight-foot-long-by-three-foot-wide pod, 22B examined the Human adolescent male it had been tasked with curating, carefully checking vital organ functions, bloodwork results, and especially his telomeres. Highlighting the telomere length results, 22B isolated the data and zoomed in on the holographic display, nodding in satisfaction. *Twelve*, it thought. *Right on schedule.* It hoped Damon would be happy. Moreover, it hoped nothing went wrong. There was still a long way to go. Lots of opportunity for things to go wrong like what happened with Mira earlier. That had been a close enough call. Best not to press luck so perilously close to the edge twice in one day.

Looking over the Human adolescent male head to toe, 22B observed its closed and unmoving eyelids. It wasn't conscious, of course—not even self-aware really, but it was alive…and quite healthy. *He lives, I live.* It was a brief thought, but a reassuring one for 22B.

Charles W. McDonald Jr.

Chapter 49: A Moment of Scale

(New Buckland Hospital, England, Earth, Very Near Future)

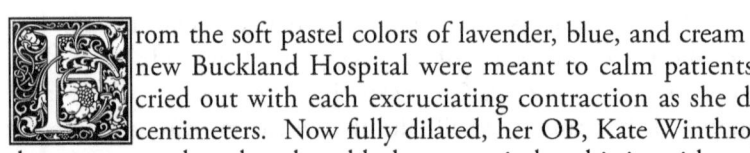rom the soft pastel colors of lavender, blue, and cream the walls of the new Buckland Hospital were meant to calm patients, but Elise still cried out with each excruciating contraction as she dilated to eleven centimeters. Now fully dilated, her OB, Kate Winthrop, called for the duty nurse—a sharp but short black woman in her thirties with raven hair down to her butt—to start wheeling Elise into OR. They were going to try vaginal delivery first, but with it being the Queen and all, they weren't taking any chances. Their new prince was on his way, and they were going to be ready!

Inside the OR, the octagonal light platform in the ceiling cast brilliant prisms of daylight-spectrum light to every nook and cranny of the octagonal-shaped sterile facility. Banks of monitors and equipment stood by, staged for a C-Section, as Elise's gurney burst through the double-door entry on the east side of the room, his majesty—Michael Anthony Day—in tow fast behind Elise. It had been a delicate ask of her OB asking him to shed his sixth-century gear—Excalibur included—for a sterile approved gown, but Michael didn't complain. He just complied, albeit with a scowl when taking in the flimsy nature of the sterile attire he was asked to wear.

The anesthesiologist, Dr. Trig Frank, tried to calm Elise, speaking in steady muted tones, "Now, Your Majesty, I'm going to give you a cocktail—just enough to take the edge off the epidural—and then we'll start that in a minute. Okay?" He didn't wait, of course, the drugs were already flowing into her IV. "We still want you to be able to feel when the contractions come so we'll know when to have you start pushing, so we're not going to numb you entirely."

Michael lovingly stroked Elise's long, strawberry-blonde hair at the head of her gurney, watching the orchestrated medical choreography going on all around them. "It'll be over before you know it," he tried to reassure his wife, but what did he know?! He'd never given birth before! He didn't know shit!

Elise chose not to reply, just a cold-stare layered over a series of breaths

Charles W. McDonald Jr.

to calm and maintain a level of control and pain management. He meant well enough—loving husband and all—but now wasn't the time for him to speak! "Ahhh…. Oh, God!" Elise felt the next wave of spasms from her contractions take over her body as Kate huddled down between her pelvis, positioning the Queen's legs in the stirrups. A visible rise in Elise's uterus told her it was time.

"Your Majesty, I'm going to need you to start pushing. A lower abdominal press just like what we discussed. Just like you're having the biggest bowel movement of your life." A swift and expert move with the scalpel, and the episiotomy was done in seconds as Kate continued to encourage, "…That's it. Keep your legs relaxed and push."

"Ughhh!! Jeeesus! Arghhh!"

"It's okay, Your Majesty. You're doing great. I've got him. I've got your son!"

A moment later, and the duty nurse, Carol, carried Michael's new son—now removed from his umbilical cord—over to a table where she worked to clean him of birth material. A brief smack to clear the airway, and the baby could be heard outside the OR—crying. In quick expertise, she had his boy cleaned and swaddled in a white hospital receiving blanket, now bringing him to the king. "Fifty-seven centimeters, three-point-four kilograms. Your prince looks terrific. Your new son, Your Majesty." Carol beamed, handing over the new prince with her long, raven hair shimmering in the light of the OR. Tears from her beautiful, bright-brown eyes fell upon the new hope of Britain as Michael Anthony Day claimed his new son.

This moment of smallness—this moment of scale—crystallized for Michael in the instant he claimed his boy, and the knowledge of what his father must have felt for him. The tears welled in his eyes beyond any control he'd hoped to measure when this moment came, and all his field experience was impotent to suppress the light of Love that now pierced his soul. "Alexander," he paused, taking in the name for the first time, "…you're named after the greatest conqueror of Man the world has ever known. With all our love and adoration, we bow at your feet, my son."

"Let…me…see…." Elise was groggy and exhausted, and barely able to feel anything going on between her legs as Kate finished up, but she wanted to see her boy as Michael held onto Alexander, showing him to Elise. "He doesn't…look like… you," she mocked, shocking him out of this incredible moment.

"WHAT?!"

"He looks better than you," she mused, smiling at her husband, her words starting to come out more smoothly—feeling as if her OB might be getting close

Charles W. McDonald Jr.

to done with her.

"Oh. Well. Yeah. Maybe." He smiled despite himself.

"I'm done down here," Kate interrupted. "We're going to wheel you back to your room where you can get some sleep. We need to borrow the Prince for a few minutes to run some routine tests, and we'll bring him right back to your room in a few minutes." The duty nurse came over, placing a tiny electronic ankle bracelet on the new prince before taking him away. "That code you have on both your bracelets is matched to his code, so you'll be able to track him just like we will. That way you'll know exactly where he is at all times." Kate reminded them of the standard neonatal practices at the hospital.

"You going to be okay if I go talk to my dad? I'll see you back in your room," Michael offered with a kiss for his still-glowing wife.

"Of course. Is everything okay?" She knew something was different in her husband but didn't know how to quantify it. Babies changed the entire landscape they were born into. She knew that, but having never experienced it before, it still took her off guard.

"I'll see you in a few...." He didn't really answer her because he didn't know how, but he knew, or felt, how this had changed him inside.

*   *   *   *

The waiting room was tense, even without the treacherous media being allowed inside. Billings, Col. Terry Goodwin, and Michael Sr. stood in a semi-circle, feigning watching CNN's coverage of the birth right down the hallway from where they now stood. Michael's footsteps had been quiet enough to get within a few feet before Michael Sr. noticed his son's presence.

"He's great. He's Alexander," Michael informed them, smiling, trying to keep himself together.

"BRAVO," Billings shouted with a diplomatic level of applause.

"Good job, Your Majesty. Congratulations," Terry offered, following up with, "How's the Queen?"

"She's fine. They're doing some routine stuff on Alexander, and they'll bring him to her room momentarily. I just wanted to...."

The sudden hug coming from his son momentarily took Michael Sr. off guard, as he put his arms around his boy in return.

"I never knew...." The muffled words spoken into Michael Sr.'s shoulders of his earth-tone tweed jacket.

"Knew what...," Sr. deflected, still patting his son's back, feeling the weight he carried upon his shoulders.

The sudden shock of the recurring vision made Michael stagger against his father, causing Michael Sr. to grab onto his son so he didn't fall. The pure, bright light with the vision of the great crystal lake and the booming voice of Creation on the other side always took Michael off guard. He didn't understand why or how the moments came to him, only that they did, and they were important. "I'm sorry. I have to go." Michael tried to get his father to let go, but his father could be persistent.

"What was that all about? You can't just leave. I want a doctor to look at you."

"Father, I'm sorry. I have to go. I'll text you when we're ready to head home. Could you handle clearing out some of this frenzy for me?"

"We're going to talk about this…. Maybe not now. I get it, and I'll handle it. But, we ARE talking about this later."

"Sure, Dad. Absolutely," Michael uncharacteristically lied, turning back to the doors that led down the neonatal corridor.

"Before you go," Billings interrupted, causing Michael to pivot back to them where he saw Billings waving in someone from the other side of the waiting area. "We thought you might like this." A young and vibrant man in his late teens with scruffy brown hair and brown eyes carried a magnificent explosion of impressionistic color on canvas housed in an elegant pewter frame with gold scrollwork all the way around, matching the style of Michael's scabbard for Excalibur. The whole painting was half the size of the boy carrying it, and Michael could tell he was struggling with it, but when the boy turned it around so Michael could see all of it, the painting knocked him from his feet right where he stood.

Brilliantly reflective, impressionistic strokes of light and shadow danced on canvas in blues, creams, browns, golds, ambers, and bursts of many other, hither and thither, illustrating Michael, Alexander, and Elise huddled in a semi-circle in front of Dover Castle. It was a Leonid Afremov—and a masterpiece at that. How he'd captured Alexander so strikingly before even a single photo of him had been released was remarkable.

"Wow! How did he even know?"

"I had it commissioned for you when you told me the sex. He said he'd be honored to have one of his paintings in the king's home—especially this one." Michael Sr. smiled, knowing how much his son loved the work of Leonid Afremov.

Rising to take the painting to Elise, he gave his father another half-hug with his free right arm as his left struggled to carry the beast of a painting back to Elise.

Charles W. McDonald Jr.

(Dover Castle, England, Earth, Near Future)

Staring at the Leonid Afremov gift from years earlier now hanging in one of the mural halls outside the master suite, but really staring through it more than anything else, Michael reassured the president, "Yes, Mr. President. You have my commitment. The Desert Rats will be there for you when you need us, sir." Getting intel on what exactly happened in the South China Sea had been difficult. Even Billings' connections at the CIA had been extremely obfuscated about it, and when could you ever trust anything coming out of the CIA, anyway? But the blinding visions had been coming more frequently, and he assumed they were leading him to this moment.

"If you don't mind me asking, Mr. President, what is our strategy after we push them back? I mean, how do we bring this to an end? You've already tried communicating with the Chinese Leadership, insisting on how this was all a misunderstanding, and they wouldn't have any of it. Did you get the sense that they would ever surrender, or capitulate, in any way? Or, did you get the feeling from your conversations with them that this was a fight to the death? That they'd made up their mind to take what they believed was theirs, no matter the cost." He didn't offer where he was getting his information from, and it was just as well the president understood Michael had his own reliable sources and information assets. Nor had he mentioned that he'd tried calling the Chinese President directly, and his calls hadn't been accepted.

The elderly but resolved masculine voice came across his Android loud and clear. "I don't want to sound like I haven't considered your question, because I have, but honestly I'm trying to push back an invading army that has cut a wide swath through my northern neighbor and is in pitched combat with us on three fronts in the open sea. My biggest concern is keeping this conventional, and not letting it escalate beyond that, but I fear that escalation may become necessary if we don't find a conventional way of halting the progress of this massive invading force. If we go nuclear to halt their advance, the whole world will lose, because they'll go nuclear. Right now, my sole focus is finding a conventional solution to halt their northern advance from Canada and keeping our nuclear silos and codes safe and under NCCS."

"I understand, Mr. President, and your priorities are correct. We need a conventional solution. I'm just wondering if there is an offer to be made that the Chinese would consider a sufficient apology for the incident."

Charles W. McDonald Jr.

"Michael…" it was the first time he'd addressed the king by name, but he needed to get his point across, "…it doesn't make a tinker's damn whose fault this is. Trust me when I tell you, they're not interested in settling. They're only interested in blood and conquest at this point. They see an opportunity to take what they have always wanted, be justified in the eyes of the UN in doing so, and they're seizing it. It's really that simple. Besides, I don't think the formal royal family was interested in hearing an apology from you for killing the former king, were they?"

An unnecessary reminder of the fatal wound he'd dealt to Harold not long ago, but he got the point. "I understand, Mr. President. I'll help you with your conventional halt to their advance. We'll be there. You can count on me."

"I've always been able to count on you. You're a good man of your word, Michael. Good evening, Your Majesty."

"Good morning and good day to you, Mr. President." Michael's eyes were heavy with the cost in blood he knew his commitment had already spilled and would spill again. Many of his men would never return home to see their wives, daughters, sons, fathers, mothers, sisters, and brothers. Many of his men were like family to him….

Ending the call and putting his Android government-issued cell in his vest pocket, Michael's eyes fell once again upon the painting of his son with Elise, knowing they, and his new baby girl, would depend on him coming home safe. There had been many other instances of a king of England leading his men into combat of course, but this wasn't the middle ages. There was a chain of command, and he hadn't been in combat for years. But these were *his* men—his brothers—going to defend a land, allied or not, that wasn't their homeland. They *did* have a dog in this fight, but it *wasn't* in their back yard.

The men would fight more fiercely if they were protecting their king, and if there was ever a battle they needed to win, it was this one. A conventional halt to their advance could end this thing before it went nuclear and tore the world apart. As he saw it, the stakes couldn't be any higher, and if the stakes were that high, he needed to be there.

Now he just needed to find a way to tell Elise he was going to New York and taking the infamous Desert Rats Armoured Division with him.

Charles W. McDonald Jr.

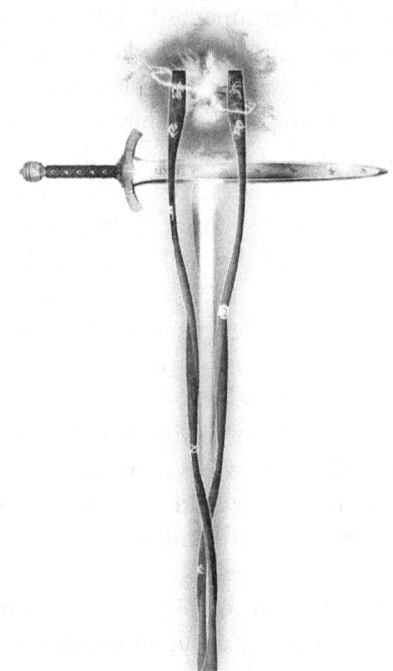

Chapter 50: Paths Destined to Cross

(Damon's Estate, Kaleion, A Very Long Time Ago)

ozens of construction workers raised the ridge spine of the new roof with brute force and a series of pulleys as Damon used his *Telekinesis* to mate rafter beams with heavy-duty trunnion joints to the ridge as he choreographed the development of what would become the finest masterpiece landmark east of the Trident. His new manor was now coming to life—from vision to reality as the dowels slammed home, creating a frame intended to last for centuries.

Damon watched from ground level as another series of heavy wood dowels joined ridge to rafter, hammered into place by the roofing team, who crawled all over the new roof like ants working with a hive-mind strategy. As he watched his vision being brought to life, realizing the amount of coin he was going through and the rate at which he was going through it, he knew he'd have to acquire more wealth, more treasure, more favors, and more allies. The Tree of Life document he'd discovered produced interesting revelations—the name 'Kellen' among them. He'd heard that name many times before. Even Illirian had mentioned it in less-than-flattering terms. Still, this was a man he needed to know—a man he needed to understand and persuade. He hoped his invitation had been received with its intended objective, but time would tell. Either way, Kellen would now be aware of him. Whether or not that was a good thing remained to be seen.

Focusing on the *Telekinesis* required to maneuver the next series of rafters into place, Damon's ears perked up at the crackling whoosh of what he knew to be a *Portal* opening and closing behind him. He couldn't drop what he was doing without killing one of the workers or destroying valuable lumber. So rather than panicking and pivoting immediately, he continued doing what he was doing, hoping the show of confidence would deter any hostile actions being considered by whomever just appeared behind him.

It wasn't like Damon, at least not by reputation, to ignore his flank as he observed the young, talented mage in charcoal-blue robes using his natural abilities to build an obscene scar upon the land east of the Trident. He considered clearing his throat to announce his presence, but he knew Damon had heard his *Portal* close. He'd heard a great deal about this…man and seeing his mastery of his natural abilities did give Kellen some pause. He had similar natural abilities, but was duly impressed with the ease, precision, and strength of the abilities Damon demonstrated before him as he maneuvered several rafters into place simultaneously, in sync with the roofers working five storeys above him.

This was the man who killed his father as a child and already made such a name for himself? The man being mentioned in hushed tones by kings and kingdoms around the planet? Kellen wasn't much for humility, but he recognized talent when he saw it. Damon could either be an enemy or an ally, but their paths were destined to cross one way or the other. The planet wasn't big enough for both of them unless they found a way to work together. Still, Kellen preferred working alone. He had risen to prominence all by his own making—a truly self-made man. He didn't need Damon. But, he also didn't need Damon to constantly be a thorn in his side either. Perhaps killing him now was the best path. As he flooded his entire body, from the tips of his toes to the edge of his black bangs, Kellen felt the lifeblood of the Arcane that filled him as he prepared to obliterate Damon with one fell swoop. "You shouldn't have left your flank so exposed," Kellen chided, his virile, youthful, medium-tone voice carried on the winds coming out of the southwest eastward toward Damon, now standing in front of him.

Charles W. McDonald Jr.

The voice came as more of a surprise than the words. He assumed it was Kellen. He'd heard a great deal about him and had imagined his voice being much deeper, closer to his own. He sounded…very young, but he knew that was a lie. He needed to respond, but he didn't want to kill his roofers by halting what he was doing and concentrating on the threat that was Kellen while simultaneously dealing with the rafters; that was a challenge for which he wasn't prepared. He knew he needed to come across both confident and non-threatening, less Kellen would seize this opportunity to eliminate him as a player on the board. "You don't want to kill me, Kellen."

"Oh…," again Kellen chided. Now more curious of Damon than before. "Why is that?"

"Because you don't have anyone you can rely on." Truth cut through bullshit faster than a hot knife through butter and Damon's frontal assault with his honesty confirmed parts of his reputation, while other parts of his own infamy usefully buttressed a safety net of mighty retribution around Damon like unto one of his protective shields.

"I don't need to rely on anyone. I work alone." It wasn't a lie exactly, but when it came to Archmages, two was a crowd—three was apocalyptic!

"We all need someone to rely on." As the final rafter he'd lifted settled into place, Damon could now release his concentration enough to pivot, facing Kellen the Destroyer for the first time. The charcoal-grey robes fit tighter against his average-sized, yet lean, body than most other mages who preferred them to move loose and fluidically about them. His were still fluid, but there was no mistaking his health and virility—nor his false age. Taut veins in his neck and hands combined with the shimmer in his bangs drooped down over bright emerald eyes, though considerably shorter and lighter than Damon, indicated this was still a formidable mage and a deadly man. There was a killer—even murderous—instinct, lustrous behind those emerald pools. Observing the shoulder-length black hair nestled around Kellen's neck, both Damon and Kellen locked eyes for the first time, taking measure of one another, both deciding in that instant not to cast.

"I'm used to working alone, Damon." Kellen's eyes watched everything about Damon. From his body language to his iron gaze. Damon wasn't afraid of him, and yet he should have been. Whether reckless or insane, Damon was living up to his reputation.

"Then why accept my invitation?" Damon's gaze locked with Kellen's—each ever more curious of the other.

A curl of Kellen's lips gave away his consideration of that question. "Why did you ask me to come see you, Damon?" Damon was a hard man to read, but

Charles W. McDonald Jr.

he had a pattern about him that he was certain he could read…in time. This was not the chaotic actor of his infamy. There was a rational logic to Damon that did *not* comport with his reputation. And he could appreciate a rational actor. Chaos didn't serve his future goals.

"Because you're Kellen of Aegenon, are you not? Kellen the Destroyer? I make it my business to know those worth knowing."

Damon had defused the tension between while stoking their curiosity in one another. Damon was calculated, thoughtful, and that made him dangerous. "I'm listening, Damon."

"You're the only living son of Hersila and Herot. Correct?" Damon's find from the Steward of Engêstal was making itself useful already.

Damon was well informed. *Now, he really is dangerous….* "Correct."

"The same Kellen being considered for appointment to the Council of Mages?"

"Correct." Kellen was wondering where this was going. Clearly Damon had him at the disadvantage by information, but Kellen wouldn't make the mistake of underestimating Damon's sources again. "Where is this going, Damon?" He didn't like Damon's knowing more about him than he knew about Damon. That could become precarious. He needed to do some research after this meeting. Kellen knew there was much to be learned in a name, but something told him there was far more to Damon than just Damon. His prior research suggested Damon wasn't even his given name, and one doesn't take on an entirely new identity without good reason. Maybe there was more than just killing his father in his history.

"I can see myself needing someone like you, and I can see myself having something to offer in return."

"Now we're getting somewhere. What is your proposal, Damon of Basrat?" A twisted smile from Kellen corroborated Kellen's interest level. Where there was profit, plunder, and upheaval, there would be Kellen the Destroyer.

"I have been to *The World Below and Between*."

"As have I." It wasn't a lie exactly. Kellen had seen the entrance to it, though he questioned the recklessness of Damon actually going inside it, given his youth and inexperience.

"I have a guide."

"You're talking about your insane cave elf friend?!"

"I am." No use in disputing that fact. Evanyil was insane. And brilliant!

"Where is this going, Damon?"

"Where indeed, is the question. I have more than just a guide." Damon could see the interest piquing in the luster of Kellen's eyes. This was where his find from Engêstal was either going to prove its worth or not. "I have a map."

"You have my attention, Damon of Basrat." Impossible! That this young mage could have found something he'd only heard of some years back. *Where was he getting his information, and where had he found this map?* Still, a map to *The World Below and Between* could be immeasurably useful—the ability to travel between worlds without magic…. If he could do that, and correlate the location, he could travel between worlds at will. He could become a god! Closing the distance of some twenty-spans between he and Damon, Kellen extended his hand to the young, resourceful mage. "Where are we going first?"

A smile from Damon as he took the dark legend's hand that was Kellen, shaking it enthusiastically as he began sharing his plan to see what was on the other side of *The World Below and Between*. He was certain there would be danger, but where there was danger there was often plunder, spoils, and more answers to an endless set of questions Damon was assembling in his ever-waking thoughts. His treasure trove of knowledge from Engêstal had raised as many questions as it had answered, but it had provided something immeasurably valuable too; it had opened his eyes to the possibilities beyond Kaleion—possibilities he did not want to share with Illirian Starfire. Not yet.

*   *   *   *

Nearly a week later, the roof now complete, Damon focused on the interior of the first floor, supervising the creation of the niches in the great foyer to display his artwork. As the construction workers flowed all around him, up and down the circular staircase to the northwest corner of his new manor, Damon noticed Kellen approaching the main entry double door casing open to the estate lands below. And he wasn't alone….

The scruffy-haired, tall, muscular man to Kellen's right would have gone almost entirely unnoticed if he hadn't been walking beside Kellen. His earth-tone pants, vest, and shirt made him blend into the surrounding landscape of the Aegen Plateau. Even though he was handsome, his features looked ordinary, if perfectly symmetrical. The bow he carried in his right hand looked…unique. Like a living rust-gold branch bent in a perfect shortbow arc, but with pointed and cupped vine-like thorn and leaves sharp enough to draw blood if the bow needed to be used in close-range combat, it was the perfect close-quarter and ranged-weapon, combined. Only when the two started to climb the makeshift construction stairs leading up to the double doors did Damon finally catch a glimmer of the quiver of arrows bristling on the back of the stranger accompanying Kellen.

Charles W. McDonald Jr.

A few more steps, and the three were standing in what would become Damon's new foyer. "Damon of Basrat, this is Goldenbow."

Goldenbow! SHIT! That name he'd heard all around the planet. *THIS was the legendary Goldenbow!* Extending his hand to shake the hand of the living legend, Damon didn't know exactly what to think. Kellen hadn't mentioned he knew Goldenbow, but this was Kellen. He probably knew everyone worth knowing. Though, it made him question how solo Kellen had truly operated in his past while achieving such fame—or rather infamy. Equivalent to his own, of course.

"I've heard about you. You took out the Steward of Engêstal recently, didn't you," Goldenbow acknowledged, taking Damon's hand to shake it, seemingly impressed.

"If we're going into the caves, we're going to need close-quarter, as well as ranged, support. I couldn't think of anyone better than Goldenbow."

"I should think not," Damon concurred, though wondering how well he'd work with Evanyil and Lorianus. After all, they weren't the most welcoming of sorts.

"Have you given more thought to my question from the other day," Kellen prompted, knowing Damon was highly intelligent, but still not really understanding the way his mind worked. It would take time and adjustment working with someone else—especially someone like Damon.

"I have. Your point was valid. There are many accounts of teams getting lost in *The World Below and Between*. It's not a place for amateurs. Many accounts of those daring the journey never being seen again, and no accounts of anyone ever returning with anything that could resemble a victory." Damon's research into *The World Below and Between* had been both grim and sobering, making him question whether he was ready for this or not, but that's where Evanyil and Kellen came in…and now Goldenbow. "The biggest difference between those expeditions that failed, and ours is A: a map; B: a bold plan; and C: an exit strategy."

"I've heard of some that entered with experienced guides and were never seen again. It's not just a matter of knowing where you're going but being prepared for what you might run into when you get where you're going." It was a fair point made by Goldenbow, who scratched his chiseled chin in reflection.

"You're not wrong about that," Damon agreed, "I think it also matters a great deal what the intended destination was. Many of those accounts gave me the impression that they were simply exploring to see what was out there rather than having a specific destination."

"And just what is our intended destination, Damon?" Kellen knew, but he hadn't bothered sharing that information with Goldenbow…yet.

Charles W. McDonald Jr.

"Destinations. Plural," Damon clarified in staccato to the surprise of both Goldenbow *and* Kellen.

Maybe Kellen didn't know after all.

A thought produced a scroll that shot forth out of Damon's charcoal-blue robes into his right hand which he quickly unfurled before both Kellen and Goldenbow.

"The Monuments of Creation," Goldenbow exhaled, reading from Damon's scroll, seemingly with a level of knowledge enough to tinge his response with reverence.

"You've heard of them." It wasn't a question from Damon, more a confirmation.

"I've heard enough to know this is no ordinary expedition...." Goldenbow paused looking carefully at the young, talented, and now obviously daring mage. "What is your intention with these monuments, Damon?"

"To know and understand more, of course."

"And plunder," Kellen interjected the obvious, with his eyes shifting between his companions.

"These monuments supposedly exist here on Kaleion.... Why go into *The World Below and Between* to get there?" It was a fair point. Goldenbow was well informed.

"Because we're going to compare them to the ones on Graelon. I want some answers to some very important questions." Damon wasn't sharing all his plundered knowledge from the steward's keep, but obviously both the steward and Illirian were trafficking in knowledge, and he wasn't about to be left out of that loop. He intended to be two moves ahead of Illirian going forward—if not four.

"So, we're going to the northern edge of the Trident then?" Kellen knew the place, of course. He'd been before. Many had. It had been thoroughly picked over for centuries. *What did Damon hope to learn from that old relic?*

"Yes, we're going to the birthplace of life on Kaleion. Then we're going to Graelon to compare the two sites."

"I have to say, Damon, this had more plunderous appeal when we spoke of it the other day." Kellen obviously beginning to doubt the necessity of his involvement in this. He wasn't much for having to go that far outside his way just for information unless that information yielded a fortune.

"I'm in," Goldenbow announced with a big smile. The smile of Goldenbow's reply could have lit up a small city. It was both genuine in friendship and simultaneously disarming of all protest.

Cornered! Kellen had brought Goldenbow into the mix. If both Goldenbow *and* Damon were going, he now *had* to go. "Fine...," Kellen capitulated, adding, "...but we better find something more interesting than old bones and broken debris."

It was a terse reference to profiteering, but Kellen had now called into question Damon's leadership, whether or not Damon had the upper hand in the knowledge of the mission. Based on that knowledge, Damon didn't feel like finding more than bones and debris would be a problem. In fact, he feared what they would find...enough to recruit Kellen.

*   *   *   *

(The Northern Trident, Kaleion, The Following Morning)

Between the Trident and Daedrid Lake along the River Tsaen, Damon, Kellen, and Goldenbow picked through the already well-picked-over ruins of the Monuments of Creation. Standing out in a majestic field of wildflowers and tall, verdant green grass, a series of nine blue-grey granite sarsen stone obelisks broken by time and weathering marched around in a three-quarter circle—surrounding a ring of nine white marble Humanoid figures. The three center stones, of nine total, bore markings: runes—one on each stone. On each of those three, just above each rune lay a slender opening: a shaft. The center of the nine bore snowy white fissures that leapt and danced with life anew in the early morning light as if rejoicing in the coming of the morning—its shaft looked to be the mate of a rod. The two Rune Stones flanking the center bore shafts more reminiscent of mating to a key.

Taking in the young, outlaw mage observing every detail of the center three Rune Stones against the backdrop of the Trident behind them, Kellen wondered where Damon was going with this. This wasn't a younger version of himself. This was someone...entirely different. This was the man whispered to sleep amongst his books, if he ever slept at all. This was the man renowned for his ruthlessness and his quest for knowledge, which Kellen could only assume was Damon's path to his own ambition. As he observed Damon, Kellen tried to understand exactly what his ambitions were....

"What is it you seek, Damon?" A multi-faceted question for certain, but Kellen wanted to know this man.

It was enough to make Damon stand upright where he had been slightly bent over, examining the center shaft of the center obelisk, just beneath its rune now dancing with life at Damon's presence. "What do you mean?"

Charles W. McDonald Jr.

"There is nothing new to learn here. As I said, this place has been picked over for centuries."

"Agreed, but has it ever been compared to the Monuments of Creation on Graelon? Did those who picked this site over even know of the existence of others like it?"

It was a question Kellen hadn't considered. Damon wasn't just here for knowledge. He was here to do something never done before. He was a pioneer at heart. That could be useful knowledge in the future, but it still didn't answer his question. "What do you hope to gain in this comparison of yours?"

"I don't believe in life from lifelessness. Creation of something from nothing. It came from somewhere. I'd like to know where, how, and why. I'd like to know the story."

"You seek the story of Creation, Damon?" Kellen's question had not been considered by Goldenbow until just now, but as Goldenbow circled the perimeter watching outwardly for threats in the nearby tree line to the east, he turned to look at Damon, and then Kellen. Kellen was onto something. Goldenbow wanted to know too. *What was Damon's larger purpose for being here?*

"I do." Damon wanted to understand how and where he came from. How and why his mother was taken from him, leaving him to be raised by a father who'd just as soon break every bone in his body as look at him. He wanted answers! He deserved answers! If there was a God of Creation, and that was a big 'IF' in his mind, then he wanted to know why this God-in-absentia didn't stand in the way of his many beatings at the hand of his merciless father. But he didn't see it that way. He expected the comparison on Graelon to reveal a more technical answer to Creation. He hoped that to be the case. Otherwise, it would mean that the God of Creation had abandoned him. He didn't want to consider the implications of what that could mean. "Why else would I have need of the great Kellen and the legendary Goldenbow?"

Damon knew how to influence people. Kellen gave him that. No one had made him smile in years…'til now. Exchanging beaming glances, Kellen and Goldenbow both looked at the young, outlaw mage, anew. This astute mage was already building alliances, the likes of which had never been seen before.

Circling around the backside of the center obelisk, Damon felt a different push-back from the ground, as if he was walking over something other than dirt and grass. It was enough to make him pause mid-track, pivoting to look down at the ground.

Kellen noticed the peculiar behavior of the young mage but chose to continue observing from a distance.

Charles W. McDonald Jr.

Using his *Telekinesis*, Damon cleared grass and dirt from the spot where he felt the unusual push-back, excavating only a small diameter hole, not much bigger than his boot-size. The large quartz stone appeared only the tip of something much larger buried deep in the ground behind the weathered circle of stones. Covering the hole immediately, he walked to the next stone over, excavating there in the same relative position as the one before.

"What are you doing, Damon?" Now Goldenbow was curious as he circled back along the outer ring of stones heading back toward Damon.

"Nothing really." He wasn't ready to share this information, but it had been mentioned in the documents he'd recovered and that's what made him look. At first, he'd assumed it had been broken, picked over, or otherwise carried off through centuries of pilfering. But, if it had been intentionally hidden, that was another story altogether, and he didn't want to question the wisdom of hiding it. Quartz was valuable and not as heavy to move as white marble or the blue-grey granite sarsens.

A quick and dirty excavation revealed another peak at the top of another quartz obelisk buried on the backside of the stone, immediately flanking the center to the west. He had the soil put back before Goldenbow made the corner to have line-of-sight on Damon and what he was doing. "I've got what I need from here. Let's meet up with Evanyil and head into the caves."

Goldenbow exchanged questioning glances with Kellen but didn't question Damon. They both knew Damon wasn't telling them everything, but this was his expedition. They both knew Damon wouldn't hide something of material value, and if it was knowledge he was hiding, well…let him keep it. Damon's passion for knowledge was an important and a necessary hunger to feed if it led them to more plunder and fame.

* * * *

Below Gravêstil Lake, between the River Tsaen and the Aegen River, along the southern border of the Trident, the physical cave entrance to *The World Below and Between* was covered in moss, flora, dogwood, and overgrown vines. One could have passed it over a hundred times and never noticed it, but Damon and Evanyil knew the place well. It was their spot, and his whole world had changed from the moment he met her. Even now, the way she stood beside him, with her dark and perfect elven skin always in contact with his, sent stimulating waves through his entire body. Even in her black bodysuit, now undone halfway to her naval to show off her taut cleavage since they'd released their sexual tension between them, she

Charles W. McDonald Jr.

still had a way of building a lasting anticipation between them he couldn't quantify or match in anyone else. Though, he wished she'd keep her right side away from him with that damnable, ever-present poisoned dagger. It made him nervous. That poison was just as lethal on a mage as it was to anyone else. Made from spider venom, it would kill in mere moments, and ate through flesh with an acidic quality.

Lorianus and Goldenbow compared bows and close-quarter weapons, then started comparing scars. *Weird,* Damon thought. Lorianus apparently, the self-proclaimed victor of that, showing off her most recent scar from the arrow wound to her tension arm as well as the scar from Horigarth's broadsword pommel smash into her chest.

Placing a signet ring on his right-hand ring finger, Damon knew enough about this place to know if you didn't have an anchor in time, there was no guarantee you'd come out relative to the time you went in. As long as they didn't become separated, they'd be fine. He was ready. Looking back at Kellen, Damon hoped he'd made the right choice.

Kellen just stood back, seemingly more comfortable taking up the flank as they began entering *The World Below and Between.* The first marker was just as described in the documentation he'd found from Engêstal. It wasn't like the language of Arcane. The symbolism was quite different from that—more technical in nature—making him question the *actual* origin of *The World Below and Between* versus the *mythical* origin. Still, this marker wasn't the one of concern. He'd been past this marker several times. It was the ones past the first waypoint, past the first underground city, that bothered him. Beyond that, he'd never been. Evanyil had—supposedly.

Passing the steps to the temple where he'd first met Evanyil and Lorianus brought back memories for Damon. He reached out to hold hands with Evanyil, and she gave him a wink and a playfully blown kiss—to a moan of disgust from Lorianus trailing behind them.

It wasn't much of a city, maybe a few hundred Humanoids at most in a few dozen buildings, huts, and other small dwellings, then they were back into the moss and fungi-laden trees, with girths the size of a titan, that made up the bulk of underground, cavernous world he'd come to know thus far. It was pitch-black down in these parts of *The World Below and Between.* So easy to get lost. Damon started producing a *Light Orb,* then stopped as soon as Evanyil squeezed his hand in response. With the *Light Orb* extinguished, he could see her naturally violet cave elf eyes glowing to life. Knowing she could see clearly, he signaled to Kellen behind him not to provide any artificial light so Evanyil and Lorianus could maintain their advantage. He'd have to rely on them to show any threats.

The splash of something just beyond Damon's vision, propelling itself through the ankle-deep water—at least he hoped it was water—raised Damon's threat-awareness level as he found himself reconsidering the *Light Orb*.

*   *   *   *

Now several days into their journey—at least Damon thought it was days; time could pass so erratically down here—Damon had followed the markers and hoped he was translating the symbols correctly. It had been a very long time since they'd seen anyone, or anything. There had been scuffles along the way, but nothing that had threatened the power they'd brought to bear on this venture. Still, he'd hoped to have a better understanding of how much further, how much longer, as he felt the patience of the group waning. Lorianus was getting on Evanyil's nerves. Evanyil was getting on Goldenbow's nerves. And Kellen…. Well, Kellen was just flat offensive! Both Evanyil and Lorianus hated him, already. Damon had heard of Kellen's exploits and assumed them to be hyperbole, but they weren't. He was just as sexist and misogynistic as touted. Damon assumed Kellen incapable of having a healthy relationship with any woman! Clearly, Kellen had as many unresolved childhood issues as Damon, if not more. Especially where it came to women.

Another splash of something flailing its body into the ankle-deep water beneath them brought Damon out of his thoughts and into the here and now, as he could see lights ahead casting shadows on the massive mushroom heads that flowered all around them, scattered between the titan-size underground trees.

Damon expected to find a measure of life in the little underground hamlet ahead, but as they approached, hut after hut was empty. Cobwebs thick as epic novels covered every surface in sight. Evanyil's violet eyes blinked, adjusting themselves to the new light conditions as they all took count of the number of massive black spiders all clearing a path for them, backing away as if more afraid of them than they were of the spiders.

"What do you make of that," Damon asked Kellen, looking back at him and Goldenbow.

"Ask her. They seem to be clearing a path for her more than they are us."

Kellen was right. Evanyil took a few steps ahead of the group, watching as she cleared a path for them, observing as they tilted their mandibles downward in reverence to her. Damon had seen that kind of behavior from familiars, but Evanyil wasn't a mage, and this was strange! This didn't make sense. Still, he kept

Charles W. McDonald Jr.

his best offensive spells at the ready, and burst a *Light Orb* into existence only to see the spiders further aggravated by it…and him. Luckily, not enough to attack. Evanyil reached out and downward, letting her fingertips trace over the web-laden ground they now walked atop. A few of them, half the size of Damon, approached Evanyil from the left and right, bowing to her before getting within a few spans of her.

"I've never seen anything like that outside the behavior of familiars," Damon proclaimed, looking back at Kellen.

"Let's just get to the other side of the village to see what the marker says." Kellen wasn't about to question Evanyil's abilities. They had bigger problems. If this wasn't the marker they expected, then they were lost, and that meant their map was wrong, which meant they'd be lucky to ever find their way back!

Moments later, on the other side of the village, the marker read:

$$\text{ˌÆ‡: ˘Œ† × ‡-}$$

"Okay, so, we all agree we want to try this exit point, right…?" Damon sounded as sure as his comment—not very. It was uncharted territory. None of them had ever gone this deep into *The World Below and Between*. It was anyone's guess what was on the other side of this exit marker.

A nod from Kellen and nocked arrows from Goldenbow and Lorianus told him to proceed, as Damon led the group out of the mouth of the tunnel, seemingly ascending in elevation as they exited to a grassy, convex-shaped plateau overlooking a far-off massive city of glass and steel with varying objects whizzing through the air all around and throughout the city. Estimating their position some twelve leagues or more away from the nearest perimeter of the city, Damon thought the city itself might have been some thirty leagues across its longest axis. Though, it wasn't a walled city, which he found interesting. Perhaps their technology made such defenses unnecessary. All Damon could do was stare in wonder and awe at what lay before them.

Evanyil came up beside Damon, holding his hand as she stood wide-eyed at the technological miracle spread across the grassy plane below.

"Wow." Kellen was at a loss for words. Unheard of, given his reputation.

Goldenbow looked around, trying to orient himself east to west, catching the setting sun in the opposite direction from which they'd come.

Lorianus came up behind Goldenbow, keeping an arrow nocked, putting her back to his to give a full-circle of defense.

Charles W. McDonald Jr.

"So, this is Graelon," Damon proclaimed, examining the dusky and majestic purple horizon over verdant green pastures dotted with several of those technological cities far off in the distance. Edging closer to the plateau's edge, Damon's soft, leather boots left footprints in the damp, tall grass that careened over the convex edge of the plateau. He felt Evanyil tugging at his left side, pulling him back from the thirty-span drop below. Still, it was an amazing view. He could see nearly a hundred leagues in every direction from this vantage point. *Surely, they knew of this entrance, as plainly as it stood out among the landscape!* He could see mountains off in the eastern distance but didn't have specific information as to the location of the Monuments of Creation on this world—only that they did exist, and he wanted to see them—in person....

Casting *Far Reaching*, Damon wanted to locate the Monuments of Creation to orient themselves to that location, so they knew where to go next.

The very next instant, six oblong, orb-shaped metallic objects with dark glass lenses, appearing as cyclops-like eyes, hovered over their plateaued position, twisting this way and that as their dark lenses...blinked from within the glass. Damon could hear mechanical noises from within the strange objects, apparently assessing their threat level. Each object couldn't have been much larger than a dwarf, but as they began extending long black barrels on either side of their chassis, Damon began to fear the worst.

"I don't think they're friendly," Kellen quipped, opening his robes as he prepared his most lethal, directed, offensive spells.

"Don't make any offensive moves, Kellen," Damon suggested, looking into those dark lenses that blinked at him again, making a mechanical noise immediately after the blink. *What are they doing?*

The object closest to Kellen opened two doors—one on either side of its chassis—releasing two more of those long black barrels.

"Fuck you!" Kellen's outburst caused amber rays of light and energy to burst out of the long, black barrels just as *Kellen's Shield Wall* simultaneously burst outward in front of Kellen, closing the distance between Kellen and the oblong-orb, extending to protect Goldenbow and Lorianus beside him. The amber energy beams bounced off of *Kellen's Shield Wall* that advanced toward them, making the invisible visible at the points of light where it met the transparent resistance, creating fissures in *Kellen's Shield Wall* where the oblong-orb was starting to penetrate. Immediately following his *Shield Wall*, Kellen cast *Kellen's Lightning Storm*, causing filaments of superheated gas to traverse across the dusky purple sky, then burst downward in a web of terror following the direction of Kellen's fingertips obliterating two of the oblong orbs.

Charles W. McDonald Jr.

Suddenly the oblong orb closest to Damon began firing its light weapon directly at him, singing Damon's robes and burning a hole in his left side. With four remaining oblong orbs and at least a dozen more on the way, rushing up from the city below, the situation was escalating fast! Wincing in pain, Damon threw up *Shields* as fast as his *Telekinesis* could snatch the scroll from his robes, then *Ball Lightning* directed at the one that shot at him, turning it into a heap of smoking metal as he watched it career into the grassy field below.

Evanyil was helpless in this kind of a fight. She didn't have a ranged weapon—nothing that would affect them as she watched the multitude of arrows from her sister and Goldenbow bounce off some invisible barrier protecting each attacking orb.

Kellen blasted another of them from the sky with a beam of fiery acid shot forth from his fingertips, causing one to slam into the ground before them on the plateau in a smoking heap.

Another volley of energy bursts from the remaining two struck Lorianus and Damon again as twelve more surged rapidly up the plateau toward them. Using his *Telekinesis* to slam the final two into one another, Damon watched as they burst into a heap of twisted burning metal on the grass before them. Now, with two of those energy wounds on his left side, Damon's body screamed in searing pain.

As the first of the twelve rushing up to them from the city below crested the convex-shaped edge of the plateau, the ground erupted all around them and Damon began thinking wiser of their situation. "Let's move! Back into the cave! NOW!!!"

"I'll cover you! Run!" Goldenbow laid down arrow fire, two arrows at a time, from a kneeling stance protecting the cave entrance. The arrows didn't penetrate, but they did cause the orbs to move, and his strategy of pinching two of them into one another worked as they slammed into one another, accidentally blasting one another with their energy weapons.

One by one, the machines pounded the group relentlessly with their energy weapons, chasing Damon, Lorianus, Evanyil, Kellen, and Goldenbow back into the mouth of the cavern entrance to *The World Below and Between.*

Rushing back to the Graelon marker, his left side throbbing to the point of making his vision spin, Damon stopped to look back. They weren't following them in. "What was that?!!"

"Your mission, Day. You tell us!" Kellen took Damon off-guard with the unexpected nickname and the twisted smile on his face. Clearly, Kellen loved combat! And, he loved a challenge even more!

Charles W. McDonald Jr.

Goldenbow laughed alongside Lorianus, but the smoke radiating off his burnt skin from the energy wound on right shoulder said he wasn't in the mood to go back and face whatever those things were again. "I haven't had to empty my quiver like that in forever, Day! Good job!" Now they were both using that nickname. He had a funny feeling it was gonna stick.

"Hey, I didn't fire first. Don't blame me! Blame Kellen!" Just talking was painful as Damon doubled over, holding his singed left side.

Clearly, he wasn't prepared for what Graelon had to offer—the mighty Kellen and Goldenbow with him or not. Still, he needed to see the other Monument of Creation. *Were there even more of them? Who had built them, and why?* He needed answers as he looked into those magnificent violet eyes of Evanyil, who opened his robes and clothes, beginning to treat his wound. His *black mirrors of the soul* locked with Evanyil's eyes as she leaned into him, under his robes, draping her soft lips across his.

"You're thinking this was a failed mission." Evanyil could read him already. They both read each other like an open book. "It wasn't. Think about what you learned from it. Use it."

An affirming nod from Damon as Evanyil snuggled into his side, getting a closer look at his wound as her violet eyes dilated in the shade of his robes. "OWWW," he screamed into her ear as she picked at his wound. "That was on purpose!"

"Sorry," she lied.

"You're not wrong though." He considered what she was suggesting. This mission might not have achieved his desired outcome, but the trip hadn't been without merit. They had successfully traveled to another world without the aid of a *Portal*, which meant he could now *Portal* back to Graelon if he so chose. But he'd have to find a way to deal with those mechanical warrior objects first. Maybe there was something in his informational treasure trove from the former steward that might explain what those things were. Perhaps he could use *The World Below and Between* to travel to other worlds, less hostile to magic. And then be able to *Portal* to and from there as well. That thought he rolled over in his mind many, many times....

"Of course, I'm not wrong," she peeked out from his left side, looking up at him, batting her beautiful eyes at him again. In a whisper only he could hear, Evanyil lifted her head to speak directly into his ear. "Sometimes the answers aren't always there in front of us, and sometimes when they are, we're too blind to see them. You may never understand the story of Creation, but that doesn't mean you should stop looking, or that I should stop looking with you. I'll go where you go

Charles W. McDonald Jr.

to help you find the answers you need, Kaylan."

Visibly recoiling at that name, Damon looked down into her stunning violet eyes still blinking at him innocently, knowing it was impossible to stay mad at her. Yes, she knew him extremely well—probably better than anyone—but that didn't give her the right to use *that* name! Still, she wasn't wrong. She was entirely too right!

(Austin, TX, Earth, Present Day)

Holding the plain silver rod again and playing back the Graelon Colonial Outpost message one more time, it was all starting to make a small measure of sense to him now…. Thinking back to his first adventure with Kellen and Goldenbow, when they sought to compare the Monuments of Creation only to have met with such fierce technical resistance upon finding their way to Graelon. His supposition led him to believe those dangerous experiments on the colonial outposts had delivered a very sobering message back to Graelon proper; enough so to make them consider Setinon may have had it right in the first place. *Maybe magic and technology couldn't coexist after all…?* But that was so long ago. That would have meant the fall of the Graelon Colonial Outpost was even further back in time than what he'd originally considered. *And was the message sent back to Graelon proper so dire that it made the descendants of the four brothers abandon their mission of delivering justice back upon the Sentinels of Setinon?!*

Clearly there were still many questions for which Damon didn't have answers. Even with this new understanding of past events, he was learning there was more out there *he didn't* understand than he *did* understand.

He still needed answers to the oldest of his questions about the Monuments of Creation. His evolving understanding of the God of Creation had filled in a great many gaps over the centuries, but the root of those old questions remained for him…. *Where had they come from, and why? Why were the Monuments of Creation built? What was their true purpose?* He had supposed they were built to summon the unmaking of Creation, or to somehow engage a series of actions to exact the brothers' revenge, but now he was far less certain. New facts cast new sunlight to dissolve layers of legend for the underlying truth.

The root of his personal struggle—dealing with the death of Seren and subsequent reckless abuse from his father—left residual and aching wounds about his soul, manifest in the scars about his chest, back, neck, and shoulders. The root of *those* questions had yet to be answered, and he'd hoped so very long ago to find some answers with Kellen and Goldenbow. Perhaps now it was time to revisit those old questions and get some *new* answers—finally!

Charles W. McDonald Jr.

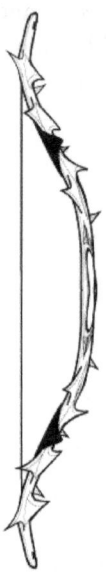

Chapter 51: The Problem with Living Legends

(The Crown of Spires, Perion, Present Day)

he cold and sterile inner sanctum of the Crown of Spires of Edinaiel was both sparse and elegant, while vast and commanding. Made inside the executive skywalk, in between the spired towers, the chamber spanned a hundred paces or more in depth by nearly three hundred paces in length. The ceiling sloped downward from the base of a three-planed crystal tower built directly over the solid ivory dais. The inner tower was more than a hundred cubits tall, while the rest of the ceiling sloped downward from the tower's base of fifty cubits. The floor was made of the same, strange diamond-shaped tiles as the divination causeways, providing a euphoric sense of being in the clouds, watching over all that ever was, or could be.

The High Seat of Thane, Edinaiel, the High Seat, and the Office of the Talon all were commanding and noble titles describing the famed Crown of Spires, but it had known only one name—one *Keeper*—in its entire existence. *Adena!*

Heavy and taut was the tension in the room as she collapsed Desindra's morning brief in her left hand. Though sitting regally, Adena appeared preoccupied in thought—perhaps driven by the tension, or perhaps her discernment of the new threat at their mighty doorstep. Shifting her seemingly delicate frame to one side of her oversized throne, her long and radiant raven hair and sapphire eyes befit her slender and seductive, youthful frame. Her gentle, loving face and her cloud-white, full-length, diaphanous dress with sleeve openings that hung to the floor were a woefully inaccurate telling of what lay beneath. It was all a lie, of course. Everything about Adena was deceiving, especially her delicate and tender appearance.

No sightings! NOT A SINGLE ONE! Where was he? She knew he would return, but like a chameleon snake slithering about the forested floor below their structure, she just didn't know when or where exactly he'd show his face. *Could the divination tiles have been wrong?* Having seen him, and the results of his toxin, they knew he wasn't to be underestimated again! *Still, where was he?!*

A sneer meant for the assassin as her eyes clipped the portrait hung in offense to warn others of the consequence of defiance, desecration, and disrespect. A thought from Adena snatched it off the wall, slamming it against the opposite wall in a thousand tiny pieces as the canvas of her distorted and disfigured likeness wrapped around the broken shards of its once beautiful, and elegant, ivory frame.

"Summon Desindra...." Adena rose in a calm and controlled—even smooth—manner, an anachronism to the display of utter frustration only a moment prior. Perhaps she hadn't controlled her temper enough as she briefly looked down to see her tea spilled—its cup shattered about the base of her dais.

Hearing and seeing the violent display, the plump, yet trustworthy, brown-eyed brunette Casiera knew Adena the cagey sort, but she'd been teetering on the edge of madness lately and she was beginning to question her own loyalties to Adena, if not to her station. Loyalties were a fickled thing; often useless when binding moments came. "Of course, Keeper." Shuffling her translucent dress with silver trim along the tiles, Casiera left the room immediately, as ordered, to fetch that hateful problem known as Desindra. *When would Adena finally kill that woman?!*

Looking down again at the spilled tea curling around the base of her dais, Adena cursed that duplicitous bitch internally. *Why did she keep Desindra around?* She had already decided her usefulness had come to an end with her dangerous use of specific written words boastfully used in her reports. Desindra couldn't be allowed to fail her again and again. It was beginning to reflect on her ability to lead. Already there were rumors. She couldn't believe them, of course. They had to be lies. Yet, if true, people—her people—were beginning to have doubts. And this... assassin wasn't helping matters! He'd managed to kill dozens of her finest assets. She'd have his scruffy cute head on a pike soon enough!

Soft, cream, elegant Elian fabric cascaded off elegant wrists that swayed side to side with Desindra's magnificent hips, as her silky, sandy-brown hair and

Charles W. McDonald Jr.

hazel eyes sparkled in the morning light that peered through the oculus at the top of the ceiling. Much like Adena, Desindra had used her skills to keep herself taut, young, and beautiful, but her mind wasn't nearly as far gone as Adena's. She still had her wits, and she'd soon need them with her now being in such proximity to Adena.

"You summoned. I am here to serve," Desindra lied, kneeling before Adena a few paces away, trying to ignore the shattered portrait frame and shattered cup on the floor.

"Then why hasn't your servitude produced the capture of this one?" A wave of Adena's left hand produced an image in the floor of the scruffy-haired, handsome blonde in earth-tone chameleon attire carrying a rust-golden vine short-bow across his right shoulder. Adena's spilled tea, still careening and making its way around the base of her dais, drew light-brown fluid lines across the stranger's face.

"He has been sly and cunning, Keeper. He will make a mistake, and we'll be ready for him when he does."

"UNACCEPTABLE! Waiting for him to make a mistake is UNAC-CEPTABLE! Find him, Desindra! Find him and bring him to me or I'll pick the flesh from your bones!" A thought slapped Desindra so hard in the face it nearly knocked her over on her left side. "GO!"

Gathering and uprighting herself slowly, as if using the lack of pace in her comportment to protest, Desindra dusted off the furls of her sleeves, walking out of the Keeper's throne room as composed as she could manage.

"AHHHH!" She'd waited for Desindra to clear the room before exploding, but Adena couldn't take it anymore, as her fury sent a massive crack-become-a-fissure racing across her throne room all the way up the wall and ceiling to the oculus. *She has to die! And, so does he!* Adena avoided looking at the scruffy-haired, handsome blonde male face still shimmering on her floor now marred with the massive fissure her hate had carved.

*　　*　　*　　*

Goldenbow knew the holotoxin had been given enough time to cause havoc and disrupt Adena's defenses, but he also knew it had signaled his arrival and penetration of their security. He knew they'd be ready for him this time, but he was equally ready. He was Goldenbow!

Precautions had been taken, but still he worked alone. No one else moved with his level of stealth, and he couldn't have someone else getting him caught.

Charles W. McDonald Jr.

Moving silently among the marsh and forestation that seemed to be immune to the Blood Night, Goldenbow's internal awareness of the exact dimensions of the famed weapon slung over his shoulder kept him from unintentionally scraping it against the branches he carefully avoided, as he made his way toward the target just above.

Getting close enough to the target should be easier with all their focus on protecting their perimeter—which had been one of the major intentions of the holotoxin. He knew there would be increased defenses around Adena as well, but he had a plan.

A look up at the divination tiles above and Goldenbow, from his previous scouting missions, already had a good measure of the exact point of entry into the massive, vaulted throne chamber built into the skywalk. It was now or never.

*   *   *   *

Two servants cleaned what they could of the mess Adena's rage had made, but there would be no fixing the massive fissure in the wall going all the way up to the oculus above. Casiera knew that would require skills beyond her capabilities as she examined the damage up close, picking at the extensive fissure in the wall, trying to ignore Adena's fury—or hoping it would look past *her*.

"Stop picking at that thing and get over here," Adena chided, summoning the last loyal 'friend' she had, if Casiera could be called that. At least, she was reliable....

"Yes, Keeper," Casiera deflected Adena's rage in calm enough tones as to be non-threatening, and just strong enough not to cower before her, which Adena detested as much, if not more, than treachery itself. Casiera's large feet flowed over the tiles smoothly and gracefully despite her awkward nature. Now fully prostrating herself before Adena, Casiera wanted to show that someone still believed in her. One had to choose sides, and Casiera wasn't in the habit of choosing the wrong ones.

Looking down the dais at Casiera, Adena was genuinely moved by the unnecessary gesture of fealty and loyalty. So much so, that the glint of morning light off the arced golden vine barely registered with Adena right before a golden arrowed shaft pierced the heart of Casiera just as she rose to face the Keeper—that arrow having been meant for her!

"GUARDS," Adena howled just before throwing up shields that deflected the next two arrows slung at her—one immediately following the next as Casiera's dying body slumped at her small, delicate feet.

Charles W. McDonald Jr.

Frustrated at the rare miss, Goldenbow loosed two more arrows, one immediately after the other, in the blink of an eye, only to see them deflect off her shield—one towards a spot on the wall looking to have held a painting for centuries, the other sticking in a massive fissure in the wall he hadn't expected to see in such a meticulously kept throne room. He had to get through her shield, and the best way was up close as he rushed Adena straight on, bringing his poisonous golden vine shortbow to bear on Adena as he rapidly closed the twenty spans between them.

Adena's eyes swelled with incredulity at the temerity of this blonde assassin, watching him rush her with a reckless abandon. *Was he insane? Capture, not kill,* was her only thought as the *Shield Cylinder* collapsed upon the would-be assassin—his inertia causing him to skid into the wall of the cylinder with a muted thud. *Caught!* But it hadn't been Adena's *Shield Cylinder* that had captured the beautiful man.

Desindra's smile could be seen from the westernmost parts of Bouschè as she confidently strutted into the throne room, locking eyes with Adena before examining her prize just a few paces from the dais. "Another few steps, and he might have had you...," Desindra's contempt causing her the slightest of pauses, "...*Keeper.*" *There,* she mulled, knowing Adena didn't deserve her skills or her contributions. Still, she was *their* leader. For now. "Hello there." Desindra smiled at the handsome, scruffy-haired catch, ticking her fingernails on the cylinder's transparent and shimmering walls.

He hadn't intended to be captured, of course, but he'd considered the very real possibility of the necessity of it, to get close enough to Adena to carry out the contract. Now, he just needed to use his charm and his wits to keep them from killing him while they held him captive. That might prove more difficult given the effectiveness of the holotoxin, but if he was reading things correctly, there might be an opportunity to get as close as he needed....

The problem with living legends was that you had to live up to expectations not your own. And, sometimes, you just might start believing your own hyperbole. If this was his end, it wouldn't be the fitting end Goldenbow had earned over centuries. *Damon owed him for this one!*

Charles W. McDonald Jr.

First there was desolation,
Then there was your smile.
Then there was uncertainty,
Answered by the loving fire behind your eyes.
Then there was doubt at being so close to your living flame,
Soothed by your presence of understanding.
Then there was the terror at staring into the abyss of love,
Resolved only in the knowledge that you were terrified too.

Charles W. McDonald Jr.

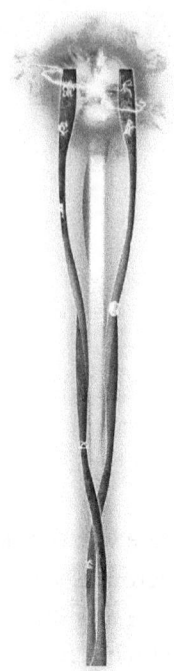

Chapter 52: The Abyss of Love

(Damon's Manor, Kaleion, A Long Time Ago)

"How did you get started? What was the one moment when you knew this was for you," Damon asked, smiling at his apprehensive and magnificent half-elven date.

"If you're asking me when I first felt it, I was probably twelve. My parents had this property near the port of Gravêstil. I would go to the port every day and watch the ships, dangling my legs over the concrete retaining wall of the main dock there, and one day I just saw this beautiful dolphin streaking through the water, and I wanted to see it jump. I don't even know how it happened. I just remember telling it 'jump now' in my thoughts, and it did. Right in front of me, and I just remember smiling from ear to ear, thinking 'do it again, do it again,' and it did. I felt this tingling all through my body like this energy was touching every part of me, and I was just hooked."

Staring into Dallia's beautiful green-gold eyes as they sat on the picnic blanket together, overlooking his vast lands and estate, Damon couldn't remember ever seeing a smile so genuine and...good. From her silver and cream translucent dress with the deep V-cut down her front, to the pop of purple and yellow wild-flower in her wavy platinum-blonde hair spilling down her back, she was...the best thing ever to happen to him.

"I remember having these visions in my sleep where I felt like the rune for source was being etched into the deepest corners of my mind shortly after that experience with the dolphin. A couple of days later, I was in a field of wildflowers and jasmine not unlike this one here." Dallia made a sweeping motion gesture with her left hand across Damon's vast estate as they faced east towards his manor with the southern tip of the Trident mountain range behind them.

Sitting amongst tall blades of grass amidst a handful of boulders and a crop of ancient trees, jasmine in bloom all around them, there couldn't have been a more perfect place on Kaleion to take this incredible woman that looked to be a part of Damon's land.

"That's when I felt 'it' for the first time...," Dallia continued after a brief pause to look into Damon's magnificent and terrifying eyes. "...the first time I drew from the source of all living things. I just redirected it into the only tree in the field, making it bigger and stronger—making the leaves bloom. Silly girl-stuff to you, I'm sure." Dallia paused again, taking in his navy cavalier shirt with grey stripes untied down to his sternum, revealing the hate he carried with him in the form of the physical scars upon his ravaged soul. "What about you," Dallia asked, before thinking about the question and who she was asking, causing an immediate awkward pause as she tried to right herself, and the conversation. "I mean you don't have to, Damon. Not if you don't want to...."

"It's okay. I'll tell you anything you want to know about me. I mean that. Anything!" Seeing her beam for him caused an almost involuntary smile for him. Dallia's happiness made him happy. *Was that a good thing?*

"The things you've heard...about my father...about what I did...that wasn't the first moment for me. That was something else."

"What do you mean?" Looking into his beautiful *black mirrors of the soul*, she wanted to know everything about him. Even the things that scared the life out of her. She *needed* to know.

"I mean. I don't know how to describe what happened in that moment. One moment I was...terrified of the next stripe across my back. Then the next I felt this.... I don't know how to describe it." He was getting frustrated. He could feel his face tightening—his whole body becoming tense. He'd never talked about it before...with anyone. Not even Evanyil, who knew way more about him than she should!

"Take your time, Damon. I'm listening. I want to know." Taking his hand in hers, resting them both on his herringbone, charcoal-blue slacks, he felt the delicate caress of her fingertips on the back of his hand in much the way Evanyil did. *Was that an elven thing*, he wondered. The only difference was it caused a deeper response from him when she did it. More than just a sexual response. It caused him to relax...a feeling of calm washing over him, simultaneous with this positive energy he couldn't describe, but his whole body was now awash in it. Emanating from her.

"I felt this...calling. This...something or someone speaking to me."

"Do you think it could have been an internal voice? I mean, he was beating you." Her eyes blinked at his in curiosity, and tenderness.

It was a diagnosis he'd considered...more than once. But.... "I don't know where it came from, but it made me reach out in thought to a lifeline I didn't know was there, and as soon as I grabbed onto it, I felt it suddenly unlock several pathways inside my mind."

"Pathways to Arcane?"

"No."

"I don't understand."

"That was the first time I used my natural abilities. It wasn't the first time I cast at all."

"Oh! Then the stories aren't true. They have it all wrong. Why don't you correct the rumors publicly? I mean..." Her eyes blinked at him again, trying to at least begin to understand the enigma who was Damon.

"Because it's nobody's business! And, that's a useful reputation."

Her smile suddenly twisted at that response. She didn't like that answer. Here was a man who leveraged and propagated his horrific reputation for his own gain. Or, maybe it was in defense. She needed to know more.

Seeing her reaction to that, he needed to correct course—fast. "The first time I cast..." He paused, making sure she was on board, and seeing her sudden smile told him she was, "...I was outside Basrat, hunting. I remember hunting with a friend of mine." He paused in reflection, and she could see the hard swallow in his throat reacting to the memory stirred. "I make it sound like he was one of many. He was my only friend. The only person who'd ever treated me with any level of care or comfort outside of my mother. Who I don't even remember.... What does that say about me?"

"It's okay, Damon. You can tell me. What you share is between us and only us."

Charles W. McDonald Jr.

"No, that's not it. I'm not concerned about you sharing this. It's just...."

"Take your time." She could see his struggle. He'd been through far more than she could imagine, and she knew it. She could feel it. Life wasn't supposed to be so harsh to a man so young. She needed to make herself vulnerable to give Damon a level of comfort. For him to not feel so alone in his struggles. This was very hard for him, and she knew he needed to share this. Moving herself to sit in his lap, she wrapped her right arm around him, laying her head against his chest while she traced his scars with the delicate fingertips of her left hand.

"We both had bows. I sucked at it, and we both knew it. We were hunting elk, and you had to be a good shot to bring one of the adults down. A good shot with some power behind the bolt. I was never going to bring one down, but I still carried that damn thing with me. And, I had the shot. I was trailing him by a good ways, spotted an elk, took a good stance and released what seemed like a great shot. The elk's head bobbed at the sound of the arrow approaching and it deflected off the elk's rack, striking my friend dead in the sternum right next to his heart."

He had to pause for a minute. He gave her a tense smile, but this was hard for him, and it was becoming harder by the moment.

"What was his name, Damon? What was your friend's name?"

"Abel. His name was Abel. He was a couple of years older than me."

"What happened to Abel, Damon?"

"I...tried to direct energy in the same way I had with *Telekinesis*, but I knew that wasn't the answer. I looked around. I could feel the life energy in the forest around us. I could see the aura of each individual lifeforces of the forest. Every single tree, bush, vine, and animal. It just sang to me and I could sense it. Like you, I felt the rune for source just kind of sear itself into my mind, but for you it was the back of your mind, for me it was right at the front of my mind—directly behind my forehead and it burned like.... I can't really describe it." A deep breath gave him the resolve to finish his story, "...I put my hand on his chest, pulled the arrow out, and tried *Healing* him."

"Damon, *Healing* takes both lots of practice and an understanding of biology. What were you thinking?"

"I was thinking I was his only chance." *What was he thinking?* He probably killed Abel—twice—once with his incompetence as an archer and once with his inexperience as a *Healer*. "He gasped. His breathing became erratic. He started to turn purple, but he seemed to be in even more pain after the *Healing*, and it was taking him a really long time to die." Damon paused again, looking away from her.

"What happened to Abel, Damon? Tell me." She didn't *want* to know. But she *had* to know. The arc of Damon's story was a treacherous road of anguish,

Charles W. McDonald Jr.

and torment. She could sense that about him, and yet she still needed to know the painful road upon which he trod with dread. Her eyes blinked expectantly. Breathlessly waiting....

"I.... I killed him. I cut his throat. He was suffering, and I killed him. People have always died around me, Dallia. I've always been a very proficient and prolific killer. A destroyer of men. I've never been good at *Healing*, or Creation or anything that could be called...good."

Her eyes stopped blinking though she couldn't tear her gaze away from him. The arc of Damon was not a sequential line of birth, life, experience, and death. It bore great and unseen traps of a tormented soul. Wrong upon wrong. Injury and injustice. A dour deliverance. Her mind worked to crawn inside his torment. To understand his impossible paradox. To give him the gift of her *hope*. "You DO have good in you, Damon. You have the biggest heart of anyone I've ever known. But.... I...don't see you as a good man. I mean, I can't...."

"It's okay. I'm not offended. It's the truth. I'm a monster."

"You ARE NOT a monster, Damon." She had to focus on keeping her eyes locked on his from her rested seat in his lap. He needed to hear this message. As did she. "You are...complicated. Conflicted. But, you ARE NOT a monster."

He didn't have a reply for that—only awkward silence.

"You've had horrific circumstances lead you to unsavory paths and circles."

"That's a political way of putting it." He was resigned, but he knew what and who he was. Who he was born to be. The great and tormented stone fate had so callously chiseled from *hate*.

"It's the truth. Where would you be if not for those horrific circumstances?"

"I don't know if I'd be a mage. I don't know if I'd want to be anyone but who I am. I love magic. I love being an Archmage of Kaleion." It was a powerful self-recognition from Damon. Originating from the deepest part of his aching soul.

"Yes, and you take great pride in that. I can see. Your identity is very much invested in that. And..." She had another message she felt both of them needed to hear, "...if I may be so bold as to speculate, I think you were very much destined to be an Archmage of Kaleion. I think you may have been destined to be one of the greatest mages of all time. And, I don't think you could get there without the burden of your past."

Moved beyond words, he was stunned. He didn't know what to say. His mouth worked, trying to come up with the words that could express his love for her acceptance of him, and all he could do was think of how she was simply the greatest thing that had ever happened to him. Time crawled as he tilted her head up toward him, carefully closing the ever so brief distance between his lips and hers. Ever so gently, he draped his lips across hers, pressing with the most tender pressure as he closed his lips around her bottom lip. And, the moment he felt her lips close over the top of his, he lost all sense of time and space as an incredible vision of light burst into the front of his mind. A booming voice of Creation calling out across a great lake of crystal seared into his mind, causing him to lose his balance. Dallia nearly fell backward out of his lap as she broke their first kiss. *What was that?*

He'd never experienced a waking vision like that before. It was soooo... real!

"Damon talk to me. Where'd you go?" Now sitting back on the picnic blanket immediately beside Damon, Dallia snapped her fingers, realizing she'd been snapping them at him for quite some time.

"Sorry, I...don't know what happened there." His eyes blinked at the far and near. At the here that was no longer there.

"Are you feeling okay? You went blank on me. Like you were suddenly somewhere else."

"Come on...," he deflected. "The sun is setting over the mountains, and I have a great view of it from my balcony. Let's go inside, and I'll give you the full tour." He managed a smile, ignoring the vision that nearly transported him, but he wasn't comfortable sharing anything else until he understood more.

Whatever he was averting must have bothered the shit out of him. She hoped he'd open back up to her. The way he had moments before. Yes, he was very dangerous, but he was also the most fascinating man she'd ever known. A great many more facets than the most beautiful diamond. She was definitely right about one thing when it came to Damon.... He *was* **complicated**.

*   *   *   *

The comfort of the balcony, outside whatever that massive, strange room Damon had going on a few spans away, provided a magnificent view of the Kaleion sunset behind the southern tip of the Trident mountain range and an intoxicating view of one moon waning and chasing the other moon, waxing over the opposite horizon. It was a beautiful piece of property, and outright stolen, if her sources were correct. Well, maybe not stolen. *Aggressively negotiated for* might have been a better description. Still, Damon wasn't delicate when it came to going after something he really wanted, and he must have really wanted this particular piece of property.

"What are you thinking about," Damon asked with his right hand falling atop her left on the stone railing as they faced one another under the Kaleion sky, dripping in dusky hues all around them. Gnats and dust-motes glinted with both the prevailing and failing light as they both competed for the magic of this moment.

"The same thing I've been thinking about for hours." It was a coy answer, if it was an answer at all, but he knew the same thing she did. She knew he felt the same thing she did. She could see it in those smoky, beautiful black gems of his, even as his black bangs tried to hide the moment, captured in his eyes.

"That's not really an answer."

"Do you believe in fate, Damon?"

Ugh. That was a toughie. He didn't know how to reply to that. "I don't know what to believe in. Or not to believe. I guess the best answer is, I don't know."

"Whatever you are, Damon, you're an honest man. I love that about you. You might be guarded, and I understand the reasons why, but your honesty is… intoxicatingly refreshing!"

"Many have come to fear my honesty."

"Should I fear you, Damon?"

"I'd harm myself before I ever harmed you."

"I believe you. And, I think I'm falling in love with you." The words escaped her lips before she could catch them. *Oh God! What have you done, you idiot?!* Quickly she moved to close what little distance still remained between them 'til her face was just beneath his—her breath on his chest—his breath in her platinum-gold bangs. Again, her fingertips went to caress the scars beneath his shirt. He didn't pull away. Just standing with his body against hers, she felt his arm flow around her waist, resting in the small of her back where he gently caressed her open back.

Slowly enunciating each careful word whispered into her ear, he let go emotionally while holding onto her physically, "I don't deserve your love, Dallia, but I'm just selfish enough to accept it if you're freely giving it to me."

"How did this happen?" She asked the question aloud, but it was really meant more for her.

"I've been asking myself that for hours," Damon admitted. Whatever Evanyil was to him, Dallia was far more. He wasn't certain if he could live without Dallia and he didn't want to find out.

She hadn't said anything, but she needed to hear him say it back to her.

Charles W. McDonald Jr.

She knew he felt it! He was such a careful man. All the rumors of his recklessness were wrong. This was a careful, orchestrated, well-structured man. How had he earned such a reckless reputation? *Ask him you dolt!* "Damon," she paused, looking into those *black mirrors of the soul.*

"Yes."

"I've been meaning to ask you…. There's so much about your reputation that is dead wrong."

"Like?"

"How did you earn such a ruthless and reckless abandon reputation? You're such a careful man."

Nodding in reflection, Damon thought even higher of her now than before…if that were possible. She was brilliant. Every bit as smart as Evanyil, and a much closer match for him. *Had she been made for him, alone?*

"Combat…," he replied confidently. Knowing further explanation was required, he continued, "…in combat, I just have this…. I don't know how to describe it. All the hate inside me comes roiling to the surface and it just takes over. I've learned to channel it—to harness it. But, it can make my actions appear both reckless and ruthless even when they're…very calculated."

Another very honest answer, and this one she didn't know what to do with. *Would she ever be on the receiving end of that hatred?* How could she be certain not to trigger those emotions? Damon was incredibly dangerous even without the hate he admittedly carried, but with it he was…. She didn't want to use that word that he'd used to describe himself. *He wasn't that! He wasn't!* "Let's talk about something else."

"Oh? Like what?"

"Liiike, you appear to be a man who has everything. What would be the nicest present you could think of ever receiving? What don't you have that you REAAALY want?"

A big smile from Damon as he considered the question. He didn't have everything. Admittedly he had a lot. Still…. "A staff…," he replied flatly, knowingly. "Not something wood…. Something durable…. Something that would last centuries…. Something terrifying and befitting The Dark Knight of Magic."

"You do love *that* title, don't you!" Her smile was sexy, cute, and simultaneously, somewhat alarming. "Besides, you're not a wood person. You're a hard man of *stone* and *metal.*"

"So, when do I get my present," he asked, prompting her with his fist balled up in the small of her back tugging her toward him.

"We'll see…." *He is super cute! Damn him!* "You *do* know my specialty is

Charles W. McDonald Jr.

enchantment, right?"

"I do."

She nodded knowingly. *Of course, he knew!* Tilting her head away from him toward the balcony railing, she tried to pull back if only for a moment to get her wits about her, as her eyes followed toward the railing—away from Damon's gaze. He had her curled around his fingers, and she was terrified.

He sensed the moment of her pulling back, causing him to look down. Do something! "I...."

"You what, Damon?" She jumped in so fast, and just like that she was back up underneath him, breathing into his sternum, inhaling his cologne.

"You're the best thing that's ever happened to me, Dallia, and I don't know how to operate around you. How to function around you. How to react or feel around you. I'm in a foreign land without knowledge of the language here." There was more. Much more. "I...fear how vulnerable you make me. I run in terrible circles of death and destruction. If you died because of me, I don't know if I could survive it."

That was so much more than an *'I love you,'* and she knew it. That was the closest thing to Damon saying he'd lay down his life for her, and she knew it to be true. "Damon, I would never ask you to change. I love you, just the way you are right now. But, what if you just pulled back a little and didn't run in those old circles as often as you do now? Just a slight difference between the way you oper-ate today. Would that seem reasonable to you? Women try to change men all the time, but you're so unique just the way you are. If I tried to change you, I might break that uniqueness, or push you away. I couldn't bear it if either of those came true!"

For the first time, Damon caressed her beautiful half-elven ears—the root of her pain and isolation as a child, hoping she wouldn't pull back again. Hoping she'd accept it the way he accepted her caress of his scars. And his torment. "I think that is a reasonable request, and with the manor built and the Council of Mages breathing down my neck, it makes sense to lay low. Not retire, mind you. It takes a lot of money to keep this place running. But, a slight pull back might be the smarter play, and would definitely be safer for both of us."

She didn't pull back. Instead, Dallia nuzzled her face and hair into Da-mon, letting him caress her ears the way she caressed his scars—delicately and with great care.

"I love you, Dallia," he whispered into her left ear, kissing its tip. In a moment of weakness turned strength as the purple rays of dusk surrendered to the blackness of the Kaleion night, Damon surrendered...completely. "In fact, I think

I adore you."

Feeling her clutch at his side as she practically tried to crawl inside him. To be a permanent part of him. Damon felt her tears streaking down her face against his chest and shirt, and hoped he was leading them down the right path—if there was a right path—for them. But, as he looked out over the edge of the great cliff of uncertainty before them, terrified for the first time since he'd been so badly beaten by his father, he felt in her the trembling terror of staring into *the abyss of love* beneath them and took comfort in being right there, with her. Alongside Dallia's *unconditional adoration* for him.

Charles W. McDonald Jr.

Chapter 53: Unconditional Adoration

(Damon's Manor, Kaleion, A Continuation, One Year Later)

t never ceased to amaze Dallia how the simple act of walking into the master bedroom threw her bearings completely off, with her thinking she should be seeing the double door entrance to the ritual room on her left as she walked into the massive rectangular master bedroom fabricated out of floorplan space that didn't exist. It almost always made her do a double-take, and Damon was only getting more and more advanced with each of his trips to other worlds. He always brought some new understanding of either magic or technology with him that made him reassess what he thought he knew. Ever the student made Damon ever the master, or the Dark Knight of Magic as he preferred. Dallia smiled, thinking of that title while her husband worked at the L-shaped desk beside the master bed simultaneously coming into view as she cleared the doorjamb, passing the six-person, dark-stained oak table centered between two L-shaped bookshelves on opposing walls of their bedroom. Taking a seat at the padded chest at the foot of their marital bed, Dallia cleared her throat,

Charles W. McDonald Jr.

seeing her husband deep in thought as he continued working, "Busy, Love...?"

Immediately stopping what he was doing to lean back in his chair, Damon looked his lovely wife over while upside down as he threatened to lean back so far in his chair as to tip over, only for her to see it come to an unnatural stop just before tilting completely over.

"You're silly," she realized, observing his excessive use of *Telekinesis*. It was one of his favorite tools—that's for certain.

Sticking his tongue out at her upside-down, he'd made his point. "When do I get my present?"

"This present...," she asked with a pause, showing him a diaphanous white dress with powder-blue flowers strategically placed throughout as she dangled the dress in front of her, modeling it for her sexy husband.

A smirk from Damon said that wasn't exactly the present he had in mind, but one he'd enjoy unwrapping, nonetheless.

A serious look on Dallia's face accompanied the note she brought him in the form of a scroll with a spider's seal. "That's four times in the last week. I think you'd better talk to her. She's not the kind of person to piss off."

"No, you're right." He grew stone quiet as he broke Evanyil's seal, unfurling her latest request to meet. *If you're quite done drilling for gold now, I'd like to talk about a job I need your help with.* No time or meeting place mentioned. Just that obtuse, terse, and crass message. Clearly Evanyil's style, though. A heavy sigh communicated more to Dallia than he'd intended.

"It's okay, Damon. Go meet with her. I trust you."

"It's not...," He paused, trying to think of how best to explain it. Dallia knew that when Damon spoke of his very dangerous circles, that Evanyil topped that list. They'd talked about it many times but blowing off Evanyil was more dangerous than talking to her—up to a point. "It's not that at all."

"Then what...?" Putting the new dress down on the chest, she approached her husband from behind, pushing his chair back forward so he didn't fall over while she started running her right hand through his long, black hair, massaging his scalp as she tried to keep him relaxed...and talking. A silent Damon was a dangerous Damon. And not good for their marriage. She'd gotten to know her husband very well over the last year, and she thought she knew him as well as just about anyone—except Evanyil.

"I'm sure she's going to want me to help her on a job." That was certain, but often her jobs caused such ripples and power vacuums, the inevitable boomerang of consequences usually came calling not long after. Always more severe each and every instance. Eventually, he'd be powerful enough to ride that out. He

Charles W. McDonald Jr.

hoped. But for now, the risk wasn't worth the reward.

"Yes, well we knew that was inevitable. I'm surprised it's taken her this long to...." she trailed off, thinking better of her next comment.

A frowning Damon finished the sentence for her in his thoughts. *Meddle in our marriage.* He knew. He could read her as well, if not better than she could read him. "I'm just saying it's our anniversary, and I was looking forward to spending it with you."

"Oh, you will! You'd better!"

He could see her playful scowl from behind him, but he could feel it.

"That's what I'm talking about. I can't make both of you happy." His relationship with Evanyil had grown...complicated. Treacherous ground. Even more so than it was, previously.

That earned him a serious frown as she mussed his hair with her hand, turning to walk away in disgust. "Go meet with Evanyil, Damon. I've still got to work on your anniversary present, and I don't want you in the house while I'm working on it. Go meet with her and have your ass back here for our anniversary dinner tonight." She felt like it was becoming a dangerous situation between him and Evanyil and didn't want it to explode all over their marriage. She knew she'd interrupted their normal routine and hoped Evanyil wasn't the jealous type. She'd heard a great deal about Evanyil and gathered all the information she could about her from Damon, but the more she learned, the more mysterious Evanyil was to her. Making her entirely unpredictable. And unpredictable was *bad*, in this situation.

He didn't like being ordered—wife or no—but he knew where she was coming from, so he'd let that one slide. Until he punished her later tonight. A smirk crossed his face at that thought as she looked back at him before she left the bedroom.

"What are you smirking at, Mister?! I know that look!"

"Oh...nothing. I'll see you tonight," he warned, smacking her bottom with his *Telekinesis* hard enough to shock her, almost knocking her into the door-jamb on her way out.

"Keep it up, Mister!" She warned, recovering before she strolled out, rubbing her now-sore bottom.

A suitable smile crossed Damon's face until he turned back to look at the fragments of wax from the broken spider seal now littering his desk. *Evanyil!*

*   *   *   *

Charles W. McDonald Jr.

(Physical Cave Entrance to The World Below and Between, Kaleion, A Few Moments Later)

Silvery blue slashes of light rent the superheated air just before Damon walked through, not expecting to see Evanyil already standing there—waiting for him.

She didn't look pissed, but she didn't look happy either. That was the worst possible look from Evanyil—feigned indifference. That was when she was most dangerous.

Looking at her beautiful, perfect, iridescent black elven skin in that black bodysuit she loved, he quickly drank in her beautiful violet eyes as he watched her balance her poison dagger on the tip of her right index finger. He needed to defuse the situation. He owed her an apology. "I'm sorry," he offered genuinely, motioning widely with both hands at the field covered in moss, flora, and overgrown vines.

"What do you have to be sorry for," she replied in the most expressionless, emotionless way her marvelous features could manage.

Now he really was worried! "You have every right to be pissed off at me, but would you like to know why I've been staying away?"

No reply. Silence. Emotionless, awkward silence. Evanyil wielded her hate like a weapon—like Damon. They learned well from one another. Of one another.

"Do you understand what this woman means to me? Do you?"

Still no reply. Only a blink of her beautiful violet eyes as she toyed with her dagger, tossing it this way and that, rolling it over her wrist then balancing it on her wrist in feigned disinterest.

"Okay…. Fine…. What did you want to talk about?"

Slipping her dagger back into its sheath, her expression moved from feigned disinterest to clear disappointment as she closed the distance, pulling out what looked like a map from between her perfect breasts.

What right did she have to be disappointed in him?! She held no claim on him!

"I believe you know this place." Batting those beautiful eyelashes at him, but still in a less than pleasant way, she looked to see his reaction as he observed the structure half-buried into the side of a mountain at the northern edge of the Trident.

"No way! That's Chara's place. I'm trying to make peace with that… woman. Find someone else if you're breaking into that place."

Charles W. McDonald Jr.

"You *owe* me, Damon."

"She's been a thorn in my side long enough, and I don't need to make more enemies right now. Find another way for me to pay you back. Name your price." He didn't have a great deal of treasure on hand right now. Upkeep on his manor was massively expensive, and he'd been avoiding pilfering and plundering to keep his enemies away from Dallia. He didn't have a lot with which to bribe Evanyil, but Dallia was more important than treasure.

"Fine," folding up the map and placing it in between her perfect breasts, Evanyil turned to head back into *The World Below and Between.*

"That's it?" Damon didn't know what to expect from Evanyil, as unpredictable as she was. She was the source of the vast majority of his reputation for being so unpredictable. But this new behavior of…whatever this was between her and him. It was…unnerving.

"That's what, Damon?"

"Clearly there's some unresolved shit between us. Let's clear it up, Evanyil. I'm here. Let's talk." His expression and his tone said he was genuine, and she of all people should have been able to tell that, but Evanyil was holding onto something, and he needed to figure out what it was—fast. "Clearly you're mad at me. Did you have some unspoken claim on me that we've never discussed?"

"No, Damon. I didn't have any claim on you." She wasn't the share my toys type, but Damon wasn't her toy. *Was he?*

"Talk to me, Evanyil. I hurt you. I'm sorry. How did I hurt you? How can I make it right?"

"A year's a long time, Damon. I'm over it."

"Bullshit! When a woman says she's over it, she's sure as fuck not!"

Blink. Blink. Blink from Evanyil, staring back at him.

"FUCK! This isn't how we fix this," Damon argued, motioning between them to drive home his point. "I'm just trying to avoid running in the old circles that would expose her to too much risk. That's why I've been quiet. It isn't because I don't care about you anymore. I DO CARE!"

"You forget, Damon. I know you. I know the real you. Does *she*?!" She paused, not wanting to address his care, or lack thereof, for her. If he cared, he wouldn't have had anything to do with that…*half-elf!* She knew the whys and wherefores, but Damon was the instigator of as many of their plans as she was. "You've been acting like a totally different person around her. Do you even know who you are, Damon of Basrat?"

"That's a fair question." It was. And a complicated one at that. He wasn't trying to be a totally different person. He was just trying to let the violence, death, and hatred take a lesser role in his life. "I wish I knew the answer to that question, Evanyil, but I don't. I know who I *was*. I know who I *am...around you*."

A nod from Evanyil acknowledged they might be getting somewhere close to her point. "Isn't that better than pretending with her?"

"I'm not pretending to be anything I'm not!" He paused, thinking about it. *Was he? Was she right?* "And, I'd do ANYTHING to be with her! ANYTHING!"

That said it all. *Her Damon was dead. Gone!* She didn't recognize whoever this man standing in front of her was. He looked like Damon. Walked and talked like Damon. He was still forthright and open with her, but deep inside, he was forcing himself to be something and someone he wasn't. That she *didn't* recognize. And couldn't respect. "I think we're done here. Go back to your wife, Damon. It's your anniversary."

Before he could even protest, she disappeared into the cavern entrance of *The World Below and Between*.

"SHIT," he thought aloud just before ripping the air in front of him into a *Portal* to his manor, in disgust.

*   *   *   *

Damon walked with a purpose and intent, radiating his tension and frustration from dealing with Evanyil as his staff avoided eye contact, watching him pace from one end of the foyer to the other, then back again as his anger cut a path of dark energy into the tile flooring of the foyer nearly visible to the naked eye.

He needed to think. He needed to find a way to make them both happy, or, at least, one happy one day, then the other happy the next. *Was Evanyil right about me? Am I becoming something and someone else just to be with Dallia? Is she changing me?* He needed an outside opinion—an opinion he could trust. He needed Goldenbow!

Dashing up the circular staircase so fast he was taking the steps two and three at a time, he quickly found himself on the fourth floor where he made the abrupt turn into the tiny decoy room that hid the secreted and protected entrance to his fourth-floor study, and master suite. Inside the study, he kicked open one of the hidden floor panels, snatching a plain metal box into the air with his *Telekinesis*, popping it open as he tilted the box toward him so he could quickly find the golden arrowhead, which his *Telekinesis* pulled from the box. A thought made the golden arrowhead burn mid-air, dripping onto the hardwood floor planks of his study.

The arrowhead was still melting when he felt the tap on the back of his

Charles W. McDonald Jr.

shoulder blade.

"Whatcha doin'," Dallia asked, wearing her traditional powder-blue traveling robes, making Damon wonder exactly where she'd been. Peeking around Damon's frame to see the gold dripping on the hardwood planks, Dallia's curiosity piqued. "You're summoning Goldenbow. Why? What's going on?"

"Just wanted his opinion on something."

"Must be something pretty important to summon him rather than just going to see him."

It was vitally important to Damon. *She* was vitally important to Damon and he needed to tell her, "You know how much I love you?"

"Of course, my Love." Taking his right hand in between hers, she brought herself close to him the way they both loved—where his chin rested on her forehead, with her body pressed close against his.

"Dallia, I adore you. I need you. And…." As he struggled to put his feelings for Dallia into words, he gently caressed the tips of her half-elven ears with the backs of his fingertips, tracing their shape around to the lobe as he felt her pulling him into her and her into him. "I don't think I could ever carry on without you." It had been an immutable fear from the moment of their first date, on that picnic blanket where they'd first kissed, that something or someone would destroy this profound thing they had built together. This collision of fate. And that he would be forced to deal with a death that might just break him—permanently.

"Am I interrupting something," Goldenbow's husky, youthful voice took them both off-guard, even though he was…expected.

"I'll let you two talk," Dallia proclaimed pulling away from Damon, but the look they shared between them said she understood. She wondered if he could tell how hard it was for her to keep herself together in this moment. She had to get out of there—fast!

Walking out of the study back out into the main fourth-floor hallway, Dallia didn't breathe until she'd cleared the staircase and taken hold of the railing on her way down to the subterranean levels, where she needed to finish her present for Damon. She couldn't stop the tears from falling on the staircase steps below as she had to hang on to the railing with everything she had just to keep herself upright. Her husband's incessant worry about her safety wasn't without merit, and she knew it. She didn't know how long they'd be allowed to have this…. Fate didn't work like that. In her experience, and his, fate had been a mostly cruel and relentless arbiter of the occlusions in one's soul. Another layer in the veil…. Until she met Damon. Until they had become one—more than the merely the sum of their individualities.

Charles W. McDonald Jr.

She needed to get to work!

"What's up, Day?" Goldenbow started, taking a seat at the table closest to the secret entrance to the master suite from Damon's study. He could already feel the tension in the room and wondered exactly why he'd been summoned. He knew he was *definitely* interrupting something. "You don't melt one of my arrowheads if it's nothing."

"It's not nothing…," Damon concurred with a pause, trying to think of how to even begin this conversation. "You know how highly I think of you."

Goldenbow only answered with that immeasurable ear-to-ear smile of his.

"It's been brought to my attention that I have changed since I've been with Dallia. Is that a true assessment, and if so, how have I changed?"

"Boy, Day! You never disappoint! You're always so damnable serious!" His grin was big. And defiant. Masquerading in lightheartedness whilst mired in the muck of Damon's foreshadowing. For all their similarities, and brotherly bond, Damon and Goldenbow were entirely unique and different people. Goldenbow could be telling a lengthy, complicated joke while silently slitting someone's throat. Damon didn't even know any good jokes. At least none Goldenbow had ever heard. Damon's humor came from his wit. And his venom.

"So, at least that hasn't changed, then." Damon smiled, though it was a tense smile, commensurate with the topic and serious tone of the conversation.

"I hope you're not asking an assassin for marital advice?!" The absurd nature of that statement rang heavy in Damon's ears.

"Ha-ha. I might only have a few friends in this life, but they're brilliant friends whose opinions I value. That's why I'm asking you."

Another bright and disarming smile from Goldenbow told Damon they were—in their own ways—good for each other. However Damon had changed due to Dallia, they were not *bad* changes. Damon was becoming more layered, more well-rounded, and more thoughtful. But in his line of work, those were not good qualities that served the task, or the moment, well. Still, for Damon and his line of work, they weren't necessarily 'bad' things. Just as an assassin, he had to keep things simple, clean, and neat. Quiet. Damon was too complex and too complicated to ever perform Goldenbow's role in life. They each had their own niche, and there was nothing wrong with that! "Very well, Damon."

Ugh…. Goldenbow used his full name. That can't be good.

Running his right hand through his scruffy hair, Goldenbow began voicing his on-the-fly analysis, "I think you understand the world, and those around you, with a great deal more…completeness. That is different, or new, depending on how you wish to look at it."

Charles W. McDonald Jr.

"I don't see that as a bad thing," Damon added, prompting Goldenbow to continue with a motion of his right hand.

"I think your love for Dallia has caused you to pull back from overtly dangerous courses of action. She's made you more reserved in action and thought. I still see the ruthless killer in you and know it is just under the surface, but before Dallia, it was prominently on display. There are new layers to you, Damon, and they are…admirable ones. It is those new layers that make up more of your surface now."

"Wow, that's a really thoughtful answer."

"You're surprised by that?"

"No…. Just impressed."

Another bolt of honesty from the legendary assassin: "I very much like this Damon as much, if not more, than the pre-Dallia Damon, but they *are* different from one another. And, you can't absorb someone as powerful as Dallia's soul into your life and not expect her to change a great many things about you. You're becoming part her, and she's becoming part you."

Wow! Again, Damon was impressed at the insight of the assassin before him. *Goldenbow was right! Evanyil was right!* Though, he cringed internally at the thought she was becoming…part him, as Goldenbow had so eloquently put it. "I need to ask a favor of you, my friend."

"Of course." He smiled again, ear to ear. They had both done a great many favors for one another, and he'd lost count of who owed whom exactly. Their relationship didn't work that way, really. It was more genuine than that.

"I still have a few enemies out there I've been unable to make peace with. You know who they are as well as I do. But, my request of you is that if you hear something—anything—that might lead you to believe they're going to act against me by getting to *her*, that you would let me know if there is time, and if there isn't time, that you would take care of that problem for me."

"Wow, that's a pretty sweeping request, Day." He wasn't saying no but thinking about how he'd reply to his friend's request. "As a professional assassin, I have to be careful about who I target and why. Bad for business and all. However, I'll make you this promise…if I hear or know of anything that would cause a conflict for me to deal with the issue, I'll try to deal with it diplomatically while simultaneously notifying you. Buy you time enough to act, so to speak. Otherwise, I'll take care of the problem outright, and immediately, for you. Fair enough?"

"More than fair. Thank you!" A genuine smile from Damon preceded a breath of relief. "If there's anything I can do in return…" He needed to be careful about how he worded this, given who—and what—he was speaking to, "…that wouldn't create the kind of problems I'm trying to avoid, I'd be happy to help."

"Absolutely, Day. You got it," Goldenbow agreed with a snap of his finger and another disarming, ear-to-ear smile. "I've gotta get back to a job in progress. Would you mind sending me back to the north side of Gravêstil?"

Opening a *Portal* for Goldenbow to walk through, Damon watched his friend—bow, quiver, and all—walk through to a forested area on the northwestern edge of Gravêstil along the Aegen River where he would have some cover.

A heavy sigh from Damon accompanied the whoosh of the closing *Portal*. He *had* changed! *So be it*! He could handle becoming part Dallia if that's what his changes meant. A broad and relieved smile from him said he could live with that just fine! It was their anniversary, and he had a very special present in mind for his wife he needed to go get.

*   *   *   *

Still sitting on the floor of Damon's hidden fourth-floor study, Dallia wondered—briefly—of the whereabouts of her wayward husband. It was nearly time for their planned anniversary dinner, and his present was finished. Well, nearly. She had only one more enchantment to perform and briefly considered how much it would take out of her to do it. *Would she even be able to walk afterwards, let alone...?* Well, she'd use whatever it took to make sure she had enough energy for *that*, later.

She needed a manuscript that Damon had been researching incessantly of late. Walking over to his desk where he'd kept it open, she took note of the strength of his writing in the margins of it—the intensity and gravity of Damon's words. This was the seriousness and dedication of the man she'd married. Damon's quest for knowledge was unparalleled, and she loved him for it. She adored him and would do whatever it took to make sure she would be there for him... despite his fears. She knew what Damon had been trying to say earlier...that only together, were they whole. Individually, they were both hurt, damaged, and very fractured souls. But, together, they were...perfect!

Taking the manuscript with her, she started reading, absorbing, and understanding the adjustments she'd need to make to her enchantments. She didn't have much time left. Damon would be back soon.

*   *   *   *

The sun was already setting over the southern tip of the Trident, off to the west as they faced one another again on that same blanket on that same hillside,

Charles W. McDonald Jr.

overlooking Damon's estate—their estate—to the east. He wore the same cavalier shirt untied down to his sternum, with the same pants he'd worn on their first date. She, on the other hand, wore the little diaphanous dress she'd been flaunting in front of him earlier that morning. Her soft, full curves and perfect legs held Damon's thoughts—and gaze—captive as she pulled the plain-white-cloth-covered *Staff of the Invoker* into her lap with a devious smile the likes of which he'd never seen on her face before.

"Do I get my present now," Damon asked, leaning forward in anticipation. Unable to take his eyes, and ear-to-ear grin, off the massive present in Dallia's lap. It had to be at least as tall as he was, maybe a little more if his guesstimate was accurate. The fact she'd been able to so easily wield it into her lap, given how massive it was, told him it must have housed tremendous enchantment.

"Yes, Love, you get your present now." She smiled, watching him eagerly burnish one hand against the other in anticipation. Still, she couldn't resist, pulling the cloth off of the *Staff of the Invoker* painfully slow, starting at the bottom of the staff, working her way slowly to the tip.

WOW! Just WOW! From the details of the acid-etched metal of the helical rods, to the perfectly terrifying charcoal-blue aura, to the runes, to the iolite gem at the tip, it was a magnificent piece of work—by far the most complex and most powerful staff he'd ever seen. "I…I…don't…."

"Don't what, Love?"

"I don't deserve it."

"Well, maybe not yet, but you can make it up to me later. Tonight…." Her sexy, knowing smile caused him to beam with pride.

What a wife!

"Would you like to hold it," she toyed, dangling it in front of him with only one hand as she gripped one of the three helical, charcoal-blue metal rods.

"In a moment," he replied to her astonishment.

Whatever could cause him….

Reaching into his back pocket to pull out a small black box roughly the length of her finger and not quite the same in width, he noticed Dallia's eyes go to the box in wonder.

It was perhaps a jewelry box? Was Damon giving her jewelry on their anniversary? That didn't seem the Damon way. Whatever it was, it must have been important to postpone his examination of the *Staff of the Invoker*. "This…," he offered, handing her the jewelry box, "…is the result of my research you've seen me buried in over the last few weeks. This is a part of me. Carry it with you always, and you'll carry with you a part of me that *only you made possible*. It's a part of my undying love for you—a part of my unconditional adoration of you."

Blink. Blink. Blink. Dallia's green-gold eyes—left dazed and confused by this other half of her who constantly surprised her—took a moment to adjust as did her fingers, unable to open the box he placed gently into her hands.

"Here." He opened it for her, showing her its contents. A satin-polished sheen on a dark-grey stone medallion roughly the size of Dallia's palm stared back at her and as she took in the embossed wildflower in the hair of her likeness on profile with the likeness of Damon's hand and fingers tracing the outline of her half-elven ear. One tear followed another, landing on the medallion.

"I…." She didn't know what to say, but her curiosity as a mage was already getting the better of her as she started to examine Damon's enchantment. *How had he even managed to do this?* Damon's strength was definitely *not* in enchantment. *Did he get help to make this?* But, as she started to probe the medallion, she felt Damon pushing back from within the medallion.

"Do you like it?"

"Damon, I don't even know what to say."

"Here." He pulled out the medallion; it looked heavy and noticeable—even from a distance—but it felt like warm air when he put it around her neck and sealed the clasp shut. Instantly, she felt its warmth against her chest as it hung between her breasts. Even having been around enchantment most of her life, she struggled to put into words what she felt from Damon's enchantment in his gift of unconditional adoration. It resonated with an indescribable energy, reaching deep inside her as if…then she felt him leave…then she felt him return…then she felt him leave again…and then return again—as if he was circling *around her*, or *through* her.

*   *   *   *

Chara reviewed the architectural plans laid out in front of her on the map table of her sitting room. Her location within the Trident was well known, and she needed a more secretive place to conduct future operations…and to hunt.

She liked what she was seeing in the design of the plans…. Directly below the battlements of the left flank eight-sided tower, Chara's new sitting room would offer a beautiful view, even through the narrow, crossed archer windows on each of the walls. It wasn't a pure octagon design, rather a rectangular construction abbreviated with four beveled edges to each wall, creating an elegant, but militarily brute construction. Location alone would make it difficult, if not impossible to siege, assuming anyone would even find her. The Valley of Deception was extremely remote.

Flipping through the architecture plans, looking for a specific profile elevation view, Chara did not expect to see the detailed biology sketch before her.

"Well, well…," Chara exhaled, taking in the detail of the filleted body, diagrammed. The closest thing she could relate it to was an autopsy, but it was very focused in detail on her chest—on her heart. It was definitely a female body, for certain. Chara's eyes traced up the victim's chest, to her neck, hair and ears. "Hmmm, a half-elf."

Chara looked around, "Useless!"

Almost instantly, Useless was in her presence, fully prostrate before her. "Someone has been in here. We have an intruder…," she paused, thinking, "…though I think they are likely gone. Still, I want to know who was in this room, and when?" She already knew the why.

Charles W. McDonald Jr.

Part 6: The Monster Revealed

Charles W. McDonald Jr.

Each day, by my own creed and ethos, will
I strive to be all I can be,
Until the monsters of hypocrisy
Reveal the monster in me.

Charles W. McDonald Jr.

Chapter 54: Fuel for the Fork

(Damon's Manor, Kaleion, Some Months Later)

She understood the need. Upkeep on their manor was draining them dry financially, and there was no way Damon would ever give up this property, nor would she *allow* him to give it up. It was as much a part of him as his limbs—as much a part of him as she. Still, they'd been avoiding disruptive behavior for a very long time and had managed to mend quite a few fences along the way. She didn't want to see any of that progress undone to aid with financial problems. Finances came and went, but burned bridges tended to stay burnt!

"So, tell me the plan then, Damon. Are we to make enemies on other worlds now?"

"Hardly." He understood her concerns because they were valid, but there was still unclaimed wealth out there. You just had to know where to look. He'd already turned hundreds of acres of his estate into valuable farmland and had hired expert staff to work that land relentlessly, but they still needed gems, diamonds,

Charles W. McDonald Jr.

precious metals, and artifacts to maintain the estate long term. Every person on Kaleion knew his name and every corner bore his likeness—such was the price of infamy. But off-world…. That was a different story. He had the advantage of a fresh reputation, which he could 'sweeten' as needed to get what he wanted, and there was always off-world mining, but that was very messy work—even for a mage. "Have faith, Love. I've been working on the perfect barter for all of our needs. All we need now is an audience."

"An audience with who, Damon?"

"King Edward of England, of course!"

(Wessex, England, Earth, December 1065)

Daily life whirled on around the frail and ailing King of England as he watched his magistrates, emissaries, nobles, and generals conduct the affairs of state in the mostly grey and earth-tone stone structure of Edward's court. A Wessex family heirloom handed down in succession, through generations dating all the way back to King Offa and King Egbert, the fortified structure wasn't really designed for the flanking fire provided in a keep with motes for defenses, but rather a state home of history and heritage that Edward the Confessor didn't want to leave. Edward the Confessor, son of Æthelred the Unready and Emma of Normandy, didn't have much time left on this Earth, and he knew it. He would pass from this Earth here in the comfort of the home of his line of succession. Still, he would see his plans for his sovereign and unified England go forth as designed. Britain worked better, operated more efficiently, and accomplished more when working as a country rather than a series of independent fiefdoms and feudal lords bent on their own ambitions. That had been the lesson since Egbert, and a lesson he intended to carry forward in his choice for succession. The country needed unified goals, and that meant it had to remain a unified people to achieve those goals.

Twirling wispy tufts of his frail and brittle, grayed, shoulder-length hair, King Edward looked, with sullen and sunken eyes, to his only trustworthy heir—Harold Godwinson—who motioned a squire to come within a few paces as he approached the king's side. In his early forties and still strapping in chest, height, and build, Harold looked the part of youthful but experienced successor, though those around him looked to each other with eyes that belied that truth. Wearing ornamental chainmail over a red tabard held by gold chain, Harold tried to remain calm when a runner preempted his conversation with King Edward, who remained bedridden beside him.

"My Lord." The teenage male messenger in light-of-foot riding attire in road-worn earth-tones was only allowed within a few spans of the royalty before him. Still short of breath, he gathered himself in front of the leadership of England. "An emissary wishes an audience."

"An emissary of who," Harold replied, looking to the king then back to the young rider.

"An emissary of the Duke of Western Francia." The rider's youthful eyes wide as silver crown coins, expectant in their expression that surely the king would want to hear from this emissary. Though his little life experience did not tell him of all the many false emissaries who'd come before.

Raised eyebrows from Harold met a frail and twisted smile from King Edward, who obviously loved the game of politics more than his body would still permit.

"Send him in…," Harold offered, anxiously awaiting what he fully expected to be a terse, if not savage, response to the messages he'd sent the descendant of Rollo. Motioning for four guards with crossbows to stand behind him, Harold remained calm until he saw the likes of the man—and woman—approaching, making their way through the double oak doors held open by a pair of English infantrymen holding long pikes. He had never seen robes of the like on this pair— the woman in beautiful, flowing V-neck, sky-blue robes with ivory runes and flowers with long, flowing, wavy platinum-blonde hair covering the tops of her ears and spilling down her back, framing a beautiful, youthful face, with a large stone medallion settled between her breasts. The man looked rugged, despite the robes, but they almost enhanced his rugged appearance—truly unusual. Clearly of wealth, his dark robes, woven in a pattern he'd never before seen, with silver and gold accents and runes, moved about him in a way that accented his physical stature, though he made no attempt to hide the scars about his chest and neck, clearly visible for all to see. *Was he proud of them*, Harold wondered. Whoever he was, he was prepared for a fight; though, Harold got the feeling with the way he held the woman's hand at his side that a fight was the last thing he sought.

Stranger in a strange land, he didn't want to intimidate or provoke, so Damon took a stance a good twenty paces from both Harold and the king, knowing they would want to hear what he had come to say. A firm press of his hand into his wife's communicated his intent to halt before getting any closer. His assumption in royalty protocol was to speak when spoken to, so he'd play along—for now.

Charles W. McDonald Jr.

Casting *Linguistics*, he was prepared to communicate in their tongue—a derivative of his own homeworld root language. He wondered what exactly that meant and hoped to find out by whatever means necessary.

"Nomrey," he heard the literal, then the translation in his thoughts, '*names?*'

"Damon, and my wife, Dallia," Damon replied using *Linguistics* to translate on the fly, motioning to Dallia on his right side. He hadn't brought the *Staff of the Invoker* with him, otherwise she'd be on his left side. They stood out enough as it was, and he didn't need that level of power—especially given Dallia's presence.

Leaning forward in his bedridden state, King Edward perked up at hearing their names. Those were not English or Welsh names, and they were not Francia names either!

"What lands do you hail from, Damon and Dallia? What are your family names?" Edward's voice might have been soft-spoken and infirm from his condition, but his mind was still sharp. Damon could see it in the king's eyes—the back-lit fire of intellect. This man hadn't risen to power by accident, and certainly hadn't unified a landscape of disparate fiefdoms and feudal lords into a country by luck. Damon's research into this world had proven useful already, based on what he was seeing. Now it was time to see if it was going to pay off or not.

"Rome," Damon replied flatly, directing his attention between Harold and Edward, but a nod of respect directed at Edward specifically as he continued in his full response, "Damon and Dallia of Rome, and while we did come from notable families, those family names are neither important, nor something we would like to share. In our trade, we find it useful to be known only by our given name. It adds more…notoriety…more legend to our names. We prefer it that way." Good. An honest answer, even though it wasn't fully what the king had asked for or wanted to hear. That would establish some credibility, if Edward didn't consider it an affront.

A nod of respect from Edward said Damon wasn't far off in his negotiating skills with this man. "And what is your trade, Damon of Rome? How is Cardinal Anselmo da Baggio by the way? I haven't spoken to him in so long, I wonder if he still remembers me." A somewhat hearty laugh from Edward caused a chorus of laughs around the room in a show of support for their ailing king, but it was clearly a test, and a bad one—ill-fatedly masked in so far as Damon could tell.

"The Holy Father, Alexander II is doing quite well, Your Majesty. In health, spirituality, and politically. But then you'd already know that, Your Majesty." A feigned frown from the frail king said that he was disappointed his ruse had been so easily cast aside by this foreigner, Damon, who clearly wasn't from Rome—

Charles W. McDonald Jr.

however knowledgeable he was. A hearty smile from Damon said he'd continue to play along for as long as Edward wished. He had the feeling the king hadn't had the opportunity to exercise his clear intellect in quite a while, so why not allow him this moment of…gamesmanship. "And, I'm certain the king *also* knows the holy father was never a cardinal before being raised to Pontiff by the conclave."

Hmmm, Edward considered, exchanging knowing glances between himself and the powerful earl, Harold…. "You didn't mention your trade, Damon of Rome." *If that's who you really are.*

"My apologies, Your Majesty. I seem to have lost my manners in your presence. Nerves, and all." Damon feigned explanation, giving Edward a knowing glance which Edward returned with a knowing smile. Clearly Edward was enjoying the gamesmanship. *Good.* That could prove useful. "Both my wife and I are…" Pausing, Damon tried to put the term into something to which the rest could relate. "…Well, Your Majesty, the closest interpretation in your culture would be druids."

Gasps from around the room confirmed everyone's suspicion as the terms, 'heretics,' 'sorcerers,' and 'witches' escaped lips around the room, but not from the king, who merely nodded knowingly—apparently not even surprised.

"A druid with such knowledge of the holy father is a formidable intellect for certain. Perhaps I've met my match." Edward chuckled, coughing into his fist, causing concerned but supportive laughs around the room. "What news do Damon and Dallia of Rome bring from our *good* friends from across the channel?"

Now they were getting somewhere. Now it was time to find out how much his information was truly worth. "I have never met, or had audience with the Duke of Francia, William, descendant of Rollo." Damon's forthright approach caused Edward's head to pull back into his pillow, considering the boldness of the man now in his court. "However, I can get an audience with anyone you wish. I know he holds claim to your throne and monitors your health from a distance. I also know he has spies in your court."

More gasps from around the room as Damon pointed to the magistrate to Harold Godwinson with a knowing look, expecting the king's men to soon find the evidence he'd just planted in the magistrate's tent. "There you will find reports of your health, written in his own handwriting. You can compare it to other letters he has made to his wife. You'll see…. They're letters to William, Your Majesty." A pinch of his wife's hand told Dallia the sacrifice of this man was necessary for credibility with Edward. Credibility couldn't be purchased…not by coin. It had to be earned by deeds—however the manner.

Harold Godwinson's magistrate, John Amos, looked both horrified and

Charles W. McDonald Jr.

amused at the ridiculous accusation. Starting to rapidly close the gap between Damon and himself, he'd see this heretic hanged before the Sun set. A motion of Edward's hand accompanied with a knowing look halted John in his tracks as three of Edward's best men seized John before he got within arresting distance of Damon.

"There is no doubt William has spies in my presence. I know this...," Edward paused, looking to Harold more suspiciously than ever before, but not entirely accusatory of his formerly trusted earl, "...however, I wasn't aware of the proximity. I'm grateful for your information...," he paused again, leaning forward again toward Damon, "...IF proven accurate."

"You will find everything I've said can be verified. I wouldn't come into your court making false claims."

"And yet you came into my court with false pretenses." Edward was still sharp, but he wasn't hostile towards Damon. He just needed an explanation.

"A fair point, Your Majesty." Damon watched as the frail, but still sharp, king relaxed back into his pillow. "I needed an audience to tell you...to see what it's worth to you, to make your William, descendant of Rollo, problem go away."

"And how might you do what my best men, resources, and negotiating skills haven't been able to do?" Edward's eyes flared, challenging this Damon of Rome from the scant distance betwixt them.

A swift motion of Damon's left hand accompanied with a mere thought invoked, by way of his *Telekinesis*, the unseen hands necessary to whisk away every single person out of the court save Damon, Dallia, and Edward, slamming the doors behind them as their bodies crashed hard up against the wall outside in the hallway. Now totally alone with the King of England, Damon could speak more freely. "*None* of them will remember a thing you've just witnessed," Damon informed, producing a static ball of lightning in his left hand, releasing Dallia with his right as she stayed behind, while Damon closed the distance between them.

"Very well, Damon of *Rome*," Edward agreed, nodding knowingly, adding a tinge of mirth with his pithy mention of Damon's alleged home. His eyes were somewhat wide at Damon's capabilities, but something had been off about Damon from the moment he walked into his court. At least now it was out in the open where he could deal with it. "I'm listening...."

Dispelling the *Ball Lightning* in his left hand, he fully closed the distance between himself and Edward, close enough to offer his right hand in open palm.

Gauging Damon carefully as he now looked into Damon's unique black eyes, Edward felt perhaps there was a play to be made here for the good of his country. Damon could be useful. In that thought, he took Damon's hand, shaking it as heartily as he could manage, in his failing condition.

Charles W. McDonald Jr.

"What would it be worth to you, King Edward?" Dispelling his formal royalty decorum along with his spells, Damon was now on higher footing with the king.

"I can't take my coin with me...," the king laughed, coughing into his fist again before he continued, clearly in thought, "...however, Harold will need treasury to maintain security and prosperity, so I can't give you everything I have. Would a tenth of my treasury in gold and silver common coins work?"

Damon considered his offer, but only for the briefest of moments before countering, "A tenth won't buy you the Duke's death, but I'll meet with him on your behalf for a tenth." *There, let the air be totally clear and in Edward's control. Let him determine how far he'd like this meeting with the Duke to go.*

"A tenth. Then we have an agreement, Damon." Edward offered his hand to Damon again for him to shake it, which Damon did as respectfully as he could without crushing the frail king's hand.

"A tenth. We have an agreement, King Edward." Pivoting toward the double doors king's guard flung open, allowing them to rush Damon, but the guards barely made it past the doorjamb before being held captive by Damon's *Telekinesis* as Damon approached each of them in turn. One by one, Damon cast *Forget*, causing each of them to collapse where they stood as the king watched wide eyed and in awe.

This was no Druid!!

Approaching Harold, Damon finally got what he'd come for, the official seal of the Earl, removing it directly from Harold's pocket just before casting *Forget*, causing him to slump back against the wall where he'd just started to regain consciousness from being slammed against the wall moments before.

Quiet all this time, Dallia approached the frail king, offering, "Thank you for meeting with us, Your Majesty." A genuine and disarming smile from Dallia produced an incredulous but warming smile from Edward, leaving him wondering what just happened and what would be the result of Damon's forthcoming meeting with the infamous William, descendant of Rollo. Pivoting to follow quick on Damon's heels, Dallia erased all traces of their magic on her way out, but she didn't know how to erase traces of Damon's natural abilities. That was something her best detection spells couldn't illustrate for her. *This would have to do*, she thought, quickly heading out into the hallway to follow her determined husband.

*　　*　　*　　*

(Rouen, Normandy, Earth, Moments Later)

Charles W. McDonald Jr.

Dallia had barely made it to within ten paces of Damon before he'd already opened the *Portal* to Francia. At least he'd had the courtesy to hold it open for her. She'd felt the restriction to her source of Arcane the minute she'd first cast here. Magic was in the throes of death here, and she wasn't sure if she could even source enough for a *Portal*, making her wonder how Damon had operated here so freely.

Hearing the whoosh of the *Portal* closing behind her, barely giving her enough time to make it through, she glowered at her impatient husband. "What was *that* all about," Dallia hissed at him, looking at the magnificent blue-grey stone structure on the hillside of their current location overlooking the Seine River, snaking its way towards Paris. It was massive! And, broodingly impressive…. "And, who is this Duke you've been talking about? Care to clue me in on your little plans here, Mister?!" She knew he'd been operating off-world quite a while, since before they'd met. Even in his first journey with Kellen, who she detested, he'd managed to lead the entire party nearly to their off-world death. *Clearly, there wasn't enough plunder or notoriety on Kaleion for Damon!*

"I don't want to make this more complicated than it has to be, Love," Damon replied, leaning into his wife, looming over her really, "…but, this conflict that's on the verge of happening would happen with, or without, my influence. My intention is just to facilitate a little profit out of the deal. And, perhaps, make it a little more swiftly executed. Less duration equals less brutality and overall body count."

Sounded harmless enough, but Damon wasn't providing all the details. He'd been back and forth between worlds many, many times—enough to pave a road of heavy magic between the two…or however many worlds he'd visited. "What aren't you telling me, Damon?"

The lack of her term of endearment for him was telling in and of itself. Clearly, he'd managed to piss off his wife already on this little adventure. They meshed well together and had proven to work well together—most of the time, though not like the way he meshed with Evanyil. Their relationship was more fluid, and very much like the dynamics of fluid, Evanyil and Damon had learned how to operate in that space of chaos created between them whereas Damon and Dallia overlapped more in their logic, often with Dallia's logic pointing in one direction while Damon's pointed in another. There was little-to-no overlap of logic between Evanyil and Damon, because there was little-to-no logic to be found *anywhere* in Evanyil. The caw of crows overhead brought Damon out of his moment of concern as he looked out over the River Seine. The naked line-of-sight from the massive keep down to their location meant their presence had already been spotted.

Charles W. McDonald Jr.

There would be armed men here any moment and, he still had a lot to do in order to make this idea of his work. He had to get his wife on board—fast...or send her home. "Look, I know you trust me, Love. Don't lose faith in me just yet. I didn't come here to wreak havoc or kill anyone." Well, technically, he had been directly responsible for hanging the magistrate that was probably on the gallows pole as he spoke, but that was a technicality.... *Right?*

"Ne bouge pas!" The gruff foreign voice glowered at them over the bolt of his crossbow, flanked by a regiment of eleven others rapidly surrounding them in a semi-circle only open to their side, facing the Seine.

Casting *Linguistics*, Damon replied in a smooth and muted tone, "We seek an audience with the Great William, descendant of Rollo, Duke of Francia. We carry a message from King Edward of England."

"And what would the King of England be doing sending two sorcerers into the court of the Duke of Francia," the guard in blues and greys accosted over the bolt of his crossbow aimed straight at Damon's black eyes.

He could destroy them all with but a thought and just start making his way up toward the keep, but he'd made a promise to his wife, and he intended to keep it. Besides, there was a diplomatic play to be made here. And money to be made. He was sure of it. "I carry a message from the Earl, Harold Godwinson, with regards to your duke's claim to the Norman Throne of England and the *legitimacy* of his claim. It is meant to be delivered directly to William, descendant of Rollo, and no one else. Not another soul. Either take me to him, or shoot me, but stop wasting our time."

That earned him a stabbing glare from his wife, who darted eyes between Damon and the guards dressed in regal blues, golds, and greys of Western Francia.

"Hands behind your back," he ordered over the bolt of his crossbow as two men, as large as Damon, closed the distance with crude iron cuffs bound together with heavy iron links, as they slammed the cuff shut on Damon and Dallia, escorting them up the hillside. To William, Duke of Francia.

A knowing wink from Damon wasn't as comforting to his wife as he'd intended. In fact, she looked even more pissed now, glowering back at him!

*   *   *   *

William's receiving room was more clean, neat, and decorated in pomp than King Edward's, with far more light shining through a series of arrow-slits running along the balcony and battlements overlooking the receiving hall floor below.

A massive mountain of a man, even bigger and broader through the shoul-

Charles W. McDonald Jr.

ders than Damon, approached, stepping down from a four-step, raised oaken dais, wearing a metallic-flavored navy royal robe over leathered sleeves of the same metallic sheen, navy with silver and gold scrolled cuffs. A decorative banner in mostly silver embroidered scrollwork ran horizontally at the bottom of the robe, a hand's span above his soft leather boots, illustrating a raised series of two lion passant family crests on a beautiful field of silver. This was the unified crest of Normandy. Damon was now in the presence of Norman royalty, watching the brute of a man close the gap between them.

Wife Matilda, of Flanders, remained seated in her slightly smaller throne chair at her husband's left side, adorned in the finest cream and gold lace, decorated with fields of flowers—some diaphanous, others more opaque on fields of gold. Occasionally hearing daily audiences, grievances, and propositions throughout western Francia with her famous husband, even Matilda could tell this was no mere audience. Whoever these foreigners were, they were dangerous—however feigningly meek their arrested appearance.

"Vous avez un message d'Edward ou Harold? Lequel est-ce?" William's powerful voice filled the receiving room chamber all the way to the ceiling some twenty spans high above them.

Damon's Linguistics still in effect, he heard the translation immediately in his thoughts, '*You have a message from Edward, or Harold? Which is it?*' He knew he had the leverage he needed with the seal by itself, but he wasn't ready to play that just yet, "Both, Your Majesty. Both. He, Edward, understands your Norman claim to the throne of England by way of your common ancestry to Edgar the Peaceful."

A knowing nod from William said that the message was well received. Good, because the rest might not be. He'd have to be...diplomatic about this, lest lots of people would die—quite possibly himself and Dallia, given the number of crossbows currently pointed at their heads, and the spears pressed against their backs. "He asks you what is it you seek out of your rule of England, *if* it were granted? What would you see become of England under your rule versus Harold's?" He knew that wasn't what he'd been sent to ask, or discuss with William, but he needed a great lever to maneuver this mountain of man and understanding him was the first step to acquiring that lever.

William smiled at the question knowing it sounded like Edward—sort of. *What game is this foreigner playing with me?* Still, he'd play along—for now. "Look around you." William motioned with both hands, obviously beaming with pride over the construction of his castle with all the latest modern defenses. "England claims to be one land, but feudal lords still battle one another across the entire landscape. This isn't the case in my lands. I'll put an end to all of that—I guar-

Charles W. M{c}Donald Jr.

antee it. Edward knows this. He only supports Harold out of loyalty, fear of the unknown, and the fact that only the strongest voice of support from him would be heard by those around him if he were to support me. In his lack of knowledge or understanding about me, he couldn't raise such a strong voice of support for my claim."

Nodding, Damon was beginning to understand this man whose brain was at least as powerful as his physical features. This was an impressive man. Looking to his wife, then to William, Damon had all but made up his mind. Now it was time to see how his plan would play out. "Your Majesty.... William, if I may□." He was taking a big chance by being so bold as to address him by name. "I have brought you two things in my robes. One for you to keep and the other for you to borrow, if only for a moment. However, the thing I brought you to borrow is incredibly valuable—so much so I won't agree to show it to you unless you ask everyone to leave the room, save only us two." Now that *was* bold, given his current disposition—and his wife's. Dallia shot him a glare like none he'd ever seen from her before, which he returned with a knowing wink. *Don't give up on me, Love. Hold tight....*

A great belly laugh from William, enough to again fill the vaulted ceiling all the way to the top, immediately preceded a deadly glare, as William's ice-blue eyes stared into Damon's *black mirrors of the soul.* William wasn't certain if this man had the balls to call him out in his own court or not, but he'd see what this man had brought him if he had to cut off his head himself to do it. Taking a gleaming longsword off his captain's side, he shouted, "OUT!"

Still handcuffed and now with a formidable longsword about to skewer his belly wide open, Damon managed a confident smile as he watched everyone, including both wives, leave the two of them alone. "Thank you, William. My name is Damon. If you'll look inside the outer right pocket of my robes, you'll find Harold's seal ring. That is yours to keep. And, if you'd like, I can forge papers from Harold, in his exact handwriting, that claim he recognizes your Norman claim to the English throne, throwing his support behind you if you agree to give him 100,000 acres of land from Glastonbury, reaching all the way to the southwestern tip of England, and from Winchester to Rochester all the way south to Sussex and Canterbury. I even took parchment from Harold's magistrate that we can use for the document. With *my* skills and *that* seal, *no one* will ever question its authenticity."

Carefully reaching into Damon's outer robe right pocket with his left hand, while William kept the tip of his longsword pointed at Damon's gut, he smiled as soon as he turned Harold's seal upside down to see the crest of the powerful Earl of

Wessex. Pulling out the parchment Damon described, William backed away from Damon, nodding at his resourcefulness. Whoever this foreigner was, William respected him. This man was a doer—a shaper of the future. He could respect that. "Damon, you said your name was…. *Why* are you here?" William hadn't bothered to ask about the other item yet, but he'd get to that.

"This fight over claims between you and Harold is going to turn to war soon enough. We both know that. Harold knows it. Edward knows it. Most of English and Norman aristocracy knows it."

Another knowing nod from William said they both saw things for what they were. Not as they would hope for them to be.

"I'm here to determine who I should throw my support behind to make this a swift and decisive victory. For a price, of course. The parchment and seal were a gift; let's call it a good faith gesture."

Dropping the point of the longsword to the floor, William liked this man. All day, every day, he dealt with people that would say or do anything to curry favor with him. That was not this Damon's style, and he found it both refreshing, and honest.

As soon as the tip of William's sword touched the floor, Damon shattered his handcuffs with a thought, breaking them off his wrists so they were free to face one another more on Damon's terms. William's ice-blue eyes turned wide as he considered calling for his guards, only to see Damon shaking his head as he waved off William's thought in protest with his right hand. "No need for that, William. If I'd wanted to kill you, you'd be dead already."

William considered using his captain's longsword to run Damon through, *but what point would that prove?! He'd only freed himself and had brought two very valuable gifts, if not a third and a fourth. Why not hear the man out? Whoever this sorcerer was?!*

"You asked *why* I was here. I'd like to know what my support is worth to you…? What would winning England in **weeks** mean to you in value? In treasure? In saved resources and men?"

"You could do this?" William's eyes walked over every inch of this tall sorcerer, wondering where his capabilities might find their limits.

Snatching William's sword with his *Telekinesis*, Damon raised the sword into the air, spinning it between them as he bent the blade over on itself using his fingers in a pincer motion until the blade snapped in half, sending shards of steel all over the stone floor.

"My soldiers are Christian. They will see such things as a work of the Devil. Are you in league with the Devil, Damon?"

"Hardly…. No." He wasn't sure if he'd emphasized that point or not. This was the descendant of Rollo. Surely, he understood more than most his men, the concept of gods beyond God the Creator. Damon could see Rollo's Norse blood and beliefs working behind the ice-blue eyes of his descendant allowing William to see Damon's powers as something other than witchcraft. "No!"

"Could you use your powers in a subtler way, so as to not raise suspicion?"

"Yes, and in fact, that was my plan all along."

Finally, they were seeing eye to eye, and William began, for the first time, considering the real possibility of a swift victory where so many others before him had failed, or made a bloody mess of the entire countryside and the people they'd intended to rule. *Sometimes the messy and more bloody way was necessary, but why not use the right tool for the right job; especially when he was standing right in front of me offering his services?!*

"And, what of this other…gift you mentioned I could borrow?"

Unseen hands snatched a plain silver rod half the length of Damon's forearm from inside his robe, landing squarely in Damon's right hand where he produced it for William to 'borrow.' He was about to see if his guess about William was right or not. "I want you to hold this for me, if you would, please."

William looked at the unremarkable rod, wondering exactly what he should expect from such a thing, carefully taking it from Damon and feeling its warmth flood his hand and forearm as soon as he took it. Wide ice-blue eyes confirmed Damon's suspicion. "That is an irreplaceable and powerful tool. It is *dangerous,* William, and I am asking you, as part of my payment, to swear to me if you ever see another one like it, you are to bury it, and I'll give you very specific instructions on *where* I want you to bury it. I have reason to believe there are one or more of these somewhere in the English countryside. Do we have an agreement, William?"

"Agreed, and the rest of your payment?" William extended his hand to Damon as they shook hands for the very first time, sealing the deal they had just struck.

As Damon, and William, the descendant of Rollo, negotiated Damon's price in the Duke's treasure and future conquest, Damon leaned into William, whispering into his ear specific instructions on where he wanted the object buried to keep it safe.

*   *   *   *

(Wessex, England, Some Hours Later)

Charles W. McDonald Jr.

It had taken quite a bit of time explaining to his wife exactly what was going on, and his agreement with William, but Damon felt confident they were getting somewhere, and now with more than a thousand new gold coins and six thousand new silver coins sitting in his foyer back home, they needed to go back to Edward and collect payment. He had only offered to *speak* to William on Edward's behalf, and he'd lived up to his side of the bargain with paperwork to prove it. William had given Damon one of Edward's messages that he'd been saving, to give to him in person once he crossed the channel to take his new English throne from the ailing king.

"Damon, why even bring me along? Clearly you don't need *me* to execute this little plan of yours...."

"Because you always complain about me running off on my own and doing my own thing even though we're supposedly married. That's one reason."

Smiling in her reply, she just shook her head, "Don't you dare blame me. What's the other reason?" Looping her arm in his as she walked by his side, she still struggled to understand this man. He was entirely too complicated!

"Because you never know what kind of problem you're going to run into, and it's just best to always have someone with you...just in case."

"Even if you're the Dark Knight of Magic," she offered with another of her beautiful, loving smiles, knowing how fond he was of that title.

"Even if you're the Dark Knight of Magic!" He just smiled, shaking his head as they both took in the fresh salt air on the northern edge of Wessex. The flash of blinding white light flooding Damon's waking vision nearly caused him to falter against his wife as he heard the booming voice of Creation just beyond his vision, across the great lake of crystal he'd seen only once before. He was still groggy, collecting his vision when he saw a familiar Humanoid figure and color off in the distance out in front of them, just before his wife collapsed, thrusting her broken body into his chest. Wide-eyed, almost to the point of her beautiful green-gold gems being hyper-extended out of their sockets, Dallia bled profusely from her chest, mouth, ears, eyes, and nose as if her entire circulatory system had just exploded internally. Collapsing to the ground, with Dallia tangled up in his love for her, Damon tried to collect himself, brushing back Dallia's radiant platinum-gold hair as he held her in his arms, watching the Light of her life, and his, rapidly fade from her eyes.

Think Damon!!! What do you need to do to save her?! Think fast! He didn't know her biology as well as Human biology, certainly not as it related to her circulatory system, and he was certain that had been shattered as he probed her body with all the Arcane Earth could afford in order to save Dallia. The valves looked misshapen, even broken and torn off at their hinges as he peered through her body and into her heart itself.

"Hang on, Dallia. Don't go. Please.... Please.... Dallia.... I need you."

Whatever this was, this wasn't a normal spell that had done this. This had been purpose-built to destroy Dallia from the inside out. Thoughts of his attempt to save Abel flooded every corner of his mind as he reached deep into Dallia with his magic, trying to fix one valve, then the next, then the next, then one chamber, then another. He had to try!!! Dallia's chest heaved as he thrust his sourced and shaped Arcane into her body with *Healing*. "Come on, Love! Come back to me!!!"

The briefest of glances up, with his vision now clear, even streaked with his tears of love for Dallia, he could clearly see the red-haired shape of Chara off in the distance—watching.

Don't think about Chara, Damon! Save Dallia first! Probing Dallia's chest for what could still be wrong he found artery after artery completely blown apart from the inside out almost through their entire length. "Oh Dallia, I'm sorry. I'm so sorry, Love. I don't know how to fix this." Memories of his very first spell fresh in his mind, he knew he didn't have it in him to kill his beloved Dallia if he accidentally prolonged her suffering—or made it even worse.

His very worst fears now realized and tangled up in his arms, Dallia's broken body started to go cold and colorless. He struggled internally with the insatiable need to leave his wife to execute Chara.

Damon's *black mirrors of the soul* were rimmed in a smoky hue of acid hatred—his irises backlit by a ring of fire threatening to consume his pupils then the whole of his eyes—if not the whole of his immortal soul. All that had been Dallia's love inside of Damon had been replaced with his *hate*. And *hate* was all he could see as Dallia took her last breath in Damon's arms.

Casting *Healing* on Dallia's eyes, enough to relocate them sufficiently to close them, Damon sent her shattered body home with a *Gate*.

That undead nemesis of abomination loomed in the distance to the northwest, by the shoreline, in a flowing bright red dress that would match the blood Damon would extract from every part of her. If it was the last thing he did, he'd see that hateful creature torn apart. Piecemeal! Rising from the ashes of all he once was, Damon felt the last vestiges of Kaylan die with his beloved Dallia. The dark monster that was Damon had been summoned and now *only* Damon remained! Only Damon was needed for Damon was the only one that could slay this grotesque abomination!

Charles W. McDonald Jr.

The crisp, cool, ocean-water-laden air made even her undead flesh tingle with anticipation as she watched from a good hundred-and-fifty paces away, as she had managed to do something far worse than kill her nemesis. She'd broken who he was. She liked this broken version of Damon better. It suited him better, as she prepared herself with protection spell after protection spell, expecting his retaliation. That was perfect. She was prepared for that. She'd been preparing for this for months! She had something special in mind for Damon—just as special as what she'd prepared for his pitiful, half-breed outcast of a wife. "That's right, Damon. Come get your revenge. Come to me. I have something for you."

Giving no thought to where he was, or even that others were not used to seeing anything like this, Damon used his *Telekinesis* to lift his body in the air on mighty unseen hands of retribution. They propelled him forward, at an altitude some thirty spans in the air, toward his collision with destiny. One protection spell after another shot forth from Damon's robes into his right hand as he discarded each after casting them in quick succession, rapidly closing the gap between him and Chara.

She'd been in combat with Damon many times before but had never seen him use the tactic of an aerial assault on her before. *Fine. So be it, Damon! Come for me! I'm here, and I'm not running! Besides, what goes up, can also be more easily brought down….*

Casting *Far Reaching*, Damon quickly followed with *Damon's Sonic Blight*, causing a massive thunderclap out of a misty, ethereal, cold sky as he directed a cone of violent sonic energy right at Chara, watching it bifurcate all around her invisible shell of protection, carving jagged craters of earth where she stood, upending her body several spans into the air. Not even waiting for her body to land, he cast *Damon's Invoking Storm*, sending Chara's body through a violent hail of lightning bolts exploding out of the ground at her even before she landed with a crushing thud. Blistering straight through all her protections, one bolt after another had charred her body—sizzling her undead flesh, keeping her body in violent convulsions suspended above ground, as she continued to get hit one after the other, until her body stopped moving after some twenty direct hits.

Now in a smoking heap on the ground, Chara still managed to open her

Charles W. McDonald Jr.

eyes in a jolt, just in time to see Damon floating above her some thirty paces in the air, and forty paces away. Gathering herself quickly, Chara cast her surprise for Damon as she felt the cold finger of death—or rather undeath—release from her right index finger in an invisible beam of doom that crept towards her arch nemesis, like unto solar waves radiating off the desert.

The sudden and unexpected sense of chilled death crept over every part of Damon's body as he plummeted to the ground, losing consciousness on the way down. He was vaguely aware of people from Wessex coming to see what wicked violence was becoming of their peaceful countryside. Blackness!

The lithe and beautiful, young, raven-haired foreigner crashed to the lush green grass below, bleeding profusely from her trachea where Chara had left her to die. A victory meal for her to savor as she watched Damon's body crash to the Earth in a defeated and broken heap.

(Damon's Manor, Kaleion, Some Weeks Later)

Damon was left still mulling over how and why he'd been left to live. Every moment of every day, when he wasn't thinking about Dallia, he was thinking about how and why Chara had let him survive. She had him right where she wanted him.

Thinking about Dallia constantly wasn't bringing her back, and each thought of her brought another knife steeped into what remained of his soul. He'd allowed himself to get soft and weak, and it had killed Dallia. His failure at *Healing* had been just as much a contributing factor to her death as was his lack of foresight to see this attack coming. Chara had the element of surprise, but he was working on a solution for that. Still, the one thing that bothered him almost as much as Dallia's death was where his medallion had gone. When he returned from Earth, it had been the only thing removed from Dallia's body—nothing else. His wife was completely intact—cold and dead, but completely undisturbed, except for the theft of his gift which symbolized his *unconditional adoration* of her.

Looking out over the majestic purple and amber hues of the Kaleion sunset over his estate, he leaned down at Dallia's headstone where he'd buried her a few weeks back, leaving another cluster of freshly gathered wildflowers to go with

Charles W. McDonald Jr.

the ones he'd picked for her yesterday. Crushing a handful of homeworld dirt in his right fist, he tossed it on Dallia's grave. "You promised me you wouldn't leave me…. And, I promised I'd protect you. I guess we both suck at keeping promises, huh?!" He used to love sunsets on his property. Now they just made him sick with loss and unending grief. "I really miss you, Love."

Turning to walk away from his wife's grave, Damon practically ran into a stunning blonde, a hand-and-a-half shorter than he in leather leggings, a leather bustier, soft leather thigh-high boots, and not much else. *Had she been watching him all this time?* He just stood there, surprised, looking at her, and *she* at him. Neither of them saying a word for the longest time. He could have sworn her eyes were gold at first, but now they were ice-blue sapphires—magnificent. She was magnificent, and he couldn't care less.

"You're still thinking about Dallia aren't you, Damon?" She broke the stalemate, never taking her beautiful eyes off his *black mirrors of the soul.*

"What else would I be thinking of?" He didn't even care enough about her to ask her name. Before Dallia he certainly would have, but there was a void inside Damon even bigger than the beautiful homeworld he so loved.

"You know even if you kill Chara, she could be brought back?" Her eyes examining every part of the man who used to be Damon. Whoever he was now.

No, he didn't know that, and if anyone could bring back Chara—regardless of why—*why couldn't they bring back Dallia?* "Who would do such a thing, and why?"

"To cause you more suffering." Again she watched him from a distance. Gauging him. Carefully.

"I deserve to suffer." His reply was as instant as his confidence in that fact. He did deserve to suffer! He was a monster! And his punishment had come home to roost in Dallia's violent death. At least the monster had a chance to destroy Chara! But he needed time to prepare. She'd be ready for him if he came after her now. He needed to do something nearly impossibly difficult right now. He needed to show some *patience* in his revenge.

"Chara succeeded in breaking you. That's clear for all to see. But, you can't let her win, Damon."

"LOOK AROUND," Damon exclaimed, motioning to Dallia's grave. "SHE'S ALREADY WON!" His black eyes were as weary as his body. Dejected. Sullen. And still *very* broken.

Her assessment of him had already returned a verdict before his last comments, but now…. "Maybe you're not who I thought you were." She was no longer confident he could become the man he was meant to be. The man she *needed* him to be. An unbreakable force forged in a *cauldron of hate*.

"Sorry to disappoint.... And who is that, anyway...? And, who the fuck are you? What do you want, and why are you on my property?"

"That's a lot of questions...." She only closed the gap between them by one full step, but it was enough for him to smell her intoxicating scent as she watched his nostrils flex, filling completely with her scent, as she took his hands into hers, delicately, slowly, non-threateningly. "You're the Dark Knight of Magic. I...am Banthis. I want you to be able to find and know happiness again, and I'm here because you won't leave your property. You haven't left your house since you came back to bury your wife."

He nodded, knowing she was correct. *But how does she know all this about me?* He'd let himself get soft and careless. He needed to be more careful now than ever. He was vulnerable, and he'd been...fortunate to survive. If he could call surviving fortunate. "Yeah, well the Dark Knight of Magic isn't in the mood for sex, so you might want to put some clothes on, Banthis."

Suddenly she was wearing an embroidered gold dress with silver and blue threads holding the dress together all the way up the front, though loose all the way down below her heavy breasts. Okay, now he was curious. "Banthis, *what* are you?"

"I'm the one you can always count on for the truth, Damon. Even if it's a truth you don't want to hear."

"Not really an answer."

"Very well, what would you have me tell you that you would believe...? You don't believe in what I am." It was true. Damon's belief systems didn't leave room for an afterlife. He wasn't even sure, as expert he was in the topic, if the soul were immortal or not. His beliefs had been shaped by horrific events, then obliterated, then misshapen again. She knew it would take time, and a great deal of her curation of him, for Damon to see clearly things as they really were. And ever could be....

"Why are you really here, and what do you really want, Banthis?"

"Damon, I'm really here to help you destroy Chara in a way she can't ever be brought back. Are you interested in what I have to tell you?"

"I'm listening, Banthis. How can we do this?"

"The book you've been studying for the last few months to make your present for your wife—The *Book of Souls* you took from the Steward of Engêstal some years ago; there are answers in that book."

"What answers?"

"Answers that can help you...help me contain Chara...permanently!

Charles W. McDonald Jr.

Would you like me to show you how?"

"What's in it for you, Banthis?"

"Damon, I think there is an opportunity for both of us to help one another achieve what we both want. What is your revenge of Dallia's death *worth* to you?"

"Everything! ANYTHING!" *Why did he feel like he was a game piece being maneuvered on a much bigger board he couldn't fully see?*

"Good, now let's go take a look at that book, so I can show you something you might have missed...." Coiling her beautiful arm in his in much the way Dallia had done only weeks before, Banthis and Damon walked side by side up the hill to the back entrance of Damon's manor as cool, blue flames left Banthis' footprints in Damon's immaculately manicured lawn, tracing their way all the way down to Dallia's grave where they were halted in their tracks by an unseen barrier before they were allowed to desecrate Dallia's remains.

(Damon's Former Estate, Kaleion, Present Day)

He swore he'd never come back, and while he'd made stipulations that made it technically not a violation of his solemn word to be back, he still cursed himself for coming back to the barren landscape that he once called home. His soft, black leather boots crunched on the dead grass that was more dirt than anything else, as he looked down at the gaping chasm that used to be the subterranean chambers of his estate. Tossing a handful of dirt down into the massive hole, he counted to thirty before he heard the first pebbles hit bottom.

Looking around at the sunset he once loved—at least it was only one sun now—he noticed the massive smoke plumes of fires burning almost everywhere he looked. Morden, and he, had done quite the job of destroying Kaleion. Off in the distance he could hear screams, but it didn't deter him from doing what he'd come to do.

Feeling the *Telekinesis* hands lift his body, carrying it over the chasm toward Dallia's grave, he allowed those unseen hands to gently set him down by what remained of her headstone—now cracked and shattered with one half leaning backward almost all the way to the ground. He hadn't had the heart to move or disturb her grave when he moved his estate, but now....

Standing there morose, in full mage regalia and carrying the mighty staff Dallia had made for him, the words came out slow and very...painfully, "I...

Charles W. McDonald Jr.

missed...you, Love." Everywhere he walked on these grounds he felt Dallia, because Dallia was still here, and it just wasn't the same on Eden without her. He could move every scrap of the subterranean levels, along with every scrap of the manor, and it still wasn't enough for him to feel her presence...except when.... *Hmmm, he'd have to examine that when he returned.*

"I told you once that I couldn't carry on without you. Well, I'm here, *carrying* on...." Searching for the words, Damon was struggling as the memories came crashing in on him one after the other. Immortality had its drawbacks. "A big part of carrying on without you was because I still had you with me—even if it was just your remains. It was still you, and it helped me. Others could leave this place without looking back. I couldn't...because you were here, and I was there, so I've come to take you to our new home...if that's okay with you." Resting his right hand on her headstone, realizing how long it had been since he'd placed flowers on Dallia's grave, he chastised himself internally. Cursing himself.

The tether he'd made in secret, suddenly snapping back on him like a rubber band across the light years of distance between worlds, snapped him out of his forlorn and deserved guilt. "Nooooooo," Damon snarled, hastily forming a *Portal* and ripping the air in front of him as he practically ran through it with his *Staff of the Invoker*, knowing he'd have to come back for Dallia another time.

Charles W. McDonald Jr.

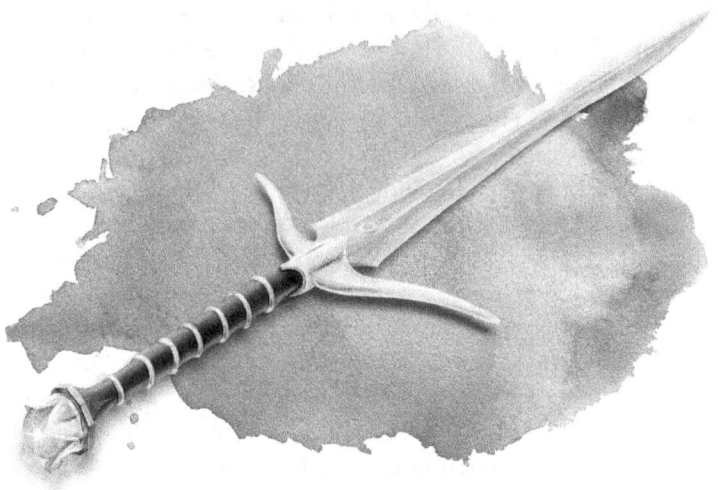

Chapter 55: The Death of Men – Part II

(Exeter, Perion, Present Day)

Brigance turned to face the hastily formed *Portal*, greeting a bruised, bloodied, and battered Radin, Michelle, Lawna, and Wraith. The look on his face said he wasn't all that shocked. He knew they'd left looking for a fight. Well, it looked like they were successful in their quest! At least they'd all returned. At least they were all still among the living. He supposed that was something positive....

"I assume the other one looks worse off," Brigance offered, managing a half-smile for them, though he didn't have the best news to report to them.

"He got away," Michelle pre-empted Radin before he'd had a chance to say anything, catching him with his mouth open. That earned a glare from Radin, followed by a flourish, prompting her to finish her report. "Sorry," she offered Radin. "...He'd seen enough and smartly decided to run. We couldn't tell where. He covered his tracks pretty well."

"Yes, well, now we know a lot more about Morden, and Damon's advice proved both helpful and accurate," Radin concluded, looking around the grounds.

Brigance wasn't sure if Radin had added that last part for his benefit or not, but he had news that they weren't going to like. "Yes, well, Talemar took a raiding party of our best men to help Royvan Miral. I haven't seen or heard from him since he left several days ago. We haven't heard from Royvan Miral in some months. We've managed to sustain eighty-five percent of our combined forces after our battle with Eldrac, but we won't be able to maintain them much longer. At this rate, there simply isn't enough food, money, and resources left on this planet to sustain such a force."

Making a smooth and vertical motion from high above his head down to his kneecaps, Radin produced a series of four chests of treasure landing with such a thud onto the crisped, dead grass of Exeter that it was nearly enough to make them shatter as two of them tilted when they landed, spilling over.

Brigance had seen that type of magic before. He thought they'd called that a *Gate*, but he'd never seen it operated like that from a remote site. Clearly Radin was growing even more powerful, and he wondered just how much of that was coming from within versus coming from…Damon. "Yes, well, that doesn't solve the food problem." He wasn't trying to be a pain in Radin's ass, nor be disrespectful or ungrateful, but this was a real issue, and, from a leadership perspective, they needed all hands on deck working the problem, or this army was doomed to disburse to the four corners of the Blood Night world.

Raised eyebrows from Radin at Brigance's comments, but he understood. They had a big army, so they had big, army-sized problems. *Could Damon help him with the food and provisions problem?* He'd have to ask. Looking around at the hundreds of military encampment tents scattered all over the estate grounds that had been killed by the Blood Night, he'd forgotten how barren his homeworld had become, but seeing Kaleion not much better off, his eyes were now fully open to the scope and scale of Damon's Master Plan. Of course, he couldn't say for sure if the End Times coming to all these worlds of Humanity simultaneously was Damon's doing or not, but it definitely had a contributing role to play. Looking to the dying tree line off to the northeast, he wondered how much game remained to hunt and how much longer they had before food would become so scarce as to cause them all to die of starvation before Damon's plan had time to run its course. "No news of the Second Seal then?"

"None. Not a word!" Brigance scratched his gruff and weathered beard, shifting in his softer and more manageable leather field armor—clearly not expecting real combat any time soon, but he still looked the part of a battle-hardened general keeping the mechanics of his army together.

"I'd like to see Elise. Is she around?" Radin's eyes darted around between the group, wondering what they thought of his relationship with Elise, but at the end of the day, you couldn't please everyone, and he knew that. They'd just have to live with it the way it was—however that was. He was just as confused about his

Charles W. McDonald Jr.

relationship with Elise as they were.

"I believe she's in her quarters. She spends most of her time in there and doesn't come out much at all. We've been making sure she's been given extra rations for the baby." Brigance's lips pursed on that last word, but he quickly forced a smile for Radin as soon as he realized it.

"I'll be back," Radin replied, starting off toward the main entrance…and Elise.

"You don't want to clean up," Lawna prompted, calling after Radin. "Geez, you don't want to send her into shock with the baby and all!"

Looking down at the cuts all over his pants and exposed, bloodied parts of his body, he realized that going directly to Elise like this probably wasn't the best idea. "Thanks," he offered, looking back at Lawna before continuing toward the main entrance, but to his quarters this time, to get cleaned up.

Lawna just shook her head, looking between Michelle, Wraith, and Brigance. *At least he was learning,* she thought. *Sort of.*

* * * *

A knock at Elise's door shook her out of her reflective moment of thought. She'd found it hard to think of much anything other than Michael since Radin had proven her worst fears realized when he gripped Excalibur only to see it not respond to him at all. "Come," she breathed aloud in a soft, exhausted tone. *Was it the baby draining all her energy?* She couldn't tell anymore. She was so emotionally drained—just completely cried out, until little else inside her remained, save the baby.

"Can I come in," Radin asked, peeking his head around the door to see her resting on the bed with her upper body propped up by a bunch of pillows.

"Sure." She didn't really want to talk to him, but he was the father of their baby. She still had feelings for him, but it was…*complicated.* She was as much to blame for the disintegration of their relationship as he was, if not more. She knew that, and it gnawed at her in the very rare moments she wasn't thinking of Michael. Still, she missed him, and she couldn't help but feel butterflies in his presence— butterflies she hadn't felt since he'd left.

Shutting the door behind them for some privacy, he slowly closed the distance between them physically and emotionally, offering, "I missed you. You look great by the way."

She didn't want to smile, but he drew it out of her regardless, with his rugged good looks and scruffy half-smile. "You look like you just cleaned up after a school-yard fight." She motioned to the cuts and bruises all over his face and the dirt he'd failed to clean from his hair.

"Yeah. Well. Sorry about that. I tried to...." *What was he doing here? What did he want?* He chastised himself internally, thinking of all this beautiful woman was going through and all she'd already been through—all that she was still about to go through with this new baby. He didn't even have the strength for it. He didn't even know how she could have the strength for it, and yet she was doing it. "I wanted to end all the secrets between us. I wanted to start over—like meeting you for the first time. Even after our last talk, I'm still confused about us. I don't know what to do. I don't want our baby to be a complication between us. I want it to be the miracle it was intended to be."

"The miracle *he* was intended to be," she corrected him aloud. There was really no point in secrets between them anymore. It wasn't useful or helpful for them *or* the baby.

There it was. Radin was going to have a boy. He'd have to let that sink in for a while. "How do you know?"

"Damon told me." Her eyes flashed at him. Accusatory in their own right, as if to say, 'if you talked to me a little more, you'd know these things.'

"Damon came to see you. Why? What else did he say?"

She didn't like that Radin seemed more interested in Damon than her.

Another knock at the door announced Brigance looking around the doorway to Radin's shock. Brigance didn't come knocking on doors personally unless it was important—otherwise he'd have sent a runner.

"What is it, General?" Radin looked between them, trying to manage a smile for Elise.

Grabbing her kneecap comfortingly, Radin offered Elise a parting smile, only to feel her grasping his wrist before he could pull away from her.

"I'm ready to tell you everything. No more secrets," she told him softly, not wanting her voice to carry to the doorway. "I want that for us...and our baby," she offered, letting him go.

"I'll be back. It's going to be okay. I promise." He didn't know what business he had making promises he wasn't even certain he could keep.

His smile was disarming, but she struggled internally, trying to map out the best way to continue their prior conversation and tell him the rest of her secrets that she had kept to herself all this time. *He deserved to know everything. Maybe it would allow them to start over—if there truly was such a thing. Maybe it would help settle her decision of whether to stay or to go.* There was no Michael anymore. He was gone, so she was leaning toward bringing her children to be with her and Radin wherever

Charles W. McDonald Jr.

they chose to live. Though she doubted very much that could, or should, be Perion or Kaleion, given what she'd seen and heard. A pensive smile from her , communicated her hope for their future when he looked back at her. Looking back was a good sign. It meant she was on his mind. Closing the door behind him, Radin followed the very serious Brigance to the map room.

*   *   *   *

His eyes went to the objects in Royvan Miral's hands—one of stone in his left and one of wood in his right—not knowing what to expect. Radin hadn't seen Royvan Miral in many months, when he left him explicit instructions to find the Second Seal no matter the outcome of the Battle of Axum. There he stood, eye to eye with his destiny in Royvan Miral's hands, and all he could do was question… everything! All his decisions. All his orders. All his plans. Radin knew himself a mountain of doubt and uncertainty for what to do next, but others were counting on him. *He* broke the Scroll of Carnac and uttered the words of God the Creator. The great unmaking begun by his own hand, whether influenced by Damon or not. And he knew it was *his* personal burden to make it right.

"He hasn't let go of the scrolls since we found them," a crowned Talemar offered, knowing the weight of those cylinders to be far greater than their wood and stone would account. "I offered to take them. But after hearing what you'd been through, he refused. He's been saving them for you."

A hard gulp from Royvan Miral as he closed the gap between himself and Radin, one very deliberate step at a time. Extending his left hand toward Radin, who just stood there, blinking and aware of the heavy burden about to befall him, Royvan couldn't let go of the stone cylinder. His hands had been clutching it so tightly for so long at the warning of Daedrin, that he too now feared the judgment of Mankind upon himself.

"It's okay," Radin offered, taking Royvan's left hand and carefully prying the stone cylinder loose from it. "Talk to me. Tell me what you know of this…and the other."

"Death," Royvan replied simply. "Death of Men," he added, shaking his head in the unknown of the moment.

"Can you help me out here," Radin asked, looking to Talemar for some greater level of explanation.

"The man who showed us the location of the scrolls, the true location of Osalin—I don't know if he was a guardian or what, but he warned us that we would be judged by Mankind and by God the Creator himself for breaking those

Seals and uttering those words within. He questioned whether or not we had the hatred in us to do such a thing, for this was the death of all men, or their salvation, depending on one's perspective."

"I can't say I like the way that sounds," Radin countered, looking at the stone cylinder in his hands, attempting to read its multi-lingual inscriptions. "What…." His doubt felt like an anvil around his neck as he rolled the cylinder in his hands, examining every line, every rune, and every symbol. He had made the decision to open the First Seal nearly alone with almost everyone else in dissenting opinion. He didn't want to make the same mistake twice. "What would you have me do with this?"

She wasn't sure what to expect, but she wanted to see Radin. She missed him and didn't want him to be out of her sight. *Admitting you miss him doesn't make you a bad person. It makes you Human. Michael is gone! You need to move on!*

Rounding the corner from the east wing, she headed down the wider hall-way leading to the map and receiving rooms, and that's when she felt it. Like a cold set of fingers reaching up inside her, yanking her baby boy downward as she felt him drop in utero with fluid running down her legs, starting to stain her dress.

Talemar looked to Brigance, Royvan, and Wraith as he now joined them. "Radin…if you're asking me what I think, the answer is outside those windows and those walls. This world is dying because of what we've done." *What Radin had done*, but he didn't want to put it that way. Radin was looking for a less painful way out, and he didn't see that as an option. There was suffering, regardless of the choice to be made here. The only question was would one path of suffering lead to a bright-er future than the other. "If you're seeking an option without more suffering, I don't see it. All paths forward include suffering. There are no paths backward. Status quo means certain withering and painful death for everyone. What other choices are there?"

"When is the last time you spoke to Damon about this, and what did he say?" Wraith, as always, sought more information. He liked to mull over every-thing in detail before committing, but once committed, he was fully so.

"I don't know if Damon has the answers for us." It was an honest assess-ment from Radin, but certainly not the one they sought. Now the glances between were heavily tinged in doubt and a weighted apprehension, as Radin's fingers felt and recognized the words etched into the cylinder, saying them *only in his thoughts*.

Charles W. McDonald Jr.

Now you see the despair of the Dragon.
Yet, the Lord of Fire,
Prince of Light, brings his justice
With sword and rod, down upon all that is Unholy in Men.
With the fire in his heart
And the light in his soul
Will he bring forth the chaos and despair of the Death of Men.

"Oh God. Nooo." Elise's voice could be heard from the hallway only a few paces away as she made her way to the map room. "No. No. No. God no...." Elise stood there helpless, shaking her head, clutching at her womb as the blood of her unborn son slowly crept over her fingers.

Rushing to her side, Radin nearly skid on the floor, coming to an abrupt stop as he saw the horrific sight of blood and shattered placenta staining Elise's silver and gold dress. A pool of blood and placenta fluids crept across the wood floor toward him in an accusation of murder—the murderer of men. The Destroyer of Men.

A cacophony of wails, moans, and screams could be heard both inside and out of the Exeter manor—all of them female, as the weight of the Death of Men crept over Exeter, and then the whole of the world, resting upon Radin's shoulders.

Standing before Elise, shaking in horror at what he'd done, Radin crushed the stone cylinder in his hands, contemplating suicide. *You just killed your own son!*

Talemar, Wraith, and Brigance skidded to a stop right beside Radin, looking at each other in shock and horror, none of them knowing what to say or do as the air rent right beside them with silvery-blue slashes of light.

"*Move*," Damon ordered, rushing to Elise as he set his right hand upon her womb, probing her deep with his Arcane, looking for his grandson and finding only horror. "THIS IS WHAT YOU MEANT! OH, YE GREATEST OF HYPOCRITES!" Damon's rage filled the room, from floor to ceiling and wall to wall as he shouted in front of a gathering crowd. "*YOU disgust me!*"

Turning to Talemar, Damon ordered, "Give me your crown!"

"Damon, I want to help you, but—" Gargled, muffled sounds were the only thing escaping from Talemar now, as Damon's shadow-mourn-glare burned right through him as Damon used his *Telekinesis* to try and choke the crowned Talemar out of existence.

"TALEMAR!" Producing a massive ball of lightning in his left hand twice the size of Talemar's head, Damon warned, "Lead, follow, or get the fuck out of

Charles W. McDonald Jr.

my way! But, *you're going to give me that crown*, or I'm going to *destroy* you with it!!!" Damon assumed his *Telekinesis* could snatch it from Talemar if necessary, but he was making a point now.

Looking between Radin and Damon, Talemar knew he wasn't ready for combat with Damon. *That was suicide!* Removing the Crystal Crown from his head, he handed it directly to Damon, who in turn handed it directly to Radin. "We're going," Damon announced to Radin.

"Going where," Radin asked incredulously, looking at Elise, completely broken at the loss of her son.

"Going to make the Creator pay for his hypocrisy!"

"The Creator didn't do this, Father. I did."

There it was. For all to hear.... Father. Radin was Damon's son! And, now they all knew, as they all began looking at Radin with new, more scrutinous eyes. All his credibility. All his leadership. It was all being brought into question in that moment.

Grabbing his son by the arm, Damon ordered, "Talemar, you'll find my grandson has severe circulatory system-wide damage. Save him if you can. If I find you gave anything less than your very best effort to save my grandson, there won't be a place in this universe you'll be able to hide from me. Understood?!"

A solitary and solemn nod from Talemar said he fully understood his task and the *consequence of disappointment* that came attached to it, as Damon and Radin simply disappeared—the Crystal Crown gone with them.

Talemar was left standing beside Elise as he probed her with his Arcane, seeing, for the first time, the impossible task that lay before him, as another female scream echoed through the halls with the death of another unborn son.

*   *   *   *

Now middle of the night in Axum, where the scars of the battle from nearly a year ago appeared still fresh in the ground, the shoreline, and the Rune Stones of the sacred ground, father and son—blackened and blinded by hate—hastily appeared on the war-wounded landscape.

"Why are we here, Father? What's happening? Why did you take me from Elise? I need to help her. I CAN help her! I should at least *try!*"

"Trust me when I tell you, Radin, you'll never be able to live with yourself if you try to save your son and fail." The words came with the look of experience behind Damon's *black mirrors of the soul.* Damon was right, and Radin knew it down to his very bones.

Charles W. McDonald Jr.

"Talemar won't summon the Chairman.... And, I can't. You have to do it," Damon informed cryptically.

"Summon the Chairman? Help me understand, Father. I don't know who the Chairman is."

"Yes, you do," Damon replied flatly and with absolute certainty, looking into the eyes of his son. "You've seen the pure light with the lake of crystal and the booming voice from the other side. You've seen it. You've seen him standing beside that booming voice. THAT is the Chairman. You knew him. You just didn't know that you knew him."

Shaking his head. *How does Damon know about these visions? What personal revenge of Damon's am I about to carry out in the sake of retribution for my unborn son?* "It's going to be difficult enough winning back trust with what I've done. They may never trust me again. What are you asking of me?"

"The Creator needs to understand he can't keep hurting the people he so claims to love. I'm the only one that can punish him for this and only if you summon the immortal shell of the Chairman. I can't do it, and Talemar won't. It's up to you, Radin. I need you to trust me. I need you to believe in your father. And, I need to punish the Creator for destroying your son—my only grandson. Are you with me, my son?"

"I'm with you, Father. *I do* believe in you." *Forgive me*, he contemplated, looking to the heavens. *Forgive me for what I'm about to do.*

"Then summon the Chairman. Summon him. Summon him. Summon him." Damon chanted in both anger and disgust, nearly hopping at the chance to vent out his righteous retribution.

Having never seen Damon like this before, Radin struggled carrying out the reprisal they both sought. *When had retribution ever yielded a better tomorrow?* But, all his thoughts were of Elise, and what used to be his living son inside her. Only the blackness remained inside him, as well as the memories of the one who risked everything and came to save him when he needed help the most, as he put on the Crystal Crown, reaching to the sky as he called out to Heaven in a voice not his own, to cancel his debt with Damon.

Charles W. McDonald Jr.

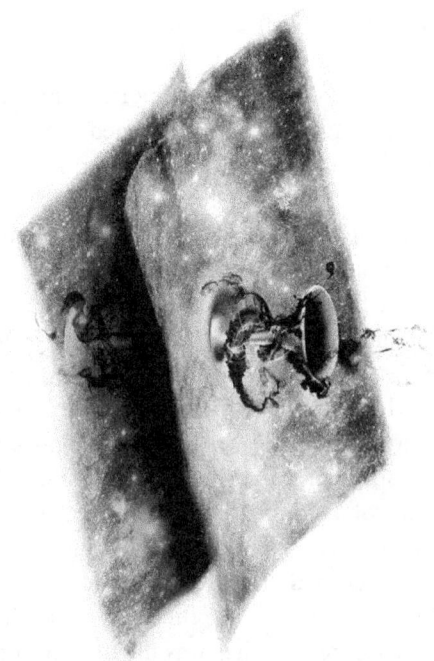

Epilogue: A Seminal Moment

(Axum, Perion, Present Day)

"I hope you can learn to forgive me, my son."

"Forgive you for what?" Damon never asked for forgiveness…for anything! *What is he doing?*

"Your friends were right about me. I *am* a monster." Casting *Far Reaching 3*, Damon reached out to all the Zero-Point he could find, going out thousands of miles in all directions as he cast *A Throne of Souls Mode 5* for the first time ever, causing a massive, charcoal-blue, radiant beam of energy to burst forth from the *Staff of the Invoker*, arcing out high in the sky—northeast and well beyond the horizon.

*   *   *   *

Charles W. McDonald Jr.

(Exeter, Perion, Moments Later)

Listening to the last of the status reports of his division's colonels, Rowarc was still trying to understand what had happened. Some forty percent of his expectant fathers reported their wives suddenly going into distress and having horrible miscarriages that defied all explanation, leaving Rowarc with only one lasting thought. *This is the end of all things.* It was coming for them, and nothing could possibly prepare them for it.

Tossing his tent flap to the side, and hurriedly exiting to salutes, he barely made it halfway to the manor's entryway when he heard a sudden thunderclap smashing into the encampment behind him. Pivoting just in time to see his entire division—some four thousand men in all—engulfed in a massive charcoal-blue aura, with screams and howls barely escaping the aura before it vanished, leaving only the tents, fires, equipment…and ash. Thousands of individual piles of ash, all of them in the shape of a symbol—a center-filled pentangle inside a pentagram inside a pentagon inside a circle. Over four thousand men—gone in an instant!!!

Rowarc had to stand there for a long moment before his combat senses kicked in, causing him to start walking the tents to see if he could find *any* of his men still alive. One tent after another was filled with nothing but ash and equipment—some with warm food in the process of being consumed. Making a symbol he hadn't made in decades, his thoughts and prayers called out skyward to the maker of all things as he fell to his knees, asking, *if this is the end, please take me now lest I see even more death.*

*   *   *   *

(Axum, Perion, Moments Later)

The amount of energy flooding him was beyond measure as he visibly watched the *Staff of the Invoker* nearly buckle—its rods expanding outward almost to the point where they couldn't flex back. He tried to steady himself as the souls came crashing inward on him by the hundreds, circling and bursting through his chest continuously, one after the other after the other, almost endlessly. He felt the energy of thousands of new souls collectively resonating throughout his body from the tips of his toes to the ends of his black bangs.

Watching the ancient and still quite capable disciple of the Creator descend from the midnight-darkened Blood Night sky on amber trumpets of light, Damon knew his anger and haste with *A Throne of Souls* had him unbalanced, but

Charles W. McDonald Jr.

he had the advantage. And now he had the power. He was as ready as he'd ever be for this ancient score that needed settling.

Landing softly and gracefully—between Damon and Radin—on the battle-scarred field of once lush green grass now poisoned and blistered by the Blood Night, the Chairman's golden-white robes with iridescent mantle glistened in the mixture of colors from the light of the twin moons, the blackness of the night, the pale-redness of the Blood Night, and the amber trumpets of his mighty arrival. Carrying only a high mountain ash walking cane, a soft, brown leather satchel slung to his left side, and an ancient shofar, his grayish-white beard down to his sternum along with his weathered and aged face belied his abilities and his health. He was in his prime, and Damon knew it. Keeping himself pointed only toward Damon, the Chairman answered his summons, "You have misused your talents and your son's by calling me here, Damon."

"I can stand no more of your master's hypocrisy, and I am calling you here to answer for it! I let you live after Dallia. I let you live after Mira. I let you live after Seren. YOU WILL ANSWER FOR THIS ABOMINATION OF PROPHESY!!! Who is this God the Creator and what right does he have to cause so much death and suffering?!" The *Staff of the Invoker's* hemispherical aura swelled to thousands of miles as it reached into Perion's stratosphere in preparation to prosecute Damon's personal indictment of God the Creator. Of the mighty Father of the Beginnings.

Shifting his shofar from his left hand to his right, the Chairman looked into and across the timelines of Creation, seeing all possible outcomes of this moment, answering, "Very well, Damon. I am here to answer for the perceived crimes of my master. What would you have me say? Your pain, most-shadow, cuts deep and vexing, my child, I don't know where to begin to assuage you of what you already know as truth. We forgive you, Damon.... For what you must do...I forgive you. But...," he paused looking at Damon eye to eye, "...things are not as you see them. Your hatred and anger has blinded you to the truth. *I* am not your enemy."

His mouth twisting in anger, in hatred, in bitterness most-dark, swallowing hard the wrongs done upon him age upon age, his only thoughts of Dallia and her broken grave, "I don't want your forgiveness, Prince of Egypt.... I've come for your soul," Damon whispered to the coldness between them. Casting *Amplify*, quickly followed by *Damon's Blistering Hatred*—an expanding conical beam of chilled blackness and death, with lightning bolts chasing down the outer perimeter of the cone, directly struck the Chairman square in the chest.

Charles W. McDonald Jr.

Seeing the child's anger shepherd the thousands of captured souls about his upper body like a great weapon of *hate*, he knew his fate, but the thrill of combat after so many millennia called to his pride...and his power as he readied his mighty shofar.

Feeling the lightning strikes all over his chest simultaneous with the chilled fingers of death crawling over every particle of his immortal shell, the Prince of Egypt fell to his knees in anguish at Damon's first powerful volley as he put the ancient shofar to his lips.

The conical wave of deafening sound cut through Damon's shields in an instant, blistering the night air so much it made ripples in the air, as it caused Damon's eardrums to explode completely, knocking him to his knees. Damon faltered as he desperately sought a level of balance that would keep him from falling over. *Another hit like that might just kill you,* he thought. *Stop toying with him! They're never going to understand what justice is unless you show it to them! NOW!*

Casting *Damon's Unrelenting Hate*, he watched the fifty fireballs simultaneously explode all around the Chairman, followed by the timed release of explosive gases turning to acid, as he prepared the *Shields* he hoped would save his life if it backfired on him again. Rising vapor from the fifty explosions quickly turned to liquid acid, falling to the ground all around the Chairman, suddenly exploding hundreds upon hundreds as each acid droplet touched the ground, blowing the Chairman's body backward into the air.

It finally worked, he thought with the briefest of smiles as he watched the shofar touch the Chairman's lips again. *Shit!*

Watching from what he hoped was a safe distance, near the shoreline of the South Sea, Radin was conflicted. *What was the right thing to do?* He heard Damon's justification and felt it. Every part of him screamed with hatred—crying out for justice that was not there, though he questioned whether any level of killing or retribution was justice enough.

Clearly Damon had grown *far* more powerful, and that evolution had been necessary, but as the explosions all around him ripped into his flesh and crushed his skeleton internally from the concussive force, but he still had a little fight left in his immortal shell. Blown backward from the last set of hundreds of explosions, he could barely hold on to the shofar, let alone pull it to his lips, but a last prayer out to his master gave him strength as he blew the last breath of air he had into the

Charles W. McDonald Jr.

ancient shofar of his heritage.

He couldn't hear anything, and was bleeding profusely from his ears and nose, but he saw the ripple coursing through the crisp midnight air as he pulled the old crest from his robes, holding it in his left hand as he hung on for dear life to the *Staff of the Invoker* with his right, casting *Portal* behind him and *A Throne of Souls Mode 4* simultaneously in front of him.

He barely had time to see the Prince of Egypt's immortal shell blown to ash and carried on the winds of his previous explosion, just before the shofar's concussive force ripped through his robes and his chest, blowing him backward through the *Portal* to Austin and he hoped…to Mira.

(Damon's House, Austin, TX, Earth, Present Day)

She didn't necessarily enjoy being back in school again after already having gone through it, but she had to keep up appearances, and she needed to get some answers for Damon and his black hole problem or else he was really going to be on to her.

Running late for class, as usual, her butt itched in her taut Lucky® brand jeans. She probably needed to wash them again to soften them up, but right now her stomach growled angrily at her neglectfulness to feed herself. There certainly wouldn't be time for eating over the next ten hours, with her heavy Tuesday and Thursday eighteen-hour class load. Tapping her heels while she waited for the ting of the microwave to present her with breakfast, she flipped through her phone, reading the latest Facebook® posts—most of them wanting pictures of Damon and her together. As if Damon was going to let that happen.

Suddenly what Mira knew as a *Portal* burned through the air between the door to the garage and the kitchen island. Hearing a thunderous cacophony of sound blaring through the *Portal*, Mira was blown backwards into the living room just in time to see Damon's blistered body thrown into the island's framework so hard he almost broke it in half, as he skidded to a stop along the floor between the kitchen and living room just inches from her.

"Damon! Oh my God!" Mira scooted her body over to his, turning him over from his face-down position to face up at her, while his body leaned up against the destroyed drywall beneath the island countertops. "Damon, I need you

Charles W. McDonald Jr.

to talk to me." Running her hands over him, looking for more wounds, she found the four-inch hole in his chest that looked like it had been cut with some sort of energy weapon. The hole in his chest was already cauterized, and his breathing was very shallow. All she could think about was losing the one man in her life that gave her the scorching and addictive love she craved for her survival. And that was unacceptable!

"Talk to me, Damon. I don't know how to fix this." She thought about calling 911, but he didn't have that kind of time left, and what would they say about these wounds even if they could save him?!

That's when she saw it…. As the strength left Damon's body, his left hand began to release its grip on the seal of a pale-pink rose with white leaves on a tan, clay-cast circle; it dropped to the floor—rolling from the kitchen toward the living room. She'd seen Damon use these before.

"Hang on, Damon. I'll be right back." Seizing up the seal with her left hand, then rushing to get a hammer from the toolbox in the garage, she was back in a flash. She slammed the seal onto what remained of the island's granite countertop, pulling the hammer high above her as Damon exhaled a final breath…his *Black Mirrors of the Soul* now extinguished….

A great thunderclap preceded Banthis' arrival in all her leathery, ribbed-winged glory before Mira could bring the hammer down on the seal. Her first time seeing Banthis in the flesh, Mira was in awe of her hard body with soft curves, seemingly more forged than formed, and basking in the fire-lit, molten glow of her fiery katana.

"STOP!" The entire house crackled with an ice-cold electricity from the echo of Banthis' command, raising the hackles on every single part of Mira's body. With hair of golden silk and abyssal, reptilian-slit eyes, her ribbed-wings cupped around her protectively as she knelt over her husband, seizing the air around the room, making it thick, like unto lava obeying her will to halt all movement in the room—save hers.

Mira didn't understand how exactly, but she couldn't move—completely frozen while the creature she assumed was Banthis knelt beside Damon—whispering into his ear as if he could hear.

"It's time for you to come home, Damon," Banthis whispered into his ear, just as the ting from the Thermador® microwave wall-oven went off, causing her to turn toward the cabinets, looking for the genesis of the strange sound.

Charles W. McDonald Jr.

'Twas only a split-second distraction, but it was just enough for Mira to feel the weighty hammer free up just a little, as if to resume falling through a slip-stream in a heavy fluid, toward the seal with the pale rose and white leaves on a tan clay circle.

Like unto an earthquake, Damon's house began to shake and moan with a dark energy of a justice long overdue. Howls and screams could be heard from what seemed to come from everywhere inside the drywall.

A standing shadow now some two feet behind Banthis' immortal shell, who was now facing Mira and the garage, called out to Mira with a complete ownership of her, to look upon her in all her dark majesty, just as chilled plumes of what appeared to be black smoke began to creep across every surface in the house emanating from her standing shadow. A knowing smile crept over Banthis' face, timed with her long-overdue call to home. An immortal creature of time, even Banthis' patience had proven not to be infinite.

Mira tried not to look at the dark, chilled shadow moving out from behind Banthis toward her. But as the sudden, stark night began creeping across the painted, textured walls of the living room and kitchen in amorphous gnarled fingers of shadow, Mira's starry-blue eyes grew wide in abject terror as a malignant smile crept over the face of the creature before her—owning Mira's essence from just a few feet away, compelling her to look upon her black and bleak destiny.

A great outwardly heave of the house itself followed by a contraction at its waistline—as if being squeezed by a great hand outside the house—cracked the framing and drywall right at the mid-point all around the perimeter of the common area while a great and guttural moan from the bowels of unearthly depths shattered picture frames, windows, and glass throughout the entire house. Everywhere, the sound of 2x6 wall-studs breaking under immense, abyssal pressure threatened to shatter Mira's eardrums as she was held captive and caged by this eternal debt come due.

Sultry yet reptilian eyes on a palette shadow lit by molten embers of Banthis' katana stared back at Mira, owning her soul, as Mira's right, hammer-laden hand struggled against this ancient *hate*.

To be continued....

Charles W. McDonald Jr.

End Book 2

of

A Throne of Souls

Charles W. McDonald Jr.

A Throne of Souls

Book 1: A Kingdom Forgotten Published September 2016
Book 2: Black Mirrors of the Soul Published April 2017
Book 3: The Fall of Hate Published June 2018
Book 4: The Rise of Hope Published December 2020

Look for *The Veil of White* 2017
The Epic Conclusion of
A Throne of Souls ®2016
Anticipated Late 2022

Charles W. McDonald Jr.

Thank you for reading *Black Mirrors of the Soul*. I hope you enjoyed it immensely, and I would be greatly honored for you to leave a review of your thoughts and impressions on either the channel of purchase and/or Goodreads. Self-published authors live and die by reviews. So, I would strongly encourage you to take a moment to leave an honest review and would greatly appreciate your time in doing so. I welcome any, and all, constructive, positive-intent feedback and would love to hear from you.

Please feel free to contact me at:
http://www.facebook.com/throneofsouls
https://www.facebook.com/royvanmiral/
https://www.athroneofsouls.com
Parler @CharlesMcDonald
Twitter @athroneofsouls
https://pilled.net/#/profile/2818 (@AThroneofSouls)
Email: royvanmiral@hotmail.com
Goodreads Author Page:
https://www.goodreads.com/author/show/16002346.Charles_W_McDonald_Jr_
Amazon Author Page:
https://www.amazon.com/-/e/B01MDPEUAW
https://itunes.apple.com/us/author/charles-w-mcdonald-jr/id1198345238?mt=11

Sincerely,

Charles W. McDonald Jr.

Charles W. McDonald Jr.

About the Author:

Charles W. McDonald Jr. was born in Oklahoma City, raised in Norman, Oklahoma, and is a graduate of the University of Oklahoma with a BBA in Management Information Systems and a Minor in Economics. He also has a background in Aerospace Engineering, High Availability Systems Engineering, Disaster Recovery, Cloud Architecture (Azure, AWS, and GCP), and DevOps. Honorably discharged from the United States Air Force Reserves, he also has a background in the armed forces and is a full member of both the AFIO (Association of Former Intelligence Officers) and NDIA (National Defense Industry Association) organizations. He lives in Roanoke, TX.

In the summer of 1995, Charles read every available book on the Wheel of Time by Robert Jordan in a couple of weeks, and later that same July awoke in the middle of the night from an incredibly immersive dream. Charles began writing, by hand, everything he could remember from that dream which became the outline for the story of A Throne of Souls. Very shortly afterwards, Charles wrote Robert Jordan directly, looking for advice and inspiration for his own work, and Robert Jordan personally responded in a three-page letter, encouraging Charles to tell his story in his way, in his voice, and in his time. The completion of A Throne of Souls is a deeply personal mission for Charles to thank the spirit of Robert Jordan.

Charles W. McDonald Jr.

Glossary of Terms

†¤‡- ‚Æ‡:ˇŒ – Earth, Graelon, Kaleion, Perion, Setinon, in that order precisely. Two icons per world.

Actual – Word used to describe the person with the actual call sign. Team members are associated with a call sign, but an individual specifically assigned that call sign is referred to as call-sign actual. This is typically, though not always, the team lead of that given unit.

APEX – 25mm high explosive round designed specifically for the J-35 Joint Strike Fighter.

ARV – Alien Reproduction Vehicle. As opposed to ETV (extraterrestrial vehicle).

AWR – Allah's Waiting Room. Squirters fleeing from a contact situation will typically gather in another structure to regroup. When an airstrike is called in on said location, it's typically referred to as AWR.

Balak – Typically a mid-to-high level demon, appearing part dragon, part man, with the head of a great wolf with a squared jaw.

BFT – Blue Force Tracker, a vitally important piece of electronic field equipment identifying friendlies (via IFF – Identify Friend or Foe) and hostiles on a battlefield.

Bigot List – A Military Industrial Complex term used to describe those who are authorized to be read into an Unacknowledged Special Access Program. Usually curated by what is called "The Watch Committee." What religious order has a periodical called "The Watch Tower?" In the Book of Enoch, what were the fallen 200 angels called? Coincidence...? Something for you to think about....

BUD/S – Basic Underwater Demolition/SEAL training.

CCP – Chinese Communist Party.

Contact – Usually a directional reference to making gunfire and/or explosive contact with hostiles.

Codenames of Presidents:

    Eagle – William Jefferson Clinton
    Deacon – Jimmy Carter
    Lancer – John F. Kennedy
    Mogul – 45
    Passkey – Gerald R. Ford

Rawhide – Ronald W. Reagan

Renegade – Barak H. Obama

Searchlight – Richard M. Nixon

Scorecard – General Dwight D. Eisenhower

Supervise – Harry S. Truman

Timberwolf – George H. W. Bush (former DCI and VP)

Trailblazer – George W. Bush

Death Blossom – When a mujahid blindly sprays automatic gunfire in a contact situation.

DNA vs RNA – AGCU = RNA (adenine, guanine, cytosine, and uracil) while AGCT (adenine, guanine, cytosine, thymine) = DNA.

Durial's Eye – See the Starlight of Immortality for one of its two definitions. The other definition refers to a scaled-up model of the first definition of Durial's Eye using the crater lake atop a dormant volcano on Eden as the eye of the scaled-up divination tool itself. Illirian Starfire was the Guardian of *Durial's Eye* until she gave it to Damon in *The Fall of Hate*. She described it to Damon in this manner, "You, of all people, are the one most like Durial, Damon. You work closely with both magic and technology, and Durial's Eye requires equal talent in both. Magic sees the future while technology refines the vision like a great and polished lens to a telescope."

EBEN – Extraterrestrial Biological Entities. EBEN. This is not a reference to ALL extraterrestrials, but of a particular race of extraterrestrials thought to be generally benevolent to, and establishing a working relationship with, Earth Humans.

Elian – A mostly diaphanous exotic textile material manufactured only by cave elves in the World Below and Between. Its exact composition is unknown, though it is often sought after by witches for reasons not known to the general public.

Entropy – An element of the Second Law of Thermodynamics describing the linearity of time as it relates to irreversible processes and their increasing levels of entropy versus reversible processes and their constant entropy (aka isentropic processes).

https://www.grc.nasa.gov/www/k-12/airplane/thermo2.html

ETV – Extraterrestrial Vehicle.

EXFIL – Exfiltrate, to leave or exit/egress a hostile zone of action.

Charles W. McDonald Jr.

Ferian – A dead language on Perion derived from Aramaic and Latin.

Forkettè – A Perion equivalent of an invocation/elemental specialist on Kaleion.

GCP – Global Consciousness Project (http://noosphere.princeton.edu/). Research data leveraged in the chapter 'Presentiment.'

Goat Trail – A fucked-up road, usually dirt, gravel, or mostly rubble from being bombed to dust.

Intelligence Categories and Terms:

    COMINT – Communications Intelligence

    DCI – Director of Central Intelligence. Usually, but not always synonymous with MJ-1.

    ELINT – Electronics Intelligence

    FISINT – Foreign Instrumentation Signals Intelligence; FISINT is intelligence from the interception of foreign electromagnetic emissions.

    GEOINT – Geospatial Intelligence

    HUMINT – Human Intelligence

    IMINT – Image(s) Intelligence; often inclusive of GEOINT.

    INTSUM – Intelligence Summary

    SIGINT – Signals Intelligence; often inclusive of COMINT and FISINT.

    MASSINT – Measurement and Signatures Intelligence; often inclusive of TELINT, SIGINT, and IMINT.

    OSINT – Open-Source Intelligence

    TELINT – Telemetry Intelligence

Goyim – A term of derision used by the Jesuits Watchtower (the Elite of the Jesuits) and Khazarian Mafia (The New World Order / Illuminati / Luciferian Cabal) to refer to the 99+% of the population, whom they do not consider worthy of having progeny or owning property of any kind.

The Haedron – See map of Kaleion. This is a sacred place with a great stone in an immense crater, presumed to have fallen from the stars and yet did not shatter or explode upon impact, suggesting its structure is incredibly dense. Perhaps more so than even iron.

Lamean – A mage on Kaleion, Graelon, or Terran system. This word is commonly associated with the general ability to cast Arcane on Perion.

Looking Glass – The US Airborne Command and Control System in

Charles W. McDonald Jr.

place 24-7-365, intended to provide a real-time, national backup to the NCA and NMCC should those ground-based systems be destroyed or rendered inoperable. In the event those ground-based systems are destroyed or rendered inoperable, the NCA would transition to the Looking Glass in real time and provide options for an immediate tactical or strategic response at the discretion of US Government Civilian Command and Control (POTUS and the National Security Team). There are actually several Looking Glass aircraft, but one is airborne at all times of the day and night protecting the United States of America and its interests around the world.

LZ – Landing Zone.

M-249/SAW – Fully-automatic-tactical-weapon-carrying member of the Teams.

MCCC - The MCCC is comprised of High-Altitude Electronic Pulse (HEMP) hardened tractor trailers enclosing a secure Command and Control (C2) network operations and communications center. The MCCC platform must be sustained to provide survivable and endurable C2 of strategic and space forces for situation monitoring, tactical warning, force management, force direction, and decision support. In addition, this contract will provide for internal integration among platform network and communication systems, as well as for external integration of these systems with other C2 systems (e.g., MILSATCOM, GCCS, and the like).(Sourced: https://www.fbo.gov/index?s=opportunity&mode=-form&id=562422c06e7019192fbe943ad51ecaf7&tab=core&_cview=1)

National Command Authority (NCA) – Within the US Government, the NCA represents the lawful and final source for any and all use of military orders, especially as they relate to the US nuclear arsenal.

National Institute of Discovery Sciences (NIDS) – A Robert Bigalow investigative unit (Est. 1994) of scientists and subject matter experts engaged in analyzing paranormal events and deriving hard, applied sciences from them. This unit dispenses with the minutiae of whether or not extraterrestrials exist. They know they do…. Their (NIDS) focus is on gaining access to metamaterials and Close Encounters of the Second Kind artifacts from which to conduct real, applied sciences to them and gain a working knowledge of how these things work in the larger whole. They have produced real, tangible scientific data results, which have been purchased by the DIA and shared on the official, secured DIA file share system for internal use and further diagnosis.

Charles W. McDonald Jr.

National Military Command Center (NMCC) – Within the US Military, the NMCC has three primary missions: 1) generate Emergency Action Messages directed to the battlefield; 2) provide solution/response options to the Joint Chiefs of Staff in response to attacks on Americans/American interests/assets around the world; 3) provide a strategic watch component monitoring nuclear weaponized activity around the world in real time.

Nuclear Command and Control Systems (NCCS) – The collective infrastructure of assets, systems, resources, and agencies that supports the President of the United States and his military chain of command with the ability to accurately direct the nation's nuclear forces in real time. The NCCS includes within its infrastructure other components and systems (ground-based, sea-based, and air-based), which include, but are not limited to, the Looking Glass/NAOC, MCCC, NMCC, NCA, and USSTRATCOM among others.

OGA – Other Government Agency (i.e. CIA).

Operator – An honored term for a special operations team member in the field.

OPORD – Operational Orders.

OSCAR MIKE – On the Move.

PCC – Pre-Combat Check.

PKM – A soviet-era general-purpose machine gun.

PLF – Programed Life Form. Typically, neutral in alignment (neither good nor evil), these semi-sentient, autonomous life forms operate similar to a cyborg but are more organic in nature.

PLUGGER – GPS Unit.

POTUS – President of the United States of America.

Raphael – Often depicted holding a staff, Raphael is considered by the three great Terran religions to be the archangel of healing but is also known to bring comfort to the dying and help transition their souls to the afterlife.

Resha – Old Tongue Ferian for The Breaker of Seals, The Destroyer of Men, and thought to be, by some, the Son of God the Creator.

Resident Identity Code Checksum – This site is designed to provide valid checksum resident identity codes for Chinese male and females. https://code-complete.com/chinaid/validids.php

Retrocausality – The concept of influencing the past from the future through communication mechanisms that cut across timelines, usually by nonlocality principles or to explain nonlocality behaviors. https://phys.org/news/2017-07-physicists-retrocausal-quantum-theory-future.html

Rose Silk – On Perion, some silkworms feed only on the nectar of roses. Their silk is often referred to as rose silk.

RPG – Rocket Propelled Grenade.

Sandbox – Operating in a theater of war associated with the Middle East or Persian Empire lands.

Shofar – A ram's-horn trumpet used by ancient Jews in religious ceremonies and in combat.

Sorians – A malevolent race of extraterrestrials, originating from the Orion star cluster and having a great empire of conquest made up of several different races from many worlds. Considered possibly synonymous with Draco and Anunnaki.

Squirter – A hostile leaving the contact zone expeditiously to avoid certain death at the hands of an Operator.

SRR – British Special Reconnaissance Regiment.

Stasis Stone – A physical gemstone imbued with the abilities to capture and maintain the immortal soul of a mortal being and to house said soul for an indefinite period of time (for safe keeping).

Staff of the Invoker – This staff was about three's—three acid-etched metal triangular helical rods, twisted in exactly three revolutions each, in a triple helix masterpiece with a massive iolite gem at its tip where the helical assembly flowered open suspending the gem in mid-air. The metallic, triple helix framework was forged in Black-Dragon fire and shaped by a great Titan, then enchanted and imbued with great powers by Dallia (Kaleion arcmage of enchantment) over the period of several days roughly a thousand years ago as a wedding present for her husband, the infamous Damon of Basrat. Specifically, its powers greatly increase the amount of energy Damon, and only Damon, can channel. The types of energy it can augment is universal. If anyone, other than Damon attempts to use it, the staff will obliterate them. It is a central artifact in this story and the story could not be told without it.

Starlight of Immortality – Small blue-green star sapphire made of supersolids materials, roughly the size of a Human palm. Neither solid nor gas nor liquid, it holds many secrets, not the least of which is to incredible longevity.

Supersolids – Wikipedia defines supersolids as: "In condensed matter physics, a supersolid is a spatially ordered material with superfluid properties. In the case of helium-4, it has been conjectured since the 1960s that it might be possible to create a supersolid.[1] Starting from 2017, a definitive proof for the existence of this state was provided by several experiments using atomic Bose-Einstein condensates.[2] The general conditions required for supersolidity to emerge in a certain substance are a topic of ongoing research."

Telomere – A telomere is a region of repetitive nucleotide sequences at each end of a chromosome, which protects the end of the chromosome from deterioration or from fusion with neighboring chromosomes. Its name is derived from the Greek nouns telos (τέλος) 'end' and meros (μέρος, root: μερ-) 'part.' (Sourced: from www.wikipedia.org). Unsourced: The telomere essentially shrinks with age, thus providing a mechanism by which we can determine biological age. For more information, go to www.teloyears.com.

The Halls of Aaramus – Created by an immeasurably powerful lich known as Aaramus. This plane of existence is time neutral, and the normal laws of physics are suspended here, as it is created out of space that does not exist in the normal/known universe; it is extra-dimensional. As such, travel here is incredibly dangerous, as one is held hostage to the rules of physics, magic, and technology allowed by Aaramus, which are dynamic to his will. *Portal /Gate* entry into the Halls of Aaramus is allowed, but *Portal /Gate* exit typically is not, at least not without the expressed permission of Aaramus himself.

The Seeds of Humanity:

Kaleion – The homeworld of Damon, Kellen, Illirian, Goldenbow, and several other characters. This world is one of the Seeds of Humanity, with twin moons, developed into an agrarian and magical society.

Perion – The homeworld of Talemar, Radin, Brigance Fireheart, and several other characters. This world is one of the seeds of Humanity, with twin moons, developed into an agrarian and magical society.

The Terran System – Also known as Earth. This is the homeworld to Michelle, Lawna, Michael, and several other characters. This world developed into a mostly technological society, though some belief in magic and witchcraft still exists, allowing some operational and effective use of same.

Graelon – One of the five homeworlds of the seeds of Humanity, Graelon is a mostly technical society where magic and witchcraft still work to a limited degree. It is the homeworld most closely associated and comparable with the Terran system. Their technology allowed them to colonize outposts where magic was more freely accepted, to disastrous outcomes in some cases.

Setinon – Possibly the oldest home of Humanity and the original seed of the Human race, Setinon is an entirely technical and highly advanced society capable of controlling planetary weather, FTL travel, and using energy directly from a star—also known as Helium 3.

Pleiadian – Introduced as a possible source world for Man pre-dating even Setinon. This is a series of seven extraordinarily bright stars arranged in a unique constellation that folds back in on itself. It is not one given solar system but a great series of solar systems 444.2 light years from the Terran solar system (Sol). https://www.gaia.com/article/who-are-the-pleiadians

UNFPA – *United Nations Population Fund.* You will not believe the evil and disgusting things this organization is involved with and responsible for until you do your own research. And just remember that any time they talk about 'voluntary' *sterilization* and/or *termination/abortion* programs, they really mean 'compulsory.'

The Void – Also known as the Nether, no one knows who, when, or why the Void was created, but it is a highly dangerous place home to souls lost between death and destiny. Large asteroids perilously collide with one another on a regular basis, making the entire Void an unstable place to visit. *Portal / Gate* entry and exit is allowed, but strongly ill-advised.

The World Below and Between – Created by unknown entities, this gateway between worlds that house the seeds of Humanity allows those who understand its navigational systems to traverse great distances in a very short period of time. Those who do not understand are permanently lost. *Portal / Gate* entry into the World Below and Between is permitted, but *Portal / Gate* exit is not. This plane of existence is time neutral.

Throne of Souls – The first Throne of Souls was made by Damon of Basrat for his wife (Banthis). There have since been others made for other entities given the travel of Damon's first spell that made such an abomination (*Damnation*). Since that time, Damon has made a highly modified version of *Damnation*, called *A Throne of Souls* that allows the caster to grant the *Throne of Souls* to himself/herself. Literally speaking, it combines some characteristics of a *Stasis Stone* in that it can

Charles W. McDonald Jr.

capture and hold inside itself the living immortal soul of a mortal being. However, unlike a *Stasis Stone*, it affords the holder of the *Throne of Souls* the living energy given off by that soul or a collection/aggregation of souls within the *Throne of Souls* itself. In other words, there is no theoretical limit to how many souls could be captured in a given Throne of Souls, so the energy output of such a device could become unfathomable. Soul energy is electromagnetic, so if one has a way to use such an energy type as a source/input, then the output of such a source could be fantastic in scale and scope.

Timeline – The timeline and location markers provided throughout the novel are intended to help the reader navigate the story. Here is a rough guideline to follow when reading these markers:

> **A Very Long Time Ago** – More than a thousand years in the past.
>
> **A Long Time Ago** – Up to one thousand years in the past.
>
> **Present Day** – Within a few months, weeks, and hours of the "now" in the timeline.
>
> **Near Future** – Within the next two to five years of the "now" in the timeline.

Uriel – The Book of Enoch declares the archangel Uriel is 'the Light of God.' Some traditions recognize Uriel as Patron Saint of the Sacrament of Confirmation. Some believe he guards the consciousness of Jesus Christ.

U.S. Strategic Command (USSTRATCOM) - USSTRATCOM combines the synergy of the U.S. legacy nuclear command and control mission with responsibility for space operations; global strike; global missile defense; and global command, control, communications, computers, intelligence, surveillance and reconnaissance (C4ISR), and combating weapons of mass destruction. This dynamic command gives national leadership a unified resource for greater understanding of specific threats around the world and the means to respond to those threats rapidly. (Sourced: http://www.stratcom.mil/About/)

Washington's Driver – A pseudo-derogatory and somewhat friendly term for a very senior Operator (i.e. He's old enough to be George Washington's driver).

Wave-Particle Duality – In experimental physics, and as evidenced by the two-slit experiment, the observation that photons behave as a wave when not observed and as a particle when observed. In other words, photon particles can behave both as a fermion and as a boson. This is the essence of the Uncertainty Principle.

Glossary of Characters

This is a 5+1-world story and as such has a plethora of characters. This glossary is my attempt to help you keep them all straight. Within this glossary, I'll show you a glimpse of the character development behind them. For example, I possess some seventy pages describing Damon of Basrat, but here you'll see a robust paragraph.

Aaramus – A lich of profound power, wealth, knowledge, and agenda. A Tier A character central to all things. Founder of The Halls of Aaramus and creator of new planes of existence that operate outside the limitations of spacetime and linear time. Allegiances unknown.

President Abel – A Tier B character and elected President of Eden's government. Has a rather extensive history with Damon and understands him better than most. He knows Damon's history—at least, as Damon has shared it with him—and is someone Damon would call a friend and ally. Whether Damon has befriended Abel because of the name and his likeness to the friend he accidentally killed so long ago is unknown, but it wasn't lost on Damon when Abel ran for and then won the presidency without his aid. Now, they work together as best they can with compartmentalized sharing of information more than occasionally getting in their way.

Armstead:

> **Pern** – Left Bouschè years ago for places and purposes unknown to his brother (Gareth). A Tier B character who finds himself in the middle of a maelstrom, raising the hidden grandson of Damon the Banished.

> **Leah** – Tier B character; wife of Pern. Adopted mother of baby Ryker.

> **Gareth** – A Tier B character whose purpose alludes him, but his belief in his grandfather's words and deeds carries the day for him, and it is in the simplicity of his guiding principles that he hopes to find the hour of his brother's greatest need and then the hour of his own.

> **Luke** – A Tier B character and a beautiful soul carried away by the archangel Raphael. His role was to teach and prepare both Pern and Gareth and to hold true the most important truths: that Humanity is not the work of the random and that both science and history will prove that

so.

Arturus Ambrosius Aurelianus – Welsh: Emrys Wledig or Romano-British: Riothamus/Supreme Leader. What fable pronounced as King Arthur.

Asamel – Tier B character. Agent of Eldrac.

Banthis – Once a modest succubus of unlimited ambition and intellect and now heir-apparent to the Dragon of Darkness. The holder of the oldest and original Throne of Souls with powers only rivaled by the Dragon of Darkness and Lilith. Current wife to Damon of Basrat. A Tier A character whose master-level manipulation is central to many parts of the storylines. The key thing to understand about Banthis is how greatly she has suffered and the lengths to which she would go to unleash and redirect that suffering upon others. The only thing or person she could ever claim she truly loved (via her own warped view of love) is Damon and, because of her love for Damon, their daughters.

Brigance Fireheart – A Tier A character of no real power save the one he makes through his sheer will. A brute of a man both broad and tall—more akin to a bear than a man in stature. Brigance is a pragmatic general of generals. Ever more scrutinizing of both Radin and especially Damon, Brigance only affords the light of realism to shine and show the way for him and his men as the Banner of Hope hangs on but a thread.

Chara – Both vampire and mage, Chara was one of the most powerful and lethal forces of Kaleion until obliterated by Damon of Basrat. Her seed and bloodline extend across multiple worlds and is considered to be the source of bloodlust across both Terran and Perion. She is the seed and fire of Damon's hate, though not the root cause.

Daedrin – Brother of Seren. Stripped Keirill of all his great powers. Allegiances unknown.

Dallia – A Tier A character of more consequence than any might understand, Dallia—The Enchantress of Winds—is the first wife and first love of Damon. His unconditional adoration of her broke his then-healing soul irreparably so. In a very short time, she wove her existence and her presence into every fiber of Damon's being. Whether a selfless act or a selfish one, she knew her time short and her love for him immortal. Her magic still lives and works itself upon Damon each and every day he draws breath. Her light and her promise are the most beautiful of all characters in the story, and her time is not yet done.

Damon of Basrat – Only child of the famed Keirill and Seren. Grandchild to Emry and Ersila, as well as Grant and Sala. Great-grandchild of Durial and Fara. Once known as Kaylan until the age of thirteen when he murdered his father. Also goes by the titles: Dark Knight of Magic, Wielder of the Staff of the Invoker, Author of Damnation, Maker and Destroyer of Worlds, and Damon the Banished. Likely the most central Tier A character in the story. A profound and prolific womanizer who has a monstrous past and has killed more than can be counted. He has an ethical compass that rarely allows him to lie, and a heart tormented by being abandoned to the hate of his father as a child. For much of Damon's life, he has been wronged by others, and now he seeks to unmake his greatest mistakes afforded by his blind ambition of avenging the death of his first wife and most precious gift of love: Dallia.

Duron of Erden – Placeholder for this character.

Dylan – Placeholder for this character.

Elise Day – Tier A character born Farelise Camden on Graelon—mage registration number: 07874376Alpha221321. Elise has been manipulated and led to the point she finds herself by the Dark Knight of Magic for purposes she's only now beginning to understand. She knows she wasn't recruited for her powers, which are significant, yet nothing compared to those of Damon. Her assumption is Damon needed a fully registered mage to help execute some part of his Master Plan, but every time she solidifies the justification of her doubt of Damon, he puts forth actions that bring her squarely back into his fold. She considers Damon a complete enigma and keeps him at arm's distance, expecting the day will come when she will be forced to pick sides—permanently so. Wife to Michael Anthony Day and lover to Radin, she left Graelon to pursue Michael Anthony Day on Earth and then left Earth to pursue the reincarnation of Michael on Perion only to find herself intimately involved with Radin, whom she considered Michael's possible kindred soul.

Emrys Wledig – Arturus Ambrosius AurElianus – Welsh: Emrys Wledig or Romano-British: Riothamus/Supreme Leader. What fable pronounced as King Arthur.

Evanyil – A dark/cave elf that is supremely capable at thievery, death, and deceit. This darkest of all pure dark elves, Evanyil is the personification of self-sustaining, self-interest. Her ever-present poisoned dagger about her right hip is one of her few constants in life, else she is as chaotic as the quantum particles Mira studies in college. Her compass is always and forever pointed in her own best interest, yet how she gets there is anything but a straight line. Straddling the fine line betwixt genius and insanity, Evanyil is just lucid enough to bring brilliant unconventional thinking to Damon's structure—making their partnership uniquely dangerous for any of their most unfortunate targets. At their peak, they pulled off some of the most legendary and atrocious acts in the history of Kaleion. Their adventures are the source of many biographical texts on Kaleion. Evanyil and Damon share a rich, passionate, and lethal history with one another and with Evanyil's sister, Lorianus. A living god now, Evanyil's ask of Damon some years back in the current continuum is the source of Damon's Master Plan and his need to grow his powers.

The Four Brothers:

Durial – Settled Kaleion with Fara. The leader of the Four Brothers. Maker and Wielder of The Starlight of Immortality, Father of Dragons, The Great Life-Bringer, and The Wellspring of Humanity.

Pierio – Settled Graelon with Ceres. The technologist and scientist of the Four Brothers, Pierio sought to recreate the conditions of Setinon where magic and technology collided, experimenting with how best to integrate and isolate the two where applicable. His foremost desire was to understand what conditions led Setinon down its path to create a more durable path for Graelon and Humanity as a whole, as well as to afford them the best opportunities to defeat the *Eye*.

Alexelio – Settled Perion with Elsa. Only second to Durial in his powers, Alexelio was the artist, the sculptor, and the creator of the Four Brothers. His bloodline created great and sweeping architectural elements inspired of wind, ocean, and starlight. He sought to keep magic, in its most powerful forms, alive at all costs—even if it meant the loss of the knowledge of science and technology. Is considered the most likely candidate for the architect of *The World Below and Between*.

Adamian – Settled Terran (Earth).

Goldenbow – Lineage unknown. Origin unknown. Kindred brother to Damon and long-time associate to Kellen the Destroyer. Tier A character whose compass and kinship closely aligns with Damon of Basrat. Professional assassin and living legend on Kaleion, Goldenbow holds a special and central place in the story, which—in time—will be revealed. He is often the source of special counsel to Damon and is Damon's most-trusted ally in all things.

Hadley Mason – Former SRI master Remote Viewer trained, like his father, by Military Intelligence before breaking away from the government's grip upon him and working alongside Ron Stencowsky after the Battle of Warwick. It should be noted Hadley is 6'1." His father, also in this story, in "The Looking Glass," is 6'2," so when you see that delta, I'm referring to the difference between father and son. These are not the same character.

Harrison – An alien hybrid son of one of the very first Men in Black and a deep black operative within one of the Secret Space Program(s).

Hersila – Placeholder for this character.

Herot – Placeholder for this character.

Iain Longbow – A Tier B character and a legendary archer on Perion and companion to Rowarc.

Illirian Starfire – Only child of Jorah and Hannah, grandchild of Grant and Sala, and great-grandchild of Durial and Fara. Born the daughter of a mariner, she often uses maritime idioms and analogies, even when not entirely appropriate. Illirian and Damon's history goes back a millennia or more as her affinity for Damon became far more dangerous over the centuries. Illirian holds many titles: 'Ruler of the Rod of the Nine,' 'Watcher of the Runes of Fate,' 'Guardian of *Durial's Eye.*' The Starlight of Immortality is synonymous with *Durial's Eye* (the original version used by the Great Durial himself), but also affords its master unlimited lifespan without the need for magic. Damon and Illirian's relationship is the definition of the word, 'complicated.' How they sort through that relationship is fundamental to the unmaking of *A Throne of Souls*. From none-too-far a distance, she both meddles and guides Damon's actions by manipulating and controlling his psyche. Some would say she keeps it on the frayed edges of sanity to keep Damon cold, calculated, and ruthless. Illirian's seal is that of a pale-pink rose with white leaves on a tan clay-cast circle. Illirian Starfire also sits on what used to be called Kaleion's Council of Mages.

Joran of Erden – A Tier B character and Royvan Miral's counterpart on Kaleion. A legend in his own right, he has a great, in-depth knowledge of both ancient and modern languages, history, lore, and relics. His power and influences come from his travels and the unearthing of secrets most profound affecting every major seat of power on Kaleion.

Keirill – One of the greatest and most powerful of all mages in history—second only to the Great Durial—Keirill tested the boundaries of what was safe and authorized to risk becoming the greatest of all. His heart was relatively pure and his compass modestly true until his greed and lust for power led him to a path of hate that would result in his hating of his own existence more than anything else. A Tier A character, Keirill's infection of the *Instrument of Humanity's Hate* both drives and vexes Damon into being. Kaylan may have been his physical progeny, but Damon was his most significant achievement for Man or Man's undoing—depending on your perspective.

Kellen the Destroyer – Child of Hersila and Herot, grandchild of Castlier and Freya, great grandchild of Durial and Fara, Kellen is a bane to all things female. There is no fouler misogynist that Kellen the Destroyer. His legendary hatred of women the only forerunner to his infamy. His actions are not entirely self-serving—at least, not on the surface—and his agenda is entirely veiled in mystery. If past is prologue, it won't be good. Like Damon, or because of Damon, he pays his debts and holds his word high in merit. Unlike Damon, he's incapable of seeing women as anything other than something to be used—usually as little more than his personal sex slaves. He has a tense but working relationship with Illirian Starfire only because of Damon's intermediary status between them. Before Damon they found themselves in combat with one another on more than one occasion but have dialed back the hostilities toward one another to see where the Master Plan is going and where they will fall on opposing sides of it. They may very well need each other, and Damon may very well need them both to work together to unmake *A Throne of Souls*. Kellen also sits on what was formerly called Kaleion's Council of Mages. A Tier A character, Kellen is one of Damon's oldest friends and Allies, but the circle of his trust with Damon has found its limits on a few occasions. He is only afforded what information Damon must provide for him to serve his function within Damon's Master Plan, and that level of trust/distrust extends in both directions, as Kellen has a great secret of his own that greatly impacts Damon and the central storylines. Kellen the Destroyer holds many titles and monikers, 'The Hate of Mankind,' 'The Midnight Morning,' and 'The Flame of Hate.'

Lis – The Genesis input of *A Throne of Souls*, though the Genesis motive stems from Dallia's death. The theft and unjust condemnation of this beautiful soul forever altered the balance of power and became the first stone cast into the pond of Creation that would present and precipitate its unmaking.

Marshall:

    Ethan – A Tier B character murdered in the first great battle for

Charles W. McDonald Jr.

Man. Ethan's contributions to that war have yet to be fulfilled.

Lynn – A Tier B character, wife to the murdered Ethan Marshall, and now love of Talemar, Lynn has advanced and grown but has stumbled along the way in her love of a baby not her own. Now the balance of her life belongs to that baby boy. Her hopes and dreams now become his.

Michael Anthony Day – Tier A character and the first love of Elise. Michael is central to many—if not all—threads of the storyline. A great many characters in *A Throne of Souls* fall into categories that are very fluid between the spectrum of good and evil. Many characters in this story are quite far from either end of that spectrum, but Michael Anthony Day is an exception. He is the most extreme example of pure goodness available in this story. He is not without flaw and certainly not without internal conflict, but his compass is the truest (morally speaking) of any character in this story. There is no moral ambiguity in the character of his soul—whatsoever. And, quite possibly, the reincarnation of Emrys Wledig.

Mira Castille – Daughter of Charles and Elizabeth Castille. Dean's list sophomore physicist at the University of Texas at Austin. Intimately close to Damon of Basrat. Mira is a foul-mouthed, mouthy preacher's daughter of a Christian parentage, naughty by nature and rebellious by necessity of survival. Her far-reaching understanding of nature described through mathematics and the laws of physics are her most trusted guide to the new realities exposed to her through Damon and his Master Plan.

Mira (Original) – Long ago, after Dallia's death, he went through many loves and lovers, but the original Mira was special. She held the same passion and mage talents as Damon—though not holding all of his natural abilities. She specialized in the same categories of magic as Damon and was nearly his equal in all things and intellect. She was murdered shortly after her visit to the Graelon Colonial Outpost, as were many of Damon's loves whose orbit was too close for their own survival. Damon and this Mira never married, but they were as close as a couple could be, and her loss took Damon centuries to fully mourn.

Mora – A significantly powerful mage and member of the former Kaleion Council of Mages, this Tier B character held ties with Eldrac, though not by choice. More of a trophy to Eldrac, she once ran in circles close to Damon and now (via Talemar's great magic) finds herself in ever tighter circles with Radin. Mora longs to chart a path for herself of her own making, but fate may have other plans for her—as may *The Eye of Time*.

Charles W. McDonald Jr.

Morden – A Tier B character and arch nemesis to Damon the Banished. He served as court arcmage to many kings and stewards and had more than one run-in with Damon that didn't fare him well. But, Morden is a powerful sorcerer, home to Kaleion, and one who has never found himself on the same side as Damon—until the latter stages of Damon's Master Plan, where Radin mended old fences of hate between the two and proposed their working together towards a common enemy. Or, enemies common to the Master Plan....

Miss X – A Tier B character high up in the directorship chain of command for Continuity of Government and COG planning.

Quincy Arthur Billings – Once the head of Whitehall and formerly the superior of Michael Anthony Day, Billings was asked by Michael to be his Senior Advisor when elevated to the throne. Since that time and Michael's death, Billings has looked after his children as Elise went in search of Michael's soul.

Quinn – A Tier B character and companion of Iain Longbow and Rowarc. A generic mage of modest-but-growing abilities and a good heart.

Radin d'Aguillon – Biological child of Damon of Basrat and Vosh. Raised by Rowarc (famed retired ranger) and Arella d'Aguillon. A Tier A character central to many threads of the storylines. Has rapidly developing powers and immeasurable potential with morals deeply conflicted by personal experiences and his proximity to Damon. The threads connecting him to his past with Rowarc fade on almost an hourly basis as he grows under Damon's wing but are more persistent than even he understands.

Rathemeer – Placeholder for this character.

Rena Rectovich – A Tier A character, born Carastovich Catarena Rectovich, she is one of a very select few surviving witnesses (other than Damon) to Dallia's death. She heads a massive corporate empire amassed over a thousand years of experience and investments. She has extensive reach—politically, influentially, and otherwise—into every major government on Earth and maintains an Immortal Army that can now operate in daylight, thanks to gene therapy of the genetic code belonging to three young babes (the Blade daughters). Catarena's agenda and Damon's may overlap at times and may conflict at others, but she has long sought out the man she saw robbed a life she thought might make him a totally different person than the man he is today.

Rena's Immortal Army:

    Michelle Alexandra Blade – A Tier A character born in Denver,

CO to Chase and Marie Blade, Michelle began a successful investigative firm that partnered closely with state and federal government officials. Discovered by and finding herself in reach of Rena's radar, Michelle was offered the opportunity to have something she'd only dreamed of before—but at an immortal price. Michelle's motives and drivers are relatively simple. She loves and adores her daughters, and that drives nearly all of her decisions. She has a healthy distrust for Rena and an even more robust distrust of Damon, but her gut and palpable instincts connect her to both and tell her to hold fast.

Lawna Blade – A Tier B character and wife to Michelle, Lawna's mistrust of Rena is almost legendary. Like Michelle, her driving force is the daughters they share, but her love for Michelle is paramount and affords with it a lethal amount of jealousy. As far as capabilities go, Lawna is likely one of the most dangerous characters in the story.

Ryker – The only child of Elise and Radin, hidden from existence for sake of his own survival. Grandson of Damon the Banished.

Ron Stencowsky – Tier B character, former M1A2 Abrams tank personnel, and now master builder and security director on Eden. Runs in circles close to Damon and is extremely limited in his trust of Damon.

Rowarc d'Aguillon – A Tier B character, he raised Radin from a baby but was and is still conflicted over his absence in Radin's life and the absence of his wife—Arella d'Aguillon. Rowarc carries a great burden of guilt extending from his wife's death and what he now knows to be the death of his biological child lost some twenty years past.

Royvan Miral – Tier A character, legendary adventurer on Perion, and crucial to the Seals thread of the storylines. Many biographical novels have been written of his adventures and his findings. He has a mind for academia, languages, and cultures. He considers himself agnostic but cannot ignore what he has seen and experienced. He's trying—greatly so—to keep an open mind in operating this close to Radin and Damon, but his reservations of Damon's Master Plan run deep.

Royvan Miral's Crew:

Kerrich – Tier B character who grew up with Radin—a man he no longer recognizes due to his close proximity to Damon and Damon's agenda. Kerrich doesn't make pretense of an agenda that he doesn't understand, but in Royvan Miral, he found a man he believes he can trust and has ascribed himself to protégé to

Charles W. McDonald Jr.

Royvan Miral as best he can. The End is upon them regardless, and the only way through this is through it. That much he agrees upon, but how we most safely get from here to the other side is a matter of the most urgent and delicate judgment, and that's where his mistrust of Damon leads him to defer to Royvan Miral—for now.

Levi – Tier B character and member of Royvan Miral's crew. Generally considered Royvan Miral's right-hand man and trusted advisor.

Ham – Tier B character and member of Royvan Miral's crew. A good and hearty soul, more in tune with the big picture than most afford him credit.

Seren – A beautiful soul compromised by hate's reach into her own life and the life of her progeny. A Tier A character whose role in this story changed everything. If not for her, there would be no Unmaking.

Silverstring:

> **Wraith** – A Tier A mage of somewhat compromised values and mysterious background wed to his fraternal twin sister. Like many characters in the story, Wraith is neither good nor evil and wouldn't even fit solidly anywhere on that spectrum. His behaviors are more fluidly fitting to the dynamics of the situations before him. He's very much an agenda-driven character, but his agenda is shut to all but his sister and wife.

> **Silura** – A Tier A very promiscuous character who is a mage and wife to her fraternal twin brother, Wraith. Even more complicated than her twin brother and husband, Silura shrouds herself in mystery and frivolity, masking intentions known only to her. With all the tact of a machine gun, Silura's brutal honesty is generally off-putting to others. As shut as Wraith is to the outside world, Silura is even more so and holds secrets, even from her husband—sometimes especially so. Both Silura and Wraith have silver locks of hair on opposing sides.

Sophia – Dean of the College of Invocation (Basrat, Kaleion). Potentially one of the incarnations of Mira Castille. One who imparted some vital information to Damon when he was but fifteen years of age and not yet a mage.

The Chairman – The right hand of God the Creator. From time immemorial, it was the Prince of Egypt until his immortal shell was slain in combat by Damon of Basrat. Now held by Illirian Starfire.

The Six:

> **Anna** – One of the Six. A Tier B character converted by Lawna

Blade into an immortal creature, Anna's history is one of a lust for both power and flesh, but her driving force now is the revenge of her affliction and it threatens to compromise her task that affords her newfound existence. As one of the Six, she has been given a mission that is expected to be carried out, and she knows herself not indispensable in that role.

Asmodeus – Prince of the Abyss. One of the Six.

Castlin – One of the Six. A Tier B character, careful and methodical and not entirely on-board or married to the role to which he was assigned. He has a long history with both Talemar and Eldrac and with Damon by reputation. His allegiances are his own, but which side he falls on may change the balance of power just enough.

Eldrac – One of the Six. Murdered by Damon the Banished.

Lilith – The Great Princess of the Abyss. One of the Six. A Tier A character, Lilith is known for an appearance so perfect and so abhorrent as to make those who look upon her physically ill. With a serpentine tail and flesh that is acidic to all living things, Lilith is a being most vile and with a contempt for Man only surpassed by her need to keep the status quo.

Xarn – One of the Six. A Tier B character, Xarn's lust for sex (with both men and women) is as legendary as her frivolity and volatility. She is quite mad and dangerously powerful with a unique gift for working massive-scale objects that will become apparent in later parts of the story. Her role is one pivotal in relation to the Monuments of Creation.

The Great Talemar – Once married with family, stranded and left behind to a fate unknown and only barely chronicled by books, half-buried by fiction, quarter-buried by time, Talemar is seeking new meaning to his life in a timeline not his own as he tries to leverage the best parts of his past to make better decisions in the future and tries to use the worst parts of his past as fuel to destroy those standing in his path. He knows himself *the One* yet is mystified by how Radin can wear his crown. He secretly seeks the answers to this question, but for now Radin has proven both powerful and useful, and he'll continue to leverage that situation for as long as need be—to buy time—as well as to understand Damon's role and Damon's Master Plan. Talemar has a great deal on his plate as he does all these things, while holding together Humanity on Perion, knowing that role will soon expand as the scrolls expound their reach throughout all the *Seeds of Humanity*. The

Charles W. McDonald Jr.

time for his greatness may have to wait, but it *is* coming.

Terry Goodwin – A Tier B character and leader of Michael Anthony Day's SRR unit on Earth.

Toblain – A Tier B character and living gold dragon.

Voltor – Once a lesser demon, Voltor ascended to great power when allying with Eldrac (and others), who afforded Voltor souls he wouldn't have otherwise held claim over. Voltor's Throne of Souls was obliterated when his immortal shell was destroyed by Damon of Basrat. Voltor is most known for his capture and torment of Radin.

Vosh – Perion arcmage and lover to Damon of Basrat (Kaleion), who together are the biological parents of Radin.

Witches:

Adena – A Tier A character, Adena is the Mother and High Seat of witches for over a thousand years. Adena ruled with the antithesis of her seemingly fragile and delicate frame. Feared by all who knew her, Adena is a formidable foe who demands utter loyalty, and one not to be taken lightly.

Desindra – A Tier B character, Desindra is a legitimate threat to Adena, Desindra's burgeoning guile finds new life in the most unlikely of sources and new-found friendships.

Silvaran – Character definitions forthcoming. As the witch thread becomes more integral in the story, you'll see many more of these characters and their development become front-and-center.

Minna – Character definitions forthcoming. As the witch thread becomes more integral in the story, you'll see many more of these characters and their development become front-and-center.

Sabine – Character definitions forthcoming. As the witch thread becomes more integral in the story, you'll see many more of these characters and their development become front and center.

Xaldran – A Tier B character and living legend of a mage on Perion though his true origins and fate were and still are unknown. Author to a great Tome of Power that articulates the history of Humanity as well as hinting to its fate, Xaldran's true purpose has yet to be fulfilled, but may yet come by that which (and who) have survived him.

Ykstherin – A Tier A character, counsel to both Radin and Talemar, whose history and future is veiled in mystery. This character hints at greatness yet yields the limelight, for it is fleeting, and he is not. Precisely who and what Ykstherin is will become known in time. Don't underestimate this character and his potential in the story.

Charles W. McDonald Jr.

www.ingramcontent.com/pod-product-compliance
Lightning Source LLC
Chambersburg PA
CBHW060756030726
47503CB00002B/263